Praise for *The Odyssey*

"Did the world need one more translation of the *Odyssey*? Yes. In Robert Fagles' lucid, muscular verse, these ancient measures stalk across the page in march time, from the first sight of 'young Dawn with her rose-red fingers' to the moment when the last suitor has been slaughtered and Odysseus takes Penelope to bed."
—*Newsweek*

"To re-create a world where everything is living, down to the chairs and table-linens, is very nearly as difficult as to create it. Fagles does this with triumphant assurance; every arrowhead flashes lightning, every bush burns: Homer is with us."
—James Dickey

"Fagles' fresh translation of Homer's classic is enough to make you tune out the Smashing Pumpkins and turn off *Melrose Place*. The peerless epic about the travels of Odysseus remains as mesmerizing as when it was first chanted on Greek hillsides almost 2,700 years ago."
—*People* magazine

"Fagles capture[s] the sheer energy of a story that sweeps on like a tidal wave over twenty-four books and 12,000 lines. He unravels Homer's complex structure like Penelope at her loom . . . compelling the reader forward. Fagles' expertise with the dialogue is unmistakable. In his hands, characters spring to life through speech."
—Josephine Balmer, *The Independent on Sunday* (London)

"Readers make their own odyssey, by now, through *Odyssey*s. This latest lap of the journey returns us quite spectrally to the *poetry* of the affair: 'So they traded stories, the two ghosts standing there in the House of Death . . .' Poetry for which, yet again, we aspirants to Homeric harness are in Robert Fagles' debt, and happy to be there."
—Richard Howard

"Fagles does justice to the narrative velocity of the poem, to its economy, and he writes a supple English that's especially pleasing when read aloud. . . . The *Odyssey* is a journey on which Robert Fagles is excellent company."
—*The Boston Globe*

"Translators have inherited from the bards and troubadours the task of making the poem new. . . . This new version is a wonderful addition to that history. Fagles has made the lines fresh again. It's as if the dew's still on them."
    —William Fiennes, *The Observer*

"A memorable achievement . . . Mr. Fagles has been remarkably successful in finding a style that is of our time and yet timeless. . . . The long and excellent Introduction by Bernard Knox is a further bonus, scholarly but also relaxed and compellingly readable. Mr. Fagles' translation of the *Iliad* was greeted by a chorus of praise when it appeared; his *Odyssey* is a worthy successor."
    —Richard Jenkyns, front page of *The New York Times Book Review*

"The other shoe has dropped, and now we have the superb Fagles/Knox *Odyssey*. If, as Robert Fagles remarks in his Postscript, Homer's work is 'a musical event,' it is Beethoven's Ninth."
    —Anthony Hecht

"In his translation of the *Odyssey*, Fagles has created in English a masterpiece of world literature, combining in his poetry the crispness and timeliness of modern colloquial speech and a timeless classical beauty and dignity. The reader is entranced with a mythical, magical world . . . in which mortal heroes and immortal gods and goddesses hold close communication."
    —*Nashville Banner*

"Robert Fagles' *Odyssey* is a splendid companion piece to his memorable English version of the *Iliad*. He has managed to create a poetic colloquial English with a timeless dignity. The sensory values of Odysseus' archaic world—the snap of the sails, the scud of seafoam, the gleam of burnished bronze—come wonderfully alive in this supple, rhythmic English."
    —Robert Alter

"As Ezra Pound said, Homer had an 'ear for the sea-surge,' and Fagles captures it superbly in images of dripping oarblades and pitchers of shining wine. . . . [He] triumphantly restores the poem to its Hellenic toughness . . . [and] breathes fantastic new life into an ancient adventure."
    —*Manchester Guardian Weekly*

"Fagles keeps taut the scenes of deception and recognition as the hero tests his family and friends, driving his lines at a surging pace. His poetic momentum does more than merely move the great battle scene in the hall to its dramatic close; it keeps the reader always on top of the action with a vantage point to see the subtlety of the actors."
    —Peter Stothard, *The Times* (London)

"It is not every day that a batter manages a Homer on each of his first two tries at the plate. But now with his *Odyssey*, as earlier with his *Iliad*, translator Robert Fagles has done just this. There is also a triumphant Introduction by Bernard Knox."
    —Maynard Mack

"Now I have Robert Fagles to thank for a new and precious gift. He has let me hear the rhapsode work his magic, and held me spellbound in those shadowy halls."
    —Peter Green, *The New Republic*

"For those bereft of Greek, the immortality of Homer, Sophocles, Aeschylus, and their compatriots has been secured through his elegant and pithy translations. We present this medal to Robert Fagles with heartfelt thanks and appreciation in lieu of a libation to the hidden muse who graces the minds of the finest translators."
    —Gregory Rabassa, Citation for the winner of the 1997
    PEN/Ralph Manheim Medal for Translation for Lifetime
    Achievement

The *Odyssey* was chosen as a main selection of The Book-of-the-Month Club, The Quality Paperback Book Club, The Canadian Book-of-the-Month Club, and as a dual main selection of The Readers Subscription Book Club (with Robert Fagles' translation of the *Iliad*). It was also chosen by The History Book Club, The Softback Preview Book Club, and The Folio Society.

THE ODYSSEY

The Greeks believed that the *Iliad* and the *Odyssey* were composed by a single poet whom they named Homer. Nothing is known of his life. While seven Greek cities claim the honor of being his birthplace, ancient tradition places him in Ionia, located in the eastern Aegean. His birthdate is undocumented as well, though most modern scholars now place the composition of the *Iliad* and the *Odyssey* in the late eighth or early seventh century B.C.

ROBERT FAGLES is Arthur W. Marks '19 Professor of Comparative Literature, Emeritus, at Princeton University. He is the recipient of the 1997 PEN/Ralph Manheim Medal for Translation and a 1996 Academy Award in Literature from the American Academy of Arts and Letters. Fagles has been elected to the Academy, the American Academy of Arts and Sciences, and the American Philosophical Society. He has translated the poems of Bacchylides. His translations of Sophocles' *Three Theban Plays*, Aeschylus' *Oresteia* (nominated for a National Book Award) and Homer's *Iliad* (winner of the 1991 Harold Morton Landon Translation Award by The Academy of American Poets, an award from The Translation Center of Columbia University, and the New Jersey Humanities Book Award) are published in Penguin Classics. His original poetry and his translations have appeared in many journals and reviews, as well as in his book of poems, *I, Vincent: Poems from the Pictures of Van Gogh*. Mr. Fagles was one of the associate editors of Maynard Mack's Twickenham Edition of Alexander Pope's *Iliad* and *Odyssey*, and, with George Steiner, edited *Homer: A Collection of Critical Essays*.

BERNARD KNOX is Director Emeritus of Harvard's Center for Hellenic Studies in Washington, D.C. His essays and reviews have appeared in numerous publications and in 1978 he won the George Jean Nathan Award for Dramatic Criticism. His works include *Oedipus at Thebes: Sophocles' Tragic Hero and His Time; The Heroic Temper: Studies in Sophoclean Tragedy; Word and Action: Essays on the Ancient Theatre; Essays Ancient and Modern* (awarded the 1989 PEN/Spielvogel-Diamonstein Award); *The Oldest Dead White European Males and Other Reflections on the Classics;* and *Backing into the Future: The Classical Tradition and its Renewal*. Mr. Knox is the editor of *The Norton Book of Classical Literature*, and has also collaborated with Robert Fagles on the *Iliad* and *The Three Theban Plays*.

Other Books by Robert Fagles

Homer: A Collection of Critical Essays
(Co-ed. with George Steiner, and contributor)

The Twickenham Edition of Pope's *Iliad* and *Odyssey*
(Assoc. Ed. among others under Maynard Mack)

I Vincent: Poems from the Pictures of Van Gogh

TRANSLATIONS

Bacchylides: *Complete Poems*
(with Adam Parry)

Aeschylus: *The Oresteia*
(with W. B. Stanford)

Sophocles: *The Three Theban Plays*
(with Bernard Knox)

Homer: *The Iliad*
(with Bernard Knox)

Other Books by Bernard Knox

Oedipus at Thebes: Sophocles' Tragic Hero and His Time

Sophocles, *Oedipus the King* (Trans.)

The Heroic Temper: Studies in Sophoclean Tragedy

Word and Action: Essays on the Ancient Theater

Essays Ancient and Modern

The Oldest Dead White European Males and Other Reflections on the Classics

The Norton Book of Classical Literature (Ed.)

Backing Into the Future: The Classical Tradition and Its Renewal

PENGUIN BOOKS

HOMER

The
Odyssey

TRANSLATED BY
Robert Fagles

INTRODUCTION AND
NOTES BY
BERNARD KNOX

PENGUIN BOOKS
Published by the Penguin Group
Penguin Group (USA) Inc., 375 Hudson Street, New York, New York 10014, U.S.A.
Penguin Group (Canada), 90 Eglinton Avenue East, Suite 700, Toronto,
    Ontario, Canada M4P 2Y3 (a division of Pearson Penguin Canada Inc.)
Penguin Books Ltd, 80 Strand, London WC2R 0RL, England
Penguin Ireland, 25 St Stephen's Green, Dublin 2, Ireland (a division of Penguin Books Ltd)
Penguin Group (Australia), 250 Camberwell Road, Camberwell,
    Victoria 3124, Australia (a division of Pearson Australia Group Pty Ltd)
Penguin Books India Pvt Ltd, 11 Community Centre,
Panchsheel Park, New Delhi – 110 017, India
Penguin Group (NZ), 67 Apollo Drive, Mairangi Bay, Auckland 1311, New Zealand
    (a division of Pearson New Zealand Ltd)
Penguin Books (South Africa) (Pty) Ltd, 24 Sturdee Avenue, Rosebank,
    Johannesburg 2196, South Africa

Penguin Books Ltd, Registered Offices: 80 Strand, London WC2R 0RL, England

First published in the United States of America by Viking Penguin
a division of Penguin Books USA Inc. 1996
Published in Penguin Books 1997

44 43 42 41 40 39 38

THE LIBRARY OF CONGRESS HAS CATALOGUED THE HARDCOVER AS FOLLOWS:
Homer.
[Odyssey. English]
The Odyssey / Homer ; translated by Robert Fagles ; introduction and notes by Bernard
Knox.
p.   cm.
Includes bibliographical references.
ISBN 0-670-82162-4 (hc.)
ISBN 978-0-14-026886-7 (pbk.)
1. Epic poetry, Greek—Translations into English.   2. Odysseus (Greek Mythology)—
Poetry.   I. Fagles, Robert.   II. Title.
PA4025.A5F34   1996
883'.01—dc20   96–17280

Printed in the United States of America
Set in Meridian
Designed by Ann Gold
Illustrations are traditional Greek motifs

For Lynne
su gar m'ebiôsao, kourê

CONTENTS

CONTENTS

INTRODUCTION

INTRODUCTION

THE ODYSSEY

"Odyssey" is a familiar English word, meaning, according to Webster, "a series of adventurous journeys usually marked by many changes of fortune." The Greek word *Odusseia*, the form from which the English word is derived, means simply "the story of Odysseus," a Greek hero of the Trojan War who took ten years to find his way back from Troy to his home on the island of Ithaca, off the western coast of mainland Greece. Homer's *Odyssey* does indeed present us with "adventurous journeys" and "changes of fortune," but it is also an epic tale of a hero's return, to find at home a situation more dangerous than anything he faced on the plains of Troy or in his wanderings over uncharted seas.

The Greek philosopher Aristotle, writing in the fourth century B.C., gives us, in his treatise known as the *Poetics*, what he considers the essence of the plot. "A certain man has been abroad many years; he is alone, and the god Poseidon keeps a hostile eye on him. At home the situation is that suitors for his wife's hand are draining his resources and plotting to kill his son. Then, after suffering storm and shipwreck, he comes home, makes himself known, attacks the suitors: he survives and they are destroyed." This terse summary is the armature of an epic poem that consists of 12,109 lines of hexameter verse composed, probably, late in the eighth century B.C. or early in the seventh, by a poet known to later ages as Homer, for whose life and activities no trustworthy information has come down to us. The poem, in other words, is some 2,700 years old. How, the reader may well ask, did it survive through such an expanse of time? By whom, for whom, and how and in what circumstances was it composed? Perhaps the best way to proceed to an exploration of these questions (no one can promise a complete and certain answer) is backward—from the text of this book.

It is a translation, by Robert Fagles, of the Greek text edited by David Monro and Thomas Allen, first published in 1908 by the Oxford University Press. This two-volume edition is printed in a Greek type, complete with lower- and uppercase letters, breathings and accents, that is based on the elegant handwriting of Richard Porson, an early-nineteenth-

3

century scholar of great brilliance, who was also an incurable alcoholic as well as a caustic wit. This was of course not the first font of Greek type; in fact, the first printed edition of Homer, issued in Florence in 1488, was composed in type that imitated contemporary Greek handwriting, with all its complicated ligatures and abbreviations. Early printers tried to make their books look like handwritten manuscripts because in scholarly circles printed books were regarded as vulgar and inferior products—cheap paperbacks, so to speak.

Back to 1488, then, there is a continuous history of the printed text of Homer, differing a little from one editor to another but essentially fixed. Before that, Homer existed only as a handwritten book. Such hand-written copies had been in circulation in Italy for a hundred years or so before the first printed edition. Petrarch had tried to learn Greek but gave up; Boccaccio succeeded and also, in 1360, had a chair of Greek founded in Florence. But before Petrarch, Dante, though he put Homer in his limbo of non-Christian poets, had never read him, and could not have read him even if he had seen a text. For the best part of a thousand years, since the end of the Roman Empire, the knowledge of Greek had been almost lost in Western Europe. In the fourteenth century it was reintro-duced into Italy from Byzantium, where a Greek-speaking Christian empire had maintained itself ever since Constantine made the city the capital of the eastern half of the Roman Empire.

The knowledge of Greek and the manuscripts of the Greek classics, Homer included, came to Italy just in time; in May 1453 Byzantium fell to the Ottoman Turks, and the Greek empire of the East came to the end of its thousand-year career. During its long life it had carefully preserved, copied and recopied a select number of the Greek masterpieces of pre-Christian times, Homer prominent among them. The immediate prede-cessors of the printed edition of Florence were bound manuscript books written on vellum or on paper in a cursive minuscule script complete with accents and breathings. These books were the final phase of the process of copying by hand that went all the way back to the ancient world. The new minuscule handwriting had been adopted in the ninth century; since it separated words, it was easier to read than its prede-cessor, a hand consisting of freestanding capital letters without word division—the standard writing of the ancient world. In the second to fifth centuries A.D., the form and material of the books had changed: parch-ment, with its longer life, had replaced papyrus, and the codex form, our book form—folded quires of paper sewn at the back—had replaced the roll. In the ancient world, the *Iliad* consisted of a number of papyrus rolls, the text written in columns on the inside surface. The rolls could not be too big (or they would break when opened for reading); a long poem like the *Odyssey* might require as many as twenty-four—in fact, it is possible that the so-called books of our text represent an original division into papyrus rolls.

In this form the poem was known to the scholars who edited and wrote commentaries on it in Alexandria, the city founded by Alexander before he set out on his epic march to India in the late fourth century B.C. And it was in this form—though, before the Alexandrian scholars made a standard edition, with many variations from one text to another—that copies were to be found all over the Greek world of the fourth and fifth centuries B.C. There must have been texts in circulation in the sixth century too, for we hear of official recitations at Athens and find echoes of Homer in sixth-century poets. By the seventh century B.C., we are moving back into the dark. In the poets of this century (whose work survives only in fragments) there are epithets, phrases and even half-lines that are also common in Homer. Though these poets—Tyrtaeus, Callinus, Alcman and Archilochus—may be using tags common to a general epic tradition, it seems more likely that these echoes betray acquaintance with the work we know as Homer's. There is also a vase, discovered on the island of Ischia, off the coast of Naples, and dated to before 700 B.C., which has an inscription that seems to refer to the famous cup of Nestor described in the *Iliad* (11.745–53).* And echoes in art are also found in the early seventh century—illustrations of scenes from the *Odyssey*, for example, on vases dated in the 670s.

But back beyond about 700 B.C. we cannot go. Evidence for this period is rare; in fact, we know very little about Greece in the eighth century, still less, if possible, about Greece in the ninth. We have only the archaeological record—geometric pots, graves, some weapons. It is the era of Greek history known, because of our almost total ignorance about it, as the Dark Age.

All we have is the tradition, what the Greeks of historical times believed they knew about Homer. Herodotus thought that he lived four hundred years, not more, before his own time; that would put him in the ninth century. The great Homeric scholar Aristarchus of Alexandria believed that he lived about one hundred forty years after the Trojan War; since the Trojan War was generally dated (in our terms) around 1200 B.C., Aristarchus' Homer was much earlier than the Homer of

---

*The line numbers here and throughout, unless otherwise indicated, refer to the Fagles translations of the *Odyssey* and the *Iliad*, where the line numbers of the Greek text will be found at the top of every page.

Herodotus. Men might disagree about his date, but everyone believed that he was blind, and though some thought he came from Chios (a so-called Homeric hymn mentions a blind singer from Chios), others traced his origin to Smyrna. It was also generally assumed that Homer, though he speaks of singing and probably did sing in performance, was a poet using the same means of composition as his fifth-century successors—that is, writing. Even those who thought that his poems were not combined into their present shape until long after his death (that, for example, the last part of the *Odyssey* is a later addition), even those who believed that different poets wrote the *Iliad* and the *Odyssey*, the so-called Separatists—all assumed that Homer was a poet who composed as all poets since have done: with the aid of writing. And so did all succeeding centuries down to the eighteenth. Pope, whose translation of the *Iliad* is the finest ever made, speaks of Homer as if he were a poet like Milton or Shakespeare or himself. "HOMER"—so begins his Preface—"is universally allow'd to have had the greatest Invention of any Writer whatever." Homer, it is taken for granted, *wrote*.

There had been one skeptic in the ancient world who thought differently. He was not a Greek but a Jew, Joseph ben Matthias. He wrote in Greek (for which, as he admits, he had a little help) a history of the Jewish rebellion against Roman rule in the first century A.D. and its savage repression by the emperor Titus—events in which he had played a prominent role. But he also wrote a pamphlet, countering the claim of a Greek writer, Apion, that the Jews had no history to speak of, since they were hardly mentioned in the works of Greek historians. Besides defending the historicity of the Old Testament chronicles, Josephus (to give him his Greek name) counterattacked by pointing out that the Greeks did not learn to write until very late in their history. The heroes of the Trojan War were "ignorant of the present-day mode of writing," he said, and even Homer "did not leave his poems in writing"; his separate songs were "transmitted by memory" and "not unified until much later."

It is true that (with one remarkable exception, which is discussed later) no one in the *Iliad* or the *Odyssey* knows how to read or write. The Mycenaean scribes had used the complicated Linear B syllabary—eighty-seven signs for different combinations of consonant and vowel. It was a system only professional scribes could handle; in any case, all memory of it was lost with the destruction of the Mycenaean centers in the twelfth century B.C. The Greeks did not learn to write again until much later. This time, they took over an alphabet of fewer than twenty-five letters from the Phoenicians, a Semitic people whose merchant ships, sailing from their cities Tyre and Sidon on the Palestinian coast, reached every island and harbor of the Mediterranean Sea. The Phoenician alphabet consisted of signs for consonants only. The Greeks appropriated their symbols (*alpha* and *beta* are meaningless words in Greek, but their Phoenician equivalents, *aleph* and *beth*, mean "ox" and "house"), but by assigning some of the letters to the vowels, they created the first efficient alphabet, a letter system that provided one, and only one, sign for each sound in the language.

Just when this creative adaptation took place is a subject of scholarly disagreement. Some of the letter shapes of the earliest Greek inscriptions look as if they had been copied from Phoenician scripts that date from as far back as the twelfth century. On the other hand, the earliest examples of Greek alphabetic writing, scratched or painted on broken pottery and found all over the Greek world from Rhodes in the east to Ischia, off the coast of Naples, in the west, are dated, by their archaeological contexts, to the last half of the eighth century B.C.

But it was not until the eighteenth century that the possibility of Homeric illiteracy was once again proposed. The English traveler Robert Wood, in his *Essay on the Original Genius of Homer* (1769), suggested that Homer had been as illiterate as his own Achilles and Odysseus. The German scholar F. A. Wolf elaborated the theory in a learned discourse entitled *Prolegomena ad Homerum*, and the Homeric Question was launched on its long and complicated career. For if Homer was illiterate, Wolf declared, he could not possibly have composed poems as long as the *Iliad* and the *Odyssey*; he must have left behind him shorter, ballad-like poems, which, preserved by memory, were later (much later, in Wolf's opinion) put together in something like the form we now possess. Wolf's thesis was almost universally accepted as soon as published. It came at the right time. Almost a century before this, the Neapolitan philosopher Giambattista Vico had claimed that the Homeric poems were the creation not of one man but of the whole Greek people. The spirit of the age now sought to find works of untutored genius, songs and ballads, the expression of a people's communal imagination—a contrast to the artificial culture and literature of the Age of Reason. The Romantic rebellion was at hand. Everywhere in Europe, scholars began to collect, record and edit popular song, ballad, epic—the German *Nibelungenlied*, the Finnish *Kalevala*, Percy's *Reliques of Ancient English Poetry*. And this was the age that saw the popularity, especially in Germany and France, of a fake collective bardic epic: the story of Ossian, a Gaelic hero, translated from the original Gaelic and collected in the Highlands by James Macpherson. In spite of the fact that Macpherson was never able to produce the originals,

"Ossian" was admired by Goethe and Schiller; it was the favorite book of Napoleon Bonaparte. They should have listened to Samuel Johnson, who called the book "as gross an imposition as ever the world was troubled with."

In such an atmosphere of enthusiasm for folk poetry, the discovery of a primitive Homer was more than welcome. And scholars, convinced that the *Iliad* and the *Odyssey* consisted of ancient shorter poems that had been sewn together by later compilers and editors, now addressed with gusto the task of deconstruction, of picking out the stitches and isolating the original "lays" or "ballads" in their primitive, pure beauty. The exercise continued throughout the whole of the nineteenth and into the twentieth century.

It continued because of course no two scholars could agree about how to take the poems apart. This was understandable, since the criteria they were using—inconsistency of character, imbalance of structure, irrelevance of theme or incident, clumsiness of transition—are notoriously subjective. At first the affair was a free-for-all; it seemed almost as if there were a competition to see who could find the greatest number of separate ballads. Karl Lachmann, in the mid-nineteenth century, after claiming that the newly discovered *Nibelungenlied* was a mosaic of short ballads (a theory now believed by no one), went on to divide the *Iliad* into eighteen original heroic songs. A similar theory of the origin of the *Chanson de Roland* was popular at about the same time. The idea was not as impossible as it now sounds; in fact, a contemporary of Lachmann, the Finnish scholar and poet Lönnrot, collected Finnish ballads on his travels as a country doctor in the most backward parts of the country and put them together to form the great Finnish epic, the *Kalevala*, a poem that has ever since been the foundation of the Finnish national consciousness. But Lachmann's analytical methods produced no agreement, only scholarly squabbles, conducted with the customary venom, about how long the pieces should be and exactly where to use the knife.

The *Iliad*, in which the action is confined to Troy and the Trojan plain and lasts for no more than a few weeks, lent itself less easily to such surgical operations than the *Odyssey*, which ranges over ten years and vast spaces. It was easy for eager analysts to detect originally separate epics and short ballads. There was a *Telemacheia* (Books 1–4), the tale of a diffident young prince's growth to full stature as a man and warrior. It contained what had originally been three separate ballads of the type known as *Nostoi* (Returns)—the voyages and homecomings of Nestor, Menelaus and Agamemnon. There was a long tale of a hero's voyage through far-off fabulous seas, like the saga of Jason's ship, the *Argo*, a song actually mentioned in the *Odyssey* (12.77). Embedded in this travel tale was a short but brilliant song about a sex scandal on Olympus—Ares and Aphrodite caught *in flagrante delicto* by her irate husband, Hephaestus. It is one of the songs of the blind bard Demodocus, who at the Phaeacian court tells also the tale of the quarrel between Achilles and Odysseus and another of Odysseus and the wooden horse that brought about the fall of Troy. There was also a full-scale *Nostos*, the return home of Odysseus, the welcome he received, and his vengeance on the suitors.

The precise dimensions of these presumably once separate components and the stages of the process that led to their amalgamation were (and in the writings of many eminent critics still are) matters for speculation and dispute. Were there three main poets—one who composed the core of the epic (the wanderings and return of Odysseus), another who sang of the coming of age and travels of Telemachus, and a third who combined the two and forged the links that bind them? Or were there only two—the poet of the voyages and homecoming, and the other who added the *Telemacheia* and Book 24 (which many scholars consider a later addition in any case)?

One obvious weakness of this line of argument is that the story of Telemachus is no fit subject for heroic song; there is nothing heroic about it until Telemachus takes his place, spear in hand, by his father's side in the palace at Ithaca. As a separate epic poem, the material of Books 1–4 is something hard to imagine in the historical context—a *Bildungsroman*, the story of a young man from a poor and backward island who asserts himself at home and visits the sophisticated courts of two rich and powerful kingdoms, to return home a grown man. Such a theme is worlds apart from the songs offered by bards in the *Odyssey* and the *Iliad*. Demodocus at the Phaeacian court tells the tale of the quarrel between Odysseus and Achilles, and later, at Odysseus' request, of the wooden horse that brought about Troy's fall. Phemius in the palace at Ithaca sings of the return of the Achaeans from Troy and the disasters inflicted on them by Athena, and when Penelope asks him to choose some other theme, she speaks of his knowledge of the "works of the gods and men that singers celebrate" (1.389). And in the *Iliad*, when the ambassadors from Agamemnon come to plead with Achilles to rejoin them on the battle line, they find him playing the lyre, "singing the famous deeds of fighting heroes" (9.228). A song celebrating the travels of Telemachus is not easy to imagine in the context of a male audience accustomed to tales of adventure and feats of arms. How would the bard begin? "Sing to me, Muse, of the coming of age of Telemachus . . ."? It seems much more likely that the *Telemacheia* was a creation of the poet who decided to

combine a tale of adventures in fabulous seas—a western voyage mod-
eled on the saga of the *Argo*'s voyage to the east—with a *Nostos*, the
return home of a hero from Troy, in this case to face a situation as dan-
gerous as that awaiting Agamemnon. For that decision forced on him a
radical departure from the traditional narrative procedure of heroic song
and confronted him with a problem for which the *Telemacheia* was a mas-
terly solution.

Epic narrative characteristically announces the point in the story at
which it begins and then proceeds in chronological order to its end. The
Iliad opens with the poet's request to the Muse: "Rage—Goddess, sing
the rage of Peleus' son Achilles"; he then tells her where to start: "Begin,
Muse, when the two first broke and clashed, / Agamemnon lord of men
and brilliant Achilles" (1.1–8). She does, and the story is told in strict
chronological order until its end: "And so the Trojans buried Hector
breaker of horses" (24.944). In the *Odyssey*, when Odysseus asks the
Phaeacian bard Demodocus to "Sing of the wooden horse / Epeus built
with Athena's help," the bard "launched out / in a fine blaze of song,
starting at just the point / where the main Achaean force, setting their
camps afire . . ." (8.552–61), and carries the story on until Troy falls. But
the prologue to the *Odyssey* abandons this traditional request to the Muse
or the singer to begin at a certain point. It begins, like the *Iliad*, with a
request to the Muse to sound a theme—the wrath of Achilles, the wan-
derings of Odysseus—but instead of telling her where to start—"Begin,
Muse, when the two first broke and clashed"—it leaves the choice to her.
"Launch out on his story, Muse, daughter of Zeus, / start from where you
will" (1.11–12). And she does. She begins, not with Odysseus' departure
from Troy (which is where he begins when he tells his story to the
Phaeacians), but in the twentieth year of his absence from home, as
Athena starts Telemachus on his journey to Pylos and Sparta and
arranges Odysseus' escape from his seven-year captivity on Calypso's
island.

The reason for this startling departure from tradition is not far to seek.
If the poet had begun at the beginning and observed a strict chronology,
he would have been forced to interrupt the flow of his narrative as soon
as he got his hero back to Ithaca, in order to explain the extremely com-
plicated situation he would have to deal with in his home. The
Telemacheia enables him to set the stage for the hero's return and to
introduce the main participants in the final scenes—Athena, Tele-
machus, Penelope, Eurycleia, Antinous, Eurymachus—as well as a group
of minor players: Medon, the servant who helped rear Telemachus;
Dolius, the servant of Laertes; Halitherses and Mentor, two old Ithacans

who disapprove of the suitors; the suitor Leocritus; and Phemius, the Ithacan bard. And the accounts of Telemachus' voyages do more than chart his progress, under Athena's guidance, from provincial diffidence to princely self-confidence in his dealings with kings; they also offer us two ideal visions of the hero's return, so different from what awaits Odysseus—Nestor among his sons, Menelaus with his wife and daughter, both of them presiding over rich kingdoms and loyal subjects.

Division into separate songs by different poets was not the only approach to dissecting the body of the *Odyssey*. The nineteenth century was the age that saw the birth of the scientific historical spirit. And also of the history of language—the discipline of linguistics. All this had a bearing on the problem. If in fact some sections of the *Odyssey* were older than others, they should contain linguistic features characteristic of an earlier stage of the language than that to be found in the more recent additions. Similarly, the later parts of the poem should contain allusions to customs, laws, objects and ideas belonging to the later historical period, and vice versa. Toward the end of the century a fresh criterion emerged for gauging the antiquity of different sections of the poem—the archaeological criterion. For with Heinrich Schliemann's excavations at Troy and Mycenae, and those of Sir Arthur Evans at Cnossos, a previously unknown civilization was revealed. If there was any historicity to Homer's account of the Achaean world that organized the attack on Troy, it must be a reference to *this* world—a world of gold masks, bronze weapons, palaces and fortifications—not to the archaeologically poverty-stricken Greece of the Dark Age. Now, by finding in Homer descriptions of objects that corresponded to something excavated from a Bronze Age site, the scholar could date a passage, because it was clear that with the destruction of the Mycenaean and Minoan palaces, all memory of that age had disappeared in Greece. Schliemann and Evans had discovered things Herodotus and Thucydides had no idea of.

Of these three approaches, the linguistic seemed the most promising, the most likely to yield objective criteria. Studies of the origins of Greek in the Indo-European family of languages had progressed along generally agreed and scientific lines: the history of the Greek language and the Greek dialects had become an exact discipline. Surely the linguistic analysis of the text would confirm or refute theories of earlier and later strata in the poems.

THE LANGUAGE OF HOMER

The language of Homer is of course a problem in itself. One thing is certain: it is not a language that anyone ever spoke. It is an artificial, poetic language—as the German scholar Witte puts it, "The language of the Homeric poems is a creation of epic verse." It was also a difficult language. For the Greeks of the great age, that fifth century we inevitably think of when we say "the Greeks," the idiom of Homer was far from limpid (they had to learn the meaning of long lists of obscure words at school), and it was brimful of archaisms—in vocabulary, syntax and grammar—and of incongruities: words and forms drawn from different dialects and different stages of the growth of the language. In fact, the language of Homer was one nobody, except epic bards, oracular priests or literary parodists would dream of using.

This does not mean that Homer was a poet known only to scholars and schoolboys; on the contrary, the Homeric epics were familiar as household words in the mouths of ordinary Greeks. They maintained their hold on the tongues and imaginations of the Greeks by their superb literary quality—the simplicity, speed and directness of the narrative technique, the brilliance and excitement of the action, the greatness and imposing humanity of the characters—and by the fact that they presented the Greek people, in memorable form, with the images of their gods and the ethical, political and practical wisdom of their cultural tradition. Homer was thus at once contemporary in content and antique in form. The texture of Homeric epic was for the classic age of Greece like that of the Elgin Marbles for us—weathered by time but speaking to us directly: august, authoritative, inimitable, a vision of life fixed forever in forms that seem to have been molded by gods rather than men.

The language of Homer is the "creation of epic verse" in a strict sense too: it is created, adapted and shaped to fit the epic meter, the hexameter. This is a line, as its name indicates, of six metrical units, which may, to put it crudely, be either dactyls (a long plus two shorts) or spondees (two longs) in the first four places but must be dactyl and spondee in that order in the last two (rarely spondee and spondee, never spondee followed by dactyl). The syllables are literally long and short; the meter is based on pronunciation time, not, as in our language, on stress. But unlike most English verse, the meter does not allow departures from the basic norms—such phenomena as the Shakespearean variations on the basic blank verse line, still less the subtleties of Eliot's prosody in *The Waste Land*.

Yet though it is always metrically regular, it never becomes monotonous; its internal variety guarantees that. This regularity imposed on variety is Homer's great metrical secret, the strongest weapon in his poetic arsenal. The long line, which no matter how it varies in the opening and middle always ends in the same way, builds up its hypnotic effect in book after book, imposing on things and men and gods the same pattern, presenting in a rhythmic microcosm the wandering course to a fixed end which is the pattern of the rage of Achilles and the travels of Odysseus, of all natural phenomena and all human destinies.

The meter itself demands a special vocabulary, for many combinations of long and short syllables that are common in the spoken language cannot be admitted to the line—any word with three consecutive short syllables, for example, any word with one short syllable between two longs. This difficulty was met by choosing freely among the many variations of pronunciation and prosody afforded by Greek dialectal differences; the epic language is a mixture of dialects. Under a light patina of Attic forms (easily removable and clearly due to the preeminence of Athens as a literary center and then of the book trade), there is an indissoluble mixture of two different dialects, Aeolic and Ionic. But the attempts of the linguists to use this criterion for early (Aeolic) and late (Ionic) ran into the dilemma that Aeolic and Ionic forms sometimes appear inextricably tangled in the same line or half-line.

The attempts to dissect the *Odyssey* along historical lines were no more satisfactory (except of course to their authors). There are indeed passages that seem to imply different historical backgrounds, but they are not passages that are identifiable as early or late by the criteria of linguistic difference or structural analysis. All through the poem, weapons and armor are made of bronze—spearheads, arrow tips, swords, helmets and breastplates; men are killed by "pitiless bronze." In superior palaces, like those of the gods or King Alcinous of the Phaeacians, bathtubs and cauldrons and even the threshold of the building are made of bronze. On the other hand, iron is used for axes and adzes; it is so familiar an item that it is constantly in use in metaphor and simile—"heart of iron," for example. But there is no way to separate Bronze Age from Iron Age layers; the two metals lie cheek by jowl, and even the distinction between bronze for weapons and iron for tools is often ignored—"Iron has powers to draw a man to ruin" is a proverbial phrase twice quoted by Odysseus (16.327, 19.14), and a man who is dipping red-hot iron in water is called a *chalkeus*, a bronze or copper worker. Early in the poem, Athena, disguised as Mentes, says that she is sailing for Temese with a cargo of iron, which she intends to trade for bronze.

But archaeological ages are not the only matter to be handled by the Muse with careless abandon. There seem to be two different marriage systems in the world of the *Odyssey*: in some passages the bride's family settles a dowry on the bride, but in others the suitor makes valuable gifts to the bride's family. "It is most probable," says a recent commentator on the *Odyssey* (West, *Commentary*, I, p. 111), "that Homeric marriage-customs represent an amalgam of practices from different historical periods and different places, further complicated, perhaps, by misconception." They are obviously not much use for dating the passages in which they appear.

It is not surprising, in view of such frustrating results, that by the beginning of the twentieth century, opinion had begun to swing away from analysis and to concentrate on the qualities of the poem itself, to stress the unity of the main action rather than the digressions and inconsistencies, above all to explore the elaborate correspondences of structure that often link scene to scene. The architecture of the poem is magnificent, and it strongly suggests the hand of one composer, but it is true that there is a certain roughness in the details of the execution. The poem does contain, in an indissoluble amalgam, material that seems linguistically and historically to span many centuries. And it does contain long digressions, and some disconcerting inconsistencies, some weaknesses of construction. What sort of poet composed it, and how did he work?

The answer was supplied by an American scholar, whose name was Milman Parry. Parry, who came from California and was an assistant professor at Harvard when he was killed in a gun accident at an early age, did his most significant work in Paris; in fact, he wrote it in French and published it in Paris in 1928. It did not appear in English until 1971, when, translated by his son, Adam Parry, it formed part of a collection of all his Homeric studies. His work was not appreciated or even fully understood until long after his death, in 1935, but once understood, it completely changed the terms of the problem.

Parry's achievement was to prove that Homer was a master of and heir to a tradition of oral epic poetry that reached back over many generations, perhaps even centuries. Parry drew attention to the so-called ornamental epithets, those long, high-sounding labels that accompany every appearance of a hero, a place, or even a familiar object. Odysseus, for example, is "much-enduring," "a man of many schemes," "godlike" and "great-hearted"; the island of Ithaca is "rocky," "seagirt" and "clear-skied"; ships are "hollow," "swift" and "well-benched," to list only some of the often polysyllabic epithets attached to them. These recurring epithets had of course been noticed before Parry, and their usefulness understood. They offer, for each god, hero or object, a choice of epithets, each one with a different metrical shape. In other words, the particular epithet chosen by the poet may have nothing to do with, for example, whether Achilles is "brilliant" or "swift-footed" at this particular point in the poem—the choice depends on which epithet fits the meter.

Parry pursued this insight of the German analytical scholars to its logical end and demonstrated that in fact there was an intricate system of metrical alternatives for the recurring names of heroes, gods and objects. It was a system that was economical—hardly any unnecessary alternatives were used—but had great scope: there was a way to fit the names into the line in any of the usual grammatical forms they would assume. Parry demonstrated that the system was more extensive and highly organized than anyone had dreamed, and he also realized what it meant. It meant that this system had been developed by and for the use of oral poets who *improvised*. In Paris he met scholars who had studied such improvising illiterate bards still performing in Yugoslavia. He went there to study their operations himself.

The Homeric epithets were created to meet the demands of the meter of Greek heroic poetry, the dactylic hexameter. They offer the improvising bard different ways of fitting the name of his god, hero, or object into whatever section of the line is left after he has, so to speak, filled up the first half (that, too, quite possibly, with another formulaic phrase). Odysseus, for example, is often described as "much-enduring, brilliant Odysseus"—*pŏlūtlās dīŏs Ŏdūssēus*—a line ending. In Book 5 Calypso, who has had Odysseus to herself on her island for seven years, is ordered by the gods to release him and tells him he can go. But he suspects a trap, and shudders. "So she spoke," says Homer, "and he shuddered"—*hōs phătŏ rīgēsēn dĕ*—and he ends with the formula "much-enduring, brilliant Odysseus"—*pŏlūtlās dīŏs Ŏdūssēus*—to form a hexameter line. A little later Calypso asks Odysseus how he can prefer his wife at home to her immortal charms, and his diplomatic answer is introduced by the formula: "and in answer he addressed her"—*tēn d' ăpŏmēibŏmĕnŏs prŏsĕphē*. But the line cannot be completed with "much-enduring, brilliant Odysseus"; that formula is too long for this position. So Odysseus ceases for the moment to be "much-enduring" and "brilliant" and becomes something that conforms to the metrical pattern: "a man of many schemes"—*pŏlŭmētĭs Ŏdūssēus*. The hero's name is especially adaptable; Homer uses two different spellings—*Odusseus* and *Oduseus*—which give the hero two different metrical identities. Often, however, the poet has to use the name in a different grammatical case from the nominative—the genitive *Ŏdŭsēŏs*, for example—and when that happens the hero becomes "blameless"—*Ŏdŭsēŏs ămŭmŏnŏs*—or, with the longer spelling of his name, "great-hearted"—*Ŏdŭssēŏs mĕgălētŏrŏs*. In the dative case he becomes "godlike"—*āntĭthĕŏ Ŏdŭsēĭ*—or "quick-minded"—*Ŏdŭsēĭ dăīphrŏnĭ*. The choice of epithet is dictated by the meter. So also the island of Ithaca is "rocky," "seagirt," "clear-skied" or "lying under Mount Neriton," depending on its grammatical case and position in the line; and under the same imperatives the Phaeacians appear as "great-hearted," "famous for ships" or "lords of the sea." As for the ships, objects as essential to the story of Odysseus as spears and swords are to that of Achilles, they are "hollow," "swift," "black," "well-benched," "well-oared," "well-worked," "scooped-out," "fast-moving," "scarlet-cheeked" and "black-prowed," to name only the principal epithets that enable the poet to use them in any grammatical case and metrical position.

This system, obviously the product of invention, refinement and elimination of superfluities over generations, could only be the work of oral bards, and in fact similar phenomena, though infinitely less sophisticated, are found in oral poetry, living and dead, in other languages. There was more to it, of course, than handy epithets. Whole lines, once honed to perfection by the bards of the tradition, became part of the repertoire; they are especially noticeable in recurring passages like descriptions of sacrifice, of communal eating and drinking. Such passages give the oral singer time to concentrate on what is coming next and, if he is a creative oral poet, to elaborate his own phrases mentally as he recites the formulas that he can sing without effort. He is helped, too, by the formulaic nature of whole themes, great type-scenes—the arming of the warrior for battle, the launching and beaching of ships. These are traditional patterns that the audience expects and the bard may vary but not radically change.

There is one aspect of Parry's discovery, however, that changed the whole problem of the nature of our Homeric text. The oral bard who uses such formulaic language is not, as scholars in the nineteenth century who struggled with the problem of illiterate bards all assumed, a poet reciting from memory a fixed text. He is improvising, along known lines, relying on a huge stock of formulaic phrases, lines and even whole scenes; but he *is* improvising. And every time he sings the poem, he may do it differently. The outline remains the same, but the text, the oral text, is flexible. The poem is new every time it is performed.

If Homer's poetry is the culmination of a long tradition of such oral composition, many of the problems that bedeviled the Analysts are solved. Over the course of generations of trial and error, formulas are introduced and rejected or retained for their usefulness in improvisation, without regard to linguistic consistency or historical accuracy. The language of the poets becomes a repository of all the combinations that have proved useful. Small wonder that Aeolic and Ionic forms appear in the same line, that a Mycenaean boar-tusk helmet can turn up in a passage in the *Iliad*, full of late linguistic forms, that people in the *Odyssey* sometimes give dowries and sometimes demand payment for their daughter's hand, that cremation and inhumation are practiced side by side. As each new generation of singers re-creates the song, new formulas may be invented, new themes and scenes introduced; reflections of contemporary reality creep into descriptions of the fighting, especially into the similes. But the dedication of epic poetry to the past and the continuing usefulness of so much traditional phraseology will slow the process of modernization and produce the unhistorical amalgam of customs, objects and linguistic forms that we find in our Homeric text.

It is the fate of most new and valuable insights to be enthusiastically developed beyond the limits of certainty, or even of probability, and Parry's demonstration that Homeric poetry had an oral base has not escaped that fate. Phrases, even whole lines, that are repeated often enough to qualify as formulaic are indeed characteristic of the poet's diction, but they do not account for more than a part of it—about one third of the whole. In an attempt to raise the formulaic element to a higher level, Parry counted as formulas expressions whose metrical pattern and position in the line were identical and that contained one word in common: for example, *tēuchĕ ĕthēkĕ; ālgĕ' ĕthēkĕ; kūdŏs ĕthēkĕ*—he "put" the arms, the sorrows, the glory on. Not content with this, Parry went on to suggest, hesitantly, the inclusion in the system of similar expressions that, however, did *not* contain one word in common: *dōkĕn hĕtāirŏ*, for example, and *tēuchĕ kŭnēssĭn*—"he gave to his comrade," "he made [him prey] for the dogs." Some of Parry's followers have been less hesitant, and by this and other extensions of the meaning of "formula" have boosted the inherited content of Homer's verse to ninety percent. This of course leaves very little room for Homer as an individual creative poet. It seems in fact to be a return to the idea of Giambattista Vico: the poems are the creation of a people, of a tradition, of generations of nameless bards.

But the argument for full formularity has feet of clay. A poet composing in a strict, demanding meter is bound to repeat syntactical combinations in identical positions, and the stricter the meter, the higher the incidence of such repeated patterns. English has no meters as precisely demanding as Homer's, but Alexander Pope, to take an example, is rich in lines that by rigid Parryite standards would qualify him as an illiterate bard:

The Smiles of Harlots, and the Tears of Heirs
The Fate of Louis *and the Fall of* Rome

Proclaim their Motions, and provoke the War
Maintain thy Honours, and enlarge thy Fame

The shining Helmet, and the pointed Spears
The silver Token, and the circled Green

Weak was his Pace, but dauntless was his Heart
Lame are their Feet, and wrinkled is their Face

Samuel Johnson, in fact, wrote a description of Pope's technique that has more than a little resemblance to Parry's conception of the oral poet. "By perpetual practice, language had in his mind a systematical arrangement; having always the same use for words, he had words so selected and combined as to be ready at his call."

Extravagant claims for the predominance of formula in Homeric poetry have now been generally discounted, and even Parry's basic theses have been shown to need modification in the light of later examination. There are many cases, for example, where a truly formulaic epithet does in fact seem to be poetically functional in its context. There are cases where verbal repetition is so poetically effective that it must be the result of poetic design rather than the working of a quasi-mechanical system. Careful investigation of the type-scenes—the ceremony of sacrifice, the arming of the warrior, and so on—has revealed that although sometimes whole verses are repeated from one scene to another, no two scenes are exactly similar. "Each occurrence," to quote a recent evaluation (Edwards, p. 72), "is unique, and often specifically adapted to its context." Even the basic concept of economy, the strict limitation of the epithets for one god or hero to those needed in different cases and positions, has been questioned: a recent study shows that in his analysis of the epithets for Achilles, Parry considered only the phrases containing the hero's name, ignoring other ways of identifying Achilles, such as "Peleus' son" (Shive, *passim*). All this, together with the monumental scale and magnificent architecture of the *Iliad*, the complex structure of the *Odyssey*, makes the image of Homer as an illiterate bard, totally dependent on ready-made formulas and stock scenes for improvised performance, hard to accept.

There is nevertheless fairly general agreement that Parry was right in one thing: Homer's unique style does show clearly that he was heir to a long tradition of oral poetry. There is, however, one problem that Parry raised but did not solve: Homer may or may not have been as illiterate as his forerunners, but at some time the *Iliad* and the *Odyssey* were written down. When, by whom, for what purpose and in what circumstances was this done?

The most likely date for the composition of the *Iliad* is the fifty years running from 725 to 675 B.C.; for the *Odyssey*, somewhat later in the period. That is also the time to which the earliest examples of Greek alphabetic writing can be dated. Did Homer take advantage of the new technique to record for future singers the huge poems he had composed without the aid of writing? Did writing perhaps play a role in its composition? To both these questions Parry's collaborator and successor, Albert Lord, gave an emphatically negative answer. "The two techniques are . . . mutually exclusive . . . It is conceivable that a man might be an oral poet in his younger years and a written poet later in life, but it is not possible that he be *both* an oral and a written poet at any given time in his career" (p. 129). Lord based this assertion on his experience with Yugoslav oral poets who, when they came in contact with literate urban societies, lost their gift for improvised recitation. He envisaged a Homer, an oral bard at the height of his powers, who dictated his poem to a scribe, one who had mastered the new art of writing. This was of course how the songs of illiterate Yugoslav bards had been written down (sometimes with the aid of recording equipment, sophisticated for its time) by Parry and Lord.

This scenario did not satisfy everyone. The analogy with modern Yugoslavia, for example, was flawed. When the bards there learned to read and write, they were immediately exposed to the corrupting influence of newspapers, magazines and cheap fiction, but if Homer learned to write in the late eighth century, there was little or nothing for him to read. Lord's generalization about the incompatibility of the two techniques has been questioned by students of oral poetry; in other parts of the world (particularly in Africa), they find no such dichotomy. "The basic point . . . is the continuity of oral and written literature. There is no deep gulf between the two: they shade into each other both in the present and over many centuries of historical development, and there are innumerable cases of poetry which has both 'oral' and 'written' elements" (Finnegan, p. 24). Furthermore, the extant specimens of alphabetic writing of the eighth and early seventh centuries B.C. make it hard to believe in a scribe of the period who could take dictation at or, for that matter, anywhere near performance speed: the letters are freestanding capitals, crudely and laboriously formed, written from right to left, or from right to left and left to right on alternate lines. One critic, in fact, irreverently conjured up a picture of Homer dictating the first line (or rather the first half-line) of the *Iliad*: "*Mênin aeide thea* . . . You got that?"

A different scenario for the transition from oral performance to written text was developed by Geoffrey Kirk. The epics were the work of an oral "monumental composer," whose version imposed itself on bards and audiences as the definitive version. They "then passed through at least a couple of generations of transmission by decadent and quasi-literate singers and rhapsodes" (Kirk, *The Iliad: A Commentary*, I, p. xxv)—that is, performers who were not themselves poets. Lord's objection to this, that memorization plays no part in the living oral tradition, was based on Yugoslav experience, but elsewhere—in Somalia, for example—very long poems are recited from memory by professional reciters who are themselves, in many cases, poets.

What neither of these theories explains, however, is the immense length of the poem. Why should an oral, illiterate poet, whose poetry exists only in its performance before an audience, create a poem so long that it would take several days to perform? For that matter, if his poetry existed only in performance, how *could* he create a poem of such length? If, on the other hand, he delivered different sections of it at different times and places, how could he have elaborated the variations on theme and formula and the inner structural correspondences that distinguish the Homeric epics so sharply from the Yugoslav texts collected by Parry and Lord?

It is not surprising that many recent scholars in the field have come to the conclusion that writing did indeed play a role in the creation of these extraordinary poems, that the phenomena characteristic of oral epic demonstrated by Parry and Lord are balanced by qualities peculiar to literary composition. They envisage a highly creative oral poet, master of the repertoire of inherited material and technique, who used the new instrument of writing to build, probably over the course of a lifetime, an epic poem on a scale beyond the imagination of his predecessors.

The last half of the eighth century was the time in which writing was coming into use all over the Greek world. Homer must have known of its existence, but the traditional nature of his material naturally forbade its appearance in the relentlessly archaic world of his heroes, who belonged to the time when men were stronger, braver and greater than men are now, a world in which men and gods spoke face-to-face. Even so, Homer does show, in one particular instance, that he was conscious of the new technique. In Book 6 of the *Iliad* Glaucus tells the story of his grandfather Bellerophon, whom Proetus, king of Argos, sent off with a message to the king of Lycia, Proetus' father-in-law; it instructed the king to kill the bearer: "[He] gave him tokens, / murderous signs, scratched in a folded tablet" (6.198–99). There has been much discussion about the nature of these signs, but the word Homer uses—*grapsas*, literally "scratching"—is later the normal word used for "writing," and *pinax*—"tablet"—is the word used by later Greeks to describe the wooden boards coated with wax that were used for short notes.

If Homer could write, what did he write on? Obviously, "tablets" would not be adequate. We do not know when papyrus, the paper of the ancient world, was first available in Greece, though we do know that it came at first not from its almost exclusive source, Egypt—which was not opened to Greek merchants until the sixth century B.C.—but from the Phoenician port the Greeks called Byblos (the Greek word for book was *biblion*—our "Bible"). Archaeological evidence for Phoenician imports into Greece dates from the ninth century B.C., and Phoenician traders are mentioned in the *Iliad* (23.828) and their operations described with a wealth of detail in the *Odyssey*. But even if papyrus was not available in quantity, there were other materials, such as animal skins. Herodotus, writing in the fifth century B.C., says that in his time the Ionian Greeks still used the word *diphthera*—"skin"—when they meant "book."

The crudity of the script in the eighth century meant that writing was a laborious business. If Homer did use writing in the composition of the poem, it is likely that the process extended over many years. Episodes from the Odyssean voyages (the one-eyed giant) or from the return of Odysseus (the slaughter in the hall) would be brought to near perfection in oral performance, perhaps combined with other episodes to form longer units for special occasions (Odysseus among the Phaeacians, the beggar in the palace) and eventually committed to writing. Gradually a complete text would be assembled, to be refined in detail and extended by insertions, the longer sections welded into unity by connecting links. It was inevitable in such a process, with writing a newly acquired skill and writing materials, papyrus or leather, not convenient for cross-reference, that the final version should contain inconsistencies. No one has ever, in spite of repeated and ingenious efforts, been able to produce a totally convincing ground plan of the palace of Odysseus; people enter and emerge from rooms that seem to shift position from one episode to the next. There are also inconsistencies in the location of the characters. In Book 15, for example, when Telemachus and Theoclymenus, the fugitive he has taken under his wing, arrive at Ithaca, they go ashore and Theoclymenus sees a hawk carry off a dove, a bird sign that he interprets as a prophecy of victory for Telemachus. But later, when he refers to this incident, he says that he saw the hawk as he "sat on the benched ship" (17.175).

These are inconsistencies typical of poetry improvised in dramatic presentation; the wonder is that there are not many more of them in so long and complex a poem. Though pointed out in scholarly commentaries, they rarely disturb the ordinary reader today, and of course Homer's original audiences, even if they had been critically disposed, would have been hard put to cite chapter and verse for their objections. But in fact the poet's listeners were not in a critical frame of mind. The word Homer uses to describe audience reaction to the longest epic recital in the *Odyssey*—the hero's tale of his wandering course from Troy to the court of the Phaeacian king, where he now sits at the banquet table—is *kêlêthmos*, "enchantment." "His story [held] them spellbound down the shadowed halls" (13.2). Many centuries later, in Plato's dialogue *Ion*, a rhapsode, a professional reciter of the Homeric epics, echoes Homer's words as he describes the audience's reaction to his performance. "I look down on them weeping, gazing at me with an awe-struck look, joining me in my astonishment at the words I am speaking."

The surprising thing is that the inconsistencies stayed in the text. If Homer, as in Lord's model, had dictated his poem, the scribe could hardly have failed to notice and correct them. In fact, Lord records such corrections in the course of dictation in Yugoslavia. And it seems hard to imagine the lines going uncorrected in Kirk's scenario of a monumental poem preserved by recitation for a generation or two before being written down. Any rhapsode (and in the earlier generation he would have been an oral poet himself) could have corrected the lines without effort and would have seen no reason not to do so. There seems to be only one possible explanation of their survival in the text: that the text was regarded as authentic, the exact words of Homer himself. And that can only mean that there was a written copy.

This is of course pure speculation, but so are all other attempts to explain the origin of the text that has come down to us. We shall never be able to answer the questions it raises with any certainty and must rest content with the fact that a great poet marshaled the resources of an age-old traditional art to create something new—the tales of the wrath of Achilles and the wanderings of Odysseus that have been models for epic poetry ever since.

THE *ODYSSEY* AND THE *ILIAD*

It has always been assumed that the *Odyssey* was composed later than the *Iliad*. One ancient critic, the author of the treatise *On the Sublime*, thought that the *Odyssey* was the product of Homer's old age, of "a mind in decline; it was a work that could be compared to the setting sun—the size remained, without the force." He did, however, temper the harshness of that judgment by adding: "I am speaking of old age—but it is the old age of Homer." What prompted his comment "without the force" is clearly his preference for the sustained heroic level of the *Iliad* over what he terms the *Odyssey*'s presentation of "the fabulous and incredible" as well as the realistic description of life in the farms and palace of Odysseus' domain, which, he says, "forms a kind of comedy of manners." His judgment is of course determined by the conception of the "sublime" which is the focus of his book, one that did not welcome scenes like those offered by Book 18 of the *Odyssey*—a fistfight between two ragged beggars, for example, or the award of a sizzling-hot goat's-blood sausage full of fat to the winner.

On the Sublime was written sometime in the first century A.D., but a different scenario for the relation of the *Iliad* to the *Odyssey* had already been proposed in the second century B.C. A number of scholars, known as *chorizontes*—"separators"—recognized that the *Odyssey* was composed later than the *Iliad* but suggested that it had a different author. This is the position taken also by many modern scholars, who find significant differences between the two poems not only in vocabulary and grammatical usage but also in what they consider development from the *Iliad* to the *Odyssey* in moral and religious ideas and attitudes. Estimates of the validity of such evidence vary, however, and there are those who find it hard to accept the idea of the emergence of two major epic poets in such a short span of time.

That the *Odyssey* was composed later than the *Iliad* can hardly be doubted. For one thing, though it takes for granted the audience's knowledge not just of the Trojan War saga but of the particular form it has been given in the *Iliad*, it carefully avoids duplicating its material. Incidents from the tale of Troy are frequently recalled, sometimes in detail and at length, but they all fall outside the time frame of the *Iliad*, occurring either before or after the period of forty-one days that began with the wrath of Achilles and ended with the burial of Hector. Demodocus at the Phaeacian court sings of the quarrel between Odysseus and Achilles (an incident not mentioned in the *Iliad* or, for that matter, anywhere else in extant Greek literature) and later of the wooden horse that brought the siege to an end. In the palace at Ithaca, the theme of the minstrel Phemius is the sufferings of the heroes on their way home from the war. Nestor at Pylos tells Telemachus how Agamemnon and Menelaus quarreled after the fall of Troy and took separate routes home. Helen and Menelaus at Sparta tell stories about Odysseus at Troy, neither of them familiar from the *Iliad*. Even when Odysseus meets the shades of his comrades Agamemnon and Achilles in Hades, Iliadic material is avoided: Agamemnon tells the story of his death at the hands of his wife and her lover, Odysseus tells Achilles about the heroic feats of arms of his son Neoptolemus and later talks to Ajax about the award of the arms of Achilles.

That the poet of the *Odyssey* knew the *Iliad* in its contemporary form is strongly suggested also by the continuity of character delineation from one poem to the other. In the *Odyssey* they are all older, those of them who are still alive, but they are recognizably the same men. Nestor is still regal, punctilious and long-winded. Menelaus' generous reaction to Telemachus' tactful refusal of his gift of chariot and horses recalls his princely response to young Antilochus' apology for his unsportsmanlike maneuver in the chariot race at the funeral games for Patroclus. Helen is still, at Sparta as she was at Troy, the poised mistress of a difficult situation. And Odysseus is still the spellbinding speaker Antenor remembered in Book 3 of the *Iliad*, whose "words came piling on like a driving winter blizzard" (3.267); he is still "the man of twists and turns" Helen identified for Priam in the same passage (3.244). And he is still the man "who says one thing but hides another in his heart" (9.379)—Achilles' description of the kind of man he hates (he is addressing Odysseus, who has come as Agamemnon's ambassador). Odysseus is still the quick-thinking and resourceful leader who by prompt action stemmed the rush for the ships caused by Agamemnon's foolish decision to test the morale of the troops by suggesting that they go home.

But in the *Odyssey* he is no longer one of many heroes fighting between the beached ships and the walls of Troy. He is on his own, first as admiral of a small fleet, then as captain of an isolated ship, and finally as a shipwrecked sailor clinging to a piece of wreckage. The scenes of his action and suffering widen to include not only the coasts and islands of the Aegean Sea and continental Greece but also, in the false travel tales he spins in his disguise as a beggar, Crete, Cyprus, Phoenicia and Sicily, and, in the stories he tells the Phaeacians at their feast, the unknown world of the western seas, full of marvels and monsters. Those ships that in the *Iliad* lie beached behind a palisade and, with Achilles out of the fighting, face the fury of Hector's assault, return in the *Odyssey* to their natural element, the wine-dark sea.

THE WESTERN SEAS

Many centuries after Homer, the Florentine Dante Alighieri, who had not read Homer and whose information about Ulysses (the Latin form of Odysseus' name) came from Virgil and Ovid, saw in the Greek hero a vision of the restless explorer, the man who, discontented with the mundane life of that home he had longed for, set off again in search of new worlds. "Neither the pleasure I took in my son," he says in the *Inferno*, "nor reverence for my aged father, nor the love I owed Penelope that should have made her joyful, could prevail against the passion I felt to win experience of the world, of human vice and worth." He sets sail for Gibraltar and launches out into the Atlantic, following the sun "to the world where no one lives." This theme was taken up in Tennyson's "Ulysses," where the hero announces his purpose "to sail beyond the sunset, and the baths / Of all the western stars . . ."

But these visions of Odysseus as the restless explorer, hungry for new worlds, have little to do with Homer's Odysseus, who wants above all things to find his way home and stay there. It is true that, as Homer tells us in the prologue, he saw "many cities of men . . . and learned their minds" (1.4); once afloat in uncharted seas, he has a thoroughly Greek curiosity about the inhabitants of the landfalls he makes, but the voyage was none of his choosing. He was "driven time and again off course, once he had plundered / the hallowed heights of Troy" (1.2–3), and far from seeking "experience of the world," he was "fighting to save his life and bring his comrades home" (1.6).

Odysseus' wanderings in the west have inspired many attempts to plot his course and identify his ports of call. This wild-goose chase had begun already in the ancient world, as we know from the brusque dismissal of such identifications by the great Alexandrian geographer Eratosthenes, who said that you would be able to chart the course of Odysseus' wanderings when you found the cobbler who sewed the bag in which Aeolus confined the winds. This of course has not deterred modern scholars and amateurs from trying; their guesses run from the possible—Charybdis as a mythical personification of whirlpools in the straits between Sicily and the toe of the Italian boot—to the fantastic: Calypso's island as Iceland. According to one investigator of the subject, "There have been some seventy theories proposed since Homer wrote the *Odyssey*, with locations bounded only by the North and South Poles and ranging within the inhabited world from Norway to South Africa and from the Canary Islands to the Sea of Azov" (Clarke, p. 251).

But even identifications that are not obviously ridiculous seem implausible in the light of Homer's confused geographical notions of areas much nearer home. He knows the Asia Minor coast and the Aegean islands: Nestor on the alternative routes from Troy across the Aegean sounds like an expert seaman. But Homer's notion of Egypt, where Menelaus was delayed by contrary winds and where Odysseus in his lying tales often lands, is, to put it mildly, vague. Menelaus describes the island of Pharos, which is one mile off the coast, as distant as far as a ship runs in a whole day with the wind behind her. And when Homer's characters move to mainland Greece and its western offshore islands, confusion reigns. His description of Ithaca is so full of contradictions that many modern scholars have proposed Leucas or Cephallenia as the real home of Odysseus rather than the island that now bears the name. Homer also displays total ignorance of the geography of mainland Greece: his Telemachus and Pisistratus go from Pylos on the west coast to Sparta in a horse-drawn chariot over a formidable mountain barrier that had no through road in ancient times.

But Homer's hazy notions of any area outside the Aegean is only one of the objections to the idea of assigning western locations to Circe's island and the land of the Lotus-eaters. A great many of the incidents in Odysseus' wanderings are obviously based on a different voyage, the voyage of the *Argo*, which, with a crew of heroes captained by Jason, sailed not the western but the eastern seas. The Laestrygonians who attack Odysseus' ships with rocks have their counterparts in the Argonauts' saga; Circe is the sister of Aeetes, keeper of the golden fleece, and Homer himself locates her island not in the west but in the east—where the sun rises. The Clashing Rocks are also a feature of Jason's voyage, and the poem that celebrates it is specifically mentioned by Homer at this point. And the Sirens appear in Apollonius' poem the *Argonautica*, which, though written in the second century B.C., certainly drew on the earlier poem to which Homer refers. What Homer has done is to transfer episodes from a mythical epic journey in eastern waters to the western seas.

It was of course a geographical imperative that if Odysseus was to be blown off course on his way home, the wind would take him west. But that imperative must have been eagerly welcomed by Homer and his audience, for the early years of the eighth century B.C. saw the beginnings of what was to become a large-scale movement of Greek traders and, later, colonists into the western Mediterranean. Odysseus, when he declines the invitation of a young Phaeacian to compete in an athletic contest, is contemptuously dismissed as no athlete but

> "some skipper of profiteers,
> roving the high seas in his scudding craft,
> reckoning up his freight with a keen eye out
> for home-cargo, grabbing the gold he can!"   (8.186–89)

The traders were soon followed by the colonists. The first settlement seems to have been Pithecusae, on the island of Ischia in the Bay of Naples; it was not a city but a trading station and is dated by archaeological evidence not later than 775 B.C. By 700 there were Greek cities in Italy: Cumae, on the mainland opposite Ischia; Rhegium (Reggio Calabria), on the toe of the Italian boot; and the proverbially wealthy city of Sybaris, on the instep, as well as Taras (Taranto) in the same area. On the neighboring island of Sicily, Syracuse and Zancle (Messina) were founded around 725. Still later were to come settlements on the southern coast of France: Massilia (Marseilles), Antipas (Antibes) and Nicaea (Nice), as well as Cyrene on the coast of what is now Libya.

Long before the first colonists set out, there must have been many voyages of trader-explorers, who no doubt brought back tales of wonders and dangers that improved in the telling. Charybdis, for example, may possibly be a fantastic version of the currents and whirlpools that are sometimes encountered in the straits between Sicily and the mainland. And though the Cyclops' gigantic size and one eye mark him as mythical, his pastoral economy and ferocity toward strangers may be a memory of the indigenous populations who opposed the intruders landing on their shores—a demonized vision of the native, like Shakespeare's Caliban. *The Tempest* was written in a similar age of exploration, and though Prospero and Ariel have powers that are not of this world, there can be no doubt that the wonders of the play are an imaginative reworking of the tall tales of the sailors and pirates who for half a century had sailed the Central American seas in search of land to settle, Spanish ships to board, Spanish towns to sack, or Spanish buyers for their cargoes of African slaves. We know, in fact, that Shakespeare must have read some of the accounts of the shipwreck of the *Sea-Venture*, the flagship of a fleet on its way to the Virginia colony, in a "dreadful and hideous storm" off the island of Bermuda, and the company's survival and eventual arrival at the colony—a series of events that one of the accounts calls "a tragical comedy."

And there is one passage in the *Odyssey* that is a clear reminiscence of Greek voyages of exploration in the west. When Odysseus comes to the land of the Cyclops, he sees a small island offshore, which is fertile and

well stocked with wild goats, but uninhabited. The Cyclops, he explains
to his Phaeacian audience,

> "have no ships with crimson prows,
> no shipwrights there to build them good trim craft . . .
> Such artisans would have made this island too
> a decent place to live in . . . No mean spot,
> it could bear you any crop you like in season.
> The water-meadows along the low foaming shore
> run soft and moist, and your vines would never flag.
> The land's clear for plowing. Harvest on harvest,
> a man could reap a healthy stand of grain—
> the subsoil's dark and rich."   (9.138–49)

It is the authentic voice of the explorer evaluating a site for settlement.

VOYAGER

Odysseus' voyage to the fabulous western seas begins in the everyday
world, as he leaves the ruins of Troy homeward bound, his ships loaded
with booty from the sack of the city. As if that booty were not enough for
him, he attacks the first settlement he comes to on his way, the town of
Ismarus on the Thracian coast opposite Troy:

> ". . . I sacked the city,
> killed the men, but as for the wives and plunder,
> that rich haul we dragged away from the place—
> we shared it round . . ."   (9.45–48)

It is sheer piracy—Ismarus was not a Trojan ally—but it is obviously an
action not unusual in its time and place; one of Odysseus' epithets is in
fact *ptoliporthos*, "sacker of cities." Nestor at Pylos politely asks Tele-
machus and Pisistratus if they are

> "Out on a trading spree or roving the waves like pirates,
> sea-wolves raiding at will, who risk their lives
> to plunder other men?"   (3.81–83)

And Polyphemus asks Odysseus the same question (9.286–88). Thucy-
dides, writing in the fifth century B.C., was probably thinking of passages

like these when, speaking of the measures taken by Minos to suppress piracy in the Aegean, he pointed out that in ancient times "this occupation was held to be honorable rather than disgraceful. This is proved . . . by the testimony of ancient poets, in whose verses newly arrived visitors are always asked whether they are pirates, a question that implies no disapproval of such an occupation on the part of either those who answer with a disclaimer or those who ask for the information." Piracy was endemic in the Aegean—a sea of islands large and small, of jagged coastlines full of hidden harbors—whenever there was no central sea power strong enough to suppress it. Long after Minos, in the fifth century, an Athenian fleet under the command of Cimon cleared out a nest of pirates on the island of Scyros. Many centuries later the young Julius Caesar was captured by pirates near the small island of Pharmacusa off the Ionian coast and held for ransom. The seas became so unsafe that in 67 B.C. Cnaeus Pompeius was given the overriding authority to deal with the problem and did so by manning 270 warships and mobilizing 100,000 troops. Whenever there was a power vacuum in the Aegean, piracy reappeared; as late as the 1820s Arab corsairs carried off the inhabitants of the Greek island of Cythera to sell in the slave market at Algiers.

Cythera is the island off Cape Malea past which Odysseus, trying to turn north toward Ithaca, was blown west for nine days, off the map, into a world of wonders and terrors, of giants and witches, goddesses and cannibals, of dangers and temptations. The tales of his landfalls and the welcomes he received differ widely in content and scope, but they are connected by a common theme, on which they are all variations. It is a theme fundamental for the *Odyssey* as a whole, pervasive not only in the wandering voyage of the hero but also in the opening books, which deal with Telemachus at home and abroad, and in the last half of the poem, which presents us with Odysseus, disguised as a ragged beggar, home at last in his own house. This theme is, briefly stated, the relation between host and guest, particularly the moral obligation to welcome and protect the stranger, an obligation imposed on civilized mankind by Zeus, one of whose many titles is *xeinios*, "protector of strangers." "Zeus of the Strangers," says Odysseus to the one-eyed giant in his cave, "guards all guests and suppliants" (9.304).

Zeus is invoked as the divine patron and enforcer of a code of conduct that helps to make travel possible in a world of piracy at sea, cattle raiding and local war by land, of anarchic competition between rival families—a world with no firm central authority to impose law and order. In such a world, a man who leaves his home depends on the kindness of strangers. Without a universally recognized code of hospitality, no man would dare travel abroad; its observance is therefore a matter of self-interest. One of its almost ritual components is the parting gift offered by the host. So when Athena, in the shape of Mentes, takes leave of Telemachus, he tells her to go back to her ship "delighted with a gift, . . . something rare and fine . . . The kind of gift / a host will give a stranger, friend to friend" (1.357–60). Athena does not wish to be burdened with the gift now; she asks him to save it for her so that she can take it on her way back. "Choose something rare and fine, and a good reward / that gift is going to bring you" (1.365–66). The reward is not a cash payment; it is the reciprocal hospitality and gift Telemachus will receive when he goes to visit Mentes. So Odysseus, in his false tale to Laertes at the end of the poem, pretends to be a man who entertained Odysseus once on his travels and loaded him with gifts. He has stopped at Ithaca now to visit Odysseus. The old man tells him Odysseus has never returned and must be dead.

> "But if you'd found him alive, here in Ithaca,
> he would have replied in kind, with gift for gift,
> and entertained you warmly . . .
> That's the old custom, when one has led the way."   (24.315–18)

The host's gift is so fixed a feature of the relationship that the guest can even ask for something else, if the proffered gift is not suitable. So Telemachus, offered a splendid chariot and team of horses by Menelaus, declines the offer. "Those horses I really cannot take to Ithaca," where there is "No running-room for mares . . . no meadows." His island is "Goat, not stallion, land" (4.676–82). Menelaus, far from being taken aback, recognizes his frankness as the mark of aristocratic birth and breeding—"Good blood runs in you, dear boy"—and offers him instead "a mixing-bowl, forged to perfection— / it's solid silver finished off with a lip of gold" (4.688–93). The bowl, he goes on to explain, was itself a gift from a host, Phaedimus, king of the Phoenician city of Sidon, with whom he stayed on his wandering course home from Troy.

Throughout his voyage, Odysseus will be dependent on the kindness of strangers, their generosity as hosts. Some of them, like the Phaeacians and Aeolus, king of the winds, will be perfect hosts, entertaining him lavishly and sending him on his way with precious gifts. Others will be savages, threatening his life and taking the lives of his crew. Still others will be importunate hosts, delaying the guest's departure—an infraction of the code. "I'd never detain you here too long," Menelaus says to Telemachus. "I'd find fault with another host . . . too warm to his guests." And taking a leaf from Pope's translation, he formulates the golden rule: " 'Welcome the coming, speed the parting guest!' " (15.74–81, see note 15.80–81). Many of Odysseus' hosts seem to have heard only the first half of that injunction. Circe is a charming hostess, but she charms her guests out of human shape and keeps them forever. Calypso too would have kept Odysseus forever, but in his own shape, perpetually young. The Sirens would have kept him forever also, but dead. Calypso and Circe, however, when the time comes to speed the parting guest, provide the requisite gifts. Calypso sends a fair wind to send his raft on its way, and Circe gives him precious instructions—how to deal with the Sirens, the warning not to kill the cattle of the Sun. Telemachus also has to deal with an importunate host. On his way back from Sparta to Pylos, he manages to evade what he fears will be an intolerable delay if he goes to Nestor's palace. "Your father's old," he says to his companion Pisistratus,

> ". . . in love with his hospitality;
> I fear he'll hold me, chafing in his palace—
> I must hurry home!"   (15.223–25)

Telemachus will return to a house where the suitors of Penelope represent an unusual infraction of the code: they are uninvited guests who abuse and waste their reluctant host's possessions. Showing their utter contempt for the idea that wanderers, beggars and suppliants are under the special protection of Zeus, they offer insults and physical violence to Odysseus, the ragged beggar who, as they will eventually find out to their cost, is their unwilling host.

Odysseus' first landfall after passing Cape Malea is the country of the Lotus-eaters, who offer three of his men food that would have kept them as permanent guests—

> "[they] lost all desire to send a message back, much less return,
> . . . all memory of the journey home
> dissolved forever."   (9.107–10)

—if Odysseus had not dragged them, weeping, back to the ships. The Lotus-eaters, as he reports, "had no notion of killing my companions" (9.104), but his next host, the Cyclops, not only kills but also eats six of them. Odysseus' invocation of Zeus as protector of strangers is met with scorn—"We Cyclops never blink at Zeus . . . or any other blessed god"

(9.309–10)—and Odysseus' request for a guest-gift is met with the concession that Odysseus will be eaten last, after all his crew. Odysseus makes his escape only because of the resourcefulness for which he is famous, but in order to trick the Cyclops he has to suppress his identity and give his name as Nobody.

Deceit is indispensable if he and his crew are to escape, but though he is master of all the arts of deceit, this particular subterfuge is one his whole nature rebels against. It is for his name and all that it means to him and his peers that he struggles to go on living and return to the world where it is known and honored. When, later, at the court of King Alcinous, he reveals his identity, he tells the banqueters, and us, not only his name but also the renown it carries. "I am Odysseus, son of Laertes, known to the world / for every kind of craft—my fame has reached the skies" (9.21–22). He speaks of his fame in an utterly objective manner, as if it were something apart from himself; his words are not a boast but a statement of the reputation, the qualities and achievements, to which he must be true. Once free of the Cyclops' cave, he insists, at great risk to himself and his ship, on telling the Cyclops who has blinded him: "Odysseus, / raider of cities, *he* gouged out your eye, / Laertes' son who makes his home in Ithaca!" (9.560–62). And this enables Polyphemus to invoke the wrath of his father, the sea god Poseidon, and ensure that Odysseus will "come home late / and come a broken man—all shipmates lost, / alone in a stranger's ship," to "find a world of pain at home" (9.592–95).

With Odysseus' next port of call, however, it begins to look as if Polyphemus' prayer will remain unanswered. Aeolus, the keeper of the winds, is a generous host and sends his guest on a magical ride—the West Wind blowing steadily toward Ithaca and all the other winds imprisoned in a bag aboard his ship. In sight of home—"we could see men tending fires" (10.34)—Odysseus, who has been at the helm for the entire voyage, finally relaxes. But the deep sleep he falls into allows the crew, suspecting that the bag contains treasure, to open it and let loose the winds. As his ships are blown back into the unknown, Odysseus faces the first of his temptations—"should I leap over the side and drown at once?" (10.56)—but resolves to stay alive, even though the hurricane winds are hurrying his ships back to Aeolus, where his plea for further aid is indignantly rejected. His next encounter is with the gigantic cannibals, the Laestrygonians, from whom he makes a narrow escape, but with the loss of all his other ships and crews. Circe's island confronts him with another danger, from which he escapes with the help of the god

Hermes, but then she turns into a temptation. Circe, after she has renounced her plan to change him and his crew into swine, becomes a perfect hostess, entertaining Odysseus in her bed and his crew at the banquet table. Odysseus, if not bewitched, is certainly charmed, for at the end of a whole year of dalliance he has to be reminded by his crew of his duty: "Captain, this is madness! / High time you thought of your own home at last" (10.520–21). Circe, unlike Calypso, is willing to release him, but tells him that he must first go down to the land of the dead to consult the ghost of the blind prophet Tiresias.

Homer's picture of the lower world is of course the model for all later Western geographies of Hell, through Virgil's sixth book of the *Aeneid* to that greatest of all visions of the life to come, the *Divina Commedia* of Dante. Quite apart from the consultation with Tiresias, the visit has a special significance for Odysseus. All through the trials of his voyage home, the temptation to find release in death has always been at hand— by suicide, as in his despair off Ithaca, or, more subtly, at any moment of tension, by simply relaxing momentarily the constant vigilance, the quick suspicion, the inexhaustible resilience and determination, that keep him alive. Anyone who has been under a continual strain in action and especially in command knows the weariness that can tempt a man to neglect precautions, take the shortcut, let things go for once; it is a mood in which the death that may result seems for the moment almost preferable to the unending bodily fatigue and mental strain. But when Odysseus sees for himself what it means to be dead, he loses any illusions he may have had that death is better than a life of unbroken tension and hardship. Homer's world of the dead is dark and comfortless; it is no place of rest and oblivion. The shades crowd round the sacrificed animals, yearning for a draft of the blood that will for a moment bring them back to life, restore memory and the power of speech. Achilles reads the lesson to Odysseus, who had congratulated him on reigning like a king over the dead:

"No winning words about death to *me*, shining Odysseus!
By god, I'd rather slave on earth for another man—
some dirt-poor tenant farmer who scrapes to keep alive—
than rule down here over all the breathless dead." (11.555–58)

The land of the dead has been hospitable, but perhaps Odysseus has overstayed his welcome, for as he waits to see still more shades of famous heroes,

"... the dead came surging round me,
hordes of them, thousands raising unearthly cries,
and blanching terror gripped me ..."   (11.723–25)

He heads for his ship and returns to Circe, who proceeds to plot them "a course and chart each seamark" (12.28) for their voyage home.

They have yet to face the Sirens, make a choice between Scylla and Charybdis, and land, against Circe's advice and Odysseus' opposition, on Thrinacia, the island where the crew will slaughter the cattle of the Sun and so seal their own fate. The Sirens are another temptation for Odysseus, perhaps the most powerful of all, for if he had not been bound to the mast, he would have gone to join the heaps of corpses that surround them. "Come closer, famous Odysseus," they sing. "We know all the pains that the Greeks and Trojans once endured / on the spreading plain of Troy" (12.200–6). Odysseus is a veteran of a ten-year war; he is on his way back to a society in which a new generation has grown up in peace. There will be no one to understand him if he talks about the war— it is significant that once home and recognized, he does not mention it to Telemachus or Penelope. Only those who shared its excitement and horrors with him can talk about it. That is perhaps why Menelaus says he would have given Odysseus an estate in his own lands if he had come home: "how often," he says, "we'd have mingled side-by-side! / Nothing could have parted us" (4.197–98). The bonds forged by fellowship in dangerous action and suffering are very strong. And that is the strength of the Sirens' appeal: "we know all the pains that Achaeans and Trojans once endured / on the spreading plain of Troy." He orders his sailors to untie him, let him go. But of course the Sirens' song is an invitation to live in the past, and that is a kind of death; the Sirens' island is piled with the bones of dead men. It was in the land of the dead that he could relive the saga of Troy, with his fellow-veterans Achilles and Agamemnon. Those days are over, and he must look forward to the future, not backward to the past.

The choice between Scylla and Charybdis is still to be made, but Odysseus will have to face both—Scylla as a ship's captain on his way to Thrinacia, and Charybdis as a lone shipwrecked sailor clinging to a piece of wreckage on the way back. Rescued by the goddess Calypso (whose name is formed from the Greek word that means "cover," "hide"), Odysseus spends seven years a virtual prisoner on her island, "unwilling lover alongside lover all too willing" (5.172). He rejects her offer to make him immortal and ageless, her husband forever. Ordered by Hermes to let him go, she reminds him of the offer and foretells the trials and tribulations that still await him on the voyage home:

> ". . . if you only knew, down deep, what pains
> are fated to fill your cup before you reach that shore,
> you'd stay right here, preside in our house with me
> and be immortal."   (5.228–31)

But he refuses.

Calypso's offer and Odysseus' refusal are an exchange unique in Greek literature and mythology. Immortality was a divine prerogative, grudgingly conferred. Heracles had to die a fiery, agonizing death to win it, and when the Dawn goddess obtained it for her mortal lover Tithonus, she forgot to ask also that he should never grow old. Now as she sets out on her route every morning, she leaves him behind in bed, where he lies inert, shriveled with age. But Calypso has offered to make Odysseus "immortal, ageless, all his days" (5.151) and invited him to live with her in a paradisal environment so enchanting that

> . . . even a deathless god
> who came upon that place would gaze in wonder,
> heart entranced with pleasure   (5.81–83)

—a place before which Hermes, messenger of Zeus, "stood . . . spellbound" (5.84). All this Odysseus rejects, though he knows that the alternative is to entrust himself again, this time alone and on a makeshift craft, to that sea about which he has no illusions. "And if a god will wreck me yet again on the wine-dark sea," he says,

> "Much have I suffered, labored long and hard by now
> in the waves and wars. Add this to the total—
> bring the trial on!"   (5.244–48)

One more offer to forget his home and his identity is made and refused before he reaches Ithaca. In the land of the Phaeacians, where he is welcomed and honored, he is offered the hand in marriage of a young and charming princess and a life of ease and enjoyment in a utopian society. The offer is made not only by the king her father—

> ". . . if only—
> seeing the man you are, seeing we think as one—
> *you* could wed my daughter and be my son-in-law
> and stay right here with us"   (7.356–59)

—but also, earlier, by the girl herself, in the subtle hints contained in her instructions to him about his approach to the city. She makes a final appeal to him as he goes to the banquet hall for the feast at which he will later identify himself and tell his story. She reminds him how much he owes her:

> "Farewell, my friend! And when you are at home,
> home in your own land, remember me at times.
> Mainly to me you owe the gift of life."   (8.518–20)

This is not quite the resigned farewell it sounds like. The word she uses for what Odysseus owes her—*zôagria*—is an Iliadic word: "the price of a life." Hephaestus uses it when Thetis comes to ask him to make new armor for Achilles; he will do anything for her, since she saved his life once—he owes her *zôagria*. Three times in the *Iliad*, Trojan warriors, disarmed and at the mercy of the victor, use the verb from which this noun is formed to offer rich ransom in exchange for their lives. Nausicaa is pressing Odysseus hard, with a word he fully understands; he had heard his captive Dolon use it to him in an appeal for his life, which was refused (*Iliad* 10.442–43). But now, reminded of how much he owes her, he tactfully evades the issue by taking her request literally; when he reaches home, he will pray to her as a deathless goddess all his days.

Loaded with treasure greater than all he had won at Troy and lost at sea, Odysseus, in a deep sleep, is transported in the magical Phaeacian ship to the real world and landed, still asleep, on the shore of Ithaca. When he wakes up, he does not recognize his own country, for Athena has cloaked the shore in a mist. Afraid that the Phaeacians have betrayed him, he repeats the agonized questions he has asked himself on so many strange shores—

> ". . . whose land have I lit on now?
> What *are* they here—violent, savage, lawless?—
> or friendly to strangers, god-fearing men?"   (13.227–29)

He has in fact reached the most dangerous of all his landfalls. To survive this last trial, he will have to call on all the qualities that mark him as a hero—the courage and martial skill of the warrior he was at Troy, but also the caution, cunning, duplicity and patience that have brought him safe to Ithaca.

HERO

"I hate that man like the very Gates of Death / who says one thing but hides another in his heart." These are the words of Achilles, the hero of the *Iliad* (9.378–79), the *chevalier sans peur et sans reproche* of the Greek aristocratic tradition. He addressed them to Odysseus, who had come as leader of a delegation charged by Agamemnon and the Achaean chieftains to persuade Achilles to rejoin them in the attack on Troy. These are strange words with which to open an answer to what seems like a generous offer of compensation for harsh words uttered in anger, but Achilles knows his man. Odysseus has told no lie, but he has concealed the truth. He has repeated verbatim the bulk of Agamemnon's message—the long list of splendid gifts, the offer of the hand of a daughter in marriage—but he has suppressed Agamemnon's reiterated claim to superiority, his relegation of Achilles to inferior rank. "Let him bow down to me! I am the greater king, / . . . the greater man" (9.192–93).

For Achilles a lie is something utterly abhorrent. But for Odysseus it is second nature, a point of pride. "I am Odysseus," he tells the Phaeacians when the time comes to reveal his identity, "known to the world / for every kind of craft" (9.21–22). The Greek word here translated "craft" is *dolos*. It is a word that can be used in praise as well as abuse. Athena uses the word when, in the guise of a handsome young shepherd, she compliments Odysseus on the complicated lie he has just told her about his identity and his past, and it is with this word that Odysseus describes the wooden horse he contrived to bring Troy down in flames. On the other hand, Athena, Menelaus and Odysseus use it of the trap Clytemnestra set for Agamemnon when he returned home, and it serves Homer as a description of the suitors' plan to ambush and kill Telemachus on his way back from Pylos. But whether complimentary or accusing, it always implies the presence of what Achilles so vehemently rejects—the intention to deceive.

Odysseus has the talent necessary for the deceiver: he is a persuasive speaker. In the *Iliad* the Trojan prince Antenor, who had listened to Odysseus when he came with an embassy to Troy, remembered the contrast between his unimpressive appearance and the powerful magic of his speech. "When *he* let loose that great voice from his chest / . . . then no man alive could rival Odysseus!" (3.266–68). And in the *Odyssey*, in the palace of Alcinous, he holds his host spellbound with the story of his adventures. When he breaks off, pleading the lateness of the hour, Alcinous begs him to go on: "what grace you give your words, and what good sense within! / You have told your story with all a singer's skill" (11.416–17). In his travels on the way to Phaeacia, Odysseus has not had much occasion to give rein to his eloquent persuasion; his skill in deception will be needed and fully revealed only when at last he reaches the shore of Ithaca, where in order to survive he has to play the role of a penniless, ragged beggar. The tales he tells, to Athena, Eumaeus, Antinous, Penelope and Laertes are brilliant fictions, tales of war, piracy, murder, blood-feuds and peril on the high seas, with a cast of rogue Phoenician captains, Cretan adventurers and Egyptian Pharaohs. They are, as Homer says, "lies like truth," thoroughly convincing, true, unlike the tale he told in Phaeacia, to the realities of life and death in the Aegean world, but nonetheless lies from beginning to end. And Homer reminds us of the contrast between Odysseus and Achilles by making Odysseus, just before he launches out on a splendidly mendacious account of his background and misfortunes, repeat the famous words Achilles addressed to him at Troy. "I hate that man like the very Gates of Death who / . . . stoops to peddling lies" (14.182–83).

The repetition of that memorable phrase makes the contrast between the two heroes explicit, but Odysseus is still, as he was in the *Iliad*, a warrior faithful to the martial ideal. He will gladly employ deceit to win victory, but if necessary he will confront mortal danger alone and unafraid. On Circe's island, when Eurylochus returns to report the disappearance of his companions inside the witch's palace and implores Odysseus not to go to their rescue but to set sail at once, he is met with a scornful refusal:

> "Eurylochus, stay right here,
> eating, drinking, safe by the black ship.
> I must be off. Necessity drives me on."   (10.299–301)

This necessity is his fidelity to that reputation, that fame among men, for which Achilles accepted an early death. This is the Odysseus of the *Iliad*, who, finding himself alone and outnumbered in a desperate struggle with the Trojans, rules out the thought of flight:

> "Cowards, I know, would quit the fighting now
> but the man who wants to make his mark in war
> must stand his ground . . ."   (11.483–85)

Odysseus shares with Achilles another characteristic of the heroic mentality: a prickly sensitivity to what he regards as a lack of respect on the part of others, an irrepressible rage against any insult to his standing as a hero. This was the motive of his near-fatal insistence on revealing his real name to Polyphemus: he could not bear the thought that the blinded giant would never know the identity or the fame of his conqueror. More cautious among the Phaeacians, he carefully remains anonymous but comes close to revealing the truth when, scorned by a young Phaeacian for his lack of athletic prowess, he hurls the discus a prodigious distance and then challenges them all—at boxing, wrestling, racing and archery. "Well I know," he tells them,

> "how to handle a fine polished bow . . .
> Philoctetes alone outshot me there at Troy
> when ranks of Achaean archers bent their bows."   (8.246–51)

The most painful insult to his honor is of course the conduct of the suitors; their three-year-long occupation of his house is an intolerable affront, compounded by their brutal treatment of him as he plays the role of Nobody once again. And their sublime confidence that even if he did return he would meet a humiliating death fighting against their superior numbers stirs in him an Achillean wrath. When he finally kills Antinous, the most violent of the suitors, and identifies himself at last—"You dogs! you never imagined I'd return from Troy" (22.36)—Eurymachus, the most deceitful of the suitors, offers full compensation and more for the damage they have done. Odysseus fiercely rejects it:

> "No, Eurymachus! Not if you paid me all your father's wealth—
> all you possess now, and all that could pour in from the world's end—
> no, not even then would I stay my hands from slaughter
> till all you suitors had paid for all your crimes!"   (22.65–68)

We have heard this note sounded before, in the voice of Achilles in the *Iliad* rejecting Agamemnon's peace offering:

> "Not if he gave me ten times as much, twenty times over, all
> he possesses now, and all that could pour in from the world's end—
> . . . no, not even then could Agamemnon
> bring my fighting spirit round until he pays me back,
> pays full measure for all his heartbreaking outrage!"   (9.464–73)

In the event, Achilles exacts full measure not from Agamemnon but from Hector, who has killed his friend Patroclus and now wears Achilles' armor. One after another he cuts down Trojan warriors, drives them into

the river to drown or die under his merciless sword, until he meets and
kills Hector, whose corpse he drags back to his camp, to lie there
unburied while he sacrifices captured Trojans to appease the spirit of
Patroclus dead. Odysseus' vindication of his honor is no less bloody and
merciless. Backed by his son and two loyal servants, he kills all the one
hundred and eight young aristocrats who have besieged his wife; his ser-
vants savagely mutilate and kill the faithless shepherd Melanthius, who
had insulted Odysseus; and Telemachus, ordered to dispatch the disloyal
maids with his sword, chooses to deny them this "clean death" (22.488)
and hangs them. All scores are paid. With interest.

Achilles' revenge ends with a compassionate gesture, the return of
Hector's body to his father, Priam, but at the end of the *Odyssey* more
blood is spilled. Eupithes, Antinous' father, leads the suitors' relatives
against Odysseus and his men, but is killed by Laertes when the battle is
joined. "They would have killed them all," says Homer (24.581), if
Athena had not ordered Odysseus back and allowed the Ithacans to run
for their lives. The description of the final battle is phrased throughout in
Iliadic phrase and formula, and as Odysseus encourages his son and
receives assurance that Telemachus will not disgrace his lineage, old
Laertes sounds the authentic heroic note: "What a day for me, dear gods!
What joy— / my son and my grandson vying over courage!" (24.567–68).

This aspect of the *Odyssey* has often been overlooked or underempha-
sized. Much, perhaps too much, has been made of Achilles' bitter rejec-
tion of Odysseus' attempt to comfort him in the world of the dead: "I'd
rather slave on earth for another man— / . . . than rule down here over
all the breathless dead" (11.556–58). His words have been interpreted as
a rejection of the heroic code of which in the *Iliad* he was the great
exemplar. But it is not so much a rejection of the everlasting glory for
which he consciously and deliberately traded his life as it is an angry
reproach to Odysseus for contrasting his own "endless trouble" (11.547)
with Achilles' great power among the dead. Achilles knew what he was
giving up when he chose an early death with glory over long life, and it
is understandable that Odysseus' specious words of comfort should
provoke an angry response. In any case, he goes on to ask for news of
his son Neoptolemus: "Did he make his way to the wars, / did the
boy become a champion—yes or no?" (11.560–61). When Achilles
hears Odysseus' answer—"scores of men he killed in bloody combat. /
How could I list them all . . . ?" (11.587–88)—and hears the tale of his
aggressive courage in the wooden horse and his safe return home,
Achilles goes off

"loping with long strides across the fields of asphodel,
triumphant in all I had told him of his son,
his gallant, glorious son."   (11.614–16)

GODS

Unlike the *Iliad*, the *Odyssey* is an epic with a thoroughly domestic base.
Except in the wanderings—and sometimes even there—we are down to
earth, whether in the full and frequent meals in the palace (Fielding
called the *Odyssey* the "eatingest epic") or in the rural domesticity of
Eumaeus' hut. Yet the poem is firmly set in what might be called "heroic
time," a time when men were stronger, braver and more eloquent than
they are now, women more beautiful, powerful and intelligent than they
have been ever since, and gods so close to human life and so involved
with individual human beings, in affection or in anger, that they inter-
vened in their lives and even appeared to them in person. The inclination
of modern critics to emphasize the unique aspect of Odyssean heroism at
the expense and often to the exclusion of the recognizably Achillean
aspects of the heroic vengeance that concludes the epic is paralleled by a
tendency to find new developments on Olympus, in the nature and
action of the gods, especially of Zeus. What has happened—according to
Alfred Heubeck in his thoughtful and valuable introduction to the
Oxford Commentary on the *Odyssey*—is nothing less than an "ethical
transformation": "With perceptiveness and wisdom Zeus now directs the
fate of the world according to moral principles, which alone create and
preserve order. The father of the gods has only a little way to go to
become the just ruler of the world" (I, p. 23).

Quite apart from the fact that it may be doubted whether Zeus ever
went that little way (even in the *Oresteia* his justice is problematic), it is
hard to find in the *Odyssey* evidence for this ethical transformation. In the
meeting on Olympus with which the poem opens, Zeus discusses the
case of Aegisthus, who, disregarding a warning delivered by Hermes, has
seduced Clytemnestra and, with her help, murdered Agamemnon. "Ah
how shameless," says Zeus,

"the way these mortals blame the gods.
From us alone, they say, come all their miseries, yes,
but they themselves, with their own reckless ways,
compound their pains beyond their proper share."   (1.37–40)

There is, as Heubeck himself points out, "nothing new in this moralizing." Zeus admits that much of humanity's suffering is the responsibility of the gods; what he is complaining about is that they compound it by reckless initiatives of their own.

This council on Olympus presents us with a situation all too familiar from the *Iliad*: gods bitterly opposed to each other over the fate of mortals. In the *Iliad* Hera and Athena are ferociously bent on Troy's destruction because of an insult to their pride and preeminence—the Judgment of Paris, the Trojan prince, which awarded the prize for beauty to Aphrodite. Poseidon, brother of Zeus, is equally intent on Troy's destruction, because the Trojan king Laomedon cheated him of payment for building the walls of Troy. Apollo, whose temple stands on the citadel of Troy, is the city's champion, and Zeus, the supreme arbiter, is partial to Troy because of the devotion of its inhabitants to his worship. The fate of the city and its women and children, as well as the lives and deaths of the warriors on both sides, are determined by the give-and-take of these divine wills in opposition, by the pattern of alliance, conflict, deceit and compromise that form their relationships.

The conflicts rarely take violent shape; on the few occasions when they do, the divine opponents are not equally matched. Athena fights Ares and Aphrodite, and easily defeats both, while Hera spanks Artemis as if she were a little girl. But among the major powers—Zeus, Hera, Athena, Poseidon, Apollo—the struggle takes different forms: retreat, deceit, compromise. When, in the climactic battles that lead up to the death of Hector, Apollo is challenged to fight by Poseidon, he declines:

"God of the earthquake—you'd think me hardly sane
if I fought with you for the sake of wretched mortals . . .
like leaves, no sooner flourishing, full of the sun's fire,
feeding on earth's gifts, than they waste away and die."   (21.527–30)

Gods may favor a hero or a city, but if that favor threatens to create a rupture between major powers, one of them may withdraw. Or they may bargain, as Zeus does with Hera when he reluctantly consents to let Troy fall. He consents, but with a proviso:

"One more thing . . .
Whenever *I* am bent on tearing down some city
filled with men you love—to please myself—
never attempt to thwart my fury . . ."   (4.46–49)

And Hera accepts; in fact, she offers him three cities instead of one:

> ". . . The three cities that I love best of all
> are Argos and Sparta, Mycenae with streets as broad as Troy's.
> Raze them . . . I will never rise in their defense . . ."   (4.60–63)

Gods may also get their way by deceit, as Hera does when she seduces Zeus and puts him to sleep so that she and Poseidon can rally the Achaeans against Hector's assault.

All three of these modes of Olympian diplomacy reappear in the *Odyssey*. Odysseus, by blinding Polyphemus, Poseidon's son, has incurred the vengeful wrath of the god who rules the waves. When the hero meets Athena on the shore of Ithaca he asks her rather brusquely why she had abandoned him during the course of his wanderings:

> ". . . I never saw you,
> never glimpsed you striding along my decks
> to ward off some disaster."   (13.361–63)

Her reply, short, obviously embarrassed, and sandwiched between fulsome compliments and the lifting of the mist to show Odysseus that he really is home, is an avowal of concession made to superior force. "I could not bring myself," she says, "to fight my Father's brother, / Poseidon" (13.388–89). And even this apology is evasive: she makes no attempt to explain why she did not help Odysseus *before* he incurred Poseidon's wrath. Not until she secures the agreement of Zeus does she take the steps that lead to Odysseus' return home. She proposes to Zeus that Odysseus be released from his seven-year confinement on Calypso's island, and she does this at a meeting on Olympus from which Poseidon is absent; he is far away, at the ends of the earth, enjoying the homage of the Ethiopians. Poseidon is, in effect, deceived; when he returns and sees Odysseus on his raft approaching the Phaeacian shore he is furious. "Outrageous! Look how the gods have changed their minds / about Odysseus—while I was off with my Ethiopians" (5.315–16). Athena would not challenge him openly; she acts behind his back.

Poseidon knows that once Odysseus reaches Phaeacia he is "fated to escape his noose of pain" (5.318), and in the event, the Phaeacians send him home on a supernaturally fast ship, loaded down with treasure greater than all he had acquired at Troy and lost at sea. Poseidon's power has been defied, his honor slighted, and someone must pay. Odysseus is now beyond his reach, but the Phaeacians are another matter. "I will lose all my honor now / among the immortals," he complains to Zeus,

> "now there are mortal men
> who show me no respect—Phaeacians, too,
> born of my own loins!"   (13.145–48)

Zeus assures him that there is no loss of respect for him on Olympus, and as for mortal men—

> "If any man, so lost in his strength
> and prowess, pays you no respect—just pay him back . . .
> Do what you like. Whatever warms your heart."   (13.162–65)

Poseidon explains his purpose: to sink the Phaeacian ship that took Odysseus home as it sails into the harbor and to "pile a huge mountain round about their port" so that "They will learn at last / to cease and desist from escorting every man alive" (13.171–73). Zeus approves, and suggests a refinement: to change the ship and, incidentally, its crew of fifty-two young men—"the best in town" (8.42)—into a rock as the Phaeacians watch it approach the harbor. Poseidon swiftly does so, and at that sight King Alcinous recognizes the fulfillment of a prophecy, which also predicted that the city would be surrounded by a great mountain. He leads his people in sacrifice and prayer to Poseidon, hoping for mercy and promising that the Phaeacians will never again give sea passage to men who come to their city.

This is the end of the great Phaeacian tradition of hospitality and help for the stranger and wayfarer. This action of Zeus casts a disturbing light on the relation between human ideals and divine conduct. If there is one stable moral criterion in the world of the *Odyssey*, it is the care taken by the powerful and well-to-do of strangers, wanderers and beggars. This code of hospitality is the one universally recognized morality. And its divine enforcer, so all mortals believe, is Zeus himself, Zeus *xeinios*, protector of stranger and suppliant. His name and title are invoked time after time, by Odysseus and also by Nausicaa, Echeneus the Phaeacian elder, Alcinous and Eumaeus.

Of all the many hosts measured by this moral standard, the Phaeacians stand out as the most generous, not only in their regal entertainment of Odysseus but also in their speedy conveyance of the hero to his own home, a service they provide for all wayfarers who reach their shore. And now they are punished by the gods for precisely this reason, since their magnanimity has made Poseidon feel that his honor—the touchy sensitivity to public opinion that in Achilles brought ten thousand woes on the Achaeans, and drove Ajax to suicide and fueled his sullenness in the underworld—has been dealt an intolerable blow. The offenders must be punished, even if their punishment displays utter indifference to the only code of moral conduct that obtains in the insecure world of the *Odyssey*. Faced with Poseidon's rage against the Phaeacians, Zeus the protector of strangers enthusiastically joins his powerful brother in his denunciation. Not only does he suggest the refinement of turning the ship to stone; he also approves of Poseidon's intention to cut the Phaeacians off from the sea forever by piling a huge mountain around the city.

This has shocked some modern translators and editors, who have accordingly followed the lead of the ancient editor Aristophanes of Byzantium. By changing three letters in the Greek, he made Zeus end his speech with the words "but do not pile a mountain round the city." The suggested petrification of the ship is a sop to gratify Poseidon and compensate him for a concession—the Phaeacians will not be cut off from the sea. Zeus *xeinios* lives up to his title; he is a Zeus who has undergone an ethical transformation.

We have no record of the reasons Aristophanes gave for his reading; though they must have been spelled out in his commentaries on the poem, our manuscript tradition preserves only the fact that he proposed it. But it does give us one more important piece of information. "Aristarchus," we are told in the same note that recorded Aristophanes' emendation, "argues against him in his dissertations." Aristarchus was the pupil of Aristophanes and was regarded as the most critical and correct of the Alexandrian editors—readers of Pope's *Dunciad* will remember that his target Richard Bentley was portrayed as "that awful Aristarch." So the suggestion was already contested in antiquity by Homer's most respected editor. And though we are told nothing about Aristophanes' reasons for suggesting the change, we may guess at them by comparing other examples of his textual criticism. He was much concerned, for example, with decorum and suspected the authenticity of lines in which royal characters fell below the level of etiquette maintained at the court of the Ptolemies. In Book 6, where Homer has Nausicaa bring her washing out of the house—"the princess brought her finery from the room / and piled it into the wagon's polished cradle" (6.84–85)—Aristophanes, with a slight alteration, produced: "Meanwhile the maids brought the finery from the room . . ." Princesses do not carry their own laundry.

He shows a similar concern for propriety when dealing with the conduct of the gods. In Book 11, when Odysseus sees the shade of Ariadne, he identifies her as

> "daughter of Minos, that harsh king. One day Theseus tried
> to spirit her off from Crete to Athens' sacred heights,
> but he got no joy from her. Artemis killed her first
> on wave-washed Dia's shores . . ."   (11.365–68)

For *ekta*, "killed," Aristophanes adopted *eschen*, "detained," thus unburdening Artemis of a killing for which no reason is given. So in that dialogue between Zeus and Poseidon, by introducing a negative, Aristophanes made Zeus, the greater god, more merciful than Poseidon.

But there is no warrant for this alteration. There is indeed a very good reason—quite apart from the fact that Aristophanes' motive is obvious—to reject it out of hand. If Homer's Zeus had really urged such a radical revision of Poseidon's plan, some sort of reply on Poseidon's part—acceptance, rejection or at least acknowledgment—would be indispensable. But he says not a word. Furthermore, if the Phaeacian city was never to be cut off by a mountain, we are left with something unprecedented in Homer, an unfulfilled prophecy—Alcinous twice mentions the prophecy of his father that one day Poseidon would ring their city with a mountain. Homer does not tell us what happened: when we see the Phaeacians for the last time, they are about to engage in sacrifice and prayer to Poseidon, hoping that he will spare them. But one thing is clear: they are done with generous hospitality and conveying strangers to their destinations. A god has forced this decision; his vindictive punishment has been fully approved by Zeus. Zeus may sometimes act as the protector of suppliants, beggars and wanderers, but human concerns and conceptions of justice fade into insignificance when the maintenance of a powerful god's prestige is the issue. Odysseus meanwhile, left asleep on the Ithacan shore with all his treasure laid out beside him, wakes to find a landscape he does not recognize—Athena has covered it in mist. He jumps to the conclusion that the Phaeacian crew has dumped him on some foreign shore. "They never kept their word," he cries,

> "Zeus of the Suppliants
> pay them back—he keeps an eye on the world of men
> and punishes all transgressors!"   (13.241–43)

He does not realize it, but Zeus of the suppliants has already paid them back. Not for breaking their word, but for keeping it.

Poseidon and Zeus are not the only Olympians to display indifference to human codes of conduct and sense of justice. Later in the poem Athena joins them. There is among the suitors one decent man, Amphinomus, who "pleased Penelope the most, / thanks to his timely words and good clear sense" (16.441–42). It is he who persuades the suitors to reject Antinous' proposal to waylay and murder Telemachus on Ithaca, now that he has evaded the ship waiting for him in ambush and returned safe home. And it is Amphinomus who, after Odysseus' victory over Irus in the boxing match, drinks his health in a golden cup and says,

> "Cheers, old friend, old father,
> saddled now as you are with so much trouble—
> here's to your luck, great days from this day on!"   (18.141–43)

Odysseus tries to save him from the imminent slaughter. He warns him solemnly that Odysseus will soon return, is now very near home, and that blood will be shed. This is dangerous ground. He calls Amphinomus by name; how could this ragged beggar who has just arrived know it? He goes even further. "You seem like a man of good sense to me," he tells him. "Just like your father." It is a slip he tries to cover at once, adding quickly, "at least I've heard his praises" (18.145–46). Homer has made it clear what a great risk Odysseus is running in his attempt to save Amphinomus' life, and he emphasizes his sincerity by having him pray for divine intervention on the suitor's behalf:

> " . . . may some power save you,
> spirit you home before you meet him face-to-face
> the moment he returns to native ground!"   (18.167–69)

Far from spiriting him home, a divine power has already passed sentence on him: "Even then Athena had bound him fast to death / at the hands of Prince Telemachus and his spear" (18.178–79). Amphinomus is the third of the suitors to die, immediately after the two principal villains, Antinous and Eurymachus.

When they are not deciding the fate of mortals, the gods live a life of their own, on Olympus, where, they say,

. . . the gods' eternal mansion stands unmoved,
never rocked by galewinds, never drenched by rains,
nor do the drifting snows assail it, no, the clear air
stretches away without a cloud, and a great radiance
plays across that world where the blithe gods
live all their days in bliss.   (6.46–51)

We are given a sample of their life of pleasure in one of the tales told by
the minstrel Demodocus in the great hall of the Phaeacian palace—the
entrapment of the adulterous pair Ares and Aphrodite in the golden net
fashioned by the wronged husband Hephaestus, and their exposure to
the prurient gaze and "uncontrollable laughter" (8.369) of the gods
whom Hephaestus has summoned to witness his wife's perfidy. (The
goddesses, we are told, stayed modestly at home.) Hephaestus himself,
when he summons the gods, refers to the spectacle he offers them as "a
sight to make you laugh" (8.349), and the comic aspect of the tale is
made plain when Apollo asks Hermes if he would like to change places
with Ares and receives the reply:

"Oh Apollo, if only! . . .
. . . bind me down with triple those endless chains!
Let all you gods look on, and all you goddesses too—
how I'd love to bed that golden Aphrodite!"   (8.381–84)

This glimpse of the private lives of the Olympians has a parallel in the
Iliad: the episode (14.187–421) in which Hera, armed with all the charms
and magic of Aphrodite, seduces Zeus, who is watching the battle from a
mountaintop, so that she can put him to sleep and then, with Poseidon,
rally the Achaean fighters against Hector's victorious assault. Zeus is
overcome with desire for his wife; his lust, he tells her, is greater than
anything he has felt in his mating with mortal women, whom he pro-
ceeds to list in a long speech that has been aptly named the "Leporello
catalogue," after the famous aria in Mozart's *Don Giovanni*.

In both epics the gods enjoy their pleasures and pursue their intrigues
on Olympus, while on earth they decide the fate of mortals and their
cities with scant regard for human conceptions of divine justice, when-
ever what is at stake is the interest or prestige of a major god. Human
beings may indeed, like the suitors and Odysseus' crew, bring disaster on
themselves "beyond their proper share" (1.40), but disaster may still
come to those who, like the Phaeacians and Amphinomus, are by human

standards admirable, and in each case it is a god who serves them their "proper share."

WOMEN AND MEN

The two Homeric epics are alike in their vision of the Olympian gods and their affirmation of the heroic code, but there is one striking difference between them. The *Iliad* celebrates the action and suffering of men at war; it is only in the poem's similes and on the shield of Achilles that we are given occasional glimpses of a world at peace. The few women who make an appearance—Briseis, Andromache, Hecuba, Helen—are secondary figures, who play no significant part in the main action. But the *Odyssey*, though its climax is a scene of furious combat and mass slaughter, presents us with a world at peace: a secure and settled peace at Pylos and Sparta, a troubled and threatened peace on Ithaca, and, in the dangers and temptations of Odysseus' voyage, intervals of peace—temptingly restful with Circe, oppressive with Calypso, and beneficent on Scheria. And almost everywhere in this peaceful world, women, human and divine, have important roles.

In Odysseus' wanderings they help, tempt or delay him. Calypso offers him immortality and keeps him for seven years but sends a favoring wind when he departs; Circe tries to keep him forever in her pigpen, does keep him for a year as her lover, but finally helps him on his way; the Sirens are his most dangerous temptation, but the sea-nymph Ino helps him land on Scheria, where Arete and Nausicaa smooth his path. There are female presences even among the monsters he has to face: Scylla, Charybdis and the gigantic wife—"huge as a mountain crag" (10.124)—of the Laestrygonian cannibal king. On the Egyptian island of Pharos, Menelaus is rescued by the minor goddess Eidothea, daughter of the Old Man of the Sea, and at Sparta, Helen gives a dazzling performance. On Ithaca, Penelope, enigmatic to the last, is the object of the suitors' desires and her son's suspicions, and it is she who precipitates the final crisis by offering to marry whichever of the suitors can string the bow of Odysseus and shoot an arrow through the axes. Eurycleia too is never far from the limelight and gets full exposure when she washes her master's feet and recognizes the scar he carries on his thigh. Meanwhile the goddess Athena encourages and supports Telemachus on his journey, and from Scheria onward she is Odysseus' helper and then fellow-conspirator in deceit and ally in battle. Besides these principal players there is a plentiful cast of female extras: the Sicilian woman who looks after old Laertes; the Phoenician nursemaid who kidnaps the young prince Eumaeus to sell him as a slave; Eurynome, Penelope's housekeeper; Melantho, the disloyal maid, lover of Antinous; Iphthime, Penelope's sister, who appears to her in a dream; and the long list of famous women Odysseus sees among the dead—Tyro, Antiope, Alcmena, Epicaste, Chloris, Leda, Iphimedeia, Phaedra, Procris, Eriphyle. It is a vision that has echoed down the centuries, that lies behind Propertius' magical line *sunt apud infernos tot milia formosarum*—"so many thousands of lovely women among the dead"—and Campion's "shades of underground . . . White Iope, blithe Helen, and the rest."

Only when the *Odyssey* turns Iliadic, as Odysseus and his son and two loyal servants face the suitors in the hall, are women offstage, and even there Athena is at hand, sustaining the morale of the hero and his party, diverting the suitors' spears from the target. Elsewhere in the poem women's voices are heard at frequent intervals and sometimes at length. Hostile critics might well be tempted to cite the defense of his tragedies Aristophanes put in the mouth of "Euripides" in the *Frogs*: "They all stepped up to speak their piece, the mistress spoke, the slave spoke too, / the master spoke, the daughter spoke, and grandma spoke." In the *Iliad*, scenes that present men in contact with women, though memorable, are rare—Helen and Paris, Hector and Andromache, Hecuba and Priam—but in the *Odyssey*, the rare exception is the scene from which women are excluded—the battle in the hall, the Cyclops in the cave. What historical reality, if any, lies behind this imagined world, so far removed from the peasant misogyny of Hesiod's near-contemporary *Works and Days*, we shall never know; perhaps it reflects an aristocratic Ionian culture like that which, a century later, saw the birth of Sappho on Lesbos.

The *Odyssey* owes much of its power to enchant so many generations of readers to its elegant exploitation of something that war temporarily suppresses or corrupts—the infinite variety of the emotional traffic between male and female. In his treatment of these relationships Homer displays an understanding of human psychology that many critics, especially those who believe in multiple authorship, but even some of those who accept a sole author yet deny him literacy, have been reluctant to recognize. A case in point is the first encounter between human beings of the opposite sex in the poem, the exchange between Telemachus and Penelope in Book 1. She has just told the bard Phemius, who is entertaining the suitors with a song about the return of the Achaeans from Troy, to change his tune, since this one pains her to the heart. Telemachus intervenes, to remind her that Phemius is not to blame for her sorrow; it is

Zeus who allots to mortals whatever destiny he pleases. But he concludes with some words that have rightly been characterized as "harsh":

> ". . . mother,
> go back to your quarters. Tend to your own tasks,
> the distaff and the loom, and keep the women
> working hard as well. As for giving orders,
> men will see to that . . ."   (1.409–13)

These same words, with "bow" replacing "giving orders" (*muthos*), recur much later in the poem, in Book 21 (389–93), where Penelope insists, in opposition to Antinous, that Eumaeus should give the bow to Odysseus; and of course they are an echo of Hector's words to Andromache in their last interview in the *Iliad*—"As for the fighting, / men will see to that" (6.587–88). In Book 21 Telemachus' words are obviously essential, for Penelope has to be removed from the hall before the fighting starts, as it will do as soon as Odysseus strings the bow. But critics have thought them out of place in Book 1; in fact, Aristarchus condemned them as an interpolation. Some modern translators (Fitzgerald, for example) have omitted them, and a recent commentator has expressed uneasiness about Telemachus' "callousness" and "adolescent rudeness." The lines have often been defended as the first manifestation of the new fighting spirit that Athena's visit has instilled in Telemachus, and though this is true, the fact is that his harshness here is consistent with the tone of nearly all the other remarks Telemachus addresses to his mother throughout the poem and of much of what he says about her to other people.

His first reference to her is, at the very least, ambiguous. Asked by Athena if he is the son of Odysseus, he replies: "Mother has always told me I'm his son, it's true, / but I am not so certain" (1.249–50). Commentators have tried to explain his remark away as "curious but perhaps conventional" and "an idea that must already have been a commonplace," but they produce little or no evidence for such a case. Telemachus is not, of course, suggesting that his mother is an adulteress but merely expressing a doubt that he is a worthy son of his great father. But he could have done so without mentioning his mother; there is a resentful tone in his voice, which sounds again when he describes for Athena the situation he faces in Ithaca:

> "she neither rejects a marriage she despises
> nor can she bear to bring the courting to an end—
> while they continue to bleed my household white."   (1.290–92)

Telemachus has grown to manhood without the correction and support of a father, an absence poignantly evoked in the words he addresses to Athena when, in the person of Mentes, she urges him to call an assembly, defy the suitors and take ship in search of news of his father. "You've counseled me with so much kindness now, / like a father to a son" (1.353–54). He has been raised by women, Eurycleia and Penelope, and it was almost inevitable that his normal adolescent rebellion would be against his mother. The first result of Athena's move to rouse Odysseus' son "to a braver pitch, inspire his heart with courage" (1.105) is this stern dismissal of his mother as he asserts his mastery in the house. Penelope has given orders to Phemius: to "break off this song" (1.391) and choose some other theme. "As for giving orders" (*muthos*), says Telemachus, "men will see to that." And as soon as she leaves, he announces that he will call an assembly where he will give his "orders" (*muthos*) to the suitors: "You must leave my palace! See to your feasting elsewhere" (1.430).

Much later, at Sparta, Athena comes to hasten his return to Ithaca; she does so by suggesting that Penelope may decide to marry, and take some treasure with her:

> "You know how the heart of a woman always works:
> she likes to build the wealth of her new groom—
> of the sons she bore, of her dear, departed husband,
> not a memory of the dead, no questions asked."   (15.23–26)

Athena is not a dream, for Telemachus is awake; she is not in disguise, as she was on Ithaca. But Telemachus makes no reply to the goddess, no acknowledgment of her presence—it is as if he had never seen or heard her. This unusual treatment of a divine epiphany may have been Homer's attempt to suggest that Athena was only enhancing in Telemachus' mind the fears and suspicions that were already there. He had, as Homer tells us, been sleepless all night, "tossing with anxious thoughts about his father" (15.9). And when he gets back to Ithaca the first thing he says to Eumaeus shows how deeply rooted are his suspicions of his mother's intentions. "I've come," he says,

> ". . . [to] learn the news—
> whether mother still holds out in the halls
> or some other man has married her at last,
> and Odysseus' bed, I suppose, is lying empty,
> blanketed now with filthy cobwebs."   (16.36–40)

At his meeting with Penelope, who weeps as she speaks of her fears that he would never return alive—she knew about the ship the suitors had sent out to waylay him—he is brusquely ungracious; he does not even answer her questions about news of Odysseus but tells her not to stir up his emotions and sends her off to her room to bathe and pray; he has business to attend to, men's business. She has to ask him later, and hesitantly, before he tells her what he learned at Sparta about her husband.

But she is not always so submissive. When she comes into the great hall after Odysseus has won his fight with Irus, she rebukes her son for exposing a stranger-guest to the risk of bodily harm. In her speech we can hear the tone of maternal reproof that Telemachus must often have heard and resented in his boyhood and adolescence:

> "Telemachus,
> your sense of balance is not what it used to be.
> When you were a boy you had much better judgment.
> Now that you've grown and reached your young prime . . .
> now your sense of fairness seems to fail you."   (18.243–49)

Telemachus' reply is, for once, conciliatory, even apologetic. He no longer feels the need to assert himself against her; his father is home, and he has been assigned a principal role in the final reckoning with the suitors. But he can still speak unflatteringly of her behind her back, as he does to Eurycleia after the nightlong interview between husband and wife:

> "Dear nurse, how did you treat the stranger in our house?
> With bed and board? Or leave him to lie untended?
> That would be mother's way—sensible as she is—
> all impulse, doting over some worthless stranger,
> turning a good man out to face the worst."   (20.145–49)

And he rebukes her to her face when she stubbornly refuses to recognize the bloodstained ragged beggar sitting opposite her as Odysseus. "Oh mother," he says,

> "cruel mother, you with your hard heart!
> Why do you spurn my father so—why don't you
> sit beside him, engage him, ask him questions?
> What other wife could have a spirit so unbending? . . .
> your heart was always harder than a rock!"   (23.111–18)

Penelope answers him gently but firmly; she denies him any competence in the matter at hand: ". . . if he is truly / Odysseus . . . we two will know each other . . . we two have secret signs" (23.121–24). And Odysseus, with a smile, sends Telemachus away.

Penelope's attitude to both the suitors and her disguised husband has given rise to much controversy and diverse interpretation. That she is faithful to Odysseus we are assured several times, as Odysseus is assured by Anticleia and Agamemnon in the world of the dead and by Eumaeus in the land of the living. On this score even Telemachus can have no doubt. It is also clear that she has done everything she can to avoid the marriage the suitors are trying to force on her. In his indictment of her before the Ithacan assembly, Antinous pays reluctant tribute to the subtlety of her delaying tactics—the shroud for old Laertes that for three years she wove at her great loom by day and unraveled by torchlight at night. Yet though her resolve to avoid marriage is firm, she would not be human if she did not feel flattered by the suitors' infatuation with her; a woman whose husband has been away for twenty years, and for whose return she has almost given up hope, could hardly remain indifferent to the ardent courtship of so many young princes. When, in Book 18, Athena inspires her with a longing "to display herself to her suitors, fan their hearts, / inflame them more" (18.183–84), she is prompting impulses that lurk dormant below the surface of Penelope's conscious mind, just as she played on Telemachus' deep suspicions of his mother's intentions in Book 15. That same hidden layer of Penelope's emotions is revealed in the dream about the pet geese slaughtered by the eagle, which she describes for Odysseus. In the dream the eagle identifies himself as Odysseus and the geese as the suitors, but not before Penelope has spoken of her delight in watching the geese and her unbridled sorrow at their destruction. In these few lines Homer shows more understanding of how dreams work than is to be found anywhere in the four books of the *Interpretation of Dreams* written by Artemidorus of Daldis in the second century of the Christian era.

None of these feelings affects Penelope's refusal to choose a husband from among the suitors, but during her long interview with Odysseus she suddenly tells him that she has decided to do so: she will marry the suitor who can string the great bow of Odysseus and shoot an arrow through the twelve axes lined up in a row. There are good reasons for yielding to the suitors' pressure at this point, and she states them clearly. After the betrayal of her delaying tactics with the shroud, she can think, she says, of no further expedient. Her parents are pressing her to remarry, and her son broods impatiently as the suitors devour his inheritance; he too, she says, beseeches her to leave. She has previously told Eurymachus what Odysseus had said to her when he left for Troy:

> " '. . . once you see the beard on the boy's cheek,
> you wed the man you like, and leave your house behind.'
> So my husband advised me then. Now it all comes true . . ."   (18.303-5)

For the plot of the *Odyssey*, of course, her decision is the turning point, the move that makes possible the long-predicted triumph of the returning hero. But why, critics have asked, does she make up her mind to do it now, when her dream clearly announces the return of Odysseus and the slaughter of the suitors, when the disguised Odysseus has convinced her that he saw Odysseus in person long ago on Crete and assured her that Odysseus had lately been seen in nearby Thesprotia and was now on his way home; when, even earlier, the prophet Theoclymenus had assured her that Odysseus was actually in Ithaca, planning destruction for the suitors? Many critics have found her decision utterly implausible. "The poet," writes one learned and influential scholar (Page, p. 123), "could not possibly have chosen a worse moment for Penelope's surrender." For those who suspect multiple authorship of the poem a simple explanation lies ready to hand: Penelope's decision comes from an alternate story line, in which husband and wife join in conspiracy to entrap the suitors. They find support for the theory in Book 24, where the shade of the suitor Amphimedon tells Agamemnon that it was Odysseus, "the soul of cunning," who "told his wife to set / the great bow and the gleaming iron axes out" (24.184–85). But it was only natural that the suitors should think so, since Penelope, at a critical moment, had argued strongly against Antinous that Odysseus should be allowed to try his hand at stringing the bow.

One modern critic (Harsh) has developed a subtly argued theory that she does in fact recognize her husband in the course of their long night interview and, while forwarding his purpose, withholds from him her realization of his identity. This reading, however, runs into an immovable obstacle in Book 23, where, to Telemachus' disgust and Odysseus' frustration, she refuses to recognize him as her husband and tests his knowledge of those "secret signs" she had mentioned before, signs "known to us both but hidden from the world" (23.124–25). Other critics have suggested that without recognizing the stranger's identity, she has been profoundly impressed by him and deeply moved by his proof that, unlike so many others who have come to her with sightings of Odysseus, he really has seen her husband. The disguised Odysseus, in the words of

56 HOMER: THE ODYSSEY

a recent sensitive interpreter (Russo, *Commentary*, III, pp. 11–12), "has come to mean much more to Penelope than would normally be possible in a relationship between a famous queen and a wandering stranger . . . an unusual and almost improper intimacy." When they go off to their separate beds, each dreams of the other. "Homer is showing us that Penelope has some kind of intuitive awareness of her husband's presence but . . . it is active on a less than conscious level." All this prompts her "to take a risk, to commit herself to life and to life's chances after years of defensive, calculated maneuvering."

This is a brilliant and attractive reading, but like many other interpretations, it does not take full account of the fact that Penelope does not have a choice in the matter. She has eloquently stated the reasons why she must decide now—pressure from her parents and her son, compounded by the threat to her son's life, demand a decision at this point. But what she proposes is not a "surrender." What the suitors have been demanding is that Penelope, or her father, choose one of them for her husband, "the best man in Achaea," the one "who offers her the most [gifts]" (16.85–86). But she faces them with something quite different: a challenge, a test in which each of them must measure himself against Odysseus by stringing his bow and shooting an arrow through the twelve axes. She is, of course, running a risk. As she tells Odysseus of her decision, she speaks as if the outcome will be the marriage she has so long avoided, and later, in her bed, she prays for death to save her from having to "warm the heart of a weaker man" (20.92). Yet she must have foreseen the possibility that none of these inferior men, youths who spend their days and nights feasting, playing board games, dancing, hurling javelin and discus, would have the strength to string the bow of Odysseus and the skill to shoot an arrow through the line of twelve axes. Antinous, in fact, though he secretly hopes to succeed, expresses a fear that they may all fail to pass the test Penelope has imposed on them:

"No easy game, I wager, to string *his* polished bow.
Not a soul in the crowd can match Odysseus—
what a man he was . . ."   (21.105–7)

Failure on the part of all the suitors might free her from their attentions; both Leodes and Eurymachus, the two suitors who try their hand and fail, speak of wooing other women elsewhere. In any case, failure would, as Eurymachus says, demonstrate their inferiority to Odysseus—"A disgrace to ring in the ears of men to come" (21.285). It would be a fatal blow to the suitors' prestige and might well turn opinion in Ithaca against them. Penelope's surprising move looks more like a counter-offensive than a surrender. She told Odysseus that after her work on Laertes' shroud was exposed as a fraud, she could not think of another "deft way out" (19.177). The word so translated is *mêtis;* it is the word that characterizes Odysseus—he is *polumêtis,* a man of many twists and turns. Penelope is from the same mold as her husband, a worthy partner—and adversary. As she demonstrates by the *mêtis* she deploys against him before she will accept him fully as her husband.

Even when he has bathed, exchanged the filthy rags of the beggar for splendid raiment, and been given the grace and beauty of an immortal by Athena, she still sits apart from him, silent. He reproaches her for her cold-ness, using words that recall what Telemachus said to her earlier: "She has a heart of iron in her breast" (23.192). He orders Eurycleia to prepare a bed for him, apart and alone. Penelope's response shows that she is almost con-vinced: "You look—how well I know—" she says, "the way he looked, / setting sail from Ithaca" (23.195–96), but nonetheless she insists on testing his knowledge of those "secret signs" she mentioned when she answered Telemachus' angry outburst. She orders Eurycleia to move Odysseus' bed out of the room. For the first and only time in the poem, Odysseus is taken aback. Up to this point he has always been the calculator, the manipulator, the dissembler, who played on the emotions of others, whether to win sympathy or to provoke hostility, but now Penelope has usurped that role. In a furious emotional outburst—"Woman—your words, they cut me to the core!" (23.205)—he tells the story of the bed's construction, and even though he realizes that he has given her the sign that she was seeking, he ends nevertheless with an accusing speculation:

"Does the bed, my lady, still stand planted firm?—
I don't know—or has someone chopped away
that olive-trunk and hauled our bedstead off?"   (23.228–30)

Penelope is convinced at last; in tears of joy she embraces him as she explains her hesitation. "In my heart of hearts I always cringed with fear / some fraud might come, beguile me with his talk" (23.242–43). Homer and his audience had not heard of Martin Guerre, but they knew the story of Alcmena and Amphitryon (both mentioned in the *Odyssey*)— how Zeus assumed the appearance and personality of Amphitryon, who was away at the wars, to lie with Alcmena and beget Heracles. In the lower world, Odysseus hears a similar story from Tyro, deceived by Poseidon, who took the form of her lover, the river Enipeus. Penelope, in fact, when Eurycleia brought her the news that the stranger was Odysseus and that he had killed all the suitors, had replied, "the story can't be true, not as you tell it, / no, it must be a god who's killed our brazen friends." (23.69–70).

Even among those who believe that the *Odyssey* is the work of one poet there may be those who doubt that an oral poet, using writing to construct, over the course of many years, a poem on the scale of the *Odyssey*, could deploy so effectively so subtle an understanding of the emotions that drive men and women together and apart. But this same sympathetic understanding of the human, especially the female, heart is at work not just in the scenes set in Ithaca but everywhere throughout the poem. Calypso, for example, when she starts Odysseus on his journey home, does not tell him that she does so under duress, on orders from Zeus, but takes credit for the action herself. And even when it is clear that he is determined to go, she cannot refrain from asking him how he can possibly prefer Penelope to her own divine person. Nausicaa on Scheria manages, with exquisite tact but in unmistakable terms, to offer her hand in marriage to Odysseus without committing herself. And at Sparta, behind the splendid facade of marital harmony in the royal palace lies the reality of subdued but barely repressed embarrassment and resentment. The embarrassment is revealed obliquely in the self-exculpatory story Helen tells of her encounter with Odysseus during the war that was fought for her sake. He came into Troy, she says, disguised as a beggar; she recognized him but helped and protected him:

> ". . . my heart had changed by now—
> I yearned
> to sail back home again! I grieved too late for the madness
> Aphrodite sent me . . ."   (4.292–94)

The resentment is clear in Menelaus' story of Odysseus at Troy; Odysseus was the one who saved their lives in the wooden horse by holding them back when Helen, imitating the voices of their wives, called on them by name to come out. What is more, she was accompanied by Deiphobus, the second Trojan prince she had married, after the death of Paris.

There are two remarks which Alexander Pope made about Homer that readers of the *Odyssey* should bear in mind. The first is that "Homer is frequently eloquent in his very Silence." And the second: "Homer has taken in all the inward Passions and Affections of Mankind to furnish his Characters."

THE END OF THE *ODYSSEY*

At the Greek line 296 of Book 23 of the *Odyssey*, husband and wife go joyfully to bed, the bed that served Penelope as the test of Odysseus' identity. We know Aristophanes and Aristarchus said that this was the "end" of the poem. We do not have their own statements, and our sources cite two different Greek words for "end." One of them, *peras*, means something like "limit" or "boundary," and the other, *telos*, besides meaning "end" in the temporal or spatial sense can often mean something more like "fulfillment," "consummation"—"end" in the Aristotelian sense. Some modern scholars have taken the words literally and pronounced the remainder of Book 23 and all of Book 24 a later addition composed by a different, and inferior, poet. They cannot, however, claim Aristarchus as their authority, for we know that he excluded the Greek lines 310–43 of Book 23 (in which Odysseus tells Penelope the tale of his travels) and lines 1–204 of Book 24 (the arrival of the shades of the suitors in the lower world). There would have been no point in doing so if he had already decided that the original poem ended at the line which put Odysseus and Penelope to bed.

In any case the poem cannot end there; too many loose ends remain to be tied up, like the consequences of the slaughter of the suitors; too many scenes have been carefully prepared for, like the meeting between Odysseus and Laertes. The first of these themes was introduced as far back as Book 20, when Odysseus discussed with Athena the plan to kill the suitors. He was appalled by the odds, one man against so many, but that is not all. "There's another worry," he tells her,

> "that haunts me even more.
> What if I kill them—thanks to you and Zeus—
> how do I run from under their avengers?"   (20.43–45)

It is with this in mind that later, in Books 22 and 23, with the corpses of the suitors cluttering the hall, he tells Telemachus to have it cleared and to organize music and dance so that passersby will guess that Penelope has at last chosen a new husband. No rumor of the truth will get out before Odysseus and his followers leave for his father's farm in the country—where Homer will stage the last of a series of recognition scenes. It is a scene for which audience expectation has been expertly aroused: in the opening book Athena-Mentes describes Laertes mourning for his son in isolation in the country, a theme taken up later by Anticleia in the world of the dead and by Eumaeus in his hut. The poem cannot end without a meeting between father and son; their reunion is in fact one of the three large units of which the final book consists.

The first, the descent of the suitors to the lower world, where they meet Agamemnon and Achilles, was condemned by Aristarchus as an interpolation. For once, we have some information about an Alexandrian editor's reason for such an opinion: the *scholia*, comments written on the margins of the medieval manuscripts, give us a selection. Some of them seem trivial; the fact that elsewhere in the poem Hermes is not called Cyllenian, for example, or the claim that a White Rock is not an appropriate landscape feature for the world of the dead. Others are more serious, such as his assertion that elsewhere in Homer the shades of the unburied are not allowed to cross the river into Hades, and the suitors' bodies are still in the hall of Odysseus' palace. It is true that in the *Iliad* the ghost of Patroclus, appearing to Achilles in a dream, tells him he cannot cross the river until Achilles gives him burial. But in the *Odyssey*, Elpenor begs Odysseus to bury his body, which has been left behind on Circe's island, and he is in Hades and makes no mention of a river. The laws and the terrain of Hades are obviously not strictly defined; they remain somewhat vague even in Virgil—it was Dante who gave Hell strict logic and a fixed geography.

Quite apart from such considerations, the descent of the suitors' ghosts to the lower world has already been foreseen in the terrifying vision that comes to Theoclymenus in the great hall in Book 20: "Ghosts, look, thronging the entrance, thronging the court, / go trooping down to the world of death and darkness!" (20.395–96). And Plato, who lived long before Aristarchus, quoted the Greek lines 6–9 of Book 24 in the *Republic*:

> [and the ghosts trailed after with high thin cries]
> as bats cry in the depths of a dark haunted cavern,
> shrilling, flittering, wild when one drops from the chain—
> slipped from the rock face, while the rest cling tight . . .
> So with their high thin cries the ghosts flocked now . . .   (24.6–10)

Like Aristarchus, he proposes to suppress them, but not because he thinks Homer did not write them—on the contrary. It is one of a list of passages Plato objects to because they will sap the morale of young men training for battle. "We shall ask Homer . . . to forgive us if we delete all passages of this kind. It is not because they are bad poetry . . . in fact the better they are as poetry . . . the less suitable they are for an audience of boys and men on whom freedom places the obligation to fear slavery more than death."

The long scene in which Odysseus reveals his identity to his father has been roundly condemned by many modern critics. The last of his auto-biographical fictions, the skillfully crafted tale he tells Laertes has been described as a "bizarre plan," as "pointless cruelty" and as a product of Odysseus' "habit of distrust." There is of course no question of real distrust; he has nothing to fear from Laertes, as he might have suspected he had from Penelope. But all these judgments should be assessed in the light not only of the difficult psychological situation Odysseus is faced with but also of Homer's imperatives as a narrative poet.

The last half of the *Odyssey* is a drama of identity disguised and revealed, a series of artful variations on the recognition scene. The first, and in some ways the strangest, of these scenes occurs in the first half of the poem, when Odysseus, waiting for the prophet Tiresias to appear, sees the ghost of his mother, Anticleia, who had still been alive when he left for Troy. He bursts into tears, but following Circe's instructions to the letter, he will not allow her to drink the sacrificial blood that would give her a semblance of life until he has heard from Tiresias. During the prophet's long speech the ghost of Anticleia sits there in silence, making no sound, showing no emotion. But once she is allowed to drink the blood, memory returns. "She knew me at once," says Odysseus, "and wailed out in grief" (11.175). Back on Ithaca, he reveals his identity to his son, but since this involves his transformation by Athena from a ragged beggar to a magnificently dressed and handsome man, Tele-machus at first (like Penelope later) is reluctant to accept him as Odysseus and thinks that he must be a god. The next recognition is one Odysseus had not planned on and that might have aroused suspicions, but his old dog Argos, recognizing his master after twenty years, is too feeble to approach him and can do no more than let his ears droop and wag his tail and then die. The next recognition, Eurycleia's discovery of the scar, might have disrupted his plans, but he forces her to keep silent. Just before the climactic moment when he gets his hands on the bow, he reveals his identity to Eumaeus and the shepherd Philoetius, enlisting them on his side, and the next revelation is also his initiative: after killing Antinous, he tells the suitors who he is and what will happen to them. "You dogs! you never imagined I'd return from Troy— / . . .

your doom is sealed!" (22.36–42). Penelope, in her turn, is unable to accept the revelation of his identity, but after he passes her test she clasps him joyfully in her arms. Only the recognition by Laertes remains.

It comes as no surprise. Not only does Odysseus tell Penelope of his intention to confront his father, but Laertes' overwhelming grief for his missing son and his withdrawal from society have been described in harrowing detail by Athena-Mentes, Anticleia and Eumaeus. The theme has been building to a climax, and something more than a simple declaration and joyful acceptance is required by the laws of storytelling. The poet's dilemma is in fact reflected in the text, put in the mouth of Odysseus. Catching sight of his father, "a man worn down with years, his heart racked with sorrow" (24.258), Odysseus

> halted under a branching pear-tree, paused and wept.
> Debating, head and heart, what should he do now?
> Kiss and embrace his father, pour out the long tale— . . .
> or probe him first and test him every way?   (24.259–63)

Like his hero, Homer decides on the second alternative.

But the choice makes sense also in terms of the persons involved. Laertes is a man to whose burden of old age has been added the loss of his only son—missing in action, no word of when, where, how or even if he died. Laertes has become a hermit, never coming into town, Athena-Mentes says in the opening book of the poem, suffering as he drags himself along the slope of his vineyard. Anticleia, his dead wife, rounds out the picture of his renunciation of civilized life: he sleeps with slaves in the ashes by the fire in winter and on fallen leaves in the summer, nursing his overwhelming grief. Eumaeus tells Odysseus that the old man prays for death as he grieves for his son and his wife, and that his reaction to the news that Telemachus has sailed off to Pylos is to refuse food and drink.

Clearly this is a case that calls for careful handling if Laertes is to be extracted from the prison of grief and self-humiliation in which he has closed himself off from the world. What Odysseus does is to bring him back to consciousness of his own dignity as a man and a king before making any mention of his son. The first part of his long, adroitly structured speech consists of what Homer calls "reproachful words." The adjective *kertomiois* is usually translated as "bantering" or "mocking," and it does often carry that meaning, but from what follows here it clearly in this case means "reproachful," as its cognate noun does in the first book of the *Iliad* (line 539 in the Greek), where it describes Hera's angry accusation that Zeus is, as usual, conspiring against her.

Odysseus' reproaches are far from gentle. He takes note of Laertes' patched and miserable garments, his fieldhand's leather shin guards and gloves, his goatskin cap. Though he starts by commending him on his work, and pays him the compliment of detecting the lineaments of royalty under his sordid appearance, he ends the first part of his speech with a question deliberately phrased for its shock effect: "whose slave are you? whose orchard are you tending?" (24.284). Nothing could more swiftly bring Laertes to a realization of the degraded condition into which he has allowed himself to fall, and Odysseus now asks another question— whether he is indeed in Ithaca. For he once befriended and helped a man from Ithaca, the son of Laertes. "By posing questions, awaking memories, and stirring long-repressed feelings," Heubeck writes in his masterly commentary on Book 24 (III, p. 390), "Odysseus forces his father not only to answer the questions put, but to ask questions in return, and so, step by step, to emerge from his self-inflicted isolation and apathy." Finally, told that the man he is talking to is Odysseus in person, he asks for a sign and is given not only the scar that Eurycleia recognized but Odysseus' enumeration of the trees his father had given him when he was a little boy—"thirteen pear, ten apple trees / and forty figs" (24.379–80). Laertes flings his arms around his long-lost son and the two of them go off to the farmhouse to join Telemachus.

There is little more to be told. The fathers of some of the dead suitors—in spite of Medon's caution that he had seen a god helping Odysseus in the fighting and old Halitherses' reminder that they were themselves to blame for not restraining their sons—arm and set out, led by Eupithes, Antinous' father, to exact vengeance from Odysseus and his party. Only one man is killed: Eupithes, at the hand of a Laertes rejuvenated by Athena. The goddess puts an end to the fighting and then, in the shape of Mentor, administers oaths to both sides as a guarantee of reconciliation and peace.

The poem ends here, but like the *Iliad*, it has already charted the future of its hero. Achilles has been told by his mother, Thetis, that his death will come soon after Hector's, but he will not renounce his passionate resolve to avenge Patroclus' death. As he prepares to take Lycaon's life, he foresees the end of his own—"There will come a dawn or sunset or high noon / when a man will take my life in battle too" (21.125–6). In the *Odyssey* the hero's death is foretold by Tiresias in the underworld. After he has killed the suitors, Tiresias tells him, he must make his peace with the god Poseidon by traveling inland, carrying an oar on his shoulder, until he reaches a people utterly ignorant of the sea and ships. When one of them asks him why he is carrying a winnowing fan on his shoulder, he is to fix the oar in the ground and make an extraordinary sacrifice—a bull, a ram and a boar—to Poseidon. Once returned home, he is to sacrifice to all the Olympian gods in turn. "And at last your own death," says Tiresias,

> "will steal upon you . . .
> a gentle, painless death, far from the sea it comes
> to take you down, borne down with the years in ripe old age
> with all your people there in blessed peace around you."   (11.153–56)

THE SPELLING AND
PRONUNCIATION OF
HOMERIC NAMES

Though the English spelling of ancient Greek names faces modern poet-translators with some difficult problems, it was not a problem at all for Shakespeare, Milton, Pope and Tennyson. Except in the case of names that had through constant use been fully Anglicized—Hector, Helen, Troy—the poets used Latin equivalents of the Greek names, which they found in the poems of Virgil and Ovid that they read in school. These are the forms we also are familiar with, from our reading of English poets through the centuries: Circe, Scylla, Sirens.

Recent poet-translators have tried to get closer to the original Greek and have transliterated the Greek names directly, not through the medium of their Latin adaptations. One translator, for example, presents his readers with Kirkê, Skylla and the Seirênês. Another shares several of these spellings but will strike a compromise at times—Circe, Skylla. All translators compromise when it comes to such fully naturalized forms as Helen, Trojans and Argives (*Helenê, Trôes* and *Argeioi* in the Greek), and they also retreat from strict transliteration in cases like Odysseus (*Odusseus*), Priam (*Priamos*) and Thrace (*Thrêikê*).

This is an area in which no one can claim perfect consistency: we too offer a compromise. Its basis, however, is a return to the traditional practice of generations of English poets—the use of Latinate spellings except for those names that have become, in their purely English forms, familiar in our mouths as household words.

Rigid adherence to this rule would of course make unacceptable demands: it would impose, for instance, Minerva instead of Athena, Ulysses for Odysseus, Jupiter or Jove for Zeus. We have preferred the Greek names, but transliterated them on Latin principles: *Hêrê*, for example, is Hera in this translation; *Athênê* is Athena. Elsewhere we have replaced the letter *k* with *c* and substituted the ending *us* for the Greek *os* in the names of persons (*Patroklos* becomes Patroclus). When, however, a personal name ends in *ros* preceded by a consonant, we have used the Latin ending *er*: Pisander for *Peisandros*. The Greek diphthongs *ai* and *oi* are represented by the Latin diphthongs *ae* and *oe* (Achaean for *Akhaian*, Euboea for *Euboia*).

This conventional Latinate spelling of the names has a traditional pronunciation system, one that corresponds with neither the Greek nor the Latin sounds. Perhaps "system" is not the best word for it, since it is full of inconsistencies. But it is the pronunciation English poets have used for centuries, the sounds they heard mentally as they composed and that they confidently expected their readers to hear in their turn. Since there seems to be no similar convention for the English pronunciation of modern transliterated Greek—is the *h* sounded in *Akhilleus?* is Diomedes pronounced *dee-oh-may'-days* or *dee-oh-mee'-deez?*—we have thought it best to work with pronunciation that Keats and Shelley would have recognized.

As in Achilles (*a-kil'-eez*), *ch* is pronounced like *k* throughout. The consonants *c* and *g* are hard (as in "cake" and "gun") before *a*—Acastus (*a-kas'-tus*), Agamemnon (*a-ga-mem'-non*); before *o*—Leucothea (*lew-ko'-the-a*), Gorgon (*gor'-gon*); before *u*—Autolycus (*aw-to'-li-kus*); and before other consonants—Patroclus (*pa-tro'-klus*), Cauconians (*kaw-kho'-ni-unz*). They are soft (as in "cinder" and "George") before *e*—Circe (*sir'-see*), Geraestus (*je-ree'-stus*); before *i*—Cicones (*si-koh'-neez*), and before *y*—Cyclops (*seye'-klops*), Gyrae (*jeye'-ree*). The final combinations *cia* and *gia* produce *sha*—Phaeacia (*fee-ay'-sha*)—and *ja*—Ortygia (*or-ti'-ja*)—respectively. There are, however, cases in which the pronunciation of the consonants does not conform to these rules. One of the names of the Greeks, for instance—Argives—is pronounced with a hard *g* (*ar'-geyevz,* not *ar'-jeyevz*), by analogy with the town of Argos.

The vowels vary in pronunciation, sometimes but not always according to the length of the Latin (or Greek) syllable, and the reader will have to find guidance in the rhythm of the English line or consult the Pronouncing Glossary at the back of the volume. Final *e* is always sounded long: Hebe (*hee'-bee*); final *es* is pronounced *eez,* as in Achilles. In other positions, the letter *e* may represent the sound heard in *sneeze* or that heard in *pet.* The letter *i* may sound as in "bit" or "bite": Antinous (*an-ti'-no-us*) or Atrides (*a-treye'-deez*). The two sounds are also found for *y*—Cythera (*si-thee'-ra*) or Cyprus (*seye'-prus*)—while *o* is pronounced as in Olympus (*o-lim'-pus*) or Dodona (*doh-doh'-na*). In this spelling system, *u* except in the ending *us* and in combination with other vowels (see below) is always long, since it represents the Greek diphthong *ou*. But it may be pronounced either *you* as in "dew"—Dulichion (*dew-li'-ki-on*)—or *oo* as in "glue"—Arethusa (*a-re-thoo'-sa*).

The diphthongs *oe* and *ae* are both pronounced *ee*—Achaeans (*a-kee'-unz*), Oenops (*ee'-nops*). The combination *aer* does not produce a diphthong: Laertes (*lay-ur'-teez*); in cases where these letters are sounded separately, a dieresis is used: Phaëthusa (*fay-e-thoo'-sa*). The diphthong *au* is pronounced *aw*—Nausicaa (*naw-si'-kay-a*)—but in name endings, Menelaus, for example, it is not a diphthong, and the vowels are pronounced separately (*me-ne-lay'-us*). Since his name is familiar to the English reader, we have thought it unnecessary to use the dieresis in such cases. The ending *ous* is similar: Pirithous (*peye-ri'-tho-us*). The ending *eus* is sounded like *yoos*—Odysseus (*o-dis'-yoos*), except in the case of the name of one river—Alpheus (*al-fee'-us*)—and one Phaeacian elder, Echeneus (*e-ken-ee'-us*).

All other vowel combinations are pronounced not as diphthongs but as separate vowels. Double *o* is pronounced *o-oh:* Thoosa (*tho-oh'-sa*). Similarly, *oi* is treated not as a diphthong but as two separate sounds—Oicles (*oh-ik'-leez*). The sequence *ei,* however, is pronounced *eye,* as in the feminine name ending *eia:* Anticleia (*an-ti-kleye'-a*), Eurycleia (*yoo-ri-kleye'-a*) and other names as well; the constellation called the Pleiades (*pleye'-a-deez*) and the sea-nymph Eidothea (*eye-do'-the-a*); but Deiphobus (*dee-i'-fo-bus*) is an exception.

Obviously we cannot claim complete consistency even within the limits we have imposed on the system. Where no Latin form exists, as in the case of Poseidon, we have used the transliterated Greek, traditionally pronounced *po-seye'-don* (not *po-see'-i-don*). But we can claim to have reduced the unsightly dieresis to a minor factor and to have given the reader who comes to Homer for the first time a guide to pronunciation that will stand him or her in good stead when reading other poets who mention Greek names. We have also provided a Pronouncing Glossary of all the proper names in the text, which indicates stress and English vowel length.

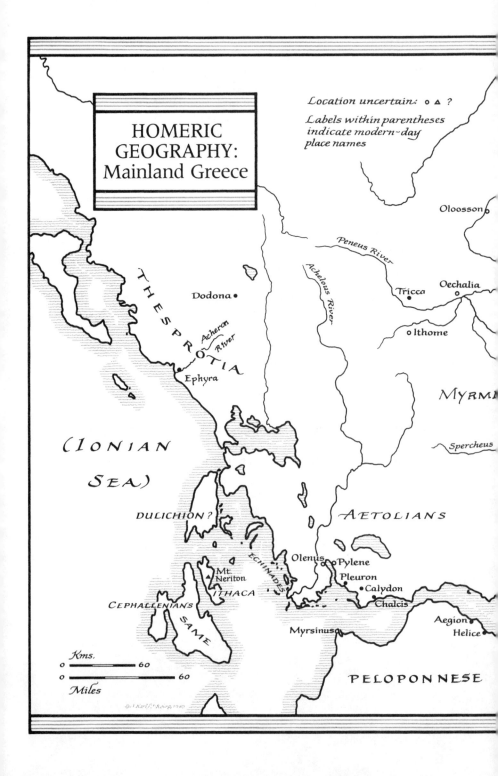

HOMERIC
GEOGRAPHY:
Mainland Greece

Location uncertain: ○ △ ?

Labels within parentheses
indicate modern-day
place names

Oloosson

Peneus River

Dodona

Acheron River

Acheron River

Tricca

Oechalia

Ithome

T H E S P R O T I A

Ephyra

MYRM

Spercheus

(IONIAN

SEA)

DULICHION?

AETOLIANS

Olenus

Pylene

Mt.
Neriton

Pleuron

ECHINADES

Calydon

ITHACA

Chalcis

CEPHALLENIANS

SAME

Aegion

Helice

Myrsinus

Kms.
0 ————— 60
0 ————— 60
Miles

PELOPONNESE

PIERIA

Mt.
Olympus ▲

Elone ○
Peneus River
○ Orthe   ▲ Mt.
○ Gyrtone   Ossa
● Argissa
                    Meliboea ●
Mt.
▲ Titanos

THESSALIAN   Lake   Thaumacia ●
                    Boebe
PLAIN
        Boebe ●
        Glaphyrae ●   Mt.
        Pherae ●   Pelion ▲
○ Ormenion   ● Iolcos
        Phylace ●

DONS   Prasus
                        Methone
        Iton ○
Enipeus River   Olizon ●
PHTHIA   Pteleos ●

        Antron ●
        Alus   Alope   Histiaea ●
River
Trachis ●   Dion ●   Cerinthus ●
Tarphe ○ Scarphe ●

        Thronion ●
LOCRIANS   ● Cynus   EUBOEA
        Opois ○

Lilaea ○ Mt.   Hyampolis ○
Parnassus ▲   ● Aspledon   Anthedon ●
PHOCIANS Orchomenos ● Copae   Chalcis ●
Crisa ●   Lake   Medeon Schoenus   Eretria ●
Pytho ○ Panopeus ● Copais   Aulis ○
Anemorea Coronea ●   Eleon ○ Hyria ○
Cyparissus Daulis   Haliartus ● Onchestus Harma ○
        Thespia ●   ● Thebes Mycalessus
BOEOTIANS   Glisas ○
        Thisbe ● Plataea ● Lutresis   Graea ○
                Erythrae ○
● Aegae   Scolus ○
                        Marathon ●   Styra ●
Hyperesia ●
                                Carystus ●

(AEGEAN
SEA)

SCYROS

N

● Athens   CAPE
                    GERAESTUS

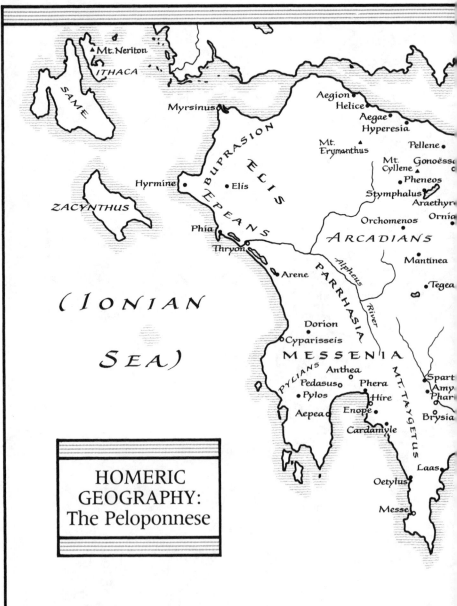

Mt. Neriton

ITHACA

SAME

ZACYNTHUS

Myrsinus

Hyrmine

Phia

Thryon

Aegion
Helice
Aegae
Hyperesia

Mt.
Erymanthus

Mt.
Cyllene

Stymphalus

Orchomenos

Pellene

Gonoëssa

Pheneos

Araethyr

Ornia

BUPRASION

ELIS

EPEANS

Elis

ARCADIANS

Mantinea

Tegea

(IONIAN

SEA)

Arene

PARRHASIA

Alpheus River

Dorion

Cyparisseis

MESSENIA

PYLIANS

Anthea

Pedasus

Phera

Pylos

Hire

Aepea

Enope

Cardamyle

MT. TAYGETUS

Spart

Amy

Phar

Brysia

Laas

Oetylus

Messe

HOMERIC
GEOGRAPHY:
The Peloponnese

Location uncertain: o *?*

*Labels within parentheses
indicate modern-day place names*

N

MAINLAND

GREECE

Styra

Carystus

on   Corinth

Athens

CAPE
GERAESTUS

Cleonae

SALAMIS

lycenae

RGOS

AEGINA

rgos

Epidaurus

Tiryns

CAPE
SOUNION

Asine

Eionae

Troezen

Mases

Hermione

EDAEMON

los

CAPE
MALEA

Kms.

0   100

0   100

CYTHERA

Miles

©A·Karl/J·Kemp 1990

CICONES

Ismarus

PAEONIANS

Axius River

THRACIANS

Aenus

SAMOTHRACE

Pityea

Mt. Athos

IMBROS

Zelea

Asca

Aesepus River

(AEGEAN

TROY

MYSIANS

See
Inset

PHRYGIAN

(SEA)

EUBOEA

SCYROS

LESBOS

Lake
Gyge?

Hermus River

PSYRIE

Mt.
Sipylus

MAEONIANS

CHIOS

CAPE MIMAS

Cayster
River

Mt.
Tmolus

Argos

SAMOS

Maeander River

ICARIA

Mt.
Mycale

CARIANS

DELOS

Miletus

CYCLADES

COS

NISYRUS

SYME

Ialysus

Camirus

RHODES

Lindos

CRETE

DIA

Amnisos

Miletus

CRAPATHUS

Cnossos

Lyctos

Lycastus

CASUS

Xanthus River

Phaestos

Gortyn

Rhytion

(MEDITERRANEAN

HOMERIC
GEOGRAPHY:
The Aegean and
Asia Minor

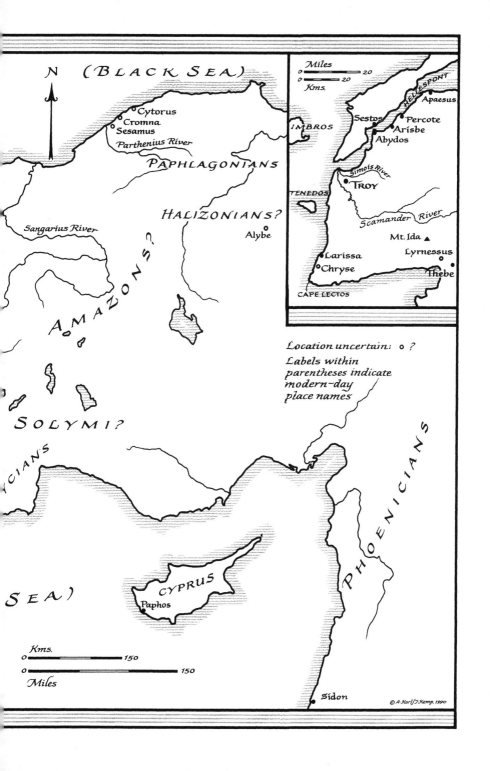

N (BLACK SEA)

Cytorus
Cromna
Sesamus
Parthenius River

PAPHLAGONIANS

Sangarius River

HALIZONIANS?

Alybe

A M A Z O N S?

S O L Y M I?

(SEA)

CYPRUS

Paphos

Sidon

Kms.
0 ——————— 150
0 ——————— 150
Miles

Miles
0 ——— 20
0 ——— 20
Kms.

IMBROS

HELLESPONT

Sestos
Abydos

Apaesus
Percote
Arisbe

Simois River
TROY

TENEDOS

Scamander River

Mt. Ida ▲

Larissa
Chryse

Lyrnessus
Thebe

CAPE LECTOS

Location uncertain: o ?
Labels within
parentheses indicate
modern–day
place names

PHOENICIANS

© A·Karl/J·Kemp, 1990

HOMER:
THE
ODYSSEY

BOOK ONE

Athena Inspires
the Prince

Sing to me of the man, Muse, the man of twists and turns
driven time and again off course, once he had plundered
the hallowed heights of Troy.
Many cities of men he saw and learned their minds,
many pains he suffered, heartsick on the open sea,
fighting to save his life and bring his comrades home.
But he could not save them from disaster, hard as he strove—
the recklessness of their own ways destroyed them all,
the blind fools, they devoured the cattle of the Sun
and the Sungod wiped from sight the day of their return.   10
Launch out on his story, Muse, daughter of Zeus,
start from where you will—sing for our time too.

　　　　　　　　　　　By now,
all the survivors, all who avoided headlong death
were safe at home, escaped the wars and waves.

But one man alone . . .
his heart set on his wife and his return—Calypso,
the bewitching nymph, the lustrous goddess, held him back,
deep in her arching caverns, craving him for a husband.
But then, when the wheeling seasons brought the year around,
that year spun out by the gods when he should reach his home,   20
Ithaca—though not even there would he be free of trials,
even among his loved ones—then every god took pity,
all except Poseidon. He raged on, seething against
the great Odysseus till he reached his native land.
                                                        But now
Poseidon had gone to visit the Ethiopians worlds away,
Ethiopians off at the farthest limits of mankind,
a people split in two, one part where the Sungod sets
and part where the Sungod rises. There Poseidon went
to receive an offering, bulls and rams by the hundred—
far away at the feast the Sea-lord sat and took his pleasure.   30
But the other gods, at home in Olympian Zeus's halls,
met for full assembly there, and among them now
the father of men and gods was first to speak,
sorely troubled, remembering handsome Aegisthus,
the man Agamemnon's son, renowned Orestes, killed.
Recalling Aegisthus, Zeus harangued the immortal powers:
"Ah how shameless—the way these mortals blame the gods.
From us alone, they say, come all their miseries, yes,
but they themselves, with their own reckless ways,
compound their pains beyond their proper share.   40
Look at Aegisthus now . . .
above and beyond *his* share he stole Atrides' wife,
he murdered the warlord coming home from Troy
though he knew it meant his own total ruin.
Far in advance we told him so ourselves,
dispatching the guide, the giant-killer Hermes.
'Don't murder the man,' he said, 'don't court his wife.
Beware, revenge will come from Orestes, Agamemnon's son,
that day he comes of age and longs for his native land.'
So Hermes warned, with all the good will in the world,   50

but would Aegisthus' hardened heart give way?
Now he pays the price—all at a single stroke."

    And sparkling-eyed Athena drove the matter home:
"Father, son of Cronus, our high and mighty king,
surely he goes down to a death he earned in full!
Let them all die so, all who do such things.
But my heart breaks for Odysseus,
that seasoned veteran cursed by fate so long—
far from his loved ones still, he suffers torments
off on a wave-washed island rising at the center of the seas.   60
A dark wooded island, and there a goddess makes her home,
a daughter of Atlas, wicked Titan who sounds the deep
in all its depths, whose shoulders lift on high
the colossal pillars thrusting earth and sky apart.
Atlas' daughter it is who holds Odysseus captive,
luckless man—despite his tears, forever trying
to spellbind his heart with suave, seductive words
and wipe all thought of Ithaca from his mind.
But he, straining for no more than a glimpse
of hearth-smoke drifting up from his own land,   70
Odysseus longs to die . . .
                        Olympian Zeus,
have you no care for *him* in your lofty heart?
Did he never win your favor with sacrifices
burned beside the ships on the broad plain of Troy?
Why, Zeus, why so dead set against Odysseus?"

    "My child," Zeus who marshals the thunderheads replied,
"what nonsense you let slip through your teeth. Now,
how on earth could I forget Odysseus? Great Odysseus
who excels all men in wisdom, excels in offerings too
he gives the immortal gods who rule the vaulting skies?   80
No, it's the Earth-Shaker, Poseidon, unappeased,
forever fuming against him for the Cyclops
whose giant eye he blinded: godlike Polyphemus,
towering over all the Cyclops' clans in power.

The nymph Thoosa bore him, daughter of Phorcys,
lord of the barren salt sea—she met Poseidon
once in his vaulted caves and they made love.
And now for his blinded son the earthquake god—
though he won't quite kill Odysseus—
drives him far off course from native land.   90
But come, all of us here put heads together now,
work out his journey home so Odysseus can return.
Lord Poseidon, I trust, will let his anger go.
How can he stand his ground against the will
of all the gods at once—one god alone?"

   Athena, her eyes flashing bright, exulted,
"Father, son of Cronus, our high and mighty king!
If now it really pleases the blissful gods
that wise Odysseus shall return—home at last—
let us dispatch the guide and giant-killer Hermes   100
down to Ogygia Island, down to announce at once
to the nymph with lovely braids our fixed decree:
Odysseus journeys home—the exile must return!
While I myself go down to Ithaca, rouse his son
to a braver pitch, inspire his heart with courage
to summon the flowing-haired Achaeans to full assembly,
speak his mind to all those suitors, slaughtering on and on
his droves of sheep and shambling longhorn cattle.
Next I will send him off to Sparta and sandy Pylos,
there to learn of his dear father's journey home.   110
Perhaps he will hear some news and make his name
throughout the mortal world."
                      So Athena vowed
and under her feet she fastened the supple sandals,
ever-glowing gold, that wing her over the waves
and boundless earth with the rush of gusting winds.
She seized the rugged spear tipped with a bronze point—
weighted, heavy, the massive shaft she wields to break the lines
of heroes the mighty Father's daughter storms against.
And down she swept from Olympus' craggy peaks
and lit on Ithaca, standing tall at Odysseus' gates,   120

the threshold of his court. Gripping her bronze spear,
she looked for all the world like a stranger now,
like Mentes, lord of the Taphians.
There she found the swaggering suitors, just then
amusing themselves with rolling dice before the doors,
lounging on hides of oxen they had killed themselves.
While heralds and brisk attendants bustled round them,
some at the mixing-bowls, mulling wine and water,
others wiping the tables down with sopping sponges,
setting them out in place, still other servants   130
jointed and carved the great sides of meat.

      First by far to see her was Prince Telemachus,
sitting among the suitors, heart obsessed with grief.
He could almost see his magnificent father, here . . .
in the mind's eye—if only *he* might drop from the clouds
and drive these suitors all in a rout throughout the halls
and regain his pride of place and rule his own domains!
Daydreaming so as he sat among the suitors,
he glimpsed Athena now
and straight to the porch he went, mortified   140
that a guest might still be standing at the doors.
Pausing beside her there, he clasped her right hand
and relieving her at once of her long bronze spear,
met her with winged words: "Greetings, stranger!
Here in our house you'll find a royal welcome.
Have supper first, then tell us what you need."

      He led the way and Pallas Athena followed.
Once in the high-roofed hall, he took her lance
and fixed it firm in a burnished rack against
a sturdy pillar, there where row on row of spears,   150
embattled Odysseus' spears, stood stacked and waiting.
Then he escorted her to a high, elaborate chair of honor,
over it draped a cloth, and here he placed his guest
with a stool to rest her feet. But for himself
he drew up a low reclining chair beside her,
richly painted, clear of the press of suitors,

concerned his guest, offended by their uproar,
might shrink from food in the midst of such a mob.
He hoped, what's more, to ask her about his long-lost father.
A maid brought water soon in a graceful golden pitcher   160
and over a silver basin tipped it out
so they might rinse their hands,
then pulled a gleaming table to their side.
A staid housekeeper brought on bread to serve them,
appetizers aplenty too, lavish with her bounty.
A carver lifted platters of meat toward them,
meats of every sort, and set beside them golden cups
and time and again a page came round and poured them wine.

   But now the suitors trooped in with all their swagger
and took their seats on low and high-backed chairs.   170
Heralds poured water over their hands for rinsing,
serving maids brought bread heaped high in trays
and the young men brimmed the mixing-bowls with wine.
They reached out for the good things that lay at hand,
and when they'd put aside desire for food and drink
the suitors set their minds on other pleasures,
song and dancing, all that crowns a feast.
A herald placed an ornate lyre in Phemius' hands,
the bard who always performed among them there;
they forced the man to sing.
                       A rippling prelude—   180
and no sooner had he struck up his rousing song
than Telemachus, head close to Athena's sparkling eyes,
spoke low to his guest so no one else could hear:
"Dear stranger, would you be shocked by what I say?
Look at them over there. Not a care in the world,
just lyres and tunes! It's easy for them, all right,
they feed on another's goods and go scot-free—
a man whose white bones lie strewn in the rain somewhere,
rotting away on land or rolling down the ocean's salty swells.
But that man—if they caught sight of him home in Ithaca,   190
by god, they'd all pray to be faster on their feet
than richer in bars of gold and heavy robes.

But now, no use, he's died a wretched death.
No comfort's left for us . . . not even if
someone, somewhere, says he's coming home.
The day of his return will never dawn.
                                        Enough.
Tell me about yourself now, clearly, point by point.
Who are you? where are you from? your city? your parents?
What sort of vessel brought you? Why did the sailors
land you here in Ithaca? Who did they say they are?   200
I hardly think you came this way on foot!
And tell me this for a fact—I need to know—
is this your first time here? Or are you a friend of father's,
a guest from the old days? Once, crowds of other men
would come to our house on visits—visitor that he was,
when he walked among the living."
                                        Her eyes glinting,
goddess Athena answered, "My whole story, of course,
I'll tell it point by point. Wise old Anchialus
was my father. My own name is Mentes,
lord of the Taphian men who love their oars.   210
And here I've come, just now, with ship and crew,
sailing the wine-dark sea to foreign ports of call,
to Temese, out for bronze—our cargo gleaming iron.
Our ship lies moored off farmlands far from town,
riding in Rithron Cove, beneath Mount Nion's woods.
As for the ties between your father and myself,
we've been friends forever, I'm proud to say,
and he would bear me out
if you went and questioned old lord Laertes.
He, I gather, no longer ventures into town   220
but lives a life of hardship, all to himself,
off on his farmstead with an aged serving-woman
who tends him well, who gives him food and drink
when weariness has taken hold of his withered limbs
from hauling himself along his vineyard's steep slopes.
And now I've come—and why? I heard that he was back . . .
your father, that is. But no, the gods thwart his passage.
Yet I tell you great Odysseus is not dead. He's still alive,

somewhere in this wide world, held captive, out at sea
on a wave-washed island, and hard men, savages,   230
somehow hold him back against his will.
                              Wait,
I'll make you a prophecy, one the immortal gods
have planted in my mind—it will come true, I think,
though I am hardly a seer or know the flights of birds.
He won't be gone long from the native land he loves,
not even if iron shackles bind your father down.
He's plotting a way to journey home at last;
he's never at a loss.
                    But come, please,
tell me about yourself now, point by point.
You're truly Odysseus' son? You've sprung up so!   240
Uncanny resemblance . . . the head, and the fine eyes—
I see him now. How often we used to meet in the old days
before he embarked for Troy, where other Argive captains,
all the best men, sailed in the long curved ships.
From then to this very day
I've not set eyes on Odysseus or he on me."

    And young Telemachus cautiously replied,
"I'll try, my friend, to give you a frank answer.
Mother has always told me I'm his son, it's true,
but I am not so certain. Who, on his own,   250
has ever really known who gave him life?
Would to god I'd been the son of a happy man
whom old age overtook in the midst of his possessions!
Now, think of the most unlucky mortal ever born—
since you ask me, yes, they say I am his son."

    "Still," the clear-eyed goddess reassured him,
"trust me, the gods have not marked out your house
for such an unsung future,
not if Penelope has borne a son like you.
But tell me about all this and spare me nothing.   260
What's this banqueting, this crowd carousing here?
And what part do you play yourself? Some wedding-feast,

some festival? Hardly a potluck supper, I would say.
How obscenely they lounge and swagger here, look,
gorging in your house. Why, any man of sense
who chanced among them would be outraged,
seeing such behavior."
                              Ready Telemachus
took her up at once: "Well, my friend,
seeing you want to probe and press the question,
once this house was rich, no doubt, beyond reproach   270
when the man you mentioned still lived here, at home.
Now the gods have reversed our fortunes with a vengeance—
wiped that man from the earth like no one else before.
I would never have grieved so much about his death
if he'd gone down with comrades off in Troy
or died in the arms of loved ones,
once he had wound down the long coil of war.
Then all united Achaea would have raised his tomb
and he'd have won his son great fame for years to come.
But now the whirlwinds have ripped him away, no fame for him!   280
He's lost and gone now—out of sight, out of mind—and I . . .
he's left me tears and grief. Nor do I rack my heart
and grieve for him alone. No longer. Now the gods
have invented other miseries to plague me.
                                        Listen.
All the nobles who rule the islands round about,
Dulichion, and Same, and wooded Zacynthus too,
and all who lord it in rocky Ithaca as well—
down to the last man they court my mother,
they lay waste my house! And mother . . .
she neither rejects a marriage she despises   290
nor can she bear to bring the courting to an end—
while they continue to bleed my household white.
Soon—you wait—they'll grind *me* down as well."
                                   "Shameful!"—
brimming with indignation, Pallas Athena broke out.
"Oh how much you need Odysseus, gone so long—
how *he*'d lay hands on all these brazen suitors!
If only he would appear, now,

at his house's outer gates and take his stand,
armed with his helmet, shield and pair of spears,
as strong as the man I glimpsed that first time   300
in our own house, drinking wine and reveling there . . .
just come in from Ephyra, visiting Ilus, Mermerus' son.
Odysseus sailed that way, you see, in his swift trim ship,
hunting deadly poison to smear on his arrows' bronze heads.
Ilus refused—he feared the wrath of the everlasting gods—
but father, so fond of him, gave him all he wanted.
If only *that* Odysseus sported with these suitors,
a blood wedding, a quick death would take the lot!
True, but all lies in the lap of the great gods,
whether or not he'll come and pay them back,   310
here, in his own house.
                           But you, I urge you,
think how to drive these suitors from your halls.
Come now, listen closely. Take my words to heart.
At daybreak summon the island's lords to full assembly,
give your orders to all and call the gods to witness:
tell the suitors to scatter, each to his own place.
As for your mother, if the spirit moves her to marry,
let her go back to her father's house, a man of power.
Her kin will arrange the wedding, provide the gifts,
the array that goes with a daughter dearly loved.
                                        For you,   320
I have some good advice, if only you will accept it.
Fit out a ship with twenty oars, the best in sight,
sail in quest of news of your long-lost father.
Someone may tell you something
or you may catch a rumor straight from Zeus,
rumor that carries news to men like nothing else.
First go down to Pylos, question old King Nestor,
then cross over to Sparta, to red-haired Menelaus,
of all the bronze-armored Achaeans the last man back.
Now, if you hear your father's alive and heading home,   330
hard-pressed as you are, brave out one more year.
If you hear he's dead, no longer among the living,
then back you come to the native land you love,

raise his grave-mound, build his honors high
with the full funeral rites that he deserves—
and give your mother to another husband.
                                        Then,
once you've sealed those matters, seen them through,
think hard, reach down deep in your heart and soul
for a way to kill these suitors in your house,
by stealth or in open combat.   340
You must not cling to your boyhood any longer—
it's time you were a man. Haven't you heard
what glory Prince Orestes won throughout the world
when he killed that cunning, murderous Aegisthus,
who'd killed his famous father?
                          And you, my friend—
how tall and handsome I see you now—be brave, you too,
so men to come will sing your praises down the years.
But now I must go back to my swift trim ship
and all my shipmates, chafing there, I'm sure,
waiting for my return. It all rests with you.   350
Take my words to heart."
                          "Oh stranger,"
heedful Telemachus replied, "indeed I will.
You've counseled me with so much kindness now,
like a father to a son. I won't forget a word.
But come, stay longer, keen as you are to sail,
so you can bathe and rest and lift your spirits,
then go back to your ship, delighted with a gift,
a prize of honor, something rare and fine
as a keepsake from myself. The kind of gift
a host will give a stranger, friend to friend."   360

    Her eyes glinting, Pallas declined in haste:
"Not now. Don't hold me here. I long to be on my way.
As for the gift—whatever you'd give in kindness—
save it for my return so I can take it home.
Choose something rare and fine, and a good reward
that gift is going to bring you."
                          With that promise,

off and away Athena the bright-eyed goddess flew
like a bird in soaring flight
but left his spirit filled with nerve and courage,
charged with his father's memory more than ever now.   370
He felt his senses quicken, overwhelmed with wonder—
this was a god, he knew it well and made at once
for the suitors, a man like a god himself.

                                      Amidst them still
the famous bard sang on, and they sat in silence, listening
as he performed The Achaeans' Journey Home from Troy:
all the blows Athena doomed them to endure.

                                           And now,
from high above in her room and deep in thought,
she caught his inspired strains . . .
Icarius' daughter Penelope, wary and reserved,
and down the steep stair from her chamber she descended,   380
not alone: two of her women followed close behind.
That radiant woman, once she reached her suitors,
drawing her glistening veil across her cheeks,
paused now where a column propped the sturdy roof,
with one of her loyal handmaids stationed either side.
Suddenly, dissolving in tears and bursting through
the bard's inspired voice, she cried out, "Phemius!
So many other songs you know to hold us spellbound,
works of the gods and men that singers celebrate.
Sing one of those as you sit beside them here   390
and they drink their wine in silence.

                                  But break off this song—
the unendurable song that always rends the heart inside me . . .
the unforgettable grief, it wounds me most of all!
How I long for my husband—alive in memory, always,
that great man whose fame resounds through Hellas
right to the depths of Argos!"

                                "Why, mother,"
poised Telemachus put in sharply, "why deny
our devoted bard the chance to entertain us
any way the spirit stirs him on?
Bards are not to blame—   400

Zeus is to blame. He deals to each and every
laborer on this earth whatever doom he pleases.
Why fault the bard if he sings the Argives' harsh fate?
It's always the latest song, the one that echoes last
in the listeners' ears, that people praise the most.
Courage, mother. Harden your heart, and listen.
Odysseus was scarcely the only one, you know,
whose journey home was blotted out at Troy.
Others, so many others, died there too.

      So, mother,
go back to your quarters. Tend to your own tasks,   410
the distaff and the loom, and keep the women
working hard as well. As for giving orders,
men will see to that, but I most of all:
I hold the reins of power in this house."

         Astonished,
she withdrew to her own room. She took to heart
the clear good sense in what her son had said.
Climbing up to the lofty chamber with her women,
she fell to weeping for Odysseus, her beloved husband,
till watchful Athena sealed her eyes with welcome sleep.

  But the suitors broke into uproar through the shadowed halls, 420
all of them lifting prayers to lie beside her, share her bed,
until discreet Telemachus took command: "You suitors
who plague my mother, you, you insolent, overweening . . .
for this evening let us dine and take our pleasure,
no more shouting now. What a fine thing it is
to listen to such a bard as we have here—
the man sings like a god.

      But at first light
we all march forth to assembly, take our seats
so I can give my orders and say to you straight out:
You must leave my palace! See to your feasting elsewhere, 430
devour your own possessions, house to house by turns.
But if you decide the fare is better, richer here,
destroying one man's goods and going scot-free,
all right then, carve away!

But I'll cry out to the everlasting gods in hopes
that Zeus will pay you back with a vengeance—all of you
destroyed in my house while I go scot-free myself!"

    So Telemachus declared. And they all bit their lips,
amazed the prince could speak with so much daring.

    Eupithes' son Antinous broke their silence: 440
"Well, Telemachus, only the gods could teach you
to sound so high and mighty! Such brave talk.
I pray that Zeus will never make *you* king of Ithaca,
though your father's crown is no doubt yours by birth."

    But cool-headed Telemachus countered firmly:
"Antinous, even though my words may offend you,
I'd be happy to take the crown if Zeus presents it.
You think that nothing worse could befall a man?
It's really not so bad to be a king. All at once
your palace grows in wealth, your honors grow as well.   450
But there are hosts of other Achaean princes, look—
young and old, crowds of them on our island here—
and any one of the lot might hold the throne,
now great Odysseus is dead . . .
But I'll be lord of my own house and servants,
all that King Odysseus won for me by force."

    And now Eurymachus, Polybus' son, stepped in:
"Surely this must lie in the gods' lap, Telemachus—
which Achaean will lord it over seagirt Ithaca.
Do hold on to your own possessions, rule your house.   460
God forbid that anyone tear your holdings from your hands
while men still live in Ithaca.
                                But about your guest,
dear boy, I have some questions. Where does he come from?
Where's his country, his birth, his father's old estates?
Did he bring some news of your father, his return?
Or did he come on business of his own?
How he leapt to his feet and off he went!

No waiting around for proper introductions.
And no mean man, not by the looks of him, I'd say."

   "Eurymachus," Telemachus answered shrewdly,   470
"clearly my father's journey home is lost forever.
I no longer trust in rumors—rumors from the blue—
nor bother with any prophecy, when mother calls
some wizard into the house to ask him questions.
As for the stranger, though,
the man's an old family friend, from Taphos,
wise Anchialus' son. He says his name is Mentes,
lord of the Taphian men who love their oars."
                                        So he said
but deep in his mind he knew the immortal goddess.
Now the suitors turned to dance and song,   480
to the lovely beat and sway,
waiting for dusk to come upon them there . . .
and the dark night came upon them, lost in pleasure.
Finally, to bed. Each to his own house.
                              Telemachus,
off to his bedroom built in the fine courtyard—
a commanding, lofty room set well apart—
retired too, his spirit swarming with misgivings.
His devoted nurse attended him, bearing a glowing torch,
Eurycleia the daughter of Ops, Pisenor's son.
Laertes had paid a price for the woman years ago,   490
still in the bloom of youth. He traded twenty oxen,
honored her on a par with his own loyal wife at home
but fearing the queen's anger, never shared her bed.
She was his grandson's escort now and bore a torch,
for she was the one of all the maids who loved
the prince the most—she'd nursed him as a baby.
He spread the doors of his snug, well-made room,
sat down on the bed and pulled his soft shirt off,
tossed it into the old woman's conscientious hands,
and after folding it neatly, patting it smooth,   500
she hung it up on a peg beside his corded bed,
then padded from the bedroom,

drawing the door shut with the silver hook,
sliding the doorbolt home with its rawhide strap.
There all night long, wrapped in a sheep's warm fleece,
he weighed in his mind the course Athena charted.

BOOK TWO

Telemachus
Sets Sail

When young Dawn with her rose-red fingers shone once more
the true son of Odysseus sprang from bed and dressed,
over his shoulder he slung his well-honed sword,
fastened rawhide sandals under his smooth feet
and stepped from his bedroom, handsome as a god.
At once he ordered heralds to cry out loud and clear
and summon the flowing-haired Achaeans to full assembly.
Their cries rang out. The people filed in quickly.
When they'd grouped, crowding the meeting grounds,
Telemachus strode in too, a bronze spear in his grip   10
and not alone: two sleek hounds went trotting at his heels.
And Athena lavished a marvelous splendor on the prince
so the people all gazed in wonder as he came forward,
the elders making way as he took his father's seat.
The first to speak was an old lord, Aegyptius,

stooped with age, who knew the world by heart.
For one dear son had sailed with King Odysseus,
bound in the hollow ships to the stallion-land of Troy—
the spearman Antiphus—but the brutal Cyclops killed him,
trapped in his vaulted cave, the last man the monster ate.   20
Three other sons he had: one who mixed with the suitors,
Eurynomus, and two kept working their father's farms.
Still, he never forgot the soldier, desolate in his grief.
In tears for the son he lost, he rose and said among them,
"Hear me, men of Ithaca. Hear what I have to say.
Not once have we held assembly, met in session
since King Odysseus sailed away in the hollow ships.
Who has summoned us now—one of the young men,
one of the old-timers? What crisis spurs him on?
Some news he's heard of an army on the march,   30
word he's caught firsthand so he can warn us now?
Or some other public matter he'll disclose and argue?
He's a brave man, I'd say. God be with him, too!
May Zeus speed him on to a happy end,
whatever his heart desires!"
                              Winning words
with a lucky ring. Odysseus' son rejoiced;
the boy could sit no longer—fired up to speak,
he took his stand among the gathered men.
The herald Pisenor, skilled in custom's ways,
put the staff in his hand, and then the prince,   40
addressing old Aegyptius first, led off with, "Sir,
that man is not far off—you'll soon see for yourself—
I was the one who called us all together.
Something wounds me deeply . . .
not news I've heard of an army on the march,
word I've caught firsthand so I can warn you now,
or some other public matter I'll disclose and argue.
No, the crisis is my own. Trouble has struck my house—
a double blow. First, I have lost my noble father
who ruled among you years ago, each of you here,   50
and kindly as a father to his children.
                              But now this,

a worse disaster that soon will grind my house down,
ruin it all, and all my worldly goods in the bargain.
Suitors plague my mother—against her will—
sons of the very men who are your finest here!
They'd sooner die than approach her father's house
so Icarius himself might see to his daughter's bridal,
hand her to whom he likes, whoever meets his fancy.
Not they—they infest our palace day and night,
they butcher our cattle, our sheep, our fat goats,   60
feasting themselves sick, swilling our glowing wine
as if there's no tomorrow—all of it, squandered.
Now we have no man like Odysseus in command
to drive this curse from the house. We ourselves?
We're hardly the ones to fight them off. All we'd do
is parade our wretched weakness. A boy inept at battle.
Oh I'd swing to attack if I had the power in me.
By god, it's intolerable, what they do—disgrace,
my house a shambles!
                          You should be ashamed yourselves,
mortified in the face of neighbors living round about!   70
Fear the gods' wrath—before they wheel in outrage
and make these crimes recoil on your heads.
I beg you by Olympian Zeus, by Themis too,
who sets assemblies free and calls us into session—
stop, my friends! Leave me alone to pine away in anguish . . .
Unless, of course, you think my noble father Odysseus
did the Achaean army damage, deliberate harm,
and to pay me back you'd do me harm, deliberately
setting these parasites against me. Better for me
if *you* were devouring all my treasure, all my cattle—   80
if you were the ones, we'd make amends in no time.
We'd approach you for reparations round the town,
demanding our goods till you'd returned the lot.
But now, look, you load my heart with grief—
there's nothing I can do!"
                          Filled with anger,
down on the ground he dashed the speaker's scepter—
bursting into tears. Pity seized the assembly.

All just sat there, silent . . .
no one had the heart to reply with harshness.
Only Antinous, who found it in himself to say,   90
"So high and mighty, Telemachus—such unbridled rage!
Well now, fling your accusations at *us?*
Think to pin the blame on *us?* You think again.
It's not the suitors here who deserve the blame,
it's your own dear mother, the matchless queen of cunning.
Look here. For three years now, getting on to four,
she's played it fast and loose with all our hearts,
building each man's hopes—
dangling promises, dropping hints to each—
but all the while with something else in mind.   100
This was her latest masterpiece of guile:
she set up a great loom in the royal halls
and she began to weave, and the weaving finespun,
the yarns endless, and she would lead us on: 'Young men,
my suitors, now that King Odysseus is no more,
go slowly, keen as you are to marry me, until
I can finish off this web . . .
so my weaving won't all fray and come to nothing.
This is a shroud for old lord Laertes, for that day
when the deadly fate that lays us out at last will take him down. 110
I dread the shame my countrywomen would heap upon me,
yes, if a man of such wealth should lie in state
without a shroud for cover.'
                              Her very words,
and despite our pride and passion we believed her.
So by day she'd weave at her great and growing web—
by night, by the light of torches set beside her,
she would unravel all she'd done. Three whole years
she deceived us blind, seduced us with this scheme . . .
Then, when the wheeling seasons brought the fourth year on,
one of her women, in on the queen's secret, told the truth   120
and we caught her in the act—unweaving her gorgeous web.
So she finished it off. Against her will. We forced her.

     Now Telemachus, here is how the suitors answer *you*—

you burn it in your mind, you and all our people:
send your mother back! Direct her to marry
whomever her father picks, whoever pleases her.
So long as she persists in tormenting us,
quick to exploit the gifts Athena gave her—
a skilled hand for elegant work, a fine mind
and subtle wiles too—we've never heard the like,   130
not even in old stories sung of all Achaea's
well-coifed queens who graced the years gone by:
Mycenae crowned with garlands, Tyro and Alcmena . . .
Not one could equal Penelope for intrigue
but in this case she intrigued beyond all limits.
So, we will devour your worldly goods and wealth
as long as *she* holds out, holds to that course
the gods have charted deep inside her heart.
Great renown she wins for herself, no doubt,
great loss for you in treasure. We'll not go back   140
to our old estates or leave for other parts,
not till she weds the Argive man she fancies."

   But with calm good sense Telemachus replied:
"Antinous, how can I drive my mother from our house
against her will, the one who bore me, reared me too?
My father is worlds away, dead or alive, who knows?
Imagine the high price I'd have to pay Icarius
if all on my own I send my mother home.
Oh what I would suffer from her father—
and some dark god would hurt me even more   150
when mother, leaving her own house behind,
calls down her withering Furies on my head,
and our people's cries of shame would hound my heels.
I will never issue that ultimatum to my mother.
And you, if you have any shame in your own hearts,
you must leave my palace! See to your feasting elsewhere,
devour your own possessions, house to house by turns.
But if you decide the fare is better, richer here,
destroying one man's goods and going scot-free,
all right then, carve away!   160

But I'll cry out to the everlasting gods in hopes
that Zeus will pay you back with a vengeance—all of you
destroyed in my house while I go scot-free myself!"

    And to seal his prayer, farseeing Zeus sent down a sign.
He launched two eagles soaring high from a mountain ridge
and down they glided, borne on the wind's draft a moment,
wing to wingtip, pinions straining taut till just
above the assembly's throbbing hum they whirled,
suddenly, wings thrashing, wild onslaught of wings
and banking down at the crowd's heads—a glaring, fatal sign—   170
talons slashing each other, tearing cheeks and throats
they swooped away on the right through homes and city.
All were dumbstruck, watching the eagles trail from sight,
people brooding, deeply, what might come to pass . . .
Until the old warrior Halitherses,
Mastor's son, broke the silence for them—
the one who outperformed all men of his time
at reading bird-signs, sounding out the omens,
rose and spoke, distraught for each man there:
"Hear me, men of Ithaca! Hear what I have to say,   180
though my revelations strike the suitors first of all—
a great disaster is rolling like a breaker toward their heads.
Clearly Odysseus won't be far from loved ones any longer—
now, right now, he's somewhere near, I tell you,
breeding bloody death for all these suitors here,
pains aplenty too for the rest of us who live
in Ithaca's sunlit air.
                          Long before that,
we must put heads together, find some way
to stop these men, or let them stop themselves.
Better for them that way, by far. I myself   190
am no stranger to prophecy—I can see it now!
Odysseus . . . all is working out for him, I say,
just as I said it would that day the Argives sailed
for Troy and the mastermind of battle boarded with them.
I said then: after many blows, and all his shipmates lost,
after twenty years had wheeled by, he would come home,

unrecognized by all . . .
and now, look, it all comes to pass!"
                              "Stop, old man!"
Eurymachus, Polybus' son, rose up to take him on.
"Go home and babble your omens to your children—   200
save *them* from some catastrophe coming soon.
I'm a better hand than you at reading portents.
Flocks of birds go fluttering under the sun's rays,
not all are fraught with meaning. Odysseus?
He's dead now, far from home—
would to god that you'd died with him too.
We'd have escaped your droning prophecies then
and the way you've loosed the dogs of this boy's anger—
your eyes peeled for a house-gift he might give you.
Here's *my* prophecy, bound to come to pass.   210
If you, you old codger, wise as the ages,
talk him round, incite the boy to riot,
he'll be the first to suffer, let me tell you.
And you, old man, we'll clap some fine on you
you'll weep to pay, a fine to crush your spirit!
                              Telemachus?
Here in front of you all, here's my advice for him.
Let him urge his mother back to her father's house—
her kin will arrange the wedding, provide the gifts,
the array that goes with a daughter dearly loved.
Not till then, I'd say, will the island princes quit   220
their taxing courtship. Who's there to fear? I ask you.
Surely not Telemachus, with all his tiresome threats.
Nor do we balk, old man, at the prophecies you mouth—
they'll come to grief, they'll make us hate you more.
The prince's wealth will be devoured as always,
mercilessly—no reparations, ever . . . not
while the queen drags out our hopes to wed her,
waiting, day after day, all of us striving hard
to win one matchless beauty. Never courting others,
bevies of brides who'd suit each noble here."   230

    Telemachus answered, firm in his resolve:

"Eurymachus—the rest of you fine, brazen suitors—
I have done with appeals to you about these matters.
I'll say no more. The gods know how things stand
and so do all the Achaeans. And now all I ask
is a good swift ship and a crew of twenty men
to speed me through my passage out and back.
I'm sailing off to Sparta, sandy Pylos too,
for news of my long-lost father's journey home.
Someone may tell me something   240
or I may catch a rumor straight from Zeus,
rumor that carries news to men like nothing else.
Now, if I hear my father's alive and heading home,
hard-pressed as I am, I'll brave out one more year.
If I hear he's dead, no longer among the living,
then back I'll come to the native land I love,
raise his grave-mound, build his honors high
with the full funeral rites that he deserves—
and give my mother to another husband."

                                        A declaration,
and the prince sat down as Mentor took the floor,   250
Odysseus' friend-in-arms to whom the king,
sailing off to Troy, committed his household,
ordering one and all to obey the old man
and he would keep things steadfast and secure.
With deep concern for the realm, he rose and warned,
"Hear me, men of Ithaca. Hear what I have to say.
Never let any sceptered king be kind and gentle now,
not with all his heart, or set his mind on justice—
no, let him be cruel and always practice outrage.
Think: not one of the people whom he ruled   260
remembers Odysseus now, that godlike man,
and kindly as a father to his children!
I don't grudge these arrogant suitors for a moment,
weaving their violent work with all their wicked hearts—
they lay their lives on the line when they consume
Odysseus' worldly goods, blind in their violence,
telling themselves that he'll come home no more.
But all the rest of you, how you rouse my fury!

Sitting here in silence . . .
never a word put forth to curb these suitors,   270
paltry few as they are and you so many."

                                "Mentor!"
Euenor's son Leocritus rounded on him, shouting,
"Rabble-rousing fool, now what's this talk?
Goading them on to try and hold us back!
It's uphill work, I warn you,
fighting a force like ours—for just a meal.
Even if Odysseus of Ithaca did arrive in person,
to find us well-bred suitors feasting in his halls,
and the man were hell-bent on routing us from the palace—
little joy would his wife derive from his return,   280
for all her yearning. Here on the spot he'd meet
a humiliating end if he fought against such odds.
You're talking nonsense—idiocy.
                            No more. Come,
dissolve the assembly. Each man return to his holdings.
Mentor and Halitherses can speed our young prince on,
his father's doddering friends since time began.
He'll sit tight a good long while, I trust,
scrabbling for news right here in Ithaca—
he'll never make that trip."

    This broke up the assembly, keen to leave.   290
The people scattered quickly, each to his own house,
while the suitors strolled back to King Odysseus' palace.

    Telemachus, walking the beach now, far from others,
washed his hands in the foaming surf and prayed to Pallas:
"Dear god, hear me! Yesterday you came to my house,
you told me to ship out on the misty sea and learn
if father, gone so long, is ever coming home . . .
Look how my countrymen—the suitors most of all,
the pernicious bullies—foil each move I make."

    Athena came to his prayer from close at hand,   300
for all the world with Mentor's build and voice,

and she urged him on with winging words: "Telemachus,
you'll lack neither courage nor sense from this day on,
not if your father's spirit courses through your veins—
now there was a man, I'd say, in words and action both!
So how can your journey end in shipwreck or defeat?
Only if you were not his stock, Penelope's too,
then I'd fear your hopes might come to grief.
Few sons are the equals of their fathers;
most fall short, all too few surpass them.   310
But you, brave and adept from this day on—
Odysseus' cunning has hardly given out in you—
there's every hope that you will reach your goal.
Put them out of your mind, these suitors' schemes and plots.
They're madmen. Not a shred of sense or decency in the crowd.
Nor can they glimpse the death and black doom hovering
just at their heads to crush them all in one short day.
But you, the journey that stirs you now is not far off,
not with the likes of me, your father's friend and yours,
to rig you a swift ship and be your shipmate too.   320
Now home you go and mix with the suitors there.
But get your rations ready,
pack them all in vessels, the wine in jars,
and barley-meal—the marrow of men's bones—
in durable skins, while I make rounds in town
and quickly enlist your crew of volunteers.
Lots of ships in seagirt Ithaca, old and new.
I'll look them over, choose the best in sight,
we'll fit her out and launch her into the sea at once!"

     And so Athena, daughter of Zeus, assured him.   330
No lingering now—he heard the goddess' voice—
but back he went to his house with aching heart
and there at the palace found the brazen suitors
skinning goats in the courtyard, singeing pigs for roasting.
Antinous, smiling warmly, sauntered up to the prince,
grasped his hand and coaxed him, savoring his name:
"Telemachus, my high and mighty, fierce young friend,
no more nursing those violent words and actions now.

Come, eat and drink with us, just like the old days.
Whatever you want our people will provide. A ship   340
and a picked crew to speed you to holy Pylos,
out for the news about your noble father."

    But self-possessed Telemachus drew the line:
"Antinous, now how could I dine with you in peace
and take my pleasure? You ruffians carousing here!
Isn't it quite enough that you, my mother's suitors,
have ravaged it all, my very best, these many years,
while I was still a boy? But now that I'm full-grown
and can hear the truth from others, absorb it too—
now, yes, that the anger seethes inside me . . .   350
I'll stop at nothing to hurl destruction at your heads,
whether I go to Pylos or sit tight here at home.
But the trip I speak of will not end in failure.
Go I will, as a passenger, nothing more,
since I don't seem to command my own crew.
That, I'm sure, is the way that suits you best."

                                          With this
he nonchalantly drew his hand from Antinous' hand
while the suitors, busy feasting in the halls,
mocked and taunted him, flinging insults now.
"God help us," one young buck kept shouting,   360
"he wants to slaughter us all!
He's off to sandy Pylos to hire cutthroats,
even Sparta perhaps, so hot to have our heads.
Why, he'd rove as far as Ephyra's dark rich soil
and run back home with lethal poison, slip it
into the bowl and wipe us out with drink!"

    "Who knows?" another young blade up and ventured.
"Off in that hollow ship of his, he just might drown,
far from his friends, a drifter like his father.
What a bore! He'd double our work for us,   370
splitting up his goods, parceling out his house
to his mother and the man who weds the queen."

                                  So they scoffed

but Telemachus headed down to his father's storeroom,
broad and vaulted, piled high with gold and bronze,
chests packed with clothing, vats of redolent oil.
And there, standing in close ranks against the wall,
were jars of seasoned, mellow wine, holding the drink
unmixed inside them, fit for a god, waiting the day
Odysseus, worn by hardship, might come home again.
Doors, snugly fitted, doubly hung, were bolted shut   380
and a housekeeper was in charge by night and day—
her care, her vigilance, guarding all those treasures—
Eurycleia the daughter of Ops, Pisenor's son.
Telemachus called her into the storeroom: "Come, nurse,
draw me off some wine in smaller traveling jars,
mellow, the finest vintage you've been keeping,
next to what you reserve for our unlucky king—
in case Odysseus might drop in from the blue
and cheat the deadly spirits, make it home.
Fill me an even dozen, seal them tightly.   390
Pour me barley in well-stitched leather bags,
twenty measures of meal, your stone-ground best.
But no one else must know. These rations now,
put them all together. I'll pick them up myself,
toward evening, just about the time that mother
climbs to her room and thinks of turning in.
I'm sailing off to Sparta, sandy Pylos too,
for news of my dear father's journey home.
Perhaps I'll catch some rumor."
                                A wail of grief—
and his fond old nurse burst out in protest, sobbing: 400
"Why, dear child, what craziness got into your head?
Why bent on rambling over the face of the earth?—
a darling only son! Your father's worlds away,
god's own Odysseus, dead in some strange land.
And these brutes here, just wait, the moment you're gone
they'll all be scheming against you. Kill you by guile,
they will, and carve your birthright up in pieces.
No, sit tight here, guard your own things here.
Don't go roving over the barren salt sea—

no need to suffer so!"
          "Courage, old woman,"   410
thoughtful Telemachus tried to reassure her,
"there's a god who made this plan.
But swear you won't say anything to my mother.
Not till ten or a dozen days have passed
or she misses me herself and learns I'm gone.
She mustn't mar her lovely face with tears."

   The old one swore a solemn oath to the gods
and vowing she would never breathe a word,
quickly drew off wine in two-eared jars
and poured barley in well-stitched leather bags.   420
Telemachus returned to the hall and joined the suitors.

   Then bright-eyed Pallas thought of one more step.
Disguised as the prince, the goddess roamed through town,
pausing beside each likely crewman, giving orders:
"Gather beside our ship at nightfall—be there."
She asked Noëmon, Phronius' generous son,
to lend her a swift ship. He gladly volunteered.

   The sun sank and the roads of the world grew dark.
Now the goddess hauled the swift ship down to the water,
stowed in her all the tackle well-rigged vessels carry,   430
moored her well away at the harbor's very mouth
and once the crew had gathered, rallying round,
she heartened every man.

   Then bright-eyed Pallas thought of one last thing.
Back she went to King Odysseus' halls and there
she showered sweet oblivion over the suitors,
dazing them as they drank, knocking cups from hands.
No more loitering now, their eyes weighed down with sleep,
they rose and groped through town to find their beds.
But calling the prince outside his timbered halls,   440
taking the build and voice of Mentor once again,
flashing-eyed Athena urged him on: "Telemachus,

your comrades-at-arms are ready at the oars,
waiting for your command to launch. So come,
on with our voyage now, we're wasting time."

    And Pallas Athena sped away in the lead
as he followed in her footsteps, man and goddess.
Once they reached the ship at the water's edge
they found their long-haired shipmates on the beach.
The prince, inspired, gave his first commands: 450
"Come, friends, get the rations aboard!
They're piled in the palace now.
My mother knows nothing of this. No servants either.
Only one has heard our plan."
                        He led them back
and the men fell in and fetched down all the stores
and stowed them briskly, deep in the well-ribbed holds
as Odysseus' son directed. Telemachus climbed aboard.
Athena led the way, assuming the pilot's seat
reserved astern, and he sat close beside her.
Cables cast off, the crew swung to the oarlocks.   460
Bright-eyed Athena sent them a stiff following wind
rippling out of the west, ruffling over the wine-dark sea
as Telemachus shouted out commands to all his shipmates:
"All lay hands to tackle!" They sprang to orders,
hoisting the pinewood mast, they stepped it firm
in its block amidships, lashed it fast with stays
and with braided rawhide halyards hauled the white sail high.
Suddenly wind hit full and the canvas bellied out
and a dark blue wave, foaming up at the bow,
sang out loud and strong as the ship made way,   470
skimming the whitecaps, cutting toward her goal.
All running gear secure in the swift black craft,
they set up bowls and brimmed them high with wine
and poured libations out to the everlasting gods
who never die—to Athena first of all,
the daughter of Zeus with flashing sea-gray eyes—
and the ship went plunging all night long and through the dawn.

BOOK THREE

King Nestor
Remembers

As the sun sprang up, leaving the brilliant waters in its wake,
climbing the bronze sky to shower light on immortal gods
and mortal men across the plowlands ripe with grain—
the ship pulled into Pylos, Neleus' storied citadel,
where the people lined the beaches,
sacrificing sleek black bulls to Poseidon,
god of the sea-blue mane who shakes the earth.
They sat in nine divisions, each five hundred strong,
each division offering up nine bulls, and while the people
tasted the innards, burned the thighbones for the god,   10
the craft and crew came heading straight to shore.
Striking sail, furling it in the balanced ship,
they moored her well and men swung down on land.
Telemachus climbed out last, with Athena far in front
and the bright-eyed goddess urged the prince along:

"Telemachus, no more shyness, this is not the time!
We sailed the seas for this, for news of your father—
where does he lie buried? what fate did he meet?
So go right up to Nestor, breaker of horses.
We'll make him yield the secrets of his heart.   20
Press him yourself to tell the whole truth:
he'll never lie—the man is far too wise."

   The prince replied, wise in his own way too,
"How can I greet him, Mentor, even approach the king?
I'm hardly adept at subtle conversation.
Someone my age *might* feel shy, what's more,
interrogating an older man."
                     "Telemachus,"
the bright-eyed goddess Athena reassured him,
"some of the words you'll find within yourself,
the rest some power will inspire you to say.   30
You least of all—I know—
were born and reared without the gods' good will."

   And Pallas Athena sped away in the lead
as he followed in her footsteps—man and goddess
gained the place where the Pylians met and massed.
There sat Nestor among his sons as friends around them
decked the banquet, roasted meats and skewered strips for broiling.
As soon as they saw the strangers, all came crowding down,
waving them on in welcome, urging them to sit.
Nestor's son Pisistratus, first to reach them,   40
grasped their hands and sat them down at the feast
on fleecy throws spread out along the sandbanks,
flanking his brother Thrasymedes and his father.
He gave them a share of innards, poured some wine
in a golden cup and, lifting it warmly toward Athena,
daughter of Zeus whose shield is storm and thunder,
greeted the goddess now with an invitation:
"Say a prayer to lord Poseidon, stranger,
his is the feast you've found on your arrival.
But once you've made your libation and your prayer—   50

all according to ancient custom—hand this cup
of hearty, seasoned wine to your comrade here
so he can pour forth too. He too, I think,
should pray to the deathless ones himself.
All men need the gods . . .
but the man is younger, just about my age.
That's why I give the gold cup first to you."

                                        With that
Pisistratus placed in her hand the cup of mellow wine
and Pallas rejoiced at the prince's sense of tact
in giving the golden winecup first to her.   60
At once she prayed intensely to Poseidon:
"Hear me, Sea-lord, you who embrace the earth—
don't deny our wishes, bring our prayers to pass!
First, then, to Nestor and all his sons grant glory.
Then to all these Pylians, for their splendid rites
grant a reward that warms their gracious hearts.
And last, Poseidon, grant Telemachus and myself
safe passage home, the mission accomplished
that sped us here in our rapid black ship."

    So she prayed, and brought it all to pass.   70
She offered the rich two-handled cup to Telemachus,
Odysseus' son, who echoed back her prayer word for word.
They roasted the prime cuts, pulled them off the spits
and sharing out the portions, fell to the royal feast.
Once they'd put aside desire for food and drink,
old Nestor the noble charioteer began, at last:
"Now's the time, now they've enjoyed their meal,
to probe our guests and find out who they are.
Strangers—friends, who are you?
Where did you sail from, over the running sea-lanes?   80
Out on a trading spree or roving the waves like pirates,
sea-wolves raiding at will, who risk their lives
to plunder other men?"
                        Poised Telemachus answered,
filled with heart, the heart Athena herself inspired,
to ask for the news about his father, gone so long,

and make his name throughout the mortal world.
"Nestor, son of Neleus, Achaea's pride and glory—
where are we from, you ask? I will tell you all.
We hail from Ithaca, under the heights of Nion.
Our mission here is personal, nothing public now.   90
I am on the trail of my father's widespread fame,
you see, searching the earth to catch some news
of great-hearted King Odysseus who, they say,
fought with you to demolish Troy some years ago.
About all the rest who fought the Trojans there,
we know where each one died his wretched death,
but father . . . even his death—
the son of Cronus shrouds it all in mystery.
No one can say for certain where he died,
whether he went down on land at enemy hands   100
or out on the open sea in Amphitrite's breakers.
That's why I've come to plead before you now,
if you can tell me about his cruel death:
perhaps you saw him die with your own eyes
or heard the wanderer's end from someone else.
More than all other men, that man was born for pain.
Don't soften a thing, from pity, respect for me—
tell me, clearly, all your eyes have witnessed.
I beg you—if ever my father, lord Odysseus,
pledged you his word and made it good in action   110
once on the fields of Troy where you Achaeans suffered,
remember his story now, tell *me* the truth."

   Nestor the noble charioteer replied at length:
"Ah dear boy, since you call back such memories,
such living hell we endured in distant Troy—
we headstrong fighting forces of Achaea—
so many raids from shipboard down the foggy sea,
cruising for plunder, wherever Achilles led the way;
so many battles round King Priam's walls we fought,
so many gone, our best and bravest fell.   120
There Ajax lies, the great man of war.

There lies Achilles too.
There Patroclus, skilled as the gods in counsel.
And there my own dear son, both strong and staunch,
Antilochus—lightning on his feet and every inch a fighter!
But so many other things we suffered, past that count—
what mortal in this wide world could tell it all?
Not if you sat and probed his memory, five, six years,
delving for all the pains our brave Achaeans bore there.
Your patience would fray, you'd soon head for home . . .   130

    Nine years we wove a web of disaster for those Trojans,
pressing them hard with every tactic known to man,
and only after we slaved did Zeus award us victory.
And no one there could hope to rival Odysseus,
not for sheer cunning—
at every twist of strategy he excelled us all.
Your father, yes, if you are in fact his son . . .
I look at you and a sense of wonder takes me.
Your way with words—it's just like his—I'd swear
no youngster could ever speak like you, so apt, so telling.   140
As long as I and great Odysseus soldiered there,
why, never once did we speak out at odds,
neither in open muster nor in royal council:
forever one in mind, in judgment balanced, shrewd,
we mapped our armies' plans so things might turn out best.
But then, once we'd sacked King Priam's craggy city,
Zeus contrived in his heart a fatal homeward run
for all the Achaeans who were fools, at least,
dishonest too, so many met a disastrous end,
thanks to the lethal rage   150
of the mighty Father's daughter. Eyes afire,
Athena set them feuding, Atreus' two sons . . .
They summoned all the Achaean ranks to muster,
rashly, just at sunset—no hour to rally troops—
and in they straggled, sodden with wine, our heroes.
The brothers harangued them, told them why they'd met:
a crisis—Menelaus urging the men to fix their minds

on the voyage home across the sea's broad back,
but it brought no joy to Agamemnon, not at all.
He meant to detain us there and offer victims,   160
anything to appease Athena's dreadful wrath—
poor fool, he never dreamed Athena would not comply.
The minds of the everlasting gods don't change so quickly.
So the two of them stood there, wrangling, back and forth
till the armies sprang up, their armor clashing, ungodly uproar—
the two plans split the ranks. That night we barely slept,
seething with hard feelings against our own comrades,
for Zeus was brooding over us, poised to seal our doom . . .
At dawn, half of us hauled our vessels down to sea,
we stowed our plunder, our sashed and lovely women.   170
But half the men held back, camped on the beach,
waiting it out for Agamemnon's next commands
while our contingent embarked—
we pushed off and sailed at a fast clip
as a god smoothed out the huge troughing swells.
We reached Tenedos quickly, sacrificed to the gods,
the crews keen for home, but a quick return was not
in Zeus's plans, not yet: that cruel power
loosed a cursed feud on us once again.
Some swung their rolling warships hard about—   180
Odysseus sailed them back, the flexible, wily king,
veering over to Agamemnon now to shore his fortunes up.
But not I. Massing the ships that came in my flotilla,
I sped away as the god's mischief kept on brewing,
dawning on me now. And Tydeus' fighting son
Diomedes fled too, rousing all his comrades.
Late in the day the red-haired Menelaus joined us,
overtook us at Lesbos, debating the long route home:
whether to head north, over the top of rocky Chios,
skirting Psyrie, keeping that island off to port   190
or run south of Chios, by Mimas' gusty cape.
We asked the god for a sign. He showed us one,
he urged us to cut out on the middle passage,
straight to Euboea now,
escape a catastrophe, fast as we could sail!

A shrilling wind came up, stiff, driving us on
and on we raced, over the sea-lanes rife with fish
and we made Geraestus Point in the dead of night.
Many thighs of bulls we offered Poseidon there—
thank god we'd crossed that endless reach of sea.   200
Then on the fourth day out the crews of Diomedes,
breaker of horses, moored their balanced ships
at Argos port, but I held course for Pylos, yes,
and never once did the good strong wind go limp
from the first day the god unleashed its blast.

    And so, dear boy, I made it home from Troy,
in total ignorance, knowing nothing of their fates,
the ones who stayed behind:
who escaped with their lives and who went down.
But still, all I've gathered by hearsay, sitting here   210
in my own house—that you'll learn, it's only right,
I'll hide nothing now.
                    They say the Myrmidons,
those savage spearmen led by the shining son
of lionhearted Achilles, traveled home unharmed.
Philoctetes the gallant son of Poias, safe as well.
Idomeneus brought his whole contingent back to Crete,
all who'd escaped the war—the sea snatched none from him.
But Atreus' son Agamemnon . . . you yourselves, even
in far-off Ithaca, must have heard how he returned,
how Aegisthus hatched the king's horrendous death.   220
But what a price he paid, in blood, in suffering.
Ah how fine it is, when a man is brought down,
to leave a son behind! Orestes took revenge,
he killed that cunning, murderous Aegisthus,
who'd killed his famous father.
                    And you, my friend—
how tall and handsome I see you now—be brave, you too,
so men to come will sing your praises down the years."

    Telemachus, weighing the challenge closely, answered,
"Oh Nestor, son of Neleus, Achaea's pride and glory,

what a stroke of revenge that was! All Achaeans   230
will spread Orestes' fame across the world,
a song for those to come.
If only the gods would arm me in such power
I'd take revenge on the lawless, brazen suitors
riding roughshod over me, plotting reckless outrage.
But for me the gods have spun out no such joy,
for my father or myself. I must bear up,
that's all."
              And the old charioteer replied,
"Now that you mention it, dear boy, I do recall
a mob of suitors, they say, besets your mother   240
there in your own house, against your will,
and plots your ruin. Tell me, though, do you
let yourself be so abused, or do people round about,
stirred up by the prompting of some god, despise you now?
Who knows if he will return someday to take revenge
on all their violence? Single-handed perhaps
or with an Argive army at his back? If only
the bright-eyed goddess chose to love you just
as she lavished care on brave Odysseus, years ago
in the land of Troy where we Achaeans struggled!   250
I've never seen the immortals show so much affection
as Pallas openly showed *him*, standing by your father—
if only she'd favor you, tend you with all her heart,
many a suitor then would lose all thought of marriage,
blotted out forever."
                   "Never, your majesty,"
Telemachus countered gravely, "that will never
come to pass, I know. What you say dumbfounds me,
staggers imagination! Hope, hope as I will,
that day will never dawn . . .
not even if the gods should will it so."
                              "Telemachus!"   260
Pallas Athena broke in sharply, her eyes afire—
"What's this nonsense slipping through your teeth?
It's light work for a willing god to save a mortal

even half the world away. Myself, I'd rather
sail through years of trouble and labor home
and see that blessed day, than hurry home
to die at my own hearth like Agamemnon,
killed by Aegisthus' cunning—by his own wife.
But the great leveler, Death: not even the gods
can defend a man, not even one they love, that day   270
when fate takes hold and lays him out at last."

                                                    "Mentor,"
wise Telemachus said, "distraught as we are for him,
let's speak of this no more. My father's return?
It's inconceivable now. Long ago the undying gods
have sealed his death, his black doom. But now
there's another question I would put to Nestor:
Nestor excels all men for sense and justice,
his knowledge of the world.
Three generations he has ruled, they say,
and to my young eyes he seems a deathless god!   280
Nestor, son of Neleus, tell me the whole story—
how did the great king Agamemnon meet his death?
Where was Menelaus? What fatal trap did he set,
that treacherous Aegisthus, to bring down a man
far stronger than himself? Was Menelaus gone
from Achaean Argos, roving the world somewhere,
so the coward found the nerve to kill the king?"

    And old Nestor the noble charioteer replied:
"Gladly, my boy, I'll tell you the story first to last . . .
Right you are, you guess what would have happened   290
if red-haired Menelaus, arriving back from Troy,
had found Aegisthus alive in Agamemnon's palace.
No barrow piled high on the earth for *his* dead body,
no, the dogs and birds would have feasted on his corpse,
sprawled on the plain outside the city gates, and no one,
no woman in all Achaea, would have wept a moment,
such a monstrous crime the man contrived!
But there we were, camped at Troy, battling out

the long hard campaign while he at his ease at home,
in the depths of Argos, stallion-country—he lay siege   300
to the wife of Agamemnon, luring, enticing her with talk.
At first, true, she spurned the idea of such an outrage,
Clytemnestra the queen, her will was faithful still.
And there was a man, what's more, a bard close by,
to whom Agamemnon, setting sail for Troy,
gave strict commands to guard his wife. But then,
that day the doom of the gods had bound her to surrender,
Aegisthus shipped the bard away to a desert island,
marooned him there, sweet prize for the birds of prey,
and swept her off to his own house, lover lusting for lover.   310
And many thighbones he burned on the gods' holy altars,
many gifts he hung on the temple walls—gold, brocades—
in thanks for a conquest past his maddest hopes.
                                              Now we,
you see, were sailing home from Troy in the same squadron,
Menelaus and I, comrades-in-arms from years of war.
But as we rounded holy Sounion, Athens' headland,
lord Apollo attacked Atrides' helmsman, aye,
with his gentle shafts he shot the man to death—
an iron grip on the tiller, the craft scudding fast—
Phrontis, Onetor's son, who excelled all men alive   320
at steering ships when gales bore down in fury.
So Menelaus, straining to sail on, was held back
till he could bury his mate with fitting rites.
But once he'd got off too, plowing the wine-dark sea
in his ribbed ships, and made a run to Malea's beetling cape,
farseeing Zeus decided to give the man rough sailing,
poured a hurricane down upon him, shrilling winds,
giant, rearing whitecaps, monstrous, mountains high.
There at a stroke he cut the fleet in half and drove
one wing to Crete, where Cydonians make their homes   330
along the Iardanus River. Now, there's a sheer cliff
plunging steep to the surf at the farthest edge of Gortyn,
out on the mist-bound sea, where the South Wind piles breakers,
huge breakers, left of the headland's horn, toward Phaestos,

with only a low reef to block the crushing tides.
In they sailed, and barely escaped their death—
the ships' crews, that is—
the rollers smashed their hulls against the rocks.
But as for the other five with pitch-black prows,
the wind and current swept them on toward Egypt.   340

    So Menelaus, amassing a hoard of stores and gold,
was off cruising his ships to foreign ports of call
while Aegisthus hatched his vicious work at home.
Seven years he lorded over Mycenae rich in gold,
once he'd killed Agamemnon—he ground the people down.
But the eighth year ushered in his ruin, Prince Orestes
home from Athens, yes, he cut him down, that cunning,
murderous Aegisthus, who'd killed his famous father.
Vengeance done, he held a feast for the Argives,
to bury his hated mother, craven Aegisthus too,   350
the very day Menelaus arrived, lord of the warcry,
freighted with all the wealth his ships could carry.
                                                    So you,
dear boy, take care. Don't rove from home too long,
too far, leaving your own holdings unprotected—
crowds in your palace so brazen
they'll carve up all your wealth, devour it all,
and then your journey here will come to nothing.
Still I advise you, urge you to visit Menelaus.
He's back from abroad at last, from people so removed
you might abandon hope of ever returning home,   360
once the winds had driven you that far off course,
into a sea so vast not even cranes could wing their way
in one year's flight—so vast it is, so awesome . . .

    So, off you go with your ships and shipmates now.
Or if you'd rather go by land, there's team and chariot,
my sons at your service too, and they'll escort you
to sunny Lacedaemon, home of the red-haired king.
Press him yourself to tell the whole truth:

he'll never lie—the man is far too wise."
                                        So he closed
as the sun set and darkness swept across the earth   370
and the bright-eyed goddess Pallas spoke for all:
"There was a tale, old soldier, so well told.
Come, cut out the victims' tongues and mix the wine,
so once we've poured libations out to the Sea-lord
and every other god, we'll think of sleep. High time—
the light's already sunk in the western shadows.
It's wrong to linger long at the gods' feast;
we must be on our way."
                              Zeus's daughter—
they all hung closely on every word she said.
Heralds sprinkled water over their hands for rinsing,   380
the young men brimmed the mixing bowls with wine,
they tipped first drops for the god in every cup
then poured full rounds for all. They rose and flung
the victims' tongues on the fire and poured libations out.
When they'd poured, and drunk to their hearts' content,
Athena and Prince Telemachus both started up
to head for their ship at once.
But Nestor held them there, objecting strongly:
"Zeus forbid—and the other deathless gods as well—
that you resort to your ship and put my house behind   390
like a rank pauper's without a stitch of clothing,
no piles of rugs, no blankets in his place
for host and guests to slumber soft in comfort.
Why, I've plenty of fine rugs and blankets here.
No, by god, the true son of my good friend Odysseus
won't bed down on a ship's deck, not while I'm alive
or my sons are left at home to host our guests,
whoever comes to our palace, newfound friends."
                                        "Dear old man,
you're right," Athena exclaimed, her eyes brightening now.
"Telemachus should oblige you. Much the better way.   400
Let him follow you now, sleep in your halls,
but I'll go back to our trim black ship,

hearten the crew and give each man his orders.
I'm the only veteran in their ranks, I tell you.
All the rest, of an age with brave Telemachus,
are younger men who sailed with him as friends.
I'll bed down there by the dark hull tonight,
at dawn push off for the proud Cauconians.
Those people owe me a debt long overdue,
and no mean sum, believe me.   410
But you, seeing my friend is now your guest,
speed him on his way with a chariot and your son
and give him the finest horses that you have,
bred for stamina, trained to race the wind."

    With that the bright-eyed goddess winged away
in an eagle's form and flight.
Amazement fell on all the Achaeans there.
The old king, astonished by what he'd seen,
grasped Telemachus' hand and cried out to the prince,
"Dear boy—never fear you'll be a coward or defenseless,   420
not if at your young age the gods will guard you so.
Of all who dwell on Olympus, this was none but she,
Zeus's daughter, the glorious one, his third born,
who prized your gallant father among the Argives.
Now, O Queen, be gracious! Give us high renown,
myself, my children, my loyal wife and queen.
And I will make you a sacrifice, a yearling heifer
broad in the brow, unbroken, never yoked by men.
I'll offer it up to you—I'll sheathe its horns in gold."

    So he prayed, and Pallas Athena heard his prayer.   430
And Nestor the noble chariot-driver led them on,
his sons and sons-in-law, back to his regal palace.
Once they reached the storied halls of the aged king
they sat on rows of low and high-backed chairs.
As they arrived the old man mixed them all a bowl,
stirring the hearty wine, seasoned eleven years
before a servant broached it, loosed its seal.

Mulling it in the bowl, old Nestor poured
a libation out, praying hard to Pallas Athena,
daughter of Zeus whose shield is storm and thunder.   440

    Once they had poured their offerings, drunk their fill,
the Pylians went to rest, each in his own house.
But the noble chariot-driver let Telemachus,
King Odysseus' son, sleep at the palace now,
on a corded bed inside the echoing colonnade,
with Prince Pisistratus close beside him there,
the young spearman, already captain of armies,
though the last son still unwed within the halls.
The king retired to chambers deep in his lofty house
where the queen his wife arranged and shared their bed.   450

    When young Dawn with her rose-red fingers shone once more
old Nestor the noble chariot-driver climbed from bed,
went out and took his seat on the polished stones,
a bench glistening white, rubbed with glossy oil,
placed for the king before his looming doors.
There Neleus held his sessions years ago,
a match for the gods in counsel,
but his fate had long since forced him down to Death.
Now royal Nestor in turn, Achaea's watch and ward,
sat there holding the scepter while his sons,   460
coming out of their chambers, clustered round him,
hovering near: Echephron, Stratius, Perseus
and Aretus, Thrasymedes like a god, and sixth,
young lord Pisistratus came to join their ranks.
They escorted Prince Telemachus in to sit beside them.
Nestor, noble charioteer, began the celebration:
"Quickly, my children, carry out my wishes now
so I may please the gods, Athena first of all—
she came to me at Poseidon's flowing feast,
Athena in all her glory!   470
Now someone go to the fields to fetch a heifer,
lead her here at once—a herdsman drive her in.
Someone hurry down to Prince Telemachus' black ship

and bring up all his crewmen, leave just two behind.
And another tell our goldsmith, skilled Laerces,
to come and sheathe the heifer's horns in gold.
The rest stay here together. Tell the maids
inside the hall to prepare a sumptuous feast—
bring seats and firewood, bring pure water too."

    They all pitched in to carry out his orders.   480
The heifer came from the fields, the crewmen came
from brave Telemachus' ship, and the smith came in
with all his gear in hand, the tools of his trade,
the anvil, hammer and well-wrought tongs he used
for working gold. And Athena came as well
to attend her sacred rites.
The old horseman passed the gold to the smith,
and twining the foil, he sheathed the heifer's horns
so the goddess' eyes might dazzle, delighted with the gift.
Next Stratius and Echephron led the beast by the horns.   490
Aretus, coming up from the storeroom, brought them
lustral water filling a flower-braided bowl,
in his other hand, the barley in a basket.
Thrasymedes, staunch in combat, stood ready,
whetted ax in his grasp to cut the heifer down,
and Perseus held the basin for the blood.
Now Nestor the old charioteer began the rite.
Pouring the lustral water, scattering barley-meal,
he lifted up his ardent prayers to Pallas Athena,
launching the sacrifice, flinging onto the fire   500
the first tufts of hair from the victim's head.

    Prayers said, the scattering barley strewn,
suddenly Nestor's son impetuous Thrasymedes
strode up close and struck—the ax chopped
the neck tendons through—
                              and the blow stunned
the heifer's strength—
                              The women shrilled their cry,
Nestor's daughters, sons' wives and his own loyal wife

Eurydice, Clymenus' eldest daughter. Then, hoisting up
the victim's head from the trampled earth, they held her fast
as the captain of men Pisistratus slashed her throat.   510
Dark blood gushed forth, life ebbed from her limbs—
they quartered her quickly, cut the thighbones out
and all according to custom wrapped them round in fat,
a double fold sliced clean and topped with strips of flesh.
And the old king burned these over dried split wood
and over the fire poured out glistening wine
while young men at his side held five-pronged forks.
Once they'd burned the bones and tasted the organs,
they sliced the rest into pieces, spitted them on skewers
and raising points to the fire, broiled all the meats.   520

   During the ritual lovely Polycaste, youngest daughter
of Nestor, Neleus' son, had bathed Telemachus.
Rinsing him off now, rubbing him down with oil,
she drew a shirt and handsome cape around him.
Out of his bath he stepped, glistening like a god,
strode in and sat by the old commander Nestor.

   They roasted the prime cuts, pulled them off the spits
and sat down to the feast while ready stewards saw
to rounds of wine and kept the gold cups flowing.
When they'd put aside desire for food and drink,   530
Nestor the noble chariot-driver issued orders:
"Hurry, my boys! Bring Telemachus horses,
a good full-maned team—
hitch them to a chariot—he must be off at once."

   They listened closely, snapped to his commands
and hitched a rapid team to a chariot's yoke in haste.
A housekeeper stowed some bread and wine aboard
and meats too, food fit for the sons of kings.
Telemachus vaulted onto the splendid chariot—
right beside him Nestor's son Pisistratus,   540
captain of armies, boarded, seized the reins,
whipped the team to a run and on the horses flew,

holding nothing back, out into open country,
leaving the heights of Pylos fading in their trail,
shaking the yoke across their shoulders all day long.

    The sun sank and the roads of the world grew dark
as they reached Phera, pulling up to Diocles' halls,
the son of Ortilochus, son of the Alpheus River.
He gave them a royal welcome; there they slept the night.

    When young Dawn with her rose-red fingers shone once more   550
they yoked their pair again, mounted the blazoned car
and out through the gates and echoing colonnade
they whipped the team to a run and on they flew,
holding nothing back—and the princes reached
the wheatlands, straining now for journey's end,
so fast those purebred stallions raced them on
as the sun sank and the roads of the world grew dark.

BOOK FOUR

The King and Queen of Sparta

At last they gained the ravines of Lacedaemon ringed by hills
and drove up to the halls of Menelaus in his glory.
They found the king inside his palace, celebrating
with throngs of kinsmen a double wedding-feast
for his son and lovely daughter. The princess
he was sending on to the son of great Achilles,
breaker of armies. Years ago Menelaus vowed,
he nodded assent at Troy and pledged her hand
and now the gods were sealing firm the marriage.
So he was sending her on her way with team and chariot,   10
north to the Myrmidons' famous city governed by her groom.
From Sparta he brought Alector's daughter as the bride
for his own full-grown son, the hardy Megapenthes,
born to him by a slave. To Helen the gods had granted
no more offspring once she had borne her first child,

the breathtaking Hermione,
a luminous beauty gold as Aphrodite.
                              So now
they feasted within the grand, high-roofed palace,
all the kin and clansmen of Menelaus in his glory,
reveling warmly here as in their midst   20
an inspired bard sang out and struck his lyre—
and through them a pair of tumblers dashed and sprang,
whirling in leaping handsprings, leading on the dance.

    The travelers, Nestor's shining son and Prince Telemachus,
had brought themselves and their horses to a standstill
just outside the court when good lord Eteoneus,
passing through the gates now, saw them there,
and the ready aide-in-arms of Menelaus
took the message through his sovereign's halls
and stepping close to his master broke the news: 30
"Strangers have just arrived, your majesty, Menelaus.
Two men, but they look like kin of mighty Zeus himself.
Tell me, should we unhitch their team for them
or send them to someone free to host them well?"

    The red-haired king took great offense at that:
"Never a fool before, Eteoneus, son of Boëthous,
now I see you're babbling like a child!
Just think of all the hospitality *we* enjoyed
at the hands of other men before we made it home,
and god save us from such hard treks in years to come.   40
Quick, unhitch their team. And bring them in,
strangers, guests, to share our flowing feast."

    Back through the halls he hurried, calling out
to other brisk attendants to follow quickly.
They loosed the sweating team from under the yoke,
tethered them fast by reins inside the horse-stalls,
tossing feed at their hoofs, white barley mixed with wheat,
and canted the chariot up against the polished walls,
shimmering in the sun, then ushered in their guests,

into that magnificent place. Both struck by the sight,   50
they marveled up and down the house of the warlord dear to Zeus—
a radiance strong as the moon or rising sun came flooding
through the high-roofed halls of illustrious Menelaus.
Once they'd feasted their eyes with gazing at it all,
into the burnished tubs they climbed and bathed.
When women had washed them, rubbed them down with oil
and drawn warm fleece and shirts around their shoulders,
they took up seats of honor next to Atrides Menelaus.
A maid brought water soon in a graceful golden pitcher
and over a silver basin tipped it out   60
so they might rinse their hands,
then pulled a gleaming table to their side.
A staid housekeeper brought on bread to serve them,
appetizers aplenty too, lavish with her bounty.
As a carver lifted platters of meat toward them,
meats of every sort, and set before them golden cups,
the red-haired king Menelaus greeted both guests warmly:
"Help yourselves to food, and welcome! Once you've dined
we'll ask you who you are. But your parents' blood
is hardly lost in you. You must be born of kings,   70
bred by the gods to wield the royal scepter.
No mean men could sire sons like you."

                                         With those words
he passed them a fat rich loin with his own hands,
the choicest part, that he'd been served himself.
They reached for the good things that lay outspread
and when they'd put aside desire for food and drink,
Telemachus, leaning his head close to Nestor's son,
spoke low to the prince so no one else could hear:
"Look, Pisistratus—joy of my heart, my friend—
the sheen of bronze, the blaze of gold and amber,   80
silver, ivory too, through all this echoing mansion!
Surely Zeus's court on Olympus must be just like this,
the boundless glory of all this wealth inside!
My eyes dazzle . . . I am struck with wonder."

    But the red-haired warlord overheard his guest

and cut in quickly with winged words for both:
"No man alive could rival Zeus, dear boys,
with his everlasting palace and possessions.
But among men, I must say, few if any
could rival *me* in riches. Believe me,   90
much I suffered, many a mile I roved to haul
such treasures home in my ships. Eight years out,
wandering off as far as Cyprus, Phoenicia, even Egypt,
I reached the Ethiopians, Sidonians, Erembians—Libya too,
where lambs no sooner spring from the womb than they grow horns.
Three times in the circling year the ewes give birth.
So no one, neither king nor shepherd could want
for cheese or mutton, or sweet milk either,
udders swell for the sucklings round the year.

    But while I roamed those lands, amassing a fortune,   100
a stranger killed my brother, blind to the danger, duped blind—
thanks to the cunning of his cursed, murderous queen!
So I rule all this wealth with no great joy.
You must have heard my story from your fathers,
whoever they are—what hardships I endured,
how I lost this handsome palace built for the ages,
filled to its depths with hoards of gorgeous things.
Well, would to god I'd stayed right here in my own house
with a third of all that wealth and they were still alive,
all who died on the wide plain of Troy those years ago,   110
far from the stallion-land of Argos.
                                   And still,
much as I weep for all my men, grieving sorely,
time and again, sitting here in the royal halls,
now indulging myself in tears, now brushing tears away—
the grief that numbs the spirit gluts us quickly—
for none of all those comrades, pained as I am,
do I grieve as much for one . . .
that man who makes sleep hateful, even food,
as I pore over his memory. No one, no Achaean
labored hard as Odysseus labored or achieved so much.   120
And how did his struggles end? In suffering for that man;

for me, in relentless, heartbreaking grief for him,
lost and gone so long now—dead or alive, who knows?
How they must mourn him too, Laertes, the old man,
and self-possessed Penelope. Telemachus as well,
the boy he left a babe in arms at home."
                                        Such memories
stirred in the young prince a deep desire to grieve
for Odysseus. Tears streamed down his cheeks
and wet the ground when he heard his father's name,
both hands clutching his purple robe before his eyes.   130
Menelaus recognized him at once but pondered
whether to let him state his father's name
or probe him first and prompt him step by step.

    While he debated all this now within himself,
Helen emerged from her scented, lofty chamber—
striking as Artemis with her golden shafts—
and a train of women followed . . .
Adreste drew up her carved reclining-chair,
Alcippe brought a carpet of soft-piled fleece,
Phylo carried her silver basket given by Alcandre,   140
King Polybus' wife, who made his home in Egyptian Thebes
where the houses overflow with the greatest troves of treasure.
The king gave Menelaus a pair of bathing-tubs in silver,
two tripods, ten bars of gold, and apart from these
his wife presented Helen her own precious gifts:
a golden spindle, a basket that ran on casters,
solid silver polished off with rims of gold.
Now Phylo her servant rolled it in beside her,
heaped to the brim with yarn prepared for weaving;
the spindle swathed in violet wool lay tipped across it.   150
Helen leaned back in her chair, a stool beneath her feet,
and pressed her husband at once for each detail:
"Do we know, my lord Menelaus, who our visitors
claim to be, our welcome new arrivals?
Right or wrong, what can I say? My heart tells me
to come right out and say I've never seen such a likeness,
neither in man nor woman—I'm amazed at the sight.

To the life he's like the son of great Odysseus,
surely he's Telemachus! The boy that hero left
a babe in arms at home when all you Achaeans   160
fought at Troy, launching your headlong battles
just for *my* sake, shameless whore that I was."

    "My dear, my dear," the red-haired king assured her,
"now that you mention it, I see the likeness too . . .
Odysseus' feet were like the boy's, his hands as well,
his glancing eyes, his head, and the fine shock of hair.
Yes, and just now, as I was talking about Odysseus,
remembering how he struggled, suffered, all for me,
a flood of tears came streaming down his face
and he clutched his purple robe before his eyes."   170

    "Right you are"—Pisistratus stepped in quickly—
"son of Atreus, King Menelaus, captain of armies:
here is the son of that great hero, as you say.
But the man is modest, he would be ashamed
to make a show of himself, his first time here,
and interrupt you. We delight in your voice
as if some god were speaking!
The noble horseman Nestor sent me along
to be his escort. Telemachus yearned to see you,
so you could give him some advice or urge some action.   180
When a father's gone, his son takes much abuse
in a house where no one comes to his defense.
So with Telemachus now. His father's gone.
No men at home will shield him from the worst."

    "Wonderful!" the red-haired king cried out.
"The son of my dearest friend, here in my own house!
That man who performed a hundred feats of arms for me.
And I swore that when he came I'd give him a hero's welcome,
him above all my comrades—if only Olympian Zeus,
farseeing Zeus, had granted us both safe passage   190
home across the sea in our swift trim ships.
Why, I'd have settled a city in Argos for him,

built him a palace, shipped him over from Ithaca,
him and all his wealth, his son, his people too—
emptied one of the cities nestling round about us,
one I rule myself. Both fellow-countrymen then,
how often we'd have mingled side-by-side!
Nothing could have parted us,
bound by love for each other, mutual delight . . .
till death's dark cloud came shrouding round us both.   200
But god himself, jealous of all this, no doubt,
robbed that unlucky man, him and him alone,
of the day of his return."
                          So Menelaus mused
and stirred in them all a deep desire to grieve.
Helen of Argos, daughter of Zeus, dissolved in tears,
Telemachus wept too, and so did Atreus' son Menelaus.
Nor could Nestor's son Pisistratus stay dry-eyed,
remembering now his gallant brother Antilochus,
cut down by Memnon, splendid son of the Morning.
Thinking of him, the young prince broke out: 210
"Old Nestor always spoke of you, son of Atreus,
as the wisest man of all the men he knew,
whenever we talked about you there at home,
questioning back and forth. So now, please,
if it isn't out of place, indulge me, won't you?
Myself, I take no joy in weeping over supper.
Morning will soon bring time enough for that.
Not that I'd grudge a tear
for any man gone down to meet his fate.
What other tribute can we pay to wretched men   220
than to cut a lock, let tears roll down our cheeks?
And I have a brother of my own among the dead,
and hardly the poorest soldier in our ranks.
You probably knew him. I never met him, never
saw him myself. But they say he outdid our best,
Antilochus—lightning on his feet and every inch a fighter!"

    "Well said, my friend," the red-haired king replied.
"Not even an older man could speak and do as well.

Your father's son you are—your words have all his wisdom.
It's easy to spot the breed of a man whom Zeus   230
has marked for joy in birth and marriage both.
Take great King Nestor now:
Zeus has blessed him, all his livelong days,
growing rich and sleek in his old age at home,
his sons expert with spears and full of sense.
Well, so much for the tears that caught us just now;
let's think again of supper. Come, rinse our hands.
Tomorrow, at dawn, will offer me and Telemachus
time to talk and trade our thoughts in full."

　　Asphalion quickly rinsed their hands with water,   240
another of King Menelaus' ready aides-in-arms.
Again they reached for the good things set before them.

　　Then Zeus's daughter Helen thought of something else.
Into the mixing-bowl from which they drank their wine
she slipped a drug, heart's-ease, dissolving anger,
magic to make us all forget our pains . . .
No one who drank it deeply, mulled in wine,
could let a tear roll down his cheeks that day,
not even if his mother should die, his father die,
not even if right before his eyes some enemy brought down   250
a brother or darling son with a sharp bronze blade.
So cunning the drugs that Zeus's daughter plied,
potent gifts from Polydamna the wife of Thon,
a woman of Egypt, land where the teeming soil
bears the richest yield of herbs in all the world:
many health itself when mixed in the wine,
and many deadly poison.
Every man is a healer there, more skilled
than any other men on earth—Egyptians born
of the healing god himself. So now Helen, once   260
she had drugged the wine and ordered winecups filled,
resuming the conversation, entertained the group:
"My royal king Menelaus—welcome guests here,
sons of the great as well! Zeus can present us

times of joy and times of grief in turn:
all lies within his power.
So come, let's sit back in the palace now,
dine and warm our hearts with the old stories.
I will tell something perfect for the occasion.
Surely I can't describe or even list them all,   270
the exploits crowding fearless Odysseus' record,
but what a feat that hero dared and carried off
in the land of Troy where you Achaeans suffered!
Scarring his own body with mortifying strokes,
throwing filthy rags on his back like any slave,
he slipped into the enemy's city, roamed its streets—
all disguised, a totally different man, a beggar,
hardly the figure he cut among Achaea's ships.
That's how Odysseus infiltrated Troy,
and no one knew him at all . . .   280
I alone, I spotted him for the man he was,
kept questioning him—the crafty one kept dodging.
But after I'd bathed him, rubbed him down with oil,
given him clothes to wear and sworn a binding oath
not to reveal him as Odysseus to the Trojans, not
till he was back at his swift ships and shelters,
then at last he revealed to me, step by step,
the whole Achaean strategy. And once he'd cut
a troop of Trojans down with his long bronze sword,
back he went to his comrades, filled with information.   290
The rest of the Trojan women shrilled their grief. Not I:
my heart leapt up—
                    my heart had changed by now—
                                        I yearned
to sail back home again! I grieved too late for the madness
Aphrodite sent me, luring me there, far from my dear land,
forsaking my own child, my bridal bed, my husband too,
a man who lacked for neither brains nor beauty."

    And the red-haired Menelaus answered Helen:
"There was a tale, my lady. So well told.
Now then, I have studied, in my time,

the plans and minds of great ones by the score.   300
And I have traveled over a good part of the world
but never once have I laid eyes on a man like him—
what a heart that fearless Odysseus had inside him!
What a piece of work the hero dared and carried off
in the wooden horse where all our best encamped,
our champions armed with bloody death for Troy . . .
when along you came, Helen—roused, no doubt,
by a dark power bent on giving Troy some glory,
and dashing Prince Deiphobus squired your every step.
Three times you sauntered round our hollow ambush,   310
feeling, stroking its flanks,
challenging all our fighters, calling each by name—
yours was the voice of all our long-lost wives!
And Diomedes and I, crouched tight in the midst
with great Odysseus, hearing you singing out,
were both keen to spring up and sally forth
or give you a sudden answer from inside,
but Odysseus damped our ardor, reined us back.
Then all the rest of the troops kept stock-still,
all but Anticlus. He was hot to salute you now   320
but Odysseus clamped his great hands on the man's mouth
and shut it, brutally—yes, he saved us all,
holding on grim-set till Pallas Athena
lured you off at last."

     But clear-sighted Telemachus ventured,
"Son of Atreus, King Menelaus, captain of armies,
so much the worse, for not one bit of that
saved *him* from grisly death . . .
not even a heart of iron could have helped.
But come, send us off to bed. It's time to rest,   330
time to enjoy the sweet relief of sleep."

     And Helen briskly told her serving-women
to make beds in the porch's shelter, lay down
some heavy purple throws for the beds themselves,
and over them spread some blankets, thick woolly robes,

a warm covering laid on top. Torches in hand,
they left the hall and made up beds at once.
The herald led the two guests on and so they slept
outside the palace under the forecourt's colonnade,
young Prince Telemachus and Nestor's shining son.   340
Menelaus retired to chambers deep in his lofty house
with Helen the pearl of women loosely gowned beside him.

    When young Dawn with her rose-red fingers shone once more
the lord of the warcry climbed from bed and dressed,
over his shoulder he slung his well-honed sword,
fastened rawhide sandals under his smooth feet,
stepped from his bedroom, handsome as a god,
and sat beside Telemachus, asking, kindly,
"Now, my young prince, tell me what brings you here
to sunny Lacedaemon, sailing over the sea's broad back.   350
A public matter or private? Tell me the truth now."

    And with all the poise he had, Telemachus replied,
"Son of Atreus, King Menelaus, captain of armies,
I came in the hope that you can tell me now
some news about my father.
My house is being devoured, my rich farms destroyed,
my palace crammed with enemies, slaughtering on and on
my droves of sheep and shambling longhorn cattle.
Suitors plague my mother—the insolent, overweening . . .
That's why I've come to plead before you now,   360
if you can tell me about his cruel death:
perhaps you saw him die with your own eyes
or heard the wanderer's end from someone else.
More than all other men, that man was born for pain.
Don't soften a thing, from pity, respect for me—
tell me, clearly, all your eyes have witnessed.
I beg you—if ever my father, lord Odysseus,
pledged you his word and made it good in action
once on the fields of Troy where you Achaeans suffered,
remember his story now, tell *me* the truth."

                              "How shameful!"   370

the red-haired king burst out in anger. "That's the bed
of a brave man of war they'd like to crawl inside,
those spineless, craven cowards!
Weak as the doe that beds down her fawns
in a mighty lion's den—her newborn sucklings—
then trails off to the mountain spurs and grassy bends
to graze her fill, but back the lion comes to his own lair
and the master deals both fawns a ghastly bloody death,
just what Odysseus will deal that mob—ghastly death.
Ah if only—Father Zeus, Athena and lord Apollo—   380
that man who years ago in the games at Lesbos
rose to Philomelides' challenge, wrestled him,
pinned him down with one tremendous throw
and the Argives roared with joy . . .
if only *that* Odysseus sported with those suitors,
a blood wedding, a quick death would take the lot!
But about the things you've asked me, so intently,
I'll skew and sidestep nothing, not deceive you, ever.
Of all he told me—the Old Man of the Sea who never lies—
I'll hide or hold back nothing, not a single word.   390

    It was in Egypt, where the gods still marooned me,
eager as I was to voyage home . . . I'd failed,
you see, to render them full, flawless victims,
and gods are always keen to see their rules obeyed.
Now, there's an island out in the ocean's heavy surge,
well off the Egyptian coast—they call it Pharos—
far as a deep-sea ship can go in one day's sail
with a whistling wind astern to drive her on.
There's a snug harbor there, good landing beach
where crews pull in, draw water up from the dark wells   400
then push their vessels off for passage out.
But here the gods becalmed me twenty days . . .
not a breath of the breezes ruffling out to sea
that speed a ship across the ocean's broad back.
Now our rations would all have been consumed,
our crews' stamina too, if one of the gods
had not felt sorry for me, shown me mercy,

Eidothea, a daughter of Proteus,
that great power, the Old Man of the Sea.
My troubles must have moved her to the heart   410
when she met me trudging by myself without my men.
They kept roaming around the beach, day in, day out,
fishing with twisted hooks, their bellies racked by hunger.
Well, she came right up to me, filled with questions:
'Are you a fool, stranger—soft in the head and lazy too?
Or do you let things slide because you *like* your pain?
Here you are, cooped up on an island far too long,
with no way out of it, none that you can find,
while all your shipmates' spirit ebbs away.'

   So she prodded and I replied at once,   420
  Let me tell you, goddess—whoever you are—
I'm hardly landlocked here of my own free will.
So I must have angered one of the deathless gods
who rule the skies up there. But you tell *me*—
you immortals know it all—which one of you
blocks my way here, keeps me from my voyage?
How can I cross the swarming sea and reach home at last?'

   And the glistening goddess reassured me warmly,
'Of course, my friend, I'll answer all your questions.
Who haunts these parts? Proteus of Egypt does,   430
the immortal Old Man of the Sea who never lies,
who sounds the deep in all its depths, Poseidon's servant.
He's my father, they say, he gave me life. And he,
if only you ambush him somehow and pin him down,
will tell you the way to go, the stages of your voyage,
how you can cross the swarming sea and reach home at last.
And he can tell you too, if you want to press him—
you are a king, it seems—
all that's occurred within your palace, good and bad,
while you've been gone your long and painful way.'   440

   'Then you are the one'—I quickly took her up.
'Show me the trick to trap this ancient power,

or he'll see or sense me first and slip away.
It's hard for a mortal man to force a god.'

   'True, my friend,' the glistening one agreed,
'and again I'll tell you all you need to know.
When the sun stands striding at high noon,
then up from the waves he comes—
the Old Man of the Sea who never lies—
under a West Wind's gust that shrouds him round   450
in shuddering dark swells, and once he's out on land
he heads for his bed of rest in deep hollow caves
and around him droves of seals—sleek pups bred
by his lovely ocean-lady—bed down too
in a huddle, flopping up from the gray surf,
giving off the sour reek of the salty ocean depths.
I'll lead you there myself at the break of day
and couch you all for attack, side-by-side.
Choose three men from your crew, choose well,
the best you've got aboard the good decked hulls.   460
Now I will tell you all the old wizard's tricks . . .
First he will make his rounds and count the seals
and once he's checked their number, reviewed them all,
down in their midst he'll lie, like a shepherd with his flock.
That's your moment. Soon as you see him bedded down,
muster your heart and strength and hold him fast,
wildly as he writhes and fights you to escape.
He'll try all kinds of escape—twist and turn
into every beast that moves across the earth,
transforming himself into water, superhuman fire,   470
but you hold on for dear life, hug him all the harder!
And when, at last, he begins to ask you questions—
back in the shape you saw him sleep at first—
relax your grip and set the old god free
and ask him outright, hero,
which of the gods is up in arms against you?
How can you cross the swarming sea and reach home at last?'

   So she urged and under the breaking surf she dove

as I went back to our squadron beached in sand,
my heart a heaving storm at every step . . .   480
Once I reached my ship hauled up on shore
we made our meal and the godsent night came down
and then we slept at the sea's smooth shelving edge.
When young Dawn with her rose-red fingers shone once more
I set out down the coast of the wide-ranging sea,
praying hard to the gods for all their help,
taking with me the three men I trusted most
on every kind of mission.
                                    Eidothea, now,
had slipped beneath the sea's engulfing folds
but back from the waves she came with four sealskins,   490
all freshly stripped, to deceive her father blind.
She scooped out lurking-places deep in the sand
and sat there waiting as we approached her post,
then couching us side-by-side she flung a sealskin
over each man's back. Now there was an ambush
that would have overpowered us all—overpowering,
true, the awful reek of all those sea-fed brutes!
Who'd dream of bedding down with a monster of the deep?
But the goddess sped to our rescue, found the cure
with ambrosia, daubing it under each man's nose—   500
that lovely scent, it drowned the creatures' stench.
So all morning we lay there waiting, spirits steeled,
while seals came crowding, jostling out of the sea
and flopped down in rows, basking along the surf.
At high noon the old man emerged from the waves
and found his fat-fed seals and made his rounds,
counting them off, counting *us* the first four,
but he had no inkling of all the fraud afoot.
Then down he lay and slept, but we with a battle-cry,
we rushed him, flung our arms around him—he'd lost nothing,   510
the old rascal, none of his cunning quick techniques!
First he shifted into a great bearded lion
and then a serpent—
                    a panther—
                            a ramping wild boar—

a torrent of water—
                    a tree with soaring branchtops—
but we held on for dear life, braving it out
until, at last, that quick-change artist,
the old wizard, began to weary of all this
and burst out into rapid-fire questions:
'Which god, Menelaus, conspired with you
to trap me in ambush? seize me against my will?   520
What on earth do you want?'
                              'You know, old man,'
I countered now. 'Why put me off with questions?
Here I am, cooped up on an island far too long,
with no way out of it, none that I can find,
while my spirit ebbs away. But you tell *me*—
you immortals know it all—which one of you
blocks my way here, keeps me from my voyage?
How can I cross the swarming sea and reach home at last?'

   'How wrong you were!' the seer shot back at once.
'You should have offered Zeus and the other gods   530
a handsome sacrifice, *then* embarked, if you ever hoped
for a rapid journey home across the wine-dark sea.
It's not your destiny yet to see your loved ones,
reach your own grand house, your native land at last,
not till you sail back through Egyptian waters—
the great Nile swelled by the rains of Zeus—
and make a splendid rite to the deathless gods
who rule the vaulting skies. Then, only then
will the gods grant you the voyage you desire.'

   So he urged, and broke the heart inside me,   540
having to double back on the mist-bound seas,
back to Egypt, that, that long and painful way . . .
Nevertheless I caught my breath and answered,
'That I will do, old man, as you command.
But tell me this as well, and leave out nothing:
Did all the Achaeans reach home in the ships unharmed,
all we left behind, Nestor and I, en route from Troy?

Or did any die some cruel death by shipwreck
or die in the arms of loved ones,
once they'd wound down the long coil of war?'   550

    And he lost no time in saying, 'Son of Atreus,
why do you ask me that? Why do you need to know?
Why probe my mind? You won't stay dry-eyed long,
I warn you, once you have heard the whole story.
Many of them were killed, many survived as well,
but only two who captained your bronze-armored units
died on the way home—you know who died in the fighting,
you were there yourself.
                      And one is still alive,
held captive, somewhere, off in the endless seas . . .

    Ajax, now, went down with his long-oared fleet.   560
First Poseidon drove him onto the cliffs of Gyrae,
looming cliffs, then saved him from the breakers—
he'd have escaped his doom, too, despite Athena's hate,
if he hadn't flung that brazen boast, the mad blind fool.
"In the teeth of the gods," he bragged, "I have escaped
the ocean's sheer abyss!" Poseidon heard that frantic vaunt
and the god grasped his trident in both his massive hands
and struck the Gyraean headland, hacked the rock in two,
and the giant stump stood fast but the jagged spur
where Ajax perched at first, the raving madman—   570
toppling into the sea, it plunged him down, down
in the vast, seething depths. And so he died,
having drunk his fill of brine.
                      Your brother?
He somehow escaped that fate; Agamemnon got away
in his beaked ships. Queen Hera pulled him through.
But just as he came abreast of Malea's beetling cape
a hurricane snatched him up and swept him way off course—
groaning, desperate—driving him over the fish-infested sea
to the wild borderland where Thyestes made his home
in the days of old and his son Aegisthus lived now.   580
But even from there a safe return seemed likely,

yes, the immortals swung the wind around to fair
and the victors sailed home. How he rejoiced,
Atrides setting foot on his fatherland once more—
he took that native earth in his hands and kissed it,
hot tears flooding his eyes, so thrilled to see his land!
But a watchman saw him too—from a lookout high above—
a spy that cunning Aegisthus stationed there,
luring the man with two gold bars in payment.
One whole year he'd watched . . .   590
so the great king would not get past unseen,
his fighting power intact for self-defense.
The spy ran the news to his master's halls
and Aegisthus quickly set his stealthy trap.
Picking the twenty best recruits from town
he packed them in ambush at one end of the house,
at the other he ordered a banquet dressed and spread
and went to welcome the conquering hero, Agamemnon,
went with team and chariot, and a mind aswarm with evil.
Up from the shore he led the king, he ushered him in—   600
suspecting nothing of all his doom—he feasted him well
then cut him down as a man cuts down some ox at the trough!
Not one of your brother's men-at-arms was left alive,
none of Aegisthus' either. All, killed in the palace.'

    So Proteus said, and his story crushed my heart.
I knelt down in the sand and wept. I'd no desire
to go on living and see the rising light of day.
But once I'd had my fill of tears and writhing there,
the Old Man of the Sea who never lies continued,
'No more now, Menelaus. How long must you weep?   610
Withering tears, what good can come of tears?
None I know of. Strive instead to return
to your native country—hurry home at once!
Either you'll find the murderer still alive
or Orestes will have beaten you to the kill.
You'll be in time to share the funeral feast.'

    So he pressed, and I felt my heart, my old pride,

for all my grieving, glow once more in my chest
and I asked the seer in a rush of winging words,
'Those two I know now. Tell me the third man's name.   620
Who is still alive, held captive off in the endless seas?
Unless he's dead by now. I want to know the truth
though it grieves me all the more.'
                              'Odysseus'—
the old prophet named the third at once—
'Laertes' son, who makes his home in Ithaca . . .
I saw him once on an island, weeping live warm tears
in the nymph Calypso's house—she holds him there by force.
He has no way to voyage home to his own native land,
no trim ships in reach, no crew to ply the oars
and send him scudding over the sea's broad back.   630
But about your own destiny, Menelaus,
dear to Zeus, it's not for you to die
and meet your fate in the stallion-land of Argos,
no, the deathless ones will sweep you off to the world's end,
the Elysian Fields, where gold-haired Rhadamanthys waits,
where life glides on in immortal ease for mortal man;
no snow, no winter onslaught, never a downpour there
but night and day the Ocean River sends up breezes,
singing winds of the West refreshing all mankind.
All this because you are Helen's husband now—   640
the gods count *you* the son-in-law of Zeus.'

    So he divined and down the breaking surf he dove
as I went back to the ships with my brave men,
my heart a rising tide at every step.
Once I reached my craft hauled up on shore
we made our meal and the godsent night came down
and then we slept at the sea's smooth shelving edge.
When young Dawn with her rose-red fingers shone once more
we hauled the vessels down to the sunlit breakers first
then stepped the masts amidships, canvas brailed—   650
the crews swung aboard, they sat to the oars in ranks
and in rhythm churned the water white with stroke on stroke.
Back we went to the Nile swelled by the rains of Zeus,

I moored the ships and sacrificed in a splendid rite,
and once I'd slaked the wrath of the everlasting gods
I raised a mound for Agamemnon, his undying glory.
All this done, I set sail and the gods sent me
a stiff following wind that sped me home,
home to the native land I love.

But come,
my boy, stay on in my palace now with me,   660
at least till ten or a dozen days have passed.
Then I'll give you a princely send-off—shining gifts,
three stallions and a chariot burnished bright—
and I'll add a gorgeous cup so you can pour
libations out to the deathless gods on high
and remember Menelaus all your days."

Telemachus,
summoning up his newfound tact, replied,
"Please, Menelaus, don't keep me quite so long.
True, I'd gladly sit beside you one whole year
without a twinge of longing for home or parents.   670
It's wonderful how you tell your stories, all you say—
I delight to listen! Yes, but now, I'm afraid,
my comrades must be restless in sacred Pylos,
and here you'd hold me just a little longer.
As for the gift you give me, let it be a keepsake.
Those horses I really cannot take to Ithaca;
better to leave them here to be your glory.
You rule a wide level plain
where the fields of clover roll and galingale
and wheat and oats and glistening full-grain barley.   680
No running-room for mares in Ithaca, though, no meadows.
Goat, not stallion, land, yet it means the world to me.
None of the rugged islands slanting down to sea
is good for pasture or good for bridle paths,
but Ithaca, best of islands, crowns them all!"

So he declared. The lord of the warcry smiled,
patted him with his hand and praised his guest, concluding,
"Good blood runs in you, dear boy, your words are proof.

Certainly I'll exchange the gifts. The power's mine.
Of all the treasures lying heaped in my palace   690
you shall have the finest, most esteemed. Why,
I'll give you a mixing-bowl, forged to perfection—
it's solid silver finished off with a lip of gold.
Hephaestus made it himself. And a royal friend,
Phaedimus, king of Sidon, lavished it on me
when his palace welcomed me on passage home.
How pleased I'd be if you took it as a gift!"

    And now as the two confided in each other,
banqueters arrived at the great king's palace,
leading their own sheep, bearing their hearty wine,   700
and their wives in lovely headbands sent along the food.
And so they bustled about the halls preparing dinner . . .
But all the while the suitors, before Odysseus' palace,
amused themselves with discus and long throwing spears,
out on the leveled grounds, free and easy as always,
full of swagger. But lord Antinous sat apart,
dashing Eurymachus beside him, ringleaders,
head and shoulders the strongest of the lot.
Phronius' son Noëmon approached them now,
quick to press Antinous with a question: 710
"Antinous, have we any notion or not
when Telemachus will return from sandy Pylos?
He sailed in a ship of mine and now I need her back
to cross over to Elis Plain where I keep a dozen horses,
brood-mares suckling some heavy-duty mules, unbroken.
I'd like to drive one home and break him in."

    That dumbfounded them both. They never dreamed
the prince had gone to Pylos, Neleus' city—
certain the boy was still nearby somewhere,
out on his farm with flocks or with the swineherd.   720

    "Tell me the truth!" Antinous wheeled on Noëmon.
"When did he go? And what young crew went with him?
Ithaca's best? Or his own slaves and servants?

Surely he has enough to man a ship.
Tell me this—be clear—I've got to know:
did he commandeer your ship against your will
or did you volunteer it once he'd won you over?"

   "I volunteered it, of course," Noëmon said.
"What else could anyone do, when such a man,
a prince weighed down with troubles,   730
asked a favor? Hard to deny him anything.
And the young crew that formed his escort? Well,
they're the finest men on the island, next to us.
And Mentor took command—I saw him climb aboard—
or a god who looked like Mentor head to foot,
and that's what I find strange. I saw good Mentor
yesterday, just at sunup, here. But clearly
he boarded ship for Pylos days ago."

   With that he headed back to his father's house,
leaving the two lords stiff with indignation.   740
They made the suitors sit down in a group
and stop their games at once. Eupithes' son
Antinous rose up in their midst to speak,
his dark heart filled with fury,
blazing with anger—eyes like searing fire:
"By god, what a fine piece of work he's carried off!
Telemachus—what insolence—and we thought his little jaunt
would come to grief. But in spite of us all, look,
the young cub slips away, just like that—
picks the best crew in the land and off he sails.   750
And this is just the start of the trouble he can make.
Zeus kill that brazen boy before he hits his prime!
Quick, fetch me a swift ship and twenty men—
I'll waylay him from ambush, board him coming back
in the straits between Ithaca and rocky Same.
This gallant voyage of his to find his father
will find *him* wrecked at last!"

   They all roared approval, urged him on,

rose at once and retired to Odysseus' palace.

But not for long was Penelope unaware   760
of the grim plots her suitors planned in secret.
The herald Medon told her. He'd overheard their schemes,
listening in outside the court while they wove on within.
He rushed the news through the halls to tell the queen
who greeted him as he crossed her chamber's threshold:
"Herald, why have the young blades sent you now?
To order King Odysseus' serving-women
to stop their work and slave to fix their feast?
I hate their courting, their running riot here—
would to god that this meal, here and now,   770
were their last meal on earth!
                              Day after day,
all of you swarming, draining our life's blood,
my wary son's estate. What, didn't you listen
to your fathers—when you were children, years ago—
telling you how Odysseus treated them, your parents?
Never an unfair word, never an unfair action
among his people here, though that's the way
of our god-appointed kings,
hating one man, loving the next, with luck.
Not Odysseus. Never an outrage done to any man alive.   780
But you, you and your ugly outbursts, shameful acts,
they're plain to see. Look at the thanks he gets
for all past acts of kindness!"
                              Medon replied,
sure of his own discretion, "Ah my queen,
if only *that* were the worst of all you face.
Now your suitors are plotting something worse,
harsher, crueler. God forbid they bring it off!
They're poised to cut Telemachus down with bronze swords
on his way back home. He's sailed off, you see . . .
for news of his father—to sacred Pylos first,   790
then out to the sunny hills of Lacedaemon."

Her knees gave way on the spot, her heart too.

She stood there speechless a while, struck dumb,
tears filling her eyes, her warm voice choked.
At last she found some words to make reply:
"Oh herald, why has my child gone and left me?
No need in the world for him to board the ships,
those chariots of the sea that sweep men on,
driving across the ocean's endless wastes . . .
Does he want his very name wiped off the earth?"   800

    Medon, the soul of thoughtfulness, responded,
"I don't know if a god inspired your son
or the boy's own impulse led him down to Pylos,
but he went to learn of his father's journey home,
or whatever fate he's met."

    Back through King Odysseus' house he went
but a cloud of heartbreak overwhelmed the queen.
She could bear no longer sitting on a chair
though her room had chairs aplenty.
Down she sank on her well-built chamber's floor,   810
weeping, pitifully, as the women whimpered round her,
all the women, young and old, who served her house.
Penelope, sobbing uncontrollably, cried out to them,
"Hear me, dear ones! Zeus has given me torment—
me above all the others born and bred in *my* day.
My lionhearted husband, lost, long years ago,
who excelled the Argives all in every strength—
that great man whose fame resounds through Hellas
right to the depths of Argos!
                                    But now my son,
my darling boy—the whirlwinds have ripped him   820
out of the halls without a trace! I never heard
he'd gone—not even from you, you hard, heartless . . .
not one of you even thought to rouse me from my bed,
though well you knew when he boarded that black ship.
Oh if only I had learned he was planning such a journey,
he would have stayed, by god, keen as he was to sail—
or left me dead right here within our palace.

Go, someone, quickly! Call old Dolius now,
the servant my father gave me when I came,
the man who tends my orchard green with trees,   830
so he can run to Laertes, sit beside him,
tell him the whole story, point by point.
Perhaps—who knows?—he'll weave some plan,
he'll come out of hiding, plead with all these people
mad to destroy his line, his son's line of kings!"

　　"Oh dear girl," Eurycleia the fond old nurse replied,
"kill me then with a bronze knife—no mercy—or let me live,
here in the palace—I'll hide nothing from you now!
I knew it all, I gave him all he asked for,
bread and mellow wine, but he made me take   840
a binding oath that I, I wouldn't tell you,
no, not till ten or a dozen days had passed
or you missed the lad yourself and learned he'd gone,
so tears would never mar your lovely face . . .
Come, bathe now, put on some fresh clothes,
climb to the upper rooms with all your women
and pray to Pallas, daughter of storming Zeus—
she may save Telemachus yet, even at death's door.
Don't worry an old man, worried enough by now.
I can't believe the blessed gods so hate   850
the heirs of King Arcesius, through and through.
One will still live on—I know it—born to rule
this lofty house and the green fields far and wide."
　　　　　　　　　　　　　　　　　　　　　　　With that
she lulled Penelope's grief and dried her eyes of tears.
And the queen bathed and put fresh clothing on,
climbed to the upper rooms with all her women
and sifting barley into a basket, prayed to Pallas,
"Hear me, daughter of Zeus whose shield is thunder—
tireless one, Athena! If ever, here in his halls,
resourceful King Odysseus   860
burned rich thighs of sheep or oxen in your honor,
oh remember it now for *my* sake, save my darling son,

defend him from these outrageous, overbearing suitors!"

She shrilled a high cry and the goddess heard her prayer
as the suitors burst into uproar through the shadowed halls
and one of the lusty young men began to brag, "Listen,
our long-courted queen's preparing us all a marriage—
with no glimmer at all
how the murder of her son has been decreed."

                                        Boasting so,
with no glimmer at all of what had been decreed.   870
But Antinous took the floor and issued orders:
"Stupid fools! Muzzle your bragging now—
before someone slips inside and reports us.
Up now, not a sound, drive home our plan—
it suits us well, we approved it one and all."

With that he picked out twenty first-rate men
and down they went to the swift ship at the sea's edge.
First they hauled the craft into deeper water,
stepped the mast amidships, canvas brailed,
made oars fast in the leather oarlock straps   880
while zealous aides-in-arms brought weapons on.
They moored her well out in the channel, disembarked
and took their meal on shore, waiting for dusk to fall.

But there in her upper rooms she lay, Penelope
lost in thought, fasting, shunning food and drink,
brooding now . . . would her fine son escape his death
or go down at her overweening suitors' hands?
Her mind in torment, wheeling
like some lion at bay, dreading gangs of hunters
closing their cunning ring around him for the finish.   890
Harried so she was, when a deep kind sleep overcame her,
back she sank and slept, her limbs feil limp and still.

And again the bright-eyed goddess Pallas thought
of one more way to help. She made a phantom now,

its build like a woman's build, Iphthime's, yes,
another daughter of generous Lord Icarius,
Eumelus' bride, who made her home in Pherae.
Athena sped her on to King Odysseus' house
to spare Penelope, worn with pain and sobbing,
further spells of grief and storms of tears.   900
The phantom entered her bedroom,
passing quickly in through the doorbolt slit
and hovering at her head she rose and spoke now:
"Sleeping, Penelope, your heart so wrung with sorrow?
No need, I tell you, no, the gods who live at ease
can't bear to let you weep and rack your spirit.
Your son will still come home—it is decreed.
He's never wronged the gods in any way."

    And Penelope murmured back, still cautious,
drifting softly now at the gate of dreams,   910
"Why have you come, my sister?
Your visits all too rare in the past,
for you make your home so very far away.
You tell me to lay to rest the grief and tears
that overwhelm me now, torment me, heart and soul?
With my lionhearted husband lost long years ago,
who excelled the Argives all in every strength?
That great man whose fame resounds through Hellas
right to the depths of Argos . . .
                                  And now my darling boy,
he's off and gone in a hollow ship! Just a youngster,   920
still untrained for war or stiff debate.
Him I mourn even more than I do my husband—
I quake in terror for all that he might suffer
either on open sea or shores he goes to visit.
Hordes of enemies scheme against him now,
keen to kill him off
before he can reach his native land again."

    "Courage!" the shadowy phantom reassured her.
"Don't be overwhelmed by all your direst fears.

He travels with such an escort, one that others   930
would pray to stand beside them. She has power—
Pallas Athena. She pities you in your tears.
She wings me here to tell you all these things."

   But the circumspect Penelope replied,
"If you *are* a god and have heard a god's own voice,
come, tell me about that luckless man as well.
Is he still alive? does he see the light of day?
Or is he dead already, lost in the House of Death?"

   "About that man," the shadowy phantom answered,
"I cannot tell you the story start to finish,   940
whether he's dead or alive.
It's wrong to lead you on with idle words."
                                 At that
she glided off by the doorpost past the bolt—
gone on a lifting breeze. Icarius' daughter
started up from sleep, her spirit warmed now
that a dream so clear had come to her in darkest night.

   But the suitors boarded now and sailed the sea-lanes,
plotting in their hearts Telemachus' plunge to death.
Off in the middle channel lies a rocky island,
just between Ithaca and Same's rugged cliffs—   950
Asteris—not large, but it has a cove,
a harbor with two mouths where ships can hide.
Here the Achaeans lurked in ambush for the prince.

BOOK FIVE

Odysseus—Nymph and Shipwreck

As Dawn rose up from bed by her lordly mate Tithonus,
bringing light to immortal gods and mortal men,
the gods sat down in council, circling Zeus
the thunder king whose power rules the world.
Athena began, recalling Odysseus to their thoughts,
the goddess deeply moved by the man's long ordeal,
held captive still in the nymph Calypso's house:
"Father Zeus—you other happy gods who never die—
never let any sceptered king be kind and gentle now,
not with all his heart, or set his mind on justice—   10
no, let him be cruel and always practice outrage.
Think: not one of the people whom he ruled
remembers Odysseus now, that godlike man,
and kindly as a father to his children.

Now
he's left to pine on an island, racked with grief
in the nymph Calypso's house—she holds him there by force.
He has no way to voyage home to his own native land,
no trim ships in reach, no crew to ply the oars
and send him scudding over the sea's broad back.
And now his dear son . . . they plot to kill the boy   20
on his way back home. Yes, he has sailed off
for news of his father, to holy Pylos first,
then out to the sunny hills of Lacedaemon."

    "My child," Zeus who marshals the thunderheads replied,
"what nonsense you let slip through your teeth. Come now,
wasn't the plan your own? You conceived it yourself:
Odysseus shall return and pay the traitors back.
Telemachus? Sail him home with all your skill—
the power is yours, no doubt—
home to his native country all unharmed   30
while the suitors limp to port, defeated, baffled men."

    With those words, Zeus turned to his own son Hermes.
"You are our messenger, Hermes, sent on all our missions.
Announce to the nymph with lovely braids our fixed decree:
Odysseus journeys home—the exile must return.
But not in the convoy of the gods or mortal men.
No, on a lashed, makeshift raft and wrung with pains,
on the twentieth day he will make his landfall, fertile Scheria,
the land of Phaeacians, close kin to the gods themselves,
who with all their hearts will prize him like a god   40
and send him off in a ship to his own beloved land,
giving him bronze and hoards of gold and robes—
more plunder than he could ever have won from Troy
if Odysseus had returned intact with his fair share.
So his destiny ordains. He shall see his loved ones,
reach his high-roofed house, his native land at last."

    So Zeus decreed and the giant-killing guide obeyed at once.

Quickly under his feet he fastened the supple sandals,
ever-glowing gold, that wing him over the waves
and boundless earth with the rush of gusting winds.   50
He seized the wand that enchants the eyes of men
whenever Hermes wants, or wakes us up from sleep.
That wand in his grip, the powerful giant-killer,
swooping down from Pieria, down the high clear air,
plunged to the sea and skimmed the waves like a tern
that down the deadly gulfs of the barren salt swells
glides and dives for fish,
dipping its beating wings in bursts of spray—
so Hermes skimmed the crests on endless crests.
But once he gained that island worlds apart,   60
up from the deep-blue sea he climbed to dry land
and strode on till he reached the spacious cave
where the nymph with lovely braids had made her home,
and he found her there inside . . .
                                A great fire
blazed on the hearth and the smell of cedar
cleanly split and sweetwood burning bright
wafted a cloud of fragrance down the island.
Deep inside she sang, the goddess Calypso, lifting
her breathtaking voice as she glided back and forth
before her loom, her golden shuttle weaving.   70
Thick, luxuriant woods grew round the cave,
alders and black poplars, pungent cypress too,
and there birds roosted, folding their long wings,
owls and hawks and the spread-beaked ravens of the sea,
black skimmers who make their living off the waves.
And round the mouth of the cavern trailed a vine
laden with clusters, bursting with ripe grapes.
Four springs in a row, bubbling clear and cold,
running side-by-side, took channels left and right.
Soft meadows spreading round were starred with violets,   80
lush with beds of parsley. Why, even a deathless god
who came upon that place would gaze in wonder,
heart entranced with pleasure. Hermes the guide,
the mighty giant-killer, stood there, spellbound . . .

But once he'd had his fill of marveling at it all
he briskly entered the deep vaulted cavern.
Calypso, lustrous goddess, knew him at once,
as soon as she saw his features face-to-face.
Immortals are never strangers to each other,
no matter how distant one may make her home.   90
But as for great Odysseus—
Hermes could not find him within the cave.
Off he sat on a headland, weeping there as always,
wrenching his heart with sobs and groans and anguish,
gazing out over the barren sea through blinding tears.
But Calypso, lustrous goddess, questioned Hermes,
seating him on a glistening, polished chair.
"God of the golden wand, why have you come?
A beloved, honored friend,
but it's been so long, your visits much too rare.   100
Tell me what's on your mind. I'm eager to do it,
whatever I *can* do . . . whatever can be done."

    And the goddess drew a table up beside him,
heaped with ambrosia, mixed him deep-red nectar.
Hermes the guide and giant-killer ate and drank.
Once he had dined and fortified himself with food
he launched right in, replying to her questions:
"As one god to another, you ask me why I've come.
I'll tell you the whole story, mince no words—
your wish is my command.   110
It was Zeus who made me come, no choice of mine.
Who would willingly roam across a salty waste so vast,
so endless? Think: no city of men in sight, and not a soul
to offer the gods a sacrifice and burn the fattest victims.
But there is no way, you know, for another god to thwart
the will of storming Zeus and make it come to nothing.
Zeus claims you keep beside you a most unlucky man,
most harried of all who fought for Priam's Troy
nine years, sacking the city in the tenth,
and then set sail for home.   120
But voyaging back they outraged Queen Athena

who loosed the gales and pounding seas against them.
There all the rest of his loyal shipmates died
but the wind drove him on, the current bore him here.
Now Zeus commands you to send him off with all good speed:
it is not his fate to die here, far from his own people.
Destiny still ordains that he shall see his loved ones,
reach his high-roofed house, his native land at last."

But lustrous Calypso shuddered at those words
and burst into a flight of indignation. "Hard-hearted   130
you are, you gods! You unrivaled lords of jealousy—
scandalized when goddesses sleep with mortals,
openly, even when one has made the man her husband.
So when Dawn with her rose-red fingers took Orion,
you gods in your everlasting ease were horrified
till chaste Artemis throned in gold attacked him,
out on Delos, shot him to death with gentle shafts.
And so when Demeter the graceful one with lovely braids
gave way to her passion and made love with Iasion,
bedding down in a furrow plowed three times—   140
Zeus got wind of it soon enough, I'd say,
and blasted the man to death with flashing bolts.
So now at last, you gods, you train your spite on *me*
for keeping a mortal man beside me. The man I saved,
riding astride his keel-board, all alone, when Zeus
with one hurl of a white-hot bolt had crushed
his racing warship down the wine-dark sea.
There all the rest of his loyal shipmates died
but the wind drove him on, the current bore him here.
And I welcomed him warmly, cherished him, even vowed   150
to make the man immortal, ageless, all his days . . .
But since there is no way for another god to thwart
the will of storming Zeus and make it come to nothing,
let the man go—if the Almighty insists, commands—
and destroy himself on the barren salt sea!
I'll send him off, but not with any escort.
I have no ships in reach, no crew to ply the oars
and send him scudding over the sea's broad back.

But I will gladly advise him—I'll hide nothing—
so he can reach his native country all unharmed."   160

   And the guide and giant-killer reinforced her words:
"Release him at once, just so. Steer clear of the rage of Zeus!
Or down the years he'll fume and make your life a hell."

   With that the powerful giant-killer sped away.
The queenly nymph sought out the great Odysseus—
the commands of Zeus still ringing in her ears—
and found him there on the headland, sitting, still,
weeping, his eyes never dry, his sweet life flowing away
with the tears he wept for his foiled journey home,
since the nymph no longer pleased. In the nights, true,   170
he'd sleep with her in the arching cave—he had no choice—
unwilling lover alongside lover all too willing . . .
But all his days he'd sit on the rocks and beaches,
wrenching his heart with sobs and groans and anguish,
gazing out over the barren sea through blinding tears.
So coming up to him now, the lustrous goddess ventured,
"No need, my unlucky one, to grieve here any longer,
no, don't waste your life away. Now I am willing,
heart and soul, to send you off at last. Come,
take bronze tools, cut your lengthy timbers,   180
make them into a broad-beamed raft
and top it off with a half-deck high enough
to sweep you free and clear on the misty seas.
And I myself will stock her with food and water,
ruddy wine to your taste—all to stave off hunger—
give you clothing, send you a stiff following wind
so you can reach your native country all unharmed.
If only the gods are willing. They rule the vaulting skies.
They're stronger than I to plan and drive things home."

   Long-enduring Odysseus shuddered at that   190
and broke out in a sharp flight of protest.
"Passage home? Never. Surely you're plotting
something else, goddess, urging me—in a raft—

to cross the ocean's mighty gulfs. So vast, so full
of danger not even deep-sea ships can make it through,
swift as they are and buoyed up by the winds of Zeus himself.
I won't set foot on a raft until you show good faith,
until you consent to swear, goddess, a binding oath
you'll never plot some new intrigue to harm me!"

He was so intense the lustrous goddess smiled,   200
stroked him with her hand, savored his name and chided,
"Ah what a wicked man you are, and never at a loss.
What a thing to imagine, what a thing to say!
Earth be my witness now, the vaulting Sky above
and the dark cascading waters of the Styx—I swear
by the greatest, grimmest oath that binds the happy gods:
I will never plot some new intrigue to harm you.
Never. All I have in mind and devise for *you*
are the very plans I'd fashion for myself
if I were in your straits. My every impulse   210
bends to what is right. Not iron, trust me,
the heart within *my* breast. I am all compassion."

And lustrous Calypso quickly led the way
as he followed in the footsteps of the goddess.
They reached the arching cavern, man and god as one,
and Odysseus took the seat that Hermes just left,
while the nymph set out before him every kind
of food and drink that mortal men will take.
Calypso sat down face-to-face with the king
and the women served her nectar and ambrosia.   220
They reached out for the good things that lay at hand
and when they'd had their fill of food and drink
the lustrous one took up a new approach. "So then,
royal son of Laertes, Odysseus, man of exploits,
still eager to leave at once and hurry back
to your own home, your beloved native land?
Good luck to you, even so. Farewell!
But if you only knew, down deep, what pains
are fated to fill your cup before you reach that shore,

you'd stay right here, preside in our house with me   230
and be immortal. Much as you long to see your wife,
the one you pine for all your days . . . and yet
I just might claim to be nothing less than she,
neither in face nor figure. Hardly right, is it,
for mortal woman to rival immortal goddess?
How, in build? in beauty?"
                                      "Ah great goddess,"
worldly Odysseus answered, "don't be angry with me,
please. All that you say is true, how well I know.
Look at my wise Penelope. She falls far short of you,
your beauty, stature. She is mortal after all   240
and you, you never age or die . . .
Nevertheless I long—I pine, all my days—
to travel home and see the dawn of my return.
And if a god will wreck me yet again on the wine-dark sea,
I can bear that too, with a spirit tempered to endure.
Much have I suffered, labored long and hard by now
in the waves and wars. Add this to the total—
bring the trial on!"
                                      Even as he spoke
the sun set and the darkness swept the earth.
And now, withdrawing into the cavern's deep recesses,   250
long in each other's arms they lost themselves in love.

    When young Dawn with her rose-red fingers shone once more
Odysseus quickly dressed himself in cloak and shirt
while the nymph slipped on a loose, glistening robe,
filmy, a joy to the eye, and round her waist
she ran a brocaded golden belt
and over her head a scarf to shield her brow,
then turned to plan the great man's voyage home.
She gave him a heavy bronze ax that fit his grip,
both blades well-honed, with a fine olive haft   260
lashed firm to its head. She gave him a polished
smoothing-adze as well and then she led the way
to the island's outer edge where trees grew tall,
alders, black poplars and firs that shot sky-high,

seasoned, drying for years, ideal for easy floating.
Once she'd shown her guest where the tall timber stood,
Calypso the lustrous goddess headed home again.
He set to cutting trunks—the work was done in no time.
Twenty in all he felled, he trimmed them clean with his ax
and split them deftly, trued them straight to the line.   270
Meanwhile the radiant goddess brought him drills—
he bored through all his planks and wedged them snugly,
knocking them home together, locked with pegs and joints.
Broad in the beam and bottom flat as a merchantman
when a master shipwright turns out her hull,
so broad the craft Odysseus made himself.
Working away at speed
he put up half-decks pinned to close-set ribs
and a sweep of gunwales rounded off the sides.
He fashioned the mast next and sank its yard in deep   280
and added a steering-oar to hold her right on course,
then he fenced her stem to stern with twigs and wicker,
bulwark against the sea-surge, floored with heaps of brush.
And lustrous Calypso came again, now with bolts of cloth
to make the sail, and he finished that off too, expertly.
Braces, sheets and brails—he rigged all fast on board,
then eased her down with levers into the sunlit sea.

       That was the fourth day and all his work was done.
On the fifth, the lovely goddess launched him from her island,
once she had bathed and decked him out in fragrant clothes.   290
And Calypso stowed two skins aboard—dark wine in one,
the larger one held water—added a sack of rations,
filled with her choicest meats to build his strength,
and summoned a wind to bear him onward, fair and warm.
The wind lifting his spirits high, royal Odysseus
spread sail—gripping the tiller, seated astern—
and now the master mariner steered his craft,
sleep never closing his eyes, forever scanning
the stars, the Pleiades and the Plowman late to set
and the Great Bear that mankind also calls the Wagon: 300
she wheels on her axis always fixed, watching the Hunter,

and she alone is denied a plunge in the Ocean's baths.
Hers were the stars the lustrous goddess told him
to keep hard to port as he cut across the sea.
And seventeen days he sailed, making headway well;
on the eighteenth, shadowy mountains slowly loomed . . .
the Phaeacians' island reaching toward him now,
over the misty breakers, rising like a shield.

But now Poseidon, god of the earthquake, saw him—
just returning home from his Ethiopian friends,   310
from miles away on the Solymi mountain-range
he spied Odysseus sailing down the sea
and it made his fury boil even more.
He shook his head and rumbled to himself,
"Outrageous! Look how the gods have changed their minds
about Odysseus—while I was off with my Ethiopians.
Just look at him there, nearing Phaeacia's shores
where he's fated to escape his noose of pain
that's held him until now. Still my hopes ride high—
I'll give that man his swamping fill of trouble!"   320

With that he rammed the clouds together—both hands
clutching his trident—churned the waves into chaos, whipping
all the gales from every quarter, shrouding over in thunderheads
the earth and sea at once—and night swept down from the sky—
East and South Winds clashed and the raging West and North,
sprung from the heavens, roiled heaving breakers up—
and Odysseus' knees quaked, his spirit too;
numb with fear he spoke to his own great heart:
"Wretched man—what becomes of me now, at last?
I fear the nymph foretold it all too well—   330
on the high seas, she said, before I can reach
my native land I'll fill my cup of pain! And now,
look, it all comes to pass. What monstrous clouds—
King Zeus crowning the whole wide heaven black—
churning the seas in chaos, gales blasting,
raging around my head from every quarter—
my death-plunge in a flash, it's certain now!

Three, four times blessed, my friends-in-arms
who died on the plains of Troy those years ago,
serving the sons of Atreus to the end. Would to god   340
I'd died there too and met my fate that day the Trojans,
swarms of them, hurled at *me* with bronze spears,
fighting over the corpse of proud Achilles!
A hero's funeral then, my glory spread by comrades—
now what a wretched death I'm doomed to die!"

    At that a massive wave came crashing down on his head,
a terrific onslaught spinning his craft round and round—
he was thrown clear of the decks—

                          the steering-oar wrenched
from his grasp—

                  and in one lightning attack the brawling
galewinds struck full-force, snapping the mast mid-shaft   350
and hurling the sail and sailyard far across the sea.
He went under a good long while, no fast way out,
no struggling up from under the giant wave's assault,
his clothing dragged him down—divine Calypso's gifts—
but at last he fought his way to the surface spewing
bitter brine, streams of it pouring down his head.
But half-drowned as he was, he'd not forget his craft—
he lunged after her through the breakers, laying hold
and huddling amidships, fled the stroke of death.
Pell-mell the rollers tossed her along down-current,   360
wild as the North Wind tossing thistle along the fields
at high harvest—dry stalks clutching each other tightly—
so the galewinds tumbled her down the sea, this way, that way,
now the South Wind flinging her over to North to sport with,
now the East Wind giving her up to West to harry on and on.

    But someone saw him—Cadmus' daughter with lovely ankles,
Ino, a mortal woman once with human voice and called
Leucothea now she lives in the sea's salt depths,
esteemed by all the gods as she deserves.
She pitied Odysseus, tossed, tormented so—   370
she broke from the waves like a shearwater on the wing,

lit on the wreck and asked him kindly, "Ah poor man,
why is the god of earthquakes so dead set against you?
Strewing your way with such a crop of troubles!
But he can't destroy you, not for all his anger.
Just do as I say. You seem no fool to me.
Strip off those clothes and leave your craft
for the winds to hurl, and swim for it now, you must,
strike out with your arms for landfall there,
Phaeacian land where destined safety waits.   380
Here, take this scarf,
tie it around your waist—it is immortal.
Nothing to fear now, neither pain nor death.
But once you grasp the mainland with your hands
untie it quickly, throw it into the wine-dark sea,
far from the shore, but you, you turn your head away!"

    With that the goddess handed him the scarf
and slipped back in the heavy breaking seas
like a shearwater once again
and a dark heaving billow closed above her.   390
But battle-weary Odysseus weighed two courses,
deeply torn, probing his fighting spirit: "Oh no—
I fear another immortal weaves a snare to trap me,
urging me to abandon ship! I won't. Not yet.
That shore's too far away—
I glimpsed it myself—where she says refuge waits.
No, here's what I'll do, it's what seems best to *me*.
As long as the timbers cling and joints stand fast,
I'll hold out aboard her and take a whipping—
once the breakers smash my craft to pieces,   400
then I'll swim—no better plan for now."

    But just as great Odysseus thrashed things out,
Poseidon god of the earthquake launched a colossal wave,
terrible, murderous, arching over him, pounding down on him,
hard as a windstorm blasting piles of dry parched chaff,
scattering flying husks—so the long planks of his boat
were scattered far and wide. But Odysseus leapt aboard

one timber and riding it like a plunging racehorse
stripped away his clothes, divine Calypso's gifts,
and quickly tying the scarf around his waist   410
he dove headfirst in the sea,
stretched his arms and stroked for life itself.
But again the mighty god of earthquakes spied him,
shook his head and grumbled deep in his spirit, "Go, go,
after all you've suffered—rove your miles of sea—
till you fall in the arms of people loved by Zeus.
Even so I can hardly think you'll find
your punishments too light!"
                              With that threat
he lashed his team with their long flowing manes,
gaining Aegae port where his famous palace stands.   420

    But Zeus's daughter Athena countered him at once.
The rest of the winds she stopped right in their tracks,
commanding them all to hush now, go to sleep.
All but the boisterous North—she whipped him up
and the goddess beat the breakers flat before Odysseus,
dear to Zeus, so he could reach the Phaeacians,
mingle with men who love their long oars
and escape his death at last.
                              Yes, but now,
adrift on the heaving swells two nights, two days—
quite lost—again and again the man foresaw his death.   430
Then when Dawn with her lovely locks brought on
the third day, the wind fell in an instant,
all glazed to a dead calm, and Odysseus,
scanning sharply, raised high by a groundswell,
looked up and saw it—landfall, just ahead.
Joy . . . warm as the joy that children feel
when they see their father's life dawn again,
one who's lain on a sickbed racked with torment,
wasting away, slowly, under some angry power's onslaught—
then what joy when the gods deliver him from his pains!   440
So warm, Odysseus' joy when he saw that shore, those trees,
as he swam on, anxious to plant his feet on solid ground again.

But just offshore, as far as a man's shout can carry,
he caught the boom of a heavy surf on jagged reefs—
roaring breakers crashing down on an ironbound coast,
exploding in fury—
                    the whole sea shrouded—
                                      sheets of spray—
no harbors to hold ships, no roadstead where they'd ride,
nothing but jutting headlands, riptooth reefs, cliffs.
Odysseus' knees quaked and the heart inside him sank;
he spoke to his fighting spirit, desperate: "Worse and worse!   450
Now that Zeus has granted a glimpse of land beyond my hopes,
now I've crossed this waste of water, the end in sight,
there's no way out of the boiling surf—I see no way!
Rugged reefs offshore, around them breakers roaring,
above them a smooth rock face, rising steeply, look,
and the surge too deep inshore, no spot to stand
on my own two legs and battle free of death.
If I clamber out, some big comber will hoist me,
dash me against that cliff—my struggles all a waste!
If I keep on swimming down the coast, trying to find   460
a seabeach shelving against the waves, a sheltered cove—
I dread it—another gale will snatch me up and haul me
back to the fish-infested sea, retching in despair.
Or a dark power will loose some monster at me,
rearing out of the waves—one of the thousands
Amphitrite's breakers teem with. Well I know
the famous god of earthquakes hates my very name!"

     Just as that fear went churning through his mind
a tremendous roller swept him toward the rocky coast
where he'd have been flayed alive, his bones crushed   470
if the bright-eyed goddess Pallas had not inspired him now.
He lunged for a reef, he seized it with both hands and clung
for dear life, groaning until the giant wave surged past
and so he escaped its force, but the breaker's backwash
charged into him full fury and hurled him out to sea.
Like pebbles stuck in the suckers of some octopus
dragged from its lair—so strips of skin torn

from his clawing hands stuck to the rock face.
A heavy sea covered him over, then and there
unlucky Odysseus would have met his death—   480
against the will of Fate—
but the bright-eyed one inspired him yet again.
Fighting out from the breakers pounding toward the coast,
out of danger he swam on, scanning the land, trying to find
a seabeach shelving against the waves, a sheltered cove,
and stroking hard he came abreast of a river's mouth,
running calmly, the perfect spot, he thought . . .
free of rocks, with a windbreak from the gales.
As the current flowed he felt the river's god and
prayed to him in spirit: "Hear me, lord, whoever you are,   490
I've come to you, the answer to all my prayers—
rescue me from the sea, the Sea-lord's curse!
Even immortal gods will show a man respect,
whatever wanderer seeks their help—like me—
I throw myself on your mercy, on your current now—
I have suffered greatly. Pity me, lord,
your suppliant cries for help!"
                                      So the man prayed
and the god stemmed his current, held his surge at once
and smoothing out the swells before Odysseus now,
drew him safe to shore at the river's mouth.   500
His knees buckled, massive arms fell limp,
the sea had beaten down his striving heart.
His whole body swollen, brine aplenty gushing
out of his mouth and nostrils—breathless, speechless,
there he lay, with only a little strength left in him,
deathly waves of exhaustion overwhelmed him now . . .
But once he regained his breath and rallied back to life,
at last he loosed the goddess' scarf from his body,
dropped it into the river flowing out to sea
and a swift current bore it far downstream   510
and suddenly Ino caught it in her hands.
Struggling up from the banks, he flung himself
in the deep reeds, he kissed the good green earth
and addressed his fighting spirit, desperate still:

"Man of misery, what next? Is this the end?
If I wait out a long tense night by the banks,
I fear the sharp frost and the soaking dew together
will do me in—I'm bone-weary, about to breathe my last,
and a cold wind blows from a river on toward morning.
But what if I climb that slope, go for the dark woods   520
and bed down in the thick brush? What if I'm spared
the chill, fatigue, and a sweet sleep comes my way?
I fear wild beasts will drag me off as quarry."

But this was the better course, it struck him now.
He set out for the woods and not far from the water
found a grove with a clearing all around and crawled
beneath two bushy olives sprung from the same root,
one olive wild, the other well-bred stock.
No sodden gusty winds could ever pierce them,
nor could the sun's sharp rays invade their depths,   530
nor could a downpour drench them through and through,
so dense they grew together, tangling side-by-side.
Odysseus crept beneath them, scraping up at once
a good wide bed for himself with both hands.
A fine litter of dead leaves had drifted in,
enough to cover two men over, even three,
in the wildest kind of winter known to man.
Long-enduring great Odysseus, overjoyed at the sight,
bedded down in the midst and heaped the leaves around him.
As a man will bury his glowing brand in black ashes,   540
off on a lonely farmstead, no neighbors near,
to keep a spark alive—no need to kindle fire
from somewhere else—so great Odysseus buried
himself in leaves and Athena showered sleep
upon his eyes . . . sleep in a swift wave
delivering him from all his pains and labors,
blessed sleep that sealed his eyes at last.

The Princess and
the Stranger

So there he lay at rest, the storm-tossed great Odysseus,
borne down by his hard labors first and now deep sleep
as Athena traveled through the countryside
and reached the Phaeacians' city. Years ago
they lived in a land of spacious dancing-circles,
Hyperia, all too close to the overbearing Cyclops,
stronger, violent brutes who harried them without end.
So their godlike king, Nausithous, led the people off
in a vast migration, settled them in Scheria,
far from the men who toil on this earth—   10
he flung up walls around the city, built the houses,
raised the gods' temples and shared the land for plowing.
But his fate had long since forced him down to Death
and now Alcinous ruled, and the gods made him wise.

Straight to his house the clear-eyed Pallas went,
full of plans for great Odysseus' journey home.
She made her way to the gaily painted room
where a young girl lay asleep . . .
a match for the deathless gods in build and beauty,
Nausicaa, the daughter of generous King Alcinous.   20
Two handmaids fair as the Graces slept beside her,
flanking the two posts, with the gleaming doors closed.
But the goddess drifted through like a breath of fresh air,
rushed to the girl's bed and hovering close she spoke,
in face and form like the shipman Dymas' daughter,
a girl the princess' age, and dearest to her heart.
Disguised, the bright-eyed goddess chided, "Nausicaa,
how could your mother bear a careless girl like you?
Look at your fine clothes, lying here neglected—
with your marriage not far off,   30
the day you should be decked in all your glory
and offer elegant dress to those who form your escort.
That's how a bride's good name goes out across the world
and it brings her father and queenly mother joy. Come,
let's go wash these clothes at the break of day—
I'll help you, lend a hand, and the work will fly!
You won't stay unwed long. The noblest men
in the country court you now, all Phaeacians
just like you, Phaeacia-born and raised. So come,
the first thing in the morning press your kingly father   40
to harness the mules and wagon for you, all to carry
your sashes, dresses, glossy spreads for your bed.
It's so much nicer for you to ride than go on foot.
The washing-pools are just too far from town."
                                                With that
the bright-eyed goddess sped away to Olympus, where,
they say, the gods' eternal mansion stands unmoved,
never rocked by galewinds, never drenched by rains,
nor do the drifting snows assail it, no, the clear air
stretches away without a cloud, and a great radiance
plays across that world where the blithe gods   50

live all their days in bliss. There Athena went,
once the bright-eyed one had urged the princess on.

    Dawn soon rose on her splendid throne and woke
Nausicaa finely gowned. Still beguiled by her dream,
down she went through the house to tell her parents now,
her beloved father and mother. She found them both inside.
Her mother sat at the hearth with several waiting-women,
spinning yarn on a spindle, lustrous sea-blue wool.
Her father she met as he left to join the lords
at a council island nobles asked him to attend.   60
She stepped up close to him, confiding, "Daddy dear,
I wonder, won't you have them harness a wagon for me,
the tall one with the good smooth wheels . . . so I
can take our clothes to the river for a washing?
Lovely things, but lying before me all soiled.
And you yourself, sitting among the princes,
debating points at your council,
you really should be wearing spotless linen.
Then you have five sons, full-grown in the palace,
two of them married, but three are lusty bachelors   70
always demanding crisp shirts fresh from the wash
when they go out to dance. Look at my duties—
that all rests on me."
                        So she coaxed, too shy
to touch on her hopes for marriage, young warm hopes,
in her father's presence. But he saw through it all
and answered quickly, "I won't deny you the mules,
my darling girl . . . I won't deny you anything.
Off you go, and the men will harness a wagon,
the tall one with the good smooth wheels,
fitted out with a cradle on the top."
                        With that   80
he called to the stablemen and they complied.
They trundled the wagon out now, rolling smoothly,
backed the mule-team into the traces, hitched them up,
while the princess brought her finery from the room

and piled it into the wagon's polished cradle.
Her mother packed a hamper—treats of all kinds,
favorite things to refresh her daughter's spirits—
poured wine in a skin, and as Nausicaa climbed aboard,
the queen gave her a golden flask of suppling olive oil
for her and her maids to smooth on after bathing.   90
Then, taking the whip in hand and glistening reins,
she touched the mules to a start and out they clattered,
trotting on at a clip, bearing the princess and her clothes
and not alone: her maids went with her, stepping briskly too.

　　Once they reached the banks of the river flowing strong
where the pools would never fail, with plenty of water
cool and clear, bubbling up and rushing through
to scour the darkest stains—they loosed the mules,
out from under the wagon yoke, and chased them down
the river's rippling banks to graze on luscious clover.   100
Down from the cradle they lifted clothes by the armload,
plunged them into the dark pools and stamped them down
in the hollows, one girl racing the next to finish first
until they'd scoured and rinsed off all the grime,
then they spread them out in a line along the beach
where the surf had washed a pebbly scree ashore.
And once they'd bathed and smoothed their skin with oil,
they took their picnic, sitting along the river's banks
and waiting for all the clothes to dry in the hot noon sun.
Now fed to their hearts' content, the princess and her retinue   110
threw their veils to the wind, struck up a game of ball.
White-armed Nausicaa led their singing, dancing beat . . .
as lithe as Artemis with her arrows striding down
from a high peak—Taygetus' towering ridge or Erymanthus—
thrilled to race with the wild boar or bounding deer,
and nymphs of the hills race with her,
daughters of Zeus whose shield is storm and thunder,
ranging the hills in sport, and Leto's heart exults
as head and shoulders over the rest her daughter rises,
unmistakable—she outshines them all, though all are lovely.   120

So Nausicaa shone among her maids, a virgin, still unwed.

But now, as she was about to fold her clothes
and yoke the mules and turn for home again,
now clear-eyed Pallas thought of what came next,
to make Odysseus wake and see this young beauty
and she would lead him to the Phaeacians' town.
The ball—
            the princess suddenly tossed it to a maid
but it missed the girl, it splashed in a deep swirling pool
and they all shouted out—
                        and that woke great Odysseus.
He sat up with a start, puzzling, his heart pounding: 130
"Man of misery, whose land have I lit on now?
What *are* they here—violent, savage, lawless?
or friendly to strangers, god-fearing men?
Listen: shouting, echoing round me—women, girls—
or the nymphs who haunt the rugged mountaintops
and the river springs and meadows lush with grass!
Or am I really close to people who speak my language?
Up with you, see how the land lies, see for yourself now . . ."

Muttering so, great Odysseus crept out of the bushes,
stripping off with his massive hand a leafy branch   140
from the tangled olive growth to shield his body,
hide his private parts. And out he stalked
as a mountain lion exultant in his power
strides through wind and rain and his eyes blaze
and he charges sheep or oxen or chases wild deer
but his hunger drives him on to go for flocks,
even to raid the best-defended homestead.
So Odysseus moved out . . .
about to mingle with all those lovely girls,
naked now as he was, for the need drove him on,   150
a terrible sight, all crusted, caked with brine—
they scattered in panic down the jutting beaches.
Only Alcinous' daughter held fast, for Athena planted
courage within her heart, dissolved the trembling in her limbs,

and she firmly stood her ground and faced Odysseus, torn now—
Should he fling his arms around her knees, the young beauty,
plead for help, or stand back, plead with a winning word,
beg her to lead him to the town and lend him clothing?
This was the better way, he thought. Plead now
with a subtle, winning word and stand well back,   160
don't clasp her knees, the girl might bridle, yes.
He launched in at once, endearing, sly and suave:
"Here I am at your mercy, princess—
are you a goddess or a mortal? If one of the gods
who rule the skies up there, you're Artemis to the life,
the daughter of mighty Zeus—I see her now—just look
at your build, your bearing, your lithe flowing grace . . .
But if you're one of the mortals living here on earth,
three times blest are your father, your queenly mother,
three times over your brothers too. How often their hearts   170
must warm with joy to see you striding into the dances—
such a bloom of beauty. True, but he is the one
more blest than all other men alive, that man
who sways you with gifts and leads you home, his bride!
I have never laid eyes on anyone like you,
neither man nor woman . . .
I look at you and a sense of wonder takes me.
                                                    Wait,
once I saw the like—in Delos, beside Apollo's altar—
the young slip of a palm-tree springing into the light.
There I'd sailed, you see, with a great army in my wake,   180
out on the long campaign that doomed my life to hardship.
That vision! Just as I stood there gazing, rapt, for hours . . .
no shaft like that had ever risen up from the earth—
so now I marvel at *you,* my lady: rapt, enthralled,
too struck with awe to grasp you by the knees
though pain has ground me down.
                                        Only yesterday,
the twentieth day, did I escape the wine-dark sea.
Till then the waves and the rushing gales had swept me on
from the island of Ogygia. Now some power has tossed me here,
doubtless to suffer still more torments on your shores.   190

I can't believe they'll stop. Long before that
the gods will give me more, still more.
                                        Compassion—
princess, please! You, after all that I have suffered,
you are the first I've come to. I know no one else,
none in your city, no one in your land.
Show me the way to town, give me a rag for cover,
just some cloth, some wrapper you carried with you here.
And may the good gods give you all your heart desires:
husband, and house, and lasting harmony too.
No finer, greater gift in the world than that . . .   200
when man and woman possess their home, two minds,
two hearts that work as one. Despair to their enemies,
a joy to all their friends. Their own best claim to glory."

    "Stranger," the white-armed princess answered staunchly,
"friend, you're hardly a wicked man, and no fool, I'd say—
it's Olympian Zeus himself who hands our fortunes out,
to each of us in turn, to the good and bad,
however Zeus prefers . . .
He gave you pain, it seems. You simply have to bear it.
But now, seeing you've reached our city and our land,   210
you'll never lack for clothing or any other gift,
the right of worn-out suppliants come our way.
I'll show you our town, tell you our people's name.
Phaeacians we are, who hold this city and this land,
and I am the daughter of generous King Alcinous.
All our people's power stems from him."

    She called out to her girls with lovely braids:
"Stop, my friends! Why run when you see a man?
Surely you don't think *him* an enemy, do you?
There's no one alive, there never will be one,   220
who'd reach Phaeacian soil and lay it waste.
The immortals love us far too much for that.
We live too far apart, out in the surging sea,
off at the world's end—
no other mortals come to mingle with us.

But here's an unlucky wanderer strayed our way
and we must tend him well. Every stranger and beggar
comes from Zeus, and whatever scrap we give him
he'll be glad to get. So, quick, my girls,
give our newfound friend some food and drink   230
and bathe the man in the river,
wherever you find some shelter from the wind."

                                               At that
they came to a halt and teased each other on
and led Odysseus down to a sheltered spot
where he could find a seat,
just as great Alcinous' daughter told them.
They laid out cloak and shirt for him to wear,
they gave him the golden flask of suppling olive oil
and pressed him to bathe himself in the river's stream.
Then thoughtful Odysseus reassured the handmaids,   240
"Stand where you are, dear girls, a good way off,
so I can rinse the brine from my shoulders now
and rub myself with oil . . .
how long it's been since oil touched my skin!
But I won't bathe in front of you. I would be embarrassed—
stark naked before young girls with lovely braids."

    The handmaids scurried off to tell their mistress.
Great Odysseus bathed in the river, scrubbed his body
clean of brine that clung to his back and broad shoulders,
scoured away the brackish scurf that caked his head.   250
And then, once he had bathed all over, rubbed in oil
and donned the clothes the virgin princess gave him,
Zeus's daughter Athena made him taller to all eyes,
his build more massive now, and down from his brow
she ran his curls like thick hyacinth clusters
full of blooms. As a master craftsman washes
gold over beaten silver—a man the god of fire
and Queen Athena trained in every fine technique—
and finishes off his latest effort, handsome work,
so she lavished splendor over his head and shoulders now.   260
And down to the beach he walked and sat apart,

glistening in his glory, breathtaking, yes,
and the princess gazed in wonder . . .
then turned to her maids with lovely braided hair:
"Listen, my white-armed girls, to what I tell you.
The gods of Olympus can't be all against this man
who's come to mingle among our noble people.
At first he seemed appalling, I must say—
now he seems like a god who rules the skies up there!
Ah, if only a man like *that* were called my husband,   270
lived right here, pleased to stay forever . . .
                                         Enough.
Give the stranger food and drink, my girls."

     They hung on her words and did her will at once,
set before Odysseus food and drink, and he ate and drank,
the great Odysseus, long deprived, so ravenous now—
it seemed like years since he had tasted food.

     The white-armed princess thought of one last thing.
Folding the clothes, she packed them into her painted wagon,
hitched the sharp-hoofed mules, and climbing up herself,
Nausicaa urged Odysseus, warmly urged her guest,   280
"Up with you now, my friend, and off to town we go.
I'll see you into my wise father's palace where,
I promise you, you'll meet all the best Phaeacians.
Wait, let's do it this way. You seem no fool to me.
While we're passing along the fields and plowlands,
you follow the mules and wagon, stepping briskly
with all my maids. I'll lead the way myself.
But once we reach our city, ringed by walls
and strong high towers too, with a fine harbor either side . . .
and the causeway in is narrow; along the road the rolling ships   290
are all hauled up, with a slipway cleared for every vessel.
There's our assembly, round Poseidon's royal precinct,
built of quarried slabs planted deep in the earth.
Here the sailors tend their black ships' tackle,
cables and sails, and plane their oarblades down.
Phaeacians, you see, care nothing for bow or quiver,

only for masts and oars and good trim ships themselves—
we glory in our ships, crossing the foaming seas!
But I shrink from all our sea-dogs' nasty gossip.
Some old salt might mock us behind our backs—   300
we have our share of insolent types in town
and one of the coarser sort, spying us, might say,
'Now who's that tall, handsome stranger Nausicaa has in tow?
Where'd she light on *him?* Her husband-to-be, just wait!
But who—some shipwrecked stray she's taken up with,
some alien from abroad? Since nobody lives nearby.
Unless it's really a god come down from the blue
to answer all her prayers, and to have her all his days.
Good riddance! Let the girl go roving to find herself
a man from foreign parts. She only spurns her own—   310
countless Phaeacians round about who court her,
nothing but our best.'
                                 So they'll scoff . . .
just think of the scandal that would face me then.
I'd find fault with a girl who carried on that way,
flouting her parents' wishes—father, mother, still alive—
consorting with men before she'd tied the knot in public.
No, stranger, listen closely to what I say, the sooner
to win your swift voyage home at my father's hands.
Now, you'll find a splendid grove along the road—
poplars, sacred to Pallas—   320
a bubbling spring's inside and meadows run around it.
There lies my father's estate, his blossoming orchard too,
as far from town as a man's strong shout can carry.
Take a seat there, wait a while, and give us time
to make it into town and reach my father's house.
Then, when you think we're home, walk on yourself
to the city, ask the way to my father's palace,
generous King Alcinous. You cannot miss it,
even an innocent child could guide you there.
No other Phaeacian's house is built like that: 330
so grand, the palace of Alcinous, our great hero.
Once the mansion and courtyard have enclosed you, go,
quickly, across the hall until you reach my mother.

Beside the hearth she sits in the fire's glare,
spinning yarn on a spindle, sea-blue wool—
a stirring sight, you'll see . . .
she leans against a pillar, her ladies sit behind.
And my father's throne is drawn up close beside her;
there he sits and takes his wine, a mortal like a god.
Go past him, grasp my mother's knees—if you want   340
to see the day of your return, rejoicing, soon,
even if your home's a world away.
If only the queen will take you to her heart,
then there's hope that you will see your loved ones,
reach your own grand house, your native land at last."

    At that she touched the mules with her shining whip
and they quickly left the running stream behind.
The team trotted on, their hoofs wove in and out.
She drove them back with care so all the rest,
maids and Odysseus, could keep the pace on foot,   350
and she used the whip discreetly.
The sun sank as they reached the hallowed grove,
sacred to Athena, where Odysseus stopped and sat
and said a prayer at once to mighty Zeus's daughter:
"Hear me, daughter of Zeus whose shield is thunder—
tireless one, Athena! Now hear my prayer at last,
for you never heard me then, when I was shattered,
when the famous god of earthquakes wrecked my craft.
Grant that here among the Phaeacian people
I may find some mercy and some love!"   360

    So he prayed and Athena heard his prayer
but would not yet appear to him undisguised.
She stood in awe of her Father's brother, lord of the sea
who still seethed on, still churning with rage against
the great Odysseus till he reached his native land.

BOOK SEVEN

Phaeacia's Halls and Gardens

Now as Odysseus, long an exile, prayed in Athena's grove,
the hardy mule-team drew the princess toward the city.
Reaching her father's splendid halls, she reined in,
just at the gates—her brothers clustering round her,
men like gods, released the mules from the yoke
and brought the clothes indoors
as Nausicaa made her way toward her bedroom.
There her chambermaid lit a fire for her—
Eurymedusa, the old woman who'd come from Apiraea
years ago, when the rolling ships had sailed her in   10
and the country picked her out as King Alcinous' prize,
for he ruled all the Phaeacians, they obeyed him like a god.
Once, she had nursed the white-armed princess in the palace.
Now she lit a fire and made her supper in the room.

At the same time, Odysseus set off toward the city.
Pallas Athena, harboring kindness for the hero,
drifted a heavy mist around him, shielding him
from any swaggering islander who'd cross his path,
provoke him with taunts and search out who he was.
Instead, as he was about to enter the welcome city,   20
the bright-eyed goddess herself came up to greet him there,
for all the world like a young girl, holding a pitcher,
standing face-to-face with the visitor, who asked,
"Little girl, now wouldn't you be my guide
to the palace of the one they call Alcinous?
The king who rules the people of these parts.
I am a stranger, you see, weighed down with troubles,
come this way from a distant, far-off shore.
So I know no one here, none at all
in your city and the farmlands round about."
                                        "Oh yes, sir,   30
good old stranger," the bright-eyed goddess said,
"I'll show you the very palace that you're after—
the king lives right beside my noble father.
Come, quietly too, and I will lead the way.
Now not a glance at anyone, not a question.
The men here never suffer strangers gladly,
have no love for hosting a man from foreign lands.
All they really trust are their fast, flying ships
that cross the mighty ocean. Gifts of Poseidon,
ah what ships they are—   40
quick as a bird, quick as a darting thought!"

     And Pallas Athena sped away in the lead
as he followed in her footsteps, man and goddess.
But the famed Phaeacian sailors never saw him,
right in their midst, striding down their streets.
Athena the one with lovely braids would not permit it,
the awesome goddess poured an enchanted mist around him,
harboring kindness for Odysseus in her heart.
And he marveled now at the balanced ships and havens,

the meeting grounds of the great lords and the long ramparts   50
looming, coped and crowned with palisades of stakes—
an amazing sight to see . . .
And once they reached the king's resplendent halls
the bright-eyed goddess cried out, "Good old stranger,
here, here is the very palace that you're after—
I've guided you all the way. Here you'll find
our princes dear to the gods, busy feasting.
You go on inside. Be bold, nothing to fear.
In every venture the bold man comes off best,
even the wanderer, bound from distant shores.   60
The queen is the first you'll light on in the halls.
Arete, she is called, and earns the name:
she answers all our prayers. She comes, in fact,
from the same stock that bred our King Alcinous.
First came Nausithous, son of the earthquake god
Poseidon and Periboea, the lovely, matchless beauty,
the youngest daughter of iron-willed Eurymedon,
king of the overweening Giants years ago.
He led that reckless clan to its own ruin,
killed himself in the bargain, but the Sea-lord   70
lay in love with Periboea and she produced a son,
Nausithous, that lionheart who ruled Phaeacia well.
Now, Nausithous had two sons, Rhexenor and Alcinous,
but the lord of the silver bow, Apollo, shot Rhexenor down—
married, true, yet still without a son in the halls,
he left one child behind, a daughter named Arete.
Alcinous made the girl his wife and honors her
as no woman is honored on this earth, of all the wives
now keeping households under their husbands' sway.
Such is her pride of place, and always will be so: 80
dear to her loving children, to Alcinous himself
and all our people. They gaze on her as a god,
saluting her warmly on her walks through town.
She lacks nothing in good sense and judgment—
she can dissolve quarrels, even among men,
whoever wins her sympathies.

If only our queen will take you to her heart,
then there's hope that you will see your loved ones,
reach your high-roofed house, your native land at last."

And with that vow the bright-eyed goddess sped away,   90
over the barren sea, leaving welcome Scheria far behind,
and reaching Marathon and the spacious streets of Athens,
entered Erechtheus' sturdy halls, Athena's stronghold.
Now as Odysseus approached Alcinous' famous house
a rush of feelings stirred within his heart,
bringing him to a standstill,
even before he crossed the bronze threshold . . .
A radiance strong as the moon or rising sun came flooding
through the high-roofed halls of generous King Alcinous.
Walls plated in bronze, crowned with a circling frieze   100
glazed as blue as lapis, ran to left and right
from outer gates to the deepest court recess,
and solid golden doors enclosed the palace.
Up from the bronze threshold silver doorposts rose
with silver lintel above, and golden handles too.
And dogs of gold and silver were stationed either side,
forged by the god of fire with all his cunning craft
to keep watch on generous King Alcinous' palace,
his immortal guard-dogs, ageless, all their days.
Inside to left and right, in a long unbroken row   110
from farthest outer gate to the inmost chamber,
thrones stood backed against the wall, each draped
with a finely spun brocade, women's handsome work.
Here the Phaeacian lords would sit enthroned,
dining, drinking—the feast flowed on forever.
And young boys, molded of gold, set on pedestals
standing firm, were lifting torches high in their hands
to flare through the nights and light the feasters down the hall.
And Alcinous has some fifty serving-women in his house:
some, turning the handmill, grind the apple-yellow grain,   120
some weave at their webs or sit and spin their yarn,
fingers flickering quick as aspen leaves in the wind
and the densely woven woolens dripping oil droplets.

Just as Phaeacian men excel the world at sailing,
driving their swift ships on the open seas,
so the women excel at all the arts of weaving.
That is Athena's gift to them beyond all others—
a genius for lovely work, and a fine mind too.

   Outside the courtyard, fronting the high gates,
a magnificent orchard stretches four acres deep   130
with a strong fence running round it side-to-side.
Here luxuriant trees are always in their prime,
pomegranates and pears, and apples glowing red,
succulent figs and olives swelling sleek and dark.
And the yield of all these trees will never flag or die,
neither in winter nor in summer, a harvest all year round
for the West Wind always breathing through will bring
some fruits to the bud and others warm to ripeness—
pear mellowing ripe on pear, apple on apple,
cluster of grapes on cluster, fig crowding fig.   140
And here is a teeming vineyard planted for the kings,
beyond it an open level bank where the vintage grapes
lie baking to raisins in the sun while pickers gather others;
some they trample down in vats, and here in the front rows
bunches of unripe grapes have hardly shed their blooms
while others under the sunlight slowly darken purple.
And there by the last rows are beds of greens,
bordered and plotted, greens of every kind,
glistening fresh, year in, year out. And last,
there are two springs, one rippling in channels   150
over the whole orchard—the other, flanking it,
rushes under the palace gates
to bubble up in front of the lofty roofs
where the city people come and draw their water.
                             Such
were the gifts, the glories showered down by the gods
on King Alcinous' realm.
               And there Odysseus stood,
gazing at all this bounty, a man who'd borne so much . . .
Once he'd had his fill of marveling at it all,

he crossed the threshold quickly,
strode inside the palace. Here he found   160
the Phaeacian lords and captains tipping out
libations now to the guide and giant-killer Hermes,
the god to whom they would always pour the final cup
before they sought their beds. Odysseus went on
striding down the hall, the man of many struggles
shrouded still in the mist Athena drifted round him,
till he reached Arete and Alcinous the king. And then,
the moment he flung his arms around Arete's knees,
the godsent mist rolled back to reveal the great man.
And silence seized the feasters all along the hall—   170
seeing him right before their eyes, they marveled,
gazing on him now as Odysseus pleaded, "Queen,
Arete, daughter of godlike King Rhexenor!
Here after many trials I come to beg for mercy,
your husband's, yours, and all these feasters' here.
May the gods endow them with fortune all their lives,
may each hand down to his sons the riches in his house
and the pride of place the realm has granted *him*.
But as for myself, grant me a rapid convoy home
to my own native land. How far away I've been   180
from all my loved ones—how long I have suffered!"

    Pleading so, the man sank down in the ashes,
just at the hearth beside the blazing fire,
while all the rest stayed hushed, stock-still.
At last the old revered Echeneus broke the spell,
the eldest lord in Phaeacia, finest speaker too,
a past master at all the island's ancient ways.
Impelled by kindness now, he rose and said,
"This is no way, Alcinous. How indecent, look,
our guest on the ground, in the ashes by the fire!   190
Your people are holding back, waiting for your signal.
Come, raise him up and seat the stranger now,
in a silver-studded chair,
and tell the heralds to mix more wine for all
so we can pour out cups to Zeus who loves the lightning,

champion of suppliants—suppliants' rights are sacred.
And let the housekeeper give our guest his supper,
unstinting with her stores."
                            Hearing that,
Alcinous, poised in all his majesty, took the hand
of the seasoned, worldly-wise Odysseus, raised him up   200
from the hearth and sat him down in a burnished chair,
displacing his own son, the courtly Lord Laodamas
who had sat beside him, the son he loved the most.
A maid brought water soon in a graceful golden pitcher
and over a silver basin tipped it out
so the guest might rinse his hands,
then pulled a gleaming table to his side.
A staid housekeeper brought on bread to serve him,
appetizers aplenty too, lavish with her bounty.
As long-suffering great Odysseus ate and drank,   210
the hallowed King Alcinous called his herald:
"Come, Pontonous! Mix the wine in the bowl,
pour rounds to all our banqueters in the house
so we can pour out cups to Zeus who loves the lightning,
champion of suppliants—suppliants' rights are sacred."

    At that Pontonous mixed the heady, honeyed wine
and tipped first drops for the god in every cup,
then poured full rounds for all. And once they'd poured
libations out and drunk to their hearts' content,
Alcinous rose and addressed his island people: 220
"Hear me, lords and captains of Phaeacia,
hear what the heart inside me has to say.
Now, our feast finished, home you go to sleep.
But at dawn we call the elders in to full assembly,
host our guest in the palace, sacrifice to the gods
and then we turn our minds to his passage home,
so under our convoy our new friend can travel back
to his own land—no toil, no troubles—soon,
rejoicing, even if his home's a world away.
And on the way no pain or hardship suffered,   230
not till he sets foot on native ground again.

There in the future he must suffer all that Fate
and the overbearing Spinners spun out on his life line
the very day his mother gave him birth . . . But if
he's one of the deathless powers, out of the blue,
the gods are working now in strange, new ways.
Always, up to now, they came to us face-to-face
whenever we'd give them grand, glorious sacrifices—
they always sat beside us here and shared our feasts.
Even when some lonely traveler meets them on the roads,   240
they never disguise themselves. We're too close kin for that,
close as the wild Giants are, the Cyclops too."

                                             "Alcinous!"
wary Odysseus countered, "cross that thought from your mind.
I'm nothing like the immortal gods who rule the skies,
either in build or breeding. I'm just a mortal man.
Whom do you know most saddled down with sorrow?
They are the ones I'd equal, grief for grief.
And I could tell a tale of still more hardship,
all I've suffered, thanks to the gods' will.
But despite my misery, let me finish dinner.   250
The belly's a shameless dog, there's nothing worse.
Always insisting, pressing, it never lets us forget—
destroyed as I am, my heart racked with sadness,
sick with anguish, still it keeps demanding,
'Eat, drink!' It blots out all the memory
of my pain, commanding, 'Fill me up!'

                                             But you,
at the first light of day, hurry, please,
to set your unlucky guest on his own home soil.
How much I have suffered . . . Oh just let me see
my lands, my serving-men and the grand high-roofed house—   260
then I can die in peace."

                    All burst into applause,
urging passage home for their newfound friend,
his pleading rang so true. And once they'd poured
libations out and drunk to their hearts' content,
each one made his way to rest in his own house.

But King Odysseus still remained at hall,
seated beside the royal Alcinous and Arete
as servants cleared the cups and plates away.
The white-armed Queen Arete took the lead;
she'd spotted the cape and shirt Odysseus wore,   270
fine clothes she'd made herself with all her women,
so now her words flew brusquely, sharply: "Stranger,
I'll be the first to question you—myself.
Who are you? Where are you from?
Who gave you the clothes you're wearing now?
Didn't you say you reached us roving on the sea?"

   "What hard labor, queen," the man of craft replied,
"to tell you the story of my troubles start to finish.
The gods on high have given me my share.
Still, this much I will tell you . . .   280
seeing you probe and press me so intently.
There is an island, Ogygia, lying far at sea,
where the daughter of Atlas, Calypso, has her home,
the seductive nymph with lovely braids—a danger too,
and no one, god or mortal, dares approach her there. But I,
cursed as I am, some power brought me to her hearth,
alone, when Zeus with a white-hot bolt had crushed
my racing warship down the wine-dark sea.
There all the rest of my loyal shipmates died
but I, locking my arms around my good ship's keel,   290
drifted along nine days. On the tenth, at dead of night,
the gods cast me up on Ogygia, Calypso's island,
home of the dangerous nymph with glossy braids,
and the goddess took me in in all her kindness,
welcomed me warmly, cherished me, even vowed
to make me immortal, ageless, all my days—
but she never won the heart inside me, never.
Seven endless years I remained there, always drenching
with my tears the immortal clothes Calypso gave me.
Then, at last, when the eighth came wheeling round,   300
she insisted that I sail—inspired by warnings sent

from Zeus, perhaps, or her own mind had changed.
She saw me on my way in a solid craft,
tight and trim, and gave me full provisions,
food and mellow wine, immortal clothes to wear
and summoned a wind to bear me onward, fair and warm.
And seventeen days I sailed, making headway well;
on the eighteenth, shadowy mountains slowly loomed . . .
your land! My heart leapt up, unlucky as I am,
doomed to be comrade still to many hardships.   310
Many pains the god of earthquakes piled upon me,
loosing the winds against me, blocking passage through,
heaving up a terrific sea, beyond belief—nor did the whitecaps
let me cling to my craft, for all my desperate groaning.
No, the squalls shattered her stem to stern, but I,
I swam hard, I plowed my way through those dark gulfs
till at last the wind and current bore me to your shores.
But here, had I tried to land, the breakers would have hurled me,
smashed me against the jagged cliffs of that grim coast,
so I pulled away, swam back till I reached a river,   320
the perfect spot at last, or so it struck me,
free of rocks, with a windbreak from the gales.
So, fighting for life, I flung myself ashore
and the godsent, bracing night came on at once.
Clambering up from the river, big with Zeus's rains,
I bedded down in the brush, my body heaped with leaves,
and a god poured down a boundless sleep upon me, yes,
and there in the leaves, exhausted, sick at heart,
I slept the whole night through
and on to the break of day and on into high noon   330
and the sun was wheeling down when sweet sleep set me free.
And I looked up, and there were your daughter's maids
at play on the beach, and she, she moved among them
like a deathless goddess! I begged her for help
and not once did her sense of tact desert her;
she behaved as you'd never hope to find
in one so young, not in a random meeting—
time and again the youngsters prove so flighty.
Not she. She gave me food aplenty and shining wine,

a bath in the river too, and gave me all this clothing.   340
That's my whole story. Wrenching to tell, but true."

    "Ah, but in one regard, my friend," the king replied,
"her good sense missed the mark, this daughter of mine.
She never escorted you to our house with all her maids
but she was the first you asked for care and shelter."

    "Your majesty," diplomatic Odysseus answered,
"don't find fault with a flawless daughter now,
not for my sake, please.
She urged me herself to follow with her maids.
I chose not to, fearing embarrassment in fact—   350
what if you took offense, seeing us both together?
Suspicious we are, we men who walk the earth."

    "Oh no, my friend," Alcinous stated flatly,
"I'm hardly a man for reckless, idle anger.
Balance is best in all things.
Father Zeus, Athena and lord Apollo! if only—
seeing the man you are, seeing we think as one—
you could wed my daughter and be my son-in-law
and stay right here with us. I'd give you a house
and great wealth—if you chose to stay, that is.   360
No Phaeacian would hold you back by force.
The curse of Father Zeus on such a thing!
And about your convoy home, you rest assured:
I have chosen the day and I decree it is tomorrow.
And all that voyage long you'll lie in a deep sleep
while my people sail you on through calm and gentle tides
till you reach your land and house, or any place you please.
True, even if landfall lies more distant than Euboea,
off at the edge of the world . . .
So say our crews, at least, who saw it once,   370
that time they carried the gold-haired Rhadamanthys
out to visit Tityus, son of Mother Earth. Imagine,
there they sailed and back they came in the same day,
they finished the homeward run with no strain at all.

You'll see for yourself how far they top the best—
my ships and their young shipmates
tossing up the whitecaps with their oars!"

So he vowed
and the long-enduring great Odysseus glowed with joy
and raised a prayer and called the god by name:
"Father Zeus on high—
may the king fulfill his promises one and all!   380
Then his fame would ring through the fertile earth
and never die—and I should reach my native land at last!"

    And now as the two men exchanged their hopes,
the white-armed queen instructed her palace maids
to make a bed in the porch's shelter, lay down
some heavy purple throws for the bed itself,
and over it spread some blankets, thick woolly robes,
a warm covering laid on top. Torches in hand,
they left the hall and fell to work at once,
briskly prepared a good snug resting-place   390
and then returned to Odysseus, urged the guest,
"Up, friend, time for sleep. Your bed is made."
How welcome the thought of sleep to that man now . . .
So there after many trials Odysseus lay at rest
on a corded bed inside the echoing colonnade.
Alcinous slept in chambers deep in his lofty house
where the queen his wife arranged and shared their bed.

BOOK EIGHT

A Day for Songs and Contests

When young Dawn with her rose-red fingers shone once more
royal Alcinous, hallowed island king, rose from bed
and great Odysseus, raider of cities, rose too.
Poised in his majesty, Alcinous led the way
to Phaeacia's meeting grounds, built for all
beside the harbored ships. Both men sat down
on the polished stone benches side-by-side
as Athena started roaming up and down the town,
in build and voice the wise Alcinous' herald,
furthering plans for Odysseus' journey home,   10
and stopped beside each citizen, urged them all,
"Come this way, you lords and captains of Phaeacia,
come to the meeting grounds and learn about the stranger!
A new arrival! Here at our wise king's palace now,
he's here from roving the ocean, driven far off course—

he looks like a deathless god!"
                           Rousing their zeal,
their curiosity, each and every man, and soon enough
the assembly seats were filled with people thronging,
gazing in wonder at the seasoned man of war . . .
Over Odysseus' head and shoulders now   20
Athena lavished a marvelous splendor, yes,
making him taller, more massive to all eyes,
so Phaeacians might regard the man with kindness,
awe and respect as well, and he might win through
the many trials they'd pose to test the hero's strength.
Once they'd grouped, crowding the meeting grounds,
Alcinous rose and addressed his island people:
"Hear me, lords and captains of Phaeacia,
hear what the heart inside me has to say.
This stranger here, our guest—   30
I don't know who he is, or whether he comes
from sunrise lands or the western lands of evening,
but he has come in his wanderings to my palace;
he pleads for passage, he begs we guarantee it.
So now, as in years gone by, let us press on
and grant him escort. No one, I tell you, no one
who comes to *my* house will languish long here,
heartsick for convoy home.
                       Come, my people!
Haul a black ship down to the bright sea,
rigged for her maiden voyage—   40
enlist a crew of fifty-two young sailors,
the best in town, who've proved their strength before.
Let all hands lash their oars to the thwarts then disembark,
come to my house and fall in for a banquet, quickly.
I'll lay on a princely feast for all. So then,
these are the orders I issue to our crews.
For the rest, you sceptered princes here,
you come to my royal halls so we can give
this stranger a hero's welcome in our palace—
no one here refuse. Call in the inspired bard   50
Demodocus. God has given the man the gift of song,

to him beyond all others, the power to please,
however the spirit stirs him on to sing."

   With those commands Alcinous led the way
and a file of sceptered princes took his lead
while the herald went to find the gifted bard.
And the fifty-two young sailors, duly chosen,
briskly following orders,
went down to the shore of the barren salt sea.
And once they reached the ship at the surf's edge,   60
first they hauled the craft into deeper water,
stepped the mast amidships, canvas brailed,
they made oars fast in the leather oarlock straps,
moored her riding high on the swell, then disembarked
and made their way to wise Alcinous' high-roofed halls.
There colonnades and courts and rooms were overflowing
with crowds, a mounting host of people young and old.
The king slaughtered a dozen sheep to feed his guests,
eight boars with shining tusks and a pair of shambling oxen.
These they skinned and dressed, and then laid out a feast   70
to fill the heart with savor.
                    In came the herald now,
leading along the faithful bard the Muse adored
above all others, true, but her gifts were mixed
with good and evil both: she stripped him of sight
but gave the man the power of stirring, rapturous song.
Pontonous brought the bard a silver-studded chair,
right amid the feasters, leaning it up against
a central column—hung his high clear lyre
on a peg above his head and showed him how
to reach up with his hands and lift it down.   80
And the herald placed a table by his side
with a basket full of bread and cup of wine
for him to sip when his spirit craved refreshment.
All reached out for the good things that lay at hand
and when they'd put aside desire for food and drink,
the Muse inspired the bard
to sing the famous deeds of fighting heroes—

the song whose fame had reached the skies those days:
The Strife Between Odysseus and Achilles, Peleus' Son . . .
how once at the gods' lavish feast the captains clashed   90
in a savage war of words, while Agamemnon, lord of armies,
rejoiced at heart that Achaea's bravest men were battling so.
For this was the victory sign that Apollo prophesied
at his shrine in Pytho when Agamemnon strode across
the rocky threshold, asking the oracle for advice—
the start of the tidal waves of ruin tumbling down
on Troy's and Achaea's forces, both at once,
thanks to the will of Zeus who rules the world.

    That was the song the famous harper sang
but Odysseus, clutching his flaring sea-blue cape   100
in both powerful hands, drew it over his head
and buried his handsome face,
ashamed his hosts might see him shedding tears.
Whenever the rapt bard would pause in the song,
he'd lift the cape from his head, wipe off his tears
and hoisting his double-handled cup, pour it out to the gods.
But soon as the bard would start again, impelled to sing
by Phaeacia's lords, who reveled in his tale,
again Odysseus hid his face and wept.
His weeping went unmarked by all the others;   110
only Alcinous, sitting close beside him,
noticed his guest's tears,
heard the groan in the man's labored breathing
and said at once to the master mariners around him,
"Hear me, my lords and captains of Phaeacia!
By now we've had our fill of food well-shared
and the lyre too, our loyal friend at banquets.
Now out we go again and test ourselves in contests,
games of every kind—so our guest can tell his friends,
when he reaches home, how far we excel the world   120
at boxing, wrestling, jumping, speed of foot."

    He forged ahead and the rest fell in behind.
The herald hung the ringing lyre back on its peg

and taking Demodocus by the hand, led him from the palace,
guiding him down the same path the island lords
had just pursued, keen to watch the contests.
They reached the meeting grounds
with throngs of people streaming in their trail
as a press of young champions rose for competition.
Topsail and Riptide rose, the helmsman Rowhard too   130
and Seaman and Sternman, Surf-at-the-Beach and Stroke-Oar,
Breaker and Bowsprit, Racing-the-Wind and Swing-Aboard
and Seagirt the son of Greatfleet, Shipwrightson
and the son of Launcher, Broadsea, rose up too,
a match for murderous Ares, death to men—
in looks and build the best of all Phaeacians
after gallant Laodamas, the Captain of the People.
Laodamas rose with two more sons of great Alcinous,
Halius bred to the sea and Clytoneus famed for ships.
And now the games began, the first event a footrace . . .   140
They toed the line—
                      and broke flat out from the start
with a fast pack flying down the field in a whirl of dust
and Clytoneus the prince outstripped them all by far,
flashing ahead the length two mules will plow a furrow
before he turned for home, leaving the pack behind
and raced to reach the crowds.
                              Next the wrestling,
grueling sport. They grappled, locked, and Broadsea,
pinning the strongest champions, won the bouts.
Next, in the jumping, Seagirt leapt and beat the field.
In the discus Rowhard up and outhurled them all by far.   150
And the king's good son Laodamas boxed them to their knees.
When all had enjoyed the games to their hearts' content
Alcinous' son Laodamas spurred them: "Come, my friends,
let's ask our guest if he knows the ropes of any sport.
He's no mean man, not with a build like that . . .
Look at his thighs, his legs, and what a pair of arms—
his massive neck, his big, rippling strength!
Nor is he past his prime,
just beaten down by one too many blows.

Nothing worse than the sea, I always say,   160
to crush a man, the strongest man alive."

    And Broadsea put in quickly,
"Well said, Laodamas, right to the point.
Go up to the fellow, challenge him yourself."

    On that cue, the noble prince strode up
before Odysseus, front and center, asking,
"Come, stranger, sir, won't you try your hand
at our contests now? If you have skill in any.
It's fit and proper for you to know your sports.
What greater glory attends a man, while he's alive,   170
than what he wins with his racing feet and striving hands?
Come and compete then, throw your cares to the wind!
It won't be long, your journey's not far off—
your ship's already hauled down to the sea,
your crew is set to sail."
                            "Laodamas,"
quick to the mark Odysseus countered sharply,
"why do you taunt me so with such a challenge?
Pains weigh on my spirit now, not your sports—
I've suffered much already, struggled hard.
But here I sit amid your assembly still,   180
starved for passage home, begging your king,
begging all your people."
                        "Oh I knew it!"
Broadsea broke in, mocking him to his face.
"I never took you for someone skilled in games,
the kind that real men play throughout the world.
Not a chance. You're some skipper of profiteers,
roving the high seas in his scudding craft,
reckoning up his freight with a keen eye out
for home-cargo, grabbing the gold he can!
You're no athlete. I see that."
                        With a dark glance   190
wily Odysseus shot back, "Indecent talk, my friend.

You, you're a reckless fool—I see *that*. So,
the gods don't hand out all their gifts at once,
not build and brains and flowing speech to all.
Oné man may fail to impress us with his looks
but a god can crown his words with beauty, charm,
and men look on with delight when he speaks out.
Never faltering, filled with winning self-control,
he shines forth at assembly grounds and people gaze
at him like a god when he walks through the streets.   200
Another man may look like a deathless one on high
but there's not a bit of grace to crown his words.
Just like you, my fine, handsome friend. Not even
a god could improve those lovely looks of yours
but the mind inside is worthless.
Your slander fans the anger in my heart!
I'm no stranger to sports—for all your taunts—
I've held my place in the front ranks, I tell you,
long as I could trust to my youth and striving hands.
But now I'm wrestled down by pain and hardship, look,   210
I've borne my share of struggles, cleaving my way
through wars of men and pounding waves at sea.
Nevertheless, despite so many blows,
I'll compete in your games, just watch. Your insults
cut to the quick—you rouse my fighting blood!"

　　Up he sprang, cloak and all, and seized a discus,
huge and heavy, more weighty by far than those
the Phaeacians used to hurl and test each other.
Wheeling round, he let loose with his great hand
and the stone whirred on—and down to ground they went,   220
those lords of the long oars and master mariners cringing
under the rock's onrush, soaring lightly out of his grip,
flying away past all the other marks, and Queen Athena,
built like a man, staked out the spot and cried
with a voice of triumph, "Even a blind man,
friend, could find your mark by groping round—
it's not mixed up in the crowd, it's far in front!

There's nothing to fear in *this* event—
no one can touch you, much less beat your distance!"

    At that the heart of the long-suffering hero laughed,   230
so glad to find a ready friend in the crowd that,
lighter in mood, he challenged all Phaeacia's best:
"Now go match *that,* you young pups, and straightaway
I'll hurl you another just as far, I swear, or even farther!
All the rest of you, anyone with the spine and spirit,
step right up and try me—you've incensed me so—
at boxing, wrestling, racing; nothing daunts me.
Any Phaeacian here except Laodamas himself.
The man's my host. Who would fight his friend?
He'd have to be good-for-nothing, senseless, yes,   240
to challenge his host and come to grips in games,
in a far-off land at that. He'd cut his own legs short.
But there are no others I'd deny or think beneath me—
I'll take on all contenders, gladly, test them head-to-head!
I'm no disgrace in the world of games where men compete.
Well I know how to handle a fine polished bow,
the first to hit my man in a mass of enemies,
even with rows of comrades pressing near me,
taking aim with our shafts to hit our targets.
Philoctetes alone outshot me there at Troy   250
when ranks of Achaean archers bent their bows.
Of the rest I'd say that I outclass them all—
men still alive, who eat their bread on earth.
But I'd never vie with the men of days gone by,
not Heracles, not Eurytus of Oechalia—archers
who rivaled immortal powers with their bows.
That's why noble Eurytus died a sudden death:
no old age, creeping upon him in his halls . . .
Apollo shot him down, enraged that the man
had challenged *him,* the Archer God.
                        As for spears,   260
I can fling a spear as far as the next man wings an arrow!
Only at sprinting I fear you'd leave me in the dust.
I've taken a shameful beating out on heavy seas,

no conditioning there on shipboard day by day.
My legs have lost their spring."

   He finished. All stood quiet, hushed.
Only Alcinous found a way to answer. "Stranger,
friend—nothing you say among us seems ungracious.
You simply want to display the gifts you're born with,
stung that a youngster marched up to you in the games,   270
mocking, ridiculing your prowess as no one would
who had some sense of fit and proper speech.
But come now, hear me out,
so you can tell our story to other lords
as you sit and feast in your own halls someday,
your own wife and your children by your side,
remembering there our island prowess here:
what skills great Zeus has given *us* as well,
down all the years from our fathers' days till now.
We're hardly world-class boxers or wrestlers, I admit,   280
but we can race like the wind, we're champion sailors too,
and always dear to our hearts, the feast, the lyre and dance
and changes of fresh clothes, our warm baths and beds.
So come—all you Phaeacian masters of the dance—
now dance away! So our guest can tell his friends,
when he reaches home, how far we excel the world
in sailing, nimble footwork, dance and song.
                       Go, someone,
quickly, fetch Demodocus now his ringing lyre.
It must be hanging somewhere in the palace."

   At the king's word the herald sprang to his feet   290
and ran to fetch the vibrant lyre from the house.
And stewards rose, nine in all, picked from the realm
to set the stage for contests: masters-at-arms who
leveled the dancing-floor to make a fine broad ring.
The herald returned and placed the ringing lyre now
in Demodocus' hands, and the bard moved toward the center,
flanked by boys in the flush of youth, skilled dancers
who stamped the ground with marvelous pulsing steps

as Odysseus gazed at their flying, flashing feet,
his heart aglow with wonder.
                                A rippling prelude—   300
now the bard struck up an irresistible song:
The Love of Ares and Aphrodite Crowned with Flowers . . .
how the two had first made love in Hephaestus' mansion,
all in secret. Ares had showered her with gifts
and showered Hephaestus' marriage bed with shame
but a messenger ran to tell the god of fire—
Helios, lord of the sun, who'd spied the couple
lost in each other's arms and making love.
Hephaestus, hearing the heart-wounding story,
bustled toward his forge, brooding on his revenge—   310
planted the huge anvil on its block and beat out chains,
not to be slipped or broken, all to pin the lovers on the spot.
This snare the Firegod forged, ablaze with his rage at War,
then limped to the room where the bed of love stood firm
and round the posts he poured the chains in a sweeping net
with streams of others flowing down from the roofbeam,
gossamer-fine as spider webs no man could see,
not even a blissful god—
the Smith had forged a masterwork of guile.
Once he'd spun that cunning trap around his bed   320
he feigned a trip to the well-built town of Lemnos,
dearest to him by far of all the towns on earth.
But the god of battle kept no blind man's watch.
As soon as he saw the Master Craftsman leave
he plied his golden reins and arrived at once
and entered the famous god of fire's mansion,
chafing with lust for Aphrodite crowned with flowers.
She'd just returned from her father's palace, mighty Zeus,
and now she sat in her rooms as Ares strode right in
and grasped her hand with a warm, seductive urging: 330
"Quick, my darling, come, let's go to bed
and lose ourselves in love! Your husband's away—
by now he must be off in the wilds of Lemnos,
consorting with his raucous Sintian friends."
                                                So he pressed

and her heart raced with joy to sleep with War
and off they went to bed and down they lay—
and down around them came those cunning chains
of the crafty god of fire, showering down now
till the couple could not move a limb or lift a finger—
then they knew at last: there was no way out, not now.   340
But now the glorious crippled Smith was drawing near . . .
he'd turned around, miles short of the Lemnos coast,
for the Sungod kept *his* watch and told Hephaestus all,
so back he rushed to his house, his heart consumed with anguish.
Halting there at the gates, seized with savage rage
he howled a terrible cry, imploring all the gods,
"Father Zeus, look here—
the rest of you happy gods who live forever—
here is a sight to make you laugh, revolt you too!
Just because I am crippled, Zeus's daughter Aphrodite   350
will always spurn me and love that devastating Ares,
just because of his striking looks and racer's legs
while I am a weakling, lame from birth, and who's to blame?
Both my parents—who else? If only they'd never bred me!
Just look at the two lovers . . . crawled inside my bed,
locked in each other's arms—the sight makes me burn!
But I doubt they'll want to lie that way much longer,
not a moment more—mad as they are for each other.
No, they'll soon tire of bedding down together,
but then my cunning chains will bind them fast   360
till our Father pays my bride-gifts back in full,
all I handed *him* for that shameless bitch his daughter,
irresistible beauty—all unbridled too!"
                              So Hephaestus wailed
as the gods came crowding up to his bronze-floored house.
Poseidon god of the earthquake came, and Hermes came,
the running god of luck, and the Archer, lord Apollo,
while modesty kept each goddess to her mansion.
The immortals, givers of all good things, stood at the gates,
and uncontrollable laughter burst from the happy gods
when they saw the god of fire's subtle, cunning work.   370
One would glance at his neighbor, laughing out,

"A bad day for adultery! Slow outstrips the Swift."

"Look how limping Hephaestus conquers War,
the quickest of all the gods who rule Olympus!"

　"The cripple wins by craft."
　　　　　　　　　　　　　"The adulterer,
he will pay the price!"
　　　　　　　　　　So the gods would banter
among themselves but lord Apollo goaded Hermes on:
"Tell me, Quicksilver, giver of all good things—
even with those unwieldy shackles wrapped around you,
how would you like to bed the golden Aphrodite?"   380

"Oh Apollo, if only!" the giant-killer cried.
"Archer, bind me down with triple those endless chains!
Let all you gods look on, and all you goddesses too—
how I'd love to bed that golden Aphrodite!"

A peal of laughter broke from the deathless ones
but not Poseidon, not a smile from him; he kept on
begging the famous Smith to loose the god of war,
pleading, his words flying, "Let him go!
I guarantee you Ares will pay the price,
whatever you ask, Hephaestus,   390
whatever's right in the eyes of all the gods."

But the famous crippled Smith appealed in turn,
"God of the earthquake, please don't urge this on me.
A pledge for a worthless man is a worthless pledge indeed.
What if he slips out of his chains—his debts as well?
How could I shackle *you* while all the gods look on?"

But the god of earthquakes reassured the Smith,
"Look, Hephaestus, if Ares scuttles off and away,
squirming out of his debt, I'll pay the fine myself."

And the famous crippled Smith complied at last: 400

"Now *there*'s an offer I really can't refuse!"

    With all his force the god of fire loosed the chains
and the two lovers, free of the bonds that overwhelmed them so,
sprang up and away at once, and the Wargod sped to Thrace
while Love with her telltale laughter sped to Paphos,
Cyprus Isle, where her grove and scented altar stand.
There the Graces bathed and anointed her with oil,
ambrosial oil, the bloom that clings to the gods
who never die, and swathed her round in gowns
to stop the heart . . . an ecstasy—a vision.   410

    That was the song the famous harper sang
and Odysseus relished every note as the islanders,
the lords of the long oars and master mariners rejoiced.

    Next the king asked Halius and Laodamas to dance,
the two alone, since none could match that pair.
So taking in hand a gleaming sea-blue ball
made by the craftsman Polybus—arching back,
one prince would hurl it toward the shadowy clouds
as the other leaping high into the air would catch it
quickly, nimbly, before his feet hit ground again.   420
Once they'd vied at throwing the ball straight up,
they tossed it back and forth in a blur of hands
as they danced across the earth that feeds us all,
while boys around the ring stamped out the beat
and a splendid rhythmic drumming sound arose
and good Odysseus looked at his host, exclaiming,
"King Alcinous, shining among your island people,
you boasted Phaeacia's dancers are the best—
they prove your point—I watch and I'm amazed!"

    His praises cheered the hallowed island king   430
who spoke at once to the master mariners around him:
"Hear me, my lords and captains of Phaeacia,
our guest is a man of real taste, I'd say. Come,
let's give him the parting gifts a guest deserves.

There are twelve peers of the realm who rule our land,
thirteen, counting myself. Let each of us contribute
a fresh cloak and shirt and a bar of precious gold.
Gather the gifts together, hurry, so our guest
can have them all in hand when he goes to dine,
his spirit filled with joy.   440
As for Broadsea, let him make amends,
man-to-man, with his words as well as gifts.
His first remarks were hardly fit to hear."

    All assented and gave their own commands,
each noble sent a page to fetch his gifts.
And Broadsea volunteered in turn, obliging:
"Great Alcinous, shining among our island people,
of course I'll make amends to our newfound friend
as you request. I'll give the man this sword.
It's solid bronze and the hilt has silver studs,   450
the sheath around it ivory freshly carved.
Here's a gift our guest will value highly."

    He placed the silver-studded sword in Odysseus' hands
with a burst of warm words: "Farewell, stranger, sir—
if any remark of mine gave you offense,
may stormwinds snatch it up and sweep it off!
May the gods grant *you* safe passage home to see your wife—
you've been so far from loved ones, suffered so!"

    Tactful Odysseus answered him in kind:
"And a warm farewell to you, too, my friend.   460
May the gods grant *you* good fortune—
may you never miss this sword, this gift you give
with such salutes. You've made amends in full."
                         With that
he slung the silver-studded sword across his shoulder.
As the sun sank, his glittering gifts arrived
and proud heralds bore them into the hall
where sons of King Alcinous took them over,
spread them out before their noble mother's feet—

a grand array of gifts. The king in all his majesty
led the rest of his peers inside, following in a file   470
and down they sat on rows of high-backed chairs.
The king turned to the queen and urged her, "Come,
my dear, bring in an elegant chest, the best you have,
and lay inside it a fresh cloak and shirt, your own gifts.
Then heat a bronze cauldron over the fire, boil water,
so once our guest has bathed and reviewed his gifts—
all neatly stacked for sailing,
gifts our Phaeacian lords have brought him now—
he'll feast in peace and hear the harper's songs.
And I will give him this gorgeous golden cup of mine,   480
so he'll remember Alcinous all his days to come
when he pours libations out in his own house
to Father Zeus and the other gods on high."

    And at that Arete told her serving-women,
"Set a great three-legged cauldron over the fire—
do it right away!"
                      And hoisting over the blaze
a cauldron, filling it brimful with bathing water,
they piled fresh logs beneath and lit them quickly.
The fire lapped at the vessel's belly, the water warmed.
Meanwhile the queen had a polished chest brought forth   490
from an inner room and laid the priceless gifts inside,
the clothes and gold the Phaeacian lords had brought,
and added her own gifts, a cloak and a fine shirt,
and gave her guest instructions quick and clear:
"Now look to the lid yourself and bind it fast
with a good tight knot, so no one can rob you
on your voyage—drifting into a sweet sleep
as the black ship sails you home."
                                    Hearing that,
the storm-tossed man secured the lid straightway,
he battened it fast with a swift, intricate knot   500
the lady Circe had taught him long ago.
And the housekeeper invited him at once
to climb into a waiting tub and bathe—

a hot, steaming bath . . .
what a welcome sight to Odysseus' eyes!
He'd been a stranger to comforts such as these
since he left the lovely-haired Calypso's house,
yet all those years he enjoyed such comforts there,
never-ending, as if he were a god . . . And now,
when maids had washed him, rubbed him down with oil   510
and drawn warm fleece and a shirt around his shoulders,
he stepped from the bath to join the nobles at their wine.
And there stood Nausicaa as he passed. Beside a column
that propped the sturdy roof she paused, endowed
by the gods with all her beauty, gazing at
Odysseus right before her eyes. Wonderstruck,
she hailed her guest with a winning flight of words:
"Farewell, my friend! And when you are at home,
home in your own land, remember me at times.
Mainly to me you owe the gift of life."   520

     Odysseus rose to the moment deftly, gently:
"Nausicaa, daughter of generous King Alcinous,
may Zeus the Thunderer, Hera's husband, grant it so—
that I travel home and see the dawn of my return.
Even at home I'll pray to you as a deathless goddess
all my days to come. You saved my life, dear girl."

     And he went and took his seat beside the king.
By now they were serving out the portions, mixing wine,
and the herald soon approached, leading the faithful bard
Demodocus, prized by all the people—seated him in a chair   530
amid the feasters, leaning it against a central column.
At once alert Odysseus carved a strip of loin,
rich and crisp with fat, from the white-tusked boar
that still had much meat left, and called the herald over:
"Here, herald, take this choice cut to Demodocus
so he can eat his fill—with warm regards
from a man who knows what suffering is . . .
From all who walk the earth our bards deserve

esteem and awe, for the Muse herself has taught them
paths of song. She loves the breed of harpers."   540

    The herald placed the gift in Demodocus' hands
and the famous blind bard received it, overjoyed.
They reached for the good things that lay outspread
and when they'd put aside desire for food and drink,
Odysseus, master of many exploits, praised the singer:
"I respect you, Demodocus, more than any man alive—
surely the Muse has taught you, Zeus's daughter,
or god Apollo himself. How true to life,
all too true . . . you sing the Achaeans' fate,
all they did and suffered, all they soldiered through,   550
as if you were there yourself or heard from one who was.
But come now, shift your ground. Sing of the wooden horse
Epeus built with Athena's help, the cunning trap that
good Odysseus brought one day to the heights of Troy,
filled with fighting men who laid the city waste.
Sing that for me—true to life as it deserves—
and I will tell the world at once how freely
the Muse gave _you_ the gods' own gift of song."

    Stirred now by the Muse, the bard launched out
in a fine blaze of song, starting at just the point   560
where the main Achaean force, setting their camps afire,
had boarded the oarswept ships and sailed for home
but famed Odysseus' men already crouched in hiding—
in the heart of Troy's assembly—dark in that horse
the Trojans dragged themselves to the city heights.
Now it stood there, looming . . .
and round its bulk the Trojans sat debating,
clashing, days on end. Three plans split their ranks:
either to hack open the hollow vault with ruthless bronze
or haul it up to the highest ridge and pitch it down the cliffs   570
or let it stand—a glorious offering made to pacify the gods—
and that, that final plan, was bound to win the day.
For Troy was fated to perish once the city lodged

inside her walls the monstrous wooden horse
where the prime of Argive power lay in wait
with death and slaughter bearing down on Troy.
And he sang how troops of Achaeans broke from cover,
streaming out of the horse's hollow flanks to plunder Troy—
he sang how left and right they ravaged the steep city,
sang how Odysseus marched right up to Deiphobus' house   580
like the god of war on attack with diehard Menelaus.
There, he sang, Odysseus fought the grimmest fight
he had ever braved but he won through at last,
thanks to Athena's superhuman power.

    That was the song the famous harper sang
but great Odysseus melted into tears,
running down from his eyes to wet his cheeks . . .
as a woman weeps, her arms flung round her darling husband,
a man who fell in battle, fighting for town and townsmen,
trying to beat the day of doom from home and children.   590
Seeing the man go down, dying, gasping for breath,
she clings for dear life, screams and shrills—
but the victors, just behind her,
digging spear-butts into her back and shoulders,
drag her off in bondage, yoked to hard labor, pain,
and the most heartbreaking torment wastes her cheeks.
So from Odysseus' eyes ran tears of heartbreak now.
But his weeping went unmarked by all the others;
only Alcinous, sitting close beside him,
noticed his guest's tears,   600
heard the groan in the man's labored breathing
and said at once to the master mariners around him,
"Hear me, my lords and captains of Phaeacia!
Let Demodocus rest his ringing lyre now—
this song he sings can hardly please us all.
Ever since our meal began and the stirring bard
launched his song, our guest has never paused
in his tears and throbbing sorrow.
Clearly grief has overpowered his heart.
Break off this song! Let us all enjoy ourselves,   610

the hosts and guest together. Much the warmer way.
All these things are performed for him, our honored guest,
the royal send-off here and gifts we give in love.
Treat your guest and suppliant like a brother:
anyone with a touch of sense knows that.
So don't be crafty now, my friend, don't hide
the truth I'm after. Fair is fair, speak out!
Come, tell us the name they call you there at home—
your mother, father, townsmen, neighbors round about.
Surely no man in the world is nameless, all told.   620
Born high, born low, as soon as he sees the light
his parents always name him, once he's born.
And tell me your land, your people, your city too,
so our ships can sail you home—their wits will speed them there.
For we have no steersmen here among Phaeacia's crews
or steering-oars that guide your common craft.
Our ships know in a flash their mates' intentions,
know all ports of call and all the rich green fields.
With wings of the wind they cross the sea's huge gulfs,
shrouded in mist and cloud—no fear in the world of foundering,   630
fatal shipwreck.
                    True, there's an old tale I heard
my father telling once. Nausithous used to say
that lord Poseidon was vexed with us because
we escorted all mankind and never came to grief.
He said that one day, as a well-built ship of ours
sailed home on the misty sea from such a convoy,
the god would crush it, yes,
and pile a huge mountain round about our port.
So the old king foretold . . . And as for the god, well,
he can do his worst or leave it quite undone,   640
whatever warms his heart.
                    But come, my friend,
tell us your own story now, and tell it truly.
Where have your rovings forced you?
What lands of men have you seen, what sturdy towns,
what men themselves? Who were wild, savage, lawless?
Who were friendly to strangers, god-fearing men? Tell me,

why do you weep and grieve so sorely when you hear
the fate of the Argives, hear the fall of Troy?
That is the gods' work, spinning threads of death
through the lives of mortal men,   650
and all to make a song for those to come . . .
Did one of your kinsmen die before the walls of Troy,
some brave man—a son by marriage? father by marriage?
Next to our own blood kin, our nearest, dearest ties.
Or a friend perhaps, someone close to your heart,
staunch and loyal? No less dear than a brother,
the brother-in-arms who shares our inmost thoughts."

BOOK NINE

In the One-Eyed
Giant's Cave

Odysseus, the great teller of tales, launched out on his story:
"Alcinous, majesty, shining among your island people,
what a fine thing it is to listen to such a bard
as we have here—the man sings like a god.
The crown of life, I'd say. There's nothing better
than when deep joy holds sway throughout the realm
and banqueters up and down the palace sit in ranks,
enthralled to hear the bard, and before them all, the tables
heaped with bread and meats, and drawing wine from a mixing-bowl
the steward makes his rounds and keeps the winecups flowing.   10
This, to my mind, is the best that life can offer.

                    But now
you're set on probing the bitter pains I've borne,
so I'm to weep and grieve, it seems, still more.
Well then, what shall I go through first,

what shall I save for last?
What pains—the gods have given me my share.
Now let me begin by telling you my name . . .
so you may know it well and I in times to come,
if I can escape the fatal day, will be your host,
your sworn friend, though my home is far from here.   20
I am Odysseus, son of Laertes, known to the world
for every kind of craft—my fame has reached the skies.
Sunny Ithaca is my home. Atop her stands our seamark,
Mount Neriton's leafy ridges shimmering in the wind.
Around her a ring of islands circle side-by-side,
Dulichion, Same, wooded Zacynthus too, but mine
lies low and away, the farthest out to sea,
rearing into the western dusk
while the others face the east and breaking day.
Mine is a rugged land but good for raising sons—   30
and I myself, I know no sweeter sight on earth
than a man's own native country.
                                        True enough,
Calypso the lustrous goddess tried to hold me back,
deep in her arching caverns, craving me for a husband.
So did Circe, holding me just as warmly in her halls,
the bewitching queen of Aeaea keen to have me too.
But they never won the heart inside me, never.
So nothing is as sweet as a man's own country,
his own parents, even though he's settled down
in some luxurious house, off in a foreign land   40
and far from those who bore him.
                                        No more. Come,
let me tell you about the voyage fraught with hardship
Zeus inflicted on me, homeward bound from Troy . . .

    The wind drove me out of Ilium on to Ismarus,
the Cicones' stronghold. There I sacked the city,
killed the men, but as for the wives and plunder,
that rich haul we dragged away from the place—
we shared it round so no one, not on my account,
would go deprived of his fair share of spoils.

Then I urged them to cut and run, set sail,   50
but would they listen? Not those mutinous fools;
there was too much wine to swill, too many sheep to slaughter
down along the beach, and shambling longhorn cattle.
And all the while the Cicones sought out other Cicones,
called for help from their neighbors living inland:
a larger force, and stronger soldiers too,
skilled hands at fighting men from chariots,
skilled, when a crisis broke, to fight on foot.
Out of the morning mist they came against us—
packed as the leaves and spears that flower forth in spring—   60
and Zeus presented us with disaster, me and my comrades
doomed to suffer blow on mortal blow. Lining up,
both armies battled it out against our swift ships,
both raked each other with hurtling bronze lances.
Long as morning rose and the blessed day grew stronger
we stood and fought them off, massed as they were, but then,
when the sun wheeled past the hour for unyoking oxen,
the Cicones broke our lines and beat us down at last.
Out of each ship, six men-at-arms were killed;
the rest of us rowed away from certain doom.   70

     From there we sailed on, glad to escape our death
yet sick at heart for the dear companions we had lost.
But I would not let our rolling ships set sail until the crews
had raised the triple cry, saluting each poor comrade
cut down by the fierce Cicones on that plain.
Now Zeus who masses the stormclouds hit the fleet
with the North Wind—
                        a howling, demonic gale, shrouding over
in thunderheads the earth and sea at once—
                                        and night swept down
from the sky and the ships went plunging headlong on,
our sails slashed to rags by the hurricane's blast!   80
We struck them—cringing at death we rowed our ships
to the nearest shoreline, pulled with all our power.
There, for two nights, two days, we lay by, no letup,
eating our hearts out, bent with pain and bone-tired.

When Dawn with her lovely locks brought on the third day,
then stepping the masts and hoisting white sails high,
we lounged at the oarlocks, letting wind and helmsmen
keep us true on course . . .
                          And now, at long last,
I might have reached my native land unscathed,
but just as I doubled Malea's cape, a tide-rip
and the North Wind drove me way off course   90
careering past Cythera.
                         Nine whole days
I was borne along by rough, deadly winds
on the fish-infested sea. Then on the tenth
our squadron reached the land of the Lotus-eaters,
people who eat the lotus, mellow fruit and flower.
We disembarked on the coast, drew water there
and crewmen snatched a meal by the swift ships.
Once we'd had our fill of food and drink I sent
a detail ahead, two picked men and a third, a runner,   100
to scout out who might live there—men like us perhaps,
who live on bread? So off they went and soon enough
they mingled among the natives, Lotus-eaters, Lotus-eaters
who had no notion of killing my companions, not at all,
they simply gave them the lotus to taste instead . . .
Any crewmen who ate the lotus, the honey-sweet fruit,
lost all desire to send a message back, much less return,
their only wish to linger there with the Lotus-eaters,
grazing on lotus, all memory of the journey home
dissolved forever. But *I* brought them back, back   110
to the hollow ships, and streaming tears—I forced them,
hauled them under the rowing benches, lashed them fast
and shouted out commands to my other, steady comrades:
'Quick, no time to lose, embark in the racing ships!'—
so none could eat the lotus, forget the voyage home.
They swung aboard at once, they sat to the oars in ranks
and in rhythm churned the water white with stroke on stroke.

    From there we sailed on, our spirits now at a low ebb,
and reached the land of the high and mighty Cyclops,

lawless brutes, who trust so to the everlasting gods   120
they never plant with their own hands or plow the soil.
Unsown, unplowed, the earth teems with all they need,
wheat, barley and vines, swelled by the rains of Zeus
to yield a big full-bodied wine from clustered grapes.
They have no meeting place for council, no laws either,
no, up on the mountain peaks they live in arching caverns—
each a law to himself, ruling his wives and children,
not a care in the world for any neighbor.
                                        Now,
a level island stretches flat across the harbor,
not close inshore to the Cyclops' coast, not too far out,   130
thick with woods where the wild goats breed by hundreds.
No trampling of men to start them from their lairs,
no hunters roughing it out on the woody ridges,
stalking quarry, ever raid their haven.
No flocks browse, no plowlands roll with wheat;
unplowed, unsown forever—empty of humankind—
the island just feeds droves of bleating goats.
For the Cyclops have no ships with crimson prows,
no shipwrights there to build them good trim craft
that could sail them out to foreign ports of call   140
as most men risk the seas to trade with other men.
Such artisans would have made this island too
a decent place to live in . . . No mean spot,
it could bear you any crop you like in season.
The water-meadows along the low foaming shore
run soft and moist, and your vines would never flag.
The land's clear for plowing. Harvest on harvest,
a man could reap a healthy stand of grain—
the subsoil's dark and rich.
There's a snug deep-water harbor there, what's more,   150
no need for mooring-gear, no anchor-stones to heave,
no cables to make fast. Just beach your keels, ride out
the days till your shipmates' spirit stirs for open sea
and a fair wind blows. And last, at the harbor's head
there's a spring that rushes fresh from beneath a cave
and black poplars flourish round its mouth.

                                                    Well,
here we landed, and surely a god steered us in
through the pitch-black night.
Not that he ever showed himself, with thick fog
swirling around the ships, the moon wrapped in clouds   160
and not a glimmer stealing through that gloom.
Not one of us glimpsed the island—scanning hard—
or the long combers rolling us slowly toward the coast,
not till our ships had run their keels ashore.
Beaching our vessels smoothly, striking sail,
the crews swung out on the low shelving sand
and there we fell asleep, awaiting Dawn's first light.

     When young Dawn with her rose-red fingers shone once more
we all turned out, intrigued to tour the island.
The local nymphs, the daughters of Zeus himself,   170
flushed mountain-goats so the crews could make their meal.
Quickly we fetched our curved bows and hunting spears
from the ships and, splitting up into three bands,
we started shooting, and soon enough some god
had sent us bags of game to warm our hearts.
A dozen vessels sailed in my command
and to each crew nine goats were shared out
and mine alone took ten. Then all day long
till the sun went down we sat and feasted well
on sides of meat and rounds of heady wine.   180
The good red stock in our vessels' holds
had not run out, there was still plenty left;
the men had carried off a generous store in jars
when we stormed and sacked the Cicones' holy city.
Now we stared across at the Cyclops' shore, so near
we could even see their smoke, hear their voices,
their bleating sheep and goats . . .
And then when the sun had set and night came on
we lay down and slept at the water's shelving edge.
When young Dawn with her rose-red fingers shone once more   190
I called a muster briskly, commanding all the hands,
'The rest of you stay here, my friends-in-arms.

I'll go across with my own ship and crew
and probe the natives living over there.
What *are* they—violent, savage, lawless?
or friendly to strangers, god-fearing men?'

    With that I boarded ship and told the crew
to embark at once and cast off cables quickly.
They swung aboard, they sat to the oars in ranks
and in rhythm churned the water white with stroke on stroke.   200
But as soon as we reached the coast I mentioned—no long trip—
we spied a cavern just at the shore, gaping above the surf,
towering, overgrown with laurel. And here big flocks,
sheep and goats, were stalled to spend the nights,
and around its mouth a yard was walled up
with quarried boulders sunk deep in the earth
and enormous pines and oak-trees looming darkly . . .
Here was a giant's lair, in fact, who always pastured
his sheepflocks far afield and never mixed with others.
A grim loner, dead set in his own lawless ways.   210
Here was a piece of work, by god, a monster
built like no mortal who ever supped on bread,
no, like a shaggy peak, I'd say—a man-mountain
rearing head and shoulders over the world.

                                        Now then,
I told most of my good trusty crew to wait,
to sit tight by the ship and guard her well
while I picked out my dozen finest fighters
and off I went. But I took a skin of wine along,
the ruddy, irresistible wine that Maron gave me once,
Euanthes' son, a priest of Apollo, lord of Ismarus,   220
because we'd rescued him, his wife and children,
reverent as we were;
he lived, you see, in Apollo's holy grove.
And so in return he gave me splendid gifts,
he handed me seven bars of well-wrought gold,
a mixing-bowl of solid silver, then this wine . . .
He drew it off in generous wine-jars, twelve in all,
all unmixed—and such a bouquet, a drink fit for the gods!

No maid or man of his household knew that secret store,
only himself, his loving wife and a single servant.   230
Whenever they'd drink the deep-red mellow vintage,
twenty cups of water he'd stir in one of wine
and what an aroma wafted from the bowl—
what magic, what a godsend—
no joy in holding back when *that* was poured!
Filling a great goatskin now, I took this wine,
provisions too in a leather sack. A sudden foreboding
told my fighting spirit I'd soon come up against
some giant clad in power like armor-plate—
a savage deaf to justice, blind to law.   240

   Our party quickly made its way to his cave
but we failed to find our host himself inside;
he was off in his pasture, ranging his sleek flocks.
So we explored his den, gazing wide-eyed at it all,
the large flat racks loaded with drying cheeses,
the folds crowded with young lambs and kids,
split into three groups—here the spring-born,
here mid-yearlings, here the fresh sucklings
off to the side—each sort was penned apart.
And all his vessels, pails and hammered buckets   250
he used for milking, were brimming full with whey.
From the start my comrades pressed me, pleading hard,
'Let's make away with the cheeses, then come back—
hurry, drive the lambs and kids from the pens
to our swift ship, put out to sea at once!'
But I would not give way—
and how much better it would have been—
not till I saw him, saw what gifts he'd give.
But he proved no lovely sight to my companions.

   There we built a fire, set our hands on the cheeses,   260
offered some to the gods and ate the bulk ourselves
and settled down inside, awaiting his return . . .
And back he came from pasture, late in the day,
herding his flocks home, and lugging a huge load

of good dry logs to fuel his fire at supper.
He flung them down in the cave—a jolting crash—
we scuttled in panic into the deepest dark recess.
And next he drove his sleek flocks into the open vault,
all he'd milk at least, but he left the males outside,
rams and billy goats out in the high-walled yard.   270
Then to close his door he hoisted overhead
a tremendous, massive slab—
no twenty-two wagons, rugged and four-wheeled,
could budge that boulder off the ground, I tell you,
such an immense stone the monster wedged to block his cave!
Then down he squatted to milk his sheep and bleating goats,
each in order, and put a suckling underneath each dam.
And half of the fresh white milk he curdled quickly,
set it aside in wicker racks to press for cheese,
the other half let stand in pails and buckets,   280
ready at hand to wash his supper down.
As soon as he'd briskly finished all his chores
he lit his fire and spied us in the blaze and
'Strangers!' he thundered out, 'now who are you?
Where did you sail from, over the running sea-lanes?
Out on a trading spree or roving the waves like pirates,
sea-wolves raiding at will, who risk their lives
to plunder other men?'
                              The hearts inside us shook,
terrified by his rumbling voice and monstrous hulk.
Nevertheless I found the nerve to answer, firmly,   290
'Men of Achaea we are and bound now from Troy!
Driven far off course by the warring winds,
over the vast gulf of the sea—battling home
on a strange tack, a route that's off the map,
and so we've come to you . . .
so it must please King Zeus's plotting heart.
We're glad to say we're men of Atrides Agamemnon,
whose fame is the proudest thing on earth these days,
so great a city he sacked, such multitudes he killed!
But since we've chanced on you, we're at your knees   300
in hopes of a warm welcome, even a guest-gift,

the sort that hosts give strangers. That's the custom.
Respect the gods, my friend. We're suppliants—at your mercy!
Zeus of the Strangers guards all guests and suppliants:
strangers are sacred—Zeus will avenge their rights!'

'Stranger,' he grumbled back from his brutal heart,
'you must be a fool, stranger, or come from nowhere,
telling *me* to fear the gods or avoid their wrath!
We Cyclops never blink at Zeus and Zeus's shield
of storm and thunder, or any other blessed god—   310
we've got more force by far.
I'd never spare you in fear of Zeus's hatred,
you or your comrades here, unless I had the urge.
But tell me, where did you moor your sturdy ship
when you arrived? Up the coast or close in?
I'd just like to know.'
                           So he laid his trap
but he never caught me, no, wise to the world
I shot back in my crafty way, 'My ship?
Poseidon god of the earthquake smashed my ship,
he drove it against the rocks at your island's far cape,   320
he dashed it against a cliff as the winds rode us in.
I and the men you see escaped a sudden death.'

Not a word in reply to that, the ruthless brute.
Lurching up, he lunged out with his hands toward my men
and snatching two at once, rapping them on the ground
he knocked them dead like pups—
their brains gushed out all over, soaked the floor—
and ripping them limb from limb to fix his meal
he bolted them down like a mountain-lion, left no scrap,
devoured entrails, flesh and bones, marrow and all!   330
We flung our arms to Zeus, we wept and cried aloud,
looking on at his grisly work—paralyzed, appalled.
But once the Cyclops had stuffed his enormous gut
with human flesh, washing it down with raw milk,
he slept in his cave, stretched out along his flocks.
And I with my fighting heart, I thought at first

to steal up to him, draw the sharp sword at my hip
and stab his chest where the midriff packs the liver—
I groped for the fatal spot but a fresh thought held me back.
There at a stroke we'd finish off ourselves as well—   340
how could *we* with our bare hands heave back
that slab he set to block his cavern's gaping maw?
So we lay there groaning, waiting Dawn's first light.

    When young Dawn with her rose-red fingers shone once more
the monster relit his fire and milked his handsome ewes,
each in order, putting a suckling underneath each dam,
and as soon as he'd briskly finished all his chores
he snatched up two more men and fixed his meal.
Well-fed, he drove his fat sheep from the cave,
lightly lifting the huge doorslab up and away,   350
then slipped it back in place
as a hunter flips the lid of his quiver shut.
Piercing whistles—turning his flocks to the hills
he left me there, the heart inside me brooding on revenge:
how could I pay him back? would Athena give me glory?
Here was the plan that struck my mind as best . . .
the Cyclops' great club: there it lay by the pens,
olivewood, full of sap. He'd lopped it off to brandish
once it dried. Looking it over, we judged it big enough
to be the mast of a pitch-black ship with her twenty oars,   360
a freighter broad in the beam that plows through miles of sea—
so long, so thick it bulked before our eyes. Well,
flanking it now, I chopped off a fathom's length,
rolled it to comrades, told them to plane it down,
and they made the club smooth as I bent and shaved
the tip to a stabbing point. I turned it over
the blazing fire to char it good and hard,
then hid it well, buried deep under the dung
that littered the cavern's floor in thick wet clumps.
And now I ordered my shipmates all to cast lots—   370
who'd brave it out with me
to hoist our stake and grind it into his eye
when sleep had overcome him? Luck of the draw:

I got the very ones I would have picked myself,
four good men, and I in the lead made five . . .

   Nightfall brought him back, herding his woolly sheep
and he quickly drove the sleek flock into the vaulted cavern,
rams and all—none left outside in the walled yard—
his own idea, perhaps, or a god led him on.
Then he hoisted the huge slab to block the door   380
and squatted to milk his sheep and bleating goats,
each in order, putting a suckling underneath each dam,
and as soon as he'd briskly finished all his chores
he snatched up two more men and fixed his meal.
But this time I lifted a carved wooden bowl,
brimful of my ruddy wine,
and went right up to the Cyclops, enticing,
'Here, Cyclops, try this wine—to top off
the banquet of human flesh you've bolted down!
Judge for yourself what stock our ship had stored.   390
I brought it here to make you a fine libation,
hoping you would pity me, Cyclops, send me home,
but your rages are insufferable. You barbarian—
how can any man on earth come visit you after *this?*
What you've done outrages all that's right!'

   At that he seized the bowl and tossed it off
and the heady wine pleased him immensely—'More'—
he demanded a second bowl—'a hearty helping!
And tell me your name now, quickly,
so I can hand my guest a gift to warm *his* heart.   400
Our soil yields the Cyclops powerful, full-bodied wine
and the rains from Zeus build its strength. But this,
this is nectar, ambrosia—this flows from heaven!'

   So he declared. I poured him another fiery bowl—
three bowls I brimmed and three he drank to the last drop,
the fool, and then, when the wine was swirling round his brain,
I approached my host with a cordial, winning word:
'So, you ask me the name I'm known by, Cyclops?

I will tell you. But you must give me a guest-gift
as you've promised. Nobody—that's my name. Nobody—   410
so my mother and father call me, all my friends.'

    But he boomed back at me from his ruthless heart,
'*Nobody?* I'll eat Nobody last of all his friends—
I'll eat the others first! That's my gift to *you!*'
                                        With that
he toppled over, sprawled full-length, flat on his back
and lay there, his massive neck slumping to one side,
and sleep that conquers all overwhelmed him now
as wine came spurting, flooding up from his gullet
with chunks of human flesh—he vomited, blind drunk.
Now, at last, I thrust our stake in a bed of embers   420
to get it red-hot and rallied all my comrades:
'Courage—no panic, no one hang back now!'
And green as it was, just as the olive stake
was about to catch fire—the glow terrific, yes—
I dragged it from the flames, my men clustering round
as some god breathed enormous courage through us all.
Hoisting high that olive stake with its stabbing point,
straight into the monster's eye they rammed it hard—
I drove my weight on it from above and bored it home
as a shipwright bores his beam with a shipwright's drill   430
that men below, whipping the strap back and forth, whirl
and the drill keeps twisting faster, never stopping—
So we seized our stake with its fiery tip
and bored it round and round in the giant's eye
till blood came boiling up around that smoking shaft
and the hot blast singed his brow and eyelids round the core
and the broiling eyeball burst—
                            its crackling roots blazed
and hissed—
            as a blacksmith plunges a glowing ax or adze
in an ice-cold bath and the metal screeches steam
and its temper hardens—that's the iron's strength—   440
so the eye of the Cyclops sizzled round that stake!
He loosed a hideous roar, the rock walls echoed round

and we scuttled back in terror. The monster wrenched the spike
from his eye and out it came with a red geyser of blood—
he flung it aside with frantic hands, and mad with pain
he bellowed out for help from his neighbor Cyclops
living round about in caves on windswept crags.
Hearing his cries, they lumbered up from every side
and hulking round his cavern, asked what ailed him:
'What, Polyphemus, what in the world's the trouble?   450
Roaring out in the godsent night to rob us of our sleep.
Surely no one's rustling your flocks against your will—
surely no one's trying to kill you now by fraud or force!'

    '*Nobody*, friends'—Polyphemus bellowed back from his cave—
'Nobody's killing me now by fraud and not by force!'

    'If you're alone,' his friends boomed back at once,
'and nobody's trying to overpower you now—look,
it must be a plague sent here by mighty Zeus
and there's no escape from *that*.
You'd better pray to your father, Lord Poseidon.'   460

    They lumbered off, but laughter filled my heart
to think how nobody's name—my great cunning stroke—
had duped them one and all. But the Cyclops there,
still groaning, racked with agony, groped around
for the huge slab, and heaving it from the doorway,
down he sat in the cave's mouth, his arms spread wide,
hoping to catch a comrade stealing out with sheep—
such a blithering fool he took me for!
But I was already plotting . . .
what was the best way out? how could I find   470
escape from death for my crew, myself as well?
My wits kept weaving, weaving cunning schemes—
life at stake, monstrous death staring us in the face—
till this plan struck my mind as best. That flock,
those well-fed rams with their splendid thick fleece,
sturdy, handsome beasts sporting their dark weight of wool:

I lashed them abreast, quietly, twisting the willow-twigs
the Cyclops slept on—giant, lawless brute—I took them
three by three; each ram in the middle bore a man
while the two rams either side would shield him well.   490
So three beasts to bear each man, but as for myself?
There was one bellwether ram, the prize of all the flock,
and clutching him by his back, tucked up under
his shaggy belly, there I hung, face upward,
both hands locked in his marvelous deep fleece,
clinging for dear life, my spirit steeled, enduring . . .
So we held on, desperate, waiting Dawn's first light.

                                                        As soon
as young Dawn with her rose-red fingers shone once more
the rams went rumbling out of the cave toward pasture,
the ewes kept bleating round the pens, unmilked,   490
their udders about to burst. Their master now,
heaving in torment, felt the back of each animal
halting before him here, but the idiot never sensed
my men were trussed up under their thick fleecy ribs.
And last of them all came my great ram now, striding out,
weighed down with his dense wool and my deep plots.
Stroking him gently, powerful Polyphemus murmured,
'Dear old ram, why last of the flock to quit the cave?
In the good old days you'd never lag behind the rest—
you with your long marching strides, first by far   500
of the flock to graze the fresh young grasses,
first by far to reach the rippling streams,
first to turn back home, keen for your fold
when night comes on—but now you're last of all.
And why? Sick at heart for your master's eye
that coward gouged out with his wicked crew?—
only after he'd stunned my wits with wine—
that, that Nobody . . .
who's not escaped his death, I swear, not yet.
Oh if only you thought like *me*, had words like *me*   510
to tell me where that scoundrel is cringing from my rage!
I'd smash him against the ground, I'd spill his brains—

flooding across my cave—and that would ease my heart
of the pains that good-for-nothing Nobody made me suffer!'

And with that threat he let my ram go free outside.
But soon as we'd got one foot past cave and courtyard,
first I loosed myself from the ram, then loosed my men,
then quickly, glancing back again and again we drove
our flock, good plump beasts with their long shanks,
straight to the ship, and a welcome sight we were   520
to loyal comrades—we who'd escaped our deaths—
but for all the rest they broke down and wailed.
I cut it short, I stopped each shipmate's cries,
my head tossing, brows frowning, silent signals
to hurry, tumble our fleecy herd on board,
launch out on the open sea!
They swung aboard, they sat to the oars in ranks
and in rhythm churned the water white with stroke on stroke.
But once offshore as far as a man's shout can carry,
I called back to the Cyclops, stinging taunts: 530
'So, Cyclops, no weak coward it was whose crew
you bent to devour there in your vaulted cave—
you with your brute force! Your filthy crimes
came down on your own head, you shameless cannibal,
daring to eat your guests in your own house—
so Zeus and the other gods have paid you back!'

That made the rage of the monster boil over.
Ripping off the peak of a towering crag, he heaved it
so hard the boulder landed just in front of our dark prow
and a huge swell reared up as the rock went plunging under—   540
a tidal wave from the open sea. The sudden backwash
drove us landward again, forcing us close inshore
but grabbing a long pole, I thrust us off and away,
tossing my head for dear life, signaling crews
to put their backs in the oars, escape grim death.
They threw themselves in the labor, rowed on fast
but once we'd plowed the breakers twice as far,
again I began to taunt the Cyclops—men around me

trying to check me, calm me, left and right:
'So headstrong—why? Why rile the beast again?'   550

    'That rock he flung in the sea just now, hurling our ship
to shore once more—we thought we'd die on the spot!'

    'If he'd caught a sound from one of us, just a moan,
he would have crushed our heads and ship timbers
with one heave of another flashing, jagged rock!'

    'Good god, the brute can throw!'
                          So they begged
but they could not bring my fighting spirit round.
I called back with another burst of anger, 'Cyclops—
if any man on the face of the earth should ask you
who blinded you, shamed you so—say Odysseus,   560
raider of cities, *he* gouged out your eye,
Laertes' son who makes his home in Ithaca!'

    So I vaunted and he groaned back in answer,
'Oh no, no—that prophecy years ago . . .
it all comes home to me with a vengeance now!
We once had a prophet here, a great tall man,
Telemus, Eurymus' son, a master at reading signs,
who grew old in his trade among his fellow-Cyclops.
All this, he warned me, would come to pass someday—
that I'd be blinded here at the hands of one Odysseus.   570
But I always looked for a handsome giant man to cross my path,
some fighter clad in power like armor-plate, but now,
look what a dwarf, a spineless good-for-nothing,
stuns me with wine, then gouges out my eye!
Come here, Odysseus, let me give you a guest-gift
and urge Poseidon the earthquake god to speed you home.
I am his son and he claims to be my father, true,
and he himself will heal me if he pleases—
no other blessed god, no man can do the work!'
                              'Heal you!'—
here was my parting shot—'Would to god I could strip you   580

of life and breath and ship you down to the House of Death
as surely as no one will ever heal your eye,
not even your earthquake god himself!'

    But at that he bellowed out to lord Poseidon,
thrusting his arms to the starry skies, and prayed, 'Hear me—
Poseidon, god of the sea-blue mane who rocks the earth!
If I really am your son and you claim to be my father—
come, grant that Odysseus, raider of cities,
Laertes' son who makes his home in Ithaca,
never reaches home. Or if he's fated to see   590
his people once again and reach his well-built house
and his own native country, let him come home late
and come a broken man—all shipmates lost,
alone in a stranger's ship—
and let him find a world of pain at home!'
                                        So he prayed
and the god of the sea-blue mane, Poseidon, heard his prayer.
The monster suddenly hoisted a boulder—far larger—
wheeled and heaved it, putting his weight behind it,
massive strength, and the boulder crashed close,
landing just in the wake of our dark stern,   600
just failing to graze the rudder's bladed edge.
A huge swell reared up as the rock went plunging under,
yes, and the tidal breaker drove us out to our island's
far shore where all my well-decked ships lay moored,
clustered, waiting, and huddled round them, crewmen
sat in anguish, waiting, chafing for our return.
We beached our vessel hard ashore on the sand,
we swung out in the frothing surf ourselves,
and herding Cyclops' sheep from our deep holds
we shared them round so no one, not on my account,   610
would go deprived of his fair share of spoils.
But the splendid ram—as we meted out the flocks
my friends-in-arms made him my prize of honor,
mine alone, and I slaughtered him on the beach
and burnt his thighs to Cronus' mighty son,
Zeus of the thundercloud who rules the world.

But my sacrifices failed to move the god:
Zeus was still obsessed with plans to destroy
my entire oarswept fleet and loyal crew of comrades.
Now all day long till the sun went down we sat   620
and feasted on sides of meat and heady wine.
Then when the sun had set and night came on
we lay down and slept at the water's shelving edge.
When young Dawn with her rose-red fingers shone once more
I roused the men straightway, ordering all crews
to man the ships and cast off cables quickly.
They swung aboard at once, they sat to the oars in ranks
and in rhythm churned the water white with stroke on stroke.
And from there we sailed on, glad to escape our death
yet sick at heart for the comrades we had lost."   630

BOOK TEN

The Bewitching
Queen of Aeaea

"We reached the Aeolian island next, the home of Aeolus,
Hippotas' son, beloved by the gods who never die—
a great floating island it was, and round it all
huge ramparts rise of indestructible bronze
and sheer rock cliffs shoot up from sea to sky.
The king had sired twelve children within his halls,
six daughters and six sons in the lusty prime of youth,
so he gave his daughters as wives to his six sons.
Seated beside their dear father and doting mother,
with delicacies aplenty spread before them,   10
they feast on forever . . . All day long
the halls breathe the savor of roasted meats
and echo round to the low moan of blowing pipes,
and all night long, each one by his faithful mate,
they sleep under soft-piled rugs on corded bedsteads.

To this city of theirs we came, their splendid palace,
and Aeolus hosted me one entire month, he pressed me for news
of Troy and the Argive ships and how we sailed for home,
and I told him the whole long story, first to last.
And then, when I begged him to send me on my way,   20
he denied me nothing, he went about my passage.
He gave me a sack, the skin of a full-grown ox,
binding inside the winds that howl from every quarter,
for Zeus had made that king the master of all the winds,
with power to calm them down or rouse them as he pleased.
Aeolus stowed the sack inside my holds, lashed so fast
with a burnished silver cord
not even a slight puff could slip past that knot.
Yet he set the West Wind free to blow us on our way
and waft our squadron home. But his plan was bound to fail,   30
yes, our own reckless folly swept us on to ruin . . .

    Nine whole days we sailed, nine nights, nonstop.
On the tenth our own land hove into sight at last—
we were so close we could see men tending fires.
But now an enticing sleep came on me, bone-weary
from working the vessel's sheet myself, no letup,
never trusting the ropes to any other mate,
the faster to journey back to native land.
But the crews began to mutter among themselves,
sure I was hauling troves of gold and silver home,   40
the gifts of open-hearted Aeolus, Hippotas' son.
'The old story!' One man glanced at another, grumbling.
'Look at our captain's luck—so loved by the world,
so prized at every landfall, every port of call.'

    'Heaps of lovely plunder he hauls home from Troy,
while we who went through slogging just as hard,
we go home empty-handed.'
                            'Now this Aeolus loads him
down with treasure. Favoritism, friend to friend!'

    'Hurry, let's see what loot is in that sack,

how much gold and silver. Break it open—now!'   50

   A fatal plan, but it won my shipmates over.
They loosed the sack and all the winds burst out
and a sudden squall struck and swept us back to sea,
wailing, in tears, far from our own native land.
And I woke up with a start, my spirit churning—
should I leap over the side and drown at once or
grit my teeth and bear it, stay among the living?
I bore it all, held firm, hiding my face,
clinging tight to the decks
while heavy squalls blasted our squadron back   60
again to Aeolus' island, shipmates groaning hard.

   We disembarked on the coast, drew water there
and crewmen snatched a meal by the swift ships.
Once we'd had our fill of food and drink
I took a shipmate along with me, a herald too,
and approached King Aeolus' famous halls and here
we found him feasting beside his wife and many children.
Reaching the doorposts at the threshold, down we sat
but our hosts, amazed to see us, only shouted questions:
'Back again, Odysseus—why? Some blustering god attacked you?   70
Surely we launched you well, we sped you on your way
to your own land and house, or any place you pleased.'

   So they taunted, and I replied in deep despair,
'A mutinous crew undid me—that and a cruel sleep.
Set it to rights, my friends. You have the power!'

   So I pleaded—gentle, humble appeals—
but our hosts turned silent, hushed . . .
and the father broke forth with an ultimatum:
'Away from my island—fast—most cursed man alive!
It's a crime to host a man or speed him on his way   80
when the blessed deathless gods despise him so.
Crawling back like this—

it proves the immortals hate you! Out—get out!'

Groan as I did, his curses drove me from his halls
and from there we pulled away with heavy hearts,
with the crews' spirit broken under the oars' labor,
thanks to our own folly . . . no favoring wind in sight.

Six whole days we rowed, six nights, nonstop.
On the seventh day we raised the Laestrygonian land,
Telepylus heights where the craggy fort of Lamus rises.   90
Where shepherd calls to shepherd as one drives in his flocks
and the other drives his out and he calls back in answer,
where a man who never sleeps could rake in double wages,
one for herding cattle, one for pasturing fleecy sheep,
the nightfall and the sunrise march so close together.
We entered a fine harbor there, all walled around
by a great unbroken sweep of sky-scraping cliff
and two steep headlands, fronting each other, close
around the mouth so the passage in is cramped.
Here the rest of my rolling squadron steered,   100
right into the gaping cove and moored tightly,
prow by prow. Never a swell there, big or small;
a milk-white calm spreads all around the place.
But I alone anchored my black ship outside,
well clear of the harbor's jaws
I tied her fast to a cliffside with a cable.
I scaled its rock face to a lookout on its crest
but glimpsed no trace of the work of man or beast from there;
all I spied was a plume of smoke, drifting off the land.
So I sent some crew ahead to learn who lived there—   110
men like us perhaps, who live on bread?
Two good mates I chose and a third to run the news.
They disembarked and set out on a beaten trail
the wagons used for hauling timber down to town
from the mountain heights above . . .
and before the walls they met a girl, drawing water,
Antiphates' strapping daughter—king of the Laestrygonians.

She'd come down to a clear running spring, Artacia,
where the local people came to fill their pails.
My shipmates clustered round her, asking questions: 120
who was king of the realm? who ruled the natives here?
She waved at once to her father's high-roofed halls.
They entered the sumptuous palace, found his wife inside—
a woman huge as a mountain crag who filled them all with horror.
Straightaway she summoned royal Antiphates from assembly,
her husband, who prepared my crew a barbarous welcome.
Snatching one of my men, he tore him up for dinner—
the other two sprang free and reached the ships.
But the king let loose a howling through the town
that brought tremendous Laestrygonians swarming up   130
from every side—hundreds, not like men, like Giants!
Down from the cliffs they flung great rocks a man could hardly hoist
and a ghastly shattering din rose up from all the ships—
men in their death-cries, hulls smashed to splinters—
They speared the crews like fish
and whisked them home to make their grisly meal.
But while they killed them off in the harbor depths
I pulled the sword from beside my hip and hacked away
at the ropes that moored my blue-prowed ship of war
and shouted rapid orders at my shipmates: 140
'Put your backs in the oars—now row or die!'
In terror of death they ripped the swells—all as one—
and what a joy as we darted out toward open sea,
clear of those beetling cliffs . . . my ship alone.
But the rest went down en masse. Our squadron sank.

    From there we sailed on, glad to escape our death
yet sick at heart for the dear companions we had lost.
We reached the Aeaean island next, the home of Circe
the nymph with lovely braids, an awesome power too
who can speak with human voice,   150
the true sister of murderous-minded Aeetes.
Both were bred by the Sun who lights our lives;
their mother was Perse, a child the Ocean bore.
We brought our ship to port without a sound

as a god eased her into a harbor safe and snug,
and for two days and two nights we lay by there,
eating our hearts out, bent with pain and bone-tired.
When Dawn with her lovely locks brought on the third day,
at last I took my spear and my sharp sword again,
rushed up from the ship to find a lookout point,   160
hoping to glimpse some sign of human labor,
catch some human voices . . .
I scaled a commanding crag and, scanning hard,
I could just make out some smoke from Circe's halls,
drifting up from the broad terrain through brush and woods.
Mulling it over, I thought I'd scout the ground—
that fire aglow in the smoke, I saw it, true,
but soon enough this seemed the better plan:
I'd go back to shore and the swift ship first,
feed the men, then send *them* out for scouting.   170
I was well on my way down, nearing our ship
when a god took pity on me, wandering all alone;
he sent me a big stag with high branching antlers,
right across my path—the sun's heat forced him down
from his forest range to drink at a river's banks—
just bounding out of the timber when I hit him
square in the backbone, halfway down the spine
and my bronze spear went punching clean through—
he dropped in the dust, groaning, gasping out his breath.
Treading on him, I wrenched my bronze spear from the wound,   180
left it there on the ground, and snapping off some twigs
and creepers, twisted a rope about a fathom long,
I braided it tight, hand over hand, then lashed
the four hocks of that magnificent beast.
Loaded round my neck I lugged him toward the ship,
trudging, propped on my spear—no way to sling him
over a shoulder, steadying him with one free arm—
the kill was so immense!
I flung him down by the hull and roused the men,
going up to them all with a word to lift their spirits: 190
'Listen to me, my comrades, brothers in hardship—
we won't go down to the House of Death, not yet,

not till our day arrives. Up with you, look,
there's still some meat and drink in our good ship.
Put our minds on food—why die of hunger here?'

  My hardy urging brought them round at once.
Heads came up from cloaks and there by the barren sea
they gazed at the stag, their eyes wide—my noble trophy.
But once they'd looked their fill and warmed their hearts,
they washed their hands and prepared a splendid meal.   200
Now all day long till the sun went down we sat
and feasted on sides of meat and seasoned wine.
Then when the sun had set and night came on
we lay down and slept at the water's shelving edge.
When young Dawn with her rose-red fingers shone once more
I called a muster quickly, informing all the crew,
'Listen to me, my comrades, brothers in hardship,
we can't tell east from west, the dawn from the dusk,
nor where the sun that lights our lives goes under earth
nor where it rises. We must think of a plan at once,   210
some cunning stroke. I doubt there's one still left.
I scaled a commanding crag and from that height
surveyed an entire island
ringed like a crown by endless wastes of sea.
But the land itself lies low, and I did see smoke
drifting up from its heart through thick brush and woods.'

  My message broke their spirit as they recalled
the gruesome work of the Laestrygonian king Antiphates
and the hearty cannibal Cyclops thirsting for our blood.
They burst into cries, wailing, streaming live tears   220
that gained us nothing—what good can come of grief?

  And so, numbering off my band of men-at-arms
into two platoons, I assigned them each a leader:
I took one and lord Eurylochus the other.
We quickly shook lots in a bronze helmet—
the lot of brave Eurylochus leapt out first.
So he moved off with his two and twenty comrades,

weeping, leaving us behind in tears as well . . .
Deep in the wooded glens they came on Circe's palace
built of dressed stone on a cleared rise of land.   230
Mountain wolves and lions were roaming round the grounds—
she'd bewitched them herself, she gave them magic drugs.
But they wouldn't attack my men; they just came pawing
up around them, fawning, swishing their long tails—
eager as hounds that fawn around their master,
coming home from a feast,
who always brings back scraps to calm them down.
So they came nuzzling round my men—lions, wolves
with big powerful claws—and the men cringed in fear
at the sight of those strange, ferocious beasts . . . But still   240
they paused at her doors, the nymph with lovely braids,
Circe—and deep inside they heard her singing, lifting
her spellbinding voice as she glided back and forth
at her great immortal loom, her enchanting web
a shimmering glory only goddesses can weave.
Polites, captain of armies, took command,
the closest, most devoted man I had: 'Friends,
there's someone inside, plying a great loom,
and how she sings—enthralling!
The whole house is echoing to her song.   250
Goddess or woman—let's call out to her now!'

    So he urged and the men called out and hailed her.
She opened her gleaming doors at once and stepped forth,
inviting them all in, and in they went, all innocence.
Only Eurylochus stayed behind—he sensed a trap . . .
She ushered them in to sit on high-backed chairs,
then she mixed them a potion—cheese, barley
and pale honey mulled in Pramnian wine—
but into the brew she stirred her wicked drugs
to wipe from their memories any thought of home.   260
Once they'd drained the bowls she filled, suddenly
she struck with her wand, drove them into her pigsties,
all of them bristling into swine—with grunts,
snouts—even their bodies, yes, and only

the men's minds stayed steadfast as before.
So off they went to their pens, sobbing, squealing
as Circe flung them acorns, cornel nuts and mast,
common fodder for hogs that root and roll in mud.

   Back Eurylochus ran to our swift black ship
to tell the disaster our poor friends had faced.   270
But try as he might, he couldn't get a word out.
Numbing sorrow had stunned the man to silence—
tears welled in his eyes, his heart possessed by grief.
We assailed him with questions—all at our wits' end—
till at last he could recount the fate our friends had met:
'Off we went through the brush, captain, as you commanded.
Deep in the wooded glens we came on Circe's palace
built of dressed stone on a cleared rise of land.
Someone inside was plying a great loom,
and how she sang—in a high clear voice!   280
Goddess or woman—we called out and hailed her . . .
She opened her gleaming doors at once and stepped forth,
inviting us all in, and in we went, all innocence.
But *I* stayed behind—I sensed a trap. Suddenly
all vanished—blotted out—not one face showed again,
though I sat there keeping watch a good long time.'

   At that report I slung the hefty bronze blade
of my silver-studded sword around my shoulder,
slung my bow on too and told our comrade,
'Lead me back by the same way that you came.'   290
But he flung both arms around my knees and pleaded,
begging me with his tears and winging words:
'Don't force me back there, captain, king—
leave me here on the spot.
You will never return yourself, I swear,
you'll never bring back a single man alive.
Quick, cut and run with the rest of us here—
we can still escape the fatal day!'

   But I shot back, 'Eurylochus, stay right here,

eating, drinking, safe by the black ship.   300
I must be off. Necessity drives me on.'

   Leaving the ship and shore, I headed inland,
clambering up through hushed, entrancing glades until,
as I was nearing the halls of Circe skilled in spells,
approaching her palace—Hermes god of the golden wand
crossed my path, and he looked for all the world
like a young man sporting his first beard,
just in the prime and warm pride of youth,
and grasped me by the hand and asked me kindly,
'Where are you going now, my unlucky friend—   310
trekking over the hills alone in unfamiliar country?
And your men are all in there, in Circe's palace,
cooped like swine, hock by jowl in the sties.
Have you come to set them free?
Well, I warn you, you won't get home yourself,
you'll stay right there, trapped with all the rest.
But wait, I can save you, free you from that great danger.
Look, here is a potent drug. Take it to Circe's halls—
its power alone will shield you from the fatal day.
Let me tell you of all the witch's subtle craft . . .   320
She'll mix you a potion, lace the brew with drugs
but she'll be powerless to bewitch you, even so—
this magic herb I give will fight her spells.
Now here's your plan of action, step by step.
The moment Circe strikes with her long thin wand,
you draw your sharp sword sheathed at your hip
and rush her fast as if to run her through!
She'll cower in fear and coax you to her bed—
but don't refuse the goddess' bed, not then, not if
she's to release your friends and treat you well yourself.   330
But have her swear the binding oath of the blessed gods
she'll never plot some new intrigue to harm you,
once you lie there naked—
never unman you, strip away your courage!'
                                                              With that
the giant-killer handed over the magic herb,

pulling it from the earth,
and Hermes showed me all its name and nature.
Its root is black and its flower white as milk
and the gods call it moly. Dangerous for a mortal man
to pluck from the soil but not for deathless gods.   340
All lies within their power.
                              Now Hermes went his way
to the steep heights of Olympus, over the island's woods
while I, just approaching the halls of Circe,
my heart a heaving storm at every step,
paused at her doors, the nymph with lovely braids—
I stood and shouted to her there. She heard my voice,
she opened her gleaming doors at once and stepped forth,
inviting me in, and in I went, all anguish now . . .
She led me in to sit on a silver-studded chair,
ornately carved, with a stool to rest my feet.   350
In a golden bowl she mixed a potion for me to drink,
stirring her poison in, her heart aswirl with evil.
And then she passed it on, I drank it down
but it never worked its spell—
she struck with her wand and 'Now,' she cried,
'off to your sty, you swine, and wallow with your friends!'
But I, I drew my sharp sword sheathed at my hip
and rushed her fast as if to run her through—
She screamed, slid under my blade, hugged my knees
with a flood of warm tears and a burst of winging words: 360
'Who are you? where are you from? your city? your parents?
I'm wonderstruck—you drank my drugs, you're not bewitched!
Never has any other man withstood my potion, never,
once it's past his lips and he has drunk it down.
You have a mind in *you* no magic can enchant!
You must be Odysseus, man of twists and turns—
Hermes the giant-killer, god of the golden wand,
he always said you'd come,
homeward bound from Troy in your swift black ship.
Come, sheathe your sword, let's go to bed together,   370
mount my bed and mix in the magic work of love—
we'll breed deep trust between us.'

                                   So she enticed
but I fought back, still wary. 'Circe, Circe,
how dare you tell me to treat you with any warmth?
You who turned my men to swine in your own house and now
you hold me here as well—teeming with treachery
you lure me to your room to mount your bed,
so once I lie there naked
you'll unman me, strip away my courage!
Mount your bed? Not for all the world. Not   380
until you consent to swear, goddess, a binding oath
you'll never plot some new intrigue to harm me!'

                                              Straightaway
she began to swear the oath that I required—never,
she'd never do me harm—and when she'd finished,
then, at last, I mounted Circe's gorgeous bed . . .

    At the same time her handmaids bustled through the halls,
four in all who perform the goddess' household tasks:
nymphs, daughters born of the springs and groves
and the sacred rivers running down to open sea.
One draped the chairs with fine crimson covers   390
over the seats she'd spread with linen cloths below.
A second drew up silver tables before the chairs
and laid out golden trays to hold the bread.
A third mulled heady, heart-warming wine
in a silver bowl and set out golden cups.
A fourth brought water and lit a blazing fire
beneath a massive cauldron. The water heated soon,
and once it reached the boil in the glowing bronze
she eased me into a tub and bathed me from the cauldron,
mixing the hot and cold to suit my taste, showering   400
head and shoulders down until she'd washed away
the spirit-numbing exhaustion from my body.
The bathing finished, rubbing me sleek with oil,
throwing warm fleece and a shirt around my shoulders,
she led me in to sit on a silver-studded chair,
ornately carved, with a stool to rest my feet.
A maid brought water soon in a graceful golden pitcher

and over a silver basin tipped it out
so I might rinse my hands,
then pulled a gleaming table to my side.   410
A staid housekeeper brought on bread to serve me,
appetizers aplenty too, lavish with her bounty.
She pressed me to eat. I had no taste for food.
I just sat there, mind wandering, far away . . .
lost in grim forebodings.

                  As soon as Circe saw me,
huddled, not touching my food, immersed in sorrow,
she sidled near with a coaxing, winged word:
'Odysseus, why just sit there, struck dumb,
eating your heart out, not touching food or drink?
Suspect me of still more treachery? Nothing to fear.   420
Haven't I just sworn my solemn, binding oath?'

   So she asked, but I protested, 'Circe—
how could any man in his right mind endure
the taste of food and drink before he'd freed
his comrades-in-arms and looked them in the eyes?
If you, you really want me to eat and drink,
set them free, all my beloved comrades—
let me feast my eyes.'
              So I demanded.
Circe strode on through the halls and out,
her wand held high in hand and, flinging open the pens,   430
drove forth my men, who looked like full-grown swine.
Facing her, there they stood as she went along the ranks,
anointing them one by one with some new magic oil—
and look, the bristles grown by the first wicked drug
that Circe gave them slipped away from their limbs
and they turned men again: younger than ever,
taller by far, more handsome to the eye, and yes,
they knew me at once and each man grasped my hands
and a painful longing for tears overcame us all,
a terrible sobbing echoed through the house . . .   440
The goddess herself was moved and, standing by me,
warmly urged me on—a lustrous goddess now:

'Royal son of Laertes, Odysseus, tried and true,
go at once to your ship at the water's edge,
haul her straight up on the shore first
and stow your cargo and running gear in caves,
then back you come and bring your trusty crew.'

    Her urging won my stubborn spirit over.
Down I went to the swift ship at the water's edge,
and there on the decks I found my loyal crew   450
consumed with grief and weeping live warm tears.
But now, as calves in stalls when cows come home,
droves of them herded back from field to farmyard
once they've grazed their fill—as all their young calves
come frisking out to meet them, bucking out of their pens,
lowing nonstop, jostling, rushing round their mothers—
so my shipmates there at the sight of my return
came pressing round me now, streaming tears,
so deeply moved in their hearts they felt as if
they'd made it back to their own land, their city,   460
Ithaca's rocky soil where they were bred and reared.
And through their tears their words went winging home:
'You're back again, my king! How thrilled we are—
as if we'd reached our country, Ithaca, at last!
But come, tell us about the fate our comrades met.'

    Still I replied with a timely word of comfort:
'Let's haul our ship straight up on the shore first
and stow our cargo and running gear in caves.
Then hurry, all of you, come along with me
to see our friends in the magic halls of Circe,   470
eating and drinking—the feast flows on forever.'

    So I said and they jumped to do my bidding.
Only Eurylochus tried to hold my shipmates back,
his mutinous outburst aimed at one and all:
'Poor fools, where are we running now?
Why are we tempting fate?—
why stumble blindly down to Circe's halls?

She'll turn us all into pigs or wolves or lions
made to guard that palace of hers—by force, I tell you—
just as the Cyclops trapped our comrades in his lair   480
with hotheaded Odysseus right beside them all—
thanks to this man's rashness they died too!'

    So he declared and I had half a mind
to draw the sharp sword from beside my hip
and slice his head off, tumbling down in the dust,
close kin that he was. But comrades checked me,
each man trying to calm me, left and right:
'Captain, we'll leave him here if you command,
just where he is, to sit and guard the ship.
Lead us on to the magic halls of Circe.'
                         With that,   490
up from the ship and shore they headed inland.
Nor did Eurylochus malinger by the hull;
he straggled behind the rest,
dreading the sharp blast of my rebuke.
                         All the while
Circe had bathed my other comrades in her palace,
caring and kindly, rubbed them sleek with oil
and decked them out in fleecy cloaks and shirts.
We found them all together, feasting in her halls.
Once we had recognized each other, gazing face-to-face,
we all broke down and wept—and the house resounded now   500
and Circe the lustrous one came toward me, pleading,
'Royal son of Laertes, Odysseus, man of action,
no more tears now, calm these tides of sorrow.
Well I know what pains you bore on the swarming sea,
what punishment you endured from hostile men on land.
But come now, eat your food and drink your wine
till the same courage fills your chests, now as then,
when you first set sail from native land, from rocky Ithaca!
Now you are burnt-out husks, your spirits haggard, sere,
always brooding over your wanderings long and hard,   510
your hearts never lifting with any joy—
you've suffered far too much.'

So she enticed
and won our battle-hardened spirits over.
And there we sat at ease,
day in, day out, till a year had run its course,
feasting on sides of meat and drafts of heady wine . . .
But then, when the year was gone and the seasons wheeled by
and the months waned and the long days came round again,
my loyal comrades took me aside and prodded,
'Captain, this is madness!   520
High time you thought of your own home at last,
if it really is your fate to make it back alive
and reach your well-built house and native land.'

  Their urging brought my stubborn spirit round.
So all that day till the sun went down we sat
and feasted on sides of meat and heady wine.
Then when the sun had set and night came on
the men lay down to sleep in the shadowed halls
but I went up to that luxurious bed of Circe's,
hugged her by the knees   530
and the goddess heard my winging supplication:
'Circe, now make good a promise you gave me once—
it's time to help me home. My heart longs to be home,
my comrades' hearts as well. They wear me down,
pleading with me whenever you're away.'
                                              So I pressed
and the lustrous goddess answered me in turn:
'Royal son of Laertes, Odysseus, old campaigner,
stay on no more in my house against your will.
But first another journey calls. You must travel down
to the House of Death and the awesome one, Persephone,   540
there to consult the ghost of Tiresias, seer of Thebes,
the great blind prophet whose mind remains unshaken.
Even in death—Persephone has given him wisdom,
everlasting vision to him and him alone . . .
the rest of the dead are empty, flitting shades.'

  So she said and crushed the heart inside me.

I knelt in her bed and wept. I'd no desire
to go on living and see the rising light of day.
But once I'd had my fill of tears and writhing there,
at last I found the words to venture, 'Circe, Circe,   550
who can pilot us on that journey? Who has ever
reached the House of Death in a black ship?'

    The lustrous goddess answered, never pausing,
'Royal son of Laertes, Odysseus, born for exploits,
let no lack of a pilot at the helm concern you, no,
just step your mast and spread your white sail wide—
sit back and the North Wind will speed you on your way.
But once your vessel has cut across the Ocean River
you will raise a desolate coast and Persephone's Grove,
her tall black poplars, willows whose fruit dies young.   560
Beach your vessel hard by the Ocean's churning shore
and make your own way down to the moldering House of Death.
And there into Acheron, the Flood of Grief, two rivers flow,
the torrent River of Fire, the wailing River of Tears
that branches off from Styx, the Stream of Hate,
and a stark crag looms
where the two rivers thunder down and meet.
Once there, go forward, hero. Do as I say now.
Dig a trench of about a forearm's depth and length
and around it pour libations out to all the dead—   570
first with milk and honey, and then with mellow wine,
then water third and last, and sprinkle glistening barley
over it all, and vow again and again to all the dead,
to the drifting, listless spirits of their ghosts,
that once you return to Ithaca you will slaughter
a barren heifer in your halls, the best you have,
and load a pyre with treasures—and to Tiresias,
alone, apart, you will offer a sleek black ram,
the pride of all your herds. And once your prayers
have invoked the nations of the dead in their dim glory,   580
slaughter a ram and a black ewe, turning both their heads
toward Erebus, but turn your head away, looking toward
the Ocean River. Suddenly then the countless shades

of the dead and gone will surge around you there.
But order your men at once to flay the sheep
that lie before you, killed by your ruthless blade,
and burn them both, and then say prayers to the gods,
to the almighty god of death and dread Persephone.
But you—draw your sharp sword from beside your hip,
sit down on alert there, and never let the ghosts   590
of the shambling, shiftless dead come near that blood
till you have questioned Tiresias yourself. Soon, soon
the great seer will appear before you, captain of armies:
he will tell you the way to go, the stages of your voyage,
how you can cross the swarming sea and reach home at last.'

   And with those words Dawn rose on her golden throne
and Circe dressed me quickly in sea-cloak and shirt
while the queen slipped on a loose, glistening robe,
filmy, a joy to the eye, and round her waist
she ran a brocaded golden belt   600
and over her head a scarf to shield her brow.
And I strode on through the halls to stir my men,
hovering over each with a winning word: 'Up now!
No more lazing away in sleep, we must set sail—
Queen Circe has shown the way.'
                      I brought them round,
my hardy friends-in-arms, but not even from there
could I get them safely off without a loss . . .
There was a man, Elpenor, the youngest in our ranks,
none too brave in battle, none too sound in mind.
He'd strayed from his mates in Circe's magic halls   610
and keen for the cool night air,
sodden with wine he'd bedded down on her roofs.
But roused by the shouts and tread of marching men,
he leapt up with a start at dawn but still so dazed
he forgot to climb back down again by the long ladder—
headfirst from the roof he plunged, his neck snapped
from the backbone, his soul flew down to Death.

   Once on our way, I gave the men their orders:

'You think we are headed home, our own dear land?
Well, Circe sets us a rather different course . . .   620
down to the House of Death and the awesome one, Persephone,
there to consult the ghost of Tiresias, seer of Thebes.'

So I said, and it broke my shipmates' hearts.
They sank down on the ground, moaning, tore their hair.
But it gained us nothing—what good can come of grief?

Back to the swift ship at the water's edge we went,
our spirits deep in anguish, faces wet with tears.
But Circe got to the dark hull before us,
tethered a ram and black ewe close by—
slipping past unseen. Who can glimpse a god   630
who wants to be invisible gliding here and there?"

BOOK ELEVEN

The Kingdom of
the Dead

"Now down we came to the ship at the water's edge,
we hauled and launched her into the sunlit breakers first,
stepped the mast in the black craft and set our sail
and loaded the sheep aboard, the ram and ewe,
then we ourselves embarked, streaming tears,
our hearts weighed down with anguish . . .
But Circe, the awesome nymph with lovely braids
who speaks with human voice, sent us a hardy shipmate,
yes, a fresh following wind ruffling up in our wake,
bellying out our sail to drive our blue prow on as we,   10
securing the running gear from stem to stern, sat back
while the wind and helmsman kept her true on course.
The sail stretched taut as she cut the sea all day
and the sun sank and the roads of the world grew dark.

And she made the outer limits, the Ocean River's bounds
where Cimmerian people have their homes—their realm and city
shrouded in mist and cloud. The eye of the Sun can never
flash his rays through the dark and bring them light,
not when he climbs the starry skies or when he wheels
back down from the heights to touch the earth once more—   20
an endless, deadly night overhangs those wretched men.
There, gaining that point, we beached our craft
and herding out the sheep, we picked our way
by the Ocean's banks until we gained the place
that Circe made our goal.
                                    Here at the spot
Perimedes and Eurylochus held the victims fast,
and I, drawing my sharp sword from beside my hip,
dug a trench of about a forearm's depth and length
and around it poured libations out to all the dead,
first with milk and honey, and then with mellow wine,   30
then water third and last, and sprinkled glistening barley
over it all, and time and again I vowed to all the dead,
to the drifting, listless spirits of their ghosts,
that once I returned to Ithaca I would slaughter
a barren heifer in my halls, the best I had,
and load a pyre with treasures—and to Tiresias,
alone, apart, I would offer a sleek black ram,
the pride of all my herds. And once my vows
and prayers had invoked the nations of the dead,
I took the victims, over the trench I cut their throats   40
and the dark blood flowed in—and up out of Erebus they came,
flocking toward me now, the ghosts of the dead and gone . . .
Brides and unwed youths and old men who had suffered much
and girls with their tender hearts freshly scarred by sorrow
and great armies of battle dead, stabbed by bronze spears,
men of war still wrapped in bloody armor—thousands
swarming around the trench from every side—
unearthly cries—blanching terror gripped me!
I ordered the men at once to flay the sheep
that lay before us, killed by my ruthless blade,   50

and burn them both, and then say prayers to the gods,
to the almighty god of death and dread Persephone.
But I, the sharp sword drawn from beside my hip,
sat down on alert there and never let the ghosts
of the shambling, shiftless dead come near that blood
till I had questioned Tiresias myself.

　　　　　　　　　　　　But first
the ghost of Elpenor, my companion, came toward me.
He'd not been buried under the wide ways of earth,
not yet, we'd left his body in Circe's house,
unwept, unburied—this other labor pressed us.　　　　　　60
But I wept to see him now, pity touched my heart
and I called out a winged word to him there: 'Elpenor,
how did you travel down to the world of darkness?
Faster on foot, I see, than I in my black ship.'

　　My comrade groaned as he offered me an answer:
'Royal son of Laertes, Odysseus, old campaigner,
the doom of an angry god, and god knows how much wine—
they were my ruin, captain . . . I'd bedded down
on the roof of Circe's house but never thought
to climb back down again by the long ladder—　　　　　　70
headfirst from the roof I plunged, my neck snapped
from the backbone, my soul flew down to Death. Now,
I beg you by those you left behind, so far from here,
your wife, your father who bred and reared you as a boy,
and Telemachus, left at home in your halls, your only son.
Well I know when you leave this lodging of the dead
that you and your ship will put ashore again
at the island of Aeaea—then and there,
my lord, remember me, I beg you! Don't sail off
and desert me, left behind unwept, unburied, don't,　　　　80
or my curse may draw god's fury on your head.
No, burn me in full armor, all my harness,
heap my mound by the churning gray surf—
a man whose luck ran out—
so even men to come will learn my story.

Perform my rites, and plant on my tomb that oar
I swung with mates when I rowed among the living.'

  'All this, my unlucky friend,' I reassured him,
'I will do for you. I won't forget a thing.'
                                        So we sat
and faced each other, trading our bleak parting words,   90
I on my side, holding my sword above the blood,
he across from me there, my comrade's phantom
dragging out his story.
                              But look, the ghost
of my mother came! My mother, dead and gone now . . .
Anticleia—daughter of that great heart Autolycus—
whom I had left alive when I sailed for sacred Troy.
I broke into tears to see her here, but filled with pity,
even throbbing with grief, I would not let her ghost
approach the blood till I had questioned Tiresias myself.

  At last he came. The shade of the famous Theban prophet,   100
holding a golden scepter, knew me at once and hailed me:
'Royal son of Laertes, Odysseus, master of exploits,
man of pain, what now, what brings you here,
forsaking the light of day
to see this joyless kingdom of the dead?
Stand back from the trench—put up your sharp sword
so I can drink the blood and tell you all the truth.'

  Moving back, I thrust my silver-studded sword
deep in its sheath, and once he had drunk the dark blood
the words came ringing from the prophet in his power: 110
'A sweet smooth journey home, renowned Odysseus,
that is what you seek
but a god will make it hard for you—I know—
you will never escape the one who shakes the earth,
quaking with anger at you still, still enraged
because you blinded the Cyclops, his dear son.
Even so, you and your crew may still reach home,
suffering all the way, if you only have the power

to curb their wild desire and curb your own, what's more,
from the day your good trim vessel first puts in   120
at Thrinacia Island, flees the cruel blue sea.
There you will find them grazing,
herds and fat flocks, the cattle of Helios,
god of the sun who sees all, hears all things.
Leave the beasts unharmed, your mind set on home,
and you all may still reach Ithaca—bent with hardship,
true—but harm them in any way, and I can see it now:
your ship destroyed, your men destroyed as well.
And even if *you* escape, you'll come home late
and come a broken man—all shipmates lost,   130
alone in a stranger's ship—
and you will find a world of pain at home,
crude, arrogant men devouring all your goods,
courting your noble wife, offering gifts to win her.
No doubt you will pay them back in blood when you come home!
But once you have killed those suitors in your halls—
by stealth or in open fight with slashing bronze—
go forth once more, you must . . .
carry your well-planed oar until you come
to a race of people who know nothing of the sea,   140
whose food is never seasoned with salt, strangers all
to ships with their crimson prows and long slim oars,
wings that make ships fly. And here is your sign—
unmistakable, clear, so clear you cannot miss it:
When another traveler falls in with you and calls
that weight across your shoulder a fan to winnow grain,
then plant your bladed, balanced oar in the earth
and sacrifice fine beasts to the lord god of the sea,
Poseidon—a ram, a bull and a ramping wild boar—
then journey home and render noble offerings up   150
to the deathless gods who rule the vaulting skies,
to all the gods in order.
And at last your own death will steal upon you . . .
a gentle, painless death, far from the sea it comes
to take you down, borne down with the years in ripe old age
with all your people there in blessed peace around you.

All that I have told you will come true.'
                                    'Oh Tiresias,'
I replied as the prophet finished, 'surely the gods
have spun this out as fate, the gods themselves.
But tell me one thing more, and tell me clearly.   160
I see the ghost of my long-lost mother here before me.
Dead, crouching close to the blood in silence,
she cannot bear to look me in the eyes—
her own son—or speak a word to me. How,
lord, can I make her know me for the man I am?'

    'One rule there is,' the famous seer explained,
'and simple for me to say and you to learn.
Any one of the ghosts you let approach the blood
will speak the truth to you. Anyone you refuse
will turn and fade away.'
                            And with those words,   170
now that his prophecies had closed, the awesome shade
of lord Tiresias strode back to the House of Death.
But I kept watch there, steadfast till my mother
approached and drank the dark, clouding blood.
She knew me at once and wailed out in grief
and her words came winging toward me, flying home:
'Oh my son—what brings you down to the world
of death and darkness? You are still alive!
It's hard for the living to catch a glimpse of this . . .
Great rivers flow between us, terrible waters,   180
the Ocean first of all—no one could ever ford
that stream on foot, only aboard some sturdy craft.
Have you just come from Troy, wandering long years
with your men and ship? Not yet returned to Ithaca?
You've still not seen your wife inside your halls?'
                                    'Mother,'
I replied, 'I had to venture down to the House of Death,
to consult the shade of Tiresias, seer of Thebes.
Never yet have I neared Achaea, never once
set foot on native ground,
always wandering—endless hardship from that day   190

I first set sail with King Agamemnon bound for Troy,
the stallion-land, to fight the Trojans there.
But tell me about yourself and spare me nothing.
What form of death overcame you, what laid you low,
some long slow illness? Or did Artemis showering arrows
come with her painless shafts and bring you down?
Tell me of father, tell of the son I left behind:
do my royal rights still lie in their safekeeping?
Or does some stranger hold the throne by now
because men think that I'll come home no more?　　　　200
Please, tell me about my wife, her turn of mind,
her thoughts . . . still standing fast beside our son,
still guarding our great estates, secure as ever now?
Or has she wed some other countryman at last,
the finest prince among them?'
　　　　　　　　　　　'Surely, surely,'
my noble mother answered quickly, 'she's still waiting
there in your halls, poor woman, suffering so,
her life an endless hardship like your own . . .
wasting away the nights, weeping away the days.
No one has taken over your royal rights, not yet.　　　　210
Telemachus still holds your great estates in peace,
he attends the public banquets shared with all,
the feasts a man of justice should enjoy,
for every lord invites him. As for your father,
he keeps to his own farm—he never goes to town—
with no bed for him there, no blankets, glossy throws;
all winter long he sleeps in the lodge with servants,
in the ashes by the fire, his body wrapped in rags.
But when summer comes and the bumper crops of harvest,
any spot on the rising ground of his vineyard rows　　　　220
he makes his bed, heaped high with fallen leaves,
and there he lies in anguish . . .
with his old age bearing hard upon him, too,
and his grief grows as he longs for your return.
And I with the same grief, I died and met my fate.
No sharp-eyed Huntress showering arrows through the halls
approached and brought me down with painless shafts,

nor did some hateful illness strike me, that so often
devastates the body, drains our limbs of power.
No, it was my longing for *you*, my shining Odysseus—   230
you and your quickness, you and your gentle ways—
that tore away my life that had been sweet.'

    And I, my mind in turmoil, how I longed
to embrace my mother's spirit, dead as she was!
Three times I rushed toward her, desperate to hold her,
three times she fluttered through my fingers, sifting away
like a shadow, dissolving like a dream, and each time
the grief cut to the heart, sharper, yes, and I,
I cried out to her, words winging into the darkness:
'Mother—why not wait for me? How I long to hold you!—   240
so even here, in the House of Death, we can fling
our loving arms around each other, take some joy
in the tears that numb the heart. Or is this just
some wraith that great Persephone sends my way
to make me ache with sorrow all the more?'

    My noble mother answered me at once:
'My son, my son, the unluckiest man alive!
This is no deception sent by Queen Persephone,
this is just the way of mortals when we die.
Sinews no longer bind the flesh and bones together—   250
the fire in all its fury burns the body down to ashes
once life slips from the white bones, and the spirit,
rustling, flitters away . . . flown like a dream.
But you must long for the daylight. Go, quickly.
Remember all these things
so one day you can tell them to your wife.'

    And so we both confided, trading parting words,
and there slowly came a grand array of women,
all sent before me now by august Persephone,
and all were wives and daughters once of princes.   260
They swarmed in a flock around the dark blood
while I searched for a way to question each alone,

and the more I thought, the more this seemed the best:
Drawing forth the long sharp sword from beside my hip,
I would not let them drink the dark blood, all in a rush,
and so they waited, coming forward one after another.
Each declared her lineage, and I explored them all.

And the first I saw there? Tyro, born of kings,
who said her father was that great lord Salmoneus,
said that she was the wife of Cretheus, Aeolus' son.   270
And once she fell in love with the river god, Enipeus,
far the clearest river flowing across the earth,
and so she'd haunt Enipeus' glinting streams,
till taking his shape one day
the god who girds the earth and makes it tremble
bedded her where the swirling river rushes out to sea,
and a surging wave reared up, high as a mountain, dark,
arching over to hide the god and mortal girl together.
Loosing her virgin belt, he lapped her round in sleep
and when the god had consummated his work of love   280
he took her by the hand and hailed her warmly:
'Rejoice in our love, my lady! And when this year
has run its course you will give birth to glorious children—
bedding down with the gods is never barren, futile—
and you must tend them, breed and rear them well.
Now home you go, and restrain yourself, I say,
never breathe your lover's name but know—
I am Poseidon, god who rocks the earth!'

With that he dove back in the heaving waves
and she conceived for the god and bore him Pelias, Neleus,   290
and both grew up to be stalwart aides of Zeus almighty,
both men alike. Pelias lived on the plains of Iolcos,
rich in sheepflocks, Neleus lived in sandy Pylos.
And the noble queen bore sons to Cretheus too:
Aeson, Pheres and Amythaon, exultant charioteer.

And after Tyro I saw Asopus' daughter Antiope,
proud she'd spent a night in the arms of Zeus himself

and borne the god twin sons, Amphion and Zethus,
the first to build the footings of seven-gated Thebes,
her bastions too, for lacking ramparts none could live   300
in a place so vast, so open—strong as both men were.

     And I saw Alcmena next, Amphitryon's wife,
who slept in the clasp of Zeus and merged in love
and brought forth Heracles, rugged will and lion heart.
And I saw Megara too, magnanimous Creon's daughter
wed to the stalwart Heracles, the hero never daunted.

     And I saw the mother of Oedipus, beautiful Epicaste.
What a monstrous thing she did, in all innocence—
she married her own son . . .
who'd killed his father, then he married *her!*   310
But the gods soon made it known to all mankind.
So he in growing pain ruled on in beloved Thebes,
lording Cadmus' people—thanks to the gods' brutal plan—
while she went down to Death who guards the massive gates.
Lashing a noose to a steep rafter, there she hanged aloft,
strangling in all her anguish, leaving her son to bear
the world of horror a mother's Furies bring to life.

     And I saw magnificent Chloris, the one whom Neleus
wooed and won with a hoard of splendid gifts,
so dazzled by her beauty years ago . . .   320
the youngest daughter of Iasus' son Amphion,
the great Minyan king who ruled Orchomenos once.
She was his queen in Pylos, she bore him shining sons,
Nestor and Chromius, Periclymenus too, good prince.
And after her sons she bore a daughter, majestic Pero,
the marvel of her time, courted by all the young lords
round about. But Neleus would not give her to any suitor,
none but the man who might drive home the herds
that powerful Iphiclus had stolen. Lurching,
broad in the brow, those longhorned beasts,   330
and no small task to round them up from Phylace.

Only the valiant seer Melampus volunteered—
he would drive them home—
but a god's iron sentence bound him fast:
barbarous herdsmen dragged him off in chains.
Yet when the months and days had run their course
and the year wheeled round and the seasons came again,
then mighty Iphiclus loosed the prophet's shackles,
once he had told him all the gods' decrees.
And so the will of Zeus was done at last.   340

   And I saw Leda next, Tyndareus' wife,
who'd borne the king two sons, intrepid twins,
Castor, breaker of horses, and the hardy boxer Polydeuces,
both buried now in the life-giving earth though still alive.
Even under the earth Zeus grants them that distinction:
one day alive, the next day dead, each twin by turns,
they both hold honors equal to the gods'.

   And I saw Iphimedeia next, Aloeus' wife,
who claimed she lay in the Sea-lord's loving waves
and gave the god two sons, but they did not live long,   350
Otus staunch as a god and far-famed Ephialtes.
They were the tallest men the fertile earth has borne,
the handsomest too, by far, aside from renowned Orion.
Nine yards across they measured, even at nine years old,
nine fathoms tall they towered. They even threatened
the deathless gods they'd storm Olympus' heights
with the pounding rush and grinding shock of battle.
They were wild to pile Ossa upon Olympus, then on Ossa
Pelion dense with timber—their toeholds up the heavens.
And they'd have won the day if they had reached peak strength   360
but Apollo the son of Zeus, whom sleek-haired Leto bore,
laid both giants low before their beards had sprouted,
covering cheek and chin with a fresh crop of down.

   Phaedra and Procris too I saw, and lovely Ariadne,
daughter of Minos, that harsh king. One day Theseus tried

to spirit her off from Crete to Athens' sacred heights
but he got no joy from her. Artemis killed her first
on wave-washed Dia's shores, accused by Dionysus.

    And I saw Clymene, Maera and loathsome Eriphyle—
bribed with a golden necklace   370
to lure her lawful husband to his death . . .
But the whole cortege I could never tally, never name,
not all the daughters and wives of great men I saw there.
Long before that, the godsent night would ebb away.
But the time has come for sleep, either with friends
aboard your swift ship or here in your own house.
My passage home will rest with the gods and you."

    Odysseus paused . . . They all fell silent, hushed,
his story holding them spellbound down the shadowed halls
till the white-armed queen Arete suddenly burst out,   380
"Phaeacians! How does this man impress you now,
his looks, his build, the balanced mind inside him?
The stranger is my guest
but each of you princes shares the honor here.
So let's not be too hasty to send him on his way,
and don't scrimp on his gifts. His need is great,
great as the riches piled up in your houses,
thanks to the gods' good will."
                                        Following her,
the old revered Echeneus added his support,
the eldest lord on the island of Phaeacia: 390
"Friends, the words of our considerate queen—
they never miss the mark or fail our expectations.
So do as Arete says, though on Alcinous here
depend all words and action."
                                        "And so it will be"—
Alcinous stepped in grandly—"sure as I am alive
and rule our island men who love their oars!
Our guest, much as he longs for passage home,
must stay and wait it out here till tomorrow,
till I can collect his whole array of parting gifts.

His send-off rests with every noble here   400
but with me most of all:
I hold the reins of power in the realm."

   Odysseus, deft and tactful, echoed back,
"Alcinous, majesty, shining among your island people,
if you would urge me now to stay here one whole year
then speed me home weighed down with lordly gifts,
I'd gladly have it so. Better by far, that way.
The fuller my arms on landing there at home,
the more respected, well received I'd be
by all who saw me sailing back to Ithaca."   410

   "Ah Odysseus," Alcinous replied, "one look at you
and we know that you are no one who would cheat us—
no fraud, such as the dark soil breeds and spreads
across the face of the earth these days. Crowds of vagabonds
frame their lies so tightly none can test them. But you,
what grace you give your words, and what good sense within!
You have told your story with all a singer's skill,
the miseries you endured, your great Achaeans too.
But come now, tell me truly: your godlike comrades—
did you see any heroes down in the House of Death,   420
any who sailed with you and met their doom at Troy?
The night's still young, I'd say the night is endless.
For us in the palace now, it's hardly time for sleep.
Keep telling us your adventures—they are wonderful.
I could hold out here till Dawn's first light
if only you could bear, here in our halls,
to tell the tale of all the pains you suffered."

   So the man of countless exploits carried on:
"Alcinous, majesty, shining among your island people,
there is a time for many words, a time for sleep as well.   430
But if you insist on hearing more, I'd never stint
on telling my own tale and those more painful still,
the griefs of my comrades, dead in the war's wake,
who escaped the battle-cries of Trojan armies

only to die in blood at journey's end—
thanks to a vicious woman's will.
                                          Now then,
no sooner had Queen Persephone driven off
the ghosts of lovely women, scattering left and right,
than forward marched the shade of Atreus' son Agamemnon,
fraught with grief and flanked by all his comrades,   440
troops of his men-at-arms who died beside him,
who met their fate in lord Aegisthus' halls.
He knew me at once, as soon as he drank the blood,
and wailed out, shrilly; tears sprang to his eyes,
he thrust his arms toward me, keen to embrace me there—
no use—the great force was gone, the strength lost forever,
now, that filled his rippling limbs in the old days.
I wept at the sight, my heart went out to the man,
my words too, in a winging flight of pity:
'Famous Atrides, lord of men Agamemnon!   450
What fatal stroke of destiny brought you down?
Wrecked in the ships when lord Poseidon roused
some punishing blast of stormwinds, gust on gust?
Or did ranks of enemies mow you down on land
as you tried to raid and cut off herds and flocks
or fought to win their city, take their women?'

    The field marshal's ghost replied at once:
'Royal son of Laertes, Odysseus, mastermind of war,
I was not wrecked in the ships when lord Poseidon
roused some punishing blast of stormwinds, gust on gust,   460
nor did ranks of enemies mow me down on land—
Aegisthus hatched my doom and my destruction,
he killed me, he with my own accursed wife . . .
he invited me to his palace, sat me down to feast
then cut me down as a man cuts down some ox at the trough!
So I died—a wretched, ignominious death—and round me
all my comrades killed, no mercy, one after another,
just like white-tusked boars
butchered in some rich lord of power's halls

for a wedding, banquet or groaning public feast.   470
You in your day have witnessed hundreds slaughtered,
killed in single combat or killed in pitched battle, true,
but if you'd laid eyes on this it would have wrenched your heart—
how we sprawled by the mixing-bowl and loaded tables there,
throughout the palace, the whole floor awash with blood.
But the death-cry of Cassandra, Priam's daughter—
the most pitiful thing I heard! My treacherous queen,
Clytemnestra, killed her over my body, yes, and I,
lifting my fists, beat them down on the ground,
dying, dying, writhing around the sword.   480
But she, that whore, she turned her back on me,
well on my way to Death—she even lacked the heart
to seal my eyes with her hand or close my jaws.
                                                So,
there's nothing more deadly, bestial than a woman
set on works like these—what a monstrous thing
she plotted, slaughtered her own lawful husband!
Why, I expected, at least, some welcome home
from all my children, all my household slaves
when I came sailing back again . . . But she—
the queen hell-bent on outrage—bathes in shame   490
not only herself but the whole breed of womankind,
even the honest ones to come, forever down the years!'

   So he declared and I cried out, 'How terrible!
Zeus from the very start, the thunder king
has hated the race of Atreus with a vengeance—
his trustiest weapon women's twisted wiles.
What armies of us died for the sake of Helen . . .
Clytemnestra schemed your death while you were worlds away!'

   'True, true,' Agamemnon's ghost kept pressing on,
'so even your own wife—never indulge her too far.   500
Never reveal the whole truth, whatever you may know;
just tell her a part of it, be sure to hide the rest.
Not that you, Odysseus, will be murdered by your wife.

She's much too steady, her feelings run too deep,
Icarius' daughter Penelope, that wise woman.
She was a young bride, I well remember . . .
we left her behind when we went off to war,
with an infant boy she nestled at her breast.
That boy must sit and be counted with the men now—
happy man! His beloved father will come sailing home   510
and see his son, and he will embrace his father,
that is only right. But *my* wife—she never
even let me feast my eyes on my own son;
she killed me first, his father!
I tell you this—bear it in mind, you must—
when you reach your homeland steer your ship
into port in secret, never out in the open . . .
the time for trusting women's gone forever!

     Enough. Come, tell me this, and be precise.
Have you heard news of my son? Where's he living now?   520
Perhaps in Orchomenos, perhaps in sandy Pylos
or off in the Spartan plains with Menelaus?
He's not dead yet, my Prince Orestes, no,
he's somewhere on the earth.'
                         So he probed
but I cut it short: 'Atrides, why ask me that?
I know nothing, whether he's dead or alive.
It's wrong to lead you on with idle words.'

     So we stood there, trading heartsick stories,
deep in grief, as the tears streamed down our faces.
But now there came the ghosts of Peleus' son Achilles,   530
Patroclus, fearless Antilochus—and Great Ajax too,
the first in stature, first in build and bearing
of all the Argives after Peleus' matchless son.
The ghost of the splendid runner knew me at once
and hailed me with a flight of mournful questions:
'Royal son of Laertes, Odysseus, man of tactics,
reckless friend, what next?

What greater feat can that cunning head contrive?
What daring brought you down to the House of Death?—
where the senseless, burnt-out wraiths of mortals make their home.'   540

    The voice of his spirit paused, and I was quick to answer:
'Achilles, son of Peleus, greatest of the Achaeans,
I had to consult Tiresias, driven here by hopes
he would help me journey home to rocky Ithaca.
Never yet have I neared Achaea, never once
set foot on native ground . . .
my life is endless trouble.
                    But you, Achilles,
there's not a man in the world more blest than you—
there never has been, never will be one.
Time was, when you were alive, we Argives   550
honored you as a god, and now down here, I see,
you lord it over the dead in all your power.
So grieve no more at dying, great Achilles.'

    I reassured the ghost, but he broke out, protesting,
'No winning words about death to *me*, shining Odysseus!
By god, I'd rather slave on earth for another man—
some dirt-poor tenant farmer who scrapes to keep alive—
than rule down here over all the breathless dead.
But come, tell me the news about my gallant son.
Did he make his way to the wars,   560
did the boy become a champion—yes or no?
Tell me of noble Peleus, any word you've heard—
still holding pride of place among his Myrmidon hordes,
or do they despise the man in Hellas and in Phthia
because old age has lamed his arms and legs?
For I no longer stand in the light of day—
the man I was—comrade-in-arms to help my father
as once I helped our armies, killing the best fighters
Troy could field in the wide world up there . . .
Oh to arrive at father's house—the man I was,   570
for one brief day—I'd make my fury and my hands,

invincible hands, a thing of terror to all those men
who abuse the king with force and wrest away his honor!'

    So he grieved but I tried to lend him heart:
'About noble Peleus I can tell you nothing,
but about your own dear son, Neoptolemus,
I can report the whole story, as you wish.
I myself, in my trim ship, I brought him
out of Scyros to join the Argives under arms.
And dug in around Troy, debating battle-tactics,   580
he always spoke up first, and always on the mark—
godlike Nestor and I alone excelled the boy. Yes,
and when our armies fought on the plain of Troy
he'd never hang back with the main force of men—
he'd always charge ahead,
giving ground to no one in his fury,
and scores of men he killed in bloody combat.
How could I list them all, name them all, now,
the fighting ranks he leveled, battling for the Argives?
But what a soldier he laid low with a bronze sword: 590
the hero Eurypylus, Telephus' son, and round him
troops of his own Cetean comrades slaughtered,
lured to war by the bribe his mother took.
The only man I saw to put Eurypylus
in the shade was Memnon, son of the Morning.
Again, when our champions climbed inside the horse
that Epeus built with labor, and I held full command
to spring our packed ambush open or keep it sealed,
all our lords and captains were wiping off their tears,
knees shaking beneath each man—but not your son.   600
Never once did I see his glowing skin go pale;
he never flicked a tear from his cheeks, no,
he kept on begging me there to let him burst
from the horse, kept gripping his hilted sword,
his heavy bronze-tipped javelin, keen to loose
his fighting fury against the Trojans. Then,
once we'd sacked King Priam's craggy city,
laden with his fair share and princely prize

he boarded his own ship, his body all unscarred.
Not a wound from a flying spear or a sharp sword,   610
cut-and-thrust close up—the common marks of war.
Random, raging Ares plays no favorites.'
                                        So I said and
off he went, the ghost of the great runner, Aeacus' grandson
loping with long strides across the fields of asphodel,
triumphant in all I had told him of his son,
his gallant, glorious son.

    Now the rest of the ghosts, the dead and gone
came swarming up around me—deep in sorrow there,
each asking about the grief that touched him most.
Only the ghost of Great Ajax, son of Telamon,   620
kept his distance, blazing with anger at me still
for the victory I had won by the ships that time
I pressed my claim for the arms of Prince Achilles.
His queenly mother had set them up as prizes,
Pallas and captive Trojans served as judges.
Would to god I'd never won such trophies!
All for them the earth closed over Ajax,
that proud hero Ajax . . .
greatest in build, greatest in works of war
of all the Argives after Peleus' matchless son.   630
I cried out to him now, I tried to win him over:
'Ajax, son of noble Telamon, still determined,
even in death, not once to forget that rage
you train on me for those accursed arms?
The gods set up that prize to plague the Achaeans—
so great a tower of strength we lost when you went down!
For *your* death we grieved as we did for Achilles' death—
we grieved incessantly, true, and none's to blame
but Zeus, who hated Achaea's fighting spearmen
so intensely, Zeus sealed your doom.   640
Come closer, king, and listen to my story.
Conquer your rage, your blazing, headstrong pride!'

    So I cried out but Ajax answered not a word.

He stalked off toward Erebus, into the dark
to join the other lost, departed dead.
Yet now, despite his anger,
he might have spoken to me, or I to him,
but the heart inside me stirred with some desire
to see the ghosts of others dead and gone.

    And I saw Minos there, illustrious son of Zeus,   650
firmly enthroned, holding his golden scepter,
judging all the dead . . .
Some on their feet, some seated, all clustering
round the king of justice, pleading for his verdicts
reached in the House of Death with its all-embracing gates.

    I next caught sight of Orion, that huge hunter,
rounding up on the fields of asphodel those wild beasts
the man in life cut down on the lonely mountain-slopes,
brandishing in his hands the bronze-studded club
that time can never shatter.
                    I saw Tityus too,   660
son of the mighty goddess Earth—sprawling there
on the ground, spread over nine acres—two vultures
hunched on either side of him, digging into his liver,
beaking deep in the blood-sac, and he with his frantic hands
could never beat them off, for he had once dragged off
the famous consort of Zeus in all her glory,
Leto, threading her way toward Pytho's ridge,
over the lovely dancing-rings of Panopeus.

    And I saw Tantalus too, bearing endless torture.
He stood erect in a pool as the water lapped his chin—   670
parched, he tried to drink, but he could not reach the surface,
no, time and again the old man stooped, craving a sip,
time and again the water vanished, swallowed down,
laying bare the caked black earth at his feet—
some spirit drank it dry. And over his head
leafy trees dangled their fruit from high aloft,
pomegranates and pears, and apples glowing red,

succulent figs and olives swelling sleek and dark,
but as soon as the old man would strain to clutch them fast
a gust would toss them up to the lowering dark clouds.   680

    And I saw Sisyphus too, bound to his own torture,
grappling his monstrous boulder with both arms working,
heaving, hands struggling, legs driving, he kept on
thrusting the rock uphill toward the brink, but just
as it teetered, set to topple over—
                                    time and again
the immense weight of the thing would wheel it back and
the ruthless boulder would bound and tumble down to the plain again—
so once again he would heave, would struggle to thrust it up,
sweat drenching his body, dust swirling above his head.

    And next I caught a glimpse of powerful Heracles—   690
his ghost, I mean: the man himself delights
in the grand feasts of the deathless gods on high,
wed to Hebe, famed for her lithe, alluring ankles,
the daughter of mighty Zeus and Hera shod in gold.
Around him cries of the dead rang out like cries of birds,
scattering left and right in horror as on he came like night,
naked bow in his grip, an arrow grooved on the bowstring,
glaring round him fiercely, forever poised to shoot.
A terror too, that sword-belt sweeping across his chest,
a baldric of solid gold emblazoned with awesome work . . .   700
bears and ramping boars and lions with wild, fiery eyes,
and wars, routs and battles, massacres, butchered men.
May the craftsman who forged that masterpiece—
whose skills could conjure up a belt like that—
never forge another!
Heracles knew me at once, at first glance,
and hailed me with a winging burst of pity:
'Royal son of Laertes, Odysseus famed for exploits,
luckless man, you too? Braving out a fate as harsh
as the fate I bore, alive in the light of day?   710
Son of Zeus that I was, my torments never ended,
forced to slave for a man not half the man I was:

he saddled me with the worst heartbreaking labors.
Why, he sent me down here once, to retrieve the hound
that guards the dead—no harder task for me, he thought—
but I dragged the great beast up from the underworld to earth
and Hermes and gleaming-eyed Athena blazed the way!'

  With that he turned and back he went to the House of Death
but I held fast in place, hoping that others might still come,
shades of famous heroes, men who died in the old days   720
and ghosts of an even older age I longed to see,
Theseus and Pirithous, the gods' own radiant sons.
But before I could, the dead came surging round me,
hordes of them, thousands raising unearthly cries,
and blanching terror gripped me—panicked now
that Queen Persephone might send up from Death
some monstrous head, some Gorgon's staring face!
I rushed back to my ship, commanded all hands
to take to the decks and cast off cables quickly.
They swung aboard at once, they sat to the oars in ranks
and a strong tide of the Ocean River swept her on downstream,   730
sped by our rowing first, then by a fresh fair wind."

BOOK TWELVE

The Cattle of
the Sun

"Now when our ship had left the Ocean River rolling in her wake
and launched out into open sea with its long swells to reach
the island of Aeaea—east where the Dawn forever young
has home and dancing-rings and the Sun his risings—
heading in we beached our craft on the sands,
the crews swung out on the low sloping shore
and there we fell asleep, awaiting Dawn's first light.

As soon as Dawn with her rose-red fingers shone again
I dispatched some men to Circe's halls to bring
the dead Elpenor's body. We cut logs in haste   10
and out on the island's sharpest jutting headland
held his funeral rites in sorrow, streaming tears.
Once we'd burned the dead man and the dead man's armor,
heaping his grave-mound, hauling a stone that coped it well,

we planted his balanced oar aloft to crown his tomb.

And so we saw to his rites, each step in turn.
Nor did our coming back from Death escape Circe—
she hurried toward us, decked in rich regalia,
handmaids following close with trays of bread
and meats galore and glinting ruddy wine.   20
And the lustrous goddess, standing in our midst,
hailed us warmly: 'Ah my daring, reckless friends!
You who ventured down to the House of Death alive,
doomed to die twice over—others die just once.
Come, take some food and drink some wine,
rest here the livelong day
and then, tomorrow at daybreak, you must sail.
But I will set you a course and chart each seamark,
so neither on sea nor land will some new trap
ensnare you in trouble, make you suffer more.'   30

Her foresight won our fighting spirits over.
So all that day till the sun went down we sat
and feasted on sides of meat and heady wine,
and then when the sun had set and night came on
the men lay down to sleep by the ship's stern-cables.
But Circe, taking me by the hand, drew me away
from all my shipmates there and sat me down
and lying beside me probed me for details.
I told her the whole story, start to finish,
then the queenly goddess laid my course: 40
'Your descent to the dead is over, true,
but listen closely to what I tell you now
and god himself will bring it back to mind.
First you will raise the island of the Sirens,
those creatures who spellbind any man alive,
whoever comes their way. Whoever draws too close,
off guard, and catches the Sirens' voices in the air—
no sailing home for him, no wife rising to meet him,
no happy children beaming up at their father's face.
The high, thrilling song of the Sirens will transfix him,   50

lolling there in their meadow, round them heaps of corpses
rotting away, rags of skin shriveling on their bones . . .
Race straight past that coast! Soften some beeswax
and stop your shipmates' ears so none can hear,
none of the crew, but if *you* are bent on hearing,
have them tie you hand and foot in the swift ship,
erect at the mast-block, lashed by ropes to the mast
so you can hear the Sirens' song to your heart's content.
But if you plead, commanding your men to set you free,
then they must lash you faster, rope on rope.   60

    But once your crew has rowed you past the Sirens
a choice of routes is yours. I cannot advise you
which to take, or lead you through it all—
you must decide for yourself—
but I can tell you the ways of either course.
On one side beetling cliffs shoot up, and against them
pound the huge roaring breakers of blue-eyed Amphitrite—
the Clashing Rocks they're called by all the blissful gods.
Not even birds can escape them, no, not even the doves
that veer and fly ambrosia home to Father Zeus: 70
even of those the sheer Rocks always pick off one
and Father wings one more to keep the number up.
No ship of men has ever approached and slipped past—
always some disaster—big timbers and sailors' corpses
whirled away by the waves and lethal blasts of fire.
One ship alone, one deep-sea craft sailed clear,
the *Argo*, sung by the world, when heading home
from Aeetes' shores. And *she* would have crashed
against those giant rocks and sunk at once if Hera,
for love of Jason, had not sped her through.   80

    On the other side loom two enormous crags . . .
One thrusts into the vaulting sky its jagged peak,
hooded round with a dark cloud that never leaves—
no clear bright air can ever bathe its crown,
not even in summer's heat or harvest-time.
No man on earth could scale it, mount its crest,

not even with twenty hands and twenty feet for climbing,
the rock's so smooth, like dressed and burnished stone.
And halfway up that cliffside stands a fog-bound cavern
gaping west toward Erebus, realm of death and darkness—   90
past it, great Odysseus, you should steer your ship.
No rugged young archer could hit that yawning cave
with a winged arrow shot from off the decks.
Scylla lurks inside it—the yelping horror,
yelping, no louder than any suckling pup
but she's a grisly monster, I assure you.
No one could look on her with any joy,
not even a god who meets her face-to-face . . .
She has twelve legs, all writhing, dangling down
and six long swaying necks, a hideous head on each,   100
each head barbed with a triple row of fangs, thickset,
packed tight—and armed to the hilt with black death!
Holed up in the cavern's bowels from her waist down
she shoots out her heads, out of that terrifying pit,
angling right from her nest, wildly sweeping the reefs
for dolphins, dogfish or any bigger quarry she can drag
from the thousands Amphitrite spawns in groaning seas.
No mariners yet can boast they've raced their ship
past Scylla's lair without some mortal blow—
with each of her six heads she snatches up   110
a man from the dark-prowed craft and whisks him off.

    The other crag is lower—you will see, Odysseus—
though both lie side-by-side, an arrow-shot apart.
Atop it a great fig-tree rises, shaggy with leaves,
beneath it awesome Charybdis gulps the dark water down.
Three times a day she vomits it up, three times she gulps it down,
that terror! Don't be there when the whirlpool swallows down—
not even the earthquake god could save you from disaster.
No, hug Scylla's crag—sail on past her—top speed!
Better by far to lose six men and keep your ship   120
than lose your entire crew.'
                        'Yes, yes,
but tell me the truth now, goddess,' I protested.

'Deadly Charybdis—can't I possibly cut and run from *her*
and still fight Scylla off when Scylla strikes my men?'

    'So stubborn!' the lovely goddess countered.
'Hell-bent yet again on battle and feats of arms?
Can't you bow to the deathless gods themselves?
Scylla's no mortal, she's an immortal devastation,
terrible, savage, wild, no fighting her, no defense—
just flee the creature, that's the only way.   130
Waste any time, arming for battle beside her rock,
I fear she'll lunge out again with all of her six heads
and seize as many men. No, row for your lives,
invoke Brute Force, I tell you, Scylla's mother—
she spawned her to scourge mankind,
she can stop the monster's next attack!

    Then you will make the island of Thrinacia . . .
where herds of the Sungod's cattle graze, and fat sheep
and seven herds of oxen, as many sheepflocks, rich and woolly,
fifty head in each. No breeding swells their number,   140
nor do they ever die. And goddesses herd them on,
nymphs with glinting hair, Phaëthusa, Lampetie,
born to the Sungod Helios by radiant Neaera.
Their queenly mother bred and reared them both
then settled them on the island of Thrinacia—
their homeland seas away—
to guard their father's sheep and longhorn cattle.
Leave the beasts unharmed, your mind set on home,
and you all may still reach Ithaca—bent with hardship,
true—but harm them in any way, and I can see it now: 150
your ship destroyed, your men destroyed as well!
And even if *you* escape, you'll come home late,
all shipmates lost, and come a broken man.'

    At those words Dawn rose on her golden throne
and lustrous Circe made her way back up the island.
I went straight to my ship, commanding all hands
to take to the decks and cast off cables quickly.

They swung aboard at once, they sat to the oars in ranks
and in rhythm churned the water white with stroke on stroke.
And Circe the nymph with glossy braids, the awesome one   160
who speaks with human voice, sent us a hardy shipmate,
yes, a fresh following wind ruffling up in our wake,
bellying out our sail to drive our blue prow on as we,
securing the running gear from stem to stern, sat back
while the wind and helmsman kept her true on course.
At last, and sore at heart, I told my shipmates,
'Friends . . . it's wrong for only one or two
to know the revelations that lovely Circe
made to me alone. I'll tell you all,
so we can die with our eyes wide open now   170
or escape our fate and certain death together.
First, she warns, we must steer clear of the Sirens,
their enchanting song, their meadow starred with flowers.
I alone was to hear their voices, so she said,
but you must bind me with tight chafing ropes
so I cannot move a muscle, bound to the spot,
erect at the mast-block, lashed by ropes to the mast.
And if I plead, commanding you to set me free,
then lash me faster, rope on pressing rope.'

So I informed my shipmates point by point,   180
all the while our trim ship was speeding toward
the Sirens' island, driven on by the brisk wind.
But then—the wind fell in an instant,
all glazed to a dead calm . . .
a mysterious power hushed the heaving swells.
The oarsmen leapt to their feet, struck the sail,
stowed it deep in the hold and sat to the oarlocks,
thrashing with polished oars, frothing the water white.
Now with a sharp sword I sliced an ample wheel of beeswax
down into pieces, kneaded them in my two strong hands   190
and the wax soon grew soft, worked by my strength
and Helios' burning rays, the sun at high noon,
and I stopped the ears of my comrades one by one.
They bound me hand and foot in the tight ship—

erect at the mast-block, lashed by ropes to the mast—
and rowed and churned the whitecaps stroke on stroke.
We were just offshore as far as a man's shout can carry,
scudding close, when the Sirens sensed at once a ship
was racing past and burst into their high, thrilling song:
'Come closer, famous Odysseus—Achaea's pride and glory—   200
moor your ship on our coast so you can hear our song!
Never has any sailor passed our shores in his black craft
until he has heard the honeyed voices pouring from our lips,
and once he hears to his heart's content sails on, a wiser man.
We know all the pains that the Greeks and Trojans once endured
on the spreading plain of Troy when the gods willed it so—
all that comes to pass on the fertile earth, we know it all!'

　　So they sent their ravishing voices out across the air
and the heart inside me throbbed to listen longer.
I signaled the crew with frowns to set me free—   210
they flung themselves at the oars and rowed on harder,
Perimedes and Eurylochus springing up at once
to bind me faster with rope on chafing rope.
But once we'd left the Sirens fading in our wake,
once we could hear their song no more, their urgent call—
my steadfast crew was quick to remove the wax I'd used
to seal their ears and loosed the bonds that lashed me.

　　We'd scarcely put that island astern when suddenly
I saw smoke and heavy breakers, heard their booming thunder.
The men were terrified—oarblades flew from their grip,   220
clattering down to splash in the vessel's wash.
She lay there, dead in the water . . .
no hands to tug the blades that drove her on.
But I strode down the decks to rouse my crewmen,
halting beside each one with a bracing, winning word:
'Friends, we're hardly strangers at meeting danger—
and this danger is no worse than what we faced
when Cyclops penned us up in his vaulted cave
with crushing force! But even from there my courage,
my presence of mind and tactics saved us all,   230

and we will live to remember *this* someday,
I have no doubt. Up now, follow my orders,
all of us work as one! You men at the thwarts—
lay on with your oars and strike the heaving swells,
trusting that Zeus will pull us through these straits alive.
You, helmsman, here's your order—burn it in your mind—
the steering-oar of our rolling ship is in your hands.
Keep her clear of that smoke and surging breakers,
head for those crags or she'll catch you off guard,
she'll yaw over there—you'll plunge us all in ruin!'   240

    So I shouted. They snapped to each command.
No mention of Scylla—how to fight that nightmare?—
for fear the men would panic, desert their oars
and huddle down and stow themselves away.
But now I cleared my mind of Circe's orders—
cramping my style, urging me not to arm at all.
I donned my heroic armor, seized long spears
in both my hands and marched out on the half-deck,
forward, hoping from there to catch the first glimpse
of Scylla, ghoul of the cliffs, swooping to kill my men.   250
But nowhere could I make her out—and my eyes ached,
scanning that mist-bound rock face top to bottom.

    Now wailing in fear, we rowed on up those straits,
Scylla to starboard, dreaded Charybdis off to port,
her horrible whirlpool gulping the sea-surge down, down
but when she spewed it up—like a cauldron over a raging fire—
all her churning depths would seethe and heave—exploding spray
showering down to splatter the peaks of both crags at once!
But when she swallowed the sea-surge down her gaping maw
the whole abyss lay bare and the rocks around her roared,   260
terrible, deafening—
                    bedrock showed down deep, boiling
black with sand—
                    and ashen terror gripped the men.
But now, fearing death, all eyes fixed on Charybdis—
now Scylla snatched six men from our hollow ship,

the toughest, strongest hands I had, and glancing
backward over the decks, searching for my crew
I could see their hands and feet already hoisted,
flailing, high, higher, over my head, look—
wailing down at me, comrades riven in agony,
shrieking out my name for one last time!   270
Just as an angler poised on a jutting rock
flings his treacherous bait in the offshore swell,
whips his long rod—hook sheathed in an oxhorn lure—
and whisks up little fish he flips on the beach-break,
writhing, gasping out their lives . . . so now they writhed,
gasping as Scylla swung them up her cliff and there
at her cavern's mouth she bolted them down raw—
screaming out, flinging their arms toward me,
lost in that mortal struggle . . .
Of all the pitiful things I've had to witness,   280
suffering, searching out the pathways of the sea,
this wrenched my heart the most.
                                        But now, at last,
putting the Rocks, Scylla and dread Charybdis far astern,
we quickly reached the good green island of the Sun
where Helios, lord Hyperion, keeps his fine cattle,
broad in the brow, and flocks of purebred sheep.
Still aboard my black ship in the open sea
I could hear the lowing cattle driven home,
the bleating sheep. And I was struck once more
by the words of the blind Theban prophet, Tiresias,   290
and Aeaean Circe too: time and again they told me
to shun this island of the Sun, the joy of man.
So I warned my shipmates gravely, sick at heart,
'Listen to me, my comrades, brothers in hardship,
let me tell you the dire prophecies of Tiresias
and Aeaean Circe too: time and again they told me
to shun this island of the Sun, the joy of man.
Here, they warned, the worst disaster awaits us.
Row straight past these shores—race our black ship on!'

    So I said, and the warnings broke their hearts.   300

But Eurylochus waded in at once—with mutiny on his mind:
'You're a hard man, Odysseus. Your fighting spirit's
stronger than ours, your stamina never fails.
You must be made of iron head to foot. Look,
your crew's half-dead with labor, starved for sleep,
and you forbid us to set foot on land, this island here,
washed by the waves, where we might catch a decent meal again.
Drained as we are, night falling fast, you'd have us desert
this haven and blunder off, into the mist-bound seas?
Out of the night come winds that shatter vessels—   310
how can a man escape his headlong death
if suddenly, out of nowhere, a cyclone hits,
bred by the South or stormy West Wind? They're the gales
that tear a ship to splinters—the gods, our masters,
willing or not, it seems. No, let's give way
to the dark night, set out our supper here.
Sit tight by our swift ship and then at daybreak
board and launch her, make for open sea!'

So Eurylochus urged, and shipmates cheered.
Then I knew some power was brewing trouble for us,   320
so I let fly with an anxious plea: 'Eurylochus,
I'm one against all—the upper hand is yours.
But swear me a binding oath, all here, that if
we come on a herd of cattle or fine flock of sheep,
not one man among us—blind in his reckless ways—
will slaughter an ox or ram. Just eat in peace,
content with the food immortal Circe gave us.'

They quickly swore the oath that I required
and once they had vowed they'd never harm the herds,
they moored our sturdy ship in the deep narrow harbor,   330
close to a fresh spring, and all hands disembarked
and adeptly set about the evening meal.
Once they'd put aside desire for food and drink,
they recalled our dear companions, wept for the men
that Scylla plucked from the hollow ship and ate alive,
and a welcome sleep came on them in their tears.

              But then,
at the night's third watch, the stars just wheeling down,
Zeus who marshals the stormclouds loosed a ripping wind,
a howling, demonic gale, shrouding over in thunderheads
the earth and sea at once—and night swept down from the sky.   340
When young Dawn with her rose-red fingers shone once more
we hauled our craft ashore, securing her in a vaulted cave
where nymphs have lovely dancing-rings and hold their sessions.
There I called a muster, warning my shipmates yet again,
'Friends, we've food and drink aplenty aboard the ship—
keep your hands off all these herds or we will pay the price!
The cattle, the sleek flocks, belong to an awesome master,
Helios, god of the sun who sees all, hears all things.'

    So I warned, and my headstrong men complied.
But for one whole month the South Wind blew nonstop,   350
no other wind came up, none but the South-southeast.
As long as our food and ruddy wine held out, the crew,
eager to save their lives, kept hands off the herds.
But then, when supplies aboard had all run dry,
when the men turned to hunting, forced to range
for quarry with twisted hooks: for fish, birds,
anything they could lay their hands on—
hunger racked their bellies—I struck inland,
up the island, there to pray to the gods.
If only one might show me some way home!   360
Crossing into the heartland, clear of the crew,
I rinsed my hands in a sheltered spot, a windbreak,
but soon as I'd prayed to all the gods who rule Olympus,
down on my eyes they poured a sweet, sound sleep . . .
as Eurylochus opened up his fatal plan to friends:
'Listen to me, my comrades, brothers in hardship.
All ways of dying are hateful to us poor mortals,
true, but to die of hunger, starve to death—
that's the worst of all. So up with you now,
let's drive off the pick of Helios' sleek herds,   370
slaughter them to the gods who rule the skies up there.
If we ever make it home to Ithaca, native ground,

erect at once a glorious temple to the Sungod,
line the walls with hoards of dazzling gifts!
But if the Sun, inflamed for his longhorn cattle,
means to wreck our ship and the other gods pitch in—
I'd rather die at sea, with one deep gulp of death,
than 'die by inches on this desolate island here!'

    So he urged, and shipmates cheered again.
At once they drove off the Sungod's finest cattle—   380
close at hand, not far from the blue-prowed ship they grazed,
those splendid beasts with their broad brows and curving horns.
Surrounding them in a ring, they lifted prayers to the gods,
plucking fresh green leaves from a tall oak for the rite,
since white strewing-barley was long gone in the ship.
Once they'd prayed, slaughtered and skinned the cattle,
they cut the thighbones out, they wrapped them round in fat,
a double fold sliced clean and topped with strips of flesh.
And since they had no wine to anoint the glowing victims,
they made libations with water, broiling all the innards,   390
and once they'd burned the bones and tasted the organs—
hacked the rest into pieces, piercing them with spits.

    That moment soothing slumber fell from my eyes
and down I went to our ship at the water's edge
but on my way, nearing the long beaked craft,
the smoky savor of roasts came floating up around me . . .
I groaned in anguish, crying out to the deathless gods:
'Father Zeus! the rest of you blissful gods who never die—
you with your fatal sleep, you lulled me into disaster.
Left on their own, look what a monstrous thing   400
my crew concocted!'
                Quick as a flash
with her flaring robes Lampetie sped the news
to the Sun on high that we had killed his herds
and Helios burst out in rage to all the immortals:
'Father Zeus! the rest of you blissful gods who never die—
punish them all, that crew of Laertes' son Odysseus—
what an outrage! They, they killed my cattle,

the great joy of my heart . . . day in, day out,
when I climbed the starry skies and when I wheeled
back down from the heights to touch the earth once more.   410
Unless they pay me back in blood for the butchery of my herds,
down I go to the House of Death and blaze among the dead!'

But Zeus who marshals the thunderheads insisted,
'Sun, you keep on shining among the deathless gods
and mortal men across the good green earth.
And as for the guilty ones, why, soon enough
on the wine-dark sea I'll hit their racing ship
with a white-hot bolt, I'll tear it into splinters.'

—Or so I heard from the lovely nymph Calypso,
who heard it herself, she said, from Hermes, god of guides.   420

As soon as I reached our ship at the water's edge
I took the men to task, upbraiding each in turn,
but how to set things right? We couldn't find a way.
The cattle were dead already . . .
and the gods soon showed us all some fateful signs—
the hides began to crawl, the meat, both raw and roasted,
bellowed out on the spits, and we heard a noise
like the moan of lowing oxen.
                                     Yet six more days
my eager companions feasted on the cattle of the Sun,
the pick of the herds they'd driven off, but then,   430
when Cronian Zeus brought on the seventh day,
the wind in its ceaseless raging dropped at last,
and stepping the mast at once, hoisting the white sail
we boarded ship and launched her, made for open sea.

But once we'd left that island in our wake—
no land at all in sight, nothing but sea and sky—
then Zeus the son of Cronus mounted a thunderhead
above our hollow ship and the deep went black beneath it.
Nor did the craft scud on much longer. All of a sudden
killer-squalls attacked us, screaming out of the west,   440

a murderous blast shearing the two forestays off
so the mast toppled backward, its running tackle spilling
into the bilge. The mast itself went crashing into the stern,
it struck the helmsman's head and crushed his skull to pulp
and down from his deck the man flipped like a diver—
his hardy life spirit left his bones behind.
Then, then in the same breath Zeus hit the craft
with a lightning-bolt and thunder. Round she spun,
reeling under the impact, filled with reeking brimstone,
shipmates pitching out of her, bobbing round like seahawks   450
swept along by the whitecaps past the trim black hull—
and the god cut short their journey home forever.

But I went lurching along our battered hulk
till the sea-surge ripped the plankings from the keel
and the waves swirled it away, stripped bare, and snapped
the mast from the decks—but a backstay made of bull's-hide
still held fast, and with this I lashed the mast and keel
together, made them one, riding my makeshift raft
as the wretched galewinds bore me on and on.

At last the West Wind quit its wild rage   460
but the South came on at once to hound me even more,
making me double back my route toward cruel Charybdis.
All night long I was rushed back and then at break of day
I reached the crag of Scylla and dire Charybdis' vortex
right when the dreadful whirlpool gulped the salt sea down.
But heaving myself aloft to clutch at the fig-tree's height,
like a bat I clung to its trunk for dear life—not a chance
for a good firm foothold there, no clambering up it either,
the roots too far to reach, the boughs too high overhead,
huge swaying branches that overshadowed Charybdis.   470
But I held on, dead set . . . waiting for her
to vomit my mast and keel back up again—
Oh how I ached for both! and back they came,
late but at last, at just the hour a judge at court,
who's settled the countless suits of brash young claimants,
rises, the day's work done, and turns home for supper—

that's when the timbers reared back up from Charybdis.
I let go—I plunged with my hands and feet flailing,
crashing into the waves beside those great beams
and scrambling aboard them fast   480
I rowed hard with my hands right through the straits . . .
And the father of men and gods did not let Scylla see me,
else I'd have died on the spot—no escape from death.

   I drifted along nine days. On the tenth, at night,
the gods cast me up on Ogygia, Calypso's island,
home of the dangerous nymph with glossy braids
who speaks with human voice, and she took me in,
she loved me . . . Why cover the same ground again?
Just yesterday, here at hall, I told you all the rest,
you and your gracious wife. It goes against my grain   490
to repeat a tale told once, and told so clearly."

Ithaca at Last

His tale was over now. The Phaeacians all fell silent, hushed,
his story holding them spellbound down the shadowed halls
until Alcinous found the poise to say, "Odysseus,
now that you have come to my bronze-floored house,
my vaulted roofs, I know you won't be driven
off your course, nothing can hold you back—
however much you've suffered, you'll sail home.
Here, friends, here's a command for one and all,
you who frequent my palace day and night and drink
the shining wine of kings and enjoy the harper's songs.   10
The robes and hammered gold and a haul of other gifts
you lords of our island council brought our guest—
all lie packed in his polished sea-chest now. Come,
each of us add a sumptuous tripod, add a cauldron!

Then recover our costs with levies on the people:
it's hard to afford such bounty man by man."

The king's instructions met with warm applause
and home they went to sleep, each in his own house.
When young Dawn with her rose-red fingers shone once more
they hurried down to the ship with handsome bronze gifts,   20
and striding along the decks, the ardent King Alcinous
stowed them under the benches, shipshape, so nothing
could foul the crewmen tugging at their oars.
Then back the party went to Alcinous' house
and shared a royal feast.
                              The majestic king
slaughtered an ox for them to Cronus' mighty son,
Zeus of the thundercloud, whose power rules the world.
They burned the thighs and fell to the lordly banquet,
reveling there, while in their midst the inspired bard
struck up a song, Demodocus, prized by all the people.   30
True, but time and again Odysseus turned his face
toward the radiant sun, anxious for it to set,
yearning now to be gone and home once more . . .
As a man aches for his evening meal when all day long
his brace of wine-dark oxen have dragged the bolted plowshare
down a fallow field—how welcome the setting sun to him,
the going home to supper, yes, though his knees buckle,
struggling home at last. So welcome now to Odysseus
the setting light of day, and he lost no time
as he pressed Phaeacia's men who love their oars,   40
addressing his host, Alcinous, first and foremost:
"Alcinous, majesty, shining among your island people,
make your libations, launch me safely on my way—
to one and all, farewell!
All is now made good, my heart's desire,
your convoy home, your precious, loving gifts,
and may the gods of Olympus bless them for me!
May I find an unswerving wife when I reach home,
and loved ones hale, unharmed! And you, my friends

remaining here in your kingdom now, may you delight   50
in your loyal wives and children! May the gods
rain down all kinds of fortune on your lives,
misfortune never harbor in your homeland!"

All burst into applause, urging passage home
for their parting guest, his farewell rang so true.
Hallowed King Alcinous briskly called his herald:
"Come, Pontonous! Mix the wine in the bowl,
pour rounds to all our banqueters in the house,
so we, with a prayer to mighty Zeus the Father,
can sail our new friend home to native land."   60

Pontonous mixed the heady, honeyed wine
and hovering closely, poured full rounds for all.
And from where they sat they tipped libations out
to the happy gods who rule the vaulting skies.
Then King Odysseus rose up from his seat
and placing his two-eared cup in Arete's hands,
addressed the queen with parting wishes on the wing:
"Your health, my queen, through all your days to come—
until old age and death, that visit all mankind,
pay you a visit too. Now I am on my way   70
but you, may you take joy in this house of yours,
in your children, your people, in Alcinous the king!"

With that the great Odysseus strode across the threshold.
And King Alcinous sent the herald off with the guest
to lead him down to the swift ship and foaming surf.
And Arete sent her serving-women, one to carry
a sea-cloak, washed and fresh, a shirt as well,
another assigned to bear the sturdy chest
and a third to take the bread and ruddy wine.

When they reached the ship at the water's edge   80
the royal escorts took charge of the gifts at once
and stores of food and wine, stowed them deep in the holds,
and then for their guest they spread out rug and sheets

on the half-deck, clear astern on the ship's hull
so he might sleep there soundly, undisturbed.
And last, Odysseus climbed aboard himself
and down he lay, all quiet
as crewmen sat to the oarlocks, each in line.
They slipped the cable free of the drilled stone post
and soon as they swung back and the blades tossed up the spray   90
an irresistible sleep fell deeply on his eyes, the sweetest,
soundest oblivion, still as the sleep of death itself . . .
And the ship like a four-horse team careering down the plain,
all breaking as one with the whiplash cracking smartly,
leaping with hoofs high to run the course in no time—
so the stern hove high and plunged with the seething rollers
crashing dark in her wake as on she surged,unwavering,
never flagging, no, not even a darting hawk,
the quickest thing on wings, could keep her pace
as on she ran, cutting the swells at top speed,   100
bearing a man endowed with the gods' own wisdom,
one who had suffered twenty years of torment, sick at heart,
cleaving his way through wars of men and pounding waves at sea
but now he slept in peace, the memory of his struggles
laid to rest.
                    And then, that hour the star rose up,
the clearest, brightest star, that always heralds
the newborn light of day, the deep-sea-going ship
made landfall on the island . . . Ithaca, at last.

    There on the coast a haven lies, named for Phorcys,
the old god of the deep—with two jutting headlands,   110
sheared off at the seaward side but shelving toward the bay,
that break the great waves whipped by the gales outside
so within the harbor ships can ride unmoored
whenever they come in mooring range of shore.
At the harbor's head a branching olive stands
with a welcome cave nearby it, dank with sea-mist,
sacred to nymphs of the springs we call the Naiads.
There are mixing-bowls inside and double-handled jars,
crafted of stone, and bees store up their honey in the hollows.

There are long stone looms as well, where the nymphs weave out   120
their webs from clouds of sea-blue wool—a marvelous sight—
and a wellspring flows forever. The cave has two ways in,
one facing the North Wind, a pathway down for mortals;
the other, facing the South, belongs to the gods,
no man may go that way . . .
it is the path for all the deathless powers.

Here at this bay the Phaeacian crew put in—
they'd known it long before—driving the ship so hard
she ran up onto the beach for a good half her length,
such way the oarsmen's brawny arms had made.   130
Up from the benches, swinging down to land,
first they lifted Odysseus off the decks—
linen and lustrous carpet too—and laid him
down on the sand asleep, still dead to the world,
then hoisted out the treasures proud Phaeacians,
urged by open-hearted Pallas, had lavished on him,
setting out for home. They heaped them all
by the olive's trunk, in a neat pile, clear
of the road for fear some passerby might spot
and steal Odysseus' hoard before he could awaken.   140
Then pushing off, they pulled for home themselves.

But now Poseidon, god of the earthquake, never once
forgetting the first threats he leveled at the hero,
probed almighty Zeus to learn his plans in full:
"Zeus, Father, I will lose all my honor now
among the immortals, now there are mortal men
who show me no respect—Phaeacians, too,
born of my own loins! I said myself
that Odysseus would suffer long and hard
before he made it home, but I never dreamed   150
of blocking his return, not absolutely at least,
once *you* had pledged your word and bowed your head.
But now they've swept him across the sea in their swift ship,
they've set him down in Ithaca, sound asleep, and loaded the man
with boundless gifts—bronze and hoards of gold and robes—

aye, more plunder than he could ever have won from Troy
if Odysseus had returned intact with his fair share!"

"Incredible," Zeus who marshals the thunderheads replied.
"Earth-shaker, you with your massive power, why moaning so?
The gods don't disrespect you. What a stir there'd be   160
if they flung abuse at the oldest, noblest of them all.
Those mortals? If any man, so lost in his strength
and prowess, pays you no respect—just pay him back.
The power is always yours.
Do what you like. Whatever warms your heart."

"King of the dark cloud," the earthquake god agreed,
"I'd like to avenge myself at once, as you advise,
but I've always feared your wrath and shied away.
But now I'll crush that fine Phaeacian cutter
out on the misty sea, now on her homeward run   170
from the latest convoy. They will learn at last
to cease and desist from escorting every man alive—
I'll pile a huge mountain round about their port!"

"Wait, dear brother," Zeus who collects the clouds
had second thoughts. "Here's what seems best to *me.*
As the people all lean down from the city heights
to watch her speeding home, strike her into a rock
that looks like a racing vessel, just offshore—
amaze all men with a marvel for the ages.
Then pile your huge mountain round about their port."   180

Hearing that from Zeus, the god of the earthquake
sped to Scheria now, the Phaeacians' island home,
and waited there till the ship came sweeping in,
scudding lightly along—and surging close abreast,
the earthquake god with one flat stroke of his hand
struck her to stone, rooted her to the ocean floor
and made for open sea.
                    The Phaeacians, aghast,
those lords of the long oars, the master mariners

traded startled glances, sudden outcries:
"Look—who's pinned our swift ship to the sea?"   190

    "Just racing for home!"
                         "Just hove into plain view!"

   They might well wonder, blind to what had happened,
till Alcinous rose and made things all too clear:
"Oh no—my father's prophecy years ago . . .
it all comes home to me with a vengeance now!
He used to say Poseidon was vexed with us because
we escorted all mankind and never came to grief.
He said that one day, as a well-built ship of ours
sailed home on the misty sea from such a convoy,
the god would crush it, yes,   200
and pile a huge mountain round about our port.
So the old king foretold. Now, look, it all comes true!
Hurry, friends, do as I say, let us all comply:
stop our convoys home for every castaway
chancing on our city! As for Poseidon,
sacrifice twelve bulls to the god at once—
the pick of the herds. Perhaps he'll pity us,
pile no looming mountain ridge around our port."

   The people, terrified, prepared the bulls at once.
So all of Phaeacia's island lords and captains,   210
milling round the altar, lifted prayers
to Poseidon, master of the sea . . .
                         That very moment
great Odysseus woke from sleep on native ground at last—
he'd been away for years—but failed to know the land
for the goddess Pallas Athena, Zeus's daughter,
showered mist over all, so under cover
she might change his appearance head to foot
as she told him every peril he'd meet at home—
keep him from being known by wife, townsmen, friends,
till the suitors paid the price for all their outrage.   220
And so to the king himself all Ithaca looked strange . . .

the winding beaten paths, the coves where ships can ride,
the steep rock face of the cliffs and the tall leafy trees.
He sprang to his feet and, scanning his own native country,
groaned, slapped his thighs with his flat palms
and Odysseus cried in anguish:
"Man of misery, whose land have I lit on now?
What *are* they here—violent, savage, lawless?
or friendly to strangers, god-fearing men?
Where can I take this heap of treasure now   230
and where in the world do I wander off myself?
If only the trove had stayed among the Phaeacians there
and I had made my way to some other mighty king
who would have hosted me well and sent me home!
But now I don't know where to stow all this,
and I can't leave it here, inviting any bandit
to rob me blind.
                    So damn those lords and captains,
those Phaeacians! Not entirely honest or upright, were they?
Sweeping me off to this, this no-man's-land, and they,
they swore they'd sail me home to sunny Ithaca—well,   240
they never kept their word. Zeus of the Suppliants
pay them back—he keeps an eye on the world of men
and punishes all transgressors!
                          Come, quickly,
I'll inspect my treasure and count it up myself.
Did they make off with anything in their ship?"

    With that he counted up the gorgeous tripods,
cauldrons, bars of gold and the lovely woven robes.
Not a stitch was missing from the lot. But still
he wept for his native country, trailing down the shore
where the wash of sea on shingle ebbs and flows,   250
his homesick heart in turmoil.
But now Athena appeared and came toward him.
She looked like a young man . . . a shepherd boy
yet elegant too, with all the gifts that grace the sons of kings,
with a well-cut cloak falling in folds across her shoulders,
sandals under her shining feet, a hunting spear in hand.

Odysseus, overjoyed at the sight, went up to meet her,
joining her now with salutations on the wing:
"Greetings, friend! Since you are the first
I've come on in this harbor, treat me kindly—   260
no cruelty, please. Save these treasures,
save me too. I pray to you like a god,
I fall before your knees and ask your mercy!
And tell me this for a fact—I need to know—
where on earth am I? what land? who lives here?
Is it one of the sunny islands or some jutting shore
of the good green mainland slanting down to sea?"

   Athena answered, her eyes brightening now,
"You must be a fool, stranger, or come from nowhere,
if you really have to ask what land this is.   270
Trust me, it's not so nameless after all.
It's known the world around,
to all who live to the east and rising sun
and to all who face the western mists and darkness.
It's a rugged land, too cramped for driving horses,
but though it's far from broad, it's hardly poor.
There's plenty of grain for bread, grapes for wine,
the rains never fail and the dewfall's healthy.
Good country for goats, good for cattle too—
there's stand on stand of timber   280
and water runs in streambeds through the year.
                                   So,
stranger, the name of Ithaca's reached as far as Troy,
and Troy, they say, is a long hard sail from Greece."

   Ithaca . . . Heart racing, Odysseus that great exile
filled with joy to hear Athena, daughter of storming Zeus,
pronounce that name. He stood on native ground at last
and he replied with a winging word to Pallas,
not with a word of truth—he choked it back,
always invoking the cunning in his heart:
"Ithaca . . . yes, I seem to have heard of Ithaca,   290
even on Crete's broad island far across the sea,

and now I've reached it myself, with all this loot,
but I left behind an equal measure for my children.
I'm a fugitive now, you see. I killed Idomeneus' son,
Orsilochus, lightning on his legs, a man who beat
all runners alive on that long island—what a racer!
He tried to rob me of all the spoil I'd won at Troy,
the plunder I went to hell and back to capture, true,
cleaving my way through wars of men and waves at sea—
and just because I refused to please his father,   300
serve under *him* at Troy. I led my own command.
So now with a friend I lay in wait by the road,
I killed him just loping in from the fields—
with one quick stroke of my bronze spear
in the dead of night, the heavens pitch-black . . .
no one could see us, spot me tearing out his life
with a weapon honed for action. Once I'd cut him down
I made for a ship and begged the Phoenician crew for mercy,
paying those decent hands a hearty share of plunder—
asked them to take me on and land me down in Pylos,   310
there or lovely Elis, where Epeans rule in power.
But a heavy galewind blew them way off course,
much against their will—
they'd no desire to cheat me. Driven afar,
we reached this island here at the midnight hour,
rowing for dear life, we made it into your harbor—
not a thought of supper, much as we all craved food,
we dropped from the decks and lay down, just like that!
A welcome sleep came over my weary bones at once,
while the crew hoisted up my loot from the holds   320
and set it down on the sand near where I slept.
They reembarked, now homeward bound for Sidon,
their own noble city, leaving me here behind,
homesick in my heart . . ."
                                   As his story ended,
goddess Athena, gray eyes gleaming, broke into a smile
and stroked him with her hand, and now she appeared a woman,
beautiful, tall and skilled at weaving lovely things.
Her words went flying straight toward Odysseus:

"Any man—any god who met you—would have to be
some champion lying cheat to get past *you*   330
for all-round craft and guile! You terrible man,
foxy, ingenious, never tired of twists and tricks—
so, not even here, on native soil, would you give up
those wily tales that warm the cockles of your heart!
Come, enough of this now. We're both old hands
at the arts of intrigue. Here among mortal men
you're far the best at tactics, spinning yarns,
and I am famous among the gods for wisdom,
cunning wiles, too.
Ah, but you never recognized me, did you?   340
Pallas Athena, daughter of Zeus—who always
stands beside you, shields you in every exploit:
thanks to me the Phaeacians all embraced you warmly.
And now I am here once more, to weave a scheme with you
and to hide the treasure-trove Phaeacia's nobles
lavished on you then—I willed it, planned it so
when you set out for home—and to tell you all
the trials you must suffer in your palace . . .
Endure them all. You must. You have no choice.
And to no one—no man, no woman, not a soul—   350
reveal that you are the wanderer home at last.
No, in silence you must bear a world of pain,
subject yourself to the cruel abuse of men."

     "Ah goddess," the cool tactician countered,
"you're so hard for a mortal man to know on sight,
however shrewd he is—the shapes you take are endless!
But I do know this: you were kind to me in the war years,
so long as we men of Achaea soldiered on at Troy.
But once we'd sacked King Priam's craggy city,
boarded ship, and a god dispersed the fleet,   360
from then on, daughter of Zeus, I never saw you,
never glimpsed you striding along my decks
to ward off some disaster. No, I wandered on,
my heart forever torn to pieces inside my chest

till the gods released me from my miseries at last,
that day in the fertile kingdom of Phaeacia when
you cheered me with words, in person, led me to their city.
But now I beg you by your almighty Father's name . . .
for I can't believe I've reached my sunny Ithaca,
I must be roaming around one more exotic land—   370
you're mocking me, I know it, telling me tales
to make me lose my way. Tell me the truth now,
have I really reached the land I love?"

    "Always the same, your wary turn of mind,"
Athena exclaimed, her glances flashing warmly.
"That's why I can't forsake you in your troubles—
you are so winning, so worldly-wise, so self-possessed!
Anyone else, come back from wandering long and hard,
would have hurried home at once, delighted to see
his children and his wife. Oh, but not you,   380
it's not your pleasure to probe for news of them—
you must put your wife to the proof yourself!
But she, she waits in your halls, as always,
her life an endless hardship . . .
wasting away the nights, weeping away the days.
I never had doubts myself, no, I knew down deep
that you would return at last, with all your shipmates lost.
But I could not bring myself to fight my Father's brother,
Poseidon, quaking with anger at you, still enraged
because you blinded the Cyclops, his dear son.   390
But come, let me show you Ithaca's setting,
I'll convince you. This haven—look around—
it's named for Phorcys, the old god of the deep,
and here at the harbor's head the branching olive stands
with the welcome cave nearby it, dank with sea-mist,
sacred to nymphs of the springs we call the Naiads.
Here, under its arching vault, time and again
you'd offer the nymphs a generous sacrifice
to bring success! And the slopes above you, look,
Mount Neriton decked in forests!"

　　　　　　　　　　　　　At those words   400
the goddess scattered the mist and the country stood out clear
and the great man who had borne so much rejoiced at last,
thrilled to see his Ithaca—he kissed the good green earth
and raised his hands to the nymphs and prayed at once,
"Nymphs of the springs, Naiads, daughters of Zeus,
I never dreamed I would see you yet again . . .
Now rejoice in my loving prayers—and later,
just like the old days, I will give you gifts
if Athena, Zeus's daughter, Queen of Armies
comes to my rescue, grants this fighter life   410
and brings my son to manhood!"
　　　　　　　　　　　"Courage!"—
goddess Athena answered, eyes afire—
"Free your mind of all that anguish now.
Come, quick, let's bury your treasures here
in some recess of this haunted hallowed cave
where they'll be safe and sound,
then we'll make plans so we can win the day."
　　　　　　　　　　　　　　　　With that
the goddess swept into the cavern's shadowed vault,
searching for hiding-places far inside its depths
while Odysseus hauled his treasures closer up,   420
the gold, durable bronze and finespun robes,
the Phaeacians' parting gifts.
Once he'd stowed them well away, the goddess,
Pallas Athena, daughter of storming Zeus,
sealed the mouth of the cavern with a stone.

　　Then down they sat by the sacred olive's trunk
to plot the death of the high and mighty suitors.
The bright-eyed goddess Athena led the way:
"Royal son of Laertes, Odysseus, old campaigner,
think how to lay your hands on all those brazen suitors,   430
lording it over your house now, three whole years,
courting your noble wife, offering gifts to win her.
But she, forever broken-hearted for your return,
builds up each man's hopes—

dangling promises, dropping hints to each—
but all the while with something else in mind."

  "God help me!" the man of intrigue broke out:
"Clearly I might have died the same ignoble death
as Agamemnon, bled white in my own house too,
if you had never revealed this to me now,   440
goddess, point by point.
Come, weave us a scheme so I can pay them back!
Stand beside me, Athena, fire me with daring, fierce
as the day we ripped Troy's glittering crown of towers down.
Stand by me—furious now as then, my bright-eyed one—
and I would fight three hundred men, great goddess,
with you to brace me, comrade-in-arms in battle!"

  Gray eyes ablaze, the goddess urged him on:
"Surely I'll stand beside you, not forget you,
not when the day arrives for us to do our work.   450
Those men who court your wife and waste your goods?
I have a feeling some will splatter your ample floors
with all their blood and brains. Up now, quickly.
First I will transform you—no one must know you.
I will shrivel the supple skin on your lithe limbs,
strip the russet curls from your head and deck you out
in rags you'd hate to see some other mortal wear;
I'll dim the fire in your eyes, so shining once—
until you seem appalling to all those suitors,
even your wife and son you left behind at home.   460
But you, you make your way to the swineherd first,
in charge of your pigs, and true to you as always,
loyal friend to your son, to Penelope, so self-possessed.
You'll find him posted beside his swine, grubbing round
by Raven's Rock and the spring called Arethusa,
rooting for feed that makes pigs sleek and fat,
the nuts they love, the dark pools they drink.
Wait there, sit with him, ask him all he knows.
I'm off to Sparta, where the women are a wonder,
to call Telemachus home, your own dear son, Odysseus.   470

He's journeyed to Lacedaemon's rolling hills
to see Menelaus, searching for news of you,
hoping to learn if you are still alive."

    Shrewd Odysseus answered her at once:
"Why not tell him the truth? You know it all.
Or is *he* too—like father, like son—condemned
to hardship, roving over the barren salt sea
while strangers devour our livelihood right here?"

    But the bright-eyed goddess reassured him firmly:
"No need for anguish, trust me, not for him—   480
I escorted your son myself
so he might make his name by sailing there.
Nor is he saddled down with any troubles now.
He sits at ease in the halls of Menelaus,
bathed in endless bounty . . . True enough,
some young lords in a black cutter lurk in ambush,
poised to kill the prince before he reaches home,
but I have my doubts they will. Sooner the earth
will swallow down a few of those young gallants
who eat you out of house and home these days!"   490

    No more words, not now—
Athena stroked Odysseus with her wand.
She shriveled the supple skin on his lithe limbs,
stripped the russet curls from his head, covered his body
top to toe with the wrinkled hide of an old man
and dimmed the fire in his eyes, so shining once.
She turned his shirt and cloak into squalid rags,
ripped and filthy, smeared with grime and soot.
She flung over this the long pelt of a bounding deer,
rubbed bare, and gave him a staff and beggar's sack,   500
torn and tattered, slung from a fraying rope.
                  All plans made,
they went their separate ways—Athena setting off
to bring Telemachus home from hallowed Lacedaemon.

BOOK FOURTEEN

The Loyal
Swineherd

So up from the haven now Odysseus climbed a rugged path
through timber along high ground—Athena had shown the way—
to reach the swineherd's place, that fine loyal man
who of all the household hands Odysseus ever had
cared the most for his master's worldly goods.

    Sitting at the door of his lodge he found him,
there in his farmstead, high-walled, broad and large,
with its long view on its cleared rise of ground . . .
The swineherd made those walls with his own hands
to enclose the pigs of his master gone for years.   10
Alone, apart from his queen or old Laertes,
he'd built them up of quarried blocks of stone
and coped them well with a fence of wild pear.

Outside he'd driven stakes in a long-line stockade,
a ring of thickset palings split from an oak's dark heart.
Within the yard he'd built twelve sties, side-by-side,
to bed his pigs, and in each one fifty brood-sows
slept aground, penned and kept for breeding.
The boars slept outside, but far fewer of them,
thanks to the lordly suitors' feasts that kept on   20
thinning the herd and kept the swineherd stepping,
sending to town each day the best fat hog in sight.
By now they were down to three hundred and sixty head.
But guarding them all the time were dogs like savage beasts,
a pack of four, reared by the swineherd, foreman of men.
The man himself was fitting sandals to his feet,
carving away at an oxhide, dark and supple.
As for his men, three were off with their pigs,
herding them here or there. Under orders he'd sent
a fourth to town, with hog in tow for the gorging suitors   30
to slaughter off and glut themselves with pork.

    Suddenly—those snarling dogs spotted Odysseus,
charged him fast—a shatter of barks—but Odysseus
sank to the ground at once, he knew the trick:
the staff dropped from his hand but here and now,
on his own farm, he might have taken a shameful mauling.
Yes, but the swineherd, quick to move, dashed for the gate,
flinging his oxhide down, rushed the dogs with curses,
scattered them left and right with flying rocks
and warned his master, "Lucky to be alive, old man—   40
a moment more, my pack would have torn you limb from limb!
Then you'd have covered me with shame. As if the gods
had never given me blows and groans aplenty . . .
Here I sit, my heart aching, broken for *him*,
my master, my great king—fattening up
his own hogs for other men to eat, while he,
starving for food, I wager, wanders the earth,
a beggar adrift in strangers' cities, foreign-speaking lands,
if he's still alive, that is, still sees the rising sun.
Come, follow me into my place, old man, so you,   50

at least, can eat your fill of bread and wine.
Then you can tell me where you're from
and all the pains you've weathered."

On that note
the loyal swineherd led the way to his shelter,
showed his guest inside and sat Odysseus down
on brush and twigs he piled up for the visitor,
flinging over these the skin of a shaggy wild goat,
broad and soft, the swineherd's own good bedding.
The king, delighted to be so well received,
thanked the man at once: "My host—may Zeus   60
and the other gods give *you* your heart's desire
for the royal welcome you have shown me here!"

    And you replied, Eumaeus, loyal swineherd,
"It's wrong, my friend, to send any stranger packing—
even one who arrives in worse shape than you.
Every stranger and beggar comes from Zeus
and whatever scrap they get from the likes of us,
they'll find it welcome. That's the best we can do,
we servants, always cowed by our high and mighty masters,
especially our young lords . . . But my old king?   70
The gods, they must have blocked his journey home.
He'd have treated me well, he would, with a house,
a plot of land and a wife you'd gladly prize.
Goods that a kind lord will give a household hand
who labors for him, hard, whose work the gods have sped,
just as they speed the work I labor at all day.
My master, I tell you, would have repaid me well
if he'd grown old right here. But now he's dead . . .
If only Helen and all her kind had died out too,
brought to her knees, just as she cut the legs   80
from under troops of men! My king among them,
he went off to the stallion-land of Troy
to fight the Trojans, save Agamemnon's honor!"

Enough—
he brusquely cinched his belt around his shirt,
strode out to the pens, crammed with droves of pigs,

picked out two, bundled them in and slaughtered both,
singed them, sliced them down, skewered them through
and roasting all to a turn, set them before Odysseus,
sizzling hot on the spits.
Then coating the meat with white barley groats   90
and mixing honeyed wine in a carved wooden bowl,
he sat down across from his guest, inviting warmly,
"Eat up now, my friend. It's all we slaves have got,
scrawny pork, while the suitors eat the fatted hogs—
no fear of the gods in their hard hearts, no mercy!
Trust me, the blessed gods have no love for crime.
They honor justice, honor the decent acts of men.
Even cutthroat bandits who raid foreign parts—
and Zeus grants them a healthy share of plunder,
ships filled to the brim, and back they head for home—   100
even their dark hearts are stalked by the dread of vengeance.
But the suitors know, they've caught some godsent rumor
of master's grisly death! That's why they have no mind
to do their courting fairly or go back home in peace.
No, at their royal ease they devour all his goods,
those brazen rascals never spare a scrap!
Not a day or a night goes by, sent down by Zeus,
but they butcher victims, never stopping at one or two,
and drain his wine as if there's no tomorrow—
swilling the last drop . . .   110
Believe me, my master's wealth was vast!
No other prince on earth could match his riches,
not on the loamy mainland or here at home in Ithaca—
no twenty men in the world could equal his great treasures!
Let me count them off for you. A dozen herds of cattle
back on the mainland, just as many head of sheep,
as many droves of pigs and goatflocks ranging free;
hired hands or his own herdsmen keep them grazing there.
Here in Ithaca, goatflocks, eleven in all, scatter
to graze the island, out at the wild end,   120
and trusty goatherds watch their every move.
And each herdsman, day after day, it never ends,

drives in a beast for the suitors—best in sight,
a sheep or well-fed goat. While I tend to these pigs,
I guard them, pick the best for those carousers
and send it to the slaughter!"
                                His voice rose
while the stranger ate his meat and drank his wine,
ravenous, bolting it all down in silence . . .
brooding on ways to serve the suitors right.
But once he'd supped and refreshed himself with food,   130
he filled the wooden bowl he'd been drinking from,
brimmed it with wine and passed it to his host
who received the offer gladly, spirit cheered
as the stranger probed him now with winging words:
"Friend, who was the man who bought you with his goods,
the master of such vast riches, powerful as you say?
You tell me he died defending Agamemnon's honor?
What's his name? I just might know such a man . . .
Zeus would know, and the other deathless gods,
if I ever saw him, if I bring you any news.   140
I've roamed the whole earth over."

    And the good swineherd answered, foreman of men,
"Old friend, no wanderer landing here with news of *him*
is likely to win his wife and dear son over.
Random drifters, hungry for bed and board,
lie through their teeth and swallow back the truth.
Why, any tramp washed up on Ithaca's shores
scurries right to my mistress, babbling lies,
and she ushers him in, kindly, pressing for details,
and the warm tears of grief come trickling down her cheeks,   150
the loyal wife's way when her husband's died abroad.
Even you, old codger, could rig up some fine tale—
and soon enough, I'd say,
if they gave you shirt and clothing for your pains.
My master? Well, no doubt the dogs and wheeling birds
have ripped the skin from his ribs by now, his life is through—
or fish have picked him clean at sea, and the man's bones

lie piled up on the mainland, buried deep in sand . . .
he's dead and gone. Aye, leaving a broken heart
for loved ones left behind, for *me* most of all.   160
Never another master kind as he!
I'll never find one—no matter where I go,
not even if I went back to mother and father,
the house where I was born and my parents reared me once.
Ah, but much as I grieve for them, much as I long
to lay my eyes on them, set foot on the old soil,
it's longing for him, him that wrings my heart—
Odysseus, lost and gone!
That man, old friend, far away as he is . . .
I can scarcely bear to say his name aloud,   170
so deeply he loved me, cared for me, so deeply.
Worlds away as he is, I call him Master, Brother!"

    "My friend," the great Odysseus, long in exile, answered,
"since you are dead certain, since you still insist
he's never coming back, still the soul of denial,
I won't simply say it—on my oath I swear
Odysseus is on his way!
Reward for such good news? Let me have it
the moment he sets foot in his own house,
dress me in shirt and cloak, in handsome clothes.   180
Before then, poor as I am, I wouldn't take a thing.
I hate that man like the very Gates of Death who,
ground down by poverty, stoops to peddling lies.
I swear by Zeus, the first of all the gods,
by this table of hospitality here, my host,
by Odysseus' hearth where I have come for help:
all will come to pass, I swear, exactly as I say.
True, this very month—just as the old moon dies
and the new moon rises into life—Odysseus will return!
He will come home and take revenge on any man   190
who offends his wedded wife and princely son!"

    "Good news," you replied, Eumaeus, loyal swineherd,

"but I will never pay a reward for *that*, old friend—
Odysseus, he'll never come home again. Never . . .
Drink your wine, sit back, let's talk of other things.
Don't remind me of all this. The heart inside me
breaks when anyone mentions my dear master.
That oath of yours, we'll let it pass—
                                        Odysseus,
oh come back!—
                just as *I* wish, I and Penelope,
old Laertes too, Telemachus too, the godlike boy.   200
How I grieve for *him* now, I can't stop—Odysseus' son,
Telemachus. The gods reared him up like a fine young tree
and I often said, 'In the ranks of men he'll match his father,
his own dear father—amazing in build and looks, that boy!'
But all of a sudden a god wrecks his sense of balance—
god or man, no matter—off he's gone to catch
some news of his father, down to holy Pylos.
And now those gallant suitors lie in wait for him,
sailing home, to tear the royal line of Arcesius
out of Ithaca, root and branch, good name and all!   210
Enough. Let *him* pass too—whether he's trapped
or the hand of Zeus will pull him through alive.
                                        Come,
old soldier, tell me the story of your troubles,
tell me truly, too, I'd like to know it well . . .
Who are you? where are you from? your city? your parents?
What sort of vessel brought you? Why did the sailors
land you here in Ithaca? Who did they say they are?
I hardly think you came this way on foot."

    The great teller of tales returned at length,
"My story—the whole truth—I'm glad to tell it all.   220
If only the two of us had food and mellow wine
to last us long, here in your shelter now,
for us to sup on, undisturbed,
while others take the work of the world in hand,
I could easily spend all year and never reach the end

of my endless story, all the heartbreaking trials
I struggled through. The gods willed it so . . .

I hail from Crete's broad land, I'm proud to say,
and I am a rich man's son. And many other sons
he brought up in his palace, born in wedlock,   230
sprung of his lawful wife. Unlike my mother.
She was a slave, a concubine he'd purchased, yes,
but he treated me on a par with all his true-born sons—
Castor, Hylax' son. I'm proud to boast his blood, that man
revered like a god throughout all Crete those days,
for wealth, power and all his glorious offspring.
But the deadly spirits soon swept him down
to the House of Death, and his high and mighty sons
carved up his lands and then cast lots for the parts
and gave me just a pittance, a paltry house as well.   240
But I won myself a wife from wealthy, landed people,
thanks to my own strong points. I was no fool
and never shirked a fight.
                         But now my heyday's gone—
I've had my share of blows. Yet look hard at the husk
and you'll still see, I think, the grain that gave it life.
By heaven, Ares gave me courage, Athena too, to break
the ranks of men wide open, once, in the old days,
whenever I picked my troops and formed an ambush,
plotting attacks to spring against our foes—
no hint of death could daunt my fighting spirit!   250
Far out of the front I'd charge and spear my man,
I'd cut down any enemy soldier backing off.
Such was I in battle, true, but I had no love
for working the land, the chores of households either,
the labor that raises crops of shining children. No,
it was always oarswept ships that thrilled my heart,
and wars, and the long polished spears and arrows,
dreadful gear that makes the next man cringe.
I loved them all—god planted that love inside me.
Each man delights in the work that suits him best.   260

Why, long before we Achaeans ever camped at Troy,
nine commands I led in our deep-sea-going ships,
raiding foreign men, and a fine haul reached my hands.
I helped myself to the lion's share and still more spoils
came by lot. And my house grew by leaps and bounds,
I walked among the Cretans, honored, feared as well.

But then, when thundering Zeus contrived that expedition—
that disaster that brought so many fighters to their knees—
and men kept pressing me and renowned Idomeneus
to head a fleet to Troy,   270
there was no way out, no denying them then,
the voice of the people bore down much too hard.
So nine whole years we Achaeans soldiered on at Troy,
in the tenth we sacked King Priam's city, then embarked
for home in the long ships, and a god dispersed the fleet.
Unlucky me. Shrewd old Zeus was plotting still more pain.
No more than a month I stayed at home, taking joy
in my children, loyal wife and lovely plunder.
But a spirit in me urged, 'Set sail for Egypt—
fit out ships, take crews of seasoned heroes!'   280
Nine I fitted out, the men joined up at once
and then six days my shipmates feasted well,
while I provided a flock of sheep to offer up
to the gods and keep the feasters' table groaning.
On the seventh we launched out from the plains of Crete
with a stiff North Wind fair astern—smooth sailing,
aye, like coasting on downstream . . .
And not one craft in our squadron foundered;
all shipshape, and all hands sound, we sat back
while the wind and helmsmen kept us true on course.   290

Five days out and we raised the great river Nile
and there in the Nile delta moored our ships of war.
God knows I ordered my trusty crews to stand by,
just where they were, and guard the anchored fleet
and I sent a patrol to scout things out from higher ground.

But swept away by their own reckless fury, the crew went berserk—
they promptly began to plunder the lush Egyptian farms,
dragged off the women and children, killed the men.
Outcries reached the city in no time—stirred by shouts
the entire town came streaming down at the break of day,   300
filling the river plain with chariots, ranks of infantry
and the gleam of bronze. Zeus who loves the lightning
flung down murderous panic on all my men-at-arms—
no one dared to stand his ground and fight,
disaster ringed us round from every quarter.
Droves of my men they hacked down with swords,
led off the rest alive, to labor for them as slaves.
And I? Zeus flashed an inspiration through my mind,
though I wish I'd died a soldier down in Egypt then!
A world of pain, you see, still lay in wait for me . . .   310
Quickly I wrenched the skullcap helmet off my head,
I tore the shield from my back and dropped my spear
and ran right into the path of the king's chariot,
hugged and kissed his knees. He pitied me, spared me,
hoisted me onto his war-car, took me home in tears.
Troops of his men came rushing after, shaking javelins,
mad to kill me—their fighting blood at the boil—
but their master drove them off.
He feared the wrath of Zeus, the god of guests,
the first of the gods to pay back acts of outrage.
                                            So,   320
there I lingered for seven years, amassing a fortune
from all the Egyptian people loading me with gifts.
Then, at last, when the eighth had come full turn,
along comes this Phoenician one fine day . . .
a scoundrel, swindler, an old hand at lies
who'd already done the world a lot of damage.
Well, he smoothly talked me round and off we sailed,
Phoenicia-bound, where his house and holdings lay.
There in his care I stayed till the year was out.
Then, when the months and days had run their course   330
and the year wheeled round and the seasons came again,
he conned me aboard his freighter bound for Libya,

pretending I'd help him ship a cargo there for sale
but in fact he'd sell *me* there and make a killing!
I suspected as much, of course, but had no choice,
so I boarded with him, yes, and the ship ran on
with a good strong North Wind gusting—
fast on the middle passage clear of Crete—
but Zeus was brewing mischief for that crew . . .
Once we'd left the island in our wake—   340
no land at all in sight, nothing but sea and sky—
then Zeus the son of Cronus mounted a thunderhead
above our hollow ship and the deep went black beneath it.
Then, then in the same breath Zeus hit the craft
with a lightning-bolt and thunder. Round she spun,
reeling under the impact, filled with reeking brimstone,
shipmates pitching out of her, bobbing round like seahawks
swept along by the breakers past the trim black hull—
and the god cut short their journey home forever.
                                                Not mine.

Zeus himself—when I was just at the final gasp—   350
thrust the huge mast of my dark-prowed vessel
right into my arms so I might flee disaster
one more time. Wrapping myself around it,
I was borne along by the wretched galewinds,
rushed along nine days—on the tenth, at dead of night,
a shouldering breaker rolled me up along Thesprotia's beaches.
There the king of Thesprotia, Phidon, my salvation,
treated me kindly, asked for no reward at all.
His own good son had found me, half-dead
from exhaustion and the cold. He raised me up   360
by the hand and led me home to his father's house
and dressed me in cloak and shirt and decent clothes.
That's where I first got wind of *him*—Odysseus . . .
The king told me he'd hosted the man in style,
befriended him on his way home to native land,
and showed me all the treasure Odysseus had amassed.
Bronze and gold and plenty of hard wrought iron,
enough to last a man and ten generations of his heirs—
so great the wealth stored up for *him* in the king's vaults!

But Odysseus, he made clear, was off at Dodona then   370
to hear the will of Zeus that rustles forth
from the god's tall leafy oak: how should he return,
after all the years away, to his own green land of Ithaca—
openly or in secret? Phidon swore to me, what's more,
as the princely man poured out libations in his house,
'The ship's hauled down and the crew set to sail,
to take Odysseus home to native land.'
                                        But I . . .
he shipped me off before. A Thesprotian cutter
chanced to be heading for Dulichion rich in wheat,
so he told the crew to take me to the king, Acastus,   380
treat me kindly, too, but it pleased them more
to scheme foul play against me,
sink me into the very depths of pain. As soon
as the ship was far off land, scudding in mid-sea,
they sprang their trap—my day of slavery then and there!
They stripped from my back the shirt and cloak I wore,
decked me out in a new suit of clothes, all rags,
ripped and filthy—the rags you see right now.
But then, once they'd gained the fields of Ithaca,
still clear in the evening light, they lashed me fast   390
to the rowing-benches, twisting a cable round me;
all hands went ashore
and rushed to catch their supper on the beach.
But the gods themselves unhitched my knots at once
with the gods' own ease. I wrapped my head in rags,
slid down the gangplank polished smooth, slipped my body
into the water, not a splash, chest-high, then quick,
launched out with both my arms and swam away—
out of the surf in no time, clear of the crew.
I clambered upland, into a flowery, fragrant brush   400
and crouched there, huddling low. They raised a hue and cry,
wildly beat the bushes, but when it seemed no use
to pursue the hunt, back they trudged again and
boarded their empty ship.
                                        The gods hid me themselves—

it's light work for them—and brought me here,
the homestead of a man who knows the world.
So it seems to be my lot that I'll live on."

      And you replied, Eumaeus, loyal swineherd,
"So much misery, friend! You've moved my heart,
deeply, with your long tale . . . such blows, such roving.   410
But one part's off the mark, I know—you'll never persuade me—
what you say about Odysseus. A man in your condition,
who are *you*, I ask you, to lie for no good reason?
Well I know the truth of my good lord's return,
how the gods detested him, with a vengeance—
never letting him go under, fighting Trojans,
or die in the arms of loved ones,
once he'd wound down the long coil of war.
Then all united Achaea would have raised his tomb
and he'd have won his son great fame for years to come.   420
But now the whirlwinds have ripped him away—no fame for him!
And I live here, cut off from the world, with all my pigs.
I never go into town unless, perhaps, wise Penelope
calls me back, when news drops in from nowhere.
There they crowd the messenger, cross-examine him,
heartsick for their long-lost lord or all too glad
to eat him out of house and home, scot-free.
But I've no love for all that probing, prying,
not since some Aetolian fooled me with his yarn.
He'd killed a man, wandered over the face of the earth,   430
stumbled onto my hut, and I received him warmly.
He told me he'd seen Odysseus
lodged with King Idomeneus down in Crete—
refitting his ships, hard-hit by the gales,
but he'd be home, he said, by summer or harvest-time,
his hulls freighted with treasure, manned by fighting crews.
So you, old misery, seeing a god has led you here to me,
don't try to charm me now, don't spellbind me with lies!
Never for *that* will I respect you, treat you kindly;
no, it's my fear of Zeus, the god of guests,   440

and because I pity you . . ."

      "Good god," the crafty man pressed on,
"what a dark, suspicious heart you have inside you!
Not even my oath can win you over, make you see the light.
Come, strike a bargain—all the gods of Olympus
witness now our pact!
If your master returns, here to your house,
dress me in shirt and cloak and send me off
to Dulichion at once, the place I long to be.
But if your master doesn't return as I predict,   450
set your men on me—fling me off some rocky crag
so the next beggar here may just think twice
before he peddles lies."
                          "Surely, friend!"—
the swineherd shook his head—"and just think
of the praise and fame I'd win among mankind,
now and for all time to come, if first I took you
under my roof, I treated you kindly as my guest
then cut you down and robbed you of your life—
how keen I'd be to say my prayers to Zeus!
But it's high time for a meal.   460
I hope the men will be home at any moment
so we can fix a tasty supper in the lodge."

      As host and guest confided back and forth
the herdsmen came in, driving their hogs up close,
penning sows in their proper sties for the night,
squealing for all they're worth, shut inside their yard,
and the good swineherd shouted to his men,
"Bring in your fattest hog!
I'll slaughter it for our guest from far abroad.
We'll savor it ourselves. All too long we've sweated   470
over these white-tusked boars—our wretched labor—
while others wolf our work down free of charge!"
                                        Calling out
as he split up kindling now with a good sharp ax
and his men hauled in a tusker five years old,

rippling fat, and stood him steady by the hearth.
The swineherd, soul of virtue, did not forget the gods.
He began the rite by plucking tufts from the porker's head,
threw them into the fire and prayed to all the powers,
"Bring him home, our wise Odysseus, home at last!"
Then raising himself full-length, with an oak log   480
he'd left unsplit he clubbed and stunned the beast
and it gasped out its life . . .
The men slashed its throat, singed the carcass,
quickly quartered it all, and then the swineherd,
cutting first strips for the gods from every limb,
spread them across the thighs, wrapped in sleek fat,
and sprinkling barley over them, flung them on the fire.
They sliced the rest into pieces, pierced them with skewers,
broiled them all to a turn and, pulling them off the spits,
piled the platters high. The swineherd, standing up   490
to share the meat—his sense of fairness perfect—
carved it all out into seven equal portions.
One he set aside, lifting up a prayer
to the forest nymphs and Hermes, Maia's son,
and the rest he handed on to each man in turn.
But to Odysseus he presented the boar's long loin
and the cut of honor cheered his master's heart.
The man for all occasions thanked his host:
"I pray, Eumaeus, you'll be as dear to Father Zeus
as you are to me—a man in my condition—   500
you honor me by giving me your best."

    You replied in kind, Eumaeus, swineherd:
"Eat, my strange new friend . . . enjoy it now,
it's all we have to offer. As for Father Zeus,
one thing he will give and another he'll hold back,
whatever his pleasure. All things are in his power."

    He burned choice parts for the gods who never die
and pouring glistening wine in a full libation,
placed the cup in his guest's hands—Odysseus,
raider of cities—and down he sat to his own share.   510

Mesaulius served them bread, a man the swineherd
purchased for himself in his master's absence—
alone, apart from his queen or old Laertes—
bought him from Taphians, bartered his own goods.
They reached out for the spread that lay at hand
and when they'd put aside desire for food and drink,
Mesaulius cleared the things away. And now, content
with bread and meat, they made for bed at once.

A foul night came on—the dark of the moon—and Zeus
rained from dusk to dawn and a sodden West Wind raged.   520
Odysseus spoke up now, keen to test the swineherd.
Would he take his cloak off, hand it to his guest
or at least tell one of his men to do the same?
He cared for the stranger so, who ventured now,
"Listen, Eumaeus, and all you comrades here,
allow me to sing my praises for a moment.
Say it's the wine that leads me on, the wild wine
that sets the wisest man to sing at the top of his lungs,
laugh like a fool—it drives the man to dancing . . . it even
tempts him to blurt out stories better never told.   530
But now that I'm sounding off, I can't hold back.
Oh make me young again, and the strength inside me
steady as a rock! Just as I was that day
we sprang a sudden ambush against the Trojans.
Odysseus led the raid with Atreus' son Menelaus.
I was third in command—they'd chosen me themselves.
Once we'd edged up under the city's steep ramparts,
crowding the walls but sinking into the thick brake,
the reeds and marshy flats, huddling under our armor
there we lay, and a foul night came on, the North Wind struck,   540
freezing cold, and down from the skies the snow fell like frost,
packed hard—the rims of our shields armored round with ice.
There all the rest of the men wore shirts and cloaks and,
hunching shields over their shoulders, slept at ease.
Not I. I'd left my cloak at camp when I set out—
idiot—never thinking it might turn cold,
so I joined in with just the shield on my back

and a shining waist-guard . . . But then at last,
the night's third watch, the stars just wheeling down—
I muttered into his ear, Odysseus, right beside me,   550
nudging him with an elbow—he perked up at once—
'Royal son of Laertes, Odysseus, full of tactics,
I'm not long for the living. The cold will do me in.
See, I've got no cloak. Some spirit's fooled me—
I came out half-dressed. Now there's no escape!'
I hadn't finished—a thought flashed in his mind;
no one could touch the man at plots or battles.
'Shhh!' he hissed back—Odysseus had a plan—
'One of our fighters over there might hear you.'
Then he propped his head on his forearm, calling out,   560
'Friends, wake up. I slept and a god sent down a dream.
It warned that we're too far from the ships, exposed.
Go, someone, tell Agamemnon, our field marshal—
he might rush reinforcements from the beach.'
Thoas, son of Andraemon, sprang up at once,
flung off his purple cloak and ran to the ships
while I, bundling into his wrap, was glad at heart
till Dawn rose on her golden throne once more.
Oh make me young again
and the strength inside me steady as a rock!   570
One of the swineherds here would lend a wrap
for love of a good soldier, respect as well.
Now they spurn me, dressed in filthy rags."

      And you replied, Eumaeus, loyal swineherd,
"Now that was a fine yarn you told, old-timer,
not without point, not without profit either.
You won't want for clothes or whatever else
is due a worn-out traveler come for help—
not for tonight at least. Tomorrow morning
you'll have to flap around in rags again.   580
Here we've got no store of shirts and cloaks,
no changes. Just one wrap per man, that's all.
But just you wait till Odysseus' dear son comes back—
that boy will deck you out in a cloak and shirt

and send you off, wherever your heart desires!"
                                             With that
he rose to his feet and laid out a bed by the fire,
throwing over it skins of sheep and goats and
down Odysseus lay. Eumaeus flung on his guest
the heavy flaring cloak he kept in reserve
to wear when winter brought some wild storm.
                                             So here   590
Odysseus slept and the young hands slept beside him.
Not the swineherd. Not his style to bed indoors,
apart from his pigs. He geared up to go outside
and it warmed Odysseus' heart,
Eumaeus cared so much for his absent master's goods.
First, over his broad shoulders he slung a whetted sword,
wrapped himself in a cloak stitched tight to block the wind,
and adding a cape, the pelt of a shaggy well-fed goat,
he took a good sharp lance to fight off men and dogs.
Then out he went to sleep where his white-tusked boars   600
had settled down for the night . . . just under
a jutting crag that broke the North Wind's blast.

BOOK FIFTEEN

The Prince Sets Sail for Home

Now south through the spacious dancing-rings of Lacedaemon
Athena went to remind the hero's princely son
of his journey home and spur him on his way.
She found him there with Nestor's gallant son,
bedded down in the porch of illustrious Menelaus—
Pisistratus, at least, overcome with deep sound sleep,
but not Telemachus. Welcome sleep could not hold him.
All through the godsent night he lay awake . . .
tossing with anxious thoughts about his father.
Hovering over him, eyes ablaze, Athena said,   10
"It's wrong, Telemachus, wrong to rove so far,
so long from home, leaving your own holdings
unprotected—crowds in your palace so brazen
they'll carve up all your wealth, devour it all,
and then your journey here will come to nothing.

Quickly, press Menelaus, lord of the warcry,
to speed you home at once, if you want to find
your irreproachable mother still inside your house.
Even now her father and brothers urge Penelope
to marry Eurymachus, who excels all other suitors   20
at giving gifts and drives the bride-price higher.
She must not carry anything off against your will!
You know how the heart of a woman always works:
she likes to build the wealth of her new groom—
of the sons she bore, of her dear, departed husband,
not a memory of the dead, no questions asked.
So sail for home, I say!
With your own hands turn over all your goods
to the one serving-woman you can trust the most,
till the gods bring to light your own noble bride.   30

    And another thing. Take it to heart, I tell you.
Picked men of the suitors lie in ambush, grim-set
in the straits between Ithaca and rocky Same,
poised to kill you before you can reach home,
but I have my doubts they will. Sooner the earth
will swallow down a few of those young gallants
who eat you out of house and home these days!
Just give the channel islands a wide berth,
push on in your trim ship, sail night and day,
and the deathless god who guards and pulls you through   40
will send you a fresh fair wind from hard astern.
At your first landfall, Ithaca's outer banks,
speed ship and shipmates round to the city side.
But you—you make your way to the swineherd first,
in charge of your pigs, and true to you as always.
Sleep the night there, send him to town at once
to tell the news to your mother, wise Penelope—
you've made it back from Pylos safe and sound."

    Mission accomplished, back she went to Olympus' heights
as Telemachus woke Nestor's son from his sweet sleep;   50
he dug a heel in his ribs and roused him briskly:

"Up, Pisistratus. Hitch the team to the chariot—
let's head for home at once!"
                                        "No, Telemachus,"
Nestor's son objected, "much as we long to go,
we cannot drive a team in the dead of night.
Morning will soon be here. So wait, I say,
wait till he loads our chariot down with gifts—
the hero Atrides, Menelaus, the great spearman—
and gives us warm salutes and sees us off like princes.
That's the man a guest will remember all his days: 60
the lavish host who showers him with kindness."

   At those words Dawn rose on her golden throne
and Menelaus, lord of the warcry, rising up from bed
by the side of Helen with her loose and lovely hair,
walked toward his guests. As soon as he saw him,
Telemachus rushed to pull a shimmering tunic on,
over his broad shoulders threw his flaring cape
and the young prince, son of King Odysseus,
strode out to meet his host: "Menelaus,
royal son of Atreus, captain of armies,   70
let me go back to my own country now.
The heart inside me longs for home at last."

   The lord of the warcry reassured the prince,
"I'd never detain you here too long, Telemachus,
not if your heart is set on going home.
I'd find fault with another host, I'm sure,
too warm to his guests, too pressing or too cold.
Balance is best in all things. It's bad either way,
spurring the stranger home who wants to linger,
holding the one who longs to leave—you know,   80
'Welcome the coming, speed the parting guest!'
But wait till I load your chariot down with gifts—
fine ones, too, you'll see with your own eyes—
and tell the maids to serve a meal at hall.
We have god's plenty here.
It's honor and glory to us, a help to you as well

if you dine in style first, then leave to see the world.
And if you're keen for the grand tour of all Hellas,
right to the depths of Argos, I'll escort you myself,
harness the horses, guide you through the towns.   90
And no host will turn us away with empty hands,
each will give us at least one gift to prize—
a handsome tripod, cauldron forged in bronze,
a brace of mules or a solid golden cup."

    Firmly resolved, Telemachus replied,
"Menelaus, royal Atrides, captain of armies,
I must go back to my own home at once.
When I started out I left no one behind
to guard my own possessions. God forbid,
searching for my great father, I lose my life   100
or lose some priceless treasure from my house!"

    As soon as the lord of the warcry heard *that,*
he told his wife and serving-women to lay out a meal
in the hall at once. They'd stores aplenty there.
Eteoneus, son of Boëthous, came to join them—
fresh from bed, he lived close by the palace.
The warlord Menelaus told him to build a fire
and broil some meat. He quickly did his bidding.
Down Atrides walked to a storeroom filled with scent,
and not alone: Helen and Megapenthes went along.   110
Reaching the spot where all the heirlooms lay,
Menelaus chose a generous two-handled cup;
he told his son Megapenthes to take a mixing-bowl,
solid silver, while Helen lingered beside the chests,
and there they were, brocaded, beautiful robes
her own hands had woven. Queenly Helen,
radiance of women, lifted one from the lot,
the largest, loveliest robe, and richly worked
and like a star it glistened, deep beneath the others.
Then all three went up and on through the halls until   120
they found Telemachus. The red-haired king spoke out:
"Oh my boy, may Zeus the Thunderer, Hera's lord,

grant you the journey home your heart desires!
Of all the treasures lying heaped in my palace
you shall have the finest, most esteemed. Look,
I'll give you this mixing-bowl, forged to perfection—
it's solid silver finished off with a lip of gold.
Hephaestus made it himself. And a royal friend,
Phaedimus, king of Sidon, lavished it on *me*
when his palace welcomed me on passage home.   130
How pleased I'd be if you took it as a gift!"

    And the warlord placed the two-eared cup
in his hands while stalwart Megapenthes carried in
the glittering silver bowl and set it down before him.
Helen, her cheeks flushed with beauty, moved beside him,
holding the robe in her arms, and offered, warmly,
"Here, dear boy, I too have a gift to give you,
a keepsake of Helen—I wove it with my hands—
for your own bride to wear
when the blissful day of marriage dawns . . .   140
Until then, let it rest in your mother's room.
And may you return in joy—my parting wish—
to your own grand house, your native land at last."
                               With that

she laid the robe in his arms, and he received it gladly.
Prince Pisistratus, taking the gifts, stowed them deep
in the chariot cradle, viewed them all with wonder.
The red-haired warlord led them back to his house
and the guests took seats on low and high-backed chairs.
A maid brought water soon in a graceful golden pitcher
and over a silver basin tipped it out   150
so they might rinse their hands,
then pulled a gleaming table to their side.
A staid housekeeper brought on bread to serve them,
appetizers aplenty too, lavish with her bounty.
Ready Eteoneus carved and passed the meat,
the son of illustrious Menelaus poured their wine.
They reached out for the good things that lay at hand
and once they'd put aside desire for food and drink,

Prince Telemachus and the gallant son of Nestor
yoked their team, mounted the blazoned car   160
and drove through the gates and echoing colonnade.
The red-haired King Menelaus followed both boys out,
his right hand holding a golden cup of honeyed wine
so the two might pour libations forth at parting.
Just in front of the straining team he strode,
lifting his cup and pledging both his guests:
"Farewell, my princes! Give my warm greetings
to Nestor, the great commander,
always kind to me as a father, long ago
when we young men of Achaea fought at Troy."   170

    And tactful Telemachus replied at once,
"Surely, my royal host, we'll tell him all,
as soon as we reach old Nestor—all you say.
I wish I were just as sure I'd find Odysseus
waiting there at home when I reach Ithaca.
I'd tell him I come from you,
treated with so much kindness at your hands,
loaded down with all these priceless gifts!"

    At his last words a bird flew past on the right,
an eagle clutching a huge white goose in its talons,   180
plucked from the household yards. And all rushed after,
shouting, men and women, and swooping toward the chariot now
the bird veered off to the right again before the horses.
All looked up, overjoyed—people's spirits lifted.
Nestor's son Pisistratus spoke out first:
"Look there! King Menelaus, captain of armies,
what, did the god send down that sign for you
or the two of us?"
             The warlord fell to thinking—
how to read the omen rightly, how to reply? . . .
But long-robed Helen stepped in well before him: 190
"Listen to me and I will be your prophet,
sure as the gods have flashed it in my mind
and it will come to pass, I know it will.

Just as the eagle swooped down from the crags
where it was born and bred, just as it snatched
that goose fattened up for the kill inside the house,
just so, after many trials and roving long and hard,
Odysseus will descend on his house and take revenge—
unless he's home already, sowing seeds of ruin
for that whole crowd of suitors!"

      "Oh if only,"   200
pensive Telemachus burst out in thanks to Helen,
"Zeus the thundering lord of Hera makes it so—
even at home I'll pray to you as a deathless goddess!"

 He cracked the lash and the horses broke quickly,
careering through the city out into open country,
shaking the yoke across their shoulders all day long.

 The sun sank and the roads of the world grew dark
as they reached Phera, pulling up to Diocles' halls,
the son of Ortilochus, son of the Alpheus River.
He gave them a royal welcome; there they slept the night. 210

 When young Dawn with her rose-red fingers shone once more
they yoked their pair again, mounted the blazoned car
and out through the gates and echoing colonnade
they whipped the team to a run and on they flew,
holding nothing back, approaching Pylos soon,
the craggy citadel. That was when Telemachus
turned to Pisistratus, saying, "Son of Nestor,
won't you do as I ask you, see it through?
We're friends for all our days now, so we claim,
thanks to our fathers' friendship. We're the same age as well 220
and this tour of ours has made us more like brothers.
Prince, don't drive me past my vessel, drop me there.
Your father's old, in love with his hospitality;
I fear he'll hold me, chafing in his palace—
I must hurry home!"

      The son of Nestor pondered . . .
how to do it properly, see it through?

Pausing a moment, then this way seemed best.
Swerving his team, he drove down to the ship
tied up on shore and loaded into her stern
the splendid gifts, the robes and gold Menelaus gave,   230
and sped his friend with a flight of winging words:
"Climb aboard now—fast! Muster all your men
before I get home and break the news to father.
With that man's overbearing spirit—I know it,
know it all too well—he'll never let you go,
he'll come down here and summon you himself.
He won't return without you, believe me—
in any case he'll fly into a rage."

    With that warning he whipped his sleek horses
back to Pylos city and reached his house in no time.   240
Telemachus shouted out commands to all his shipmates:
"Stow our gear, my comrades, deep in the holds
and board at once—we must be on our way!"

    His shipmates snapped to orders,
swung aboard and sat to the oars in ranks.
But just as Telemachus prepared to launch,
praying, sacrificing to Pallas by the stern,
a man from a far-off country came toward him now,
a fugitive out of Argos: he had killed a man . . .
He was a prophet, sprung of Melampus' line of seers,   250
Melampus who lived in Pylos, mother of flocks, some years ago,
rich among his Pylians, at home in his great high house.
But then he was made to go abroad to foreign parts,
fleeing his native land and hot-blooded Neleus—
most imperious man alive—who'd commandeered
his vast estate and held it down by force
for one entire year. That year Melampus,
bound by cruel chains in the halls of Phylacus,
suffered agonies—all for Neleus' daughter Pero,
that and the mad spell a Fury, murderous spirit,   260
cast upon his mind. But the seer worked free of death

and drove the lusty, bellowing cattle out of Phylace,
back to Pylos. There he avenged himself on Neleus
for the shameful thing the king had done to him,
and escorted Pero home as his brother's bride.
But he himself went off to a distant country,
Argos, land of stallions—his destined home
where he would live and rule the Argive nation.
Here he married a wife and built a high-roofed house
and sired Antiphates and Mantius, two staunch sons.   270
Antiphates fathered Oicles, gallant heart,
Oicles fathered Amphiaraus, driver of armies,
whom storming Zeus and Apollo loved intensely,
showering him with every form of kindness.
But he never reached the threshold of old age,
he died at Thebes—undone by a bribe his wife accepted—
leaving behind his two sons, Alcmaeon and Amphilochus.
On his side Mantius sired Polyphides and Clitus both
but Dawn of the golden throne whisked Clitus away,
overwhelmed by his beauty,   280
so the boy would live among the deathless gods.
Yet Apollo made magnanimous Polyphides a prophet—
after Amphiaraus' death—the greatest seer on earth.
But a feud with his father drove him off to Hyperesia
where he made his home and prophesied to the world . . .

     This prophet's son it was—Theoclymenus his name—
who approached Telemachus now and found him pouring
wine to a god and saying prayers beside his ship.
"Friend," he said in a winging supplication,
"since I find you burning offerings here,   290
I beg you by these rites and the god you pray to,
then by your own life and the lives of all the men
who travel with you—tell me truly, don't hold back,
who are you? where are you from? your city? your parents?"

     "Of course, stranger," the forthright prince responded,
"I will tell you everything, clearly as I can.

Ithaca is my country. Odysseus is my father—
there was a man, or was he all a dream? . . .
but he's surely died a wretched death by now.
Yet here I've come with my crew and black ship,   300
out for news of my father, lost and gone so long."

    And the godlike seer Theoclymenus replied,
"Just like you, I too have left my land—
I because I killed a man of my own tribe.
But he has many brothers and kin in Argos,
stallion-land, who rule the plains in force.
Fleeing death at their hands, a dismal fate,
I am a fugitive now,
doomed to wander across this mortal world.
So take me aboard, hear a fugitive's prayer: 310
don't let them kill me—they're after me, well I know!"

    "So desperate!" thoughtful Telemachus exclaimed.
"How could I drive you from my ship? Come sail with us,
we'll tend you at home, with all we can provide."

    And he took the prophet's honed bronze spear,
laid it down full-length on the rolling deck,
swung aboard the deep-sea craft himself,
assuming the pilot's seat reserved astern
and put the seer beside him. Cables cast off,
Telemachus shouted out commands to all his shipmates: 320
"All lay hands to tackle!" They sprang to orders,
hoisting the pinewood mast, they stepped it firm
in its block amidships, lashed it fast with stays
and with braided rawhide halyards hauled the white sail high.
Now bright-eyed Athena sent them a stiff following wind
blustering out of a clear sky, gusting on so the ship
might run its course through the salt sea at top speed—
and past the Springs she raced and the Chalcis' rushing stream
as the sun sank and the roads of the world grew dark and
on she pressed for Pheae, driven on by a wind from Zeus   330
and flew past lovely Elis, where Epeans rule in power,

and then Telemachus veered for the Jagged Islands,
wondering all the way—
would he sweep clear of death or be cut down?

    The king and loyal swineherd, just that night,
were supping with other fieldhands in the lodge.
And once they'd put aside desire for food and drink,
Odysseus spoke up, eager to test the swineherd,
see if he'd stretch out his warm welcome now,
invite him to stay on in the farmstead here   340
or send him off to town. "Listen, Eumaeus,
all you comrades here—at the crack of dawn
I mean to go to town and do my begging,
not be a drain on you and all your men.
But advise me well, give me a trusty guide
to see me there. And then I'm on my own
to roam the streets—I must, I have no choice—
hoping to find a handout, just a crust or cupful.
I'd really like to go to the house of King Odysseus
and give my news to his cautious queen, Penelope.   350
Why, I'd even mix with those overweening suitors—
would they spare me a plateful? Look at all they have!
I'd do good work for them, promptly, anything they want.
Let me tell you, listen closely, catch my drift . . .
Thanks to Hermes the guide, who gives all work
of our hands the grace and fame that it deserves,
no one alive can match me at household chores:
building a good fire, splitting kindling neatly,
carving, roasting meat and pouring rounds of wine . . .
anything menials do to serve their noble masters."   360

    "God's sake, my friend!" you broke in now,
Eumaeus, loyal swineherd, deeply troubled.
"What's got into your head, what crazy plan?
You must be hell-bent on destruction, on the spot,
if you're keen to mingle with that mob of suitors—
their pride and violence hit the iron skies!
They're a far cry from you,

the men who do their bidding. Young bucks,
all rigged out in their fine robes and shirts,
hair sleeked down with oil, faces always beaming,   370
the ones who slave for *them!* The tables polished,
sagging under the bread and meat and wine.
No, stay here. No one finds you a burden,
surely not I, nor any comrade here.
You wait till Odysseus' dear son comes back—
that boy will deck you out in a cloak and shirt
and send you off, wherever your heart desires!"

    "If only, Eumaeus," the wayworn exile said,
"you were as dear to Father Zeus as you are to me!
You who stopped my pain, my endless, homesick roving.   380
Tramping about the world—there's nothing worse for a man.
But the fact is that men put up with misery
to stuff their cursed bellies.
But seeing you hold me here, urging me now
to wait for *him*, the prince who's on his way,
tell me about the mother of King Odysseus, please,
the father he left as well—on the threshold of old age—
when he sailed off to war. Are they still alive,
perhaps, still looking into the light of day?
Or dead by now, and down in Death's long house?"
                                            "Friend,"   390

the swineherd, foreman of men, assured his guest,
"I'll tell you the whole story, point by point.
Laertes is still alive, but night and day
he prays to Zeus, waiting there in his house,
for the life breath to slip away and leave his body.
His heart's so racked for his son, lost and gone these years,
for his wife so fine, so wise—*her* death is the worst blow
he's had to suffer—it made him old before his time.
She died of grief for her boy, her glorious boy,
it wore her down, a wretched way to go.   400
I pray that no one I love dies such a death,
no island neighbor of mine who treats me kindly!
While she was still alive, heartsick as she was,

it always moved me to ask about her, learn the news.
She'd reared me herself, and right beside her daughter,
Ctimene, graceful girl with her long light gown,
the youngest one she'd borne . . .
Just the two of us, growing up together,
the woman tending me almost like her child,
till we both reached the lovely flush of youth   410
and then her parents gave her away in marriage, yes,
to a Samian man, and a haul of gifts they got.
But her mother decked me out in cloak and shirt,
good clothing she wrapped about me—gave me sandals,
sent me here, this farm. She loved me from the heart.
Oh how I miss her kindness now! The happy gods
speed the work that I labor at, that gives me
food and drink to spare for the ones I value.
But from Queen Penelope I never get a thing,
never a winning word, no friendly gesture,   420
not since this, this plague has hit the house—
these high and mighty suitors. Servants miss it,
terribly, gossiping back and forth with the mistress,
gathering scraps of news, a snack and a cup or two,
then taking home to the fields some little gift.
It never fails to cheer a servant's heart."

    "Imagine that," his canny master said,
"you must have been just a little fellow, Eumaeus,
when you were swept so far from home and parents.
Come, tell me the whole story, truly too.   430
Was your city sacked?—
some city filled with people and wide streets
where your father and your mother made their home?
Or were you all alone, herding your sheep and cattle,
when pirates kidnapped, shipped and sold you off
to this man's house, who paid a healthy price?"

    "My friend," the swineherd answered, foreman of men,
"you really want my story? So many questions—well,
listen in quiet, then, and take your ease, sit back

and drink your wine. The nights are endless now.   440
We've plenty of time to sleep or savor a long tale.
No need, you know, to turn in before the hour.
Even too much sleep can be a bore.
But anyone else who feels the urge
can go to bed and then, at the crack of dawn,
break bread, turn out and tend our master's pigs.
We two will keep to the shelter here, eat and drink
and take some joy in each other's heartbreaking sorrows,
sharing each other's memories. Over the years, you know,
a man finds solace even in old sorrows, true, a man   450
who's weathered many blows and wandered many miles.
My own story? This will answer all your questions . . .

    There's an island, Syrie—you may have heard of it—
off above Ortygia, out where the sun wheels around.
Not so packed with people, still a good place, though,
fine for sheep and cattle, rich in wine and wheat.
Hunger never attacks the land, no sickness either,
that always stalks the lives of us poor men.
No, as each generation grows old on the island,
down Apollo comes with his silver bow, with Artemis,   460
and they shoot them all to death with gentle arrows.
Two cities there are, that split the land in half,
and over them both my father ruled in force—
Ormenus' son Ctesius, a man like a deathless god.
                                        One day
a band of Phoenicians landed there. The famous sea-dogs,
sharp bargainers too, the holds of their black ship
brimful with a hoard of flashy baubles. Now,
my father kept a Phoenician woman in his house,
beautiful, tall and skilled at weaving lovely things,
and her rascal countrymen lusted to seduce her, yes,   470
and lost no time—she was washing clothes when one of them
waylaid her beside their ship, in a long deep embrace
that can break a woman's will, even the best alive.
And then he asked her questions . . .
her name, who was she, where did she come from?

She waved at once to my father's high-roofed house—
'But I'm proud to hail from Sidon paved in bronze,' she said,
'and Arybas was my father, a man who rolled in wealth.
I was heading home from the fields when Taphian pirates
snatched me away, and they shipped and sold me here   480
to this man's house. He paid a good stiff price!'

    The sailor, her secret lover, lured her on:
'Well then, why don't you sail back home with us?—
see your own high house, your father and mother there.
They're still alive, and people say they're rich!'

    'Now there's a tempting offer,' she said in haste,
'if only you sailors here would swear an oath
you'll land me safe at home without a scratch.'

    Those were her terms, and once they vowed to keep them,
swore their oaths they'd never do her harm,   490
the woman hatched a plan: 'Now not a word!
Let none of your shipmates say a thing to me,
meeting me on the street or at the springs.
Someone might go running off to the house
and tell the old king—he'd think the worst,
clap me in cruel chains and find a way to kill you.
So keep it a secret, down deep, get on with buying
your home cargo, quickly. But once your holds
are loaded up with goods, then fast as you can
you send the word to me over there at the palace.   500
I'll bring you all the gold I can lay my hands on
and something else I'll give you in the bargain,
fare for passage home . . .
I'm nurse to my master's son in the palace now—
such a precious toddler, scampering round outside,
always at my heels. I'll bring him aboard as well.
Wherever you sell him off, whatever foreign parts,
he'll fetch you quite a price!'

                           Bargain struck,
back the woman went to our lofty halls

and the rovers stayed on with us one whole year,   510
bartering, piling up big hoards in their hollow ship,
and once their holds were loaded full for sailing
they sent a messenger, fast, to alert the woman.
This crafty bandit came to my father's house,
dangling a golden choker linked with amber beads,
and while the maids at hall and my noble mother
kept on fondling it—dazzled, feasting their eyes
and making bids—he gave a quiet nod to my nurse,
he gave her the nod and slunk back to his ship.
Grabbing my hand, she swept me through the house   520
and there in the porch she came on cups and tables
left by the latest feasters, father's men of council
just gone off to the meeting grounds for full debate—
and quick as a flash she snatched up three goblets,
tucked them into her bosom, whisked them off
and I tagged along, lost in all my innocence!
The sun sank, the roads of the world grew dark
and both on the run, we reached the bay at once
where the swift Phoenician ship lay set to sail.
Handing us up on board, the crewmen launched out   530
on the foaming lanes and Zeus sent wind astern.
Six whole days we sailed, six nights, nonstop
and then, when the god brought on the seventh day,
Artemis showering arrows came and shot the woman—
headfirst into the bilge she splashed like a diving tern
and the crewmen heaved her body over, a nice treat
for the seals and fish, but left me all alone,
cowering, sick at heart . . .
                               Until, at last,
the wind and current bore us on to Ithaca,
here where Laertes bought me with his wealth.   540
And so I first laid eyes on this good land."

   And royal King Odysseus answered warmly,
"Eumaeus, so much misery! You've moved my heart,
deeply, with your long tale—such pain, such sorrow.
True, but look at the good fortune Zeus sends you,

hand-in-hand with the bad. After all your toil
you reached the house of a decent, kindly man
who gives you all you need in meat and drink—
he's seen to that, I'd say—
it's a fine life you lead! Better than mine . . .   550
I've been drifting through cities up and down the earth
and now I've landed here."
                              So guest and host
confided through the night until they slept,
a little at least, not long.
Dawn soon rose and took her golden throne.
                                        That hour
Telemachus and his shipmates raised the coasts of home,
they struck sail and lowered the mast, smartly,
rowed her into a mooring under oars.
Out went the bow-stones, cables fast astern,
the crew themselves swung out in the breaking surf,   560
they got a meal together and mixed some ruddy wine.
And once they'd put aside desire for food and drink,
clear-headed Telemachus gave the men commands:
"Pull our black ship round to the city now—
I'm off to my herdsmen and my farms. By nightfall,
once I've seen to my holdings, I'll be down in town.
In the morning I'll give you wages for the voyage,
a handsome feast of meat and hearty wine."

    The seer Theoclymenus broke in quickly,
"Where shall I go, dear boy? Of all the lords   570
in rocky Ithaca, whose house shall I head for now?
Or do I go straight to your mother's house and yours?"

    "Surely in better times," discreet Telemachus replied,
"I would invite you home. Our hospitality never fails
but now, I fear, it could only serve you poorly.
I'll be away, and mother would never see you.
She rarely appears these days,
what with those suitors milling in the hall;
she keeps to her upper story, weaving at her loom.

But I'll mention someone else you might just visit: 580
Eurymachus, wise Polybus' fine, upstanding son.
He's the man of the hour! Our island people
look on him like a god—the prince of suitors,
hottest to wed my mother, seize my father's powers.
But god knows—Zeus up there in his bright Olympus—
whether or not before that wedding day arrives
he'll bring the day of death on all their heads!"

    At his last words a bird flew past on the right,
a hawk, Apollo's wind-swift herald—tight in his claws
a struggling dove, and he ripped its feathers out   590
and they drifted down to earth between the ship
and the young prince himself . . .
The prophet called him aside, clear of his men,
and grasped his hand, exclaiming, "Look, Telemachus,
the will of god just winged that bird on your right!
Why, the moment I saw it, here before my eyes,
I knew it was a sign. No line more kingly than yours
in all of Ithaca—yours will reign forever!"
                                  "If only, friend,"
alert Telemachus answered, "all you say comes true!
You'd soon know my affection, know my gifts.   600
Any man you meet would call you blest."

    He turned to a trusted friend and said, "Piraeus,
son of Clytius, you are the one who's done my bidding,
more than all other friends who sailed with me to Pylos.
Please, take this guest of mine to your own house,
treat him kindly, host him with all good will
till I can come myself."
                        "Of course, Telemachus,"
Piraeus the gallant spearman offered warmly:
"Stay up-country just as long as you like.
I'll tend the man, he'll never lack a lodging."   610

    Piraeus boarded ship and told the crew
to embark at once and cast off cables quickly—

they swung aboard and sat to the oars in ranks.
Telemachus fastened rawhide sandals on his feet
and took from the decks his rugged bronze-tipped spear.
The men cast off, pushed out and pulled for town
as Telemachus ordered, King Odysseus' son.
The prince strode out briskly,
legs speeding him on till he reached the farm
where his great droves of pigs crowded their pens   620
and the loyal swineherd often slept beside them,
always the man to serve his masters well.

BOOK SIXTEEN

Father and Son

As dawn came into the lodge, the king and loyal swineherd
set out breakfast, once they had raked the fire up
and got the herdsmen off with droves of pigs.
And now Telemachus . . .
the howling dogs went nuzzling up around him,
not a growl as he approached. From inside
Odysseus noticed the pack's quiet welcome,
noticed the light tread of footsteps too
and turned to Eumaeus quickly, winged a word:
"Eumaeus, here comes a friend of yours, I'd say.   10
Someone you know, at least. The pack's not barking,
must be fawning around him. I can hear his footfall."

The words were still on his lips when his own son
stood in the doorway, there. The swineherd started up,

amazed, he dropped the bowls with a clatter—he'd been busy
mixing ruddy wine. Straight to the prince he rushed
and kissed his face and kissed his shining eyes,
both hands, as the tears rolled down his cheeks.
As a father, brimming with love, welcomes home
his darling only son in a warm embrace—   20
what pain he's borne for him and him alone!—
home now, in the tenth year from far abroad,
so the loyal swineherd hugged the beaming prince,
he clung for dear life, covering him with kisses, yes,
like one escaped from death. Eumaeus wept and sobbed,
his words flew from the heart: "You're home, Telemachus,
sweet light of my eyes! I never thought I'd see you again,
once you'd shipped to Pylos! Quick, dear boy, come in,
let me look at you, look to my heart's content—
under my own roof, the rover home at last.   30
You rarely visit the farm and men these days,
always keeping to town, as if it *cheered* you
to see them there, that infernal crowd of suitors!"

    "Have it your way," thoughtful Telemachus replied.
"Dear old man, it's all for you that I've come,
to see you for myself and learn the news—
whether mother still holds out in the halls
or some other man has married her at last,
and Odysseus' bed, I suppose, is lying empty,
blanketed now with filthy cobwebs."
                                "Surely,"   40
the foreman of men responded, "she's still waiting
there in your halls, poor woman, suffering so,
her life an endless hardship . . .
wasting away the nights, weeping away the days."
                                                With that
he took the bronze spear from the boy, and Telemachus,
crossing the stone doorsill, went inside the lodge.
As he approached, his father, Odysseus, rose
to yield his seat, but the son on his part
waved him back: "Stay where you are, stranger.

I know we can find another seat somewhere,   50
here on our farm, and here's the man to fetch it."

    So Odysseus, moving back, sat down once more,
and now for the prince the swineherd strewed a bundle
of fresh green brushwood, topped it off with sheepskin
and there the true son of Odysseus took his place.
Eumaeus set before them platters of roast meat
left from the meal he'd had the day before;
he promptly served them bread, heaped in baskets,
mixed their hearty wine in a wooden bowl
and then sat down himself to face the king.   60
They reached for the good things that lay at hand,
and when they'd put aside desire for food and drink
Telemachus asked his loyal serving-man at last,
"Old friend, where does this stranger come from?
Why did the sailors land him here in Ithaca?
Who did they say they are?
I hardly think he came this way on foot."

    You answered him, Eumaeus, loyal swineherd,
"Here, my boy, I'll tell you the whole true story.
He hails from Crete's broad land, he's proud to say,   70
but he claims he's drifted round through countless towns of men,
roaming the earth . . . and so a god's spun out his fate.
He just now broke away from some Thesprotian ship
and came to my farm. I'll put him in *your* hands,
you tend to him as you like.
He counts on you, he says, for care and shelter."

    "Shelter? Oh Eumaeus," Telemachus replied,
"that word of yours, it cuts me to the quick!
How can I lend the stranger refuge in my house?
I'm young myself. I can hardly trust my hands   80
to fight off any man who rises up against me.
Then my mother's wavering, always torn two ways:
whether to stay with me and care for the household,
true to her husband's bed, the people's voice as well,

or leave at long last with the best man in Achaea
who courts her in the halls, who offers her the most.
But our new guest, since he's arrived at your house,
I'll give him a shirt and cloak to wear, good clothing,
give him a two-edged sword and sandals for his feet
and send him off, wherever his heart desires.   90
Or if you'd rather, keep him here at the farmstead,
tend to him here, and I'll send up the clothes
and full rations to keep the man in food;
he'll be no drain on you and all your men.
But I can't let him go down and join the suitors.
They're far too abusive, reckless, know no limits:
they'll make a mockery of him—that would break my heart.
It's hard for a man to win his way against a mob,
even a man of iron. They are much too strong."

    "Friend"—the long-enduring Odysseus stepped in—   100
"surely it's right for *me* to say a word at this point.
My heart, by god, is torn to pieces hearing this,
both of you telling how these reckless suitors,
there in your own house, against your will,
plot your ruin—a fine young prince like you.
Tell me, though, do you let yourself be so abused
or do people round about, stirred up by the prompting
of some god, despise you? Or are your brothers at fault?
Brothers a man can trust to fight beside him, true,
no matter what deadly blood-feud rages on.   110
Would I were young as you, to match my spirit now,
or I were the son of great Odysseus, or the king himself
returned from all his roving—there's still room for hope!
Then let some foreigner lop my head off if I failed
to march right into Odysseus' royal halls
and kill them all. And what if I went down,
crushed by their numbers—I, fighting alone?
I'd rather die, cut down in my own house
than have to look on at their outrage day by day.
Guests treated to blows, men dragging the serving-women   120
through the noble house, exploiting them all, no shame,

and the gushing wine swilled, the food squandered—
gorging for gorging's sake—
and the courting game goes on, no end in sight!"

    "You're right, my friend," sober Telemachus agreed.
"Now let me tell you the whole story, first to last.
It's not that all our people have turned against me,
keen for a showdown. Nor have I any brothers at fault,
brothers a man can trust to fight beside him, true,
no matter what deadly blood-feud rages on . . .   130
Zeus made our line a line of only sons.
Arcesius had only one son, Laertes,
and Laertes had only one son, Odysseus,
and I am Odysseus' only son. He fathered me,
he left me behind at home, and from me he got no joy.
So now our house is plagued by swarms of enemies.
All the nobles who rule the islands round about,
Dulichion, and Same, and wooded Zacynthus too,
and all who lord it in rocky Ithaca as well—
down to the last man they court my mother,   140
they lay waste my house! And mother . . .
she neither rejects a marriage she despises
nor can she bear to bring the courting to an end—
while they continue to bleed my household white.
Soon—you wait—they'll grind *me* down as well!
But all lies in the lap of the great gods.
                                        Eumaeus,
good old friend, go, quickly, to wise Penelope.
Tell her I'm home from Pylos safe and sound.
I'll stay on right here. But you come back
as soon as you've told the news to her alone.   150
No other Achaean must hear—
all too many plot to take my life."
                                "I know,"
you assured your prince, Eumaeus, loyal swineherd.
"I see your point—there's sense in this old head.
One thing more, and make your orders clear.

On the same trip do I go and give the news
to King Laertes too? For many years, poor man,
heartsick for his son, he'd always keep an eye
on the farm and take his meals with the hired hands
whenever he felt the urge to. Now, from the day   160
you sailed away to Pylos, not a sip or a bite
he's touched, they say, not as he did before,
and his eyes are shut to all the farmyard labors.
Huddled over, groaning in grief and tears,
he wastes away—the man's all skin and bones."

   "So much the worse," Telemachus answered firmly.
"Leave him alone; though it hurts us now, we must.
If men could have all they want, free for the taking,
I'd take first my father's journey home. So,
you go and give the message, then come back,   170
no roaming over the fields to find Laertes.
Tell my mother to send her housekeeper,
fast as she can, in secret—
she can give the poor old man the news."

   That roused Eumaeus. The swineherd grasped his sandals,
strapped them onto his feet and made for town.
His exit did not escape Athena's notice . . .
Approaching, closer, now she appeared a woman,
beautiful, tall and skilled at weaving lovely things.
Just at the shelter's door she stopped, visible to Odysseus   180
but Telemachus could not see her, sense her there—
the gods don't show themselves to every man alive.
Odysseus saw her, so did the dogs; no barking now,
they whimpered, cringing away in terror through the yard.
She gave a sign with her brows, Odysseus caught it,
out of the lodge he went and past the high stockade
and stood before the goddess. Athena urged him on:
"Royal son of Laertes, Odysseus, old campaigner,
now is the time, now tell your son the truth.
Hold nothing back, so the two of you can plot   190

the suitors' doom and then set out for town.
I myself won't lag behind you long—
I'm blazing for a battle!"

    Athena stroked him with her golden wand.
First she made the cloak and shirt on his body
fresh and clean, then made him taller, supple, young,
his ruddy tan came back, the cut of his jawline firmed
and the dark beard clustered black around his chin.
Her work complete, she went her way once more
and Odysseus returned to the lodge. His own son   200
gazed at him, wonderstruck, terrified too, turning
his eyes away, suddenly—
                            this must be some god—
and he let fly with a burst of exclamations:
"Friend, you're a new man—not what I saw before!
Your clothes, they've changed, even your skin has changed—
surely you are some god who rules the vaulting skies!
Oh be kind, and we will give you offerings,
gifts of hammered gold to warm your heart—
spare us, please, I beg you!"
                            "No, I am not a god,"
the long-enduring, great Odysseus returned.   210
"Why confuse me with one who never dies?
No, I am your father—
the Odysseus you wept for all your days,
you bore a world of pain, the cruel abuse of men."

    And with those words Odysseus kissed his son
and the tears streamed down his cheeks and wet the ground,
though before he'd always reined his emotions back.
But still not convinced that it was his father,
Telemachus broke out, wild with disbelief,
"No, you're not Odysseus! Not my father!   220
Just some spirit spellbinding me now—
to make me ache with sorrow all the more.
Impossible for a mortal to work such marvels,
not with his own devices, not unless some god

comes down in person, eager to make that mortal
young or old—like that! Why, just now
you were old, and wrapped in rags, but *now,* look,
you seem like a god who rules the skies up there!"

    "Telemachus," Odysseus, man of exploits, urged his son,
"it's wrong to marvel, carried away in wonder so   230
to see your father here before your eyes.
No other Odysseus will ever return to you.
That man and I are one, the man you see . . .
here after many hardships,
endless wanderings, after twenty years
I have come home to native ground at last.
My changing so? Athena's work, the Fighter's Queen—
she has that power, she makes me look as she likes,
now like a beggar, the next moment a young man,
decked out in handsome clothes about my body.   240
It's light work for the gods who rule the skies
to exalt a mortal man or bring him low."
                                                     At that
Odysseus sat down again, and Telemachus threw his arms
around his great father, sobbing uncontrollably
as the deep desire for tears welled up in both.
They cried out, shrilling cries, pulsing sharper
than birds of prey—eagles, vultures with hooked claws—
when farmers plunder their nest of young too young to fly.
Both men so filled with compassion, eyes streaming tears,
that now the sunlight would have set upon their cries   250
if Telemachus had not asked his father, all at once,
"What sort of ship, dear father, brought you here?—
Ithaca, at last. Who did the sailors say they are?
I hardly think you came back home on foot!"

    So long an exile, great Odysseus replied,
"Surely, my son, I'll tell you the whole story now.
Phaeacians brought me here, the famous sailors
who ferry home all men who reach their shores.
They sailed me across the sea in their swift ship,

they set me down in Ithaca, sound asleep, and gave me   260
glittering gifts—bronze and hoards of gold and robes.
All lie stowed in a cave, thanks to the gods' help,
and Athena's inspiration spurred me here, now,
so we could plan the slaughter of our foes.
Come, give me the full tally of these suitors—
I must know their numbers, gauge their strength.
Then I'll deploy this old tactician's wits,
decide if the two of us can take them on,
alone, without allies,
or we should hunt reserves to back us up."

                                "Father,"   270
clear-headed Telemachus countered quickly,
"all my life I've heard of your great fame—
a brave man in war and a deep mind in counsel—
but what you say dumbfounds me, staggers imagination!
How on earth could two men fight so many and so strong?
These suitors are not just ten or twenty, they're far more—
you count them up for yourself now, take a moment . . .
From Dulichion, fifty-two of them, picked young men,
six servants in their troop; from Same, twenty-four,
from Zacynthus, twenty Achaeans, nobles all,   280
and the twelve best lords from Ithaca itself.
Medon the herald's with them, a gifted bard,
and two henchmen, skilled to carve their meat.
If we pit ourselves against all these in the house,
I fear the revenge you come back home to take
will recoil on our heads—a bitter, deadly blow.
Think: can you come up with a friend-in-arms?
Some man to fight beside us, some brave heart?"

   "Let me tell you," the old soldier said,
"bear it in mind now, listen to me closely.   290
Think: will Athena flanked by Father Zeus
do for the two of us?
Or shall I rack my brains for another champion?"

   Telemachus answered shrewdly, full of poise,

"Two great champions, those you name, it's true.
Off in the clouds they sit
and they lord it over gods and mortal men."

   "Trust me," his seasoned father reassured him,
"they won't hold off long from the cries and clash of battle,
not when we and the suitors put our fighting strength   300
to proof in my own halls! But now, with daybreak,
home you go and mix with that overbearing crowd.
The swineherd will lead me into the city later,
looking old and broken, a beggar once again.
If they abuse me in the palace, steel yourself,
no matter what outrage I must suffer, even
if they drag me through our house by the heels
and throw me out or pelt me with things they hurl—
you just look on, endure it. Prompt them to quit
their wild reckless ways, try to win them over   310
with friendly words. Those men will never listen,
now the day of doom is hovering at their heads.
One more thing. Take it to heart, I urge you.
When Athena, Queen of Tactics, tells me it is time,
I'll give you a nod, and when you catch that signal
round up all the deadly weapons kept in the hall,
stow them away upstairs in a storeroom's deep recess—
all the arms and armor—and when the suitors miss them
and ask you questions, put them off with a winning story:
'I stowed them away, clear of the smoke. A far cry   320
from the arms Odysseus left when he went to Troy,
fire-damaged equipment, black with reeking fumes.
And a god reminded me of something darker too.
When you're in your cups a quarrel might break out,
you'd wound each other, shame your feasting here
and cast a pall on your courting.
Iron has powers to draw a man to ruin.'
                       Just you leave
a pair of swords for the two of us, a pair of spears
and a pair of oxhide bucklers right at hand so we
can break for the weapons, seize them! Then Athena,   330

Zeus in his wisdom—they will daze the suitors' wits.
Now one last thing. Bear it in mind. You must.
If you are my own true son, born of my blood,
let no one hear that Odysseus has come home.
Don't let Laertes know, not Eumaeus either,
none in the household, not Penelope herself.
You and I alone will assess the women's mood
and we might test a few of the serving-men as well:
where are the ones who still respect us both,
who hold us in awe? And who shirk their duties?—   340
slighting you because you are so young."

    "Soon enough, father," his gallant son replied,
"you'll sense the courage inside me, that I know—
I'm hardly a flighty, weak-willed boy these days.
But I think your last plan would gain us nothing.
Reconsider, I urge you.
You'll waste time, roaming around our holdings,
probing the fieldhands man by man, while the suitors
sit at ease in our house, devouring all our goods—
those brazen rascals never spare a scrap!   350
But I do advise you to sound the women out:
who are disloyal to you, who are guiltless?
The men—I say no to testing them farm by farm.
That's work for later, if you have really seen
a sign from Zeus whose shield is storm and thunder."

    Now as father and son conspired, shaping plans,
the ship that brought the prince and shipmates back
from Pylos was just approaching Ithaca, home port.
As soon as they put in to the harbor's deep bay
they hauled the black vessel up onto dry land   360
and eager deckhands bore away their gear
and rushed the priceless gifts to Clytius' house.
But they sent a herald on to Odysseus' halls at once
to give the news to thoughtful, cautious Penelope
that Telemachus was home—just up-country now
but he'd told his mates to sail across to port—

so the noble queen would not be seized with fright
and break down in tears. And now those two men met,
herald and swineherd, both out on the same errand,
to give the queen the news. But once they reached   370
the house of the royal king the herald strode up,
into the serving-women's midst, and burst out,
"Your beloved son, my queen, is home at last!"
Eumaeus though, bending close to Penelope,
whispered every word that her dear son
entrusted him to say. Message told in full,
he left the halls and precincts, heading for his pigs.

But the news shook the suitors, dashed their spirits.
Out of the halls they crowded, past the high-walled court
and there before the gates they sat in council.   380
Polybus' son Eurymachus opened up among them:
"Friends, what a fine piece of work he's carried off!
Telemachus—what insolence—and we thought his little jaunt
would come to grief! Up now, launch a black ship,
the best we can find—muster a crew of oarsmen,
row the news to our friends in ambush, fast,
bring them back at once."
                                And just then—
he'd not quite finished when Amphinomus,
wheeling round in his seat,
saw their vessel moored in the deep harbor,   390
their comrades striking sail and hoisting oars.
He broke into heady laughter, called his friends:
"No need for a message now. They're home, look there!
Some god gave them the news, or they saw the prince's ship
go sailing past and failed to overtake her."

Rising, all trooped down to the water's edge
as the crew hauled the vessel up onto dry land
and the hot-blooded hands bore off their gear.
Then in a pack they went to the meeting grounds,
suffering no one else, young or old, to sit among them.   400
Eupithes' son Antinous rose and harangued them all:

"What a blow! See how the gods have saved this boy
from bloody death? And our lookouts all day long,
stationed atop the windy heights, kept watch,
shift on shift; and once the sun went down
we'd never sleep the night ashore, never,
always aboard our swift ship, cruising till dawn,
patrolling to catch Telemachus, kill him on the spot,
and all the while some spirit whisked him home!
So here at home we'll plot his certain death: 410
he must never slip through our hands again,
that boy—while he still lives,
I swear we'll never bring our venture off.
The clever little schemer, he does have his skills,
and the crowds no longer show us favor, not at all.
So act! before he can gather his people in assembly.
He'll never give in an inch, I know, he'll rise
and rage away, shouting out to them all how we,
we schemed his sudden death but never caught him.
Hearing of our foul play, they'll hardly sing our praises.   420
Why, they might do us damage, run us off our lands,
drive us abroad to hunt for strangers' shores.
Strike first, I say, and kill him!—
clear of town, in the fields or on the road.
Then we'll seize his estates and worldly goods,
carve them up between us, share and share alike.
But as for his palace, let his mother keep it,
she and the man she weds.
                           There's my plan.
If you find it offensive, if you want him
living on—in full command of his patrimony—   430
gather here no more then, living the life of kings,
consuming all his wealth. Each from his own house
must try to win her, showering her with gifts.
Then she can marry the one who offers most,
the man marked out by fate to be her husband."

    That brought them all to a hushed, stunned silence
till Amphinomus rose to have his say among them—

the noted son of Nisus, King Aretias' grandson,
the chief who led the suitors from Dulichion,
land of grass and grains,   440
and the man who pleased Penelope the most,
thanks to his timely words and good clear sense.
Concerned for their welfare now, he stood and argued:
"Friends, I've no desire to kill Telemachus, not I—
it's a terrible thing to shed the blood of kings.
Wait, sound out the will of the gods—that first.
If the decrees of mighty Zeus commend the work,
I'll kill the prince myself and spur on all the rest.
If the gods are against it, then I say hold back!"

    So Amphinomus urged, and won them over.   450
They rose at once, returned to Odysseus' palace,
entered and took their seats on burnished chairs.

    But now an inspiration took the discreet Penelope
to face her suitors, brutal, reckless men.
The queen had heard it all . . .
how they plotted inside the house to kill her son.
The herald Medon told her—he'd overheard their schemes.
And so, flanked by her ladies, she descended to the hall.
That luster of women, once she reached her suitors,
drawing her glistening veil across her cheeks,   460
paused now where a column propped the sturdy roof
and rounding on Antinous, cried out against him:
"You, Antinous! Violent, vicious, scheming—
you, they say, are the best man your age in Ithaca,
best for eloquence, counsel. You're nothing of the sort!
Madman, why do you weave destruction for Telemachus?—
show no pity to those who need it?—those over whom
almighty Zeus stands guard. It's wrong, unholy, yes,
weaving death for those who deserve your mercy!
Don't you know how your father fled here once?   470
A fugitive, terrified of the people, up in arms
against him because he'd joined some Taphian pirates
out to attack Thesprotians, sworn allies of ours.

The mobs were set to destroy him, rip his life out,
devour his vast wealth to their heart's content,
but Odysseus held them back, he kept their fury down.
And this is the man whose house you waste, scot-free,
whose wife you court, whose son you mean to kill—
you make my life an agony! Stop, I tell you,
stop all this, and make the rest stop too!"   480

    But Polybus' son Eurymachus tried to calm her:
"Wise Penelope, daughter of Icarius, courage!
Disabuse yourself of all these worries now.
That man is not alive—
he never will be, he never can be born—
who'll lift a hand against Telemachus, your son,
not while *I* walk the land and I can see the light.
I tell you this—so help me, it will all come true—
in an instant that man's blood will spurt around my spear!
My spear, since time and again Odysseus dandled me   490
on his knees, the great raider of cities fed me
roasted meat and held the red wine to my lips.
So to *me* your son is the dearest man alive,
and I urge the boy to have no fear of death,
not from the suitors at least.
What comes from the gods—there's no escaping that."

    Encouraging, all the way, but all the while
plotting the prince's murder in his mind . . .
The queen, going up to her lofty well-lit room,
fell to weeping for Odysseus, her beloved husband,   500
till watchful Athena sealed her eyes with welcome sleep.

    Returning just at dusk to Odysseus and his son,
the loyal swineherd found they'd killed a yearling pig
and standing over it now were busy cooking supper.
But Athena had approached Laertes' son Odysseus,
tapped him with her wand and made him old again.
She dressed him in filthy rags too, for fear Eumaeus,
recognizing his master face-to-face, might hurry

back to shrewd Penelope, blurting out the news
and never hide the secret in his heart.   510

    Telemachus was the first to greet the swineherd:
"Welcome home, my friend! What's the talk in town?
Are the swaggering suitors back from ambush yet—
or still waiting to catch me coming home?"

    You answered the prince, Eumaeus, loyal swineherd,
"I had no time to go roaming all through town,
digging round for that. My heart raced me on
to get my message told and rush back here.
But I met up with a fast runner there,
sent by your crew, a herald,   520
first to tell your mother all the news.
And this I know, I saw with my own eyes—
I was just above the city, heading home,
clambering over Hermes' Ridge, when I caught sight
of a trim ship pulling into the harbor, loaded down
with a crowd aboard her, shields and two-edged spears.
I *think* they're the men you're after—I'm not sure."

    At that the young prince Telemachus smiled,
glancing toward his father, avoiding Eumaeus' eyes.
                             And now,
with the roasting done, the meal set out, they ate well   530
and no one's hunger lacked a proper share of supper.
When they'd put aside desire for food and drink,
they remembered bed and took the gift of sleep.

Stranger at
the Gates

When young Dawn with her rose-red fingers shone once more
Telemachus strapped his rawhide sandals to his feet
and the young prince, the son of King Odysseus,
picked up the rugged spear that fit his grip
and striking out for the city, told his swineherd,
"I'm off to town, old friend, to present myself to mother.
She'll never stop her bitter tears and mourning,
well I know, till she sees me face-to-face.
And for you I have some orders—
take this luckless stranger to town, so he can beg   10
his supper there, and whoever wants can give the man
some crumbs and a cup to drink. How can *I* put up with
every passerby? My mind's weighed down with troubles.
If the stranger resents it, all the worse for him.
I like to tell the truth and tell it plainly."

"My friend,
subtle Odysseus broke in, "I've no desire, myself,
to linger here. Better that beggars cadge their meals
in town than in the fields. Some willing soul
will see to my needs. I'm hardly fit, at my age,
to keep to a farm and jump to a foreman's every order.   20
Go on then. This man will take me, as you've told him,
once I'm warm from the fire and the sun's good and strong.
Look at the clothing on my back—all rags and tatters.
I'm afraid the frost at dawn could do me in,
and town, you say, is a long hard way from here."

     At that Telemachus strode down through the farm
in quick, firm strides, brooding death for the suitors.
And once he reached his well-constructed palace,
propping his spear against a sturdy pillar
and crossing the stone threshold, in he went.   30

     His old nurse was the first to see him, Eurycleia,
just spreading fleeces over the carved, inlaid chairs.
Tears sprang to her eyes, she rushed straight to the prince
as the other maids of great Odysseus flocked around him,
hugged him warmly, kissed his head and shoulders.

     Now down from her chamber came discreet Penelope,
looking for all the world like Artemis or golden Aphrodite—
bursting into tears as she flung her arms around her darling son
and kissed his face and kissed his shining eyes and sobbed,
"You're home, Telemachus!"—words flew from her heart—   40
"sweet light of my eyes! I never thought I'd see you again,
once you shipped to Pylos—against my will, so secret,
out for news of your dear father. Quick tell me,
did you catch sight of the man—meet him—what?"

     "Please, mother," steady Telemachus replied,
"don't move me to tears, don't stir the heart inside me.
I've just escaped from death. Sudden death.
No. Bathe now, put on some fresh clothes,

go up to your own room with your serving-women,
pray, and promise the gods a generous sacrifice   50
to bring success, if Zeus will ever grant us
the hour of our revenge. I myself am off
to the meeting grounds to summon up a guest
who came with me from abroad when I sailed home.
I sent him on ahead with my trusted crew.
I told Piraeus to take him to his house,
treat him well, host him with all good will
till I could come myself."

                        Words to the mark
that left his mother silent . . .
She bathed now, put on some fresh clothes,   60
prayed, and promised the gods a generous sacrifice
to bring success, if Zeus would ever grant
the hour of their revenge.

                        Spear in hand,
Telemachus strode on through the hall and out,
and a pair of sleek hounds went trotting at his heels.
And Athena lavished a marvelous splendor on the prince
so the people all gazed in wonder as he came forward.
The swaggering suitors clustered, milling round him,
welcome words on their lips, and murder in their hearts.
But he gave them a wide berth as they came crowding in   70
and there where Mentor sat, Antiphus, Halitherses too—
his father's loyal friends from days gone by—
he took his seat as they pressed him with their questions.
And just then Piraeus the gallant spearman approached,
leading the stranger through the town and out onto
the meeting grounds. Telemachus, not hanging back,
went right up to greet Theoclymenus, his guest,
but Piraeus spoke out first: "Quickly now,
Telemachus, send some women to my house
to retrieve the gifts that Menelaus gave you."   80

   "Wait, Piraeus," wary Telemachus cautioned,
"we've no idea how all of this will go.

If the brazen suitors cut me down in the palace—
off guard—and carve apart my father's whole estate,
I'd rather you yourself, or one of his friends here,
keep those gifts and get some pleasure from them.
But if I can bring down slaughter on that crew,
you send the gifts to my house—we'll share the joy."

     Their plans made, he led the wayworn stranger home
and once they reached the well-constructed palace,   90
spreading out their cloaks on a chair or bench,
into the burnished tubs they climbed and bathed.
When women had washed them, rubbed them down with oil
and drawn warm fleece and shirts around their shoulders,
out of the baths they stepped and sat on high-backed chairs.
A maid brought water soon in a graceful golden pitcher
and over a silver basin tipped it out
so they might rinse their hands,
then pulled a gleaming table to their side.
A staid housekeeper brought on bread to serve them,   100
appetizers aplenty too, lavish with her bounty.
Penelope sat across from her son, beside a pillar,
leaning back on a low chair and winding finespun yarn.
They reached out for the good things that lay at hand
and when they'd put aside desire for food and drink,
the queen, for all her composure, said at last,
"Telemachus, I'm going back to my room upstairs
and lie down on my bed . . .
that bed of pain my tears have streaked, year in,
year out, from the day Odysseus sailed away to Troy   110
with Atreus' two sons.
                        But you, you never had the heart—
before those insolent suitors crowd back to the house—
to tell me clearly about your father's journey home,
if you've heard any news."
                        "Of course, mother,"
thoughtful Telemachus reassured her quickly,
"I will tell you the whole true story now.

We sailed to Pylos, to Nestor, the great king,
and he received me there in his lofty palace,
treated me well and warmly, yes, as a father treats
a long-lost son just home from voyaging, years abroad: 120
such care he showered on me, he and his noble sons.
But of strong, enduring Odysseus, dead or alive,
he's heard no news, he said, from any man on earth.
He sent me on to the famous spearman Atrides Menelaus,
on with a team of horses drawing a bolted chariot.
And there I saw her, Helen of Argos—all for her
Achaeans and Trojans suffered so much hardship,
thanks to the gods' decree . . .
The lord of the warcry, Menelaus, asked at once
what pressing need had brought me to lovely Lacedaemon,   130
and when I told him the whole story, first to last,
the king burst out, 'How shameful! That's the bed
of a brave man of war they'd like to crawl inside,
those spineless, craven cowards!
Weak as the doe that beds down her fawns
in a mighty lion's den—her newborn sucklings—
then trails off to the mountain spurs and grassy bends
to graze her fill, but back the lion comes to his own lair
and the master deals both fawns a ghastly bloody death,
just what Odysseus will deal that mob—ghastly death.   140
Ah if only—Father Zeus, Athena and lord Apollo—
that man who years ago in the games at Lesbos
rose to Philomelides' challenge, wrestled him,
pinned him down with one tremendous throw
and the Argives roared with joy . . .
if only *that* Odysseus sported with those suitors,
a blood wedding, a quick death would take the lot!
But about the things you've asked me, so intently,
I'll skew and sidestep nothing, not deceive you, ever.
Of all he told me—the Old Man of the Sea who never lies—   150
I'll hide or hold back nothing, not a single word.
He said he'd seen Odysseus on an island,
ground down in misery, off in a goddess' house,

the nymph Calypso, who holds him there by force.
He has no way to voyage home to his own native land,
no trim ships in reach, no crew to ply the oars
and send him scudding over the sea's broad back.'

　So Menelaus, the famous spearman, told me.
My mission accomplished, back I came at once,
and the gods sent me a stiff following wind　　　　　　160
that sped me home to the native land I love."

　His reassurance stirred the queen to her depths
and the godlike seer Theoclymenus added firmly,
"Noble lady, wife of Laertes' son, Odysseus,
Menelaus can have no perfect revelations;
mark *my* words—I will make you a prophecy,
quite precise, and *I*'ll hold nothing back.
I swear by Zeus, the first of all the gods,
by this table of hospitality here, my host,
by Odysseus' hearth where I have come for help—　　　170
I swear Odysseus *is* on native soil, here and now!
Poised or on the prowl, learning of these rank crimes
he's sowing seeds of ruin for all your suitors.
So clear, so true, that bird-sign I saw
as I sat on the benched ship
and sounded out the future to the prince!"

　"If only, my friend," reserved Penelope exclaimed,
"everything you say would come to pass!
You'd soon know my affection, know my gifts.
Any man you meet would call you blest."　　　　　　180

　And so the three confided in the halls
while all the suitors, before Odysseus' palace,
amused themselves with discus and long throwing spears,
out on the leveled grounds, free and easy as always,
full of swagger. When the dinner-hour approached
and sheep came home from pastures near and far,

driven in by familiar drovers,
Medon called them all, their favorite herald,
always present at their meals: "My young lords,
now you've played your games to your hearts' content,   190
come back to the halls so we can fix your supper.
Nothing's better than dining well on time!"

    They came at his summons, rising from the games
and now, bustling into the well-constructed palace,
flinging down their cloaks on a chair or bench,
they butchered hulking sheep and fatted goats,
full-grown hogs and a young cow from the herd,
preparing for their feast.
                        At the same time
the king and his loyal swineherd geared to leave
the country for the town. Eumaeus, foreman of men,   200
set things in motion: "Friend, I know you're keen
on going down to town today, just as my master bid,
though I'd rather you stay here to guard the farm.
But I prize the boy, I fear he'll blame me later—
a dressing-down from your master's hard to bear.
So off we go now. The shank of the day is past.
You'll find it colder with nightfall coming on."

    "I know, I see your point," the crafty man replied.
"There's sense in this old head. So let's be off.
And from now on, you lead me all the way.   210
Just give me a stick to lean on,
if you have one ready-cut. You say the road
is treacherous, full of slips and slides."
                           With that
he flung his beggar's sack across his shoulders—
torn and tattered, slung from a fraying rope.
Eumaeus gave him a staff that met his needs.
Then the two moved out, leaving behind them
dogs and herdsmen to stay and guard the farm.
And so the servant led his master toward the city,
looking for all the world like an old and broken beggar   220

hunched on a stick, his body wrapped in shameful rags . . .

    Down over the rugged road they went till hard by town
they reached the stone-rimmed fountain running clear
where the city people came and drew their water.
Ithacus built it once, with Neritus and Polyctor.
Round it a stand of poplar thrived on the dank soil,
all in a nestling ring, and down from a rock-ledge overhead
the cold water splashed, and crowning the fountain
rose an altar-stone erected to the nymphs,
where every traveler paused and left an offering.   230
Here Dolius' son, Melanthius, crossed their path,
herding his goats with a pair of drovers' help,
the pick of his flocks to make the suitors' meal.
As soon as he saw them there he broke into a flood
of brutal, foul abuse that made Odysseus' blood boil.
"Look!"—he sneered—"one scum nosing another scum along,
dirt finds dirt by the will of god—it never fails!
Wretched pig-boy, where do you take your filthy swine,
this sickening beggar who licks the pots at feasts?
Hanging round the doorposts, rubbing his back,   240
scavenging after scraps,
no hero's swords and cauldrons, not for *him*.
Hand him over to me—I'll teach him to work a farm,
muck out my stalls, pitch feed to the young goats;
whey to drink will put some muscle on his hams!
Oh no, he's learned his lazy ways too well,
he's got no itch to stick to good hard work,
he'd rather go scrounging round the countryside,
begging for crusts to stuff his greedy gut!
Let me tell you—so help me it's the truth—   250
if he sets foot in King Odysseus' royal palace,
salvos of footstools flung at his head by all the lords
will crack his ribs as he runs the line of fire through the house!"

    Wild, reckless taunts—and just as he passed Odysseus
the idiot lurched out with a heel and kicked his hip
but he couldn't knock the beggar off the path,

he stood his ground so staunchly. Odysseus was torn . . .
should he wheel with his staff and beat the scoundrel senseless?—
or hoist him by the midriff, split his skull on the rocks?
He steeled himself instead, his mind in full control.   260
But Eumaeus glared at the goatherd, cursed him to his face,
then lifted up his hands and prayed his heart out:
"O nymphs of the fountain, daughters of Zeus—
if Odysseus ever burned you the long thighs
of lambs or kids, covered with rich fat,
now bring my prayer to pass!
Let that man come back—some god guide him now!
He'd toss to the winds the flashy show you make,
Melanthius, so cocksure—always strutting round the town
while worthless fieldhands leave your flocks a shambles!"   270

    "Listen to him!" the goatherd shouted back.
"All bark and no bite from the vicious mutt!
One fine day I'll ship him out in a black lugger,
miles from Ithaca—sell him off for a good stiff price!
Just let Apollo shoot Telemachus down with his silver bow,
today in the halls, or the suitors snuff his life out—
as sure as I know the day of the king's return
is blotted out, the king is worlds away!"

    With his parting shot he left them trudging on
and went and reached the royal house in no time.   280
Slipping in, he took his seat among the suitors,
facing Eurymachus, who favored him the most.
The carvers set before him his plate of meat,
a staid housekeeper brought the man his bread.

    And now at last the king and loyal swineherd,
drawing near the palace, halted just outside
as the lyre's rippling music drifted round them—
Phemius, striking up a song for assembled guests—
and the master seized his servant's hand, exclaiming,
"Friend, what a noble house! Odysseus' house, it must be!   290
No mistaking it—you could tell it among a townful, look.

One building linked to the next, and the courtyard wall
is finished off with a fine coping, the double doors
are battle-proof—no man could break them down!
I can tell a crowd is feasting there in force—
smell the savor of roasts . . . the ringing lyre, listen,
the lyre that god has made the friend of feasts."

    "An easy guess," you said, Eumaeus, swineherd,
"for a man as keen as you at every turn.
Put heads together. What do we do next?   300
Either you're the first one into the palace—
mix with the suitors, leave me where I am.
Or if you like, stay put, and I'll go first myself.
Don't linger long. Someone might spot you here outside,
knock you down or pelt you. Mark my words. Take care."

    The man who'd borne long years abroad replied,
"Well I know. Remember? There's sense in this old head.
You go in, you first, while I stay here behind.
Stones and blows and I are hardly strangers.
My heart is steeled by now,   310
I've had my share of pain in the waves and wars.
Add this to the total. Bring the trial on.
But there's no way to hide the belly's hungers—
what a curse, what mischief it brews in all our lives!
Just for hunger we rig and ride our long benched ships
on the barren salt sea, speeding death to enemies."

    Now, as they talked on, a dog that lay there
lifted up his muzzle, pricked his ears . . .
It was Argos, long-enduring Odysseus' dog
he trained as a puppy once, but little joy he got   320
since all too soon he shipped to sacred Troy.
In the old days young hunters loved to set him
coursing after the wild goats and deer and hares.
But now with his master gone he lay there, castaway,
on piles of dung from mules and cattle, heaps collecting
out before the gates till Odysseus' serving-men

could cart it off to manure the king's estates.
Infested with ticks, half-dead from neglect,
here lay the hound, old Argos.
But the moment he sensed Odysseus standing by   330
he thumped his tail, nuzzling low, and his ears dropped,
though he had no strength to drag himself an inch
toward his master. Odysseus glanced to the side
and flicked away a tear, hiding it from Eumaeus,
diverting his friend in a hasty, offhand way:
"Strange, Eumaeus, look, a dog like this,
lying here on a dung-hill . . .
what handsome lines! But I can't say for sure
if he had the running speed to match his looks
or he was only the sort that gentry spoil at table,   340
show-dogs masters pamper for their points."

   You told the stranger, Eumaeus, loyal swineherd,
"Here—it's all too true—here's the dog of a man
who died in foreign parts. But if he had now
the form and flair he had in his glory days—
as Odysseus left him, sailing off to Troy—
you'd be amazed to see such speed, such strength.
No quarry he chased in the deepest, darkest woods
could ever slip this hound. A champion tracker too!
Ah, but he's run out of luck now, poor fellow . . .   350
his master's dead and gone, so far from home,
and the heartless women tend him not at all. Slaves,
with their lords no longer there to crack the whip,
lose all zest to perform their duties well. Zeus,
the Old Thunderer, robs a man of half his virtue
the day the yoke clamps down around his neck."

   With that he entered the well-constructed palace,
strode through the halls and joined the proud suitors.
But the dark shadow of death closed down on Argos' eyes
the instant he saw Odysseus, twenty years away.   360

   Now Prince Telemachus, first by far to note

the swineherd coming down the hall, nodded briskly,
called and waved him on. Eumaeus, glancing about,
picked up a handy stool where the carver always sat,
slicing meat for the suitors feasting through the house.
He took and put it beside the prince's table, facing him,
straddled it himself as a steward set a plate of meat
before the man and served him bread from trays.

    Right behind him came Odysseus, into his own house,
looking for all the world like an old and broken beggar   370
hunched on a stick, his body wrapped in shameful rags.
Just in the doorway, just at the ashwood threshold,
there he settled down . . .
leaning against the cypress post a master joiner
planed smooth and hung with a plumb line years ago.
Telemachus motioned the swineherd over now,
and choosing a whole loaf from a fine wicker tray
and as much meat as his outstretched hands could hold,
he said, "Now take these to the stranger, tell him too
to make the rounds of the suitors, beg from one and all.   380
Bashfulness, for a man in need, is no great friend."

    And Eumaeus did his bidding, went straight up
to the guest and winged a greeting: "Here, stranger,
Prince Telemachus sends you these, and tells you too
to make the rounds of the suitors, beg from one and all.
Bashfulness for a beggar, he says, is no great friend."

    "Powerful Zeus!" the crafty king responded,
"grant that your prince be blest among mankind—
and all his heart's desires come to pass!"

    Taking the food in both hands, setting it down,   390
spread out on his filthy sack before his feet,
the beggar fell to his meal
as the singer raised a song throughout the house.
Once he'd supped and the stirring bard had closed,
the suitors broke into uproar down along the hall.

And now Athena came to the side of Laertes' royal son
and urged him, "Go now, gather crusts from all the suitors,
test them, so we can tell the innocent from the guilty."
But not even so would Athena save one man from death.
Still, off he went, begging from each in turn,   400
circling left to right, reaching out his hand
like a beggar from the day that he was born.
They pitied him, gave him scraps, were puzzled too,
asking each other, "Who is this?" "Where's he from?"
Till the goatherd Melanthius shouted out in their midst,
"Listen to me, you lords who court our noble queen—
I'll tell you about the stranger. I've seen him before.
I know for a fact the swineherd led him in,
though I have no idea who the fellow is
or where he thinks he comes from."

                                        At that   410
Antinous wheeled on Eumaeus, lashing out at him:
"Your highness, swineherd—why drag *this* to town?
Haven't we got our share of vagabonds to deal with,
disgusting beggars who lick the feasters' plates?
Isn't it quite enough, these swarming crowds
consuming your master's bounty—
must you invite this rascal in the bargain?"

                                        "Antinous,
highborn as you are," you told the man, Eumaeus,
"that was a mean low speech!
Now who'd go out, who on his own hook—   420
not I—and ask a stranger in from nowhere
unless he had some skills to serve the house?
A prophet, a healer who cures disease, a worker in wood
or even a god-inspired bard whose singing warms the heart—
they're the ones asked in around the world. A beggar?
Who'd invite a beggar to bleed his household white?
You, you of all the suitors are always roughest
on the servants of our king, on me most of all.
Not that I care, no, so long as his queen,
his wise queen, is still alive in the palace,   430

Prince Telemachus too."
                              "Stop, Eumaeus,"
poised Telemachus broke in quickly now,
"don't waste so much breath on Antinous here.
It's just his habit to bait a man with abuse
and spur the rest as well."
                              He wheeled on the suitor,
letting loose: "How kind you are to me, Antinous,
kind as a father to his son! Encouraging me
to send this stranger packing from my house
with a harsh command! I'd never do it. God forbid.
Take and give to the beggar. I don't grudge it—   440
I'd even urge you on. No scruples now,
never fear your gifts will upset my mother
or any servant in King Odysseus' royal house.
But no such qualm could enter that head of yours,
bent on feeding your own face, not feeding strangers!"

     Antinous countered the young prince in kind:
"So high and mighty, Telemachus—such unbridled rage!
If all the suitors gave him the sort of gift I'll give,
the house would be rid of *him* for three whole months!"
With that, from under his table he seized the stool   450
that propped his smooth feet as he reveled on—
just lifting it into view . . .
                              But as for the rest,
all gave to the beggar, filled his sack with handouts,
bread and meat. And Odysseus seemed at the point
of getting back to his doorsill,
done with testing suitors, home free himself
when he stopped beside Antinous, begging face-to-face:
"Give me a morsel, friend. You're hardly the worst
Achaean here, it seems. The noblest one, in fact.
You look like a king to me!   460
So you should give a bigger crust than the rest
and I will sing your praises all across the earth.
I too once lived in a lofty house that men admired;

rolling in wealth, I'd often give to a vagabond like myself,
whoever he was, whatever need had brought him to my door.
And crowds of servants I had, and lots of all it takes
to live the life of ease, to make men call you rich.
But Zeus ruined it all—god's will, no doubt—
when he shipped me off with a roving band of pirates
bound for Egypt, a long hard sail, to wreck my life.   470
There in the Nile delta I moored our ships of war.
God knows I ordered my trusty crews to stand by,
just where they were, and guard the anchored fleet
and I sent a patrol to scout things out from higher ground.
But swept away by their own reckless fury, the crew went berserk—
they promptly began to plunder the lush Egyptian farms,
dragged off the women and children, killed the men.
Outcries reached the city in no time—stirred by shouts
the entire town came streaming down at the break of day,
filling the river plain with chariots, ranks of infantry   480
and the gleam of bronze. Zeus who loves the lightning
flung down murderous panic on all my men-at-arms—
no one dared to stand his ground and fight,
disaster ringed us round from every quarter.
Droves of my men they hacked down with swords,
led off the rest alive, to labor for them as slaves.
Myself? They passed me on to a stranger come their way,
to ship me to Cyprus—Iasus' son Dmetor it was,
who ruled Cyprus then with an iron fist.
And from there I sailed to Ithaca,   490
just as you see me now, ground down by pain and sorrow—"

   "Good god almighty!" Antinous cut the beggar short.
"What spirit brought this pest to plague our feast?
Back off! Into the open, clear of my table, or you,
you'll soon land in an Egypt, Cyprus, to break your heart!
What a brazen, shameless beggar! Scrounging food
from each man in turn, and look at their handouts,
reckless, never a qualm, no holding back, not
when making free with the next man's goods—
each one's got plenty here."

"Pity, pity,"   500
the wry Odysseus countered, drawing away.
"No sense in your head to match your handsome looks.
You'd grudge your servant a pinch of salt from your own larder,
you who lounge at the next man's board but lack the heart
to tear a crust of bread and hand it on to me,
though there's god's plenty here."
                              Boiling over
Antinous gave him a scathing look and let fly,
"*Now* you won't get out of the hall unscarred, I swear,
not after such a filthy string of insults!"
                              With that
he seized the stool and hurled it—
                              Square in the back   510
it struck Odysseus, just under the right shoulder
but he stood up against it—steady as a rock,
unstaggered by Antinous' blow—just shook his head,
silent, his mind churning with thoughts of bloody work.
Back he went to the doorsill, crouched, and setting down
his sack about to burst, he faced the suitors, saying,
"Hear me out, you lords who court the noble queen,
I must say what the heart inside me urges.
There's nothing to groan about, no hurt, when a man
takes a blow as he fights to save his own possessions,   520
cattle or shining flocks. But Antinous struck me
all because of my good-for-nothing belly—that,
that curse that makes such pain for us poor men.
But if beggars have their gods and Furies too,
let Antinous meet his death before he meets his bride!"

"Enough, stranger!" Antinous volleyed back.
"Sit there and eat in peace—or go get lost! Or else,
for the way you talk, these young men will hale you
up and down the halls by your hands or feet
until you're skinned alive!"
                              Naked threats—   530
but the rest were outraged, even those brash suitors.
One would say to another, "Look, Antinous,

that was a crime, to strike the luckless beggar!"

   "Your fate is sealed if he's some god from the blue."

   "And the gods do take on the look of strangers
dropping in from abroad—"
                "Disguised in every way
as they roam and haunt our cities, watching over us—"

   "All our foul play, all our fair play too!"

   So they warned, but Antinous paid no heed.
And the anguish welled up in Telemachus' breast   540
for the blow his father took, yet he let no tears
go rolling down his face—he just shook his head,
silent, his mind churning with thoughts of bloody work.

   But then, when cautious Queen Penelope heard
how Antinous struck the stranger, there in the halls,
she cried out, with her serving-women round her,
"May Apollo the Archer strike you just as hard!"
And her housekeeper Eurynome added quickly,
"If only our prayers were granted—
then not one of the lot would live to see   550
Dawn climb her throne tomorrow!"
                "Dear old woman,"
alert Penelope replied, "they're all hateful,
plotting their vicious plots. But Antinous
is the worst of all—he's black death itself.
Here's this luckless stranger, wandering down
the halls and begging scraps—hard-pressed by need—
and the rest all give the man his fill of food
but that one gives him a footstool
hurled at his right shoulder, hits his back!"

   While she exclaimed among her household women,   560
sitting there in her room, Odysseus bent to supper.

Penelope called the swineherd in and gave instructions:
"Go, good Eumaeus, tell the stranger to come at once.
I'd like to give him a warm welcome, ask the man
if he's heard some news about my gallant husband
or seen him in the flesh . . .
He seems like one who's roved around the world."

    "My queen," you answered, Eumaeus, loyal swineherd,
"if only the lords would hold their peace a moment!
Such stories he tells—he'd charm you to your depths.   570
Three nights, three days I kept him in my shelter;
I was the first the fellow stumbled onto,
fleeing from some ship. But not even so
could he bring his tale of troubles to an end.
You know how you can stare at a bard in wonder—
trained by the gods to sing and hold men spellbound—
how you can long to sit there, listening, all your life
when the man begins to sing. So he charmed my heart,
I tell you, huddling there beside me at my fire.
He and Odysseus' father go way back, he says,   580
sworn friends, and the stranger hails from Crete
where the stock of old King Minos still lives on,
and from Crete he made his way, racked by hardship,
tumbling on like a rolling stone until he turned up here.
He swears he's heard of Odysseus—just in reach,
in rich Thesprotian country—still alive,
laden with treasure, heading home at last!"
                                              "Go,"
the cautious queen responded, "call him here
so he can tell me his own tale face-to-face.
Our friends can sit at the gates or down the halls   590
and play their games, debauched to their hearts' content.
Why not? Their own stores, their bread and seasoned wine,
lie intact at home; food for their serving-men alone.
But they, they infest our palace day and night,
they butcher our cattle, our sheep, our fat goats,
feasting themselves sick, swilling our glowing wine

as if there's no tomorrow—all of it, squandered.
No, there is no man like Odysseus in command
to drive this curse from the house. Dear god,
if only Odysseus came back home to native soil now,   600
he and his son would avenge the outrage of these men—like that!"

   At her last words Telemachus shook with a lusty sneeze
like a thunderclap resounding up and down the halls.
The queen was seized with laughter, calling out
to Eumaeus winged words: "Quickly, go!
Bring me this stranger now, face-to-face!
You hear how my son sealed all I said with a sneeze?
So let death come down with grim finality on these suitors—
one and all—not a single man escape his sudden doom!
And another thing. Mark my words, I tell you.   610
If I'm convinced that all he says is true,
I'll dress him in shirt and cloak, in handsome clothes."

   Off the swineherd went, following her instructions,
made his way to the stranger's side and winged a word:
"Old friend—our queen, wise Penelope, summons you,
the prince's mother! The spirit moves her now,
heartsick as she is,
to ask a question or two about her husband.
And if she's convinced that all you say is true,
she'll dress you in shirt and cloak. That's what you need,   620
that most of all now. Bread you can always beg
around the country, fill your belly well—
they'll give you food, whoever has a mind to."

   "Gladly, Eumaeus," the patient man replied,
"I'll tell her the whole truth and nothing but,
Icarius' daughter, your wise queen Penelope.
I know all about that man . . .
it's been my lot to suffer what he's suffered.
But I fear the mob's abuse, those rough young bucks,
their pride and violence hit the iron skies!   630

Just now that scoundrel—as I went down the halls,
harming no one—up and dealt me a jolting blow,
and who would raise a hand to save me? Telemachus?
Anyone else? No one. So tell Penelope now,
anxious as she may be, to wait in the halls
until the sun goes down. Then she can ask me
all she likes about her husband's journey home.
But let her give me a seat close by the fire.
The clothes on my back are tatters. Well you know—
you are the first I begged for care and shelter."   640

   Back the swineherd went, following his instructions.
Penelope, just as he crossed her threshold, broke out,
"Didn't you bring him? What's in the vagrant's mind?
Fear of someone? Embarrassed by something else,
here in the house? Is the fellow bashful?
A bashful man will make a sorry beggar."

   You answered your queen, Eumaeus, loyal swineherd,
"He talks to the point—he thinks as the next man would
who wants to dodge their blows, that brutal crew.
He tells you to wait here till the sun goes down.   650
It's better for you, my queen. Then you can talk
with the man in private, hear the stranger's news."

   "Nobody's fool, that stranger," wise Penelope said,
"he sees how things could go. Surely no men on earth
can match that gang for reckless, deadly schemes."

   So she agreed, and now, mission accomplished,
back the loyal swineherd went to mix with the suitors.
Moving next to the prince, he whispered a parting word,
their heads close together so no one else could hear.
"Dear boy, I must be off, to see to the pigs   660
and the whole farm—your living, mine as well.
You're the one to tend to all things here.
Look out for your own skin first,

374 HOMER: THE ODYSSEY

do take care, you mustn't come to grief.
Crowds of your own countrymen plot your death—
let Zeus wipe out the lot before they kill us all!"

    "Right you are, old friend," the canny prince replied.
"Now off you go, once you've had your supper.
But come back bright and early,
bring some good sound boars for slaughter. Yes,   670
I'll tend to all things here, I and the deathless gods."

    And the swineherd sat down again on his polished stool
and once he'd supped and drunk to his heart's content,
back he went to his pigs, leaving the royal precincts
still filled with feasters, all indulging now
in the joys of dance and song.
The day was over. Dusk was falling fast.

BOOK EIGHTEEN

The Beggar-King
of Ithaca

Now along came this tramp, this public nuisance
who used to scrounge a living round the streets of Ithaca—
notorious for his belly, a ravenous, bottomless pit
for food and drink, but he had no pith, no brawn,
despite the looming hulk that met your eyes.
Arnaeus was his name,
so his worthy mother called him at birth,
but all the young men called him Irus for short
because he'd hustle messages at any beck and call.
Well *he* came by to rout the king from his own house   10
and met Odysseus now with a rough, abusive burst:
"Get off the porch, you old goat, before I haul you
off by the leg! Can't you see them give me the wink,
all of them here, to drag you out—and so I would
but I've got some pangs of conscience. Up with you, man,

375

or before you know it, we'll be trading blows!"

                                        A killing look,
and the wily old soldier countered, "Out of your mind?
What damage have I done *you?* What have I said?
I don't grudge you anything,
not if the next man up and gives you plenty.   20
This doorsill is big enough for the both of us—
you've got no call to grudge me what's not yours.
You're another vagrant, just like me, I'd say,
and it lies with the gods to make us rich or poor. So,
keep your fists to yourself, don't press your luck, don't rile me,
or old as I am, I'll bloody your lip, splatter your chest
and buy myself some peace and quiet for tomorrow.
I doubt you'll ever come lumbering back again
to the halls of Laertes' royal son Odysseus."

    "Look who's talking!" the beggar rumbled in anger.   30
"How this pot-bellied pig runs off at the mouth—
like an old crone at her oven!
Well *I've* got a knock-out blow in store for *him*—
I'll batter the tramp with both fists, crack every tooth
from his jaws, I'll litter the ground with teeth
like a rogue sow's, punished for rooting corn!
Belt up—so the lords can see us fight it out.
How can you beat a champion half your age?"

    Tongue-lashing each other, tempers flaring,
there on the polished sill before the lofty doors.   40
And Antinous, that grand prince, hearing them wrangle,
broke into gloating laughter, calling out to the suitors,
"Friends, nothing like this has come our way before—
what sport some god has brought the palace now!
The stranger and Irus, look,
they'd battle it out together, fists flying.
Come, let's pit them against each other—fast!"

    All leapt from their seats with whoops of laughter,

clustering round the pair of ragged beggars there
as Eupithes' son Antinous planned the contest.   50
"Quiet, my fine friends. Here's what I propose.
These goat sausages sizzling here in the fire—
we packed them with fat and blood to have for supper.
Now, whoever wins this bout and proves the stronger,
let that man step up and take his pick of the lot!
What's more, from this day on he feasts among us—
no other beggar will we allow inside
to cadge his meals from us!"
                                        They all cheered
but Odysseus, foxy veteran, plotted on . . .
"Friends, how can an old man, worn down with pain,   60
stand up to a young buck? It's just this belly of mine,
this trouble-maker, tempts me to take a licking.
So first, all of you swear me a binding oath:
come, not one of you steps in for Irus here,
strikes me a foul blow to pull him through
and lays me in the dust."
                                        And at that
they all mouthed the oath that he required,
and once they vowed they'd never interfere,
Prince Telemachus drove the matter home:
"Stranger, if your spine and fighting pride   70
prompt you to go against this fellow now,
have no fear of any suitor in the pack—
whoever fouls you will have to face a crowd.
Count on *me*, your host. And two lords back me up,
Antinous and Eurymachus—both are men of sense."

    They all shouted approval of the prince
as Odysseus belted up, roping his rags around his loins,
baring his big rippling thighs—his boxer's broad shoulders,
his massive chest and burly arms on full display
as Athena stood beside him,   80
fleshing out the limbs of the great commander . . .
Despite their swagger, the suitors were amazed,

gaping at one another, trading forecasts:
"Irus will soon be ironed out for good!"

   "He's in for the beating he begged for all along."

   "Look at the hams on that old-timer—"
                                   "Just under his rags!"

   Each outcry jolted Irus to the core—too late.
The servants trussed his clothes up, dragged him on,
the flesh on his body quaking now with terror.
Antinous rounded on him, flinging insults: 90
"You, you clumsy ox, you're better off dead
or never born at all, if you cringe at *him,*
paralyzed with fear of an old, broken hulk,
ground down by the pains that hound his steps.
Mark my word—so help me I'll make it good—
if that old relic whips you and wins the day,
I'll toss you into a black ship and sail you off
to Echetus, the mainland king who wrecks all men alive!
He'll lop your nose and ears with his ruthless blade,
he'll rip your privates out by the roots, he will,   100
and serve them up to his dogs to bolt down raw!"

   That threat shook his knees with a stronger fit
but they hauled him into the ring. Both men put up their fists—
with the seasoned fighter Odysseus deeply torn now . . .
should he knock him senseless, leave him dead where he dropped
or just stretch him out on the ground with a light jab?
As he mulled things over, that way seemed the best:
a glancing blow, the suitors would not detect him.
The two men squared off—
                            and Irus hurled a fist
at Odysseus' right shoulder as *he* came through   110
with a hook below the ear, pounding Irus' neck,
smashing the bones inside—
                            suddenly red blood

came spurting out of his mouth, and headlong down
he pitched in the dust, howling, teeth locked in a grin,
feet beating the ground—
                              and the princely suitors,
flinging their hands in the air, died laughing.
Grabbing him by the leg, Odysseus hauled him
through the porch, across the yard to the outer gate,
heaped him against the courtyard wall, sitting slumped,
stuck his stick in his hand and gave him a parting shot: 120
"Now hold your post—play the scarecrow to all the pigs and dogs!
But no more lording it over strangers, no more playing
the beggar-king for you, you loathsome fool,
or you'll bring down something worse around your neck!"

    He threw his beggar's sack across his shoulders—
torn and tattered, slung from a fraying rope—
then back he went to the sill and took his seat.
The suitors ambled back as well, laughing jauntily,
toasting the beggar warmly now, those proud young blades,
one man egging the other on: "Stranger, friend, may Zeus   130
and the other deathless gods fill up your sack with blessings!"

    "All your heart desires!"
                              "You've knocked him out of action,
that insatiable tramp—"
                              "That parasite on the land!"

    "Ship him off to Echetus, fast—the mainland king
who wrecks all men alive!"
                              Welcome words
and a lucky omen too—Odysseus' heart leapt up.
Antinous laid before him a generous goat sausage,
bubbling fat and blood. Amphinomus took two loaves
from the wicker tray and set them down beside him,
drank his health in a golden cup and said,   140
"Cheers, old friend, old father,
saddled now as you are with so much trouble—

here's to your luck, great days from this day on!"

    And the one who knew the world replied at length,
"Amphinomus, you seem like a man of good sense to me.
Just like your father—at least I've heard his praises,
Nisus of Dulichion, a righteous man, and rich.
You're his son, they say, you seem well-spoken, too.
So I will tell you something. Listen. Listen closely.
Of all that breathes and crawls across the earth,   150
our mother earth breeds nothing feebler than a man.
So long as the gods grant him power, spring in his knees,
he thinks he will never suffer affliction down the years.
But then, when the happy gods bring on the long hard times,
bear them he must, against his will, and steel his heart.
Our lives, our mood and mind as we pass across the earth,
turn as the days turn . . .
as the father of men and gods makes each day dawn.
I too seemed destined to be a man of fortune once
and a wild wicked swath I cut, indulged my lust for violence,   160
staking all on my father and my brothers.
                                        Look at me now.
And so, I say, let no man ever be lawless all his life,
just take in peace what gifts the gods will send.
                                        True,
but here I see you suitors plotting your reckless work,
carving away at the wealth, affronting the loyal wife
of a man who won't be gone from kin and country long.
I say he's right at hand—and may some power save you,
spirit you home before you meet him face-to-face
the moment he returns to native ground!
Once under his own roof, he and your friends,   170
believe you me, won't part till blood has flowed."
                                        With that
he poured out honeyed wine to the gods and drank deeply,
then restored the cup to the young prince's hands.
Amphinomus made his way back through the hall,
his heart sick with anguish, shaking his head,
fraught with grave forebodings . . .

but not even so could he escape his fate.
Even then Athena had bound him fast to death
at the hands of Prince Telemachus and his spear.
Now back he went to the seat that he'd left empty.   180

But now the goddess Athena with her glinting eyes
inspired Penelope, Icarius' daughter, wary, poised,
to display herself to her suitors, fan their hearts,
inflame them more, and make her even more esteemed
by her husband and her son than she had been before.
Forcing a laugh, she called her maid: "Eurynome,
my spirit longs—though it never did till now—
to appear before my suitors, loathe them as I do.
I'd say a word to my son too, for his own good,
not to mix so much with that pernicious crowd,   190
so glib with their friendly talk
but plotting wicked plots they'll hatch tomorrow."

"Well said, my child," the old woman answered,
"all to the point. Go to the boy and warn him now,
hold nothing back. But first you should bathe yourself,
give a gloss to your face. Don't go down like that—
your eyes dimmed, your cheeks streaked with tears.
It makes things worse, this grieving on and on.
Your son's now come of age—your fondest prayer
to the deathless gods, to see him wear a beard."   200

"Eurynome," discreet Penelope objected,
"don't try to coax me, care for me as you do,
to bathe myself, refresh my face with oils.
Whatever glow I had died long ago . . .
the gods of Olympus snuffed it out that day
my husband sailed away in the hollow ships.
But please, have Autonoë and Hippodameia come
and support me in the hall. I'll never brave
those men alone. I'd be too embarrassed."

Now as the old nurse bustled through the house   210

to give the women orders, call them to the queen,
the bright-eyed goddess thought of one more thing.
She drifted a sound slumber over Icarius' daughter,
back she sank and slept, her limbs fell limp and still,
reclining there on her couch, all the while Athena,
luminous goddess, lavished immortal gifts on her
to make her suitors lose themselves in wonder . . .
The divine unguent first. She cleansed her cheeks,
her brow and fine eyes with ambrosia smooth as the oils
the goddess Love applies, donning her crown of flowers   220
whenever she joins the Graces' captivating dances.
She made her taller, fuller in form to all men's eyes,
her skin whiter than ivory freshly carved, and now,
Athena's mission accomplished, off the bright one went
as bare-armed maids came in from their own quarters,
chattering all the way, and sleep released the queen.
She woke, touched her cheek with a hand, and mused,
"Ah, what a marvelous gentle sleep, enfolding me
in the midst of all my anguish! Now if only
blessed Artemis sent me a death as gentle, now,   230
this instant—no more wasting away my life,
my heart broken in longing for my husband . . .
He had every strength,
rising over his countrymen, head and shoulders."

        Then, leaving her well-lit chamber, she descended,
not alone: two of her women followed close behind.
That radiant woman, once she reached her suitors,
drawing her glistening veil across her cheeks,
paused now where a column propped the sturdy roof,
with one of her loyal handmaids stationed either side.   240
The suitors' knees went slack, their hearts dissolved in lust—
all of them lifted prayers to lie beside her, share her bed.
But turning toward her son, she warned, "Telemachus,
your sense of balance is not what it used to be.
When you were a boy you had much better judgment.
Now that you've grown and reached your young prime
and any stranger, seeing how tall and handsome you are,

would think you the son of some great man of wealth—
now your sense of fairness seems to fail you.
Consider the dreadful thing just done in our halls—   250
how you let the stranger be so abused! Why,
suppose our guest, sitting here at peace,
here in our own house,
were hauled and badly hurt by such cruel treatment?
You'd be shamed, disgraced in all men's eyes!"

    "Mother . . ." Telemachus paused, then answered.
"I cannot fault your anger at all this.
My heart takes note of everything, feels it, too,
both the good and the bad—the boy you knew is gone.
But how can I plan my world in a sane, thoughtful way?   260
These men drive me mad, hedging me round, right and left,
plotting their lethal plots, and no one takes my side.
Still, this battle between the stranger and Irus
hardly went as the suitors might have hoped:
the stranger beat him down!
If only—Father Zeus, Athena and lord Apollo—
these gallants, now, this moment, here in our house,
were battered senseless, heads lolling, knees unstrung,
some sprawled in the courtyard, some sprawled outside!
Slumped like Irus down at the front gates now,   270
whipped, and his head rolling like some drunk.
He can't stand up on his feet and stagger home,
whatever home he's got—the man's demolished."

    So Penelope and her son exchanged their hopes
as Eurymachus stepped in to praise the queen.
"Ah, daughter of Icarius, wise Penelope,
if all the princes in Ionian Argos saw you now!
What a troop of suitors would banquet in your halls
tomorrow at sunrise! You surpass all women
in build and beauty, refined and steady mind."   280

    "Oh no, Eurymachus," wise Penelope demurred,
"whatever form and feature I had, what praise I'd won,

the deathless gods destroyed that day the Achaeans
sailed away to Troy, my husband in their ships,
Odysseus—if *he* could return to tend my life
the renown I had would only grow in glory.
Now my life is torment . . .
look at the griefs some god has loosed against me!
I'll never forget the day he left this land of ours;
he caught my right hand by the wrist and said, gently,   290
'Dear woman, I doubt that every Achaean under arms
will make it home from Troy, all safe and sound.
The Trojans, they say, are fine soldiers too,
hurling javelins, shooting flights of arrows,
charioteers who can turn the tide—like that!—
when the great leveler, War, brings on some deadlock.
So I cannot tell if the gods will sail me home again
or I'll go down out there, on the fields of Troy,
but all things here must rest in your control.
Watch over my father and mother in the palace,   300
just as now, or perhaps a little more,
when I am far from home.
But once you see the beard on the boy's cheek,
you wed the man you like, and leave your house behind.'
So my husband advised me then. Now it all comes true . . .
a night will come when a hateful marriage falls my lot—
this cursed life of mine! Zeus has torn away my joy.
But there's something else that mortifies me now.
Your way is a far cry from the time-honored way
of suitors locked in rivalry, striving to win   310
some noble woman, a wealthy man's daughter.
They bring in their own calves and lambs
to feast the friends of the bride-to-be, yes,
and shower her with gleaming gifts as well.
They don't devour the woman's goods scot-free."

    Staunch Odysseus glowed with joy to hear all this—
his wife's trickery luring gifts from her suitors now,
enchanting their hearts with suave seductive words
but all the while with something else in mind.

"Gifts?"

Eupithes' son Antinous took her point at once.   320
"Daughter of Icarius, sensible Penelope,
whatever gifts your suitors would like to bring,
accept them. How ungracious to turn those gifts away!
We won't go back to our own estates, or anywhere else,
till you have wed the man you find the best."

So he proposed, and all the rest agreed.
Each suitor sent a page to go and get a gift.
Antinous' man brought in a grand, resplendent robe,
stiff with embroidery, clasped with twelve gold brooches,
long pins that clipped into sheathing loops with ease.   330
Eurymachus' man brought in a necklace richly wrought,
gilded, strung with amber and glowing like the sun.
Eurydamas' two men came with a pair of earrings,
mulberry clusters dangling in triple drops
with a glint to catch the heart.
From the halls of lord Pisander, Polyctor's son,
a servant brought a choker, a fine, gleaming treasure.
And so each suitor in turn laid on a handsome gift.
Then the noble queen withdrew to her upper room,
her file of waiting ladies close behind her,   340
bearing the gorgeous presents in their arms.

Now the suitors turned to dance and song,
to the lovely beat and sway,
waiting for dusk to come upon them there . . .
and the dark night came upon them, lost in pleasure.
They rushed to set up three braziers along the walls
to give them light, piled them high with kindling,
sere, well-seasoned, just split with an ax,
and mixed in chips to keep the torches flaring.
The maids of Odysseus, steady man, took turns   350
to keep the fires up, but the king himself,
dear to the gods and cunning to the core,
gave them orders brusquely: "Maids of Odysseus,
your master gone so long—quick now, off you go

to the room where your queen and mistress waits.
Sit with her there and try to lift her spirits,
combing wool in your hands or spinning yarn.
But I will trim the torches for all her suitors,
even if they would like to revel on till Morning
mounts her throne. They'll never wear me down.   360
I have a name for lasting out the worst."

                                   At that
the women burst into laughter, glancing back and forth.
Flushed with beauty, Melantho mocked him shamelessly—
Dolius was her father but Penelope brought her up;
she treated her like her own child and gave her toys
to cheer her heart. But despite that, her heart
felt nothing for all her mistress' anguish now.
She was Eurymachus' lover, always slept with him.
She was the one who mocked her king and taunted,
"Cock of the walk, did someone beat your brains out?   370
Why not go bed down at the blacksmith's cozy forge?
Or a public place where tramps collect? Why here—
blithering on, nonstop,
bold as brass in the face of all these lords?
No fear in your heart? Wine's got to your wits?—
or do you always play the fool and babble nonsense?
Lost your head, have you, because you drubbed that hobo Irus?
You wait—a better man than Irus will take you on,
he'll box both sides of your skull with heavy fists
and cart you from the palace gushing blood!"

                                   "*You* wait,   380
you bitch"—the hardened veteran flashed a killing look.
"I'll go straight to the prince with your foul talk.
The prince will chop you to pieces here and now!"

    His fury sent the women fluttering off, scattering
down the hall with panic shaking every limb—
they knew he spoke the truth.
But he took up his post by the flaring braziers,
tending the fires closely, looking after them all,

though the heart inside him stirred with other things,
ranging ahead, now, to all that must be done . . . 390

But Athena had no mind to let the brazen suitors
hold back now from their heart-rending insults—
she meant to make the anguish cut still deeper
into the core of Laertes' son Odysseus.
Polybus' son Eurymachus launched in first,
baiting the king to give his friends a laugh:
"Listen to me, you lords who court our noble queen!
I simply have to say what's on my mind. Look,
surely the gods have fetched this beggar here
to Odysseus' house. At least our torchlight *seems* 400
to come from the sheen of the man's own head—
there's not a hair on his bald pate, not a wisp!"

Then he wheeled on Odysseus, raider of cities:
"Stranger, how would you like to work for me
if I took you on—I'd give you decent wages—
picking the stones to lay a tight dry wall
or planting tall trees on the edge of my estate?
I'd give you rations to last you year-round,
clothes for your body, sandals for your feet.
Oh no, you've learned your lazy ways too well, 410
you've got no itch to stick to good hard work,
you'd rather go scrounging round the countryside,
begging for crusts to stuff your greedy gut!"

"Ah, Eurymachus," Odysseus, master of many exploits,
answered firmly, "if only the two of us *could* go
man-to-man in the labors of the field . . .
In the late spring, when the long days come round,
out in the meadow, I swinging a well-curved scythe
and you swinging yours—we'd test our strength for work,
fasting right till dusk with lots of hay to mow. 420
Or give us a team of oxen to drive, purebreds,
hulking, ruddy beasts, both lusty with fodder,

paired for age and pulling-power that never flags—
with four acres to work, the loam churning under the plow—
you'd see what a straight unbroken furrow I could cut you then.
Or if Zeus would bring some battle on—out of the blue,
this very day—and give me a shield and two spears
and a bronze helmet to fit this soldier's temples,
then you'd see me fight where front ranks clash—
no more mocking this belly of mine, not then.   430
Enough. You're sick with pride, you brutal fool.
No doubt you count yourself a great, powerful man
because you sport with a puny crowd, ill-bred to boot.
If only Odysseus came back home and stood right here,
in a flash you'd find those doors—broad as they are—
too cramped for your race to safety through the porch!"

      That made Eurymachus' fury seethe and burst—
he gave the beggar a dark look and let fly, "You,
you odious—I'll make you pay for your ugly rant!
Bold as brass in the face of all these lords?   440
No fear in your heart? Wine's got to your wits?—
or do you always play the fool and babble nonsense?
Lost your head, have you, because you drubbed that hobo Irus?"

      As he shouted out he seized a stool, but Odysseus,
fearing the blow, crouched at Amphinomus' knees
as Eurymachus hurled and hit the wine-steward,
clipping his right hand—
his cup dropped, clattered along the floor
and flat on his back he went, groaning in the dust.
The suitors broke into uproar through the shadowed halls,   450
glancing at one another, trading angry outcries:
"Would to god this drifter had dropped dead—"

      "Anywhere else before he landed here!"

      "Then he'd never have loosed such pandemonium."

      "Now we're squabbling over *beggars!*"

                                        "No more joy
in the sumptuous feast . . ."
                                "Now riot rules the day!"

    But now Prince Telemachus dressed them down:
"Fools, you're out of your minds! No hiding it,
food and wine have gone to your heads. Some god
has got your blood up. Come, now you've eaten well   460
go home to bed—when the spirit moves, that is.
I, for one, I'll drive no guest away."

    So he declared. And they all bit their lips,
amazed the prince could speak with so much daring.
At last Amphinomus rose to take the floor,
the noted son of Nisus, King Aretias' grandson.
"Fair enough, my friends; when a man speaks well
we have no grounds for wrangling, no cause for abuse.
Hands off the stranger! And any other servant
in King Odysseus' palace. Come, steward,   470
pour first drops for the god in every cup;
let's make libations, then go home to bed.
The stranger? Leave him here in Odysseus' halls
and have his host, Telemachus, tend him well—
it's the prince's royal house the man has reached."

    So he said. His proposal pleased them all.
And gallant Mulius, a herald of Dulichion,
a friend-in-arms of lord Amphinomus too,
mixed the men a bowl and, hovering closely,
poured full rounds for all. They tipped cups   480
to the blissful gods and then, libations made,
they drank the heady wine to their hearts' content
and went their ways to bed, each suitor to his house.

BOOK NINETEEN

Penelope and Her Guest

That left the great Odysseus waiting in his hall
as Athena helped him plot the slaughter of the suitors.
He turned at once to Telemachus, brisk with orders:
"Now we must stow the weapons out of reach, my boy,
all the arms and armor—and when the suitors miss them
and ask you questions, put them off with a winning story:
'I stowed them away, clear of the smoke. A far cry
from the arms Odysseus left when he went to Troy,
fire-damaged equipment, black with reeking fumes.
And a god reminded me of something darker too.   10
When you're in your cups a quarrel might break out,
you'd wound each other, shame your feasting here
and cast a pall on your courting.
Iron has powers to draw a man to ruin.' "

Telemachus did his father's will at once,
calling out to his old nurse Eurycleia: "Quick,
dear one, close the women up in their own quarters,
till I can stow my father's weapons in the storeroom.
Splendid gear, lying about, neglected, black with soot
since father sailed away. I was only a boy then.   20
Now I must safeguard them from the smoke."

"High time, child," the loving nurse replied.
"If only you'd bother to tend your whole house
and safeguard *all* your treasures. Tell me,
who's to fetch and carry the torch for you?
You won't let out the maids who'd light your way."

"Our friend here will," Telemachus answered coolly.
"I won't put up with a man who shirks his work,
not if he takes his ration from my stores,
even if he's miles away from home."   30

That silenced the old nurse.
She barred the doors that led from the long hall—
and up they sprang, Odysseus and his princely son,
and began to carry off the helmets, studded shields
and pointed spears, and Pallas Athena strode before them,
lifting a golden lamp that cast a dazzling radiance round about.
"Father," Telemachus suddenly burst out to Odysseus,
"oh what a marvel fills my eyes! Look, look there—
all the sides of the hall, the handsome crossbeams,
pinewood rafters, the tall columns towering—   40
all glow in my eyes like flaming fire!
Surely a god is here—
one of those who rule the vaulting skies!"

"Quiet," his father, the old soldier, warned him.
"Get a grip on yourself. No more questions now.
It's just the way of the gods who rule Olympus.
Off you go to bed. I'll stay here behind
to test the women, test your mother too.

She in her grief will ask me everything I know."

Under the flaring torchlight, through the hall   50
Telemachus made his way to his own bedroom now,
where he always went when welcome sleep came on him.
There he lay tonight as well, till Dawn's first light.
That left the great king still waiting in his hall
as Athena helped him plot the slaughter of the suitors . . .

Now down from her chamber came reserved Penelope,
looking for all the world like Artemis or golden Aphrodite.
Close to the fire her women drew her favorite chair
with its whorls of silver and ivory, inlaid rings.
The craftsman who made it years ago, Icmalius,   60
added a footrest under the seat itself,
mortised into the frame,
and over it all was draped a heavy fleece.
Here Penelope took her place, discreet, observant.
The women, arms bared, pressing in from their quarters,
cleared away the tables, the heaped remains of the feast
and the cups from which the raucous lords had drunk.
Raking embers from the braziers onto the ground,
they piled them high again with seasoned wood,
providing light and warmth.
                                And yet again   70
Melantho lashed out at Odysseus: "You still here?—
you pest, slinking around the house all night,
leering up at the women?
Get out, you tramp—be glad of the food you got—
or we'll sling a torch at you, rout you out at once!"

A killing glance, and the old trooper countered,
"What's possessed you, woman? Why lay into me? Such abuse!
Just because I'm filthy, because I wear such rags,
roving round the country, living hand-to-mouth.
But it's fate that drives me on: 80
that's the lot of beggars, homeless drifters.
I too once lived in a lofty house that men admired;

rolling in wealth, I'd often give to a vagabond like myself,
whoever he was, whatever need had brought him to my door.
And crowds of servants I had, and lots of all it takes
to live the life of ease, to make men call you rich.
But Zeus ruined it all—god's will, no doubt.
So beware, woman, or one day you may lose it all,
all your glitter that puts your work-mates in the shade.
Or your mistress may just fly in a rage and dress you down　　90
or Odysseus may return—there's still room for hope!
Or if he's dead as you think and never coming home,
well there's his son, Telemachus . . .
like father, like son—thanks to god Apollo.
No women's wildness here in the house escapes
the prince's eye. He's come of age at last."

　　So he warned, and alert Penelope heard him,
wheeled on the maid and tongue-lashed her smartly:
"Make no mistake, you brazen, shameless bitch,
none of your ugly work escapes me either—　　100
you will pay for it with your life, you will!
How well you knew—you heard from my own lips—
that I meant to probe this stranger in our house
and ask about my husband . . . my heart breaks for him."

　　She turned to her housekeeper Eurynome and said,
"Now bring us a chair and spread it soft with fleece,
so our guest can sit and tell me his whole story
and hear me out as well.
I'd like to ask him questions, point by point."

　　Eurynome bustled off to fetch a polished chair　　110
and set it down and spread it soft with fleece.
Here Odysseus sat, the man of many trials,
as cautious Penelope began the conversation:
"Stranger, let me start our questioning myself . . .
Who are you? where are you from? your city? your parents?"

　　"My good woman," Odysseus, master of craft, replied,

"no man on the face of the earth could find fault with *you.*
Your fame, believe me, has reached the vaulting skies.
Fame like a flawless king's who dreads the gods,
who governs a kingdom vast, proud and strong—   120
who upholds justice, true, and the black earth
bears wheat and barley, trees bow down with fruit
and the sheep drop lambs and never fail and the sea
teems with fish—thanks to his decent, upright rule,
and under his sovereign sway the people flourish.
So then, here in your house, ask me anything else
but don't, please, search out my birth, my land,
or you'll fill my heart to overflowing even more
as I bring back the past . . .
I am a man who's had his share of sorrows.   130
It's wrong for me, in someone else's house,
to sit here moaning and groaning, sobbing so—
it makes things worse, this grieving on and on.
One of your maids, or you yourself, might scold me,
think it's just the wine that had doused my wits
and made me drown in tears."

     "No, no, stranger," wise Penelope demurred,
"whatever form and feature I had, what praise I'd won,
the deathless gods destroyed that day the Achaeans
sailed away to Troy, my husband in their ships,   140
Odysseus—if *he* could return to tend my life
the renown I had would only grow in glory.
Now my life is torment . . .
look at the griefs some god has loosed against me!
All the nobles who rule the islands round about,
Dulichion, Same, and wooded Zacynthus too,
and all who lord it in sunny Ithaca itself—
they court me against my will, they lay waste my house.
So I pay no heed to strangers, suppliants at my door,
not even heralds out on their public errands here—   150
I yearn for Odysseus, always, my heart pines away.
They rush the marriage on, and I spin out my wiles.
A god from the blue it was inspired me first

to set up a great loom in our royal halls
and I began to weave, and the weaving finespun,
the yarns endless, and I would lead them on: 'Young men,
my suitors, now that King Odysseus is no more,
go slowly, keen as you are to marry me, until
I can finish off this web . . .
so my weaving won't all fray and come to nothing.   160
This is a shroud for old lord Laertes, for that day
when the deadly fate that lays us out at last will take him down.
I dread the shame my countrywomen would heap upon me,
yes, if a man of such wealth should lie in state
without a shroud for cover.'
                    My very words,
and despite their pride and passion they believed me.
So by day I'd weave at my great and growing web—
by night, by the light of torches set beside me,
I would unravel all I'd done. Three whole years
I deceived them blind, seduced them with this scheme.   170
Then, when the wheeling seasons brought the fourth year on
and the months waned and the long days came round once more,
then, thanks to my maids—the shameless, reckless creatures—
the suitors caught me in the act, denounced me harshly.
So I finished it off. Against my will. They forced me.
And now I cannot escape a marriage, nor can I contrive
a deft way out. My parents urge me to tie the knot
and my son is galled as they squander his estate—
he sees it all. He's a grown man by now, equipped
to tend to his own royal house and tend it well: 180
Zeus grants my son that honor . . .
But for all that—now tell me who you are.
Where do you come from? You've hardly sprung
from a rock or oak like some old man of legend."

   The master improviser answered, slowly,
"My lady . . . wife of Laertes' son, Odysseus,
will your questions about my family never end?
All right then. Here's my story. Even though
it plunges me into deeper grief than I feel now.

But that's the way of the world, when one has been   190
so far from home, so long away as I, roving over
many cities of men, enduring many hardships.

                              Still,

my story will tell you all you need to know.

    There is a land called Crete . . .
ringed by the wine-dark sea with rolling whitecaps—
handsome country, fertile, thronged with people
well past counting—boasting ninety cities,
language mixing with language side-by-side.
First come the Achaeans, then the native Cretans,
hardy, gallant in action, then Cydonian clansmen,   200
Dorians living in three tribes, and proud Pelasgians last.
Central to all their cities is magnificent Cnossos,
the site where Minos ruled and each ninth year
conferred with almighty Zeus himself. Minos,
father of my father, Deucalion, that bold heart.
Besides myself Deucalion sired Prince Idomeneus,
who set sail for Troy in his beaked ships of war,
escorting Atreus' sons. My own name is Aethon.
I am the younger-born;
my older brother's a better man than I am.   210
Now, it was there in Cnossos that I saw him . . .
Odysseus—and we traded gifts of friendship.
A heavy gale had landed him on our coast,
driven him way off course, rounding Malea's cape
when he was bound for Troy. He anchored in Amnisus,
hard by the goddess' cave of childbirth and labor,
that rough harbor—barely riding out the storm.
He came into town at once, asking for Idomeneus,
claiming to be my brother's close, respected friend.
Too late. Ten or eleven days had already passed   220
since he set sail for Troy in his beaked ships.
So I took Odysseus back to my own house,
gave him a hero's welcome, treated him in style—
stores in our palace made for princely entertainment.
As for his comrades, all who'd shipped with him,

I dipped into public stock to give them barley,
ruddy wine and fine cattle for slaughter,
beef to their hearts' content. A dozen days
they stayed with me there, those brave Achaeans,
penned up by a North Wind so stiff that a man,   230
even on dry land, could never keep his feet—
some angry spirit raised that blast, I'd say.
Then on the thirteenth day the wind died down
and they set sail for Troy."

                         Falsehoods all,
but he gave his falsehoods all the ring of truth.
As she listened on, her tears flowed and soaked her cheeks
as the heavy snow melts down from the high mountain ridges,
snow the West Wind piles there and the warm East Wind thaws
and the snow, melting, swells the rivers to overflow their banks—
so she dissolved in tears, streaming down her lovely cheeks,   240
weeping for him, her husband, sitting there beside her.
Odysseus' heart went out to his grief-stricken wife
but under his lids his eyes remained stock-still—
they might have been horn or iron—
his guile fought back his tears. And she,
once she'd had her fill of grief and weeping,
turned again to her guest with this reply:
"Now, stranger, I think I'll test you, just to see
if there in your house, with all his friends-in-arms,
you actually entertained my husband as you say.   250
Come, tell me what sort of clothing he wore,
what cut of man was he?
What of the men who followed in his train?"

                             "Ah good woman,"
Odysseus, the great master of subtlety, returned,
"how hard it is to speak, after so much time
apart . . . why, some twenty years have passed
since he left my house and put my land behind him.
Even so, imagine the man as I portray him—
I can see him now.

               King Odysseus . . .
he was wearing a heavy woolen cape, sea-purple   260

in double folds, with a golden brooch to clasp it,
twin sheaths for the pins, on the face a work of art:
a hound clenching a dappled fawn in its front paws,
slashing it as it writhed. All marveled to see it,
solid gold as it was, the hound slashing, throttling
the fawn in its death-throes, hoofs flailing to break free.
I noticed his glossy tunic too, clinging to his skin
like the thin glistening skin of a dried onion,
silky, soft, the glint of the sun itself.
Women galore would gaze on it with relish.   270
And this too. Bear it in mind, won't you?
I've no idea if Odysseus wore these things at home
or a comrade gave him them as he boarded ship,
or a host perhaps—the man was loved by many.
There were few Achaeans to equal him . . . and I?
I gave him a bronze sword myself, a lined cloak,
elegant, deep red, and a fringed shirt as well,
and I saw him off in his long benched ship of war
in lordly style.
                      Something else. He kept a herald
beside him, a man a little older than himself.   280
I'll try to describe him to you, best I can.
Round-shouldered he was, swarthy, curly-haired.
His name? Eurybates. And Odysseus prized him
most of all his men. Their minds worked as one."

   His words renewed her deep desire to weep,
recognizing the strong clear signs Odysseus offered.
But as soon as she'd had her fill of tears and grief,
Penelope turned again to her guest and said,
"Now, stranger, much as I pitied you before,
now in my house you'll be my special friend,   290
my honored guest. I am the one, myself,
who gave him the very clothes that you describe.
I brought them up from the storeroom, folded them neatly,
fastened the golden brooch to adorn my husband,
Odysseus—never again will I embrace him,
striding home to his own native land.

A black day it was
when he took ship to see that cursed city . . .
Destroy, I call it—I hate to say its name!"

    "Ah my queen," the man of craft assured her,   300
"noble wife of Laertes' son, Odysseus,
ravage no more your lovely face with tears
or consume your heart with grieving for your husband.
Not that I'd blame you, ever. Any woman will mourn
the bridegroom she has lost, lain with in love
and borne his children too. Even though he
was no Odysseus—a man like a god, they say.
But dry your tears and take my words to heart.
I will tell you the whole truth and hide nothing:
I have heard that Odysseus now, at last, is on his way,   310
he's just in reach, in rich Thesprotian country—
the man is still alive
and he's bringing home a royal hoard of treasure,
gifts he won from the people of those parts.
His crew? He's lost his crew and hollow ship
on the wine-dark waters off Thrinacia Island.
Zeus and Helios raged, dead set against Odysseus
for his men-at-arms had killed the cattle of the Sun,
so down to the last hand they drowned in crashing seas.
But not Odysseus, clinging tight to his ship's keel—   320
the breakers flung him out onto dry land, on Scheria,
the land of Phaeacians, close kin to the gods themselves,
and with all their hearts they prized him like a god,
showered the man with gifts, and they'd have gladly
sailed him home unscathed. In fact Odysseus
would have been here beside you long ago
but he thought it the better, shrewder course
to recoup his fortunes roving through the world.
At sly profit-turning there's not a man alive
to touch Odysseus. He's got no rival there.   330
So I learned from Phidon, king of Thesprotia,
who swore to me as he poured libations in his house,
'The ship's hauled down and the shipmates set to sail,

to take Odysseus home to native land.'
                                But I . . .
he shipped me off before. A Thesprotian cutter
chanced to be heading for Dulichion rich in wheat.
But he showed me all the treasure Odysseus had amassed,
enough to last a man and ten generations of his heirs—
so great the wealth stored up for *him* in the king's vaults!
But Odysseus, he made clear, was off at Dodona then   340
to hear the will of Zeus that rustles forth
from the god's tall leafy oak: how should he return,
after all the years away, to his own beloved Ithaca,
openly or in secret?
                      And so the man is safe,
as you can see, and he's coming home, soon,
he's close, close at hand—
he won't be severed long from kin and country,
no, not now. I give you my solemn, binding oath.
I swear by Zeus, the first, the greatest god—
by Odysseus' hearth, where I have come for help: 350
all will come to pass, I swear, exactly as I say.
True, this very month—just as the old moon dies
and the new moon rises into life—Odysseus will return!"

   "If only, my friend," reserved Penelope exclaimed,
"everything you say would come to pass!
You'd soon know my affection, know my gifts.
Any man you meet would call you blest.
But my heart can sense the way it all will go.
Odysseus, I tell you, is never coming back,
nor will you ever gain your passage home,   360
for we have no masters in our house like him
at welcoming in or sending off an honored guest.
Odysseus. There was a man, or was he all a dream?
But come, women, wash the stranger and make his bed,
with bedding, blankets and lustrous spreads to keep him warm
till Dawn comes up and takes her golden throne.
Then, tomorrow at daybreak, bathe him well
and rub him down with oil, so he can sit beside

Telemachus in the hall, enjoy his breakfast there.
And anyone who offends our guest beyond endurance—   370
he defeats himself; he's doomed to failure here,
no matter how raucously he raves and blusters on.
For how can you know, my friend, if I surpass
all women in thoughtfulness and shrewd good sense,
if I'd allow you to take your meals at hall
so weatherbeaten, clad in rags and tatters?
Our lives are much too brief . . .
If a man is cruel by nature, cruel in action,
the mortal world will call down curses on his head
while he is alive, and all will mock his memory after death.   380
But then if a man is kind by nature, kind in action,
his guests will carry his fame across the earth
and people all will praise him from the heart."

    "Wait, my queen," the crafty man objected,
"noble wife of Laertes' son, Odysseus—
blankets and glossy spreads? They're not my style.
Not from the day I launched out in my long-oared ship
and the snowy peaks of Crete went fading far astern.
I'll lie as I've done through sleepless nights before.
Many a night I've spent on rugged beds afield,   390
waiting for Dawn to mount her lovely throne.
Nor do I pine for any footbaths either.
Of all the women who serve your household here,
not one will touch my feet. Unless, perhaps,
there is some old retainer, the soul of trust,
someone who's borne as much as I have borne . . .
I wouldn't mind if she would touch my feet."

                          "Dear friend,"
the discreet Penelope replied, "never has any man
so thoughtful—of all the guests in my palace
come from foreign parts—been as welcome as you . . .   400
so sensible, so apt, is every word you say.
I have just such an old woman, seasoned, wise,
who carefully tended my unlucky husband, reared him,
took him into her arms the day his mother bore him—

frail as the woman is, she'll wash your feet.
Up with you now, my good old Eurycleia,
come and wash your master's . . . equal in years.
Odysseus must have feet and hands like his by now—
hardship can age a person overnight."

At that name
the old retainer buried her face in both hands,   410
burst into warm tears and wailed out in grief,
"Oh my child, how helpless I am to help you now!
How Zeus despised you, more than all other men,
god-fearing man that you were . . .
Never did any mortal burn the Old Thunderer
such rich thighbones—offerings charred and choice—
never as many as *you* did, praying always to reach
a ripe old age and raise a son to glory. Now,
you alone he's robbed of your home-coming day!
Just so, the women must have mocked my king,   420
far away, when he'd stopped at some fine house—
just as all these bitches, stranger, mock you here.
And because you shrink from their taunts, their wicked barbs,
you will not let them wash you. The work is mine—
Icarius' daughter, wise Penelope, bids me now
and I am all too glad. I will wash your feet,
both for my own dear queen and for yourself—
your sorrows wring my heart . . . and why?
Listen to me closely, mark my words.
Many a wayworn guest has landed here   430
but never, I swear, has one so struck my eyes—
your build, your voice, your feet—you're like Odysseus . . .
to the life!"

"Old woman," wily Odysseus countered,
"that's what they all say who've seen us both.
We bear a striking resemblance to each other,
as you have had the wit to say yourself."

    The old woman took up a burnished basin
she used for washing feet and poured in bowls
of fresh cold water before she stirred in hot.

Odysseus, sitting full in the firelight, suddenly   440
swerved round to the dark, gripped by a quick misgiving—
soon as she touched him she might spot the scar!
The truth would all come out.

                                    Bending closer
she started to bathe her master . . . then,
in a flash, she knew the scar—

                            that old wound
made years ago by a boar's white tusk when Odysseus
went to Parnassus, out to see Autolycus and his sons.
The man was his mother's noble father, one who excelled
the world at thievery, that and subtle, shifty oaths.
Hermes gave him the gift, overjoyed by the thighs   450
of lambs and kids he burned in the god's honor—
Hermes the ready partner in his crimes. Now,
Autolycus once visited Ithaca's fertile land,
to find his daughter's son had just been born.
Eurycleia set him down on the old man's knees
as he finished dinner, urging him, "Autolycus,
you must find a name for your daughter's darling son.
The baby comes as the answer to her prayers."

                                            "You,
my daughter, and you, my son-in-law," Autolycus replied,
"give the boy the name I tell you now. Just as I   460
have come from afar, creating pain for many—
men and women across the good green earth—
so let his name be *Odysseus* . . .
the Son of Pain, a name he'll earn in full.
And when he has come of age and pays his visit
to Parnassus—the great estate of his mother's line
where all my treasures lie—I will give him enough
to cheer his heart, then speed him home to you."

                                            And so,
in time, Odysseus went to collect the splendid gifts.
Autolycus and the sons of Autolycus warmed him in   470
with eager handclasps, hearty words of welcome.
His mother's mother, Amphithea, hugged the boy
and kissed his face and kissed his shining eyes.

Autolycus told his well-bred sons to prepare
a princely feast. They followed orders gladly,
herded an ox inside at once, five years old,
skinned it and split the carcass into quarters,
deftly cut it in pieces, skewered these on spits,
roasted all to a turn and served the portions out.
So all day long till the sun went down they feasted,   480
consuming equal shares to their hearts' content.
Then when the sun had set and night came on
they turned to bed and took the gift of sleep.

                                                      As soon
as young Dawn with her rose-red fingers shone once more
they all moved out for the hunt, hounds in the lead,
Autolycus' sons and Prince Odysseus in their ranks.
Climbing Parnassus' ridges, thick with timber,
they quickly reached the mountain's windy folds
and just as the sun began to strike the plowlands,
rising out of the deep calm flow of the Ocean River,   490
the beaters came to a wooded glen, the hounds broke,
hot on a trail, and right behind the pack they came,
Autolycus' sons—Odysseus out in front now,
pressing the dogs, brandishing high his spear
with its long shadow waving. Then and there
a great boar lay in wait, in a thicket lair so dense
that the sodden gusty winds could never pierce it,
nor could the sun's sharp rays invade its depths
nor a downpour drench it through and through,
so dense, so dark, and piled with fallen leaves.   500
Here, as the hunters closed in for the kill,
crowding the hounds, the tramp of men and dogs
came drumming round the boar—he crashed from his lair,
his razor back bristling, his eyes flashing fire
and charging up to the hunt he stopped, at bay—
and Odysseus rushed him first,
shaking his long spear in a sturdy hand,
wild to strike but the boar struck faster,
lunging in on the slant, a tusk thrusting up
over the boy's knee, gouging a deep strip of flesh   510

but it never hit the bone—
                          Odysseus thrust and struck,
stabbing the beast's right shoulder—
                          a glint of bronze—
the point ripped clean through and down in the dust he dropped,
grunting out his breath as his life winged away.
The sons of Autolycus, working over Odysseus,
skillfully binding up his open wound—
the gallant, godlike prince—
chanted an old spell that stanched the blood
and quickly bore him home to their father's palace.
There, in no time, Autolycus and the sons of Autolycus   520
healed him well and, showering him with splendid gifts,
sped Odysseus back to his native land, to Ithaca,
a young man filled with joy. His happy parents,
his father and noble mother, welcomed him home
and asked him of all his exploits, blow-by-blow:
how did he get that wound? He told his tale with style,
how the white tusk of a wild boar had gashed his leg,
hunting on Parnassus with Autolycus and his sons . . .
                                      That scar—
as the old nurse cradled his leg and her hands passed down
she felt it, knew it, suddenly let his foot fall—   530
down it dropped in the basin—the bronze clanged,
tipping over, spilling water across the floor.
Joy and torment gripped her heart at once,
tears rushed to her eyes—voice choked in her throat
she reached for Odysseus' chin and whispered quickly,
"Yes, yes! you are *Odysseus*—oh dear boy—
I couldn't know you before . . .
not till I touched the body of my king!"

     She glanced at Penelope, keen to signal her
that here was her own dear husband, here and now,   540
but she could not catch the glance, she took no heed,
Athena turned her attention elsewhere. But Odysseus—
his right hand shot out, clutching the nurse's throat,
with his left he hugged her to himself and muttered,

"Nurse, you want to kill me? You suckled me yourself
at your own breast—and now I'm home, at last,
after bearing twenty years of brutal hardship,
home, on native ground. But now you know,
now that a god has flashed it in your mind,
quiet! not a word to anyone in the house.   550
Or else, I warn you—and I mean business too—
if a god beats down these brazen suitors at my hands,
I will not spare you—my old nurse that you are—
when I kill the other women in my house."

      "Child," shrewd old Eurycleia protested,
"what nonsense you let slip through your teeth!
You know *me*—I'm stubborn, never give an inch—
I'll keep still as solid rock or iron.
One more thing. Take it to heart, I tell you.
If a god beats down these brazen suitors at your hands,   560
I'll report in full on the women in your house:
who are disloyal to you, who are guiltless."

      "Nurse," the cool tactician Odysseus said,
"why bother to count them off? A waste of breath.
I'll observe them, judge each one myself.
Just be quiet. Keep your tales to yourself.
Leave the rest to the gods."
                              Hushed so,
the old nurse went padding along the halls
to fetch more water—her basin had all spilled—
and once she'd bathed and rubbed him down with oil,   570
Odysseus drew his chair up near the fire again,
trying to keep warm,
but he hid his scar beneath his beggar's rags
as cautious Penelope resumed their conversation:
"My friend, I have only one more question for you,
something slight, now the hour draws on for welcome sleep—
for those who can yield to sweet repose, that is,
heartsick as they are. As for myself, though,
some god has sent me pain that knows no bounds.

All day long I indulge myself in sighs and tears   580
as I see to my tasks, direct the household women.
When night falls and the world lies lost in sleep,
I take to my bed, my heart throbbing, about to break,
anxieties swarming, piercing—I may go mad with grief.
Like Pandareus' daughter, the nightingale in the green woods
lifting her lovely song at the first warm rush of spring,
perched in the treetops' rustling leaves and pouring forth
her music shifting, trilling and sinking, rippling high to burst
in grief for Itylus, her beloved boy, King Zethus' son
whom she in innocence once cut down with bronze . . .   590
so my wavering heart goes shuttling, back and forth:
Do I stay beside my son and keep all things secure—
my lands, my serving-women, the grand high-roofed house—
true to my husband's bed, the people's voice as well?
Or do I follow, at last, the best man who courts me
here in the halls, who gives the greatest gifts?
My son—when he was a boy and lighthearted—
urged me not to marry and leave my husband's house.
But now he has grown and reached his young prime,
he begs me to leave our palace, travel home.   600
Telemachus, so obsessed with his own estate,
the wealth my princely suitors bleed away.

                              But please,
read this dream for me, won't you? Listen closely . . .
I keep twenty geese in the house, from the water trough
they come and peck their wheat—I love to watch them all.
But down from a mountain swooped this great hook-beaked eagle,
yes, and he snapped their necks and killed them one and all
and they lay in heaps throughout the halls while he,
back to the clear blue sky he soared at once.
But I wept and wailed—only a dream, of course—   610
and our well-groomed ladies came and clustered round me,
sobbing, stricken: the eagle killed my geese. But down
he swooped again and settling onto a jutting rafter
called out in a human voice that dried my tears,
'Courage, daughter of famous King Icarius!
This is no dream but a happy waking vision,

real as day, that will come true for you.
The geese were your suitors—I was once the eagle
but now I am your husband, back again at last,
about to launch a terrible fate against them all!'   620
So he vowed, and the soothing sleep released me.
I peered around and saw my geese in the house,
pecking at their wheat, at the same trough
where they always took their meal."

                                        "Dear woman,"
quick Odysseus answered, "twist it however you like,
your dream can only mean one thing. Odysseus
told you himself—he'll make it come to pass.
Destruction is clear for each and every suitor;
not a soul escapes his death and doom."

     "Ah my friend," seasoned Penelope dissented,   630
"dreams are hard to unravel, wayward, drifting things—
not all we glimpse in them will come to pass . . .
Two gates there are for our evanescent dreams,
one is made of ivory, the other made of horn.
Those that pass through the ivory cleanly carved
are will-o'-the-wisps, their message bears no fruit.
The dreams that pass through the gates of polished horn
are fraught with truth, for the dreamer who can see them.
But I can't believe my strange dream has come that way,
much as my son and I would love to have it so.   640
One more thing I'll tell you—weigh it well.
The day that dawns today, this cursed day,
will cut me off from Odysseus' house. Now,
I mean to announce a contest with those axes,
the ones he would often line up here inside the hall,
twelve in a straight unbroken row like blocks to shore a keel,
then stand well back and whip an arrow through the lot.
Now I will bring them on as a trial for my suitors.
The hand that can string the bow with greatest ease,
that shoots an arrow clean through all twelve axes—   650
he's the man I follow, yes, forsaking this house
where I was once a bride, this gracious house

so filled with the best that life can offer—
I shall always remember it, that I know . . .
even in my dreams."
                              "Oh my queen,"
Odysseus, man of exploits, urged her on,
"royal wife of Laertes' son, Odysseus, now,
don't put off this test in the halls a moment.
Before that crew can handle the polished bow,
string it taut and shoot through all those axes—   660
Odysseus, man of exploits, will be home with you!"

    "If only, my friend," the wise Penelope replied,
"you were willing to sit beside me in the house,
indulging me in the comfort of your presence,
sleep would never drift across my eyes.
But one can't go without one's sleep forever.
The immortals give each thing its proper place
in our mortal lives throughout the good green earth.
So now I'm going back to my room upstairs
and lie down on my bed,   670
that bed of pain my tears have streaked, year in,
year out, from the day Odysseus sailed away to see . . .
Destroy, I call it—I hate to say its name!
There I'll rest, while you lie here in the hall,
spreading your blankets somewhere on the floor,
or the women will prepare a decent bed."
                                        With that
the queen went up to her lofty well-lit room
and not alone: her women followed close behind.
Penelope, once they reached the upper story,
fell to weeping for Odysseus, her beloved husband,   680
till watchful Athena sealed her eyes with welcome sleep.

Portents Gather

Off in the entrance-hall the great king made his bed,
spreading out on the ground the raw hide of an ox,
heaping over it fleece from sheep the suitors
butchered day and night, then Eurynome threw
a blanket over him, once he'd nestled down.
And there Odysseus lay . . .
plotting within himself the suitors' death—
awake, alert, as the women slipped from the house,
the maids who whored in the suitors' beds each night,
tittering, linking arms and frisking as before.   10
The master's anger rose inside his chest,
torn in thought, debating, head and heart—
should he up and rush them, kill them one and all
or let them rut with their lovers one last time?
The heart inside him growled low with rage,

as a bitch mounting over her weak, defenseless puppies
growls, facing a stranger, bristling for a showdown—
so he growled from his depths, hackles rising at their outrage.
But he struck his chest and curbed his fighting heart:
"Bear up, old heart! You've borne worse, far worse,   20
that day when the Cyclops, man-mountain, bolted
your hardy comrades down. But you held fast—
Nobody but your cunning pulled you through
the monster's cave you thought would be your death."

    So he forced his spirit into submission,
the rage in his breast reined back—unswerving,
all endurance. But he himself kept tossing, turning,
intent as a cook before some white-hot blazing fire
who rolls his sizzling sausage back and forth,
packed with fat and blood—keen to broil it quickly,   30
tossing, turning it, this way, that way—so he cast about:
how could he get these shameless suitors in his clutches,
one man facing a mob? . . . when close to his side she came,
Athena sweeping down from the sky in a woman's build
and hovering at his head, the goddess spoke:
"Why still awake? The unluckiest man alive!
Here is your house, your wife at home, your son,
as fine a boy as one could hope to have."

                                        "True,"
the wily fighter replied, "how right you are, goddess,
but still this worry haunts me, heart and soul—   40
how can I get these shameless suitors in my clutches?
Single-handed, braving an army always camped inside.
There's another worry, that haunts me even more.
What if I kill them—thanks to you and Zeus—
how do I run from under their avengers?
Show me the way, I ask you."

                                "Impossible man!"
Athena bantered, the goddess' eyes ablaze.
"Others are quick to trust a weaker comrade,
some poor mortal, far less cunning than I.
But I am a goddess, look, the very one who   50

guards you in all your trials to the last.
I tell you this straight out:
even if fifty bands of mortal fighters
closed around us, hot to kill us off in battle,
still you could drive away their herds and sleek flocks!
So, surrender to sleep at last. What a misery,
keeping watch through the night, wide awake—
you'll soon come up from under all your troubles."

    With that she showered sleep across his eyes
and back to Olympus went the lustrous goddess.   60
As soon as sleep came on him, loosing his limbs,
slipping the toils of anguish from his mind,
his devoted wife awoke and,
sitting up in her soft bed, returned to tears.
When the queen had wept to her heart's content
she prayed to the Huntress, Artemis, first of all:
"Artemis—goddess, noble daughter of Zeus, if only
you'd whip an arrow through my breast and tear my life out,
now, at once! Or let some whirlwind pluck me up
and sweep me away along those murky paths and   70
fling me down where the Ocean River running
round the world rolls back upon itself!
                            Quick
as the whirlwinds swept away Pandareus' daughters—
years ago, when the gods destroyed their parents,
leaving the young girls orphans in their house.
But radiant Aphrodite nursed them well
on cheese and luscious honey and heady wine,
and Hera gave them beauty and sound good sense,
more than all other women—virgin Artemis made them tall
and Athena honed their skills to fashion lovely work.   80
But then, when Aphrodite approached Olympus' peaks
to ask for the girls their crowning day as brides
from Zeus who loves the lightning—Zeus who knows all,
all that's fated, all not fated, for mortal man—
then the storm spirits snatched them away

and passed them on to the hateful Furies,
yes, for all their loving care.
                                        Just so
may the gods who rule Olympus blot me out!
Artemis with your glossy braids, come shoot me dead—
so I can plunge beneath this loathsome earth   90
with the image of Odysseus vivid in my mind.
Never let me warm the heart of a weaker man!
Even grief is bearable, true, when someone weeps
through the days, sobbing, heart convulsed with pain
yet embraced by sleep all night—sweet oblivion, sleep
dissolving all, the good and the bad, once it seals our eyes—
but even my dreams torment me, sent by wicked spirits.
Again—just this night—someone lay beside me . . .
like Odysseus to the life, when he embarked
with his men-at-arms. My heart raced with joy.   100
No dream, I thought, the waking truth at last!"
                                        At those words
Dawn rose on her golden throne in a sudden gleam of light.
And great Odysseus caught the sound of his wife's cry
and began to daydream—deep in his heart it seemed
she stood beside him, knew him, now, at last . . .
Gathering up the fleece and blankets where he'd slept,
he laid them on a chair in the hall, he took the oxhide out
and spread it down, lifted his hands and prayed to Zeus:
"Father Zeus, if you really willed it so—to bring me
home over land and sea-lanes, home to native ground   110
after all the pain you brought me—show me a sign,
a good omen voiced by someone awake indoors,
another sign, outside, from Zeus himself!"

    And Zeus in all his wisdom heard that prayer.
He thundered at once, out of his clear blue heavens
high above the clouds, and Odysseus' spirit lifted.
Then from within the halls a woman grinding grain
let fly a lucky word. Close at hand she was,
where the good commander set the handmills once

and now twelve women in all performed their tasks,   120
grinding the wheat and barley, marrow of men's bones.
The rest were abed by now—they'd milled their stint—
this one alone, the frailest of all, kept working on.
Stopping her mill, she spoke an omen for her master:
"Zeus, Father! King of gods and men, now *there*
was a crack of thunder out of the starry sky—
and not a cloud in sight!
Sure it's a sign you're showing someone now.
So, poor as I am, grant *me* my prayer as well:
let this day be the last, the last these suitors   130
bolt their groaning feasts in King Odysseus' house!
These brutes who break my knees—heart-wrenching labor,
grinding their grain—now let them eat their last!"

    A lucky omen, linked with Zeus's thunder.
Odysseus' heart leapt up, the man convinced
he'd grind the scoundrels' lives out in revenge.

                                        By now
the other maids were gathering in Odysseus' royal palace,
raking up on the hearth the fire still going strong.
Telemachus climbed from bed and dressed at once,
brisk as a young god—   140
over his shoulder he slung his well-honed sword,
he fastened rawhide sandals under his smooth feet,
he seized his tough spear tipped with a bronze point
and took his stand at the threshold, calling Eurycleia:
"Dear nurse, how did you treat the stranger in our house?
With bed and board? Or leave him to lie untended?
That would be mother's way—sensible as she is—
all impulse, doting over some worthless stranger,
turning a good man out to face the worst."

    "Please, child," his calm old nurse replied,   150
"don't blame *her*—your mother's blameless this time.
He sat and drank his wine till he'd had his fill.
Food? He'd lost his hunger. But she asked him.

And when it was time to think of turning in,
she told the maids to spread a decent bed, but he—
so down-and-out, poor soul, so dogged by fate—
said no to snuggling into a bed, between covers.
No sir, the man lay down in the entrance-hall,
on the raw hide of an ox and sheep's fleece,
and we threw a blanket over him, so we did."
                                    Hearing that,   160
Telemachus strode out through the palace, spear in hand,
and a pair of sleek hounds went trotting at his heels.
He made for the meeting grounds to join the island lords
while Eurycleia the daughter of Ops, Pisenor's son,
that best of women, gave the maids their orders:
"Quick now, look alive, sweep out the house,
wet down the floors!
                      You, those purple coverlets,
fling them over the fancy chairs!
                                   All those tables,
sponge them down—scour the winebowls, burnished cups!
The rest—now off you go to the spring and fetch some water,   170
fast as your legs can run!
Our young gallants won't be long from the palace,
they'll be bright and early—today's a public feast."

      They hung on her words and ran to do her bidding.
Full twenty scurried off to the spring's dark water,
others bent to the housework, all good hands.
Then in they trooped, the strutting serving-men,
who split the firewood cleanly now as the women
bustled in from the spring, the swineherd at their heels,
driving three fat porkers, the best of all his herds.   180
And leaving them to root in the broad courtyard,
up he went to Odysseus, hailed him warmly:
"Friend, do the suitors show you more respect
or treat you like the dregs of the earth as always?"

      "Good Eumaeus," the crafty man replied,

"if only the gods would pay back their outrage!
Wild and reckless young cubs, conniving here
in another's house. They've got no sense of shame."

     And now as the two confided in each other,
the goatherd Melanthius sauntered toward them,   190
herding his goats with a pair of drovers' help,
the pick of his flocks to make the suitors' meal.
Under the echoing porch he tethered these, then turned
on Odysseus once again with cutting insults: "Still alive?
Still hounding your betters, begging round the house?
Why don't you cart yourself away? Get out!
We'll never part, I swear,
till we taste each other's fists. Riffraff,
you and your begging make us sick! Get out—
we're hardly the only banquet on the island."   200

     No reply. The wily one just shook his head,
silent, his mind churning with thoughts of bloody work . . .

     Third to arrive was Philoetius, that good cowherd,
prodding in for the crowd a heifer and fat goats.
Boatmen had brought them over from the mainland,
crews who ferry across all travelers too,
whoever comes for passage.
Under the echoing porch he tethered all heads well
and then approached the swineherd, full of questions:
"Who's this stranger, Eumaeus, just come to the house?   210
What roots does the man claim—who are his people?
Where are his blood kin? his father's fields?
Poor beggar. But what a build—a royal king's!
Ah, once the gods weave trouble into our lives
they drive us across the earth, they drown us all in pain,
even kings of the realm."
                              And with that thought
he walked up to Odysseus, gave him his right hand
and winged a greeting: "Cheers, old friend, old father,
here's to your luck, great days from this day on—

saddled now as you are with so much trouble.   220
Father Zeus, no god's more deadly than you!
No mercy for men, you give them life yourself
then plunge them into misery, brutal hardship.
I broke into sweat, my friend, when I first saw you—
see, my eyes still brim with tears, remembering *him*,
Odysseus . . . He must wear such rags, I know it,
knocking about, drifting through the world
if he's still alive and sees the light of day.
If he's dead already, lost in the House of Death,
my heart aches for Odysseus, my great lord and master.   230
He set me in charge of his herds, in Cephallenian country,
when I was just a youngster. How they've grown by now,
past counting! No mortal on earth could breed
a finer stock of oxen—broad in the brow,
they thrive like ears of corn. But just look,
these interlopers tell me to drive them in
for their own private feasts. Not a thought
for the young prince in the house, they never flinch—
no regard for the gods' wrath—in their mad rush
to carve up his goods, my master gone so long!   240
I'm tossed from horn to horn in my own mind . . .
What a traitor I'd be, with the prince still alive,
if I'd run off to some other country, herds and all,
to a new set of strangers. Ah, but isn't it worse
to hold out here, tending the herds for upstarts,
not their owners—suffering all the pains of hell?
I could have fled, ages ago, to some great king
who'd give me shelter. It's unbearable here.
True, but I still dream of my old master,
unlucky man—if only *he*'d drop in from the blue   250
and drive these suitors all in a rout throughout the halls!"

     "Cowherd," the cool tactician Odysseus answered,
"you're no coward, and nobody's fool, I'd say.
Even I can see there's sense in that old head.
So I tell you this on my solemn, binding oath:
I swear by Zeus, the first of all the gods—

by the table of hospitality waiting for us,
by Odysseus' hearth where I have come for help,
Odysseus will come home while you're still here.
You'll see with your own eyes, if you have the heart,   260
these suitors who lord it here cut down in blood."

    "Stranger, if only," the cowherd cried aloud,
"if only Zeus would make that oath come true—
you'd see my power, my fighting arms in action!"

    Eumaeus echoed his prayer to all the gods
that their wise king would soon come home again.

    Now as they spoke and urged each other on,
and once more the suitors were plotting certain doom
for the young prince—suddenly, banking high on the left
an omen flew past, an eagle clutching a trembling dove.   270
And Amphinomus rose in haste to warn them all,
"My friends, we'll never carry off this plot
to kill the prince. Let's concentrate on feasting."

    His timely invitation pleased them all.
The suitors ambled into Odysseus' royal house
and flinging down their cloaks on a chair or bench,
they butchered hulking sheep and fatted goats,
full-grown hogs and a young cow from the herd.
They roasted all the innards, served them round
and filled the bowls with wine and mixed it well.   280
Eumaeus passed out cups; Philoetius, trusty herdsman,
brought on loaves of bread in ample wicker trays;
Melanthius poured the wine. The whole company
reached out for the good things that lay at hand.

    Telemachus, maneuvering shrewdly, sat his father down
on the stone threshold, just inside the timbered hall,
and set a rickety stool and cramped table there.
He gave him a share of innards, poured his wine

in a golden cup and added a bracing invitation:
"Now sit right there. Drink your wine with the crowd.   290
I'll defend you from all their taunts and blows,
these young bucks. This is no public place,
this is *Odysseus'* house—
my father won it for me, so it's mine.
You suitors, control yourselves. No insults now,
no brawling, no, or it's war between us all."

   So he declared. And they all bit their lips,
amazed the prince could speak with so much daring.
Only Eupithes' son Antinous ventured,
"Fighting words, but do let's knuckle under—   300
to our *prince*. Such abuse, such naked threats!
But clearly Zeus has foiled us. Or long before
we would have shut his mouth for him in the halls,
fluent and flowing as he is."
                              So he mocked.
Telemachus paid no heed.
                              And now through the streets
the heralds passed, leading the beasts marked out
for sacrifice on Apollo's grand festal day,
and the islanders with their long hair were filing
into the god's shady grove—the distant deadly Archer.

   Those in the palace, once they'd roasted the prime cuts,   310
pulled them off the spits and, sharing out the portions,
fell to the royal feast . . .
The men who served them gave Odysseus his share,
as fair as the helping they received themselves.
So Telemachus ordered, the king's own son.

   But Athena had no mind to let the brazen suitors
hold back now from their heart-rending insults—
she meant to make the anguish cut still deeper
into the core of Laertes' son Odysseus.
There was one among them, a lawless boor—   320

Ctesippus was his name, he made his home in Same,
a fellow so impressed with his own astounding wealth
he courted the wife of Odysseus, gone for years.
Now the man harangued his swaggering comrades:
"Listen to me, my fine friends, here's what I say!
From the start our guest has had his fair share—
it's only right, you know.
How impolite it would be, how wrong to scant
whatever guest Telemachus welcomes to his house.
Look here, I'll give him a proper guest-gift too,   330
a prize he can hand the crone who bathes his feet
or a tip for another slave who haunts the halls
of our great king Odysseus!"
                              On that note,
grabbing an oxhoof out of a basket where it lay,
with a brawny hand he flung it straight at the king—
but Odysseus ducked his head a little, dodging the blow,
and seething just as the oxhoof hit the solid wall
he clenched his teeth in a wry sardonic grin.
Telemachus dressed Ctesippus down at once:
"Ctesippus, you can thank your lucky stars   340
you missed our guest—he ducked your blow, by god!
Else I would have planted my sharp spear in your bowels—
your father would have been busy with your funeral,
not your wedding here. Enough.
Don't let me see more offenses in my house,
not from anyone! I'm alive to it all, now,
the good and the bad—the boy you knew is gone.
But I still must bear with this, this lovely sight . . .
sheepflocks butchered, wine swilled, food squandered—
how can a man fight off so many single-handed?   350
But no more of your crimes against me, please!
Unless you're bent on cutting me down, now,
and I'd rather die, yes, better that by far
than have to look on at your outrage day by day:
guests treated to blows, men dragging the serving-women
through our noble house, exploiting them all, no shame!"

Dead quiet. The suitors all fell silent, hushed.
At last Damastor's son Agelaus rose and said,
"Fair enough, my friends; when a man speaks well
we have no grounds for wrangling, no cause for abuse.   360
Hands off this stranger! Or any other servant
in King Odysseus' palace. But now a word
of friendly advice for Telemachus and his mother—
here's hoping it proves congenial to them both.
So long as your hearts still kept a spark alive
that Odysseus would return—that great, deep man—
who could blame you, playing the waiting game at home
and holding off the suitors? The better course, it's true.
What if Odysseus had returned, had made it home at last?
But now it's clear as day—the man will come no more.   370
So go, Telemachus, sit with your mother, coax her
to wed the best man here, the one who offers most,
so you can have and hold your father's estate,
eating and drinking here, your mind at peace
while mother plays the wife in another's house."

The young prince, keeping his poise, replied,
"I swear by Zeus, Agelaus, by all my father suffered—
dead, no doubt, or wandering far from Ithaca these days—
I don't delay my mother's marriage, not a moment,
I press her to wed the man who takes her heart.   380
I'll shower her myself with boundless gifts.
But I shrink from driving mother from our house,
issuing harsh commands against her will.
God forbid it ever comes to that!"
                                        So he vowed
and Athena set off uncontrollable laughter in the suitors,
crazed them out of their minds—mad, hysterical laughter
seemed to break from the jaws of strangers, not their own,
and the meat they were eating oozed red with blood—
tears flooded their eyes, hearts possessed by grief.
The inspired seer Theoclymenus wailed out in their midst,   390
"Poor men, what terror is this that overwhelms you so?

Night shrouds your heads, your faces, down to your knees—
cries of mourning are bursting into fire—cheeks rivering tears—
the walls and the handsome crossbeams dripping dank with blood!
Ghosts, look, thronging the entrance, thronging the court,
go trooping down to the world of death and darkness!
The sun is blotted out of the sky—look there—
a lethal mist spreads all across the earth!"

                                        At that
they all broke into peals of laughter aimed at the seer—
Polybus' son Eurymachus braying first and foremost,   400
"Our guest just in from abroad, the man is raving!
Quick, my boys, hustle him out of the house,
into the meeting grounds, the light of day—
everything *here* he thinks is dark as night!"

    "Eurymachus," the inspired prophet countered,
"when I want your escort, I'll ask for it myself.
I have eyes and ears, and both my feet, still,
and a head that's fairly sound,
nothing to be ashamed of. These will do
to take me past those doors . . .
                         Oh I can see it now—   410
the disaster closing on you all! There's no escaping it,
no way out—not for a single one of you suitors,
wild reckless fools, plotting outrage here,
the halls of Odysseus, great and strong as a god!"

    With that he marched out of the sturdy house
and went home to Piraeus, the host who warmed him in.
Now all the suitors, trading their snide glances, started
heckling Telemachus, made a mockery of his guests.
One or another brash young gallant scoffed,
"Telemachus, no one's more unlucky with his guests!"   420

    "Look what your man dragged in—this mangy tramp
scraping for bread and wine!"
                         "Not fit for good hard work,

the bag of bones—"
                    "A useless dead weight on the land!"

   "And then this charlatan up and apes the prophet."

   "Take it from me—you'll be better off by far—
toss your friends in a slave-ship—"
                                "Pack them off
to Sicily, fast—they'll fetch you one sweet price!"

   So they jeered, but the prince paid no attention . . .
silent, eyes riveted on his father, always waiting
the moment he'd lay hands on that outrageous mob.   430

   And all the while Icarius' daughter, wise Penelope,
had placed her carved chair within earshot, at the door,
so she could catch each word they uttered in the hall.
Laughing rowdily, men prepared their noonday meal,
succulent, rich—they'd butchered quite a herd.
But as for supper, what could be less enticing
than what a goddess and a powerful man
would spread before them soon? A groaning feast—
for they'd been first to plot their vicious crimes.

BOOK TWENTY-ONE

Odysseus Strings
His Bow

The time had come. The goddess Athena with her blazing eyes
inspired Penelope, Icarius' daughter, wary, poised,
to set the bow and the gleaming iron axes out
before her suitors waiting in Odysseus' hall—
to test their skill and bring their slaughter on.
Up the steep stairs to her room she climbed
and grasped in a steady hand the curved key—
fine bronze, with ivory haft attached—
and then with her chamber-women made her way
to a hidden storeroom, far in the palace depths,   10
and there they lay, the royal master's treasures:
bronze, gold and a wealth of hard wrought iron
and there it lay as well . . . his backsprung bow
with its quiver bristling arrows, shafts of pain.
Gifts from the old days, from a friend he'd met

424

in Lacedaemon—Iphitus, Eurytus' gallant son.
Once in Messene the two struck up together,
in sly Ortilochus' house, that time Odysseus
went to collect a debt the whole realm owed him,
for Messenian raiders had lifted flocks from Ithaca,   20
three hundred head in their oarswept ships, the herdsmen too.
So his father and island elders sent Odysseus off,
a young boy on a mission,
a distant embassy made to right that wrong.
Iphitus went there hunting the stock that *he* had lost,
a dozen mares still nursing their hardy suckling mules.
The same mares that would prove his certain death
when he reached the son of Zeus, that iron heart,
Heracles—the past master of monstrous works—
who killed the man, a guest in his own house.   30
Brutal. Not a care for the wrathful eyes of god
or rites of hospitality he had spread before him,
no, he dined him, then he murdered him, commandeered
those hard-hoofed mares for the hero's own grange.
Still on the trail of these when he met Odysseus,
Iphitus gave him the bow his father, mighty Eurytus,
used to wield as a young man, but when he died
in his lofty house he left it to his son.
In turn, Odysseus gave his friend a sharp sword
and a rugged spear to mark the start of friendship,   40
treasured ties that bind. But before they got to know
the warmth of each other's board, the son of Zeus
had murdered Iphitus, Eurytus' magnificent son
who gave the prince the bow.
                          That great weapon—
King Odysseus never took it abroad with him
when he sailed off to war in his long black ships.
He kept it stored away in his stately house,
guarding the memory of a cherished friend,
and only took that bow on hunts at home.
                          Now,
the lustrous queen soon reached the hidden vault   50
and stopped at the oaken doorsill, work an expert

sanded smooth and trued to the line some years ago,
planting the doorjambs snugly, hanging shining doors.
At once she loosed the thong from around its hook,
inserted the key and aiming straight and true,
shot back the bolts—and the rasping doors groaned
as loud as a bull will bellow, champing grass at pasture.
So as the key went home those handsome double doors
rang out now and sprang wide before her.
She stepped onto a plank where chests stood tall,   60
brimming with clothing scented sweet with cedar.
Reaching, tiptoe, lifting the bow down off its peg,
still secure in the burnished case that held it,
down she sank, laying the case across her knees,
and dissolved in tears with a high thin wail
as she drew her husband's weapon from its sheath . . .
Then, having wept and sobbed to her heart's content,
off she went to the hall to meet her proud admirers,
cradling her husband's backsprung bow in her arms,
its quiver bristling arrows, shafts of pain.   70
Her women followed, bringing a chest that held
the bronze and the iron axes, trophies won by the master.
That radiant woman, once she reached her suitors,
drawing her glistening veil across her cheeks,
paused now where a column propped the sturdy roof,
with one of her loyal handmaids stationed either side,
and delivered an ultimatum to her suitors:
"Listen to me, my overbearing friends!
You who plague this palace night and day,
drinking, eating us out of house and home   80
with the lord and master absent, gone so long—
the only excuse that you can offer is your zest
to win me as your bride. So, to arms, my gallants!
Here is the prize at issue, right before you, look—
I set before you the great bow of King Odysseus now!
The hand that can string this bow with greatest ease,
that shoots an arrow clean through all twelve axes—
he is the man I follow, yes, forsaking this house
where I was once a bride, this gracious house

so filled with the best that life can offer—   90
I shall always remember it, that I know . . .
even in my dreams."
                              She turned to Eumaeus,
ordered the good swineherd now to set the bow
and the gleaming iron axes out before the suitors.
He broke into tears as he received them, laid them down.
The cowherd wept too, when he saw his master's bow.
But Antinous wheeled on both and let them have it:
"Yokels, fools—you can't tell night from day!
You mawkish idiots, why are you sniveling here?
You're stirring up your mistress! Isn't she drowned   100
in grief already? She's lost her darling husband.
Sit down. Eat in peace, or take your snuffling
out of doors! But leave that bow right here—
our crucial test that makes or breaks us all.
No easy game, I wager, to string *his* polished bow.
Not a soul in the crowd can match Odysseus—
what a man he was . . .
I saw him once, remember him to this day,
though I was young and foolish way back then."
                                        Smooth talk,
but deep in the suitor's heart his hopes were bent   110
on stringing the bow and shooting through the axes.
Antinous—fated to be the first man to taste
an arrow whipped from great Odysseus' hands,
the king he mocked, at ease in the king's house,
egging comrades on to mock him too.
                              "Amazing!"
Prince Telemachus waded in with a laugh:
"Zeus up there has robbed me of my wits.
My own dear mother, sensible as she is,
says she'll marry again, forsake our house,
and look at *me*—laughing for all I'm worth,   120
giggling like some fool. Step up, my friends!
Here is the prize at issue, right before you, look—
a woman who has no equal now in all Achaean country,
neither in holy Pylos, nor in Argos or Mycenae,

not even Ithaca itself or the loamy mainland.
You know it well. Why sing my mother's praises?
Come, let the games begin! No dodges, no delays,
no turning back from the stringing of the bow—
we'll see who wins, we will.
I'd even take a crack at the bow myself . . .   130
If I string it and shoot through all the axes,
I'd worry less if my noble mother left our house
with another man and left me here behind—man enough
at last to win my father's splendid prizes!"
                                                        With that
he leapt to his feet and dropped his bright-red cloak,
slipping the sword and sword-belt off his shoulders.
First he planted the axes, digging a long trench,
one for all, and trued them all to a line
then tamped the earth to bed them. Wonder took
the revelers looking on: his work so firm, precise,   140
though he'd never seen the axes ranged before.
He stood at the threshold, poised to try the bow . . .
Three times he made it shudder, straining to bend it,
three times his power flagged—but his hopes ran high
he'd string his father's bow and shoot through every iron
and now, struggling with all his might for the fourth time,
he would have strung the bow, but Odysseus shook his head
and stopped him short despite his tensing zeal.
"God help me," the inspired prince cried out,
"must I be a weakling, a failure all my life?   150
Unless I'm just too young to trust my hands
to fight off any man who rises up against me.
Come, my betters, so much stronger than I am—
try the bow and finish off the contest."

    He propped his father's weapon on the ground,
tilting it up against the polished well-hung doors
and resting a shaft aslant the bow's fine horn,
then back he went to the seat that he had left.
"Up, friends!" Antinous called, taking over.
"One man after another, left to right,   160

starting from where the steward pours the wine."

    So Antinous urged and all agreed.
The first man up was Leodes, Oenops' son,
a seer who could see their futures in the smoke,
who always sat by the glowing winebowl, well back,
the one man in the group who loathed their reckless ways,
appalled by all their outrage. His turn first . . .
Picking up the weapon now and the swift arrow,
he stood at the threshold, poised to try the bow
but failed to bend it. As soon as he tugged the string   170
his hands went slack, his soft, uncallused hands,
and he called back to the suitors, "Friends,
I can't bend it. Take it, someone—try.
Here is a bow to rob our best of life and breath,
all our best contenders! Still, better be dead
than live on here, never winning the prize
that tempts us all—forever in pursuit,
burning with expectation every day.
If there's still a suitor here who hopes,
who aches to marry Penelope, Odysseus' wife,   180
just let him try the bow; he'll see the truth!
He'll soon lay siege to another Argive woman
trailing her long robes, and shower her with gifts—
and then our queen can marry the one who offers most,
the man marked out by fate to be her husband."

    With those words he thrust the bow aside,
tilting it up against the polished well-hung doors
and resting a shaft aslant the bow's fine horn,
then back he went to the seat that he had left.
But Antinous turned on the seer, abuses flying: 190
"Leodes! what are you saying? what's got past your lips?
What awful, grisly nonsense—it shocks me to hear it—
'here is a bow to rob our best of life and breath!'
Just because *you* can't string it, you're so weak?
Clearly your genteel mother never bred her boy
for the work of bending bows and shooting arrows.

We have champions in our ranks to string it quickly.
Hop to it, Melanthius!"—he barked at the goatherd—
"Rake the fire in the hall, pull up a big stool,
heap it with fleece and fetch that hefty ball   200
of lard from the stores inside. So we young lords
can heat and limber the bow and rub it down with grease
before we try again and finish off the contest!"

   The goatherd bustled about to rake the fire
still going strong. He pulled up a big stool,
heaped it with fleece and fetched the hefty ball
of lard from the stores inside. And the young men
limbered the bow, rubbing it down with hot grease,
then struggled to bend it back but failed. No use—
they fell far short of the strength the bow required.   210
Antinous still held off, dashing Eurymachus too,
the ringleaders of all the suitors,
head and shoulders the strongest of the lot.

                                               But now
the king's two men, the cowherd and the swineherd,
had slipped out of the palace side-by-side
and great Odysseus left the house to join them.
Once they were past the courtyard and the gates
he probed them deftly, surely: "Cowherd, swineherd,
what, shall I blurt this out or keep it to myself?
No, speak out. The heart inside me says so.   220
How far would you go to fight beside Odysseus?
Say he dropped like *that* from a clear blue sky
and a god brought him back—
would you fight for the suitors or your king?
Tell me how you feel inside your hearts."

   "Father Zeus," the trusty cowherd shouted,
"bring my prayer to pass! Let the master come—
some god guide him now! You'd see my power,
my fighting arms in action!"

   Eumaeus echoed his prayer to all the gods   230

that their wise king would soon come home again.
Certain at least these two were loyal to the death,
Odysseus reassured them quickly: "I'm right here,
here in the flesh—myself—and home at last,
after bearing twenty years of brutal hardship.
Now I know that of all my men you two alone
longed for my return. From the rest I've heard
not one real prayer that I come back again.
So now I'll tell you what's in store for *you.*
If a god beats down the lofty suitors at my hands,   240
I'll find you wives, both of you, grant you property,
sturdy houses beside my own, and in my eyes you'll be
comrades to Prince Telemachus, brothers from then on.
Come, I'll show you something—living proof—
know me for certain, put your minds at rest.

                                        This scar,
look, where a boar's white tusk gored me, years ago,
hunting on Parnassus, Autolycus' sons and I."

                                        With that,
pushing back his rags, he revealed the great scar . . .
And the men gazed at it, scanned it, knew it well,
broke into tears and threw their arms around their master—   250
lost in affection, kissing his head and shoulders,
and so Odysseus kissed their heads and hands.
Now the sun would have set upon their tears
if Odysseus had not called a halt himself.
"No more weeping. Coming out of the house
a man might see us, tell the men inside.
Let's slip back in—singly, not in a pack.
I'll go first. You're next. Here's our signal.
When all the rest in there, our lordly friends,
are dead against my having the bow and quiver,   260
good Eumaeus, carry the weapon down the hall
and put it in my hands. Then tell the serving-women
to lock the snugly fitted doors to their own rooms.
If anyone hears from there the jolting blows
and groans of men, caught in our huge net,
not one of them show her face—

sit tight, keep to her weaving, not a sound.
You, my good Philoetius, here are your orders.
Shoot the bolt of the courtyard's outer gate,
lock it, lash it fast."
                        With that command   270
the master entered his well-constructed house
and back he went to the stool that he had left.
The king's two men, in turn, slipped in as well.

     Just now Eurymachus held the bow in his hands,
turning it over, tip to tip, before the blazing fire
to heat the weapon. But he failed to bend it even so
and the suitor's high heart groaned to bursting.
"A black day," he exclaimed in wounded pride,
"a blow to myself, a blow to each man here!
It's less the marriage that mortifies me now—   280
that's galling too, but lots of women are left,
some in seagirt Ithaca, some in other cities.
What breaks my heart is the fact we fall so short
of great Odysseus' strength we cannot string his bow.
A disgrace to ring in the ears of men to come."

     "Eurymachus," Eupithes' son Antinous countered,
"it will never come to that, as you well know.
Today is a feast-day up and down the island
in honor of the Archer God. Who flexes bows today?
Set it aside. Rest easy now. And all the axes,   290
let's just leave them planted where they are.
Trust me, no one's about to crash the gates
of Laertes' son and carry off these trophies.
Steward, pour some drops for the god in every cup,
we'll tip the wine, then put the bow to bed.
And first thing in the morning have Melanthius
bring the pick of his goats from all his herds
so we can burn the thighs to Apollo, god of archers—
then try the bow and finish off the contest."

     Welcome advice. And again they all agreed.   300

Heralds sprinkled water over their hands for rinsing,
the young men brimmed the mixing bowls with wine,
they tipped first drops for the god in every cup,
then poured full rounds for all. And now, once
they'd tipped libations out and drunk their fill,
the king of craft, Odysseus, said with all his cunning,
"Listen to me, you lords who court the noble queen.
I have to say what the heart inside me urges.
I appeal especially to Eurymachus, and you,
brilliant Antinous, who spoke so shrewdly now.   310
Give the bow a rest for today, leave it to the gods—
at dawn the Archer God will grant a victory
to the man he favors most.
                              For the moment,
give me the polished bow now, won't you? So,
to amuse you all, I can try my hand, my strength . . .
is the old force still alive inside these gnarled limbs?
Or has a life of roaming, years of rough neglect,
destroyed it long ago?"
                        Modest words
that sent them all into hot, indignant rage,
fearing he just might string the polished bow.   320
So Antinous rounded on him, dressed him down:
"Not a shred of sense in your head, you filthy drifter!
Not content to feast at your ease with us, the island's pride?
Never denied your full share of the banquet, never,
you can listen in on our secrets. No one else
can eavesdrop on our talk, no tramp, no beggar.
The wine has overpowered you, heady wine—
the ruin of many another man, whoever
gulps it down and drinks beyond his limit.
Wine—it drove the Centaur, famous Eurytion,   330
mad in the halls of lionhearted Pirithous.
There to visit the Lapiths, crazed with wine
the headlong Centaur bent to his ugly work
in the prince's own house! His hosts sprang up,
seized with fury, dragged him across the forecourt,
flung him out of doors, hacking his nose and ears off

with their knives, no mercy. The creature reeled away,
still blind with drink, his heart like a wild storm,
loaded with all the frenzy in his mind!
                                        And so
the feud between mortal men and Centaurs had its start.   340
But the drunk was first to bring disaster on himself
by drowning in his cups. You too, I promise you
no end of trouble if you should string that bow.
You'll meet no kindness in our part of the world—
we'll sail you off in a black ship to Echetus,
the mainland king who wrecks all men alive.
Nothing can save you from his royal grip!
So drink, but hold your peace,
don't take on the younger, stronger men."

   "Antinous," watchful Penelope stepped in,   350
"how impolite it would be, how wrong, to scant
whatever guest Telemachus welcomes to his house.
You really think—if the stranger trusts so to his hands
and strength that he strings Odysseus' great bow—
he'll take me home and claim me as his bride?
He never dreamed of such a thing, I'm sure.
Don't let that ruin the feast for any reveler here.
Unthinkable—nothing, nothing could be worse."

   Polybus' son Eurymachus had an answer:
"Wise Penelope, daughter of Icarius, do we really   360
expect the man to wed you? Unthinkable, I know.
But we do recoil at the talk of men and women.
One of the island's meaner sort will mutter,
'Look at the riffraff courting a king's wife.
Weaklings, look, they can't even string his bow.
But along came this beggar, drifting out of the blue—
strung his bow with ease and shot through all the axes!'
Gossip will fly. We'll hang our heads in shame."

   "Shame?" alert Penelope protested—

"How can you hope for any public fame at all?   370
You who disgrace, devour a great man's house and home!
Why hang your heads in shame over next to nothing?
Our friend here is a strapping, well-built man
and claims to be the son of a noble father.
Come, hand him the bow now, let's just see . . .
I tell you this—and I'll make good my word—
if he strings the bow and Apollo grants him glory,
I'll dress him in shirt and cloak, in handsome clothes,
I'll give him a good sharp lance to fight off men and dogs,
give him a two-edged sword and sandals for his feet   380
and send him off, wherever his heart desires."
                                                    "Mother,"
poised Telemachus broke in now, "my father's bow—
no Achaean on earth has more right than I
to give it or withhold it, as I please.
Of all the lords in Ithaca's rocky heights
or the islands facing Elis grazed by horses,
not a single one will force or thwart my will,
even if I decide to give our guest this bow—
a gift outright—to carry off himself.
                                        So, mother,
go back to your quarters. Tend to your own tasks,   390
the distaff and the loom, and keep the women
working hard as well. As for the bow now,
men will see to that, but I most of all:
I hold the reins of power in this house."
                                        Astonished,
she withdrew to her own room. She took to heart
the clear good sense in what her son had said.
Climbing up to the lofty chamber with her women,
she fell to weeping for Odysseus, her beloved husband,
till watchful Athena sealed her eyes with welcome sleep.

    And now the loyal swineherd had lifted up the bow,   400
was taking it toward the king, when all the suitors
burst out in an ugly uproar through the palace—

brash young bullies, this or that one heckling,
"Where on earth are you going with that bow?"

"You, you grubby swineherd, are you crazy?"

"The speedy dogs you reared will eat your corpse—"

"Out there with your pigs, out in the cold, alone!"

"If only Apollo and all the gods shine down on us!"

Eumaeus froze in his tracks, put down the bow,
panicked by every outcry in the hall.   410
Telemachus shouted too, from the other side,
and full of threats: "Carry on with the bow, old boy!
If you serve too many masters, you'll soon suffer.
Look sharp, or I'll pelt you back to your farm
with flying rocks. I may be younger than you
but I'm much stronger. If only I had that edge
in fists and brawn over all this courting crowd,
I'd soon dispatch them—licking their wounds at last—
clear of our palace where they plot their vicious plots!"

His outburst sent them all into gales of laughter,   420
blithe and oblivious, that dissolved their pique
against the prince. The swineherd took the bow,
carried it down the hall to his ready, waiting king
and standing by him, placed it in his hands,
then he called the nurse aside and whispered,
"Good Eurycleia—Telemachus commands you now
to lock the snugly fitted doors to your own rooms.
If anyone hears from there the jolting blows
and groans of men, caught in our huge net,
not one of you show your face—   430
sit tight, keep to your weaving, not a sound."

That silenced the old nurse—
she barred the doors that led from the long hall.

The cowherd quietly bounded out of the house
to lock the gates of the high-stockaded court.
Under the portico lay a cable, ship's tough gear:
he lashed the gates with this, then slipped back in
and ran and sat on the stool that he'd just left,
eyes riveted on Odysseus.
                    Now *he* held the bow
in his own hands, turning it over, tip to tip,   440
testing it, this way, that way . . . fearing worms
had bored through the weapon's horn with the master gone abroad.
A suitor would glance at his neighbor, jeering, taunting,
"Look at our connoisseur of bows!"
                       "Sly old fox—
maybe he's got bows like it, stored in *his* house."

  "That or he's bent on making one himself."

  "Look how he twists and turns it in his hands!"

  "The clever tramp means trouble—"

  "I wish him luck," some cocksure lord chimed in,
"as good as his luck in bending back that weapon!"   450

    So they mocked, but Odysseus, mastermind in action,
once he'd handled the great bow and scanned every inch,
then, like an expert singer skilled at lyre and song—
who strains a string to a new peg with ease,
making the pliant sheep-gut fast at either end—
so with his virtuoso ease Odysseus strung his mighty bow.
Quickly his right hand plucked the string to test its pitch
and under his touch it sang out clear and sharp as a swallow's cry.
Horror swept through the suitors, faces blanching white,
and Zeus cracked the sky with a bolt, his blazing sign,   460
and the great man who had borne so much rejoiced at last
that the son of cunning Cronus flung that omen down for *him*.
He snatched a winged arrow lying bare on the board—
the rest still bristled deep inside the quiver,

soon to be tasted by all the feasters there.
Setting shaft on the handgrip, drawing the notch
and bowstring back, back . . . right from his stool,
just as he sat but aiming straight and true, he let fly—
and never missing an ax from the first ax-handle
clean on through to the last and out   470
the shaft with its weighted brazen head shot free!

                                        "Telemachus,"

Odysseus looked to his son and said, "your guest,
sitting here in your house, has not disgraced you.
No missing the mark, look, and no long labor spent
to string the bow. My strength's not broken yet,
not quite so frail as the mocking suitors thought.
But the hour has come to serve our masters right—
supper in broad daylight—then to other revels,
song and dancing, all that crowns a feast."

He paused with a warning nod, and at that sign   480
Prince Telemachus, son of King Odysseus,
girding his sharp sword on, clamping hand to spear,
took his stand by a chair that flanked his father—
his bronze spearpoint glinting now like fire . . .

BOOK TWENTY-TWO

Slaughter in the Hall

Now stripping back his rags Odysseus master of craft and battle
vaulted onto the great threshold, gripping his bow and quiver
bristling arrows, and poured his flashing shafts before him,
loose at his feet, and thundered out to all the suitors:
"Look—your crucial test is finished, now, at last!
But another target's left that no one's hit before—
we'll see if *I* can hit it—Apollo give me glory!"

    With that he trained a stabbing arrow on Antinous . . .
just lifting a gorgeous golden loving-cup in his hands,
just tilting the two-handled goblet back to his lips,   10
about to drain the wine—and slaughter the last thing
on the suitor's mind: who could dream that one foe
in that crowd of feasters, however great his power,
would bring down death on himself, and black doom?

But Odysseus aimed and shot Antinous square in the throat
and the point went stabbing clean through the soft neck and out—
and off to the side he pitched, the cup dropped from his grasp
as the shaft sank home, and the man's life-blood came spurting
from his nostrils—
        thick red jets—
              a sudden thrust of his foot—
he kicked away the table—
           food showered across the floor,   20
the bread and meats soaked in a swirl of bloody filth.
The suitors burst into uproar all throughout the house
when they saw their leader down. They leapt from their seats,
milling about, desperate, scanning the stone walls—
not a shield in sight, no rugged spear to seize.
They wheeled on Odysseus, lashing out in fury:
"Stranger, shooting at men will cost your life!"

  "Your game is over—you, you've shot your last!"

  "You'll never escape your own headlong death!"

  "You killed the best in Ithaca—our fine prince!"   30

  "Vultures will eat your corpse!"
               Groping, frantic—
each one persuading himself the guest had killed
the man by chance. Poor fools, blind to the fact
that all their necks were in the noose, their doom sealed.
With a dark look, the wily fighter Odysseus shouted back,
"You dogs! you never imagined I'd return from Troy—
so cocksure that you bled my house to death,
ravished my serving-women—wooed my wife
behind my back while I was still alive!
No fear of the gods who rule the skies up there,   40
no fear that men's revenge might arrive someday—
now all your necks are in the noose—your doom is sealed!"

  Terror gripped them all, blanched their faces white,

each man glancing wildly—how to escape his instant death?
Only Eurymachus had the breath to venture, "If you,
you're truly Odysseus of Ithaca, home at last,
you're right to accuse these men of what they've done—
so much reckless outrage here in your palace,
so much on your lands. But here he lies,
quite dead, and he incited it all—Antinous—   50
look, the man who drove us all to crime!
Not that he needed marriage, craved it so;
he'd bigger game in mind—though Zeus barred his way—
he'd lord it over Ithaca's handsome country, king himself,
once he'd lain in wait for your son and cut him down!
But now he's received the death that he deserved.
So spare your own people! Later we'll recoup
your costs with a tax laid down upon the land,
covering all we ate and drank inside your halls,
and each of us here will pay full measure too—   60
twenty oxen in value, bronze and gold we'll give
until we melt your heart. Before we've settled,
who on earth could blame you for your rage?"

    But the battle-master kept on glaring, seething.
"No, Eurymachus! Not if you paid me all your father's wealth—
all you possess now, and all that could pour in from the world's end—
no, not even then would I stay my hands from slaughter
till all you suitors had paid for all your crimes!
Now life or death—your choice—fight me or flee
if you hope to escape your sudden bloody doom!   70
I doubt one man in the lot will save his skin!"

    His menace shook their knees, their hearts too
but Eurymachus spoke again, now to the suitors: "Friends!
This man will never restrain his hands, invincible hands—
now that he's seized that polished bow and quiver, look,
he'll shoot from the sill until he's killed us all!
So fight—call up the joy of battle! Swords out!
Tables lifted—block his arrows winging death!
Charge him, charge in a pack—

try to rout the man from the sill, the doors,   80
race through town and sound an alarm at once—
our friend would soon see he's shot his bolt!"

                              Brave talk—
he drew his two-edged sword, bronze, honed for the kill
and hurled himself at the king with a raw savage cry
in the same breath that Odysseus loosed an arrow
ripping his breast beside the nipple so hard
it lodged in the man's liver—
out of his grasp the sword dropped to the ground—
over his table, head over heels he tumbled, doubled up,
flinging his food and his two-handled cup across the floor—   90
he smashed the ground with his forehead, writhing in pain,
both feet flailing out, and his high seat tottered—
the mist of death came swirling down his eyes.

    Amphinomus rushed the king in all his glory,
charging him face-to-face, a slashing sword drawn—
if only he could force him clear of the doorway, now,
but Telemachus—too quick—stabbed the man from behind,
plunging his bronze spear between the suitor's shoulders
and straight on through his chest the point came jutting out—
down he went with a thud, his forehead slammed the ground.   100
Telemachus swerved aside, leaving his long spearshaft
lodged in Amphinomus—fearing some suitor just might
lunge in from behind as he tugged the shaft,
impale him with a sword or hack him down,
crouching over the corpse.
He went on the run, reached his father at once
and halting right beside him, let fly, "Father—
now I'll get you a shield and a pair of spears,
a helmet of solid bronze to fit your temples!
I'll arm myself on the way back and hand out   110
arms to the swineherd, arm the cowherd too—
we'd better fight equipped!"

                        "Run, fetch them,"
the wily captain urged, "while I've got arrows left
to defend me—or they'll force me from the doors

while I fight on alone!"

   Telemachus moved to his father's orders smartly.
Off he ran to the room where the famous arms lay stored,
took up four shields, eight spears, four bronze helmets
ridged with horsehair crests and, loaded with these,
ran back to reach his father's side in no time.   120
The prince was first to case himself in bronze
and his servants followed suit—both harnessed up
and all three flanked Odysseus, mastermind of war,
and he, as long as he'd arrows left to defend himself,
kept picking suitors off in the palace, one by one
and down they went, corpse on corpse in droves.
Then, when the royal archer's shafts ran out,
he leaned his bow on a post of the massive doors—
where walls of the hallway catch the light—and armed:
across his shoulder he slung a buckler four plies thick,   130
over his powerful head he set a well-forged helmet,
the horsehair crest atop it tossing, bristling terror,
and grasped two rugged lances tipped with fiery bronze.

   Now a side-door was fitted into the main wall—
right at the edge of the great hall's stone sill—
and led to a passage always shut by good tight boards.
But Odysseus gave the swineherd strict commands
to stand hard by the side-door, guard it well—
the only way the suitors might break out.
Agelaus called to his comrades with a plan: 140
"Friends, can't someone climb through the hatch?—
tell men outside to sound the alarm, be quick—
our guest would soon see he'd shot his last!"

   The goatherd Melanthius answered, "Not a chance,
my lord—the door to the courtyard's much too near,
dangerous too, the mouth of the passage cramped.
One strong man could block us, one and all!
No, I'll fetch you some armor to harness on,
out of the storeroom—there, nowhere else, I'm sure,

the king and his gallant son have stowed their arms!"   150

    With that the goatherd clambered up through smoke-ducts
high on the wall and scurried into Odysseus' storeroom,
bundled a dozen shields, as many spears and helmets
ridged with horsehair crests and, loaded with these,
rushed back down to the suitors, quickly issued arms.
Odysseus' knees shook, his heart too, when he saw them
buckling on their armor, brandishing long spears—
here was a battle looming, well he knew.
He turned at once to Telemachus, warnings flying:
"A bad break in the fight, my boy! One of the women's   160
tipped the odds against us—or could it be the goatherd?"

    "My fault, father," the cool clear prince replied,
"the blame's all mine. That snug door to the vault,
I left it ajar—they've kept a better watch than I.
Go, Eumaeus, shut the door to the storeroom,
check and see if it's one of the women's tricks
or Dolius' son Melanthius. He's our man, I'd say."

    And even as they conspired, back the goatherd
climbed to the room to fetch more burnished arms,
but Eumaeus spotted him, quickly told his king   170
who stood close by: "Odysseus, wily captain,
there he goes again, the infernal nuisance—
just as we suspected—back to the storeroom.
Give me a clear command!
Do I kill the man—if I can take him down—
or drag him back to you, here, to pay in full
for the vicious work he's plotted in your house?"

    Odysseus, master of tactics, answered briskly,
"I and the prince will keep these brazen suitors
crammed in the hall, for all their battle-fury.   180
You two wrench Melanthius' arms and legs behind him,
fling him down in the storeroom—lash his back to a plank
and strap a twisted cable fast to the scoundrel's body,

hoist him up a column until he hits the rafters—
let him dangle in agony, still alive,
for a good long time!"

   They hung on his orders, keen to do his will.
Off they ran to the storeroom, unseen by him inside—
Melanthius, rummaging after arms, deep in a dark recess
as the two men took their stand, either side of the doorposts,   190
poised till the goatherd tried to cross the doorsill . . .
one hand clutching a crested helmet, the other
an ample old buckler blotched with mildew,
the shield Laertes bore as a young soldier once
but there it lay for ages, seams on the handstraps split—
Quick, they rushed him, seized him, haled him back by the hair,
flung him down on the floor, writhing with terror, bound him
hand and foot with a chafing cord, wrenched his limbs
back, back till the joints locked tight—
just as Laertes' cunning son commanded—   200
they strapped a twisted cable round his body,
hoisted him up a column until he hit the rafters,
then you mocked him, Eumaeus, my good swineherd:
"Now stand guard through the whole night, Melanthius—
stretched out on a soft bed fit for *you*, your highness!
You're bound to see the Morning rising up from the Ocean,
mounting her golden throne—at just the hour you always
drive in goats to feast the suitors in the hall!"

   So they left him, trussed in his agonizing sling;
they clapped on armor again, shut the gleaming doors   210
and ran to rejoin Odysseus, mastermind of war.
And now as the ranks squared off, breathing fury—
four at the sill confronting a larger, stronger force
arrayed inside the hall—now Zeus's daughter Athena,
taking the build and voice of Mentor, swept in
and Odysseus, thrilled to see her, cried out,
"Rescue us, Mentor, now it's life or death!
Remember your old comrade—all the service
I offered you! We were boys together!"

So he cried
yet knew in his bones it was Athena, Driver of Armies.   220
But across the hall the suitors brayed against her,
Agelaus first, his outburst full of threats:
"Mentor, never let Odysseus trick you into
siding with *him* to fight against the suitors.
Here's our plan of action, and we will see it through!
Once we've killed them both, the father and the son,
we'll kill you too, for all you're bent on doing
here in the halls—you'll pay with your own head!
And once our swords have stopped your violence cold—
all your property, all in your house, your fields,   230
we'll lump it all with Odysseus' rich estate
and never let your sons live on in your halls
or free your wife and daughters to walk through town!"

    Naked threats—and Athena hit new heights of rage,
she lashed out at Odysseus now with blazing accusations:
"Where's it gone, Odysseus—your power, your fighting heart?
The great soldier who fought for famous white-armed Helen,
battling Trojans nine long years—nonstop, no mercy,
mowing their armies down in grueling battle—
you who seized the broad streets of Troy   240
with your fine strategic stroke! How can you—
now you've returned to your own house, your own wealth—
bewail the loss of your combat strength in a war with *suitors*?
Come, old friend, stand by me! You'll see action now,
see how Mentor the son of Alcimus, that brave fighter,
kills your enemies, pays you back for service!"
                                                  Rousing words—
but she gave no all-out turning of the tide, not yet,
she kept on testing Odysseus and his gallant son,
putting their force and fighting heart to proof.
For all the world like a swallow in their sight   250
she flew on high to perch
on the great hall's central roofbeam black with smoke.

    But the suitors closed ranks, commanded now by Damastor's son

Agelaus, flanked by Eurynomus, Demoptolemus and Amphimedon,
Pisander, Polyctor's son, and Polybus ready, waiting—
head and shoulders the best and bravest of the lot
still left to fight for their lives,
now that the pelting shafts had killed the rest.
Agelaus spurred his comrades on with battle-plans:
"Friends, at last the man's invincible hands are useless!   260
Mentor has mouthed some empty boasts and flitted off—
just four are left to fight at the front doors. So now,
no wasting your long spears—all at a single hurl,
just six of us launch out in the first wave!
If Zeus is willing, we may hit Odysseus,
carry off the glory! The rest are nothing
once the captain's down!"
                              At his command,
concentrating their shots, all six hurled as one
but Athena sent the whole salvo wide of the mark—
one of them hit the jamb of the great hall's doors,   270
another the massive door itself, and the heavy bronze point
of a third ashen javelin crashed against the wall.
Seeing his men untouched by the suitors' flurry,
steady Odysseus leapt to take command:
"Friends! now it's for *us* to hurl at them, I say,
into this ruck of suitors! Topping all their crimes
they're mad to strip the armor off our bodies!"

    Taking aim at the ranks, all four let fly as one
and the lances struck home—Odysseus killed Demoptolemus,
Telemachus killed Euryades—the swineherd, Elatus—   280
and the cowherd cut Pisander down in blood.
They bit the dust of the broad floor, all as one.
Back to the great hall's far recess the others shrank
as the four rushed in and plucked up spears from corpses.

    And again the suitors hurled their whetted shafts
but Athena sent the better part of the salvo wide—
one of them hit the jamb of the great hall's doors,
another the massive door itself, and the heavy bronze point

of a third ashen javelin crashed against the wall.
True, Amphimedon nicked Telemachus on the wrist—   290
the glancing blade just barely broke his skin.
Ctesippus sent a long spear sailing over
Eumaeus' buckler, grazing his shoulder blade
but the weapon skittered off and hit the ground.
And again those led by the brilliant battle-master
hurled their razor spears at the suitors' ranks—
and now Odysseus raider of cities hit Eurydamas,
Telemachus hit Amphimedon—Eumaeus, Polybus—
and the cowherd stabbed Ctesippus
right in the man's chest and triumphed over his body: 300
"Love your mockery, do you? Son of that blowhard Polytherses!
No more shooting off your mouth, you idiot, such big talk—
leave the last word to the gods—they're much stronger!
Take this spear, this guest-gift, for the cow's hoof
you once gave King Odysseus begging in his house!"

So the master of longhorn cattle had his say—
as Odysseus, fighting at close quarters, ran Agelaus
through with a long lance—Telemachus speared Leocritus
so deep in the groin the bronze came punching out his back
and the man crashed headfirst, slamming the ground full-face.   310
And now Athena, looming out of the rafters high above them,
brandished her man-destroying shield of thunder, terrifying
the suitors out of their minds, and down the hall they panicked—
wild, like herds stampeding, driven mad as the darting gadfly
strikes in the late spring when the long days come round.
The attackers struck like eagles, crook-clawed, hook-beaked,
swooping down from a mountain ridge to harry smaller birds
that skim across the flatland, cringing under the clouds
but the eagles plunge in fury, rip their lives out—hopeless,
never a chance of flight or rescue—and people love the sport—   320
so the attackers routed suitors headlong down the hall,
wheeling into the slaughter, slashing left and right
and grisly screams broke from skulls cracked open—
the whole floor awash with blood.
                                              Leodes now—

he flung himself at Odysseus, clutched his knees,
crying out to the king with a sudden, winging prayer:
"I hug your knees, Odysseus—mercy! spare my life!
Never, I swear, did I harass any woman in your house—
never a word, a gesture—nothing, no, I tried
to restrain the suitors, whoever did such things.   330
They wouldn't listen, keep their hands to themselves—
so reckless, so they earn their shameful fate.
But I was just their prophet—
my hands are clean—and I'm to die their death!
Look at the thanks I get for years of service!"

   A killing look, and the wry soldier answered,
"Only a priest, a prophet for this mob, you say?
How hard you must have prayed in my own house
that the heady day of my return would never dawn—
my dear wife would be yours, would bear your children!   340
For that there's no escape from grueling death—you die!"

   And snatching up in one powerful hand a sword
left on the ground—Agelaus dropped it when he fell—
Odysseus hacked the prophet square across the neck
and the praying head went tumbling in the dust.

                                        Now one was left,
trying still to escape black death. Phemius, Terpis' son,
the bard who always performed among the suitors—
they forced the man to sing . . .
There he stood, backing into the side-door,
still clutching his ringing lyre in his hands,   350
his mind in turmoil, torn—what should he do?
Steal from the hall and crouch at the altar-stone
of Zeus who Guards the Court, where time and again
Odysseus and Laertes burned the long thighs of oxen?
Or throw himself on the master's mercy, clasp his knees?
That was the better way—or so it struck him, yes,
grasp the knees of Laertes' royal son. And so,
cradling his hollow lyre, he laid it on the ground
between the mixing-bowl and the silver-studded throne,

then rushed up to Odysseus, yes, and clutched his knees,   360
singing out to his king with a stirring, winged prayer:
"I hug your knees, Odysseus—mercy! spare my life!
What a grief it will be to you for all the years to come
if you kill the singer now, who sings for gods and men.
I taught myself the craft, but a god has planted
deep in my spirit all the paths of song—
songs I'm fit to sing for you as for a god.
Calm your bloodlust now—don't take my head!
He'd bear me out, your own dear son Telemachus—
never of *my* own will, never for any gain did I   370
perform in your house, singing after the suitors
had their feasts. They were too strong, too many—
they forced me to come and sing—I had no choice!"

    The inspired Prince Telemachus heard his pleas
and quickly said to his father close beside him,
"Stop, don't cut him down! This one's innocent.
So is the herald Medon—the one who always
tended me in the house when I was little—
spare him too. Unless he's dead by now,
killed by Philoetius or Eumaeus here—   380
or ran into *you* rampaging through the halls."

    The herald pricked up his anxious ears at that . . .
cautious soul, he cowered, trembling, under a chair—
wrapped in an oxhide freshly stripped—to dodge black death.
He jumped in a flash from there, threw off the smelly hide
and scuttling up to Telemachus, clutching his knees,
the herald begged for life in words that fluttered:
"Here I am, dear boy—spare me! Tell your father,
flushed with victory, not to kill me with his sword—
enraged as he is with these young lords who bled   390
his palace white and showed you no respect,
the reckless fools!"
                    Breaking into a smile
the canny Odysseus reassured him, "Courage!
The prince has pulled you through, he's saved you now

so you can take it to heart and tell the next man too:
clearly doing good puts doing bad to shame.
Now leave the palace, go and sit outside—
out in the courtyard, clear of the slaughter—
you and the bard with all his many songs.
Wait till I've done some household chores   400
that call for my attention."

    The two men scurried out of the house at once
and crouched at the altar-stone of mighty Zeus—
glancing left and right,
fearing death would strike at any moment.

    Odysseus scanned his house to see if any man
still skulked alive, still hoped to avoid black death.
But he found them one and all in blood and dust . . .
great hauls of them down and out like fish that fishermen
drag from the churning gray surf in looped and coiling nets   410
and fling ashore on a sweeping hook of beach—some noble catch
heaped on the sand, twitching, lusting for fresh salt sea
but the Sungod hammers down and burns their lives out . . .
so the suitors lay in heaps, corpse covering corpse.
At last the seasoned fighter turned to his son:
"Telemachus, go, call the old nurse here—
I must tell her all that's on my mind."

    Telemachus ran to do his father's bidding,
shook the women's doors, calling Eurycleia:
"Come out now! Up with you, good old woman!   420
You who watch over all the household hands—
quick, my father wants you, needs to have a word!"

    Crisp command that left the old nurse hushed—
she spread the doors to the well-constructed hall,
slipped out in haste, and the prince led her on . . .
She found Odysseus in the thick of slaughtered corpses,
splattered with bloody filth like a lion that's devoured
some ox of the field and lopes home, covered with blood,

his chest streaked, both jaws glistening, dripping red—
a sight to strike terror. So Odysseus looked now,   430
splattered with gore, his thighs, his fighting hands,
and she, when she saw the corpses, all the pooling blood,
was about to lift a cry of triumph—here was a great exploit,
look—but the soldier held her back and checked her zeal
with warnings winging home: "Rejoice in your heart,
old woman—peace! No cries of triumph now.
It's unholy to glory over the bodies of the dead.
These men the doom of the gods has brought low,
and their own indecent acts. They'd no regard
for any man on earth—good or bad—   440
who chanced to come their way. And so, thanks
to their reckless work, they met this shameful fate.
Quick, report in full on the women in my halls—
who are disloyal to me, who are guiltless?"

                                            "Surely, child,"
his fond old nurse replied, "now here's the truth.
Fifty women you have inside your house,
women we've trained to do their duties well,
to card the wool and bear the yoke of service.
Some dozen in all went tramping to their shame,
thumbing their noses at me, at the queen herself!   450
And Telemachus, just now come of age—his mother
would never let the boy take charge of the maids.
But let me climb to her well-lit room upstairs
and tell your wife the news—
some god has put the woman fast asleep."

    "Don't wake her yet," the crafty man returned,
"you tell those women to hurry here at once—
just the ones who've shamed us all along."

    Away the old nurse bustled through the house
to give the women orders, rush them to the king.   460
Odysseus called Telemachus over, both herdsmen too,
with strict commands: "Start clearing away the bodies.
Make the women pitch in too. Chairs and tables—

scrub them down with sponges, rinse them clean.
And once you've put the entire house in order,
march the women out of the great hall—between
the roundhouse and the courtyard's strong stockade—
and hack them with your swords, slash out all their lives—
blot out of their minds the joys of love they relished
under the suitors' bodies, rutting on the sly!"   470

      The women crowded in, huddling all together . . .
wailing convulsively, streaming live warm tears.
First they carried out the bodies of the dead
and propped them under the courtyard colonnade,
standing them one against another. Odysseus
shouted commands himself, moving things along
and they kept bearing out the bodies—they were forced.
Next they scrubbed down the elegant chairs and tables,
washed them with sopping sponges, rinsed them clean.
Then Telemachus and the herdsmen scraped smooth   480
the packed earth floor of the royal house with spades
as the women gathered up the filth and piled it outside.
And then, at last, once the entire house was put in order,
they marched the women out of the great hall—between
the roundhouse and the courtyard's strong stockade—
crammed them into a dead end, no way out from there,
and stern Telemachus gave the men their orders:
"No clean death for the likes of them, by god!
Not from me—they showered abuse on my head,
my mother's too!
                    You sluts—the suitors' whores!"   490

      With that, taking a cable used on a dark-prowed ship
he coiled it over the roundhouse, lashed it fast to a tall column,
hoisting it up so high no toes could touch the ground.
Then, as doves or thrushes beating their spread wings
against some snare rigged up in thickets—flying in
for a cozy nest but a grisly bed receives them—
so the women's heads were trapped in a line,
nooses yanking their necks up, one by one

so all might die a pitiful, ghastly death . . .
they kicked up heels for a little—not for long.

Melanthius?   500

They hauled him out through the doorway, into the court,
lopped his nose and ears with a ruthless knife,
tore his genitals out for the dogs to eat raw
and in manic fury hacked off hands and feet.

Then,

once they'd washed their own hands and feet,
they went inside again to join Odysseus.
Their work was done with now.
But the king turned to devoted Eurycleia, saying,
"Bring sulfur, nurse, to scour all this pollution—
bring me fire too, so I can fumigate the house.   510
And call Penelope here with all her women—
tell all the maids to come back in at once."

    "Well said, my boy," his old nurse replied,
"right to the point. But wait,
let me fetch you a shirt and cloak to wrap you.
No more dawdling round the palace, nothing but rags
to cover those broad shoulders—it's a scandal!"

    "Fire first," the good soldier answered.
"Light me a fire to purify this house."

    The devoted nurse snapped to his command,   520
brought her master fire and brimstone. Odysseus
purged his palace, halls and court, with cleansing fumes.

    Then back through the royal house the old nurse went
to tell the women the news and bring them in at once.
They came crowding out of their quarters, torch in hand,
flung their arms around Odysseus, hugged him, home at last,
and kissed his head and shoulders, seized his hands, and he,
overcome by a lovely longing, broke down and wept . . .
deep in his heart he knew them one and all.

The Great
Rooted Bed

U p to the rooms the old nurse clambered, chuckling all the way,
to tell the queen her husband was here now, home at last.
Her knees bustling, feet shuffling over each other,
till hovering at her mistress' head she spoke:
"Penelope—child—wake up and see for yourself,
with your own eyes, all you dreamed of, all your days!
He's here—Odysseus—he's come home, at long last!
He's killed the suitors, swaggering young brutes
who plagued his house, wolfed his cattle down,
rode roughshod over his son!"   10

   "Dear old nurse," wary Penelope replied,
"the gods have made you mad. They have that power,
putting lunacy into the clearest head around

or setting a half-wit on the path to sense.
They've unhinged you, and you were once so sane.
Why do you mock me?—haven't I wept enough?—
telling such wild stories, interrupting my sleep,
sweet sleep that held me, sealed my eyes just now.
Not once have I slept so soundly since the day
Odysseus sailed away to see that cursed city . . .   20
Destroy, I call it—I hate to say its name!
Now down you go. Back to your own quarters.
If any other woman of mine had come to me,
rousing me out of sleep with such a tale,
I'd have her bundled back to her room in pain.
It's only your old gray head that spares you that!"

    "Never"—the fond old nurse kept pressing on—
"dear child, I'd never mock you! No, it's all true,
he's here—Odysseus—he's come home, just as I tell you!
He's the stranger they all manhandled in the hall.   30
Telemachus knew he was here, for days and days,
but he knew enough to hide his father's plans
so *he* could pay those vipers back in kind!"

    Penelope's heart burst in joy, she leapt from bed,
her eyes streaming tears, she hugged the old nurse
and cried out with an eager, winging word,
"Please, dear one, give me the whole story.
If he's really home again, just as you tell me,
how did he get those shameless suitors in his clutches?—
single-handed, braving an army always camped inside."   40

    "I have no idea," the devoted nurse replied.
"I didn't see it, I didn't ask—all I heard
was the choking groans of men cut down in blood.
We crouched in terror—a dark nook of our quarters—
all of us locked tight behind those snug doors
till your boy Telemachus came and called me out—
his father rushed him there to do just that. And then
I found Odysseus in the thick of slaughtered corpses;

there he stood and all around him, over the beaten floor,
the bodies sprawled in heaps, lying one on another . . .   50
How it would have thrilled your heart to see him—
splattered with bloody filth, a lion with his kill!
And now they're all stacked at the courtyard gates—
he's lit a roaring fire,
he's purifying the house with cleansing fumes
and he's sent me here to bring you back to him.
Follow me down! So now, after all the years of grief,
you two can embark, loving hearts, along the road to joy.
Look, your dreams, put off so long, come true at last—
he's back alive, home at his hearth, and found you,   60
found his son still here. And all those suitors
who did him wrong, he's paid them back, he has,
right in his own house!"

                    "Hush, dear woman,"
guarded Penelope cautioned her at once.
"Don't laugh, don't cry in triumph—not yet.
You know how welcome the sight of him would be
to all in the house, and to me most of all
and the son we bore together.
But the story can't be true, not as you tell it,
no, it must be a god who's killed our brazen friends—   70
up in arms at their outrage, heartbreaking crimes.
They'd no regard for any man on earth—
good or bad—who chanced to come their way. So,
thanks to their reckless work they die their deaths.
Odysseus? Far from Achaea now, he's lost all hope
of coming home . . . he's lost and gone himself."

    "Child," the devoted old nurse protested,
"what nonsense you let slip through your teeth.
Here's your husband, warming his hands at his own hearth,
here—and you, you say he'll never come home again,   80
always the soul of trust! All right, this too—
I'll give you a sign, a proof that's plain as day.
That scar, made years ago by a boar's white tusk—
I spotted the scar myself, when I washed his feet,

and I tried to tell you, ah, but he, the crafty rascal,
clamped his hand on my mouth—I couldn't say a word.
Follow me down now. I'll stake my life on it:
if I am lying to *you*—
kill me with a thousand knives of pain!"

   "Dear old nurse," composed Penelope responded,   90
"deep as you are, my friend, you'll find it hard
to plumb the plans of the everlasting gods.
All the same, let's go and join my son
so I can see the suitors lying dead
and see . . . the one who killed them."

                           With that thought
Penelope started down from her lofty room, her heart
in turmoil, torn . . . should she keep her distance,
probe her husband? Or rush up to the man at once
and kiss his head and cling to both his hands?
As soon as she stepped across the stone threshold,   100
slipping in, she took a seat at the closest wall
and radiant in the firelight, faced Odysseus now.
There he sat, leaning against the great central column,
eyes fixed on the ground, waiting, poised for whatever words
his hardy wife might say when she caught sight of him.
A long while she sat in silence . . . numbing wonder
filled her heart as her eyes explored his face.
One moment he seemed . . . Odysseus, to the life—
the next, no, he was not the man she knew,
a huddled mass of rags was all she saw.   110

   "Oh mother," Telemachus reproached her,
"cruel mother, you with your hard heart!
Why do you spurn my father so—why don't you
sit beside him, engage him, ask him questions?
What other wife could have a spirit so unbending?
Holding back from her husband, home at last for *her*
after bearing twenty years of brutal struggle—
your heart was always harder than a rock!"

                       "My child,"

Penelope, well-aware, explained, "I'm stunned with wonder,
powerless. Cannot speak to him, ask him questions,   120
look him in the eyes . . . But if he is truly
Odysseus, home at last, make no mistake:
we two will know each other, even better—
we two have secret signs,
known to us both but hidden from the world."

   Odysseus, long-enduring, broke into a smile
and turned to his son with pointed, winging words:
"Leave your mother here in the hall to test me
as she will. She soon will know me better.
Now because I am filthy, wear such grimy rags,   130
she spurns me—your mother still can't bring herself
to believe I am her husband.
                    But you and I,
put heads together. What's our best defense?
When someone kills a lone man in the realm
who leaves behind him no great band of avengers,
still the killer flees, goodbye to kin and country.
But *we* brought down the best of the island's princes,
the pillars of Ithaca. Weigh it well, I urge you."

   "Look to it all yourself now, father," his son
deferred at once. "You are the best on earth,   140
they say, when it comes to mapping tactics.
No one, no mortal man, can touch you there.
But we're behind you, hearts intent on battle,
nor do I think you'll find us short on courage,
long as our strength will last."
                       "Then here's our plan,"
the master of tactics said. "I think it's best.
First go and wash, and pull fresh tunics on
and tell the maids in the hall to dress well too.
And let the inspired bard take up his ringing lyre
and lead off for us all a dance so full of heart   150
that whoever hears the strains outside the gates—
a passerby on the road, a neighbor round about—

will think it's a wedding-feast that's under way.
No news of the suitors' death must spread through town
till we have slipped away to our own estates,
our orchard green with trees. There we'll see
what winning strategy Zeus will hand us then."

They hung on his words and moved to orders smartly.
First they washed and pulled fresh tunics on,
the women arrayed themselves—the inspired bard   160
struck up his resounding lyre and stirred in all
a desire for dance and song, the lovely lilting beat,
till the great house echoed round to the measured tread
of dancing men in motion, women sashed and lithe.
And whoever heard the strains outside would say,
"A miracle—someone's married the queen at last!"

"One of her hundred suitors."
                    "That callous woman,
too faithless to keep her lord and master's house
to the bitter end—"
                    "Till he came sailing home."

So they'd say, blind to what had happened: 170
the great-hearted Odysseus was home again at last.
The maid Eurynome bathed him, rubbed him down with oil
and drew around him a royal cape and choice tunic too.
And Athena crowned the man with beauty, head to foot,
made him taller to all eyes, his build more massive,
yes, and down from his brow the great goddess
ran his curls like thick hyacinth clusters
full of blooms. As a master craftsman washes
gold over beaten silver—a man the god of fire
and Queen Athena trained in every fine technique—   180
and finishes off his latest effort, handsome work . . .
so she lavished splendor over his head and shoulders now.
He stepped from his bath, glistening like a god,
and back he went to the seat that he had left
and facing his wife, declared,

"Strange woman! So hard—the gods of Olympus
made you harder than any other woman in the world!
What other wife could have a spirit so unbending?
Holding back from her husband, home at last for *her*
after bearing twenty years of brutal struggle.   190
Come, nurse, make me a bed, I'll sleep alone.
She has a heart of iron in her breast."

                                        "Strange *man,*"
wary Penelope said. "I'm not so proud, so scornful,
nor am I overwhelmed by your quick change . . .
You look—how well I know—the way he looked,
setting sail from Ithaca years ago
aboard the long-oared ship.

                              Come, Eurycleia,
move the sturdy bedstead out of our bridal chamber—
that room the master built with his own hands.
Take it out now, sturdy bed that it is,   200
and spread it deep with fleece,
blankets and lustrous throws to keep him warm."

     Putting her husband to the proof—but Odysseus
blazed up in fury, lashing out at his loyal wife:
"Woman—your words, they cut me to the core!
Who could move my bed? Impossible task,
even for some skilled craftsman—unless a god
came down in person, quick to lend a hand,
lifted it out with ease and moved it elsewhere.
Not a man on earth, not even at peak strength,   210
would find it easy to prise it up and shift it, no,
a great sign, a hallmark lies in its construction.
I know, I built it myself—no one else . . .
There was a branching olive-tree inside our court,
grown to its full prime, the bole like a column, thickset.
Around it I built my bedroom, finished off the walls
with good tight stonework, roofed it over soundly
and added doors, hung well and snugly wedged.
Then I lopped the leafy crown of the olive,
clean-cutting the stump bare from roots up,   220

planing it round with a bronze smoothing-adze—
I had the skill—I shaped it plumb to the line to make
my bedpost, bored the holes it needed with an auger.
Working from there I built my bed, start to finish,
I gave it ivory inlays, gold and silver fittings,
wove the straps across it, oxhide gleaming red.
There's our secret sign, I tell you, our life story!
Does the bed, my lady, still stand planted firm?—
I don't know—or has someone chopped away
that olive-trunk and hauled our bedstead off?"

                                               Living proof—   230

Penelope felt her knees go slack, her heart surrender,
recognizing the strong clear signs Odysseus offered.
She dissolved in tears, rushed to Odysseus, flung her arms
around his neck and kissed his head and cried out,
"Odysseus—don't flare up at me now, not you,
always the most understanding man alive!
The gods, it was the gods who sent us sorrow—
they grudged us both a life in each other's arms
from the heady zest of youth to the stoop of old age.
But don't fault me, angry with me now because I failed,   240
at the first glimpse, to greet you, hold you, so . . .
In my heart of hearts I always cringed with fear
some fraud might come, beguile me with his talk;
the world is full of the sort,
cunning ones who plot their own dark ends.
Remember Helen of Argos, Zeus's daughter—
would *she* have sported so in a stranger's bed
if she had dreamed that Achaea's sons were doomed
to fight and die to bring her home again?
Some god spurred her to do her shameless work.   250
Not till then did her mind conceive that madness,
blinding madness that caused her anguish, ours as well.
But now, since you have revealed such overwhelming proof—
the secret sign of our bed, which no one's ever seen
but you and I and a single handmaid, Actoris,
the servant my father gave me when I came,

who kept the doors of our room you built so well . . .
you've conquered my heart, my hard heart, at last!"

The more she spoke, the more a deep desire for tears
welled up inside his breast—he wept as he held the wife   260
he loved, the soul of loyalty, in his arms at last.
Joy, warm as the joy that shipwrecked sailors feel
when they catch sight of land—Poseidon has struck
their well-rigged ship on the open sea with gale winds
and crushing walls of waves, and only a few escape, swimming,
struggling out of the frothing surf to reach the shore,
their bodies crusted with salt but buoyed up with joy
as they plant their feet on solid ground again,
spared a deadly fate. So joyous now to her
the sight of her husband, vivid in her gaze,   270
that her white arms, embracing his neck
would never for a moment let him go . . .
Dawn with her rose-red fingers might have shone
upon their tears, if with her glinting eyes
Athena had not thought of one more thing.
She held back the night, and night lingered long
at the western edge of the earth, while in the east
she reined in Dawn of the golden throne at Ocean's banks,
commanding her not to yoke the windswift team that brings men light,
Blaze and Aurora, the young colts that race the Morning on.   280
Yet now Odysseus, seasoned veteran, said to his wife,
"Dear woman . . . we have still not reached the end
of all our trials. One more labor lies in store—
boundless, laden with danger, great and long,
and I must brave it out from start to finish.
So the ghost of Tiresias prophesied to me,
the day that I went down to the House of Death
to learn our best route home, my comrades' and my own.
But come, let's go to bed, dear woman—at long last
delight in sleep, delight in each other, come!"   290

    "If it's bed you want," reserved Penelope replied,

"it's bed you'll have, whenever the spirit moves you,
now that the gods have brought you home again
to native land, your grand and gracious house.
But since you've alluded to it,
since a god has put it in your mind,
please, tell me about this trial still to come.
I'm bound to learn of it later, I am sure—
what's the harm if I hear of it tonight?"

                              "Still so strange,"
Odysseus, the old master of stories, answered.   300
"Why again, why force me to tell you all?
Well, tell I shall. I'll hide nothing now.
But little joy it will bring you, I'm afraid,
as little joy for me.
                The prophet said
that I must rove through towns on towns of men,
that I must carry a well-planed oar until
I come to a people who know nothing of the sea,
whose food is never seasoned with salt, strangers all
to ships with their crimson prows and long slim oars,
wings that make ships fly. And here is my sign,   310
he told me, clear, so clear I cannot miss it,
and I will share it with you now . . .
When another traveler falls in with me and calls
that weight across my shoulder a fan to winnow grain,
then, he told me, I must plant my oar in the earth
and sacrifice fine beasts to the lord god of the sea,
Poseidon—a ram, a bull and a ramping wild boar—
then journey home and render noble offerings up
to the deathless gods who rule the vaulting skies,
to all the gods in order.   320
And at last my own death will steal upon me . . .
a gentle, painless death, far from the sea it comes
to take me down, borne down with the years in ripe old age
with all my people here in blessed peace around me.
All this, the prophet said, will come to pass."

  "And so," Penelope said, in her great wisdom,

"if the gods will really grant a happier old age,
there's hope that we'll escape our trials at last."

So husband and wife confided in each other,
while nurse and Eurynome, under the flaring brands,   330
were making up the bed with coverings deep and soft.
And working briskly, soon as they'd made it snug,
back to her room the old nurse went to sleep
as Eurynome, their attendant, torch in hand,
lighted the royal couple's way to bed and,
leading them to their chamber, slipped away.
Rejoicing in each other, they returned to their bed,
the old familiar place they loved so well.

Now Telemachus, the cowherd and the swineherd
rested their dancing feet and had the women do the same,   340
and across the shadowed hall the men lay down to sleep.

But the royal couple, once they'd reveled in all
the longed-for joys of love, reveled in each other's stories,
the radiant woman telling of all she'd borne at home,
watching them there, the infernal crowd of suitors
slaughtering herds of cattle and good fat sheep—
while keen to win her hand—
draining the broached vats dry of vintage wine.
And great Odysseus told his wife of all the pains
he had dealt out to other men and all the hardships   350
he'd endured himself—his story first to last—
and she listened on, enchanted . . .
Sleep never sealed her eyes till all was told.

He launched in with how he fought the Cicones down,
then how he came to the Lotus-eaters' lush green land.
Then all the crimes of the Cyclops and how he paid him back
for the gallant men the monster ate without a qualm—
then how he visited Aeolus, who gave him a hero's welcome
then he sent him off, but the homeward run was not his fate,
not yet—some sudden squalls snatched him away once more   360

and drove him over the swarming sea, groaning in despair.
Then how he moored at Telepylus, where Laestrygonians
wrecked his fleet and killed his men-at-arms.
He told her of Circe's cunning magic wiles
and how he voyaged down in his long benched ship
to the moldering House of Death, to consult Tiresias,
ghostly seer of Thebes, and he saw old comrades there
and he saw his mother, who bore and reared him as a child.
He told how he caught the Sirens' voices throbbing in the wind
and how he had scudded past the Clashing Rocks, past grim Charybdis,
past Scylla—whom no rover had ever coasted by, home free—
and how his shipmates slaughtered the cattle of the Sun
and Zeus the king of thunder split his racing ship
with a reeking bolt and killed his hardy comrades,
all his fighting men at a stroke, but he alone
escaped their death at sea. He told how he reached
Ogygia's shores and the nymph Calypso held him back,
deep in her arching caverns, craving him for a husband—
cherished him, vowed to make him immortal, ageless, all his days,
yes, but she never won the heart inside him, never . . .   380
then how he reached the Phaeacians—heavy sailing there—
who with all their hearts had prized him like a god
and sent him off in a ship to his own beloved land,
giving him bronze and hoards of gold and robes . . .
and that was the last he told her, just as sleep
overcame him . . . sleep loosing his limbs,
slipping the toils of anguish from his mind.

    Athena, her eyes afire, had fresh plans.
Once she thought he'd had his heart's content
of love and sleep at his wife's side, straightaway   390
she roused young Dawn from Ocean's banks to her golden throne
to bring men light and roused Odysseus too, who rose
from his soft bed and advised his wife in parting,
"Dear woman, we both have had our fill of trials.
You in our house, weeping over my journey home,
fraught with storms and torment, true, and I,
pinned down in pain by Zeus and other gods,

for all my desire, blocked from reaching home.
But now that we've arrived at our bed together—
the reunion that we yearned for all those years—   400
look after the things still left me in our house.
But as for the flocks those brazen suitors plundered,
much I'll recoup myself, making many raids;
the rest our fellow-Ithacans will supply
till all my folds are full of sheep again.
But now I must be off to the upland farm,
our orchard green with trees, to see my father,
good old man weighed down with so much grief for me.
And you, dear woman, sensible as you are,
I would advise you, still . . .   410
quick as the rising sun the news will spread
of the suitors that I killed inside the house.
So climb to your lofty chamber with your women.
Sit tight there. See no one. Question no one."

   He strapped his burnished armor round his shoulders,
roused Telemachus, the cowherd and the swineherd,
and told them to take up weapons honed for battle.
They snapped to commands, harnessed up in bronze,
opened the doors and strode out, Odysseus in the lead.
By now the daylight covered the land, but Pallas,   420
shrouding them all in darkness,
quickly led the four men out of town.

BOOK TWENTY-FOUR

Peace

Now Cyllenian Hermes called away the suitors' ghosts,
holding firm in his hand the wand of fine pure gold
that enchants the eyes of men whenever Hermes wants
or wakes us up from sleep.
With a wave of this he stirred and led them on
and the ghosts trailed after with high thin cries
as bats cry in the depths of a dark haunted cavern,
shrilling, flittering, wild when one drops from the chain—
slipped from the rock face, while the rest cling tight . . .
So with their high thin cries the ghosts flocked now   10
and Hermes the Healer led them on, and down the dank
moldering paths and past the Ocean's streams they went
and past the White Rock and the Sun's Western Gates and past
the Land of Dreams, and they soon reached the fields of asphodel

where the dead, the burnt-out wraiths of mortals, make their home.

     There they found the ghosts of Peleus' son Achilles,
Patroclus, fearless Antilochus—and Great Ajax too,
the first in stature, first in build and bearing
of all the Argives after Peleus' matchless son.
They had grouped around Achilles' ghost, and now   20
the shade of Atreus' son Agamemnon marched toward them—
fraught with grief and flanked by all his comrades,
troops of his men-at-arms who died beside him,
who met their fate in lord Aegisthus' halls.
Achilles' ghost was first to greet him: "Agamemnon,
you were the one, we thought, of all our fighting princes
Zeus who loves the lightning favored most, all your days,
because you commanded such a powerful host of men
on the fields of Troy where we Achaeans suffered.
But you were doomed to encounter fate so early,   30
you too, yet no one born escapes its deadly force.
If only you had died your death in the full flush
of the glory you had mastered—died on Trojan soil!
Then all united Achaea would have raised your tomb
and you'd have won your son great fame for years to come.
Not so. You were fated to die a wretched death."

     And the ghost of Atrides Agamemnon answered,
"Son of Peleus, great godlike Achilles! Happy man,
you died on the fields of Troy, a world away from home,
and the best of Trojan and Argive champions died around you,   40
fighting for your corpse. And you . . . there you lay
in the whirling dust, overpowered in all your power
and wiped from memory all your horseman's skills.
That whole day we fought, we'd never have stopped
if Zeus had not stopped *us* with sudden gales.
Then we bore you out of the fighting, onto the ships,
we laid you down on a litter, cleansed your handsome flesh
with warm water and soothing oils, and round your body
troops of Danaans wept hot tears and cut their locks.

Hearing the news, your mother, Thetis, rose from the sea,   50
immortal sea-nymphs in her wake, and a strange unearthly cry
came throbbing over the ocean. Terror gripped Achaea's armies,
they would have leapt in panic, boarded the long hollow ships
if one man, deep in his age-old wisdom, had not checked them:
Nestor—from the first his counsel always seemed the best,
and now, concerned for the ranks, he rose and shouted,
'Hold fast, Argives! Sons of Achaea, don't run now!
This is Achilles' mother rising from the sea
with all her immortal sea-nymphs—
she longs to join her son who died in battle!'   60
That stopped our panicked forces in their tracks
as the Old Man of the Sea's daughters gathered round you—
wailing, heartsick—dressed you in ambrosial, deathless robes
and the Muses, nine in all, voice-to-voice in choirs,
their vibrant music rising, raised your dirge.
Not one soldier would you have seen dry-eyed,
the Muses' song so pierced us to the heart.
For seventeen days unbroken, days and nights
we mourned you—immortal gods and mortal men.
At the eighteenth dawn we gave you to the flames   70
and slaughtered around your body droves of fat sheep
and shambling longhorn cattle, and you were burned
in the garments of the gods and laved with soothing oils
and honey running sweet, and a long cortege of Argive heroes
paraded in review, in battle armor round your blazing pyre,
men in chariots, men on foot—a resounding roar went up.
And once the god of fire had burned your corpse to ash,
at first light we gathered your white bones, Achilles,
cured them in strong neat wine and seasoned oils.
Your mother gave us a gold two-handled urn,   80
a gift from Dionysus, she said,
a masterwork of the famous Smith, the god of fire.
Your white bones rest in that, my brilliant Achilles,
mixed with the bones of dead Patroclus, Menoetius' son,
apart from those of Antilochus, whom you treasured
more than all other comrades once Patroclus died.
Over your bones we reared a grand, noble tomb—

devoted veterans all, Achaea's combat forces—
high on its jutting headland over the Hellespont's
broad reach, a landmark glimpsed from far out at sea   90
by men of our own day and men of days to come.

                                        And then
your mother, begging the gods for priceless trophies,
set them out in the ring for all our champions.
You in your day have witnessed funeral games
for many heroes, games to honor the death of kings,
when young men cinch their belts, tense to win some prize—
but if you'd laid eyes on these it would have thrilled your heart,
magnificent trophies the goddess, glistening-footed Thetis,
held out in your honor. You were dear to the gods,
so even in death your name will never die . . .   100
Great glory is yours, Achilles,
for all time, in the eyes of all mankind!

                          But I?
What joy for *me* when the coil of war had wound down?
For my return Zeus hatched a pitiful death
at the hands of Aegisthus—and my accursed wife."

    As they exchanged the stories of their fates,
Hermes the guide and giant-killer drew up close to both,
leading down the ghosts of the suitors King Odysseus killed.
Struck by the sight, the two went up to them right away
and the ghost of Atreus' son Agamemnon recognized   110
the noted prince Amphimedon, Melaneus' dear son
who received him once in Ithaca, at his home,
and Atrides' ghost called out to his old friend now,
"Amphimedon, what disaster brings you down to the dark world?
All of you, good picked men, and all in your prime—
no captain out to recruit the best in any city
could have chosen better. What laid you low?
Wrecked in the ships when lord Poseidon roused
some punishing blast of gales and heavy breakers?
Or did ranks of enemies mow you down on land   120
as you tried to raid and cut off herds and flocks
or fought to win their city, take their women?

Answer me, tell me. I was once your guest.
Don't you recall the day I came to visit
your house in Ithaca—King Menelaus came too—
to urge Odysseus to sail with us in the ships
on our campaign to Troy? And the long slow voyage,
crossing wastes of ocean, cost us one whole month.
That's how hard it was to bring him round,
Odysseus, raider of cities."

                "Famous Atrides!"   130
Amphimedon's ghost called back. "Lord of men, Agamemnon,
I remember it all, your majesty, as you say,
and I will tell you, start to finish now,
the story of our death,
the brutal end contrived to take us off.
We were courting the wife of Odysseus, gone so long.
She neither spurned nor embraced a marriage she despised,
no, she simply planned our death, our black doom!
This was her latest masterpiece of guile:
she set up a great loom in the royal halls   140
and she began to weave, and the weaving finespun,
the yarns endless, and she would lead us on: 'Young men,
my suitors, now that King Odysseus is no more,
go slowly, keen as you are to marry me, until
I can finish off this web . . .
so my weaving won't all fray and come to nothing.
This is a shroud for old lord Laertes, for that day
when the deadly fate that lays us out at last will take him down.
I dread the shame my countrywomen would heap upon me,
yes, if a man of such wealth should lie in state   150
without a shroud for cover.'
                Her very words,
and despite our pride and passion we believed her.
So by day she'd weave at her great and growing web—
by night, by the light of torches set beside her,
she would unravel all she'd done. Three whole years
she deceived us blind, seduced us with this scheme . . .
Then, when the wheeling seasons brought the fourth year on
and the months waned and the long days came round once more,

one of her women, in on the queen's secret, told the truth
and we caught her in the act—unweaving her gorgeous web.   160
So she finished it off. Against her will. We forced her.
But just as she bound off that great shroud and washed it,
spread it out—glistening like the sunlight or the moon—
just then some wicked spirit brought Odysseus back,
from god knows where, to the edge of his estate
where the swineherd kept his pigs. And back too,
to the same place, came Odysseus' own dear son,
scudding home in his black ship from sandy Pylos.
The pair of them schemed our doom, our deathtrap,
then lit out for town—   170
Telemachus first in fact, Odysseus followed,
later, led by the swineherd, and clad in tatters,
looking for all the world like an old and broken beggar
hunched on a stick, his body wrapped in shameful rags.
Disguised so none of us, not even the older ones,
could spot that tramp for the man he really was,
bursting in on us there, out of the blue. No,
we attacked him, blows and insults flying fast,
and he took it all for a time, in his own house,
all the taunts and blows—he had a heart of iron.   180
But once the will of thundering Zeus had roused his blood,
he and Telemachus bore the burnished weapons off
and stowed them deep in a storeroom, shot the bolts
and he—the soul of cunning—told his wife to set
the great bow and the gleaming iron axes out
before the suitors—all of us doomed now—
to test our skill and bring our slaughter on . . .
Not one of us had the strength to string that powerful weapon,
all of us fell far short of what it took. But then,
when the bow was coming round to Odysseus' hands,   190
we raised a hue and cry—he must not have it,
no matter how he begged! Only Telemachus
urged him to take it up, and once he got it
in his clutches, long-suffering great Odysseus
strung his bow with ease and shot through all the axes,
then, vaulting onto the threshold, stood there poised, and pouring

his flashing arrows out before him, glaring for the kill,
he cut Antinous down, then shot his painful arrows
into the rest of us, aiming straight and true,
and down we went, corpse on corpse in droves.   200
Clearly a god was driving him and all his henchmen,
routing us headlong in their fury down the hall,
wheeling into the slaughter, slashing left and right
and grisly screams broke from skulls cracked open—
the whole floor awash with blood.
                                    So we died,
Agamemnon . . . our bodies lie untended even now,
strewn in Odysseus' palace. They know nothing yet,
the kin in our houses who might wash our wounds
of clotted gore and lay us out and mourn us.
These are the solemn honors owed the dead."
                                    "Happy Odysseus!"   210
Agamemnon's ghost cried out. "Son of old Laertes—
mastermind—what a fine, faithful wife you won!
What good sense resided in your Penelope—
how well Icarius' daughter remembered you,
Odysseus, the man she married once!
The fame of her great virtue will never die.
The immortal gods will lift a song for all mankind,
a glorious song in praise of self-possessed Penelope.
A far cry from the daughter of Tyndareus, Clytemnestra—
what outrage she committed, killing the man *she* married once!—   220
yes, and the song men sing of her will ring with loathing.
She brands with a foul name the breed of womankind,
even the honest ones to come!"
                                    So they traded stories,
the two ghosts standing there in the House of Death,
far in the hidden depths below the earth.

    Odysseus and his men had stridden down from town
and quickly reached Laertes' large, well-tended farm
that the old king himself had wrested from the wilds,
years ago, laboring long and hard. His lodge was here
and around it stretched a row of sheds where fieldhands,   230

bondsmen who did his bidding, sat and ate and slept.
And an old Sicilian woman was in charge,
who faithfully looked after her aged master
out on his good estate remote from town.
Odysseus told his servants and his son,
"Into the timbered lodge now, go, quickly,
kill us the fattest porker, fix our meal.
And I will put my father to the test,
see if the old man knows me now, on sight,
or fails to, after twenty years apart."   240

    With that he passed his armor to his men
and in they went at once, his son as well. Odysseus
wandered off, approaching the thriving vineyard, searching,
picking his way down to the great orchard, searching,
but found neither Dolius nor his sons nor any hand.
They'd just gone off, old Dolius in the lead,
to gather stones for a dry retaining wall
to shore the vineyard up. But he did find
his father, alone, on that well-worked plot,
spading round a sapling—clad in filthy rags,   250
in a patched, unseemly shirt, and round his shins
he had some oxhide leggings strapped, patched too,
to keep from getting scraped, and gloves on his hands
to fight against the thorns, and on his head
he wore a goatskin skullcap
to cultivate his misery that much more . . .
Long-enduring Odysseus, catching sight of him now—
a man worn down with years, his heart racked with sorrow—
halted under a branching pear-tree, paused and wept.
Debating, head and heart, what should he do now?   260
Kiss and embrace his father, pour out the long tale—
how he had made the journey home to native land—
or probe him first and test him every way?
Torn, mulling it over, this seemed better:
test the old man first,
reproach him with words that cut him to the core.
Convinced, Odysseus went right up to his father.

Laertes was digging round the sapling, head bent low
as his famous offspring hovered over him and began,
"You want no skill, old man, at tending a garden.   270
All's well-kept here; not one thing in the plot,
no plant, no fig, no pear, no olive, no vine,
not a vegetable, lacks your tender, loving care.
But I must say—and don't be offended now—
your plants are doing better than yourself.
Enough to be stooped with age
but look how squalid you are, those shabby rags.
Surely it's not for sloth your master lets you go to seed.
There's nothing of slave about your build or bearing.
I have eyes: you look like a king to me. The sort   280
entitled to bathe, sup well, then sleep in a soft bed.
That's the right and pride of you old-timers.
Come now, tell me—in no uncertain terms—
whose slave are you? whose orchard are you tending?
And tell me this—I must be absolutely sure—
this place I've reached, is it truly Ithaca?
Just as that fellow told me, just now . . .
I fell in with him on the road here. Clumsy,
none too friendly, couldn't trouble himself
to hear me out or give me a decent answer   290
when I asked about a long-lost friend of mine,
whether he's still alive, somewhere in Ithaca,
or dead and gone already, lost in the House of Death.
Do you want to hear his story? Listen. Catch my drift.
I once played host to a man in my own country;
he'd come to my door, the most welcome guest
from foreign parts I ever entertained.
He claimed he came of good Ithacan stock,
said his father was Arcesius' son, Laertes.
So I took the new arrival under my own roof,   300
I gave him a hero's welcome, treated him in style—
stores in our palace made for princely entertainment.
And I gave my friend some gifts to fit his station,
handed him seven bars of well-wrought gold,
a mixing-bowl of solid silver, etched with flowers,

a dozen cloaks, unlined and light, a dozen rugs
and as many full-cut capes and shirts as well,
and to top it off, four women, perfect beauties
skilled in crafts—he could pick them out himself."

    "Stranger," his father answered, weeping softly,   310
"the land you've reached is the very one you're after,
true, but it's in the grip of reckless, lawless men.
And as for the gifts you showered on your guest,
you gave them all for nothing.
But if you'd found him alive, here in Ithaca,
he would have replied in kind, with gift for gift,
and entertained you warmly before he sent you off.
That's the old custom, when one has led the way.
But tell me, please—in no uncertain terms—
how many years ago did you host the man,   320
that unfortunate guest of yours, my son . . .
there was a son, or was he all a dream?
That most unlucky man, whom now, I fear,
far from his own soil and those he loves,
the fish have swallowed down on the high seas
or birds and beasts on land have made their meal.
Nor could the ones who bore him—mother, father—
wrap his corpse in a shroud and mourn him deeply.
Nor could his warm, generous wife, so self-possessed,
Penelope, ever keen for her husband on his deathbed,   330
the fit and proper way, or close his eyes at last.
These are the solemn honors owed the dead.
But tell me your own story—that I'd like to know:
Who are you? where are you from? your city? your parents?
Where does the ship lie moored that brought you here,
your hardy shipmates too? Or did you arrive
as a passenger aboard some stranger's craft
and men who put you ashore have pulled away?"
                                                "The whole tale,"
his crafty son replied, "I'll tell you start to finish.
I come from Roamer-Town, my home's a famous place,   340
my father's Unsparing, son of old King Pain,

and my name's Man of Strife . . .
I sailed from Sicily, aye, but some ill wind
blew me here, off course—much against my will—
and my ship lies moored off farmlands far from town.
As for Odysseus, well, five years have passed
since he left my house and put my land behind him,
luckless man! But the birds were good as he launched out,
all on the right, and I rejoiced as I sent him off
and he rejoiced in sailing. We had high hopes   350
we'd meet again as guests, as old friends,
and trade some shining gifts."

                              At those words
a black cloud of grief came shrouding over Laertes.
Both hands clawing the ground for dirt and grime,
he poured it over his grizzled head, sobbing, in spasms.
Odysseus' heart shuddered, a sudden twinge went shooting up
through his nostrils, watching his dear father struggle . . .
He sprang toward him, kissed him, hugged him, crying,
"Father—I am your son—myself, the man you're seeking,
home after twenty years, on native ground at last!   360
Hold back your tears, your grief.
Let me tell you the news, but we must hurry—
I've cut the suitors down in our own house,
I've paid them back their outrage, vicious crimes!"

                                          "Odysseus . . ."
Laertes, catching his breath, found words to answer.
"You—you're truly my son, Odysseus, home at last?
Give me a sign, some proof—I must be sure."

                                    "This scar first,"
quick to the mark, his son said, "look at this—
the wound I took from the boar's white tusk
on Mount Parnassus. There you'd sent me, you   370
and mother, to see her fond old father, Autolycus,
and collect the gifts he vowed to give me, once,
when he came to see us here.

                          Or these, these trees—
let me tell you the trees you gave me years ago,
here on this well-worked plot . . .

I begged you for everything I saw, a little boy
trailing you through the orchard, picking our way
among these trees, and you named them one by one.
You gave me thirteen pear, ten apple trees
and forty figs—and promised to give me, look,   380
fifty vinerows, bearing hard on each other's heels,
clusters of grapes year-round at every grade of ripeness,
mellowed as Zeus's seasons weigh them down."

                                        Living proof—
and Laertes' knees went slack, his heart surrendered,
recognizing the strong clear signs Odysseus offered.
He threw his arms around his own dear son, fainting
as hardy great Odysseus hugged him to his heart
until he regained his breath, came back to life
and cried out, "Father Zeus—
you gods of Olympus, you still rule on high   390
if those suitors have truly paid in blood
for all their reckless outrage! Oh, but now
my heart quakes with fear that all the Ithacans
will come down on us in a pack, at any time,
and rush the alarm through every island town!"

   "There's nothing to fear," his canny son replied,
"put it from your mind. Let's make for your lodge
beside the orchard here. I sent Telemachus on ahead,
the cowherd, swineherd too, to fix a hasty meal."

   So the two went home, confiding all the way   400
and arriving at the ample, timbered lodge,
they found Telemachus with the two herdsmen
carving sides of meat and mixing ruddy wine.
Before they ate, the Sicilian serving-woman
bathed her master, Laertes—his spirits high
in his own room—and rubbed him down with oil
and round his shoulders drew a fresh new cloak.
And Athena stood beside him, fleshing out the limbs
of the old commander, made him taller to all eyes,
his build more massive, stepping from his bath,   410

so his own son gazed at him, wonderstruck—
face-to-face he seemed a deathless god . . .
"Father"—Odysseus' words had wings—"surely
one of the everlasting gods has made you
taller, stronger, shining in my eyes!"

    Facing his son, the wise old man returned,
"If only—Father Zeus, Athena and lord Apollo—
I were the man I was, king of the Cephallenians
when I sacked the city of Nericus, sturdy fortress
out on its jutting cape! If I'd been young in arms   420
last night in our house with harness on my back,
standing beside you, fighting off the suitors,
how many I would have cut the knees from under—
the heart inside you would have leapt for joy!"

    So father and son confirmed each other's spirits.
And then, with the roasting done, the meal set out,
the others took their seats on chairs and stools,
were just putting their hands to bread and meat
when old Dolius trudged in with his sons,
worn out from the fieldwork.   430
The old Sicilian had gone and fetched them home,
the mother who reared the boys and tended Dolius well,
now that the years had ground the old man down . . .
When they saw Odysseus—knew him in their bones—
they stopped in their tracks, staring, struck dumb,
but the king waved them on with a warm and easy air:
"Sit down to your food, old friend. Snap out of your wonder.
We've been cooling our heels here long enough,
eager to get our hands on all this pork,
hoping you'd all troop in at any moment."   440

    Spreading his arms, Dolius rushed up to him,
clutched Odysseus by the wrist and kissed his hand,
greeting his king now with a burst of winging words:
"Dear master, you're back—the answer to our prayers!
We'd lost all hope but the gods have brought you home!

Welcome—health! The skies rain blessings on you!
But tell me the truth now—this I'd like to know—
shrewd Penelope, has she heard you're home?
Or should we send a messenger?"

                  "She knows by now,
old man," his wily master answered brusquely.   450
"Why busy yourself with that?"

    So Dolius went back to his sanded stool.
His sons too, pressing around the famous king,
greeted Odysseus warmly, grasped him by the hand
then took their seats in order by their father.

    But now, as they fell to supper in the lodge,
Rumor the herald sped like wildfire through the city,
crying out the news of the suitors' bloody death and doom,
and massing from every quarter as they listened, kinsmen milled
with wails and moans of grief before Odysseus' palace.   460
And then they carried out the bodies, every family
buried their own, and the dead from other towns
they loaded onto the rapid ships for crews
to ferry back again, each to his own home . . .
Then in a long, mourning file they moved to assembly
where, once they'd grouped, crowding the meeting grounds,
old lord Eupithes rose in their midst to speak out.
Unforgettable sorrow wrung his heart for his son,
Antinous, the first that great Odysseus killed.
In tears for the one he lost, he stood and cried,   470
"My friends, what a mortal blow this man has dealt
to all our island people! Those fighters, many and brave,
he led away in his curved ships—he lost the ships
and he lost the men and back he comes again
to kill the best of our Cephallenian princes.
Quick, after him! Before he flees to Pylos
or holy Elis, where Epeans rule in power—
up, attack! Or we'll hang our heads forever,
all disgraced, even by generations down the years,
if we don't punish the murderers of our brothers and our sons!   480

Why, life would lose its relish—for me, at least—
I'd rather die at once and go among the dead.
Attack!—before the assassins cross the sea
and leave us in their wake."
                              He closed in tears
and compassion ran through every Achaean there.
Suddenly Medon and the inspired bard approached them,
fresh from Odysseus' house, where they had just awakened.
They strode into the crowds; amazement took each man
but the herald Medon spoke in all his wisdom:
"Hear me, men of Ithaca. Not without the hand   490
of the deathless gods did Odysseus do these things!
Myself, I saw an immortal fighting at his side—
like Mentor to the life. I saw the same god,
now in front of Odysseus, spurring him on,
now stampeding the suitors through the hall,
crazed with fear, and down they went in droves!"

    Terror gripped them all, their faces ashen white.
At last the old warrior Halitherses, Mastor's son—
who alone could see the days behind and days ahead—
rose up and spoke, distraught for each man there: 500
"Hear me, men of Ithaca. Hear what I have to say.
Thanks to your own craven hearts these things were done!
You never listened to me or the good commander Mentor,
you never put a stop to your sons' senseless folly.
What fine work they did, so blind, so reckless,
carving away the wealth, affronting the wife
of a great and famous man, telling themselves
that he'd return no more! So let things rest now.
Listen to me for once—I say don't attack!
Else some will draw the lightning on their necks."
                              So he urged   510
and some held fast to their seats, but more than half
sprang up with warcries now. They had no taste
for the prophet's sane plan—winning Eupithes
quickly won them over. They ran for armor
and once they'd harnessed up in burnished bronze

they grouped in ranks before the terraced city.
Eupithes led them on in their foolish, mad campaign,
certain he would avenge the slaughter of his son
but the father was not destined to return—
he'd meet his death in battle then and there.   520

    Athena at this point made appeals to Zeus:
"Father, son of Cronus, our high and mighty king,
now let me ask you a question . . .
tell me the secrets hidden in your mind.
Will you prolong the pain, the cruel fighting here
or hand down pacts of peace between both sides?"

    "My child," Zeus who marshals the thunderheads replied,
"why do you pry and probe me so intently? Come now,
wasn't the plan your own? You conceived it yourself:
Odysseus should return and pay the traitors back.   530
Do as your heart desires—
but let me tell you how it should be done.
Now that royal Odysseus has taken his revenge,
let both sides seal their pacts that he shall reign for life,
and let us purge their memories of the bloody slaughter
of their brothers and their sons. Let them be friends,
devoted as in the old days. Let peace and wealth
come cresting through the land."
                 So Zeus decreed
and launched Athena already poised for action—
down she swept from Olympus' craggy peaks.   540

    By then Odysseus' men had had their fill
of hearty fare, and the seasoned captain said,
"One of you go outside—see if they're closing in."
A son of Dolius snapped to his command,
ran to the door and saw them all too close
and shouted back to Odysseus,
"They're on top of us! To arms—and fast!"
Up they sprang and strapped themselves in armor,
the three men with Odysseus, Dolius' six sons

and Dolius and Laertes clapped on armor too,   550
gray as they were, but they would fight if forced.
Once they had all harnessed up in burnished bronze
they opened the doors and strode out, Odysseus in the lead.

    And now, taking the build and voice of Mentor,
Zeus's daughter Athena marched right in.
The good soldier Odysseus thrilled to see her,
turned to his son and said in haste, "Telemachus,
you'll learn soon enough—as you move up to fight
where champions strive to prove themselves the best—
not to disgrace your father's line a moment.   560
In battle prowess we've excelled for ages
all across the world."
                          Telemachus reassured him,
"Now you'll see, if you care to watch, father,
now I'm fired up. Disgrace, you say?
I won't disgrace your line!"

    Laertes called out in deep delight,
"What a day for me, dear gods! What joy—
my son and my grandson vying over courage!"
                                              "Laertes!"
Goddess Athena rushed beside him, eyes ablaze:
"Son of Arcesius, dearest of all my comrades,   570
say a prayer to the bright-eyed girl and Father Zeus,
then brandish your long spear and wing it fast!"

    Athena breathed enormous strength in the old man.
He lifted a prayer to mighty Zeus's daughter,
brandished his spear a moment, winged it fast
and hit Eupithes, pierced his bronze-sided helmet
that failed to block the bronze point tearing through—
down Eupithes crashed, his armor clanging against his chest.
Odysseus and his gallant son charged straight at the front lines,
slashing away with swords, with two-edged spears and now   580
they would have killed them all, cut them off from home
if Athena, daughter of storming Zeus, had not cried out

in a piercing voice that stopped all fighters cold,
"Hold back, you men of Ithaca, back from brutal war!
Break off—shed no more blood—make peace at once!"

    So Athena commanded. Terror blanched their faces,
they went limp with fear, weapons slipped from their hands
and strewed the ground at the goddess' ringing voice.
They spun in flight to the city, wild to save their lives,
but loosing a savage cry, the long-enduring great Odysseus,   590
gathering all his force, swooped like a soaring eagle—
just as the son of Cronus hurled a reeking bolt
that fell at her feet, the mighty Father's daughter,
and blazing-eyed Athena wheeled on Odysseus, crying,
"Royal son of Laertes, Odysseus, master of exploits,
hold back now! Call a halt to the great leveler, War—
don't court the rage of Zeus who rules the world!"

    So she commanded. He obeyed her, glad at heart.
And Athena handed down her pacts of peace
between both sides for all the years to come—   600
the daughter of Zeus whose shield is storm and thunder,
yes, but the goddess still kept Mentor's build and voice.

NOTES

TRANSLATOR'S
POSTSCRIPT

"*Homer* makes us Hearers," Pope has said, "and *Virgil* leaves us Readers." So the great translator of Homer, no doubt unknowingly, set at odds the claims of an oral tradition and those of a literary one, as we would call the two traditions now. Homer's work is a performance, even in part a musical event. Perhaps that is the source of his speed, directness and simplicity, that Matthew Arnold praised—and his nobility too, elusive yet undeniable, that Arnold pursued but never really caught. Surely it is a major source of Homer's energy, the loft and carry of his imagination that sweeps along the listener together with the performer. For there is a power in Homer's song, and whether it is "that unequal'd Fire and Rapture" that Pope found in the *Iliad* or the glow of the setting sun that Longinus found in the *Odyssey*, it brings to light the Homeric Question facing all translators: how to convey the force of his performance in the quieter medium of writing? "*Homer* makes us Hearers, and *Virgil* leaves us Readers."

Yet the contrast may be too extreme. Virgil the writer was certainly no stranger to recitation. Homer the performer, as Bernard Knox conjectures in his Introduction, may have known a rudimentary form of writing. And writing may have lent his work some qualities we associate with written works in general—idiosyncrasies at times, and pungency and wit—and with the *Iliad* and the *Odyssey* in particular, their architectonics, their magnificent scale, and the figures of Achilles and Hector, Odysseus and Penelope. But even if Homer never used an alphabet himself, he now seems less the creature of an oral tradition whom Milman Parry discovered, and more and more its master, as envisioned by Adam, Parry's son, and as others have agreed. A brilliant improviser, Homer deployed the stock, inherited features of this tradition with all the individual talent he could muster. Never more so, in fact, than in his use of the fixed and formulaic, frequently repeated phrase. Not only is Homer often less formulaic than might appear, but the formulas themselves are often more resonant, more apt and telling in their contexts, than the "hard Parryites" argued for at first. So the original form of Homer's work, though a far cry from a work of literature as we know it now, is not exactly a song, pure and simple, either. It may be more the record of a song, building, perhaps, over the poet's entire lifetime—not spontaneity outright but what Marianne Moore would call "a simulacrum of spontaneity."

Writing at a far remove from Homer, my approach in this translation has been the one I took in a version of the *Iliad*. With the *Odyssey*, however, I have tried to vary my voice in even more ways, modulating it to fit the postwar world, the more domestic, more intimate world of the later poem; yet raising it when an occasion calls—when Homer returns to heroic action or a fabulous encounter or an emotional crescendo—as a reminder that a related voice runs through both poems. That, taken as a sequel to the *Iliad*, the *Odyssey* would celebrate, in Wallace Stevens' phrase, "war's miracle begetting that of peace." And both of my translations share a related impulse, too. Again I have tried to find a middle ground (and not a no-man's-land, if I can help it) between the features of Homer's performance and the expectations of a contemporary reader. Not a line-by-line translation, my version of the *Odyssey* is, I hope, neither so literal in rendering Homer's language as to cramp and distort my own—though I want to convey as much of what he says as possible—nor so literary as to brake his energy, his forward drive, though I want my work to be literate and clear. For the more literal approach would seem to be too little English, and the more literary seems too little Greek. What I have tried to find is a cross between the two, a modern English Homer.

Of course, it is a risky business, stating what one had tried to do or, worse, the principles one has used (petards that will probably hoist the writer later). But a few words of explanation seem in order, and the first of them refer to the more fixed and formulaic parts of Homer. Again I have treated them in a flexible, discretionary way, not incompatible with Homer's way, I like to think—especially when his formulas are functional as well as fixed—yet also answering to the ways we read today. It is a matter of "riding easy in the harness," as Robert Frost once said of democracy, and my practice ranges from the pliant to the fairly strict.

With one of the most frequently repeated phrases, for example—the line that introduces many individual speeches—I have been the freest, trying to hint at the speaker's nuance of the moment while retaining, at least, the habit of an introductory line for every speech. When Homer begins a speech of "winged words," however, I rarely omit the well-known phrase, yet I like the flight of the words to vary, with a sudden burst at times and a longer drift at others, depending on the words a character has to say. And so with the epithets that cling to the leading figures as closely as their names. According to what *perifrôn* Penelope is doing at the time, the sense of the epithet may go from the heroine's guardedness, her circumspection, to her self-possession, to her gift for great good wisdom, and her willingness to give that wisdom voice. With *pepnumenos* Telemachus, many qualities, from his wariness, to his growing poise, to his level-headed sense in action as well as speech, may be involved. And with *polumêtis* Odysseus, the epithet may extend from the hero's craft and cunning (murderous cunning when required), to his skill of hand or expertise at quick disguise and spinning yarns, to his zest for exploit and adventure. Odysseus, the virtuoso of sometimes doubtful virtue, is short on "character" in the sense of habitual goodness but long on "character" as John Crowe Ransom has described "the Shake-spearean, modern, passionately cherished, almost religious sense of the total individuality of a person who is rich in vivid yet contingent traits, even physical traits, that are not ethical at all." And as Ransom con-cludes, "this kind of character engages an auditor's love, and that is more than his ethical approval." Fullness of personality would seem to be essential, particularly for the "polytropic" hero, "the man of twists and turns"—the beggar-king who moves at will from self-effacement to self-assertion, from *mê tis* to *mêtis*, from Nobody to Odysseus, the wily raider of cities. (See notes 9.410 and 19.463–64.) In sum, as each Homeric epi-thet recurs, within its family of meanings I try to find a kindred English word that suits the character and the context.

Yet with longer repetitions in the *Odyssey* I like to repeat my English version closely, especially if the context shifts the function of the passage, and the opportunities for irony may be ample. For instance, the rituals prior to dining—rinsing the hands, serving the appetizers and the bread, and drawing a table toward a guest—recur, hospitably, in Ithaca and Sparta and Phaeacia, but in Circe's house they are part of her seductions, all of which Odysseus resists until the witch, who turned his shipmates into pigs, turns them back again to men. With one of the longest recur-rent passages in the poem, Penelope's deception of her suitors, the trans-lation, like Homer's original, repeats almost verbatim the weaving and unweaving of her web. First Antinous describes it in Book 2.101–22, indicting Penelope before the Ithacan assembly while, as the Introduc-tion observes, paying "reluctant tribute to the subtlety of her delaying tactics." Then when she describes her weaving in Book 19.153–75—adding her own words of indignation in 173–74—she defends herself, her fidelity and her finesse before the nameless stranger, though some suggest she is also secretly appealing to the man she senses is Odysseus. And finally in Book 24.139–61, a leading suitor, Amphimedon—killed by Odysseus and new to the world of the dead—cries out against Penelope's duplicity to the ghost of Agamemnon, who had been murdered by

Clytemnestra, his duplicitous wife. The suitor may trust that the warlord will be outraged when he hears of another wife's deceptions, but of course the wife of Odysseus, deliberately or not, sped the work of her avenging husband. That's what impresses Agamemnon, and so he calls for "a glorious song in praise of self-possessed Penelope" (24.218, see note 1.34–55)—the song that Homer has provided in the *Odyssey*. All in all, then, I have tried for repetition with a difference when variation seems of use, yet for virtual repetition in the longer passages, particularly when the weave of right and wrong, the Homeric moral fabric, is at issue.

Turning briefly to Homer's metrics, I would also like to hold a middle ground, here between his spacious hexameter line—his "ear, ear for the sea-surge," as Pound once heard it—and a tighter line more native to English verse. If, as Knox suggests, the strongest weapon in Homer's poetic arsenal is variety within a metrical norm, the translation opts for a freer give-and-take between the two, and one that offers more variety than uniformity in the end. Working from a five- or six-beat line while leaning more to six, I expand at times to seven beats—to convey the reach of a simile or the vehemence of a storm at sea or a long-drawn-out conclusion to a story—or I contract at times to three, to give a point in speech or action sharper stress. Free as it is, such interplay between variety and norm results, I suppose, from a kind of tug-of-war peculiar to translation: in this case, trying to capture the meaning of the Greek on the one hand, trying to find a cadence for one's English on the other, yet joining hands, if possible, to make a line of verse. I hope, at any rate, not only to give my own language a slight stretching now and then, but also to lend Homer the sort of range in rhythm, pace and tone that may make an *Odyssey* engaging to the reader.

And I would like to suggest, again at a far remove, another tension in Homer's metrics, his blend of mass and movement both—his lines have so much body or *ongkos* yet so much grace and speed. And so I have tried to make my own lines as momentarily end-stopped, and yet as steadily ongoing too, as English syntax and the breathing marks of punctuation will allow. My hope has been that each turn in the verse might mark a fresh beginning, moving toward a fresh conclusion, turning and returning, like a version in minuscule of a familiar Odyssean rhythm. In other words, I have tried to keep the master's voice in mind and to offer, if nothing more, a partial, distant echo of it in the reader's ear. But Homer's line is the line beyond compare, and I would only remind the reader of the Introduction's fine description: "The long line, which no matter how it varies in the opening and middle always ends in the same way, builds up its hypnotic effect in book after book, imposing on things and men and gods the same pattern, presenting in a rhythmic microcosm the wandering course to a fixed end which is the pattern of the rage of Achilles and the travels of Odysseus, of all natural phenomena and all human destinies."

In aiming for these and other objectives in a version of the *Odyssey*, I have had many kinds of help. The greatest has come from my collaborator, Bernard Knox, whom I would rather call a comrade. As we worked together on Sophocles and the *Iliad*, so we have done on the *Odyssey* as well. Not only has he written the Introduction and Notes on the Translation, but he has commented on my drafts for many years. And when I leaf through the pages now, his commentary seems to ring my typescript so completely that I might be looking at a worse-for-wear, dog-eared manuscript encircled by a scholiast's remarks. Yet Knox's gifts are larger, for he has offered me what Yeats would call Platonic tolerance and Doric discipline, and something even more basic to the *Iliad* and the *Odyssey*. Athena, disguised as Mentor, encourages Telemachus to live up to Odysseus, "a man . . . in words and action both" (2.305). My good fortune has been to work with such a man.

Several modern scholars and critics, cited among the further readings, have helped as well, and so have several modern translators of the *Odyssey*. Each has introduced me to a new aspect of the poem, another potential for the present. "For if it is true," as Maynard Mack proposes, "that what we translate from a given work is what, wearing the spectacles of our time, we see in it, it is also true that we see in it what we have the power to translate." So the help I have derived from others is considerable, and I would like to say my thanks to them, dividing them for convenience into groups. First the ones who have translated the *Odyssey* into prose: from Samuel Butler, A. T. Murray, revised by George E. Dimock, and George Herbert Palmer, to W. H. D. Rouse and R. D. Dawe, and in particular to Walter Shewring and to D. C. H. Rieu who, in consultation with Peter V. Jones, has revised the earlier work of his father, E. V. Rieu. Each presents an example of accuracy as well as grace, and the stronger that example, the more instructive each has been in bringing me somewhat closer to the Greek. And next the translators who have turned the *Odyssey* into verse: from Albert Cook to Ennis Rees to Richmond Lattimore, Allen Mandelbaum, Oliver Taplin and Robert Fitzgerald. Each presents a kind of aspiration, and I have learned from each, probably most from Fitzgerald, since he would persuade us that Homer is, as he described him, "a living presence bringing into life his great company of imagined persons." And finally there are the unapproachables, who either are too remote (and so to me, at least, examples not to follow), like certain Victorians, and Cowper, and Chapman—pace Keats—or are impossible to equal, like T. E. Lawrence at his best or Pope in the dozen books of the *Odyssey* that he produced himself.

Only a few of the recent translators have I known in person, yet we all may know each other in a way, having trekked across the same territory, perhaps having experienced the same nightmare that harried Pope throughout his Homeric efforts. "He was engaged in a long journey," as Joseph Spence reports Pope's dream, "puzzled which way to take, and full of fears" that it would never end. And if you reach the end, the fears may start in earnest. Your best hope, I suppose, and a distant one at that, is the one held out by Walter Benjamin in his essay "The Task of the Translator," where he writes, "even the greatest translation is destined to become part of the growth of its own language and eventually to be absorbed by its renewal."

Many friends have come to my side, some by reading, some by listening to me read, the work-in-progress, and responding with criticism or encouragement or a healthy blend of both. Most encouraging of all, none has asked me, "Why another *Odyssey*?" Each has understood, it seems, that if Homer was a performer, his translator might aim to be one as well; and no two performances of the same work—surely not of musical composition, so probably not of a work of language either—will ever be the same. The timbre and tempo of each will be distinct, let alone its deeper resonance, build and thrust. My thanks, then, to André Aciman, Clarence Brown, Andrew Ford, Rachel Hadas, Robert Hollander, David Lenson, Earl Miner, Sarah Nelson, Joyce Carol Oates, Jacqueline Savini, Ben Sonnenberg and Theodore Weiss. And I also thank the ones who invited me to try the work in public, and improve it in the bargain: Peter Bien at Dartmouth College, Ward Briggs III at the University of South Carolina, Larry Carver and Paul Woodruff at the University of Texas in Austin, and Karl Kirchwey at the Unterberg Poetry Center of the 92nd Street Y. And philhellenic thanks should go to Edmund Keeley, the English voice of the great modern Greek poets, for he accompanied me on Homer's *nostos*, reacting line by line and knowing well, with his Cavafy, that only Ithaca can give you "the marvelous journey" in the first place.

Several classicists have offered information and advice: Marilyn Arthur Katz, John Keaney, Richard Martin, Georgia Nugent, John Peradotto, Pietro Pucci and Froma Zeitlin. Together with the lexicons, Homeric and ancient Greek in general, the commentaries of other scholars have been my vade mecums: those on other English translations of the *Odyssey*—Ralph Hexter's on Robert Fitzgerald's and Peter Jones's on Richmond Lattimore's—and those on Homer's text itself: A. F.

Garvie's on Books 6 through 8 and R. B. Rutherford's on 19 and 20; the complete three-volume Oxford commentary compiled by M. Fernández-Galiano, J. B. Hainsworth, A. Heubeck, A. Hoekstra, J. Russo and S. West; and W. B. Stanford's edition of the *Odyssey* with his commentary on the poem. The first incentive for translating Homer came from the late Stanford, who, one afternoon in County Wicklow many years ago, sketched out a route for returning to the source. And in pursuit of it, I have often consulted the familiar spirits of Anne and Adam Parry.

The roofs of some great houses have extended welcome shelter to the translator and his work. Mary and Theodore Cross have turned Nantucket into Ithaca West with their Homeric hospitality. Princeton University gave me generous leaves of absence in the spring of 1992 and, adding a McCosh Faculty Fellowship for good measure, throughout the spring and fall semesters three years later. More important, the University has enabled me to study Homer with students who have been an education to me. The Program in Hellenic Studies appointed me to a Stanley J. Seeger Fellowship, which took me to the Ionian islands in the summer of 1994 (and persuaded me that unless Cephallenia—lying "low and away, the farthest out to sea" [9.27]—was actually Ithaca, Odysseus may never have got home at all). The Rockefeller Foundation provided Bernard Knox with a resident fellowship at the Villa Serbelloni in April 1991, when he began to write the Introduction. And the staff of Comparative Literature at Princeton, Carol Szymanski and Cass Garner, have been invaluable to us both as we prepared the work for publication.

To produce the book at hand, my editor, Kathryn Court, assisted by Laurie Walsh, has treated the writing and the writer, too, with insight, affection and address. As my manuscript editor, Beena Kamlani's efforts to tame and train a fairly unruly piece of work have been heroic. The good people at Viking Penguin—Barbara Grossman, Cathy Hemming, Paul Slovak, Leigh Butler—all have been loyal allies in New York, where Peter Mayer—like Peter Carson and Paul Keegan in London—has been a gracious host to the latest Homer in the house. Ann Gold with all her artistry, in coordination with Junie Lee, has designed a volume to companion the *Iliad* that came before it, and Maggie Payette and Neil Stuart have created its handsome jacket. Roni Axelrod and Cynthia Achar oversaw the production of the book, and Marjorie Horvitz's sharp eye was helpful to the text. Dan Lundy, Mary Sunden and Maria Barbieri have labored long and hard with Joe Marcey and Peter Smith to find this version of the *Odyssey* some readers. Mark Stafford, Susan Mosakowski and Mary Kohl have done the same to find some listeners, too, producing the Penguin Audiobook, read by Ian McKellen, who performs the translation as if he were personifying Homer. My former editor Alan Williams, who saw me through the straits of Aeschylus and Sophocles, gave my plans a timely push toward Troy, then home again to Greece with the old dog Argos as our guide. And through it all, without the unfailing stay and strategies of my friend and agent Georges Borchardt, assisted by Cindy Klein for several years, this translation might not have seen the light.

The *Odyssey*, the perennial poem of adventure, stops but never really ends. Seen in one way, Odysseus is forever outward bound, off to another country to appease Poseidon in the future, and changing through the centuries as he goes, "the man of twists and turns," of many incarnations, with as many destinations. Among them are Virgil's Aeneas, who makes his way toward Rome, and Dante's Ulysses moving toward "the world where no one lives," and Milton's Adam toward "a paradise within thee, happier far," and Tennyson's restless mariner toward "the baths / of all the western stars," and Joyce's Bloom toward the New Bloomusalem, until he settles for dear dirty Dublin and the moly that is Molly. For as Joyce makes clear, an equal adventure lies within the bounds of Homer's poem itself. There, after twenty years of warfaring and wayfaring, Odysseus circles back toward Penelope, and the two together reach their resting place and share a kingdom with their offspring, as if to say, with great good spirit, that life continues here and now at home. If the translation offers any sense of this, the translator thanks his daughters, Katya and Nina, and first and last the Muse he calls on in the dedication, Lynne.

R. F.

Princeton, N.J.
June 17, 1996

A NOTE ON THIS PRINTING:

This printing contains minor revisions of the text.

R.F. and B.K.

June 2001

THE GENEALOGY
OF THE ROYAL HOUSE
OF ODYSSEUS

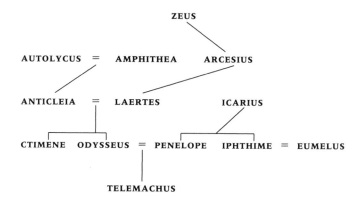

THE GENEALOGY
OF THE ROYAL HOUSE
OF PHAEACIA

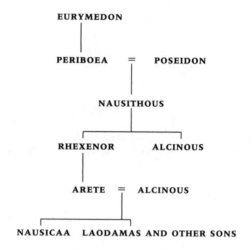

THE GENEALOGY
OF THEOCLYMENUS

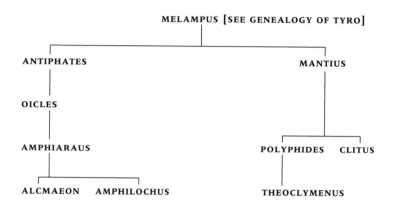

MELAMPUS [SEE GENEALOGY OF TYRO]

ANTIPHATES

OICLES

AMPHIARAUS

ALCMAEON   AMPHILOCHUS

MANTIUS

POLYPHIDES   CLITUS

THEOCLYMENUS

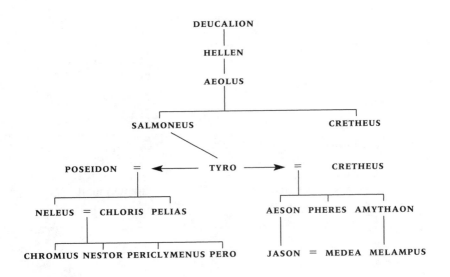

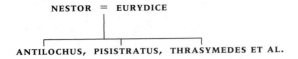

TEXTUAL VARIANTS FROM
THE OXFORD CLASSICAL TEXT

2.11	*duô*		9.199	*paisi*
2.191	Omitted		9.483	Omitted
3.131	Omitted		13.400	*anthrôpon*
4.399	*xeine*		15.345	Omitted
4.465	*ereeineis*		18.402	*metheêke*
4.783	Omitted		23.320	Omitted
5.91	Omitted			

NOTES ON
THE TRANSLATION

(Here and throughout the Pronouncing Glossary that follows, line numbers refer to the translation, where the line numbers of the Greek text will be found at the top of every page.)

1.20 *that year spun out by the gods when he should reach his home:* The tenth year since the sack of Troy, the twentieth year since Odysseus left Ithaca.

1.34–55 *Aegisthus, / the man Agamemnon's son, renowned Orestes, killed:* Throughout the *Odyssey*, the events in the House of Atreus will provide a continuous background to Homer's narrative. Taken in sequence, these events begin with the successful vengeance of Orestes—which is chosen by Zeus as an example of justice (1.34–55)—then are used by Athena to rouse the courage of Telemachus (1.341–47), and then by Nestor (3.289–357) not only to encourage the prince but also to caution him with the additional stories of Clytemnestra's infidelity and the wanderings of Menelaus, absent from Argos when Agamemnon was assassinated. Next Menelaus tells Telemachus how Proteus informed him of Agamemnon's murder by Aegisthus (4.573–604); and the crime is dramatized when, in the underworld, Odysseus learns from the ghost of Agamemnon how both he and Cassandra were murdered by his wife together with her lover (11.457–98). However optimistic the climax of Orestes' vengeance, in other words, each version of Agamemnon's death presents a greater darkness, and so a starker foil for the luminous reunion of Odysseus and Penelope; until at the end of the *Odyssey* (24.210–23) Agamemnon's ghost calls for a song to immortalize the virtue of Penelope and another to condemn the perfidy of Clytemnestra. As W. B. Stanford observes (his note 24.196–98), Homer has provided the first, and Aeschylus, in the *Oresteia*, the second. See note 4.590.

1.62 *Atlas, wicked Titan:* In other accounts, Atlas is a giant who holds up the sky "with his hard and unwearying hands" (Hesiod, *Theogony* 519). Here he apparently stands in the sea and supports pillars that perform the same function. His location in the sea rather than on land (as in Hesiod) may be due to influence from Near Eastern myths. Why he is called "wicked" we do not know.

1.375 *The Achaeans' Journey Home from Troy:* Phemius' song is one of those poems (now lost) that the Greeks called *Nostoi*—Returns Home. During the capture and sack of Troy, Ajax, son of Oileus (not the Great Ajax, son of Telamon, who had killed himself before Troy fell: see 11.620–45 and note 11.625), attempted to rape Cassandra, King Priam's daughter, in the temple of Athena, where she had taken refuge. The Achaeans failed to punish him for this offense, and Athena retaliated by arranging for storm winds to blow most of them off course on their way home. Ajax was killed by Poseidon when he had almost reached home (see 4.560–73), Menelaus wandered for seven years, Odysseus for ten.

1.443 *king of Ithaca:* The Greek word translated as "king," *basileus,* does not carry the connotation of hereditary monarchical rule inherent in the English word. In the kingdom of Phaeacia, Alcinous announces: "There are twelve peers of the realm who rule our land, / thirteen, counting myself" (8.435–36). The word he uses is *basilêes.* They are all kings, but he is, so to speak, top king. That is why Telemachus can say: "I'd be happy to take the crown if Zeus presents it" (1.447). It is a position won by acclaim and superior wealth and achievement, and clearly Antinous, as the leader of the suitors, thinks himself in line for the position once he marries Penelope.

2.172 *they swooped away on the right:* The lucky side for omens, lucky at least for Telemachus in this case. The idea that signs on the right are lucky and on the left unlucky is common in many cultures and languages: our word "sinister," for example, is the Latin word for "left." See 15.179–84, 588–98, 20.269, 24.348–50.

2.371 *splitting up his goods:* In the event of Telemachus' death, the palace and all its property would revert to Penelope and whichever of the suitors she chose to marry. The suitor here seems to be suggesting a division of Telemachus' property as a consolation prize for those who do not win Penelope's hand. The speech emphasizes once again the reckless illegality of the suitors' proceedings. See Introduction, pp. 31, 39.

3.46 *daughter of Zeus whose shield is storm and thunder:* The shield is the aegis (literally "goatskin"). It is sometimes displayed by Zeus himself, and by Apollo, as well as by Athena. Its shape is not easily determined from the text: at times it seems to be a shield, for the figure of the Gorgon's head and other forms of terror appear on it. Its effect seems to be to stiffen morale among those it is raised to protect and inspire terror in those who face it.

3.81–83 *roving the waves like pirates:* See Introduction, pp. 28–29.

3.121–25 *There Ajax lies ... Achilles ... Patroclus ... Antilochus:* Ajax, son of Telamon, the greatest of the Achaean warriors after Achilles, killed himself when the arms and armor of the dead Achilles, offered by his mother, Thetis, as a prize to the bravest champion, were given to Odysseus (see 11.620–45 and note 11.625). Achilles was killed by an arrow shot by Paris, son of Priam; Patroclus, his closest friend, was killed by Euphorbus, Hector and Apollo. Antilochus, who had come to the aid of his father, Nestor, was killed by the Ethiopian prince Memnon, an ally of the Trojans.

3.150 *[Athena's] rage:* See note 1.375.

3.213–14 *the shining son / of lionhearted Achilles:* Neoptolemus (whose name means "new war") came to Troy after Achilles' death and, together with Philoctetes, who wielded the unerring bow of Heracles, led the fight against the Trojans (see 11.583–606). Idomeneus, a Cretan king, is often mentioned later in Odysseus' false travel tales (see 13.294, 14.269, 19.218).

3.215 *Philoctetes:* His safe return concludes a well-known story about the final phase of the Trojan War. The Achaeans, unable to take Troy, learned of a prophecy that they would be able to do so only with the aid of Philoctetes and his bow, a famous weapon that he had inherited from Heracles. They had to send an embassy to Lemnos to persuade him to come and help them. This embassy is the subject of Sophocles' tragedy *Philoctetes*.

3.346–47 *Orestes / home from Athens:* In Athenian tragedy, he always comes home from Phocis, in central Greece. This may be due to the fact that Aeschylus, in the last play of the *Oresteia* (458 B.C.), brings him to Athens to stand trial for his mother's murder—a *coup de théâtre* that would have been spoiled if he had come from there in the first place.

3.373 *cut out the victims' tongues:* The tongues of the sacrificed animals, like the thighbones, are reserved for the gods. In this case they were cut out when the bulls were sacrificed in the morning (3.6–10) but put aside as a late evening offering. The first drops of wine are for the libation: the wine poured on the fire for the gods.

3.423 *Zeus's daughter . . . his third born:* This is a literal rendering of Athena's title *Tritogeneia*, but the meaning of the word is disputed. Some ancient sources connect it with Lake Tritonis in Libya, where Zeus sent Athena to be reared, or with the river Triton in Boeotia. A modern explanation compares the Athenian *Tritopateres*, i.e., genuine ancestors: this would give the meaning "genuine daughter of Zeus."

3.485–520 *Athena came . . . / to attend her sacred rites:* What happens in the following passage is a sacrifice to the gods that is also a feast for the human worshipers (this was the way meat was eaten in the ancient world). The animal is placed at the altar, and the sacrificers wash their hands to establish purity for the ritual. They scatter barley on the victim, then stun the animal with a blow on the head, pull back its head and cut its throat over the altar. The animal's skin is taken off and a portion of the meat prepared for the gods. This is a choice portion, the meat of the thighbones: it is wrapped in a double fold of fat and the outside covered with small pieces of meat from different parts of the animal. This portion is burned over the fire—the smoke and savor go up to the gods above. Wine is poured over it, a libation. The sacrificers at last begin their meal—with the entrails, which they have roasted on forks over the fire. They then carve the carcass and roast portions of meat on spits and set them out for the feast.

4.6 *the son of great Achilles:* Neoptolemus, who married Hermione, the daughter of Helen and Menelaus. See 11.576ff. and note 3.213–14.

4.96 *Three times in the circling year the ewes give birth:* A typical traveler's yarn about a far-off region—it is an impossibility for ewes to bear three cycles of lambs in every year, since the gestation period for sheep is about 150 days.

4.106 *I lost this handsome palace built for the ages:* Presumably because he did not see it for seventeen years; but also because Paris and Helen, when they left, stripped it of all its treasures. In the *Iliad* the terms of the duel between Menelaus and Paris in Book 3 are that if Paris wins he will keep "Helen and all her wealth"; if not, the Trojans will surrender Helen and "those treasures" (3.86–88).

4.144 *tripods:* Large metal pots or cauldrons standing on three legs so they can straddle a fire. Often highly ornamented for presentation as a gift or prize, they were unusually valuable and rare.

4.165 *Odysseus' feet were like the boy's:* Since ancient Greeks went barefoot or wore sandals most of the time, familiarity with the shape of someone else's foot was nothing strange. In Aeschylus' tragedy *The Libation Bearers* Electra recognizes the footprints left on the ground by her brother Orestes.

4.304–6 *What a piece of work the hero dared:* Odysseus' most famous exploit, celebrated in song at the court of Alcinous (8.559–84) and invoked by Athena disguised as Mentor to spur him on in the fight against the suitors (22.236–41), was to plan and participate in the stratagem that brought about the fall of Troy—the wooden horse in which he and a band of Achaean heroes were concealed while the Trojans brought it into the city as an offering to Athena.

4.454 *his lovely ocean-lady:* The wife of Proteus, who is either Thetis or Amphitrite.

4.560–73 *Ajax . . . went down:* Little Ajax, son of Oileus. See note 1.375.

4.574–86 *Agamemnon got away / in his beaked ships:* This passage shows Homer's uncertain grasp of the geography of the western side of the Aegean Sea. Agamemnon's home is Argos; he would have no reason to sail as far south as Cape Malea on his way home. Furthermore, the prevailing wind at the cape is NE; it is the wind that blows Odysseus' ship SW into the unknown world. It is also far from clear exactly where Aegisthus' home is. It must be close to Agamemnon's if Aegisthus is able to prepare an ambush in his palace, then go out to meet the king as soon as his spy reports his arrival, yet at 581–83 it sounds as if it were far away. The confusion here may stem from the amalgamation of two different accounts of Agamemnon's return home. See Introduction, p. 26.

4.590 *One whole year he'd watched:* Presumably Aegisthus posted the watchman during the tenth year of the Trojan War, the year that Calchas has prophesied would see the city's fall. A simple hireling of Aegisthus in the *Odyssey*, the watchman becomes a loyal servant of Agamemnon in Aeschylus' *Oresteia*, where he unwittingly ensures the king's death by rushing the news of his arrival to Clytemnestra, his queen.

4.632–41 *it's not for you to die:* This special dispensation for Menelaus has nothing to do with merit: he qualifies for Elysium simply because he is the husband of Helen, who will later be worshiped as a goddess at Sparta and elsewhere in Greece.

4.663 *three stallions and a chariot:* Two under the yoke and a third to serve as a trace horse.

4.738 *he boarded ship for Pylos days ago:* Actually Athena did, disguised as Mentor, and the goddess set sail with Telemachus for Pylos four days before.

4.857 *sifting barley into a basket:* Barley is scattered on the sacrificial animal before it is killed (see 3.498–502). We do not know what Penelope intends to do with it: pour it out as a sort of libation? offer it to the goddess?

5.60 *that island worlds apart:* Ogygia, home of Calypso.

5.134–40 *Orion . . . Demeter . . . Iasion:* Orion was a giant huntsman with whom Eos, the dawn goddess, fell in love; after his death he became a constellation. Demeter was the goddess of the crops and especially of wheat; the place where she made love with Iasion was a field ritually plowed with a triple furrow at the beginning of the plowing season.

5.161 *the guide and giant-killer:* In the Greek, two regular epithets of Hermes. He is called the guide or escort (the meaning of the word is disputed) because he is often sent by Zeus to act in that role, as at the start of Book 24, when he escorts the dead souls of the suitors to the underworld. The other epithet refers to the fact that, at the request of Zeus, Hermes killed a monster of immense strength called Argos, who had eyes all over his body, so that he could keep some of them open when he slept. He was killed because Hera had sent him to guard Io, a woman Zeus was in love with, whom Hera had changed into a cow.

5.205 *the Styx:* The main river of the underworld was the guarantor of oaths sworn by the gods. Any one of the gods, Hesiod tells us (*Theogony* 793–806), who pours a libation of the river's water and swears falsely is paralyzed for one year and for nine years after that is excluded from the feasts and assemblies of the gods. See note 10.563–65.

5.299–302 *the stars . . . the Plowman . . . the Great Bear . . . the Hunter:* "Plowman" is the English equivalent of the Greek name *Boötes*, a constellation that sets in the late evening. "The Wagon" is the constellation also known as the Big Dipper and the Great Bear. As seen from the northern hemisphere, it never disappears below the horizon or, as Homer puts it, "plunge[s] in the Ocean's baths." The Great Bear is referred to as "she" (301) because she was originally the nymph Callisto, who ranged the woods as one of the virgin companions of the goddess Artemis. Zeus made her pregnant, and when this could no longer be concealed, Artemis changed her into a bear and killed her. Zeus in turn changed her into the constellation. The Hunter is Orion.

5.367 *Ino, a mortal woman once:* Ino, daughter of Cadmus, jumped into the sea at Corinth with her infant son in her arms, in flight from her insane husband, Athamas. Her new name—Leucothea—means "white goddess."

6.156–57 *fling his arms around her knees . . . / plead for help:* What Odysseus declines to adopt is the position of the suppliant—kneeling, clasping the knees of the person supplicated, reaching up to his (or her) chin. It is a gesture that symbolizes the utter helplessness of the suppliant, his abject dependence, but at the same time applies a physical and moral constraint on the person so addressed. The Greeks believed that Zeus was the protector and champion of suppliants. See 10.359, 530.

6.245 *I would be embarrassed:* He has of course been naked all along, but shielding his privates with the olive branch—"the first gentleman in Europe," as Joyce described Odysseus in this scene. Since, however, men are regularly bathed by young women elsewhere in the poem (3.521–24, 4.56–57), his modesty here seems strange. It may be due to the fact that, unlike Telemachus when he is bathed by Nestor's youngest daughter and Odysseus himself when bathed by Circe's handmaids, he is now "a terrible sight . . . all crusted, caked with brine." From Homer's point of view, of course, it is necessary to get him off by himself so that Athena can make him "taller to all eyes, / his build more massive now."

7.62–63 *Arete, she is called, and earns the name: / she answers all our prayers:* The name brings to mind the Greek verb *araomai,* "pray," which suggests the meaning "prayed for" (by her parents) as well as "prayed to" (by suppliants like Odysseus).

7.64 *the same stock that bred our King Alcinous:* See Genealogy (adapted from Garvie), p. 498.

7.233 *Spinners:* The Fates. They were visualized as three women spinning thread, a normal household occupation for Greek women: the thread was a human life. After Homer they were given names: Clotho ("Spinner"), Lachesis ("Allotter"—she decided how long the thread should be), and Atropos ("one who cannot be turned back"), who cuts the thread.

7.368 *more distant than Euboea:* A long, narrow island off the eastern coast of Greece; for the Phaeacians, who apparently live in the fabulous west, it is "off at the edge of the world" (369).

7.371–72 *Rhadamanthys . . . Tityus:* Rhadamanthys was a legendary Cretan king who after his death went to Elysium (4.635). Tityus was one of the great legendary sinners; for his attempt to rape the goddess Leto, the mother of Apollo and Artemis, he was eternally tortured in the lower world (11.660–68). Why Rhadamanthys went to Euboea to visit him we do not know.

8.41 *a crew of fifty-two young sailors:* The ship is apparently a penteconter, and so requires fifty oarsmen plus two officers.

8.89–98 *The Strife Between Odysseus and Achilles:* Our sources do not explain the cause of the strife between the two. See Introduction, p. 23.

8.129–39 *young champions rose for competition:* The translation attempts to gloss the Homeric names of the Phaeacian competitors in terms of their root meanings in Greek, all of them fittingly nautical for a seafaring people. In doing so, the translator has followed the lead of earlier translators of the *Odyssey*, W. H. D. Rowse (1937) and Robert Fitzgerald (1961), as well as his own practice in glossing the names of the Nereids in the *Iliad* (18.43–56). The translator uses the same strategy with other, though far from all, "significant names" in the *Odyssey*: with those of Odysseus' forebears, for example, as Autolycus cites them in Book 19.460–64, and with Odysseus' fictitious parents in Book 24.340–42. See notes 9.410, 10.563–65, 19.299, 19.460–64, 24.341–42.

8.144 *the length two mules will plow a furrow:* This length (*ouron*) is the customary length Greek plowmen went before turning; we have no accurate figure for it, and the usual guess is 30 to 40 meters.

8.302–410 *The Love of Ares and Aphrodite:* Hephaestus, the smith god, is lame. This may be a reflection of the fact that in a community where agriculture and war are the predominant features in the life of its men, someone with weak legs and strong arms would probably become a blacksmith. He seems to have been lame from birth: in the *Iliad* (18.461–64) he says that his mother, Hera, threw him out of Olympus because of this defect.

8.321–22 *Lemnos:* A center of the cult of Hephaestus, Lemnos was an island noted for its volcanic gas and inhabited by people whom Homer identifies as Sintians (see 8.334), who rescued Hephaestus after his fall from Mount Olympus.

8.361 *our Father:* Zeus, the father of both Aphrodite and Hephaestus.

9.27 *[Ithaca] lies low and away, the farthest out to sea:* For the vagueness of Homeric geography see Introduction, p. 26, and note 4.574–86.

9.74 *the triple cry:* A funeral rite, presumably a farewell to the dead; three times presumably to make sure the dead hear the cry.

9.232 *twenty cups of water he'd stir in one of wine:* A powerful wine indeed. Ancient Greeks drank their wine diluted with water (as do many modern Greeks), but the usual proportions of water to wine were 3:1 or 3:2.

9.410 *Nobody—that's my name:* The Greek word *outis*, the name Odysseus gives himself, is formed from the normal Greek locution for "nobody"—*ou tis*, "not anybody." This enables Homer to make brilliant use of wordplay that cannot be adequately reproduced in English. When his fellow Cyclops ask Polyphemus why he is making such an uproar and he tells them "Nobody's killing me now by fraud and not by force," they naturally misunderstand it and reply, "*If . . . nobody's trying to overpower you . . .*" (456–57). But in Greek their reply has a different form for "no one": not *ou tis* but *mê tis*, the usual form for use after the word "if." But *mê tis*, "not anyone," sounds exactly the same as *mêtis*, a key word of the *Odyssey*, the main characteristic of its hero: craft, cunning. And Polyphemus is in fact being overpowered by the *mêtis*, the craft and cunning of Odysseus. See, for example, 4.119, 8.229, 9.452–63, 508–14, 573, 20.23, 23.142.

9.560–62 *Odysseus, / raider of cities . . . / Laertes' son who makes his home in Ithaca:* For the importance of Odysseus' declaration of his name, see Introduction, pp. 32, 39.

9.590–95 *if he's fated to see / his people once again . . . let him find a world of pain at home:* Polyphemus' curse will be repeated by Tiresias as prophecy in the underworld (11.125–35) and by Circe as a solemn warning on the island of Aeaea (12.148–53).

10.563–65 *there into Acheron . . . rivers flow:* The names Acheron and Styx are glossed in the translation; the Greek name of the River of Fire is Pyriphlegethon and that of the River of Tears, Cocytus. Milton has made their names and etymologies resound in *Paradise Lost*:

> . . . four infernal Rivers that disgorge
> Into the burning Lake their baleful streams:
> Abhorred *Styx* the flood of deadly hate,
> Sad *Acheron* of sorrow, black and deep;
> *Cocytus*, nam'd of lamentation loud
> Heard on the rueful stream; fierce *Phlegeton*
> Whose waves of torrent fire inflame with rage.   2.575–81

11.146 *a fan to winnow grain:* Before the invention of a threshing machine in 1784, grain was beaten on a flat surface on a windy hill; it was then thrown up into the wind to blow away the chaff in a shallow basket fixed to the end of a long handle, a winnowing fan.

11.154 *a gentle, painless death, far from the sea:* Aeschylus and Sophocles may have understood the words as "out of the sea," for they both wrote tragedies based on a legend that Odysseus was killed by a fishbone, either through blood poisoning from a scratch or as the result of a wound inflicted by a spear tipped with fishbone, which Telegonus, his son by Circe, wielded. But the words "a gentle, painless death" tell against this interpretation.

11.268 *Tyro:* Among her descendants are Nestor, Jason, the leader of the Argonauts, and Melampus, the grandfather of Theoclymenus. For Tyro's line, see Introduction, p. 26, and Genealogies (adapted from Jones and Stanford), pp. 499, 500.

11.307 *Epicaste:* She is called Iocaste (Jocasta) in Sophocles' play *Oedipus the King*, in which Oedipus, when he learns the truth, blinds himself and leaves Thebes, in exile.

11.318 *Chloris:* Daughter of Amphion of Orchomenos (not the Amphion who founded Thebes; see 11.298). She was married to Neleus, father of Nestor. Neleus would give the hand of their daughter Pero only to the man who could recover his stolen cattle from Iphiclus, who had driven the herd from Pylos to his home at Phylace in Thessaly. Melampus, captured in an attempt to recover the cattle, was imprisoned but released because of his prophetic skills. A different form of the story is given at 15.250–85. See note ad loc., and Genealogies, pp. 499, 500.

11.343 *Castor ... Polydeuces:* Twin sons of Leda, who are often referred to as the Dioscuri—"sons of Zeus." The extraordinary privilege granted them—that they should come back to life on alternate days—was attributed to the fact that one was the son of Zeus and the other of Tyndareus, Leda's human husband. (The usual English form of Polydeuces is Pollux.)

11.351 *Otus ... Ephialtes:* The best-known version of the story is that they piled Mount Pelion on Mount Ossa in Thessaly to reach Mount Olympus, the home of the gods; here the gods are imagined as living in the sky.

11.364 *Ariadne:* She helped Theseus kill the Minotaur and left Crete with him but, according to the usual version of the story, was abandoned by him on the island of Dia off the northern shore of Crete (on the island of Naxos in other accounts), where Dionysus came to take her as his bride, and she "play[ed] the queen," as Robert Graves has said, "to nobler company." Why the god denounced her in Homer's version we do not know.

11.369 *Eriphyle:* She accepted from Polynices, leader of the Seven Against Thebes, a necklace as a bribe for persuading her husband, the prophet Amphiaraus, to join the expedition, in which he met his death.

11.591 *Eurypylus:* Like Amphiaraus, he lost his life as the result of a bribe, this time one accepted from King Priam of Troy by his mother, who persuaded her son to fight on the Trojan side.

11.625 *Pallas and captive Trojans served as judges:* The captured sons of the Trojans would obviously be competent judges of the fighting qualities of their opponents. Athena, however, who favored Odysseus in all things, was hardly an impartial judge. The unexpected decision was such a shock to Ajax that he went berserk and tried to kill Agamemnon, Menelaus and Odysseus but, thwarted, killed himself instead. His suicide is the subject of Sophocles' tragedy *Ajax*. See note 3.121–25.

11.660–68 *Tityus:* See note 7.371–72.

11.669–80 *Tantalus:* Homer takes for granted the audience's knowledge of Tantalus' offense. Later accounts of it differ in detail, but food and drink play a part in most of them. One version has Tantalus, who was a confidant and often invited guest of the gods, invite them to his palace for a feast and serve up to them the cooked flesh of his son Pelops, as a test of their divine powers of perception. They all refused the meat, except Demeter, who gnawed on a shoulder. After Tantalus was dispatched to his everlasting punishment in Hades—doomed, fittingly enough, to eternal thirst and hunger—Pelops was put back together again and brought to life; the missing part of his shoulder was replaced by a marble prosthesis, which was on display centuries later at Olympia, the site of the games founded by Pelops.

11.681–89 *Sisyphus:* A great trickster (in some accounts he is the real father of Odysseus), who tricked even the God of Death. On his deathbed he told his wife not to perform the funeral rituals for him. Once in Hades, he complained that his wife had left him unburied and asked permission to return and persuade her to do her duty. Permission was given, but once at home, he refused to return and lived on to a ripe old age.

11.690–718 *Heracles:* The greatest of the Greek heroes, Heracles eventually, after his death, became an immortal god. He was the son of Zeus and a mortal woman, Alcmena. Zeus intended that he should lord it over all who dwell around him, but Zeus's jealous wife, Hera, contrived to have that destiny conferred on Eurystheus, king of Argos, to whom Heracles was to be subject. At Eurystheus' command, Heracles performed the famous twelve labors: among them was the capture of the three-headed dog, Cerberus, the guardian of the entrance to the underworld. Homer attributes Heracles' death to Hera's anger, but in other poets' versions of his death Hera plays no part. See notes 3.213–14, 3.215.

12.68 *Clashing Rocks:* The Greek word Homer uses means something like "Wandering Rocks" but clearly he is drawing on the story of the Symplegades (a word which *does* mean Clashing Rocks), between which even the doves bringing ambrosia to Zeus could get caught. They are a prominent feature of the story of Jason and the Argonauts, which is mentioned as a well-known theme for song at 12.76–80. See Introduction, p. 26.

12.285 *Hyperion:* A name which, whatever its true etymology, suggests the meaning "the one who goes above," and is another name of Helios, the sun.

12.337 *the night's third watch:* The night was divided into three parts, each approximately four hours long.

12.384 *fresh green leaves ... for the rite:* A substitute for the barley scattered over the sacrificial animal. Later, lacking wine, they made libations with water. It is appropriate that, since the slaughter of the cattle is an offense to the god, the ritual should fall far short of proper procedure.

13.180 *Then pile your huge mountain round about their port:* For Zeus's encouragement of Poseidon here, see Introduction, pp. 43–47.

14.63 *And you replied, Eumaeus, loyal swineherd:* Homer is fond of introducing Eumaeus in the second person, as he often does Patroclus and Menelaus in the *Iliad.* It may be a metrical convenience or a vestige of older, bardic practice or here, as Stanford (in his note 14.55), referring to Eustathius, reports, "a mark of the poet's special affection for Eumaeus"—an idea which Stanford rejects, but some other commentators accept.

14.494 *the forest nymphs and Hermes:* One share of Eumaeus' supper is set aside for a local cult of the wood nymphs, another share for Hermes, in his role as patron god of herdsmen.

15.21 *bride-price:* See 8.361 and Introduction, pp. 14, 17.

15.80–81 *you know, / 'Welcome the coming, speed the parting guest!':* This is Pope's translation of the line, adopted here but enclosed in quotation marks as if, by a spin of reverse English, it had become proverbial in our language, even though spoken by Menelaus centuries before. Pope in his Horatian Imitations (*Satires* II.ii.160), introducing it as "sage Homer's rule," later revised the line to read "welcome the coming, speed the going guest." This translator prefers the Odyssean version. See Introduction, p. 31.

15.250–85 *Melampus' line of seers:* A different version of the story told at 11.318–40. Here Neleus drives Melampus out and confiscates his property. We do not know why Phylacus (Iphiclus in the other version) imprisoned Melampus, nor why he was persecuted by the Furies, nor how he avenged himself on Neleus. In this version he wins Neleus' daughter Pero not for himself but for his brother. Homer does not mention it, but we learn from Hesiod that Melampus, who could understand the speech of birds and animals, was released from prison because he had heard worms in the palace roofbeams discussing how thoroughly they had undermined the structure, and so Melampus warned his captor that the building would soon collapse. See Genealogies, pp. 499, 500, and note 11.318.

15.276 *undone by a bribe his wife accepted:* See note 11.369.

16.131–35 *Zeus made our line a line of only sons:* See Genealogy, p. 497.

17.602–9 *Telemachus shook with a lusty sneeze:* Ancient Greeks regarded a sneeze as an omen, since it is something a human being can neither produce at will nor control when it arrives. Hence it must be the work of a god.

18.6–9 *Arnaeus ... Irus:* Arnaeus is called Irus presumably because, like Iris the messenger of the gods, he runs errands for the suitors.

18.277 *Ionian Argos:* The adjective usually designates Greek settlements on the Aegean islands and what is now the western coast of Turkey, whose inhabitants spoke a dialect known as Ionian. Argos is in the Peloponnese, but there is good evidence for an Ionian presence there in very early times.

19.94 *thanks to god Apollo:* In his aspect of *Apollo kourotrophos,* the rearer of young men.

19.203–5 *Minos:* The legendary king of Crete, whose name has been given to the civilization unearthed by archaeologists in the early years of our century. Minos ruled Crete either in nine-year cycles or, as Plato understood the Homeric line, went every ninth year to the cave of Zeus to confer with the god and bring back laws for his people. Together with another Cretan king, Rhadamanthys, he is sometimes mentioned as one of the judges in the world of the dead. See 11.650–55.

19.299 Destroy, *I call it—I hate to say its name:* "desTroy" is T.E. Lawrence's rendering of a remarkable turn of phrase in Penelope's speech: she calls the city she does not wish to mention *kakoilion,* combining the Greek word for evil—*kakos*—with the name *Ilion,* an alternative name for Troy. See 19.673, 23.21.

19.407 *your master's . . . equal in years:* The pause indicated in the translation, allowing the reader to imagine for a second that Penelope has penetrated Odysseus' disguise, attempts to reproduce a similar effect that Homer produced for the ears of his audience, but through Greek word order rather than a pause.

19.463–64 Odysseus . . . / *the Son of Pain, a name he'll earn in full:* The name "Odysseus" may be associated with the Greek verb *odussomai*—to feel anger toward, to rage or hate. The verb, however, appears to function in the middle voice, a cross between the active and the passive, implying that Odysseus is not only an agent of rage or hatred but its target too. Particularly to the point are the discussions by John Peradotto (pp. 129–34) and George Dimock (pp. 257–63), who suggest that Odysseus suffers for making others suffer, not as an end in itself but, insofar as *odussomai* brings to mind the verb *ôdinô*—to suffer pain, especially the pain of labor—as the rigors by which the hero brings his identity to life. Consequently Dimock proposes that we translate "Odysseus" as "man of pain"— active and passive, doing and done to, agent and victim both, inflicting and bearing pain yet somehow born himself in the process. That is the version which this translator adopts and adapts throughout his work. Yet when Homer intends a pun between the root of the hero's name and the hostility he arouses in others, the translator tries to develop some wordplay, wherever possible, between "Odysseus" and those "dead set" against him. See 1.75, 5.373, 19.317; and, as variations on the theme, 3.106, 4.364, 5.467, 23.349–51, 24.341–42.

19.585–90 *Pandareus' daughter, the nightingale:* Her name was Aedon (which is the Greek word for nightingale). She had only one son, but her sister-in-law Niobe had many; in a fit of jealous rage, she tried to kill Niobe's eldest son but by mistake killed her own son, Itylus. Zeus turned her into a nightingale, mourning her son in song forever. There is a different version of the story that is familiar to us from the Latin and our own poets, in which Procne, an Athenian princess, married Tereus, a Thracian king. Tereus raped Procne's sister, Philomela, and then cut out her tongue to prevent her from denouncing him to her sister. But Philomela wove the story into a tapestry to show Procne, who then killed Itys, her son by Tereus, cooked the flesh and served it to her husband, who ate it. When told what he had eaten, Tereus tried to kill both sisters, but Zeus turned them all into birds: Procne became the nightingale, eternally mourning Itys, Philomela the swallow and Tereus the hoopoe.

19.633–38 *Two gates . . . for our evanescent dreams:* Why the ivory gate should be the exit for false dreams and the gate of horn for true has never been satisfactorily explained.

19.644 *a contest with those axes:* There has been much controversy about the axes and still no agreement. When in 21.137–41 Telemachus sets them up for the contest, he digs a trench in the dirt floor of the hall, plants them in it in a straight line and stamps the earth down to hold them firm. Many editors have assumed that what he planted in the trench were the ax blades, with the holes for the helves lined up. But to shoot an arrow through such a lineup, the archer would have to be lying on the floor, an impossible position from which to draw the bow, not to mention making such a difficult shot. In any case, we are told (21.467–68) that when Odysseus does shoot an arrow through the axes he is sitting on a stool. So the holes the arrow goes through must be at least two feet off the ground. The only possible solution seems to be that the axes all have a metal ring on the end of the helve, presumably so that the ax could be hung on a nail in the wall.

20.73–87 *the whirlwinds swept away Pandareus' daughters:* This story of the death of Pandareus' daughters, none of them named, seems to have no connection with the tale of the nightingale. See 19.585–90 and note ad loc.

20.307 *Apollo's grand festal day:* It is a significant coincidence that the archery contest, which will bring about the deaths of the suitors and Odysseus' reinstatement in his own home, is to take place on the festival day of Apollo, the archer god. See 8.246–60 and note 21.16.

20.395 *Ghosts, look:* Presumably those of the suitors, glimpsed here in a visionary, prophetic way but clearly present, following their slaughter in Book 22, at the beginning of Book 24.

21.16 *Eurytus:* One of the great archers Odysseus mentions when he claims mastery of the bow among the Phaeacians (8.246–60). Eurytus had even challenged Apollo to a contest, an insult for which the god killed him. According to later sources, Apollo had given him a bow and trained him in its use; if so, the bow Iphitus gave Odysseus comes from the hand of the archer god himself, to be used against the suitors on Apollo's feast day. See note 20.307.

21.55 *inserted the key and aiming straight and true, / shot back the bolts:* The mechanism of Homeric doorlocks is so mysterious that Joyce's parody in *Ulysses* may be the best commentary on this passage:

> How did the centripetal remainer afford egress to the centrifugal departer?
> By inserting the barrel of an arruginated male key in the hole of an unstable female lock, obtaining a purchase on the bow of the key and turning its wards from right to left, withdrawing a bolt from its staple, pulling inward spasmodically an obsolescent unhinged door and revealing an aperture for free egress and free ingress.

21.331–40 *Pirithous:* A friend of Theseus and his companion on many of his exploits, he was king of the Lapiths, a tribe living in Thessaly, a country famous for its horses. He invited to his wedding with Hippodameia the Centaurs, who were later visualized as half man and half horse but whom Homer describes in the *Iliad* (1.312) as "wild brutes of the mountains." Their leader, Eurytion, got drunk at the feast and tried to rape the bride (whose name, incidentally, means "tamer of horses"). The resultant battle was a favorite theme for temple sculpture (it is featured, for example, on the west pediment of the temple of Zeus at Olympia); it symbolized the fight between civilized Greeks and savage barbarians.

22.134–36 *a side-door was fitted into the main wall:* Commentators have puzzled over the architectural details of the palace in vain. The confusion is probably the result of a combination of different bardic formulas over time, which became the standard version. In any case, the original audience, swept along by the performance, would not have worried too much about the details. See Introduction, p. 21.

22.241 *your fine strategic stroke:* Odysseus' stratagem of the Trojan Horse, which held the Achaean force that leveled Troy. See note 4.304–6.

24.126 *to urge Odysseus to sail:* In a later epic poem, the *Cypria,* we are told that Odysseus, unwilling to leave his wife and baby son, feigned madness to escape the summons to the war against Troy. He drove his plow, harnessed to an ass and an ox, sowing salt in the furrows. Palamedes, the cleverest of the chiefs assembled for the expedition, put Odysseus' baby son in the path of the plow; Odysseus reined it in, his deceit exposed. "But once at the war," as Joyce reminded Frank Budgen, "the conscientious objector became a *jusqu'auboutist.*"

24.341–42 *my father's Unsparing, son of old King Pain, / and my name's Man of Strife . . . :* See note 19.463–64.

SUGGESTIONS FOR FURTHER READING

I. Texts and Commentaries

Homeri Opera. Ed. by T. W. Allen. 2d ed., Vols. III and IV. Oxford Classical Texts. London and New York, 1917.

The Odyssey. Ed. with Introduction, Commentary and Indexes by W. B. Stanford. 2d ed., 2 vols. London and New York, reprinted with alterations and additions, 1967.

A Commentary on Homer's Odyssey. Vol. I: Books I–VIII, A. Heubeck, S. West, J. B. Hainsworth. Vol. II: Books IX–XVI, A. Heubeck, A. Hoekstra. Vol. III: Books XVII–XXIV, J. Russo, M. Fernández-Galiano, A. Heubeck. New York and Oxford, 1988–92.

Homer, Odyssey: Books XIX and XX. Ed. R. B. Rutherford. Cambridge Greek and Latin Classics. Cambridge, England, 1992.

Homer, Odyssey: Books VI–VIII. Ed. A. F. Garvie. Cambridge Greek and Latin Classics. Cambridge, England, 1994.

Homer, The Odyssey. Ed. with English translation by A. T. Murray, revised by George E. Dimock. 2 vols. The Loeb Classical Library. Cambridge, Mass., and London, 1995.

II. Critical Works

Ahl, Frederick, and Hanna M. Roisman. *The Odyssey Re-Formed.* Ithaca, 1996.

Arnold, Matthew. "On Translating Homer." In *On the Classical Tradition,* ed. R. H. Super. Ann Arbor and London, 1960.

Atchity, Kenneth, ed. *Critical Essays on Homer.* Boston, 1987.

Auerbach, Erich. *Mimesis: The Representation of Reality in Western Literature.* Trans. Willard Trask. Chapter 1, "Odysseus' Scar." Princeton, 1953.

Austin, Norman. *Archery at the Dark of the Moon: Poetic Problems in Homer's Odyssey.* Berkeley, Los Angeles and London, 1975.

Bakker, Egbert, and Ahuvia Kahane, eds. *Written Voices, Spoken Signs: Tradition, Performance, and the Epic Text.* Cambridge, Mass., 2000.

Beissinger, Margaret, Jane Tylus, and Susanne Wofford, eds. *Epic Traditions in the Contemporary World: The Poetics of Community.* Berkeley, 1999.

Benardete, Seth. *The Bow and the Lyre: A Platonic Reading of the Odyssey.* New York and London, 1997.

Beye, Charles R. *The Iliad, the Odyssey, and the Epic Tradition.* New York and London, 1966.

Bloom, Harold, ed. *Homer's Odyssey*. New York, 1996.

Brann, Eva. *Homeric Moments: Clues to Delight in Reading the Odyssey and the Iliad*. Philadelphia, 2002.

Bremer, J. M., I. J. F. de Jong, and J. Kalff, eds. *Homer: Beyond Oral Poetry. Recent Trends in Homeric Interpretation*. Amsterdam, 1987.

Buitron, Diana, and Beth Cohen, eds. *The Odyssey and Ancient Art: An Epic in Word and Image*. The Edith C. Blum Art Institute, Bard College, Annandale-on-Hudson, New York, 1992.

Camps, W. A. *An Introduction to Homer*. Oxford, 1980.

Carpenter, Rhys. *Folk Tale, Fiction, and Saga in the Homeric Epics*. Berkeley, 1946.

Carter, Jane B., and Sarah P. Morris, eds. *The Ages of Homer: A Tribute to Emily Townsend Vermeule*. Austin, 1995.

Chadwick, John. *The Mycenaean World*. London and New York, 1976.

Clarke, Howard. *Homer's Readers: A Historical Introduction to the Iliad and the Odyssey*. Newark, Del., 1981.

Clay, Jenny Strauss. *The Wrath of Athena: Gods and Men in the Odyssey*. Princeton, 1983.

Cohen, Beth, ed. *The Distaff Side: Representing the Female in Homer's Odyssey*. New York and London, 1995.

Cook, Erwin F. *The "Odyssey" in Athens: Myths of Cultural Origins*. Ithaca and London, 1996.

Crotty, Kevin. *The Poetics of Supplication: Homer's Iliad and Odyssey*. Ithaca and London, 1994.

Dawe, R. D. *The Odyssey: Translation and Analysis*. Sussex, 1993.

Dimock, George E. *The Unity of the Odyssey*. Amherst, 1989.

Edwards, Mark W. *Homer: Poet of the Iliad*. Baltimore and London, 1987.

Felson-Rubin, Nancy. *Regarding Penelope: From Character to Poetics*. Princeton, 1994.

Fenik, Bernard. *Studies in the Odyssey*. Hermes Einzelschrift 30. Wiesbaden, 1974.

Ferrucci, Franco. *The Poetics of Disguise: The Autobiography of the Work in Homer, Dante, and Shakespeare*. Trans. A. Dunnigan. Ithaca, 1980.

Finley, John H., Jr. *Homer's Odyssey*. Cambridge, Mass., and London, 1978.

Finley, Sir Moses. *The World of Odysseus*. 2d rev. ed. Harmondsworth, 1979.

Finnegan, Ruth. *Oral Poetry: Its Nature, Significance, and Social Context*. Cambridge, England, 1977.

Ford, Andrew. *Homer: The Poetry of the Past*. Ithaca and London, 1992.

Frame, Douglas. *The Myth of Return in Early Greek Epic*. New Haven, 1978.

Greene, Thomas M. *The Descent from Heaven: A Study in Epic Continuity*. Chapter 4, "Form and Craft in the *Odyssey*." New Haven, 1963.

Griffin, Jasper. *Homer on Life and Death*. Oxford, 1980.

———. *Homer: The Odyssey*. Landmarks of World Literature. Cambridge, England, and New York, 1987.

Guthrie, W. K. C. *The Greeks and Their Gods*. London, 1949; repr. Boston, 1950.

Hexter, Ralph. *A Guide to the Odyssey: A Commentary on the English Translation of Robert Fitzgerald*. New York, 1993.

Jenkyns, Richard. *Classical Epic: Homer and Virgil*. Bristol Classical World series. London, 1992.

Jones, Peter V. *Homer's Odyssey: A Companion to the Translation of Richmond Lattimore*. Carbondale and Bristol, 1988.

Katz, Marylin A. *Penelope's Renown: Meaning and Indeterminacy in the Odyssey*. Princeton, 1991.

Kirk, G. S. *The Songs of Homer*. Cambridge, England, 1962.

Lamberton, Robert. *Homer the Theologian: Neoplatonist Allegorical Reading and the Growth of the Epic Tradition*. Berkeley, Los Angeles and London, 1986.

——, and J. J. Keaney, eds. *Homer's Ancient Readers: The Hermeneutics of Greek Epic's Earliest Exegetes*. Princeton, 1992.

Lloyd-Jones, Sir Hugh. *The Justice of Zeus*. 2d ed. Sather Classical Lectures, Vol. 41. Berkeley, Los Angeles and London, 1983.

Lord, Albert. *The Singer of Tales*. Cambridge, Mass., 1960.

Louden, Bruce. *The Odyssey: Structure, Narration, and Meaning*. Baltimore and London, 1999.

Martin, Richard. *The Language of Heroes: Speech and Performance in the Iliad*. Ithaca, 1989.

McAuslan, Ian, and Peter Walcot, eds. *Homer*. Oxford and New York, 1998.

Morris, Ian, and Barry Powell, eds. *A New Companion to Homer*. Leiden and New York, 1997.

Moulton, Carroll. *Similes in the Homeric Poems*. Göttingen, 1977.

Mueller, Martin, *The Iliad*. Unwin Critical Library, ed. Claude Rawson. London, 1984.

Murnaghan, Sheila. *Disguise and Recognition in the Odyssey*. Princeton, 1987.

Myrsiades, Kostas, ed. *Approaches to Teaching Homer's Iliad and Odyssey*. New York, 1987.

Nagy, Gregory. *The Best of the Achaeans: Concepts of the Hero in Archaic Greek Poetry*. Baltimore and London, 1979.

Olson, S. Douglas. *Blood and Iron: Stories and Storytelling in Homer's Odyssey*. Leiden, New York, Köln, 1995.

Page, Sir Denys. *Folktales in Homer's Odyssey*. Cambridge, Mass., 1973.

——. *The Homeric Odyssey*. Oxford, 1955.

Parry, Adam M. Foreword by Sir Hugh Lloyd-Jones. *The Language of Achilles and Other Papers*. Oxford, 1989.

Parry, Milman. *The Making of Homeric Verse: The Collected Papers of Milman Parry*. Ed. Adam Parry. Oxford, 1971.

Peradotto, John. *Man in the Middle Voice: Name and Narration in the Odyssey*. Martin Classical Lectures, New Series, Vol. 1. Princeton, 1990.

Pucci, Pietro. *Odysseus Polutropos: Intertextual Readings in the Odyssey and the Iliad*. 2d ed. Ithaca, 1995.

Rubens, Beaty, and Oliver Taplin. *An Odyssey Round Odysseus: The Man and His Story Traced Through Time and Place*. London, 1989.

Rubino, Carl A., and Cynthia W. Shelmerdine, eds. *Approaches to Homer*. Austin, 1983.

Schein, Seth L., ed. *Reading the Odyssey: Selected Interpretive Essays*. Princeton, 1995.

Scully, Stephen. *Homer and the Sacred City*. Ithaca and London, 1990.

Segal, Charles. *Singers, Heroes, and Gods in the Odyssey*. Ithaca, 1994.

Shive, David M. *Naming Achilles*. New York and Oxford, 1987.

Stanford, W. B. *The Ulysses Theme: A Study in the Adaptability of a Traditional Hero*. 2d. ed. Oxford, 1968.

Steiner, George, and Robert Fagles, eds. *Homer: A Collection of Critical Essays*. Twentieth Century Views, ed. Maynard Mack. Englewood Cliffs, 1962.

———, ed., with Aminadov Dykman. *Homer in English*. Penguin Poets in Translation, ed. Christopher Ricks. Harmondsworth, 1996.

Suzuki, Mihoko. *Metamorphoses of Helen: Authority, Difference, and the Epic*. Chapter 2, *"The Odyssey."* Ithaca and London, 1989.

Taylor, Charles H., Jr., ed. *Essays on the Odyssey: Selected Modern Criticism*. Indianapolis, 1963.

Thalmann, William G. *The Odyssey: An Epic of Return*. Twayne Publishers, New York, 1992.

———. *The Swineherd and the Bow: Representations of Class in the Odyssey*. Ithaca, N.Y., 1998.

Thornton, Agathe. *People and Themes in Homer's Odyssey*. London, 1970.

Tracy, Stephen V. *The Story of the Odyssey*. Princeton, 1990.

———. *Greece in the Bronze Age*. Chicago and London, 1964.

Vermeule, Emily. *Aspects of Death in Early Greek Art and Poetry*. Sather Classical Lectures, Vol. 46. Berkeley, Los Angeles and London, 1979.

Vivante, Paolo. *Homer*. Hermes Books, ed. John Herington. New Haven and London, 1985.

Wace, Alan J. B., and Frank Stubbings. *A Companion to Homer*. London, 1962.

Wender, Dorothea. *The Last Scenes of the Odyssey*. Mnemosyne Supplement 52. Leiden, 1978.

Whitman, Cedric H. *Homer and the Heroic Tradition*. Chapter 12, "The *Odyssey* and Change." Cambridge, Mass., and London, 1958.

Wood, Robert. *An Essay on the Original Genius and Writings of Homer*. London, 1769; rep. Philadelphia, 1976.

Woodhouse, W. J. *The Composition of Homer's Odyssey*. Oxford, 1930.

PRONOUNCING GLOSSARY

The main purpose of this glossary is to indicate pronunciation. Identifications are brief, and only the first appearance of a name is listed.

Phonetic Equivalents:

a as in *cat*	*o* as in *pot*
ay as in *day*	*oh* as in *bone*
aw as in *raw*	*oo* as in *boot*
ai as in *air*	*or* as in *bore*
ah as in *father*	
e as in *pet*	*s* as in *hiss*
ee as in *feet*	*th* as in *thin*
i as in *bit*	*u* as in *us*
eye as in *bite*	*ur* as in *burst*

Stress is indicated by an apostrophe *after* the stressed syllable (*af'-ter*).

ACASTUS (*a-kas'-tus*): king of Dulichion, 14.380.

ACHAEA (*a-kee'-a*): general, collective name for mainland Greece, 1.278.

ACHAEANS (*a-kee'-unz*): collective name for all Greek people, including the citizens of Ithaca, 1.106.

ACHERON (*a'-ker-on*): a river in the underworld, 10. 563. See note ad loc.

ACHILLES (*a-kil'-eez*): son of Peleus and Thetis, grandson of Aeacus, and commander of the Myrmidons, Achaean allies, at Troy, 3.118.

ACTORIS (*ak'-to-ris*): maid of Penelope, 23.255.

ADRESTE (*a-drees'-tee*): maid of Helen, 4.138.

AEACUS (*ee'-a-kus*): son of Zeus, father of Peleus, grandfather of Achilles, 11.613.

AEAEA (*ee-ee'-a*): island home of Circe, 9.36.

AEETES (*ee-ee'-teez*): brother of Circe, 10.151.

AEGAE (*ee'-jee*): Achaean city in the northern Peloponnese and sacred to Poseidon, 5.420.

AEGISTHUS (*ee-jis'-thus*): son of Thyestes, seducer of Clytemnestra and murderer of Agamemnon, killed by Orestes, 1.34. See note ad loc.

AEGYPTIUS (*ee-jip'-shus*): Ithacan elder, father of Eurynomus, 2.15.

AEOLIA (*ee-oh'-li-a*): island ruled by Aeolus, 10.1.

AEOLUS (*ee'-oh-lus*): (1) master of the winds, 10.1. (2) Father of Cretheus, 11.270.

AESON (*ee'-son*): son of Tyro and Cretheus, father of Jason, 11.295.

AETHON (*ee'-thon*): name assumed by Odysseus, disguised as a beggar, 19.208.

AETOLIA (*ee-toh'-li-a*): region in west-central Greece, 14.429.

AGAMEMNON (*a-ga-mem'-non*): king of Mycenae, son of Atreus, husband of Clytemnestra, murdered by her and Aegisthus; brother of Menelaus, supreme commander of all Achaea's armies and leader of the largest contingent at Troy, 1.35. See note 1.34–55.

AGELAUS (*a-je-lay'-us*): suitor, son of Damastor, killed by Odysseus, 20.358.

AJAX (*ay'-jax*): (1) Achaean, son of Telamon, Telamonian or Great Ajax, defeated by Odysseus in the contest for Achilles' armor, 3.121. See notes ad loc. and 11.625. (2) Achaean, son of Oileus, Oilean or Little Ajax, 4.560. See notes 1.375, 4.560–73.

ALCANDRE (*al-kan'-dree*): lady of Egyptian Thebes, wife of Polybus, 4.140.

ALCIMUS (*al'-si-mus*): father of Mentor, 22.245.

ALCINOUS (*al-si'-no-us*): king of the Phaeacians, husband of Arete, father of Nausicaa, 6.14.

ALCIPPE (*al-si'-pee*): maid of Helen, 4.139.

ALCMAEON (*alk-mee'-on*): son of Amphiaraus, 15.277.

ALCMENA (*alk-mee'-na*): mother of Heracles by Zeus, 2.133. See note 11.690–718.

ALECTOR (*a-lek'-tor*): Spartan, whose daughter married Megapenthes, 4.12.

ALOEUS (*a-lee'-us*): husband of Iphimedeia, supposed father of Otus and Ephialtes, 11.348.

ALPHEUS (*al-fee'-us*): river in the western Peloponnese, 3.548.

AMNISUS (*am-ni'-sus*): port city of Cnossos, on the northern coast of Crete, 19.215.

AMPHIARAUS (*am-fi-a-ray'-us*): prophet and king of Argos, son of Oicles, grandfather of Theoclymenus, and one of the Seven Against Thebes who fought and died there, 15.272. See note 11.369.

AMPHILOCHUS (*am-fi'-lo-kus*): son of Amphiaraus, 15.277.

AMPHIMEDON (*am-fi'-me-don*): suitor killed by Telemachus; in the underworld his ghost reports the death of all the suitors to the ghost of Agamemnon, 22.254.

AMPHINOMUS (*am-fi'-no-mus*): a suitor killed by Telemachus, and a favorite of Penelope, 16.388.

AMPHION (*am-feye'-on*): (1) son of Zeus and Antiope; co-founder of Thebes (2) with his brother Zethus, 11.298. (2) King of Orchomenos, son of Iasus (1) and father of Chloris, 11.321.

AMPHITHEA (*am-fi'-the-a*): wife of Autolycus, mother of Anticleia, grandmother of Odysseus, 19.472.

AMPHITRITE (*am-fi-treye'-tee*): queen of the sea, 3.101.

AMPHITRYON (*am-fi'-tri-on*): husband of Alcmena, supposed father of Heracles, 11.302.

AMYTHAON (*a-mi-thay'-on*): son of Tyro and Cretheus, 11.295.

ANCHIALUS (*an-keye'-a-lus*): father of Mentes, 1.208.

ANDRAEMON (*an-dree'-mon*): father of Thoas, 14.565.

ANTICLEIA (*an-ti-kleye'-a*): daughter of Autolycus, wife of Laertes, mother of Odysseus, 11.95.

ANTICLUS (*an'-ti-klus*): one of the Achaean soldiers in the Trojan horse, 4.320.

ANTILOCHUS (*an-ti'-lo-kus*): son of Nestor, brother of Pisistratus and Thrasymedes; killed by Memnon at Troy, 3.125. See note 3.121–25.

ANTINOUS (*an-ti'-no-us*): son of Eupithes, one of the two leading suitors, 1.440. See note 1.443.

ANTIOPE (*an-teye'-o-pee*): daughter of Asopos, mother by Zeus of Amphion and Zethus, 11.296.

ANTIPHATES (*an-ti'-fa-teez*): (1) king of the Laestrygonians, 10.117. (2) Son of Melampus, father of Oicles, 15.270.

ANTIPHUS (*an'-ti-fus*): (1) son of Aegyptius, companion of Odysseus, killed by the Cyclops, 2.19. (2) Ithacan elder, 17.71.

APHRODITE (*a-fro-deye'-tee*): goddess of love, daughter of Zeus and wife of Hephaestus, 4.17. See note 8.361.

APIRAEA (*a-peye-ree'-a*): home of Eurymedusa, servant of Nausicaa, 7.9.

APOLLO (*a-pol'-oh*): son of Zeus and Leto, patron of the arts, especially music and poetry, and the god of archery—"lord of the silver bow"—whose arrows are a metaphor for the onset of a plague, and whose festival day in Ithaca is the day on which Odysseus kills the suitors, 3.317. See notes, passim.

ARCESIUS (*ar-see'-si-us*): son of Zeus, father of Laertes, grandfather of Odysseus, 4.851.

ARES (*ai'-reez*): son of Zeus and Hera, god of war, lover of Aphrodite, 8.135.

ARETE (*a-ree'-tee*): queen of Phaeacia, wife of Alcinous, mother of Nausicaa, 7.62. See note ad loc.

ARETHUSA (*a-re-thoo'-sa*): spring in Ithaca, 13.465.

ARETIAS (*a-ree'-ti-as*): grandfather of Amphinomus, 16.438.

ARETUS (*a-ree'-tus*): son of Nestor, 3.463.

ARGIVES (*ar'-geyevz*): alternate name for the Achaeans, 1.243.

ARGO (*ar'-goh*): the ship of the Argonauts, 12.77. See note 12.68.

ARGOS (*ar'-gos*): city or district in the northeastern Peloponnese, or the general region of the Achaeans, mainland Greece, 1.397.

ARGOS (*ar'-gos*): dog of Odysseus, 17.319.

ARIADNE (*a-ri-ad'-nee*): daughter of Minos, killed by Artemis, 11.364. See note ad loc.

ARNAEUS (*ar-nee'-us*): true name of the beggar Irus, 18.6.

ARTACIA (*ar-tay'-sha*): a spring on the island of the Laestrygonians, 10.118.

ARTEMIS (*ar'-te-mis*): daughter of Zeus and Leto, sister of Apollo, goddess of childbirth and hunting, 4.136. See note 5.299–302.

ARYBAS (*a'-ri-bas*): a lord of Sidon, father of Eumaeus' nurse, 15.478.

ASOPUS (*a-soh'-pus*): river in Boeotia; as a river god, the father of Antiope, 11.296.

ASPHALION (*as-fa'-li-on*): attendant of Menelaus, 4.240.

ASTERIS (*as'-ter-is*): small island south of Ithaca, 4.951.

ATHENA (*a-thee'-na*): or Pallas Athena, goddess, daughter of Zeus, defender of the Achaeans. A patron of human ingenuity and resourcefulness, whether exemplified by handicrafts, such as spinning and weaving, or by skill in human relations, such as that possessed by Odysseus, her favorite among the Greeks, 1.53. See notes, passim.

ATHENS (*a'-thenz*): the great city of Erechtheus and Athena, located in Attica, in east-central Greece, 3.316.

ATLAS (*at'-las*): Titan who upholds the pillars separating the earth and sky; father of Calypso, 1.62. See note ad loc.

ATREUS (*ay'-tryoos*): father of Agamemnon and Menelaus, 4.172.

ATRIDES (*a-treye'-deez*): "son of Atreus," patronymic of Agamemnon or Menelaus, 1.42.

AUTOLYCUS (*aw-to'-li-kus*): "the wolf himself," father of Anticleia, maternal grandfather of Odysseus, 11.95.

AUTONOË (*aw-to'-no-ee*): maid of Penelope, 18.207.

BOËTHOUS (*boh-ee'-tho-us*): father of Eteoneus, 4.36.

CADMUS (*kad'-mus*): founder of Thebes, father of Ino Leucothea, 5.366.

CALYPSO (*ka-lip'-soh*): goddess-nymph, daughter of Atlas, who makes her home on the island of Ogygia, 1.16.

CASSANDRA (*ka-san'-dra*): daughter of Priam, lover of Agamemnon, and murdered with him by Aegisthus and Clytemnestra, 11.476. See note 1.375.

CASTOR (*kas'-tor*): (1) son of Zeus and Leda, brother of Helen and Polydeuces, 11.343. See note ad loc. (2) Son of Hylax, fictitious father of Odysseus, 14.234.

CAUCONIANS (*kaw-koh'-ni-unz*): a tribe southwest of Pylos, 3.408.

CENTAURS (*sen'-tawrz*): wild creatures, part man and part horse, who live in the vicinity of Mount Pelion, 21.340. See note ad loc.

CEPHALLENIANS (*se-fa-lee'-ni-unz*): 20.231, general name for the subjects of Odysseus as well as for the people of **CEPHALLENIA** (*se-fa-lee'-ni-a*), an island off the coast of Greece, to the west of Ithaca, in the kingdom of Odysseus, 20.231.

CETEANS (*se-tee'-unz*): the people led by Eurypylus, 11.592.

CHALCIS (*kal'-sis*): a stream south of the mouth of the Alpheus, off the western coast of the Peloponnese, 15.328.

CHARYBDIS (*ka-rib'-dis*): monster in the form of a giant whirlpool, located across from Scylla, 12.115.

CHIOS (*kee'-os*): large Aegean island off the coast of Asia Minor, 3.189.

CHLORIS (*kloh'-ris*): wife of Neleus, mother of Nestor, 11.318.

CHROMIUS (*kro'-mi-us*): son of Neleus and Chloris, brother of Nestor, 11.324.

CICONES (*si-koh'-neez*): Trojan allies, living in Thrace, to the north of Troy, 9.45.

CIMMERIANS (*si-mer'-i-unz*): people living near the kingdom of the dead, 11.16.

CIRCE (*sir'-see*): goddess and enchantress of Aeaea, who changes men to swine, 8.501. See note 11.154.

CLASHING ROCKS: legendary and lethal rocks or cliffs, near Scylla and Charybdis, which menace sailors, 12.68. See note ad loc.

CLITUS (*kleye'-tus*): son of Mantius, abducted by the Dawn, 15.278.

CLYMENE (*kli'-men-ee*): heroine seen by Odysseus in the underworld, 11.369.

CLYMENUS (*kli'-men-us*): father of Eurydice, 3.508.

CLYTEMNESTRA (*kleye-tem-nes'-tra*): daughter of Leda and Tyndareus, queen of Argos, wife of Agamemnon, lover of Aegisthus, and mother of Orestes, 3.303. See note 1.34–55.

CLYTIUS (*kli'-ti-us*): father of Piraeus, 15.603.

CLYTONEUS (*kli-to-nee'-us*): son of Alcinous and Arete, 8.139.

CNOSSOS (*knos'-os*): principal city of Crete, 19.202.

CREON (*kree'-on*): king of Thebes, father of Megara, 11.305.

CRETANS (*kree'-tunz*): 14.266, people of **CRETE** (*kreet*), the large island south of the Peloponnese in the Aegean, the kingdom of Idomeneus, 11.366.

CRETHEUS (*kree'-thyoos*): son of Aeolus (2), husband of Tyro, 11.270.

CRONUS (*kro'-nus*): god, son of Uranus, father of Zeus, Hades, Poseidon, Hera, Demeter, 1.54.

CTESIPPUS (*ktee-si'-pus*): suitor killed by Philoetius, 20.321.

CTESIUS (*ktee'-si-us*): father of Eumaeus, 15.464.

CTIMENE (*kti'-me-nee*): younger sister of Odysseus, 15.406.

CYCLOPS (*seye'-klops*): a cannibal clan of one-eyed giants; also a name for Polyphemus in particular, 1.82. See note 9.410.

CYDONIANS (*si-doh'-ni-unz*): a people of Crete, 3.330.

CYLLENE (*seye-lee'-nee*): a mountain in northern Arcadia, the site of Hermes' birth and sacred to the god, 24.1.

CYPRUS (*seye'-prus*): large island in the eastern Mediterranean, 4.93.

CYTHERA (*si-thee'-ra*): island off the southeastern coast of the Peloponnese, 9.92.

DAMASTOR (*da-mas'-tor*): father of Agelaus, 20.358.

DANAANS (*da'-nay-unz*): alternative name for the Achaeans, 24.49.

DAWN: goddess of the morning, wife of Tithonus, 2.1.

DEATH: Hades, god of the dead, son of Cronus and Rhea, brother of Zeus, Demeter and Poseidon, 3.269.

DEIPHOBUS (*dee-i'-fo-bus*): son of Priam; commander in chief of the Trojans after Hector's death; consort of Helen after the death of Paris, 4.309.

DELOS (*dee'-los*): Aegean island in the Cyclades, sacred to Apollo, 6.178.

DEMETER (*dee-mee'-tur*): goddess of the grain crops, sister of Zeus and mother of Persephone, 5.138. See note 11.669–80.

DEMODOCUS (*dee-mo'-do-kus*): blind singer of the Phaeacians, 8.51.

DEMOPTOLEMUS (*dee-mop-to'-le-mus*): suitor killed by Odysseus, 22.254.

DEUCALION (*dew-kay'-li-on*): king of Crete, son of Minos, father of Idomeneus, 19.205.

DIA (*deye'-ah*): a small island off the northern shore of Crete, 11.368.

DIOCLES (*deye'-o-kleez*): son of Ortilochus, king of Phera, 3.547.

DIOMEDES (*deye-o-mee'-deez*): son of Tydeus, king of Argos, 3.186.

DIONYSUS (*deye-o-neye'-sus*): son of Zeus and Semele, the god of ecstatic release, especially associated with wine, 11.368.

DMETOR (*dmee'-tor*): son of Iasus (2), king of Cyprus, 17.488.

DODONA (*doh-doh'-na*): site in Thesprotia, in northwestern Greece; the sanctuary of an oracle of Zeus, whose prophecies were communicated through the rustling of the leaves of a great oak, 14.370.

DOLIUS (*do'-li-us*): an old manservant, attached to Penelope, father of Melanthius and Melantho, 4.828.

DORIANS (*doh'-ri-unz*): a people identified as Cretans by Odysseus, 19.201.

DULICHION (*dew-li'-ki-on*): island near Ithaca, off the western coast of Greece, 1.286.

DYMAS (*deye'-mas*): Phaeacian noble, 6.25.

EARTH: mother of Tityus, 7.372.

ECHENEUS (*e-ke-nee'-us*): Phaeacian elder, 7.185.

ECHEPHRON (*e-ke'-fron*): son of Nestor, 3.462.

ECHETUS (*e'-ke-tus*): brutal king, perhaps in western Greece, 18.98.

EGYPT: the country in Africa, 3.340.

EIDOTHEA (*eye-do'-the-a*): sea-nymph, daughter of Proteus, 4.408.

ELATUS (*e'-la-tus*): suitor killed by Eumaeus, 22.280.

ELIS (*ee'-lis*): realm of the Epeans, in the northwestern Peloponnese, bordering Nestor's Pylos, 4.714.

ELPENOR (*el-pee'-nor*): companion of Odysseus, 10.608.

ELYSIAN FIELDS (*ee-li'-zhun*): distant home of the fortunate after death, 4.635.

ENIPEUS (*e-neye'-pyoos*): river in Thessaly, 11.271.

EPEANS (*e-pee'-unz*): people of Elis and Buprasion, in the northwestern Peloponnese, 13.311.

EPEUS (*e-pee'-us*): builder of the Trojan horse, 8.553.

EPHIALTES (*e-fi-al'-teez*): giant, son of Iphimedeia and Poseidon, brother of Otus, killed by Apollo, 11.351. See note ad loc.

EPHYRA (*e'-fi-ra*): city in Thesprotia, in northwestern Greece, 1.302.

EPICASTE (*e-pi-kas'-tee*): Jocasta, mother and wife of Oedipus, 11.307. See note ad loc.

EREBUS (*e'-re-bus*): the underworld, 10.582.

ERECHTHEUS (*e-rek'-thyoos*): first king of Athens, reared by Athena, 7.93.

EREMBIANS (*e-rem'-bi-unz*): people visited by Menelaus, 4.94.

ERIPHYLE (*e-ri-feye'-lee*): wife of Amphiaraus, 11.369. See note ad loc.

ERYMANTHUS (*e-ri-man'-thus*): mountain in the northwest Peloponnese, 6.114.

ETEONEUS (*ee-tee-ohn'-yoos*): attendant of Menelaus, 4.26.

ETHIOPIANS (*ee-thee-oh'-pi-unz*): 1.25, people of **ETHIOPIA** (*ee-thee-oh'-pi-a*), a far-off country to the east and a favorite haunt of Poseidon, 5.310.

EUANTHES (*yoo-an'-theez*): father of Maron, 9.220.

EUBOEA (*yoo-bee'-a*): large island lying off the coast of eastern Greece, 3.194.

EUENOR (*yoo-ee'-nor*): father of Leocritus, 2.272.

EUMAEUS (*yoo-mee'-us*): swineherd of Odysseus, 14.63. See note ad loc.

EUMELUS (*yoo-mee'-lus*): husband of Iphthime, brother-in-law of Penelope, 4.897.

EUPITHES (*yoo-peye'-theez*): father of Antinous, killed by Laertes, 1.440.

EURYADES (*yoo-reye'-a-deez*): suitor killed by Telemachus, 22.280.

EURYBATES (*yoo-ri'-ba-teez*): herald of Odysseus, 19.283.

EURYCLEIA (*yoo-ri-kleye'-a*): the old nurse of Odysseus and Telemachus, attendant of Penelope, 1.489.

EURYDAMAS (*yoo-ri'-da-mas*): suitor killed by Odysseus, 18.333.

EURYDICE (*yoo-ri'-di-see*): daughter of Clymenus, wife of Nestor, 3.508.

EURYLOCHUS (*yoo-ri'-lo-kus*): kin of Odysseus, and his second in command, 10.224.

EURYMACHUS (*yoo-ri'-ma-kus*): one of the two leading suitors, son of Polybus, and killed by Odysseus, 1.457.

EURYMEDON (*yoo-ri'-me-don*): king of the Giants, father of Periboea, 7.67.

EURYMEDUSA (*yoo-ri-me-doo'-sa*): nurse and servant of Nausicaa, 7.9.

EURYMUS (*yoo'-ri-mus*): father of Telemus, prophet of the Cyclops, 9.567.

EURYNOME (*yoo-ri'-no-mee*): housekeeper of Penelope, 17.548.

EURYNOMUS (*yoo-ri'-no-mus*): suitor, son of Aegyptius, 2.22.

EURYPYLUS (*yoo-ri'-pi-lus*): son of Telephus, leader of the Ceteans, 11.591.

EURYTION (*yoo-ri'-ti-on*): drunken Centaur, 21.330.

EURYTUS (*yoo'-ri-tus*): king of Oechalia, archer killed by Apollo, 8.255.

FURIES: avenging spirits whose task it is to exact blood for blood when no human avenger is left alive. They are particularly concerned with injuries done by one member of a family to another; and they have regulatory powers as well, as when they punish Oedipus for marrying his mother and driving her to suicide; 2.152, see 11.317.

GERAESTUS (*je-ree'-stus*): promontory on the island of Euboea, 3.198.

GORGON (*gor'-gon*): fabulous female monster whose glance could turn a person into stone, 11.726. See note 3.46.

GORTYN (*gor'-tin*): city in Crete, 3.332.

GRACES: attendant goddesses, daughters of Zeus who personify beauty and charm, often associated with the arts and the Muses, 6.21.

GREAT BEAR: constellation, also called the Wagon and the Big Dipper, 5.300. See note 5.299–302.

GYRAE (*jeye'-ree*): rocky headland somewhere in the Aegean Sea, 4.561.

HALITHERSES (*ha-li-thur'-seez*): Ithacan elder with prophetic powers, 2.175.

HALIUS (*ha'-li-us*): Phaeacian, son of Alcinous and Arete, 8.139.

HEBE (*hee'-bee*): goddess of youth, daughter of Zeus and Hera, servant of the gods, 11.693.

HELEN (*he'-len*): daughter of Zeus and Leda, wife of Menelaus, consort of Paris; her abduction by him from Sparta caused the Trojan War, 4.14. See notes 4.106, 4.632–41.

HELIOS (*hee'-li-os*): the Sun, 8.307. See note 12.285.

HELLAS (*hel'-as*): the district ruled by Achilles, later called Thessaly, as well as a name for Greece in general, 1.396.

HELLESPONT (*hel'-es-pont*): strait between the Troad and Thrace (the Dardanelles), 24.89.

HEPHAESTUS (*he-fees'-tus*): god of fire, the great artificer, son of Hera, husband of Aphrodite, 4.694. See notes 8.302–410, 8.321–22.

HERA (*hee'-ra*): goddess, daughter of Cronus and Rhea, wife and sister of Zeus, 4.575. See notes 5.161, 11.690–718.

HERACLES (*her'-a-kleez*): son of Zeus and Alcmena; the hero of the Labors, who after death divides his time between the underworld and Olympus, 8.255. See notes 3.215, 11.690–718.

HERMES (*hur'-meez*): god, son of Zeus and Maia, messenger of the gods, giant-killer, and guide of dead souls to the underworld, 1.46. See notes 5.161, 14.494.

HERMIONE (*hur-meye'-o-nee*): daughter of Menelaus and Helen, 4.16.

HIPPODAMEIA (*hi-po-da-meye'-a*): maid of Penelope, 18.207.

HIPPOTAS (*hip'-o-tas*): father of Aeolus, 10.2.

HUNTER: constellation (otherwise called Orion), 5.301. See note 5.299–302.

HYLAX (*heye'-lax*): fictitious father of Castor (2), 14.234.

HYPERESIA (*hi-pe-ree'-si-a*): city in Achaea, home of Polyphides, 15.284.

HYPERIA (*hi-pe-reye'-a*): former land of the Phaeacians, near to the Cyclops, 6.6.

HYPERION (*heye-pee'-ri-on*): alternative name of the sungod, Helios, 12.285. See note ad loc.

IARDANUS (*i-ar'-da-nus*): river in Crete, 3.331.

IASION (*eye-a'-si-on*): son of Zeus and Electra, loved by Demeter, 5.139. See note 5.134–40.

IASUS (*eye'-a-sus*): (1) father of Amphion (2), 11.321. (2) Father of Dmetor, 17.488.

ICARIUS (*eye-ka'-ri-us*): father of Penelope and brother of Tyndareus, 1.379.

ICMALIUS (*ik-ma'-li-us*): Ithacan craftsman who made Penelope's chair, 19.60.

IDOMENEUS (*eye-do'-men-yoos*): Achaean, son of Deucalion, commander of the Cretan contingent at Troy, 3.216. See note 3.213–14.

ILIUM (*il'-i-um*): Troy, the city of Ilus, 9.44.

ILUS (*eye'-lus*): lord of Ephyra, son of Mermerus, 1.302.

INO (*eye'-noh*): (Leucothea), daughter of Cadmus, once a mortal and now a sea-nymph, 5.367. See note ad loc.

IOLCOS (*i-ol'-kos*): city in Thessaly, home of Pelias, where Jason sought the golden fleece, 11.292.

IPHICLUS (*eye'-fi-klus*): king of Phylace, 11.329.

IPHIMEDEIA (*eye-fi-me-deye'-a*): wife of Aloeus, mother of Otus and Ephialtes by Poseidon, 11.348.

IPHITUS (*eye'-fi-tus*): son of Eurytus, killed by Heracles, 21.16.

IPHTHIME (*if-theye'-mee*): wife of Eumelus, sister of Penelope, 4.895.

IRUS (*eye'-rus*): nickname of Ithacan beggar whose true name is Arnaeus, 18.8. See note 18.6–9.

ISMARUS (*iz'-ma-rus*): Thracian city, home of the Cicones, 9.44.

ITHACANS (*ith'-a-kunz*): 23.404, people of **ITHACA** (*ith'-a-ka*), home of Odysseus, Ionian island off the western coast of Greece, 1.21.

ITHACUS (*ith'-a-kus*): builder of a well on Ithaca, 17.225.

ITYLUS (*it'-i-lus*): son of Zethus and Pandareus' daughter, who was transformed into a nightingale, 19.589. See note 19.585–90.

JAGGED ISLANDS: a cluster of islands between Elis and Ithaca, 15.332.

JASON (*jay'-son*): leader of the Argonauts and captain of the ship *Argo*, 12.80. See notes 11.268, 12.68.

LACEDAEMON (*la-se-dee'-mon*): city and kingdom of Menelaus, in the southern Peloponnese, 3.367.

LAERCES (*lay-er'-seez*): goldsmith in Pylos, 3.475.

LAERTES (*lay-er'-teez*): son of Arcesius, husband of Anticleia, father of Odysseus, 1.219.

LAESTRYGONIANS (*lee-stri-goh'-ni-unz*): legendary clan of giant cannibals, 10.117.

LAMPETIE (*lam-pe'-ti-ee*): nymph, daughter of Helios and Neaera, 12.142.

LAMUS (*lam'-us*): either the founding king of the Laestrygonians or their major city, 10.90.

LAODAMAS (*lay-o'-da-mas*): Phaeacian, son of Alcinous and Arete, 7.202.

LAPITHS (*la'-piths*): Thessalian tribe, led by Pirithous, 21.332. See note 21.331–40.

LEDA (*lee'-da*): wife of Tyndareus and mother of Clytemnestra; mother by Zeus of Castor, Helen and Polydeuces, 11.341. See note 11.343.

LEMNOS (*lem'-nos*): island in the northeastern Aegean, 8.321. See note ad loc.

LEOCRITUS (*lee-o'-kri-tus*): suitor killed by Telemachus, 2.272.

LEODES (*lee-oh'-deez*): suitor with prophetic gifts, killed by Odysseus, 21.163.

LESBOS (*lez'-bos*): island and city off the coast of Asia Minor, south of Troy, 3.188.

LETO (*lee'-toh*): goddess, mother of Apollo and Artemis by Zeus, 6.118.

LEUCOTHEA (*lew-ko'-the-a*): Ino's name after she became a divinity, 5.368.

LIBYA: the country in Africa as well as a general name for the continent itself, 4.94.

LOTUS-EATERS: legendary people visited by Odysseus, they live on a plant whose fruit induces stupor and forgetfulness of home, 9.95.

MAERA (*mee'-ra*): heroine seen by Odysseus in the underworld, 11.369.

MAIA (*may'-a*): mother of Hermes, 14.494.

MALEA (*ma-lee'-a*): stormy southeastern cape of the Peloponnese, 3.325.

MANTIUS (*man'-shus*): prophet, son of Melampus, grandfather of Theoclymenus, 15.270.

MARATHON (*ma'-ra-thon*): village in Attica near Athens, 7.92.

MARON (*mah'-ron*): son of Euanthes, priest of Apollo at Ismarus, 9.219.

MASTOR (*mas'-tor*): father of Halitherses, 2.176.

MEDON (*mee'-don*): herald of Odysseus in Ithaca, 4.762.

MEGAPENTHES (*me-ga-pen'-theez*): son of Menelaus by a slave woman, 4.13.

MEGARA (*me'-ga-ra*): daughter of Creon, wife of Heracles, 11.305.

MELAMPUS (*me-lam'-pus*): famous seer, 11.332. See note ad loc.

MELANEUS (*me'-lan-yoos*): father of Amphimedon, 24.111.

MELANTHIUS (*me-lan'-thi-us*): son of Dolius, goatherd, 17.231.

MELANTHO (*me-lan'-thoh*): daughter of Dolius, maid of Penelope, 18.363.

MEMNON (*mem'-non*): son of Tithonus and Dawn, 4.209. See note 3.121–25.

MENELAUS (*me-ne-lay'-us*): son of Atreus, king of Lacedaemon, brother of Agamemnon, husband of Helen, 1.328. See notes, passim.

MENOETIUS (*me-nee'-shus*): father of Patroclus, 24.84.

MENTES (*men'-teez*): son of Anchialus, king of the Taphians, name assumed by Athena in Ithaca, 1.123.

MENTOR (*men'-tor*): son of Alcimus, Ithacan friend of Odysseus, often impersonated by Athena, 2.250. See notes 4.304–6, 4.738.

MERMERUS (*mur'-me-rus*): father of Ilus, 1.302.

MESAULIUS (*me-saw'-li-us*): servant of Eumaeus, 14.511.

MESSENIANS (*me-see'-ni-unz*): 21.20, people of **MESSENE** (*me-see'-nee*), a city in Lacedaemon, 21.17.

MIMAS (*meye'-mas*): craggy promontory of Asia Minor opposite the island of Chios, 3.191.

MINOS (*meye'-nos*): son of Zeus and Europa, king of Crete, father of Deucalion, 11.365. See note 19.203–5.

MINYANS (*min'-yunz*): people of Orchomenos in east-central Greece, 11.322.

MULIUS (*moo'-li-us*): Dulichian herald of Amphinomus, 18.477.

MUSE: goddess, daughter of Zeus, one of the nine, all told, who preside over literature and the arts and are the sources of artistic inspiration, 1.1.

MYCENAE (*meye-see'-nee*): (1) legendary heroine from whom the Argive city took its name, 2.133. (2) City in the Argolid, Agamemnon's capital, just to the north of the city of Argos, 3.344.

MYRMIDONS (*mur'-mi-donz*): people of Phthia, in southern Thessaly, ruled by King Peleus and commanded at Troy by Achilles, 3.212.

NAIADS (*neye'-adz*): water-nymphs, 13.117.

NAUSICAA (*naw-si'-kay-a*): daughter of Alcinous and Arete, 6.20.

NAUSITHOUS (*naw-si'-tho-us*): son of Poseidon, father of Alcinous and Rhexenor, founder of the Phaeacian settlement on Scheria, 6.8.

NEAERA (*ne-ee'-ra*): wife of Helios, mother of Lampetie and Phaëthusa, 12.143.

NION (*neye'-on*): alternative name of Mount Neriton, on Ithaca, 1.215.

NELEUS (*neel'-yoos*): son of Poseidon and Tyro, father of Nestor, former king of Pylos, 3.4.

NEOPTOLEMUS (*nee-op-to'-le-mus*): son of Achilles; married to Hermione, daughter of Helen and Menelaus, 11.576. See note 3.213–14.

NERICUS (*nee'-ri-cus*): town on the western coast of Greece, captured by Laertes, 24.419.

NERITON (*nee'-ri-ton*): mountain on Ithaca, 9.24.

NERITUS (*nee'-ri-tus*): builder of a well on Ithaca, 17.225.

NESTOR (*nes'-tor*): son of Neleus, king of the Pylians, father of Antilochus, Pisistratus, Thrasymedes and others; the oldest of the Achaean chieftains, 3.19.

NILE: the famous river of Egypt, 4.536.

NISUS (*neye'-sus*): king of Dulichion, father of Amphinomus, 16.438.

NOËMON (*no-ee'-mon*): Ithacan, son of Phronius, 2.426.

OCEAN: the great river that surrounds the world and the god who rules its waters, 4.638.

ODYSSEUS (*o-dis'-yoos*): grandson of Arcesius and Autolycus, son of Laertes and Anticleia, husband of Penelope, father of Telemachus, king of Ithaca and the surrounding islands, 1.24. See notes, passim.

OECHALIA (*ee-kay'-li-a*): Thessalian city of Eurytus, 8.255.

OEDIPUS (*ee'-di-pus*): son of Laius and Jocasta (Epicaste), her husband as well, and king of Thebes (2), 11.307. See note ad loc.

OENOPS (*ee'-nops*): Ithacan, father of Leodes, 21.163.

OGYGIA (*oh-ji'-ja*): island in the center of the sea and home of Calypso, 1.101.

OICLES (*oh-i'-kleez*): father of Amphiaraus, 15.271.

OLYMPUS (*o-lim'-pus*): mountain in northeastern Thessaly, the home of the gods, 1.119.

ONETOR (*o-nee'-tor*): father of Phrontis, 3.320.

OPS (*ops*): son of Pisenor, father of Eurycleia, 1.489.

ORCHOMENOS (*or-ko'-men-os*): city of the Minyans, in east-central Greece, bordering on Boeotia, 11.322.

ORESTES (*o-res'-teez*): son of Agamemnon and Clytemnestra, and the avenger of his father, 1.35. See notes 1.34–55, 3.346–47, 4.165.

ORION (*o-reye'-on*): mythical hunter, loved by the Dawn, murdered by Artemis; and the constellation in his name, 5.134. See note 5.299–302.

ORMENUS (*or'-men-us*): father of Ctesius, grandfather of Eumaeus, 15.464.

ORSILOCHUS (*or-si'-lo-kus*): son of Idomeneus, 13.295.

ORTILOCHUS (*or-ti'-lo-kus*): father of Diocles, 3.548.

ORTYGIA (*or-ti'-ja*): legendary place where Artemis killed Orion, an island sometimes identified as Delos, 15.454.

OSSA (*os'-a*): mountain in Thessaly, 11.358.

OTUS (*oh'-tus*): giant, son of Iphimedeia and Poseidon, brother of Ephialtes, killed by Apollo, 11.351. See note ad loc.

PALLAS (*pal'-as*): epithet of Athena, 1.147.

PANDAREUS (*pan-dar'-yoos*): father of the nightingale, whose daughters were snatched away by the whirlwinds, 19.585. See note ad loc.

PANOPEUS (*pan'-op-yoos*): city in Phocis, 11.668.

PAPHOS (*pa'-fos*): city in Cyprus and a favorite haunt of Aphrodite, 8.405.

PARNASSUS (*par-nas'-us*): great mountain in central Greece, on the north side of the Gulf of Corinth; the oracle of Delphi was situated on its southern slope, 19.447.

PATROCLUS (*pa-tro'-klus*): son of Menoetius, brother-in-arms of Achilles, killed by Hector at Troy, 3.123. See note 3.121–25.

PELASGIANS (*pe-laz'-junz*): Trojan allies, a tribe located in Asia Minor, 19.201.

PELEUS (*peel'-yoos*): father by Thetis of Achilles, 8.89.

PELIAS (*pe'-li-as*): son of Poseidon and Tyro, king of Iolcus, 11.290.

PELION (*pee'-li-on*): mountain in Thessaly, home of the Centaurs, 11.359.

PENELOPE (*pe-ne'-lo-pee*): daughter of Icarius, wife of Odysseus, mother of Telemachus, queen of Ithaca, 1.259. See notes, passim.

PERIBOEA (*pe-ri-bee'-a*): daughter of Eurymedon, mother by Poseidon of Nausithous, 7.66.

PERICLYMENUS (*per-ri-kli'-men-us*): son of Neleus and Chloris, brother of Nestor, 11.324.

PERIMEDES (*per-ri-mee'-deez*): companion of Odysseus, 11.26.

PERO (*pee'-roh*): daughter of Neleus and Chloris, 11.325.

PERSE (*pur'-see*): nymph, daughter of Ocean, wife of Helios, mother of Aeetes and Circe, 10.153.

PERSEPHONE (*pur-se'-fo-nee*): goddess of the underworld, daughter of Demeter, and wife of Hades, 10.540.

PERSEUS (*purs'-yoos*): son of Nestor, 3.462.

PHAEACIANS (*fee-ay'-shunz*): 5.39, people of Alcinous and Arete, inhabitants of **PHAEACIA** (*fee-ay'-sha*), a kingdom whose alternative name is Scheria, 5.317.

PHAEDIMUS (*fee'-di-mus*): king of the Sidonians, friend of Menelaus, 4.695.

PHAEDRA (*fee'-dra*): wife of Theseus, heroine seen by Odysseus in the underworld, 11.364.

PHAESTOS (*fees'-tos*): city in Crete, 3.334.

PHAËTHUSA (*fay-e-thoo'-sa*): nymph, daughter of Helios and Neaera, 12.142.

PHAROS (*fa'-ros*): island off the mouth of the Nile where Menelaus subdued Proteus, 4.396.

PHEAE (*fe'-ee*): town in Elis, 15.330.

PHEMIUS (*fee'-mi-us*): son of Terpis, Ithacan bard, 1.178.

PHERA (*fee'-ra*): town between Pylos and Sparta, the home of Diocles, 3.547.

PHERAE (*fee'-ree*): town in Thessaly, the home of Eumelus, 4.897.

PHERES (*fe'-reez*): son of Cretheus and Tyro, 11.295.

PHIDON (*feye'-don*): king of Thesprotia, 14.357.

PHILOCTETES (*fi-lok-tee'-teez*): son of Poias, the great archer of the Trojan War, commander of the Thessalians, marooned on Lemnos suffering from an infected snakebite, 3.215. See note ad loc.

PHILOETIUS (*fi-lee'-shus*): cowherd loyal to Odysseus, 20.203.

PHILOMELIDES (*fi-lo-me-leye'-deez*): wrestler in Lesbos, thrown by Odysseus, 4.382.

PHOEBUS (*fee'-bus*): epithet of Apollo, translated as Lord Apollo, 3.317.

PHOENICIANS (*fee-ni'-shunz*): 13.308, people of **PHOENICIA** (*fee-ni'-sha*), a country on the coast of Syria, 4.93.

PHORCYS (*for'-seez*): an old god of the sea, father of Thoosa, 1.85.

PHRONIUS (*fron'-i-us*): father of Noëmon, 2.426.

PHRONTIS (*fron'-tis*): son of Onetor, helmsman of Menelaus, 3.320.

PHTHIA (*ftheye'-a*): sector of southern Thessaly, kingdom of Peleus and home of Achilles, 11.564.

PHYLACE (*fil'-a-see*): home of Iphiclus in Thessaly, 11.331.

PHYLACUS (*fil'-a-kus*): hero of Phylace, 15.258.

PHYLO (*feye'-loh*): handmaid of Helen, 4.140.

PIERIA (*pi-e'-ree-a*): area north of Mount Olympus in Thessaly, 5.54.

PIRAEUS (*peye-ree'-us*): Ithacan, friend of Telemachus, host of Theoclymenus, 15.602.

PIRITHOUS (*peye-ri'-tho-us*): son of Zeus, king of the Lapiths, 21.331. See note ad loc.

PISANDER (*peye-san'-der*): suitor, son of Polyctor, killed by Philoetius, 18.336.

PISENOR (*peye-see'-nor*): (1) father of Ops, 1.489. (2) Ithacan herald, 2.39.

PISISTRATUS (*peye-si'-stra-tus*): son of Nestor, who accompanies Telemachus to Sparta, 3.40.

PLEIADES (*pleye'-a-deez*): constellation, 5.299. See note ad loc.

PLOWMAN: constellation, 5.299. See note ad loc.

POIAS (*poi'-as*): father of Philoctetes, 3.215

POLITES (*po-leye'-teez*): companion of Odysseus, 10.246.

POLYBUS (*pol'-i-bus*): (1) father of Eurymachus, 1.457. (2) A man of Egyptian Thebes, visited by Menelaus and Helen, 4.141. (3) Phaeacian craftsman, 8.417. (4) Suitor killed by Eumaeus, 22.255.

POLYCASTE (*po-li-kas'-tee*): youngest daughter of Nestor, 3.521.

POLYCTOR (*po-lik'-tor*): (1) builder of a well on Ithaca, 17.225. (2) Father of Pisander, 18.336.

POLYDAMNA (*po-li-dam'-na*): wife of Thon, an Egyptian, 4.253.

POLYDEUCES (*po-li-dyoo'-seez*): brother of Helen and Castor (1), 11.343. See note ad loc.

POLYPHEMUS (*po-li-fee'-mus*): Cyclops, son of Poseidon and Thoosa, blinded by Odysseus, 1.83.

POLYPHIDES (*po-li-feye'-deez*): son of the prophet Mantius, and father of Theoclymenus, 15.278.

POLYTHERSES (*po-li-thur'-seez*): father of Ctesippus, 22.301.

PONTONOUS (*pon-ton'-o-us*): herald of Alcinous, 7.212.

POSEIDON (*po-seye'-don*): god of the sea, son of Cronus and Rhea, younger brother of Zeus, father of Polyphemus, throughout the *Odyssey* an inveterate enemy of Odysseus, 1.23.

PRAMNIAN WINE (*pram'-ni-an*): dispensed by Circe, and a wine often used medicinally, 10.258.

PRIAM (*preye'-am*): king of Troy, son of Laomedon of the line of Dardanus, father of Hector and Paris, 3.119. See note 11.591.

PROCRIS (*pro'-kris*): daughter of Erechtheus, king of Athens, and seen by Odysseus in the underworld, 11.364.

PROTEUS (*proh'-tyoos*): the Old Man of the Sea, servant of Poseidon and father of Eidothea, 4.408.

PSYRIE (*psi'-ri-ee*): island off the northern coast of Chios, 3.190.

PYLIANS (*peye'-li-unz*): 3.35, people of **PYLOS** (*peye'-los*), Nestor's capital city and also the region surrounding it in the southwestern Peloponnese, 1.109.

PYTHO (*peye'-thoh*): place in Phocis sacred to Apollo, his sanctuary and oracle on the slopes of Mount Parnassus, and later called Delphi, 8.94.

RHADAMANTHYS (*ra-da-man'-this*): son of Zeus and Europa, brother of Minos, and the justicer who rules the Elysian Fields, 4.635.

RHEXENOR (*rex-ee'-nor*): son of Nausithous, brother of Alcinous, father of Arete, 7.73.

RITHRON (*reye'-thron*): harbor on the coast of Ithaca, 1.215.

RUMOR: personified as the messenger of Zeus, 24.457.

SALMONEUS (*sal-mohn'-yoos*): son of Aeolus (2), father of Tyro, 11.269.

SAME (*sam'-ee*): island off the western coast of Greece (later called Cephallenia), near Ithaca in the kingdom of Odysseus, 1.286.

SCHERIA (*ske'-ri-a*): island of the Phaeacians, 5.38.

SCYLLA (*sil'-a*): man-eating monster that lives in a cliffside cavern opposite the whirlpool of Charybdis, 12.94.

SCYROS (*skeye'-ros*): island in the central Aegean off the coast of Euboea, 11.579.

SICILIANS: 20.427, people of **SICILY**, the large island just off the southern tip of Italy in the Mediterranean, 24.343.

SIDONIANS (*seye-do'-ni-unz*): 4.94, people of **SIDON** (*seye'-don*), a city in Phoenicia, 13.322.

SINTIANS (*sin'-chunz*): friends of Hephaestus in Lemnos, 8.334.

SIRENS: enchantresses of the sea, whose song can tempt a sailor to his ruin, 12.44.

SISYPHUS (*sis'-i-fus*): legendary figure doomed in the underworld to rolling a boulder up an incline and forever failing to surmount its crest, 11.681. See note ad loc.

SOLYMI (*so'-li-meye*): Lycian mountain range in Asia Minor, 5.311.

SOUNION (*soon'-yun*): southeasternmost cape of Attica, near Athens, 3.316.

SPARTA (*spar'-ta*): capital city of Lacedaemon, the home of Menelaus and Helen, 1.109.

SPRINGS: place on the western coast of Greece, across from Ithaca, 15.328.

STRATIUS (*stra'-shus*): son of Nestor, 3.462.

STYX (*stix*): river in the underworld, by which the gods swear their binding oaths, 5.205. See notes ad loc. and 10.563–65.

SYRIE (*si'-ri-ee*): place of unknown location, perhaps an island, perhaps a country; the original home of Eumaeus, 15.453.

TANTALUS (*tan'-ta-lus*): legendary figure doomed to eternal thirst and hunger in the underworld, 11.669. See note ad loc.

TAPHIANS (*ta'-fi-unz*): 1.123, sea-trading people of **TAPHOS** (*ta'-fos*), uncertainly located on or near the western coast of Greece, 1.476.

TAYGETUS (*tay-i'-ge-tus*): mountain range in Lacedaemon, 6.114.

TELAMON (*tel'-a-mon*): father of Great Ajax, 11.620.

TELEMACHUS (*te-lem'-a-kus*): grandson of Laertes and Anticleia, son of Odysseus and Penelope, heir to the throne of Ithaca, 1.132. See notes, passim.

TELEMUS (*tee'-le-mus*): prophet of the Cyclops, 9.567.

TELEPHUS (*tee'-le-fus*): father of Eurypylus, 11.591.

TELEPYLUS (*tee-le'-pi-lus*): city of the Laestrygonians, 10.90.

TEMESE (*te'-me-see*): place of unknown location, perhaps in Cyprus, and invented by Athena disguised as Mentes, 1.213.

TENEDOS (*ten'-e-dos*): island in the northeastern Aegean off the coast of Troy, 3.176.

TERPIS (*ter'-pis*): father of Phemius, 22.346.

THEBES (*theebz*): (1) city in Egypt, famous for its wealth and hundred gates, 4.141. (2) Seven-gated city in Boeotia, 10.541.

THEMIS (*the'-mis*): goddess whose province is established law and custom, 2.73.

THEOCLYMENUS (*the-o-kli'-men-us*): Argive seer of prophetic lineage, son of Polyphides, 15.286.

THESEUS (*thees'-yoos*): son of Aegeus, king of Athens, who abducted Ariadne from Crete, 11.365.

THESPROTIANS (*thes-proh'-shunz*): 16.473, people of **THESPROTIA** (*thes-proh'-sha*), a district in northwestern Greece, 14.356.

THETIS (*the'-tis*): sea-goddess, daughter of Nereus, married to Peleus and by him the mother of Achilles, 24.50.

THOAS (*thoh'-as*): Achaean, son of Andraemon, commander of the Aetolians at Troy, 14.565.

THON (*thohn*): Egyptian, husband of Polydamna, 4.253.

THOOSA (*tho-oh'-sa*): sea-nymph, daughter of Phorcys, mother by Poseidon of Polyphemus, 1.85.

THRACE (*thrays*): a country north of the Aegean and the Hellespont, 8.404.

THRASYMEDES (*thra-si-mee'-deez*): son of Nestor, brother of Antilochus and Pisistratus, 3.43.

THRINACIA (*thri-nay'-sha*): mythical island of Helios, the sungod, where he pastured his sacred cattle, 11.121.

THYESTES (*theye-es'-teez*): brother of Atreus, father of Aegisthus, 4.579.

TIRESIAS (*teye-ree'-si-as*): blind seer of Thebes (2), who retains his prophetic powers even in the underworld, 10.541.

TITHONUS (*ti-thoh'-nus*): husband of the Dawn, son of Laomedon and elder brother of Priam, 5.1.

TITYUS (*ti'-ti-yus*): legendary figure doomed to eternal torture in the underworld for having violated Leto, mother of Artemis and Apollo, 7.372. See note ad loc.

TROJANS (*troh'-junz*): 3.95, people of the Troad and their allies arrayed against the Achaeans in the Trojan War; as well as the people of **TROY** (*troy*), capital city of the Troad, and alternatively called Ilium, 1.3.

TYDEUS (*teye'-dyoos*): son of Oeneus, father of Diomedes, 3.185.

TYNDAREUS (*tin-dar'-yoos*): husband of Leda, father of Clytemnestra, Castor and Polydeuces, 11.341.

TYRO (*teye'-roh*): daughter of Salmoneus, wife of Cretheus, mother by Poseidon of Pelias and Neleus, 2.133.

WAGON: constellation, also called the Great Bear and the Big Dipper, 5.300. See note 5.299–302.

ZACYNTHUS (*za-kin'-thus*): island off the western coast of Greece, south of Ithaca, in the kingdom of Odysseus, 1.286.

ZETHUS (*zee'-thus*): son of Zeus and Antiope, builder of Thebes (2) with his brother Amphion (1), and father of Itylus, 11.298.

ZEUS (*zyoos*): king of the gods, son of Cronus and Rhea, brother and husband of Hera, father of the Olympians and many mortals too. His spheres include the sky and the weather, hospitality and the rights of guests and suppliants, the punishment of injustice, the sending of omens, and the governance of the universe, controlled to some extent by Fate as well, 1.11. See notes, passim.

AVAILABLE FROM PENGUIN

TRANSLATED BY ROBERT FAGLES

The Aeneid
Virgil
Introduction by Bernard Knox
ISBN 978-0-14-310629-6

The Aeneid
Virgil
(Penguin Classics Deluxe Edition)
Introduction by Bernard Knox
ISBN 978-0-14-310513-8

The Iliad
Homer
Introduction and Notes by
Bernard Knox
ISBN 978-0-14-044592-3

The Iliad
Homer
(Penguin Classics Deluxe Edition)
Introduction and Notes by
Bernard Knox
ISBN 978-0-14-027536-0

The Odyssey
Homer
Introduction and Notes by
Bernard Knox
ISBN 978-0-14-303995-2

The Odyssey
Homer
(Penguin Classics Deluxe Edition)
Introduction and Notes by
Bernard Knox
ISBN 978-0-14-026886-7

The Oresteia
Agamemnon; The Libation Bearers;
The Eumenides
Aeschylus
Introduction, Notes, and Glossary
by Robert Fagles and W. B. Stanford
ISBN 978-0-14-044333-2

The Three Theban Plays
Antigone; Oedipus the King;
Oedipus at Colonus
Sophocles
Introduction and Notes by
Bernard Knox
ISBN 978-0-14-044425-4

PENGUIN
CLASSICS